Country Lovers

First published in the UK in 2019 by Head of Zeus Ltd

9 7 5 3 1 2 4 6 8

A catalogue record for this book is available from the British Library.

Typeset by Silicon Chips

ISBN (HB): 9781784977276
ISBN (XTPB): 9781784977283
ISBN (E): 9781784977269

Printed and bound in Great Britain by CPI Group (UK) Ltd, Croydon, CR0 4YY

Head of Zeus Ltd
5–8 Hardwick Street
London EC1R 4RG

WWW.HEADOFZEUS.COM

Country Lovers

Fiona Walker is the bestselling author of nineteen novels. She lives in Warwickshire with her partner and two children plus an assortment of horses and dogs. Visit Fiona's website at www.fionawalker.com.

By Fiona Walker

French Relations
Kiss Chase
Well Groomed
Snap Happy
Between Males
Lucy Talk
Lots of Love
Tongue in Cheek
Four Play
Love Hunt
Kiss and Tell
The Love Letter
Sealed with a Kiss
The Summer Wedding
The Country Escape
The Woman Who Fell in Love for a Week
The Weekends of You and Me
The Country Set
The Country Lovers

To the OM Sisterhood: SP, LB and HB
(my brilliant divorce lawyer), on all of whose wise
shoulders I cried more than once while writing this,
in laughter as much as frustration.

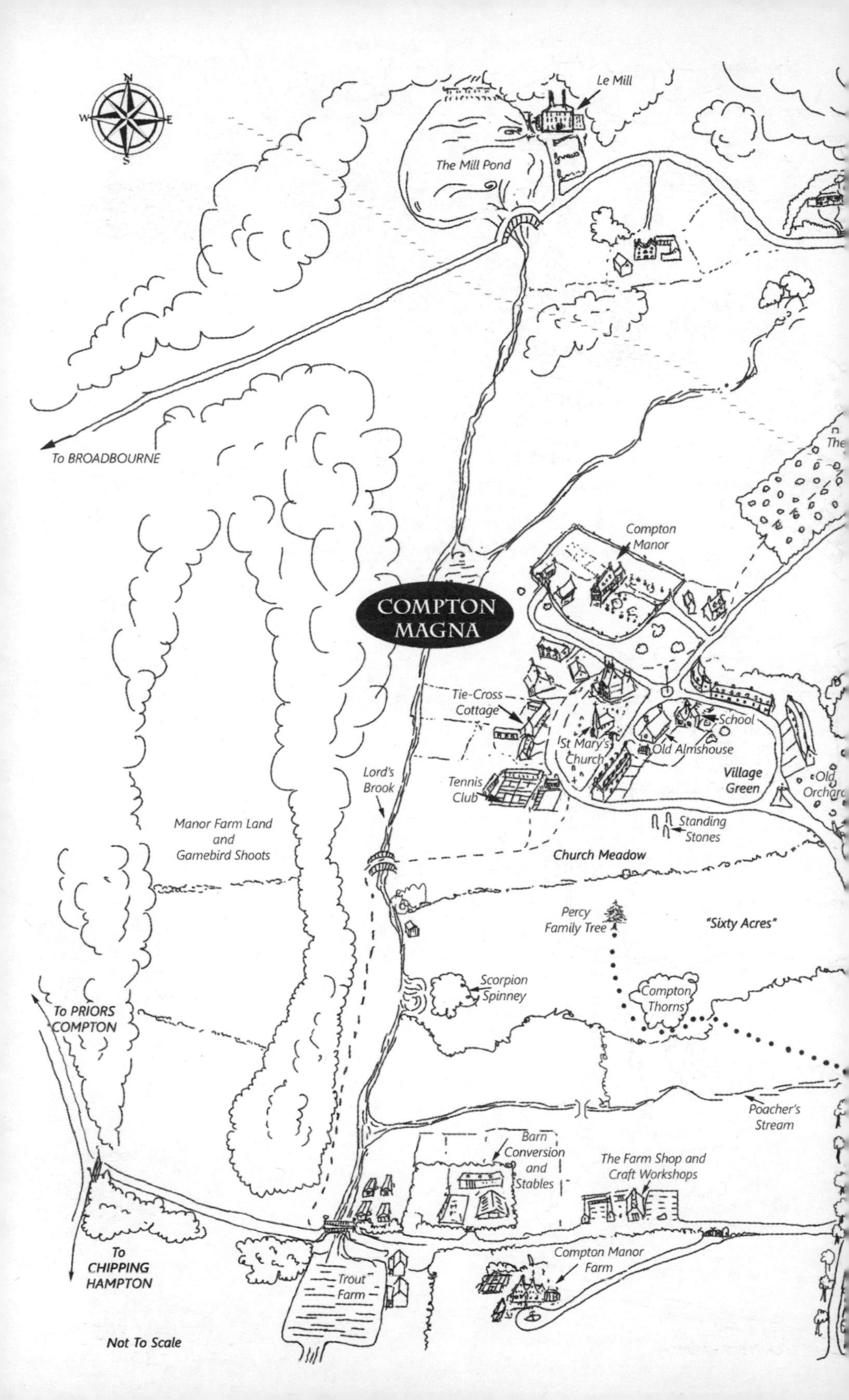

N
W
E
S
Le Mill
The Mill Pond
To BROADBOURNE
COMPTON MAGNA
Compton Manor
Tie-Cross Cottage
St Mary's Church
School
Old Almshouse
Village Green
Old Orchard
Lord's Brook
Tennis Club
Standing Stones
Manor Farm Land and Gamebird Shoots
Church Meadow
Percy Family Tree
"Sixty Acres"
Scorpion Spinney
Compton Thorns
To PRIORS COMPTON
Poacher's Stream
Barn Conversion and Stables
The Farm Shop and Craft Workshops
Compton Manor Farm
To CHIPPING HAMPTON
Trout Farm
Not To Scale

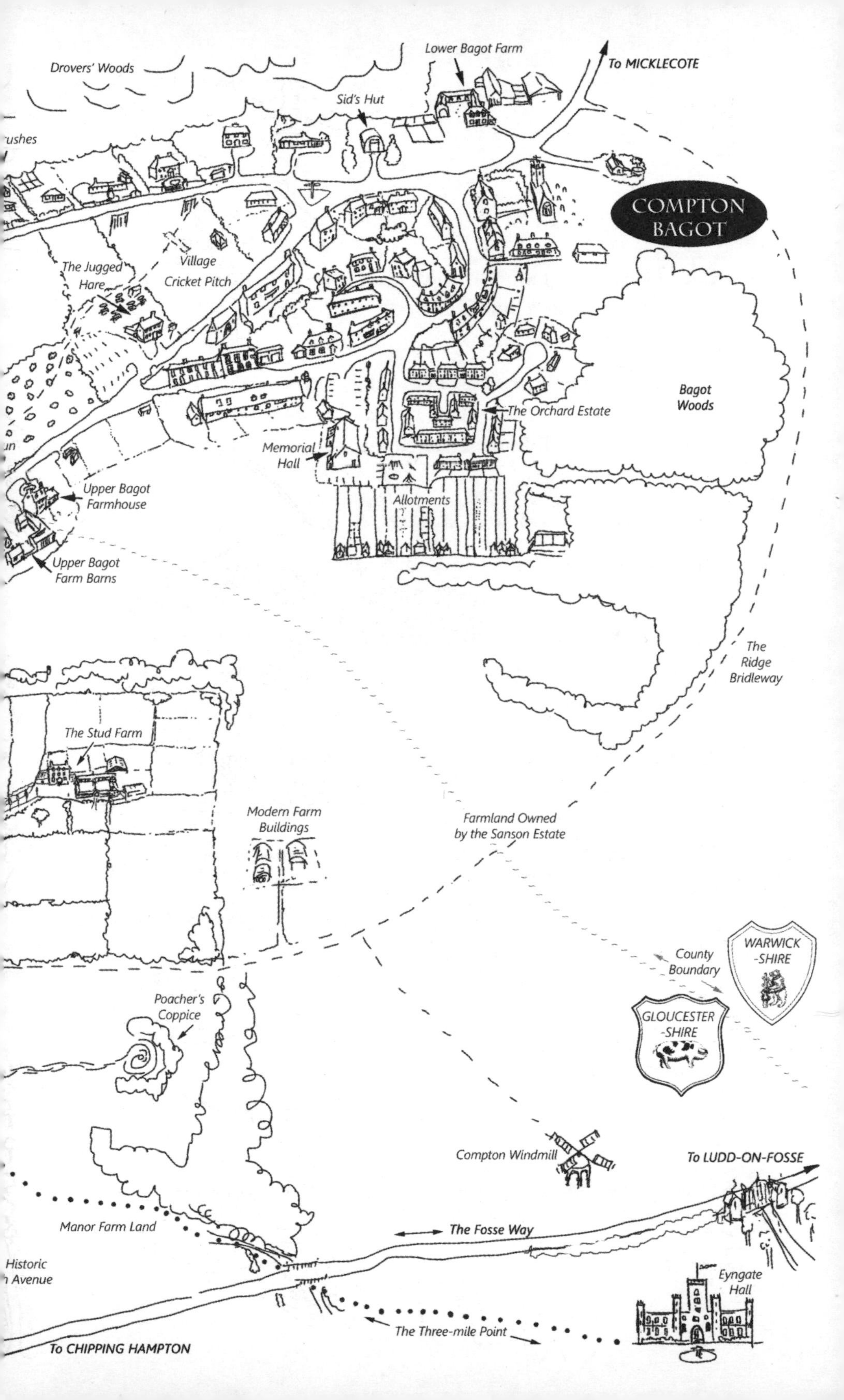

Drovers' Woods
Lower Bagot Farm
To MICKLECOTE
Sid's Hut
COMPTON BAGOT
The Jugged Hare
Village Cricket Pitch
Bagot Woods
The Orchard Estate
Memorial Hall
Upper Bagot Farmhouse
Allotments
Upper Bagot Farm Barns
The Ridge Bridleway
The Stud Farm
Modern Farm Buildings
Farmland Owned by the Sanson Estate
County Boundary
WARWICK -SHIRE
GLOUCESTER -SHIRE
Poacher's Coppice
Compton Windmill
To LUDD-ON-FOSSE
Manor Farm Land
The Fosse Way
Eyngate Hall
The Three-mile Point
To CHIPPING HAMPTON

DRAMATIS PERSONAE

Luca O'Brien: a globe-trotting rider and Irish charmer with a heart-breaking reputation, known throughout the equestrian world as the Horsemaker.

Veronica 'Ronnie Percy' Ledwell: chatelaine of Compton Magna Stud, a fast-riding blonde whose ill-fated marriage to handsome Johnny Ledwell ended with a swift exit in a lover's sports car.

Alice Petty: her estranged daughter, a bossy Pony Club stalwart.

Tim Ledwell: Ronnie's son, a debonair wine merchant with a complicated love life in South Africa.

Patricia 'Pax' Forsyth: their younger sister, the family peace-maker whose marriage to tough Scot Mack is a battlefield.

Kes: their five-year-old son.

Muir and Mairi: Mack's parents, granite-faced puritans.

Lizzie: Pax's friend from junior eventing days.

Lester: the stud's tight-lipped stallion man, dedicated to his horses, his routine and a quiet life.

Blair Robertson: craggy Australian three-day-event rider known as 'Mr Sit Tight'.

Verity Verney: his wife, a reclusive Wiltshire landowner.

Carly Turner: animal-loving young mum, adjusting to village life and job juggling.

Ash Turner: her ex-soldier husband whose family rule the Orchard Estate.

Ellis, Sienna and baby Jackson: their three children.

Country Lovers

Janine Turner: Ash's older sister, queen of cleaning and nail art empires.

'Social' Norm: the emphysemic Turner family patriarch, a settled Romany.

Ink and Hardcase: Ash's old school friends and drinking buddies.

Flynn the farrier: another childhood friend, the Bon Jovi of the anvil.

Skully: a wily operator and unofficial medicine man.

Auriol Bullock: battle-axe headmistress of Compton Magna Primary School.

Helen Beadle: divorce lawyer and sharp-minded chairman of the school's PTA.

Bridget Mazur: Belfast-born member of the village's Saddle Bags, a hipster young mum married to volatile Polish builder, Aleš.

Flavia and Zak: their two young children.

Petra Gunn: historical novelist and neglected wife, founder of the Saddle Bags whose gossipy hacks keep her sane.

Gill Walcote: straight-talking member of the Saddle Bags who runs a local veterinary practice with Kiwi husband.

Mo Dawkins: the jolliest of the Saddle Bags, a tirelessly hard-working farmer's daughter.

Bay Austen: dashing agricultural entrepreneur, hunt thruster and serial flirt.

Monique Austen: his steely Dutch wife.

Suzy 'Sous Vide' David: an on-trend schleb chef and new proprietor of The Jugged Hare.

Animals

Beck: an explosive warmblood stallion, once Germany's hotly-tipped new star, as stunning as he is screwed up.

Cruisoe: the stud's foundation stallion whose winning progeny inherit his lion heart.

Spirit: a wall-eyed colt with a big man attitude and a bright future.

The stud's broodmares: an opinionated bunch of matriarchs.

Craic: Bridge's nervouscited Connemara pony.

The Redhead: Petra's rabble-rousing mare.

Coll: her sidekick, a brutish greedy Shetland.

Lester's cob: as mannerly and well-turned-out as its rider.

Olive and Enid: Ronnie's sprightly little Lancashire Heelers, a squabbling mother and daughter.

Stubbs: Lester's unswervingly loyal fox terrier.

Knott: Pax's cautious deerhound puppy.

Pricey: a bull lurcher bred for coursing.

Laurence: a rescued fox cub.

Barista and Jam: the Mazurs' cats.

Prologue

2012

Fresh from the deep freeze, the vodka bottle opened with a satisfying crack of metal seal and a vaporous curl of condensing air.

If Luca had come to work in the Middle East with the intention of sobering up, he wasn't doing a very good job. In the eight weeks he'd been here, he'd barely seen the wagon amid all the chauffeur-driven luxury and million-dollar horseflesh, let alone got on it. All the westerners he'd got to know – and there were many on the showjumping circuit – drank like fish behind closed doors. A man with a habit and a broken heart could only swim against the tide for so long in a dry country.

The frozen vodka poured thick as oil, the toxic nectar which had made his host country among the wealthiest horse-loving nations.

'*Skål!*'

'*Sláinte.*' Luca tipped his glass against that of his companion, a pretty Swedish event rider called Signe who he knew vaguely from the European circuit, also attracted by the heat and money. Like him she was a work rider, hired to mentor a young member of the extended royal family – in her case their boss's oldest granddaughter, a teenage princess with her ambitions set on being the first Arab winner of Badminton. Today she'd told Signe that the world's biggest pop pin-up, a snake-hipped American youth with twenty million Twitter followers, had been booked by her indulgent grandfather to sing at her sixteenth birthday party, his fee big enough to buy a superyacht for every day of the week.

'It's so crazy, the money here!' Signe exclaimed, playing with Luca's hair. They had slept together the previous week – he'd been very drunk, full of determined charm, and only had partial recall – and now that seemed to give her permission to stroke him all the time, like a pet dog. He couldn't decide whether he liked it. 'If you could have any musician play at your birthday, who would it be?' she asked.

'Leonard Cohen.'

'Depressing duh?' She had a cute huck to her laugh. He missed a lover's laughter. 'Shouldn't you have an Irish singer?'

'That's like saying you have to choose Abba because you're Swedish.'

'I *would* choose Abba.'

'Good on ya.'

'Only they split up before I was born.' She pulled a sad face.

'Too bad.'

'I bet the boss here could pay enough for Abba to get back together.' She sighed, eyes sparkling.

Luca doubted that, his own battered heart heavy at being bought. Taking on this contract, he'd imagined that immersing himself in patriarchal, male-dominated isolation would be cathartic, a *marche ou crève* crusade, far from the woman he loved but could never have. Instead, living in a country so controlling it kept its mothers, wives and daughters behind veils and closed doors, felt like joining a cult of perdition. The expat women like Signe, with their deep tans, white teeth and tight breeches, were a predatory, self-protective tribe, equally bad for his health.

Blue-eyed, ruddy-faced and athletically seductive, Signe was like a lot of horse professionals Luca knew, who rode hard all day and viewed recreational sex as the after-party. They were cut from the same cloth, nomadic work riders who followed the competition seasons round all continents, love and commitment top-shelved. Probably in her early thirties, she was old enough to know what she was doing and was good company, with her melodic voice, upbeat attitude and ready laugh. The perfect no-strings fling was being dangled in front of his eyes, had he not been so tied up in knots, counting the days until he was free from his royal noose.

Keeping his head down and grafting harder than ever, Luca was determined to stick it out. He was here to help the most talented horse he'd ever worked with get to the Olympics – and he was being paid a lot to do it. His only obstacle was the lad who would be riding him there.

'Golden boy fall off again today?' asked Signe, unbuttoning his shirt as deftly as she plaited a mane.

'Yep. That's five days in a row. They're competing again tomorrow, so they are.'

'Your accent is such a turn-on.' Her kiss tasted of vodka. He liked that. Grey Goose, the kick pure as sea surf in this hotbed of fake rain, steel high rise and plastic trees.

Coming up for air and turning away to refill their glasses, he dwelt reluctantly on the memory of the boy at his last competition, unable to get the horse out of the collecting ring, dumped in the silica sand at the FEI official's feet. Luca had worked the stallion for an hour beforehand, privileged to be balanced on a fast-thinking powerhouse, the rocket detonating over practice fences, a warhorse ready to lay down his life to win, his trust total. But when the boy had taken over, his skills sketchy and his nerves tight, his faith was not in the horse or in Luca, but in a birthright and advantage beyond their reach. Luca couldn't have done any more to help, short of brainwashing the stallion to believe that the kid could ride.

'Mishaal needs to learn more feel.' He let the second vodka burn into him. 'Right now, he thinks showjumping is just about steering and staying on.' The thirteenth child of a high-ranking royal, the young prince was a go-cart driver with a Grand Prix ego.

'If anyone can teach feel, you can, yes?' Signe slapped her small palm against Luca's, fingers interlacing to draw his hand to her mouth, bonbon blue eyes gazing up into his. He sensed she knew exactly how cute she looked.

'As Mishaal keeps reminding me, his showjumping coach is a four-time gold-medallist from California.' He gently removed his forefinger from her mouth, its soft, wet suck too fast-track. 'I'm just here to warm up the saddle for him.'

'You're *way* more than that.' Signe was indignant. 'You are the Horsemaker. Does golden boy have any idea how lucky that makes him?'

Luca was grateful to her, cupping her face, tipping his twice-broken nose against her upturned one, then ducking away from another kiss to finish his vodka shot.

Luca O'Brien – known to all as the Horsemaker – had a well-renowned knack for settling difficult horses, making his home wherever he laid his Samshield helmet. It had kept him packing light and flying long haul for a decade, a literal globetrotter.

The horse he'd accompanied on this job was more difficult than most: Bechstein was named after the exquisite handmade concert piano, which was fitting given that it took a virtuoso to get a tune out of him. Highly strung, sensitive, headstrong and explosive as a Zeppelin, he was also off-the-scale talented. Produced by Gestüt Fuchs, one of Germany's top studs, the stallion had been hothoused to jump at the highest level, achieving his first Olympic qualification at just seven. With his distinctive dappled-grey coat like filigree silver, pure white mane and flamboyant style, he'd already earned a fan club in

Europe, a collective roar of outrage going up when he'd been sold six months ahead of the London Olympics for a record-breaking amount. Although his youth and volatility had kept him from selection at home, his qualification for the games was a golden ticket.

Somewhat astonishingly, nineteen-year-old Prince Mishaal had an Olympic qualification of his own, achieved on a horse so experienced he could have taken a toddler round a World Cup track blindfold, but also so pensionable the veterinary team could no longer keep him legally sound. To continue his son's Olympic dream, Mishaal's father had not only bought the most hotly tipped showjumper in the world, but also the only rider who could keep the horse sane enough for a rookie to compete. It wasn't a job Luca would normally have taken, however fat the cheque; if he hadn't been carrying a big open wound in his heart, he'd be spending winter somewhere with unspoilt young horses to break and snow on the ground as crisp and crunchy as the crystals in the vodka bottle. But somehow, head spinning from hung-up calls and hangovers, he'd let himself be talked into it, hoping six months of baking heat might finally hang his heart out to dry.

Instead, he found himself boiling over with exasperation, and knew getting drunk with pretty girls wasn't the solution. He wasn't sure how much longer he could rein in his temper with the reckless young prince, though certainly longer than Bechstein.

Having worked with the stallion since he was an unbacked three-year-old, Luca knew the key to riding him was lightness, those pianist's fingers *leggerissimamente* on the reins, seat-bones tucked beneath like coat-tails, the weight in the stirrups equally balanced between soft and sustain. But Prince Mishaal – who saw Luca as tuner and page-turner, hired to keep the sound sweet for the big concerto – only knew how to play 'Chopsticks' whilst bouncing on the piano stool like Elton John.

The young prince's relationship with Bechstein had been on a collision course from the start, Luca's role conflicted as he was forced to watch horse and rider in discord – one as arrogant, unbalanced and hard-handed as the other was instinctive and knife-edge brilliant.

'The two of them looked great to start with,' Signe pointed out. 'What's gone wrong?'

'The same thing as most relationships – they got to know one another better.'

It was true that the stallion's exuberance had thrilled the handsome young prince at first, throwing his new superhorse over fences fearlessly, accustomed to forgiving schoolmasters who made no more effort than necessary to clear them. It was kamikaze stuff, but they had won two Grand Prix classes in their first outings, the home press going wild as they predicted an Arab gold in London. Bechstein, who didn't know how to lose, had never had a fence down in his life, no matter that he was being galloped at them like a jouster's charger at an opponent's lance.

But the stallion had been confused and in shock from the start, relying on the Horsemaker to pick him up and put him right again each time. He was a strong, excitable horse and the more he was jabbed in the mouth and spurred in the sides, the hotter-headed he became.

Away from the public eye, the wheels were quick to come off. At home, he was soon refusing to stand still for the boy to mount, then napping, rearing, twisting himself inside out to be rid of the devil on his back. Every day, Luca had to ride him in longer to settle him. And with each passing day, Luca had seen the horse pick up more of his rider's aggressive tension. Jab, jab, jab went the reins, Bechstein now trussed in all manner of harsh tack like a BDSM gimp, his sides raw with spur marks, eyes blank with pain. As falls followed failure, Mishaal's fear and anger had escalated, humiliation curdling spitefully. The prince's new horse had gone from plaything to broken toy and it was inevitable that Bechstein would eventually throw a tantrum at a competition, as he had last week. The team line was that the horse had been stung by a bee just before his round, but Luca feared for next time. He didn't doubt there would be a next time.

Earlier that week the boy had been badly dragged in yet another fall in the school at home. Smashed against the kick boards so hard his ribs bruised, he'd cursed all manner of deadly oaths in Arabic, and Luca was certain he'd witnessed the 'click' moment when an animal makes man his foe: Bechstein, a horse who had only known the very best of handlers and most skilful of riders in his short life, hated the prince.

In training today, the boy had been unable to get him to jump a single fence.

'He's competing the stallion again tomorrow.' Luca rubbed his face tiredly. 'His father's booked a hospitality tent.'

'You serious?'

'He's hosting lunch for eighty. My arse is for the firing squad if the horse kicks off.'

'No shit!'

'If only the boy listened. He's got enough talent. He's just a total brat.'

'He's not so bad,' Signe volunteered. 'Mishaal is always nice to me; he has good manners and knows lots about Sweden. He has a crush, I think.' She eyed him for reaction.

'Probably wants to make you his cougar Queen Noor.'

She looked rather taken with the idea. 'I could have a string of four-star eventers.'

'You'd have to share golden boy with his other wives.'

'As long as I didn't have to share the horses, that's cool by me.' That hucking laugh.

This time, Luca had no desire to share it.

'His father will buy him another horse, maybe?' Signe seemed to think the answer to everything lay in the patriarch's bottomless pockets. 'You can ask him to. You are his pet.'

'Since when did you do what your pet told you?' Luca felt powerless, his advice ignored, royal pride intractable in both father and son; those early wins had been taken as proof that the millions spent were justified. Luca must work the horse better, that's all. Whilst the father – a jovial, Hibernophile racing fanatic – had favourited the Irish rider from day one, the message was clear: you will get this partnership to the Olympics, Horsemaker. Luca was a courtier. His smiling, fiddle-playing Irish charm was mandatory; having an opinion was not. They were all courtiers, the legion of brash horsey westerners with their loose morals and fast jump-offs.

Signe's lips were on his right ear now, her little tongue working it like an oyster shell. His stomach curled, torn between pleasure and unease.

'It was fun last time, hey?' she purred into his ear, but instead of finding it arousing, he just felt worse that he couldn't remember. They'd talked and laughed more last time, surely? Drunk more, certainly.

He tried not to let his mind drift back to that angry little figure picking himself out of the sand last week, whip arm raised to bring it down on the horse, enraged when Luca had stepped forward to snatch it away with a firm 'no'.

They were in Signe's staff apartment, which was neater and sweeter-smelling than his; she'd put on music he didn't recognise, a clubby trance thing that she got up to dance a few steps to.

'Ørjan Nilsen featuring Neev Kennedy, "Anywhere But Here",' she told him, hands on her head, hips gyrating. 'She's Irish too.'

'No kidding.'

He looked around the room. The staff apartments were all identical, white sarcophagus cells with brightly polished floors and windows too high to look through. No bigger than a single garage, cupboard doors mirrored to give the impression of space, the icy cold air conditioning made it feel more like living in an igloo than an accommodation block in a scorching equestrian oasis. Signe had personalised hers with a framed photograph of her ruddy-faced blonde family, a Swedish flag throw over the sofa back, the glacially white shelves jewelled with colourful boxes and bottles bought at the souk. Her love of shopping was a running joke on the yard, the tax-free earnings that others saved up going through her fingers like sand.

Signe sat back down astride him. He rolled her off, deflective smile at the ready. 'Let's have another vodka.'

'Have as many as you like, *sötnos*.' She picked up the bottle, unruffled. 'I have more in the freezer: Beluga Noble.'

'Only the best black markets for you.'

She unscrewed the lid with a wink.

'Don't you ever find this place soulless?' he asked her.

'Not any more. After four or five months, you stop noticing the hypocrisy: that the Indians are bussed in from camps to work like slaves, that the ecology is totally fucked and the malls are full of zombies with credit cards buying pret-a-porter Stella McCartney like it's an H&M sale. This place buys your skill and sells your soul. And they get the *best* horses.' She whistled. 'They just keep arriving like drugs. Watching you on that stallion is something else, Mr Horsemaker. You make him look like Pegasus.'

'He's better.'

She handed him a brimming shot glass, blue eyes gleaming.

'He flies without wings.' He drank the vodka in one.

While it burned his lips and throat, he saw all too clearly through his own evasion. Tonight, he needed sleep, not drunken sex he wouldn't remember. He couldn't make the boy ride any better, but if he put his mind to it, perhaps he could stop the horse self-destructing.

He cast Signe an apologetic smile. 'I'm going back to crash out.'

'Stay and talk just a little longer, hey.' With a mischievous smile, she refilled his glass so fast it overflowed.

He stared at it, wishing he had the willpower to push it away. 'Just one more then.'

She was playing with his collar now, head tilted prettily. 'What are you, Luca, twenty-eight, thirty?'

'Thereabouts.'

'Good-looking man like you must have broken a lot of hearts.'

He smiled, shaking his head. She had a lovely, lively face, and he was reminded again of somebody he'd once known; her eyes had the same roundness and sparkle, the way they drank him in with that live-for-the-moment vivid blue. But he wasn't about to share his shadowed soul. Looking away, he caught his own reflection staring back at him from one of the mirrored doors, a clean-cut stranger. Luca's royal employers, who liked their staff immaculately presented, sent in a barber every fortnight to keep the team's hair trimmed. He looked as if he was in the army, his shorn hair bleached white by the sun.

He turned as he heard shot glasses being refilled yet again. 'I've had enough.'

'Nonsense. I want you to tell me everything, mysterious Mr Horsemaker.' Handing him one, Signe wriggled closer. She'd changed the music streaming to something bluesier, a saxophone ripping through some bass notes. 'Ever fallen in love with someone you shouldn't?'

'Buzzcocks, 1978,' he deflected.

'I've done it plenty,' she sighed, lifting her shot and squinting into its clear depths, quite drunk now. 'It's like falling off a horse, they say – do it seven times and you can call yourself a pro.'

'And what number are you up to?' he humoured her.

She held up a Victory V with the hand holding the glass, then lifted the other to add five more fingers. 'You're looking at a pro. You?'

Just one woman. Not mine to keep. 'Signe, I'm not looking for any sort of relationship right now. I'm only just out of something that did my head in, you know?' Leaving the final shot untouched, Luca planted a modest kiss on her cheek. 'I gotta go.'

'Hey, you're safe.' She caught hold of his shirt collar. 'I'm not in the market for number eight. Let's change the subject, okay?' She played with the lapel. 'Stay a while.' She drew him closer. 'We'll just fuck, no more talking.'

'Another time.'

She looked crestfallen when he stood up, her face unguarded for once. 'I need company tonight.'

Luca kept his guilt in check. It could be a lonely life for a gypsy in Konig boots, trick riders living off their wits. But the cardinal rule of the job was that horses always came first. He reached back down to extract his phone and keys from the coffee table.

She was too quick for him, grabbing them and dancing off behind the big carved wooden screen that divided the room from the sleeping area. 'You'll need to do better than that!'

'Signe, this isn't funny.'

'At least stay for a blow job.' She headed into the bathroom with another husky laugh. 'You know I'm good!'

Luca glanced at his watch impatiently. It was past midnight. He wanted to look in on the stallion. The stable hand on nightshift was his least favourite, a surly Bangladeshi, always sloping off for a cigarette when he wasn't napping in the office with the CCTV screens. He didn't check the horses often enough. Bechstein, who box-walked endlessly, and had to have automatic drinkers turned off because they freaked him out, would almost certainly need his water bucket topped up.

He could hear Signe peeing, the door open out of sight as she carried on talking. 'You're a boring old man, Luca,' she shouted brightly. 'You promised me you'd let me play your fiddle!'

Had he drunkenly offered to teach her a jig last time, he wondered as he pulled on his trainers by the door, or was that a sexual innuendo?

When Signe reappeared around the screen, she was naked, his keys in one hand, phone in the other. 'Ready to fiddle?'

Innuendo, then. Luca eyed her warily. Hair tousled and lips glossed, she was propping one arm up on the wall and striking a *Playboy* pose. She had a chandelier tattoo beneath her breasts. With a flash of clarity, he remembered burying his forehead drunkenly into it, calling her by somebody else's name.

His groin – no great judge of one-liners, but a rapid response unit to full frontal – was stirring obligingly, and he forced himself to think about the boy spitting out sand, the undiluted fury in his face. Mishaal would never bear the shame of such dishonour if his father was there to witness it with eighty close friends and business allies. Luca had to ensure it didn't happen by getting up at dawn tomorrow to work the horse in. 'Signe, I really can't stay.'

'Of course you can.' She weaved towards him, chandelier swinging as her hips swayed exaggeratedly, holding his keys and phone behind her back now.

'Put some clothes on, please.' He reached round her to take them, finding himself trapped in an octopus tangle of naked Signe clinch. 'Seriously, I'm away to my bed.'

'Away to mine instead,' she said, mocking his accent breathily, arms curling around him.

If it was difficult to take one's leave with a small, naked and remarkably strong Swedish woman grappling to undo one's fly buttons, it was harder still with door double-locked.

'How do I undo this fucking thing?'

Signe was on his belt buckle now, kissing his chest where his shirt was still open from all her unbuttoning earlier.

'For the love of God, Signe, will you get off me! What's got into you?'

She backed off reluctantly, holding her hands up. 'Okay! So you don't want sex?'

'You're beautiful and you're fun, but no. Not right now.'

She looked suddenly vulnerable, crossing her arms over her

breasts. 'Just stay and sleep here tonight, will you? No sex, I promise.'

Again, Luca sought to shrug off the yoke of obligation from his shoulders. 'Sure, you'll be fine. Nobody's going to get in past this thing, if that's what you're worried about.' He spun the lock again. 'Will you let me out? I have to check on Bechstein.'

'Why?' she demanded, anxious white rims round the blue eyes. 'The nightman's there.'

'I don't trust him.'

'The dogs will be loose.'

'Sure, they don't bother me. C'mon, Signe, stop mucking about.'

Looking even more agitated, she reversed to the sofa to wrap herself in the Swedish flag. 'I think it's best you stay here, Luca, for your own sake.'

This was starting to get seriously weird. Guessing that she'd double-locked the door, Luca started searching for her keys. In a large glass bowl beside him, amongst loose change, hairclips and lanyarded competition passes, was a man's watch, a chunky Patek Phillipe, its three-dial face familiar. He'd stared it in its face at wither height more than once, the crocodile strap wrapped around the sinewy wrist of a petulant young horseman born to the sort of outrageous privilege that meant his timepieces were worth more than Irish country houses set amid rolling acres, and yet could be casually left forgotten on a washbasin rim or in a member of staff's flat.

Suspicion gripped him, chaotic as smoke at first. Was it stolen? A bribe? Surely not something left behind by a lover? Signe might eat cavalier young riders for *frokost*, but Mishaal was barely legal.

'What is going on, Signe?' The expensive imported vodka, the dedicated seduction, the lock-in. It all added up. 'What's Mishaal up to?'

'I don't know what you're talking about.' She kept her head turned away. She had another tattoo at the top of her spine, an intricately lacy dreamcatcher. Luca would have given anything to wake up right now and find this was all a nightmare.

'He's doing something to the horse, isn't he? To Bechstein?'

She let out a guilty whimper, covering her mouth with her hand.

'Just fucking tell me! What's Mishaal up to?'

'I'm supposed to keep you busy,' she whispered. 'I think he's paid the nightman to dope him. That's all I know.'

He turned and sprinted towards the fire escape. For a moment a Swedish flag blocked his way and Signe begged him to stay, pleading that she would be fired.

'It's only a bit of dope!' she protested, believing it.

But Luca had seen the boy's humiliation and anger close up, how incensed he was that the horse refused to jump for him. He was a vindictive character whose cruelty to his sisters, staff and horses Luca had witnessed more than once. To spare his own dishonour, Mishaal would make sure Bechstein could jump for no man.

He pushed Signe aside and clambered out onto the fire escape at the back of the staff accommodation, a narrow first-floor walkway that connected all the apartments, overshadowed by the big American barn housing the most valuable competition horses in state-of-the-art, temperature-controlled luxury.

As he sprinted along towards the ladder, Luca could hear an eerie, feral sound coming from inside the building. It was something he'd heard only a few times, always a precursor to tragedy. A horse screaming, terrified and in pain.

The stallion was fighting for his life.

PART ONE

1

It was New Year's Eve, and the Saddle Bags were hacking around the village of Compton Bagot. Bright winter sunshine had burned off the early frost, the quartet of long shadows mounted on giant black silhouette horses far slimmer than the four women felt.

Bridge Mazur's shadow – a head shorter and a lot hairier than the others thanks to her helmet bobble and fake fur jacket – was bouncing around a lot as her grey Connemara pony Craic took exception to the flashing icicle lights around the eaves of the Old Post Office.

'I swear I'm still sweating cream liqueur,' Petra complained beside her.

'I've got a muffin top – and bottom,' panted Mo from behind.

'Let's step this up, shall we?' Front rider Gill led them into a vigorous rising trot. 'There's half a stone of cheese, assorted nuts and Shiraz on each of these thighs.'

'I raise you two loosened belt notches in honour of *jakbłecznik* and *makowiec*,' Bridge said as Craic bunny-hopped forwards, vying to be in front.

'Are those more of Aleš's cousins?' Petra's unruly chestnut mare charged past them all.

'Polish cakes,' she explained, clinging onto the reins. 'Make my old ma's fifteens look like diet food. I'm amazed Ryanair didn't charged me excess baggage on these Michelins.' She patted her belly, ignoring the crabby looks from her fellow riders who knew she was the only one amongst them whose gym membership card got swiped regularly.

Yet for all her air of sharp hipster cool, Bridge liked sweet things: Haribos, mojitos, Gil Elvgren illustrations, sticky desserts and unicorns. Her husband Aleš – typically Polish, romantic and soppily sentimental – was very sweet when he wasn't being oafish or sulky, their little Cotswold cottage with beams so low he bumped his head every day was sweet, their chubby-wristed toddler Flavia and curly-haired tot Zak were both sweet, and Bridge's dappled grey pony was sugar-spun perfection. Wise enough to see that amongst her village riding friends, her comparative youth and inexperience was also sweet, Bridge was nonetheless a competitive soul who found failure a bitter pill to swallow.

Bridge had flown home two days earlier than planned, summoned back from Krakow to the Cotswolds by an eleventh-hour job interview. Abandoning Aleš and the children to see in Nowego Roku without her, she'd been almost as excited by the prospect of a rare chance to be Zen in their cluttered little cottage – and to ride – as in her bid to return to work after her long baby sabbatical. As it turned out, the attempt at a career reboot was a waste of dry cleaning. Running the business administration side of a chain of Cotswold gastro pubs owned by a self-absorbed daytime telly star was always going to be a tall order for a straight-talking Belfast woman like Bridge. She didn't suffer fools, especially matcha and redbean ones topped with black sesame Yatsuhashi.

'How did the interview go?' Mo asked eagerly, red-faced from the effort of kicking her coloured cob along to keep up with the others. 'Is the Sous Vide as mad as they say?'

'Madder,' Bridge grumbled, thinking back to the breathless half hour spent following the glow of Suzy David's famously bleached white crew cut and perpetually animated iPad around the village pub. 'We could have done the whole thing on Skype. She needs common sense, not an HR consultant. D'you know she's dropping the "Jugged" from "Hare" because she thinks it has unfortunate beer and boob connotations? I said, "Queen, it's a country pub. Boozing and tit-ogling are still legal blood sports round here."'

'You didn't!'

Utterly professional in work mode, Bridge had waited to say it into her hall mirror afterwards, but she winked now, satisfied it was God's truth. She had a reputation to protect; her three riding friends delighted in being shocked by their Belfast black sheep. Youngest and most urban of the four, and with the shortest and hottest marriage, Bridge's chippy streak meant she took on the plums in her fellow riders' mouths with her pierced tongue. She considered it her duty to be the naughty kid at the back of the middle class. Historical novelist Petra, Yorkshire-born and determinedly left wing, might fancy herself the arty boho outsider, but she had a barrister husband, independently educated children and a working gun dog. Farmer's daughter Mo – perpetually broke, always dealing with a family crisis and juggling three jobs – ate home-reared guinea fowl and hunted twice a week. And Gill, grey-haired, gung-ho equine vet, mother of three and Laura Ashley devotee, was an original Sloane Ranger, if endearingly supportive. They were all diamonds, this mounted big-sisterhood, whose kindness and honesty had seen Bridge through giddying ups and downs during her first year in the village, their endless good humour and wise counsel keeping her sane, their poshness a running joke to a dock-worker's daughter from Ardoyne.

It riled rebel-hearted Bridge that her family now accused *her* of being the snob, especially sister Bernie, who claimed this was because they were born either side of midnight on the twenty-first of March, meaning she, as the older twin, was a generous, broad-minded Pisces while Bridge was a tough, ambitious Aries. 'That's also why you argue with everyone,' Bernie had insisted when they'd last spoken across whatever time zone divided them, 'it's star-crossed.'

Bridge – who held no truck with astrology – thought she argued with everyone because she was just plain cross. There nothing starry about Bridge Mazur.

'Sous Vide can stuff her fecking job.' She thrust her chin up, still smarting from the rejection. She'd never dream of telling the Bags that the cook had accused her of being out of touch, finding every hole in her CV and tripping her up on her data protection know-how.

'Good for you!' Gill rallied.

'She doesn't deserve me.' Bridge summoned a big smile to show the others she wasn't bothered, turning to look at the pretty old limestone inn as they trotted past it. The painted hoarding boasted a grand reopening of 'Suzy David's The Hare at Compton' on Burns Night. 'Which is a pain in the arse because it's fecking well-paid and practically next door.'

'Utter hell to work for, I should imagine,' Gill reassured her as they slowed back to walk at the junction. 'They said that poor little Russian she danced with on *Strictly* had to go into therapy afterwards.'

'I feel much the same after taking to the dance floor to "Come on Eileen" with my husband,' Petra pointed out. 'And Charlie can't rustle up a seared plantain black rice risotto afterwards.'

'Is it going to be all veggie food, then?' Mo read the hoarding in alarm.

'Vegan.' Gill shuddered. 'Her raw food fine-dining restaurants are all the rage: Cirencester, Cheltenham and Chippy have one. The Bardswolds are the last preserved limestone outpost south of Birmingham. *Sous Vide vient ici. Allumez les feux, mes copains*!'

'Is that one of her dishes?' Mo sniffed.

'It's all smoke and mirror glazes.' Petra winked at Bridge.

'Gill's saying light the fires in French, queen,' she translated for Mo's benefit.

Of all the corners of the Cotswolds, the Fosse Hills were the one restaurateurs always found hardest to crack. Known as the Bardswolds for its proximity to Shakespeare's Stratford-upon-Avon, its wealthy home crowd was less fashion-led and London-centric than the other wolds, strong-willed Midlanders and old money, taste buds still craving comfort food and hearty British puddings. Eating remained a noisy, sociable recreation around here, not an on-trend artform.

'When Suzy asked me if I preferred kimchi to kefir, I thought she was talking about Greek fecking islands,' Bridge admitted. 'Not my thing, all that sour grub. And I can't imagine any locals popping in for wood-aged single-hop organic craft beer at a tenner a pop, can you?'

'What's the use of all that trendy nonsense round here?' chuckled Mo. 'It'll go out of fashion before the blackthorn loses its blossom. We'll get the old Jug back by the time the spring lambs are ready to roast, ladies.'

'I plan to have thighs like a whippet and a washboard stomach by then,' Gill said through gritted teeth.

'Eat at the village pub and you will!' Mo's chuckle turned into a big guffaw.

Bridge – who was prone to grand pronouncements – had worked her way up to a New Year's Eve one as, standing in her stirrups, she declared, 'Ladies, if I don't have meaningful employment by the time that fecking pub opens, I'm setting up a kebab van opposite. You heard it here first.'

It was only when her three companions whooped in delight, taking turns to high five her, that it occurred to Bridge they might just hold her to the wager. Her Saddle Bags honour was at stake. She had to get a job, and fast.

*

'Blast the blasted thing!' Ronnie waved her phone around, failing to get the thinnest wedge of a signal. She'd tried all the usual sweet spots – the top coppice, the watchtower over the furthest stable-yard arch and the gate by the walled garden – and now she'd even come up to the dust-festooned attic in the hope it might have reception, but there was nothing. Pulling her reading glasses from crown to nose, she frowned at the screen.

Her reply to Blair's text was still there with a red unsent cross beside it: *Happy New Year*. A bland, innocent-looking greeting to an outsider, but loaded with meaning for two on-off lovers, one of them married, the other under disapproving family scrutiny, their five-year love affair date-stamped with just such messages.

When Off, no phone calls was the unspoken rule. Calling was pressing the red button. They'd last spoken just days ago, but he'd believed that she was leaving the country then. Now Ronnie's plans had changed, the trip switch on their volatile relationship had been reset. Blair's text message was testing the circuit. Picked up in a momentary patch of phone signal, it had made her morning. Now she couldn't reply in kind.

Damn this rural go slow. Her late father's refusal to allow a cellular mast on his land must have scuppered many a love affair in mobile-blackspot Compton Magna. With just one business landline and no Internet – also a legacy from the intransigent Captain Percy – the village's stud was still in the communication dark ages. Taking no notice of stallion-man Lester's proclamations that the world wide web was full of Russian spies, Ronnie had ordered the cheapest broadband deal available weeks ago. Multiple cancelled engineers' visits later, the cabinet, telegraph pole and copper wire in the lane had all been pronounced inadequate, another engineer booked for February. How could anyone hope to sell horses with no mobile signal or Internet, she wanted to wail, let alone commit adultery?

Her son-in-law, a bullish property developer, had spent

much of last week's Boxing Day family get-together trying to persuade Ronnie to hire the 'smart-home nerd' who connected up the luxurious houses he and Pax renovated, installing all sorts of fibre-optic wizardry so that they were practically supercomputers with a roof. It sounded ridiculously expensive, and Ronnie could tell from Pax's fixed-on-fingernails glare that she didn't agree with the idea.

Her youngest daughter had looked thin and drawn that day, drinking too much and saying little. Although Pax smoothly denied anything was wrong, Ronnie read something into the fact she wasn't joining her in-laws in Scotland this New Year, insisting she could usefully cover the yard while her mother visited old friends, adding candidly, 'It's easier being there when you're not around.' Their relationship was butterfly-wing fragile, upsetting it likely to ripple out through the family. Of Ronnie's children, all trustees of the stud with her, only Pax supported keeping the business running; the other two wanted it sold off. The trio judged her harshly for past mistakes, and rightly so Ronnie felt. She had a lot to prove.

It was probably a good reason for keeping her nose clean with Blair. None of her children approved of their close friendship, even though the only reason the stud could pay its feed bill this winter was because he'd done her a favour and bought a lorry full of unbroken four-year-olds in the autumn. The reason he could afford to do that, they'd no doubt point out, was because he was married to a woman rich enough to pay.

Blair Robertson, legendary Australian rider, had been a close friend of Ronnie's for over three decades, one of the loyal brigade to stand by her when she'd fled her marriage, just as she had defended him in the nineties when he'd shocked the eventing world by running off with the wife of one of its greatest aristocratic patrons, a ravishing countess twenty years his senior. It had taken 'Mr Sit Tight' a great many hard-won championships, team medals and feats of bravery to reclaim his reputation as the daring darling of the sport, as famously hot-headed with rivals as he was cool-headed with his horses. By then, Ronnie had become a near neighbour of the Robertsons' big yard in Wiltshire, one of the few to know the tragic truth behind the great love story: Verity's ill health had stolen her away from Blair just a few years after their marriage, early onset Alzheimer's gradually depriving her of almost all memory of him. He cared for her stoically, helped by a small team at home, but he'd long since lost the woman he'd risked everything to love. His affair with Ronnie, born of friendship and forged by intense physical attraction, had knocked them both for six. Passionate, mutually adoring, it was soul-deep in affection and allegiance, but it would devastate Verity's family and friends if they ever found out about it.

Conscience pricked, Ronnie tapped her phone against her chin. Let her reply wait until she drove out of the blackspot. Dangerous enough to be celebrating New Year in their former stomping ground, partying just a few fields from Blair's farm. Not that their paths would cross; Blair was an honourable absentee from the old Wiltshire set these days, his once-sociable wife no longer able to remember who her neighbours were.

'Blast it!' She stalked to one of the little windows, slapping the phone down on the sill, unable to fool herself. They both had their fingers hovering over the red button, she and Blair: Ronnie deliberately tempting fate by agreeing to the Wiltshire invitation, his message sent to test her reaction time. Without a laggy signal, it would have been less than a minute.

He knew how she ticked. Tough, no-nonsense Ronnie, serial survivor, was struggling to close the lid on this one, no matter how explosive and impossible the match. They'd flirted through nearly four decades of friendship before becoming lovers. Blair's obstinate, bloody-minded possessiveness held no surprises. And whether fifteen or fifty-something, her Percy pride hadn't changed either – nothing short of tragedy would compel her to pick up the phone and call him. That old-fashioned purring landline. It had once rung non-stop: clients, villagers, friends, hunt members, salesmen, boyfriends. Silent more days than not, now. They didn't even get ambulance chasers or PPI cold calls. And nobody had rung enquiring about putting a mare to a Percy stallion or buying a youngster in months.

She wiped condensation off one of the windowpanes with a finger, its glass a rain-stained sepia from lack of cleaning. These attic rooms offered the best view across two beautiful hidden Cotswolds valleys: the Comptons from the other side, Eynhope Park from this, once the stately seat of far grander Percy ancestors. The stud's undulating, wood-fringed land in the foreground always lifted her spirits, even at its monochrome, muddy winter worst, and with hundreds of its acres long since sold off by her father. A lion's mane of winter wheat now surrounded the remaining fields and paddocks, but the Percy pride still roared at its heart.

Convinced the stud's revival would bring her family closer together, Ronnie refused to be daunted by the hard work needed to make it profitable by the trustees' deadline. She just had to attract owners, generate stud fees and sell horses fast. Horse-trading was in her blood.

Behind her, Ronnie's two small dogs were rooting round the skirting boards on the hunt for mice, sneezing at the dust. Tough, low-slung black and tans – mother and daughter Lancashire Heelers – their tails gyrated at a fresh scent.

'Catch 'em, girls,' she urged. 'Got to make this place habitable.' She glanced round the room, part of a long-neglected staff flat. Blast the housekeeper for going AWOL just when they needed her most, a handwritten note delivered last week to say she was fed up working for nothing.

Well, she couldn't afford to buy Pip back when she had a new work rider to pay.

Hired before she'd changed her mind about staying on, Luca O'Brien was an added expense Ronnie knew she must justify. Having poached him from a big Canadian showjumping yard, she'd vetoed both daughters' demands to withdraw the job offer at the last minute. No rider could make a horse look as good as Luca; added to which he wasn't afraid to muck in and get his hands dirty, could manage a yard, and never stopped smiling. Lester had his teeth gritted too tightly in disapproval to muster much joy these days.

She watched the small, bowed figure in the distance, throwing open the gate to the winter turn-out then limping back to the broad-span barn to let out a stampede of yak-like woolly beasts, kicking and squealing as they charged into the field to shake off the straw, playfight and roll. Somewhere beneath all the matted hair and mud were some decent youngsters, she hoped. And whinnying furiously from his stallion box in the yard, trumpeting his superiority, her beautiful grey powerhouse would wow fellow breeders just as soon as she figured out how to defuse the bomb in his head.

Her phone face lit up on the windowsill, notifications pinging. 'At last!'

Happy New Year had a green tick beside it now. A moment later, *How are you keeping?* appeared in a bubble below it, followed by, *O'Brien there yet?* The prospect of Ronnie sharing close quarters with a cavalier young globetrotter had irritated Blair from the start. So that's why he was marking his territory.

About to reply with a cool 'not yet' – flying out of Ontario today, Luca had a forty-eight-hour Dublin stop-off to see family – Ronnie realised the signal was lost again. Leave it there, she told herself firmly, pocketing her phone. He'll get the message.

Having worked off more Christmas pounds cantering around the set-aside field beside the cricket pitch, Bridge felt her spirits rallying as the Bags started discussing New Year's Resolutions.

'Being a feck-off high flyer again by Easter,' she told them.

'Mine's to meet my deadline for once,' Petra vowed.

'I want a new SMC,' sighed Mo. 'Jed Turner's lost his sparkle since the conviction.'

The SMC – or Safe Married Crush – was a Saddle Bag rite of passage, the mainstay of the frustrated Cotswold wife, a fairy-tale fantasy about somebody out of reach, conveniently close to home.

'Our local member has lost his too,' muttered Gill whose comedy crush on the Fosse Vale MP – which all the Bags knew was a smokescreen for her far more heartfelt crush on local weekending theatre director, Kit Donne – had been flushed out further by inappropriate behaviour rumours on social media involving a Business Enterprise drinks party, an Arab strap and a junior secretary called Justin.

'Let's all nominate new ones!' Petra's eyes lit up.

'Bagsy me the hunky husband from Well Cottage.' Bridge, more competitive than carnal, laid her claim before Petra could. She'd never really got the point of the SMC, but she enjoyed beating the others to a new object of desire.

'Say who?' Mo loved fresh blood.

Bridge exchanged a glance with Petra, WhatsApp emojis already hot-swapped on the subject. 'They're renting the holiday let while Aleš builds them a house on the Broadbourne Road.'

'Not that modern monstrosity we all objected to?' Gill looked disapproving. 'Replacing old Mr Noakes's bungalow?'

'It's carbon-neutral, stripped-back modern living,' Bridge insisted. The award-winning eco architect, who granted Aleš a lot of tenders, helped pay their mortgage, even if his houses all looked like shoeboxes.

'Bet they're bloody vegans,' Mo shuddered.

'Excellent SMC choice, Bridge,' Petra clicked approvingly. 'Think young Mel Gibson, ladies.'

'Ew!' Bridge recoiled. 'Put me off him, why don't you?'

'*Young*. *Mad Max* era but without the mullet. Heartbreakingly sexy eyes. Builds bespoke aircraft.'

'How d'you know that?' she asked jealously.

'We met them at Rowles's drinks party.'

Bridge scowled. Petra somehow always managed to be Prima Bag: hers was the biggest house and family (albeit with a barely-there marriage); she was a social butterfly who walked dogs with aristocratic stud owner, Ronnie Percy, and flirted with the local farming heartthrob (even if Petra wanted to sack Bay Austen as her SMC, he remained the sexiest man in the village); she was excitingly careered up (even if she grumbled that her books were no longer stocked in Tesco), and she looked like Nigella, albeit in her curvier days. Now she'd staked out the Well Cottage hunk.

'If he's into planes, then he's more Harrison Ford than Mel,' Gill suggested eagerly.

'Harrison's always been crumbly,' Petra countered. 'Well, Cottage Man is *not* crumbly.'

'Mel's a Wensleydale of crumbliness,' insisted Mo. 'Bridge deserves better.'

Bridge tuned out of the argument. Petra was welcome to Well Cottage Man. It was all just for show, and she was happy enough to stay loyal to her original SMC and next-door neighbour, Flynn, a Lothario farrier with the flirtiest eyes in the Bardswolds, the only man in Back Lane brave enough to park in the space Aleš Mazur liked to leave his van.

Her thoughts returned to her career, a driving force in her life, currently SORNed.

Bridge's ascent into office management was a subject upon which she'd always been jokingly sardonic, her vocation accidental. It was a far cry from the creative dreams she and Bernie had shared when first leaving Belfast to take up their places at the London College of Fashion, one set on being the next Orla Kiely, the other a cutting-edge make-up artist. Being a material girl had always been an important part of Bridge's fabric, the office temping jobs she'd taken on to pay her way through her textile degree proving so profitable, it was hard to give up the money after graduating. Whereas laidback Bernie had been happy to drift artfully from party to club to unpaid work experience, wearing the longest false eyelashes in Marylebone in search of a break as a make-up artist, Bridge had always put graft before craft. And when both girls wanted to stay on in London after graduating, it was Bridge's 'straight' job that earned their way. Her court shoe on the property ladder had come long before her peers'; promotions followed, her ever-fattening salary funding parties, exotic holidays, a flashy car, designer clothes. Looking back now, Bridge wished she'd stopped to enjoy the view more often.

'My Barry is definitely Emmental.' The Bags were now comparing husbands to cheeses, Mo's red-faced husband typecast in wax. 'Mild and nutty.'

'Charlie's Stilton – blue-veined and at his best after dinner,' Petra said loyally. 'What about Paul, Gill?'

'Dairylea slice,' said Gill dismissively.

They all looked at Bridge, expecting her to come up with an unpronounceable Polish mountain cheese with a complicated flavour, as deep and smoky as her giant of a husband.

'Cheddar,' she said firmly. 'Delicious, popular and versatile.'

The pragmatic, no-nonsense attitude that had propelled Bridge into management in her early twenties had also lent her a common-sense romantic outlook. By twenty-five, reluctant to follow her alter-ego twin into dating a series of heartbreaking deviants, Bridge had a strict wish list: he had to be tall, practical, funny and hard-working, like to get drunk, and shag well. Upgrading from Kilburn flat to Harlesden townhouse, she'd hired the sexiest Polish builder in town to convert her loft, soon ticking all the boxes before earning herself another top-floor promotion, this time from girlfriend to wife.

Five years later she was a stay-at-home mother of two, riding around the Home Counties with three middle-aged women, wondering who had hijacked her life. She'd gone from high flying to autopilot. She had to figure out how to take back the controls.

If her fellow Bags could all juggle career, families and horses, Bridge knew she had no excuse, no matter that the climb back up the career ladder was far harder with a child on both hips. It had been straightforward after Flavia was born three years ago, maternity leave guaranteeing her return to the personnel department of a blue-chip logistics company. But she'd taken voluntary redundancy when they'd moved to the Cotswolds so that Aleš could go into partnership with his brother, and then she'd fallen pregnant again.

Aleš was very vocal in his belief that his wife had no need to work; his business was doing well enough for money not to be a worry, and he preferred Bridge at home with the kids, doing his bookkeeping for nothing, making more babies soon if he had his way. But Bridge craved a life beyond motherhood.

Her greatest freedom already came at a cost that was holding her to ransom: Aleš resented the money that went on Craic. It didn't help that she had never discussed horses with her husband before buying one on their credit card. Craic had been the ultimate impulse buy. They'd just moved into the village, the need for a new sofa great. Like Jack and the Beanstalk, she'd gone to market focussed on cowhide, and got distracted on the way. While her head was saying vintage leather button-back chesterfield, the sight of a poster for a Horse and Pony Sale at the local auction room made her heart take over. A day later, Bridge was the owner of an unbroken Connemara pony, fresh off the boat from Ireland. For a young mum who'd had a handful of riding lessons, it was undoubtedly a crazy thing to do, but Bridge didn't regret it for a minute. Craic made her feel alive.

She laughed as the little grey tearaway shot sideways, her rollercoaster ride of beating heart and flight instinct, her hand on his neck stilling him, the black-tipped ears flicking back.

They were passing the Bernard Ugger Memorial Hall, known to locals as the 'Bugger All' after the antisocial local coach entrepreneur whose legacy to the village had been the slab-like, brightly lit eyesore, a pleasure palace of punch-ups and late-night police raids. While the others ambled past its 'New Years' Eve Disco Tonite' banner, talking about their plans for later, Bridge reminded herself why she needed a job, and fast. Worried about her husband's ever-louder objections to the smell of horse and the cost of keeping one in oats, she had vowed to pay for Craic herself. And the craic. It was time to shake off the guilt and the hormones and earn her spurs.

Mo drew alongside, breathlessly enthusiastic, 'I meant to say, they're looking for someone to run the office at the village school. The Head's a bit of a battleaxe, but soft as putty underneath. I can put a word in, if you like?'

Bridge stared at the black-tipped ears in front of her, feeling her ego quietly fold into an origami warrior and commit hara-kiri. She mustn't be proud. Sous Vide had made it clear she'd dropped a pay grade with each pregnancy. 'That's kind of you.'

Mo puffed with laughter. 'It was a joke! You're a high flyer, you.'

Bridge forced a smile, curling her fingers through Craic's mane, grateful at least that he made her feel miles high. 'Sure I am.'

Peeling off his yard gloves in his small cottage kitchen, Lester fetched Stubbs's feed bowl, shaking in the kibble and breaking an egg on top, before dousing it all with a splash of water from the kettle that he now refilled and switched on.

'You'll have to wait,' he reminded the little fox terrier as it danced from paw to paw below, Lloyd George eyebrows shifting.

Lester folded the metal mesh rack around his slice of bread and wedged it between Rayburn range plate and lid. Leaving it to toast, he headed outside to fill the bowl in the hutch by the back door. Two vulpine eyes gleamed back at him.

Laurence the fox. The stud's housekeeper Pip had named it – she was a big fan of the television series *Lewis*, starring an actor by that name.

Compton Magna Stud had been manned by an increasingly paltry staff in recent years, the breeding enterprise downscaled in the shadow of family tragedy, ill health and economic recession. Lester, recruited by the late Captain Jocelyn Percy during his national service days with the Household Cavalry, had worked there for over fifty years, and been stallion man for twenty, outstaying all others. Now, even the eager local housekeeper appeared to have deserted the sinking ship, claiming to be far too busy over Christmas to help out.

Despite finding chatty little Pip very wearying, Lester missed her baking. He hoped she would be back in the New Year, although Ronnie seemed to have the impression Pip was taking up a new career in private detection, no doubt inspired by her taste in small-screen whodunnits. Lester had never heard anything so ludicrous.

Then again, if such a far-fetched thing were true, he might be grateful for her services. Some strange things were going on around here. Initially relieved that Ronnie had decided to stay on in Compton Magna to take up the reins of her late father's enterprise – pleased would be pushing it – Lester was extremely annoyed that she'd hired a stud manager who was coming over from Canada to run it with her for six months, no doubt bringing newfangled ideas and gadgetry. Moreover, while the man had yet to arrive, his possessions had been turning up throughout the Christmas period. First had been the mysterious boxes that had been delivered by international movers, sent by shipping container weeks ago, then a horsebox had rolled up to drop off more bags and boxes, an eventer friend laughingly sharing the joke with Ronnie that a rolling stone like Luca O'Brien gathered no moss because he left it all in other people's barns.

There had been several phone calls to the stud's landline at very antisocial hours: a seductive female voice asking whether Luca had arrived yet; another, male and menacing, possibly South African, enquiring whether a Mr O'Brien worked there. And out hunting with the Fosse yesterday, Lester had found himself the focus of yet more unwanted attention.

'Is it true Smiley O'Reilly is coming to the Wolds?' the MFH, Bay Austen, had demanded at check.

'I think his name is O'Brien, sir.'

'Ha!' Bay's frosty Dutch-born wife had ridden between them. 'When I trained in Limburg, Luca was based at Gestüt Fuchs, just over the German border, okay. That place is so huge, nobody remembers names, but he was not so easy to forget. He could ride any horse, however crazy, played the violin like a gypsy and everybody there was in love with him. They all called him Smiley.'

'Could be because he was a spy, I suppose?' Bay had looked amused.

'He left under a *very* dark cloud.' Monique could slay a reputation in a breath. 'I heard it was something to do with a stallion he handled that was injured. That wiped the smile off all their faces. It was no accident, perhaps.'

Lester had felt his blood quicken. If anybody mistreated his beloved stallion Cruisoe, he'd slay them. Or indeed the grey beast of Ronnie's, who for all his delinquency, was the best-looking horse Compton Magna Stud had seen in a century.

The hunting field exchange unsettled Lester, although he normally took no heed of tittle-tattle. He wouldn't dream of saying anything to Ronnie – in fact, he derived a certain amount of pride in the fact that he had managed to get within days of the man's arrival having not once referred to him by name, nickname or reputation – but he felt a deep-seated need for allies.

'Nobody's fiddling while Rome burns around here,' he muttered to Lawrence before following the smell of burned toast back inside. The infernal phone was ringing again. Lester shared the stud's landline with the office in the main house, from which his late employer, the Captain, had shouted at bookmakers, friends and relatives. Having none of these himself, Lester rarely had use of it and was damned if he was going to answer it when he knew there was someone at home to do so.

As he set down Stubbs' feed bowl, however, a flash of blonde, bright as the sun, appeared in the small rectangular window above his front door followed by a familiar, percussive rap.

Ronnie was on his doorstep, dressed up in her best fur-trimmed tweed coat and pearls, wearing make-up for once. She still knocked the rest dead, Lester thought, wondering if she was going to see her fancy man.

'I have to set out now or I'll miss this bloody lunch in Wilts,' she said, glancing instinctively up at the clock over the stable-yard arch, although it had been saying half past ten for six years. 'I'd bow out, but Bunny's invited a bunch of owners and breeders especially, and lord knows we need the business. Pax should be here by now to help you. Did you take that call? Was it her?' She plucked out her mobile phone, no more than a glorified clock on days like today when their patchy rural signal thinned to nothing, sighing at its blank face.

He cleared his throat. 'I can cope.'

'Can you?' The bluest eyes in the Cotswolds, ever amused, regarded him shrewdly as he shuffled aside to let the younger of her little black-and-tan dogs bustle in to lick Stubbs' now empty bowl.

Not for the first time, he sensed she knew precisely how much his hips hurt, how bad his eyesight was, how hard he found it to push a full barrow up the muck plank these days. 'Done it long enough.'

'That's the point. You're supposed to start easing off a bit now I'm here; you're too valuable.' Laying down her phone and handbag, she stooped to help her elderly dog over the front step.

'If you say so.'

'I do, Lester, I do. Pax should be here.' She glanced over her shoulder at the stud's drive as if willing her daughter to appear. 'Damn. I wanted to talk to her before I set off, too. I don't buy this story about not going to Scotland for Hogmanay because of the puppy, do you? I mean it's jolly lovely that she's offered to help here while I'm gallivanting, but it's not like her to let Kes out of her sight. Alice could have the puppy. *We* could have him here, come to that.'

Listening to the snarling and snapping coming from his kitchen, Lester was grateful, at least, that Ronnie's heelers were going with her, their manners as tenacious as their mistress's. Pax's Scottish deerhound puppy – a Christmas present to her husband that Lester suspected was really to herself – was already bigger than Stubbs, to which the little bearded terrier took great umbrage, as well as its sharp teeth and general clumsy larkiness. Lester was rather hoping Pax would leave it in the car. Like Ronnie, he didn't believe the Hogmanay story either. Those big hare eyes had too many unspilled tears in them.

'I've suggested she stays here in the house tonight,' Ronnie told him. 'No point shivering in that tin box alone, and the ghastly M and Ms won't let the puppy in their bungalow because of their cat.'

Ronnie was talking about Muir and Mairi Forsyth, Pax's hollow cheeked in-laws. Lester thought the nickname very disrespectful. Straight-backed and snowy-haired, the Forsyths struck him as show-bred examples of parsimonious, doughty Scots, unlike their fast-talking and profligate son, Mack. *He* was the reason his wife and child were enduring a second winter in a static caravan in the shadow of the gutted shell of an old Cotswold rectory they were renovating to live in. Pax was loyally tight-lipped, but her sister Alice didn't mind who knew that Mack Forsyth – who Alice claimed fleeced local farmers by underpaying for development projects – had blown the budget on half a dozen million-pound barn conversions they now couldn't sell. Mack's parents, who had moved down from Scotland to rent nearby, were helping keep the ship afloat as far as Lester could tell. Pax should be grateful, not listen to Ronnie pouring scorn with her usual disrespect for seniority.

'You'll see in the New Year with her, won't you?' Ronnie demanded now.

'She won't stay.'

'Oh, I know she's not ready to spend a night under the same roof as this Scarlet Harlot of the Wolds, Lester.' Ronnie laughed throatily. 'I'm staying in Wiltshire. Bunny's been banging on about the Bretts' party again, and it's another good place to plug the stud. Lots of old chums. But I don't want to desert you; I'll be back by eight thirty tomorrow morning latest. You're hunting, I take it?'

Lester nodded. 'You should be too.'

'Oh, I am.' She winked, picking up her bag. 'Hunting for clients. Wiltshire horsemen have very deep pockets.' As she turned away with a wave, calling her dogs, he caught a breath of her scent, sweet and light as winter jasmine.

Lester narrowed his eyes. She was definitely seeing the fancy man.

Bridge made light of Craic's hysterical attempts to reverse through a hedge at the sight of fly-tipped litter in a gateway – like a Womble having a panic attack – despite the Bags well-meaning advice.

'Kick him on!'

'Give him a slap!'

'You need the Horsemaker, darling!'

When not telling her to keep her heels down and leg on, they had moved on to discuss the object of Petra's new Safe Married Crush, an international man of mystery not even in the country yet.

'Ronnie has promised me Luca O'Brien is totally TDF DDG,' she said in her breathy posh Yorkshire voice.

'Tiny dull fogey dealing dodgy gee-gees?' Bridge suggested with a cynical snort as Craic burst from the hedge.

'To Die For, Drop Dead Gorgeous,' Mo told her helpfully, she and Petra both mothers of nine-year-old *Dork Diaries* addicts.

'No man's so gorgeous that you'd die for him,' Bridge argued.

'The French call an orgasm *la petite mort*,' said Petra, 'the little death.'

Bridge laughed. 'In that case I die for Aleš all the fecking time! I should be demanding a marble plaque and flowers.'

Petra and Gill's smiles developed a frozen, jealous look.

'*La petite mort*,' she repeated, liking the dangerously sacrificial, all-absorbing sound of it, and the way it made the others uncomfortable.

'Oh, Barry gave me some of those at Christmas.' Mo panted alongside. 'From Aldi, they were. We gave Gill one when she came round. She wouldn't stop going on about how good it was.'

'Petit *four*, Mo. You gave me a petit *four*.'

'Did Ronnie Percy really use the phrase "drop dead gorgeous"?' Bridge asked Petra, having imagined something far cooler from the Bardswold Bolter, Ronnie's nickname earned after a dramatic departure in a sports car from the village and her marriage in her twenties.

'She actually said the Horsemaker is the Angel Gabriel in breeches, Lucifer out of them.'

'Better than Mel Gibson or Harrison Ford,' Bridge muttered. Petra turned everything into romantic melodrama, a side-effect of penning so many Georgian virgins about to have their bodices ripped off.

The imminent arrival of Luca 'the Horsemaker' O'Brien

was *the* most anticipated thing in this village if Petra was to be believed. Hired by Ronnie Percy to try to turn around the fortunes of her family's failing stud, the Irish-Italian stallion man with the battered passport was purportedly a globetrotting stud in his own right.

'One can't deny Ronnie has a good eye for men as well as horses,' Gill conceded, adding beadily, 'Is it currently on or off between her and Mr Sit Tight do we know?'

'No idea.' Petra flashed her big, easy smile.

The cause of much fascination, stud owner Ronnie was a Percy family prodigal, her scurrilous past, forthright presence and uncertain future keeping tongues wagging.

These days the Bags rarely rode past the stud without standing up in their stirrups to take a better look, especially since Petra, who regularly dog walked with Ronnie, had hinted at a clandestine affair with three-day eventing's sexiest silver fox and six-time Olympian, craggy sexpot Blair Robertson.

'The Bolter won't stay single for long,' Gill predicted.

'I heard she got very pally with your Shakespeare director from the Old Almshouse over Christmas.' Mo gave Gill one of her *Carry On* winks.

'They're hardly a good match,' Gill dismissed, guarding her secret crush fiercely. 'Kit's an academic, so not nearly he-man enough for the Bardswold Bolter. She's bringing this lusty young horse-whisperer over for herself, mark my words.'

'When does Horse Boy arrive?' asked Bridge, who had a vision of Poldark in Pikeur, all dark, thrusting good looks.

'The Horsemaker,' Petra corrected. 'Later this week, I think Ronnie said. One touch of his hand makes horses follow him like disciples, apparently,' she sighed, clearly in the Poldark zone too. 'Goodness knows, they need him. The stud's really short-staffed now Pip's stopped going in to help.'

'No bad thing; silly woman was a menace around those horses,' Gill said chippily. 'Ronnie's obviously cash-strapped.

We all know old Lester's superhuman at seventy-whatever, and Ronnie's no shirker, but they've got far too many horses.'

They were passing the open gateway of the stud farm drive now, all the Bags glancing up the long, poplar-lined stretch of tarmac to its golden-faced house and two interconnected Cotswold stone stable yards, the weathervane glinting above one of the arches, pointing north as the wind stripped their faces.

'Pax has been helping out a bit,' said Petra.

'That's one of the daughters, right?' Bridge, whose only knowledge of the Percy family came from the others gossiping, knew that Ronnie had been estranged from all three of her children for years. 'Is she the redhead we keep seeing parked up in a Noddy car in village lay-bys, shouting into her Bluetooth?'

'The same.'

Mo bustled alongside Petra again, loving village drama. 'She and the Scottish husband do up big old Cotswold piles and sell them for a fortune, don't they?'

'Places like Petra's, you mean,' Bridge snorted.

'*Much* smarter.' Petra took it in good cheer.

'Playpens for pop stars, footballers and city boys.' Sounding highly disapproving, Gill signalled for single file as a car approached, the quartet moving up onto the verge and waving thanks to weekenders from one of the thatched cottages on The Green as they edged past in an immaculately clean Audi, eyeing the horses with trepidation. 'Mack Forsyth's a shark,' she told the others over her shoulder. 'He's quite a bit older than Pax – closer to Ronnie's age. Obvious father figure; never seen him out of a suit.'

The riders waited for a big pickup to come the other way.

'His first wife took off with the kids to live in Australia, which is pretty ouch,' Petra let slip.

'He sounds a right one,' Mo tutted.

'Don't you feel sorry for him?' Bridge was surprised.

'Mothers don't put continents between kiddies and their dads without good reason.'

'Mack looks like George Clooney, mind you.' Gill raised her crop hand in thanks as the pickup passed.

'Jimmy Nesbit,' Petra downgraded.

'Not more geriatric pin-ups!' grumbled Bridge, noticing Petra sucking in her plump lips, clearly party to the inside story thanks to her dog-walking alliance with Ronnie.

As a third car appeared over the hill, trapping them all on the verge longer, Petra cracked, 'He's a terrible control freak and his parents are Presbyterian zealots; Ronnie thinks that when the in-laws moved down from Aviemore last summer to rule the roost from a neighbouring bungalow, Pax went from fed up to clinically depressed.'

Bridge let a sarcastic huff escape her lips, her eyes drifting back across to the beautiful golden stud, unable to imagine feeling miserable when you could escape there.

'So she's spending more time with Mummy and the horses?' She feigned a cut-glass accent, sitting tight as Craic took objection to the approaching car's roof box.

Mo chuckled. 'You've got the right hump today, Mrs Mazur.'

'I just don't see what's special about having a selfish husband and mad in-laws. Sure, we've all got those.' The chip on her shoulder sizzled. 'At least he's a snappy dresser, this silver fox of hers. Aleš has been trending plaster-encrusted joggers and trainers for years, *and* his parents are certifiable – but you don't catch me doing the shouty Bluetooth thing or running home to Mammy, do you? Sure, she'd just tell me to get down on my knees, and not to pray: every Walsh woman learns early on that to have a good marriage you need to give him lip and head in equal measure.' Craic spun round as the offending roof box whooshed past, cannoning into Mo's good-natured cob who flattened its ears, his rider's face puce.

Chastened, Bridge apologised. 'Sorry. Horse and mouth running away with me again.' She had no bate with Ronnie's daughter; she didn't know the woman. Today's bad temper was entirely directed at herself.

'We can't all have your exciting love life, Bridge duck,' Mo sighed. 'When Barry gets up my nose, *I* spend time with Mum and the horses. Bloody muddy and hard work it is too. You try mucking out ten when it's so cold you can't feel your fingers.'

Smarting quietly because Craic was one of those ten kept at the little livery yard Mo ran from her parents' farm, Bridge remembered Aleš arguing against paying the extra for him to be stabled in winter ('He should live in field. You treat that fucking animal like baby. You want another baby, let's make another baby, baby.' His Bond baddie way of talking, once so endearing, now got firmly on her nerves).

'Yeah, well not all of us have a mammy we can run to.' She shrugged, mustering the sardonic smile. 'Some of us just take it on the chin. And I genuinely find spunk's better than Protect & Perfect serum for fine lines and eye bags.'

'That's a Bridge too far.' Gill looked shocked. 'Put those heels down and sit up. Another quick pipe-opener, ladies?'

The riders cut through the Church Meadows, cantering up to the still-frosted standing stones before dropping back to walk along the narrow track between the old kennels and the tennis club, Craic on springs.

Belly still fluttering with the thrill of the quick-speed fix, Bridge cursed her forked tongue again. In truth, it was a tongue that had been nowhere near Aleš's dick in weeks; a ban imposed after some petty row about him not pulling his weight around the house had turned nasty, a stubborn stand-off she regretted every time he stood up to magnificent attention. In retaliation, his beard was no longer tracing its way between her thighs either.

Although still far more active than the other Bags, their sex life was definitely on the wane, a bedtime routine made ever more time-saving and point-scoring, like hastily loading their dinner plates in the dishwasher when they'd once spent a giggly, messy, foamy hour washing up. Add on a passion-killing fortnight with his close-knit family in Poland, crammed on an inflatable mattress between a travel cot and a bunk, and her mojo was twitching for better times. Bridge sympathised with Petra's desire for a healing touch, but not from a TDF, DDG fantasy figure. Hers was still six-feet-four Aleš with his gunmetal eyes and Atlas shoulders. But even if she'd die for him, a *petit mort* at a time, that wasn't a reason not to start living again. They all deserved a life beyond marriage, even depressed redheads.

'Whatshername – Pax,' she said. 'She needs a SMC.'

'She's not having the Horsemaker,' growled Petra.

It was only when he was pulling his yard boots on after breakfast that Lester spotted Ronnie's little black phone still on his hall table. Tutting, he put a flat cap over it and pulled on the fur trapper hat Pax had bought him for Christmas, a masterful invention for keeping his ears warm.

The landline was ringing again. Confounded thing! Knowing it might be Pax, he reluctantly plucked the receiver from the wall and lifted a furry ear flap.

'Stud.'

'Ronnie there?' Man's voice, sleepy and peaty, not British.

'No.'

'Luca O'Brien.'

'*He's* not here either,' he growled.

There was a loudspeaker announcement in the background at the other end, a different foreign accent. 'Listen, I'm about to board. My flight details have now changed, yeah?'

'*Yes*,' Lester corrected. The Captain had loathed 'yeah'.

'I transfer in Schiphol, not Dublin, so I'll not be staying the night in Ireland now.'

This peaty voice was Irish, Lester realised, closing his eyes in disappointment. Deep and dulcet. He'd been expecting a reedy jockey's whine, not a husky baritone. *This* was Luca.

'I'll be with yous all tonight.'

'Be with *you* tonight,' he corrected again, mind racing.

'Good to hear it. Flight KL1435, Birmingham. I should be through customs twenty-two thirty. Will it be yourself or Ronnie meeting me, Lester?'

Hearing his name, so affably spoken by this stranger to whom he had never been introduced, Lester stiffened further. He could no longer trust his eyes with night driving – a fact he had yet to acquaint Ronnie with – and he certainly had no intention of setting out in sub-zero temperatures to fetch the enemy home.

'Not myself,' he said, glancing at the flat cap. 'We'll see what we can do. Someone will be there.' Perhaps Pip could be persuaded?

'Great. Looking forward to meeting ya.'

'Looking forward to meeting *you*.' He rang off briskly.

When Lester called Pip, it went straight to voice mail. The same with Pax. He tried Alice next. Her reaction was predictable. 'Absolutely not. We've a house full of teenagers, cows to milk first thing tomorrow, then hunting. Sod Mummy's bad logistics. Come to supper.'

She sounded more like her grandmother Ann every year, he thought, politely declining the offer.

Grumbling under his breath to Stubbs that this was not his responsibility, Lester took the stud's battered old hardback telephone book containing at least four generations of Percy handwriting listing contact details of all manner of professional equestrians. There was no record of a 'Bunny' in Wiltshire, which was the only name Lester had ever heard Ronnie use to refer to her former landlord, host of a large horse trials and a big eventing mover-shaker. There were, however, several entries for three-day-event rider Blair Robertson who had been buying and selling horses since he first got off the boat from

Australia almost forty years earlier. Lester dialled the one number not crossed out, a mobile.

It was answered in two rings.

'Ronnie.' The low growl was pure sex-fuelled testosterone. If Luca was husky Gaelic gold, Aussie Blair was diamond-mine deep and rough-hewn.

'It's Compton Magna Stud. We need to get a message to Mrs Ledwell.'

'Ooooookay.'

'She will be with you later, I believe.'

'Why's she coming here?' The voice rumbled like distant thunder. Was it anger?

Lester realised that perhaps he'd misread the situation, the love affair still in deep winter hibernation.

There was a click of tongue against palate, Blair's hoarse voice cynical. 'Don't tell me, Bunny's convinced her to join him for his end-of-year lunch?'

'I believe so. Will you be attending?'

'Not my bag, mate. I wondered why the old sod was being so coy. I bet he's taking her to the Bretts' bash too.'

'Perhaps you have a telephone number on which I can contact Mr Bunny?'

He laughed again. 'Tell me the message. I'll make sure she gets it.'

'Her friend arrives tonight. The Irish gentleman.'

The call was abruptly ended.

2

The Saddle Bags said farewell to Gill at her sprawling cottage in the wooded shadows behind St Mary's church, her daughters' ponies bellowing unseen for attention, the huge yews still spun with jewelled spiders' webs. Soon afterwards, Petra headed through the electric gates to her handsome farmhouse. Cotswold vales laid out like giant, misty watercolour paintings to either side, it sat isolated on high ground midway between Compton Magna and Compton Bagot, on the orchard-skirted lane known as Plum Run, a runway from one village's picture-postcard perfection to the other's workmanlike hotchpotch of artisan and eyesore. With its Georgian face, Tudor flank and barn conversions sold off to rich Londoners, the farmhouse was a lifetime away from its agricultural roots, and hard to imagine it was anything like the ramshackle working farm belonging to Mo's parents, where Bridge kept Craic on livery.

'Byeeeee! Happy New Year!' Petra waved over her shoulder, disappearing behind a high Cotswold wall, many-paned windows glinting beyond. She was always so upbeat, radiating naughty jollity and optimism, a state of mind Bridge envied far more than her big pretend farmhouse.

As the last two Bags headed home, the Jugged Hare's hoarding ahead of them, she felt gloom descending.

Mo's big, kind face turned to study her. 'What is it, love? Not just the interview, I reckon.'

'It's nothing.'

'Spit it out.'

'It's all good.' Bridge was well-accustomed to glossing over her crabbier moments. 'Only, don't you sometimes just want the "old me" back, y'know?'

'That never happens, love. We're heading in opposite directions; the old me is always getting younger as we grow older. You're closer to yours than the rest of us, mind you.'

Bridge thought of Bernie, whose old and new selves remained one and the same, and she felt another familiar, soul-deep pang of missing her twin. This Christmas, with one in the States and the other in Poland, the Walsh girls hadn't got together in Belfast with their band of siblings. Both were comforted by the prospect of hosting a joint thirtieth birthday party here in the Cotswolds in March, but it still felt wrong.

'You're missing your Aleš and the kiddies, that's what it is. No time to be alone, New Year.'

Bridge rolled her eyes at Craic's ears. Whilst she did miss her babies terribly, they'd be asleep by six, after which the Mazur family traditionally endured indigestion from *Bigos* stew, wind from gassy beer, aching cheeks from showing good cheer, sore feet from dancing and ringing ears from enduring Aleš's gregariously tuneless singing. Her eyelids prickled. Mo was right. She wished she was still there.

'Come round to us if you like. Barry's got a keg in and I've made cottage pie. We've always a fair few over, farming folk mostly.'

'Thanks, but I've got plans.' She was looking forward to her Cowshed bath oil, bottle of wine and luxury ready meal for one.

'When does Aleš get back?' Mo always pronounced it 'Alice' no matter how often she heard the correct 'Alesh', making

Bridge envisage her husband in shock-rock leather and eyeliner singing 'School's Out for Summer'.

'Day after tomorrow.' She was surprised again by how sharp the pinch from missing him felt.

Now in Compton Bagot village, the two riders spotted a small, comically curvy car parked outside the memorial hall ahead of them, a solitary figure inside waving her hands around, mouth moving.

Pax Forsyth, all copper curls, long limbs and fragile bone structure, like Satine in *Moulin Rouge*.

'It's a four-wheeled phone booth, that car.' Bridge nodded in its direction.

'Who d'you suppose she parks up to talk to?'

'Her lover?' Bridge suggested in a 'duh?' voice.

Mo's kind, wide face unfolded into spherical shock. 'Valerie Benson's hubby used to stop his Jag here every night to call his bit on the side before old Mr Coles overheard him having phone sex on his air-traffic radio band. That was a way back, mind you.'

'D'you think it's anyone we know?' Bridge whispered.

'My bet's on one of the Chipping Norton set.' Mo embraced the idea with surprising enthusiasm. 'Could never resist them fiery redheads. She mixes in high circles, I heard.'

Bridge gazed at the figure in the car, undeniably beautiful and foxily sylvan in an oversized tartan scarf, eyes huge, lips dewy buds, pale freckled neck swan-long, the sort of woman red-blooded country types inevitably wanted to devour. The chip on her shoulder sizzled hotly again.

'Always was the prettiest of the Captain's grandkids,' Mo sighed.

At that moment, Pax put her head in her hands, shoulders shaking, grief-stricken. The two women looked hastily away, guilty eyes trained on the Old Post Office's flashing icicles.

'Make the most of tonight, duck.' Kindly Mo groped for a distracting platitude. 'Last night of the year is always special.'

'Especially when your husband is nine hundred miles away and the farrier next door's having open house.'

'Are you sure going there is wise?'

'Mo, I'll be tucked up in bed in a onesie watching Jools from eleven. I rave vicariously through the party wall these days.'

'One more night to blow the diet before I actually start the diet,' Mo said cheerfully as they rode on.

Glancing over her shoulder at Pax, Bridge saw the redhead was raking her hair back from her wide-eyed face, talking again.

Her own phone started ringing in her pocket, her husband's handsome, bearded mug on its screen when she pulled it out.

'We miss you, *kochanie*!' Aleš boomed in her ear. 'Tomorrow, I try to change flights, yes? Come home early?'

'Absolutely not. It'll cost too much.'

'You are worth every euro, *moja kochana. Marzę o twoim dotyku.*'

'I dream of your touch too, baby, but—'

'Is that horse feet?'

'What?'

'I hear horse hoofs. *Jazda konna*? You are riding?'

'Yes.' She pulled up and Craic whinnied throatily as his cob friend carried on. 'So?'

'You do not want us home sooner because you want to be with horse, yes?'

'Don't be silly, Aleš. Last time we changed flights home, it cost five hundred euro.'

'Your horse cost more than that every month!'

'Sure, it's way less than that.' Ahead of her, Mo had pulled up too, looking round questioningly.

'You rather play with horse than see your family?' he accused. Although Aleš wasn't Craic's biggest fan – and he was always more hot-blooded at home in Poland – she had a shrewd suspicion he was also pretty keen to get away from his mother.

Smiling reassuringly at Mo, she muttered through gritted teeth, 'I love you more than life, my darling. Now stop being such a fecking dick, enjoy *Sylwester* with your family and hurry home. I miss you all.'

There were kissing noises in her ear. 'Okay. I am dick. *Kocham cię*. I love you.'

'Love you too. We'll talk later,' she rang off.

You are going to earn your spurs and enjoy the Craic, Bridge reminded herself, kicking on to catch Mo up. Without thinking, she glanced over her shoulder again at the Noddy car. Two pale, wet amber eyes were watching her now, the mouth moving fast.

Feeling awkward, she smiled and waved. Pax looked away without reacting.

'Stuck-up bitch.' Bridge turned back and trotted on.

Pax usually parked in the tree-shrouded lay-by on Luddford Hill to listen to her husband shouting at her on hands-free. There, she could get a four-bar signal and privacy. But today she'd been turning into Compton Bagot when Mack called, and by the time she'd passed the Old Post Office, the light-up icicles had been a blur. Tears still stung, hot and wet on her cheeks, the lump in her throat like a clenched fist.

'– you have no *idea* how *damaging* this is –' Mack bellowed on '– the sheer *madness* of this *whole* fucking *week*.' He hammered the emphasis every few words like a Scottish Peston. Pax tried not to jump each time.

The two women on horses were riding away now. How she envied them their freedom. When she'd ridden, all those years ago, she'd felt mythical, like a female Centaur. She wanted to gallop very fast in open country right now, not feel buried up to her neck in a toxic relationship.

A marriage breaking up over Christmas was such a cliché. It happened in soap operas, not to a calm, well-brought-up family tactician like Pax. The festive fight was so not her style, that crazy, wine-fuelled argument in paper hats that ended with the scream, 'This marriage is over!'

This year, however, Pax Forsyth had, in her husband's words 'completely lost it'.

Every day that had passed since made bigger strangers of them. Their week of putting on the ultimate pantomime.

At the most sociable time of year, with its stack of invitations, play dates and family commitments, the 'Christmas Day Episode' as Mack called it, had been kept rigidly hidden from view while the Forsyths spread Tidings of Comfort and Joy around their Cotswolds circle with boxes of Prestat and bottles of Moët, but it was a wound bleeding beneath the Boden perfection.

Even at home, they'd remained acidly polite, putting on a united front in front of five-year-old Kes, whilst studiously avoiding being alone together. Pax spent late evenings on the running machine in the garage; Mack glared at a screen or retreated to his parents' bungalow in the neighbouring village to lick his wounds. He was waiting for a retraction she refused to issue. Not Talking About It was a tacit pact. But as soon as she left the house alone, stepped out of the Safe Zone, he seemed to snap. First came texts, offended questions – *Have you really thought about this? Do you realise what you stand to destroy? What do you think you're doing to our son? Is there someone else?* – followed by the call, a sanctimonious monologue.

Today's, delivered from the loo of the sleeper to Edinburgh, was typical.

'– you've said that you would *never* put Kes through what *you* went through when *your mother* abandoned you, and now *this*?'

Pax listened, tearfully watching the two riders disappearing from view.

'After *all* that I've *done* for you, saving you from rock *bottom*, giving you *everything* you could *want* or *need*—'

'On the seventh Day of Christmas, my true love gave to me,' she murmured, 'seven sleepless nights, six of the best, fiiiive old sins.'

'I might have *guessed* spending time with your *mother* would lead to something like this!'

'Four cruel words, three Scottish Glens, two hurtful loves and a—'

'Tishy, are you *even* fucking *LISTENING*?'

His voice had conjured Ewan McGregor the first time they'd met, she remembered. Close your eyes and he was no longer a black-haired, rugby-mad civil engineer from Argyll, he was Obi-Wan Kenobi. How naïve was that?

'I just need some space to think, Mack.'

'FUCKING WELL *THINK FAST*!'

'I am.' Her calmness infuriated him, she knew, but in her head her outwardly honey-soft words shrilled. Her mind was constantly whirring, her senses heightened, like exam week at university. 'I think about nothing else.'

She could hear him breathing deeply, that annoying wheeze that signalled a mood change, followed by the gruff laugh she'd loved so unquestioningly once, all fresh air and heather. 'C'mon, Tishy. Let's make up, eh?' Never Pax. Mack had rebranded her when they'd first met, taking old-fashioned Patricia that she'd been christened with and, for a long while, making her feel safe. Tishy was loved. Then, as now, he'd been utterly dogmatic.

'Let's stop this silliness.' His voice was brusque. 'It's a new year, a new start.'

She could almost swear she could hear '... and I'm feeeeeling good' in the back of his throat. It was typical of Mack, impatiently expecting her to snap out of it, to fix her charming wife smile back on, show her class. He was always happier north of the border, almost child-like with homecoming joy.

'We'll talk about it when you get back,' she said stiffly. 'Talk properly, just you and me.'

'Who says I *am* coming back?'

She rolled her eyes and threw up her hands with an irritated growl, making the puppy in the back of her car lift its head. This was typical posturing. 'Don't let's go there, Mack. Just don't.'

The laughter vanished from his voice. 'Six days ago, you said – and I quote – "this marriage is over".'

Four words spoken in the heat of the moment had changed everything between them.

Where had her lava of repressed anger erupted from after the Stilton and figs? Yes, she'd drunk too much that day; they'd both overdone the Christmas cognac, but that usually anaesthetised her discontent. Besides which, it was something of a personal challenge to get tight in her in-laws' bungalow, where the spirits tantalus – kept under lock and key – had not been topped up since the Scottish referendum. There was no blue flame above the discount supermarket Christmas pudding when the Forsyths hosted.

The countdown to Pax's outburst had been more dyspeptic than distraught. No secrets uncovered, no love affairs, no explosive *Who's Afraid Of Virginia Wolf* whisky-slinging. Just the annual skin-grating ennui of a loveless marriage at Christmas. Their relationship had been as stale as Mairi Forsyth's oatcakes for years. It hardly ever went from dead water to tempest, and although it had been on the rocks more than once before, they knew how to patch up the hull and sail on. Business partners as well as life ones, the couple were adept at keeping up a good show.

Christmas morning had gone much as she expected; Kes opening his stocking at dawn, lots of 'ooohs' and 'aaaahs' and 'good for Santa!', her hangover thumping; losing the fight for the shower (only one hot one possible on their tiny tank);

Mack chivvying her to hurry up, his parents looking pointedly at their watches as they waited on their bungalow doorstep at ten; strong tea and shortbread in place of Prosecco and blinis, the Forsyths' gifts wrapped in last year's paper – a mountain of Lego for Kes, a set of golf clubs and lesson vouchers for Mack, and bath salts for her, discount price tag still on.

Pax had been no more hurt than usual that her husband was unimpressed by her over-generous gift to him – the still-unnamed deerhound puppy, now asleep in the back of her car – and he'd plainly forgotten that the huge slab of KitchenAid gadgetry he'd given her, for which they had no space in the static caravan, was a duplicate of his gift last year, its twin still in its box in the shipping container that they used as storage. At least they'd both made an effort, and they had lavished Kes with treats. Their one point of mutual, passionate affection was their five-year-old son, as dark-haired and devilishly handsome as his daddy, so hard-won after eight rounds of IVF. The couple's sexual spark might have died somewhere between laboratory and labour, but a fierce bonfire of parental love had blazed into life with Kes's arrival, burning their path onwards.

Pax never anticipated that this Christmas she would douse the fire so instantly. Her calmness was legendary. Pax the peacemaker; Pax the level-headed negotiator; Pax who never got angry.

She'd been doing so well, enduring her in-laws' miserly hosting: folding up paper for next year, a bracing walk, a thimble of Madeira. Thank God she'd brought a hip flask. She'd tolerated Mairi being a well-meaning bully in the kitchen with quiet dignity, undermining her greater culinary expertise ('*this* is how Forsyths make bread sauce, Patricia – now chop faster, girl, and I need you to grate that swede next.'). That Mairi had been complimented so effusively over her cold, dry turkey, over-boiled and over-salted veg and Aunt Bessie's cook-from-frozen roasties, blackened to coal bricks, had admittedly been a surprise, both son and husband in paroxysms of joy ('You're the best, Mum!' 'Mairi, you have triumphed again!'), her own smile fixed, because relieved as she was that her mother-in-law took all the credit for its awfulness, the food really was *awful*. But she understood that Mack lavished praise on Mairi because, like all good sons, he loved her so much that she could do no wrong in his eyes. And like all bored husbands, he no longer noticed much of what Pax did. By contrast, every single thing Mack did that day seemed to irritate his wife more than ever.

The way he ate so noisily, talked with his mouth full, filled his own glass and not hers, spoke over everyone, laughed too loudly. The way he encouraged his father to tell those interminable golfing anecdotes, flattered his mother ridiculously, forced both parents to feign interest in his sports bike customisation, every technical detail described in condescendingly over-explained minutiae. His over-competitive cracker-pulling, his badgering insistence Kes try a soggy parsnip until the boy wept. The 'I think you've drunk enough, Tishy' had been particularly infuriating, as had his pompous 'Tishy and I will clear up this feast – least we can do after you've done all the hard work, Mum.' It was teeth-grindingly annoying when he handed her back each of the pans she'd washed up to do again. His nasal hum made her want to scream. His lack of eye contact irked her, the way he loaded the dishwasher knives blade up, the sprouts' fart he let out then blamed on the puppy, his hair combed spivvily sideways, his awful Christmas jumper worn with a *suit*, his red ears – *HIM*.

And yet none of that really justified 'This marriage is over!' did it? Wasn't he just having fun while she was a being a miserable, buttoned-up Scrooge?

The petty row had started over fat in the gravy strainer. He wanted her to rinse it down the sink; she insisted it would block the drains, their voices *sotto*. Next door, Kes was elbow-deep in Lego, the Forsyths watching the Queen's Speech – volume mercifully high because Muir stubbornly refused to wear a hearing aid. It was Mack who started ramping up the stealth fight, always more combative than she, taunting with his tea-towel matador cloak, goading and arrogant. Talking in undertones, they'd hissed and dismissed, the argument gaining momentum, the venom and despair all too soon pouring forth, hers forty percent proof and 100 per cent truth.

Within just a few short word associations, they'd moved rapidly past the plumbing faults of the eighties bungalow, through how much his parents hated the Cotswolds, touched upon the still unfinished Rectory renovation, the loathsome mobile home, Mack's aggressive business tactics and the expensive school Kes had yet to settle in, dwelt far too long on her interfering friends, then paid lip duty to their lousy sex life, her drinking, his lack of affection, her mother. Her bloody awful mother whose ridiculously selfish behaviour had fucked up her childhood and killed her father. His words, delivered as dispassionately as a busy oncologist telling a patient they have a large tumour.

'Maybe being married to you has helped me understand why she left him!' Out it came, seemingly from nowhere, the first steam of the volcano erupting from beneath the calm blue ocean. The end of the marriage was the one thing she'd sworn never to even threaten, the very last thing she would ever want to do to Kes. Yet it felt like the truth the moment she said it. Breaking the seal on the pressure cooker.

'Now that's fucking uncalled for,' Mack had snarled. 'But I'm prepared to forgive you because I know how dysfunctional your family are.' His eyes were osprey-like, unblinkingly fixed and predatory, revealing just how shocked he was. 'Is that why you were so jealous of Mum's lovely spread today, you daft wee bird? Those Christmases at the stud were so bloody feudal, you have no idea what it's like to be civilised.'

Christmases in Compton Magna had been sacrosanct. Adults drunken and laughing, children riotous, music and merrymaking, horses and dogs centre stage, and so much food. Her grandmother Ann had been a glorious cook, Pax at her side, standing on a chair, her kitchen assistant, brining and basting and chopping and whisking just as tirelessly as she had for Mairi, the succulent gamey goose and deeply sweet red beef they'd brought to the table a legend.

At that moment the lonely grief of an unhappy wife had hit her like a tidal wave, carrying all that had been good about her grandparents' marriage – their companionship, their generosity, their fierce good spirits, their shared passion for horse and country – and smashing it against the rocks of her own hard place.

Thoughts that had been shifting like sea-sucked shingle for months gathered force, that ever-louder shanty echoing through her mind: *You don't love him, you don't love him, this can't go on, he undermines you, you don't love him, leave him, leave him, leave him.*

I will never again love Mack, she finally admitted to herself. I don't even like him.

Their drifting, shipwreck marriage splintered in front of her eyes.

Awash with hip flask Cointreau, post-lunch Armagnac and most of Mairi's cooking sherry, she'd gulped for air, a silent storm raging, sentimentality and regret wrenching great rips through her calm surface.

Barely able to breathe, she'd watched Mack take the turkey fat and pour it down the sink with a self-important swagger, saying over his shoulder, 'You sound like you're coming down with a cold, wee bird.'

'This marriage is over!'

'You'll regret saying that.' Placing the gravy strainer carefully on the draining board, he'd left the room.

That night, he'd slept in his parents' spare room.

In the Mack Shack, Pax had let Kes crawl into bed with her and cuddled his small, solid warmth tightly, anticipating a sleepless night of guilt and turmoil, but instead she'd slept better than she had in months. Just briefly, the answer was so simple. All she had to do was stick to her word.

Gazing unseeing at the lane ahead, hearing her husband breathing heavily, Pax berated herself for joining in the pretence that she'd never said it, for her overwhelming need to keep the peace.

Just a few hours later, on the other side of her hangover, in the cold light of day and after a muttered apology from both sides, they had called a truce of sorts to be on show for her family at the stud, too shell-shocked to do anything other than carry on with the festivities.

This, the first Christmas since the legendary Captain's death, had been the first without a traditional Percy family gathering on the day itself, no Grumps carving the meat in the green-walled dining room. Instead, Pax's prodigal mother was back, and while Ronnie had wanted all her children to join her at the stud, those bridges would take a long time to build. The hastily cobbled Boxing Day get-together in Compton Magna had been fraught with tension, Pax wearing a fixed smile throughout, 'This marriage is over!' still ringing in her ears, grudgingly grateful to Mack and his parents for behaving impeccably amid the cross-currents.

The gathering had deepened her sense of isolation. She needed the stud to stay in the family; it was her bedrock, and her mother's decision to stay changed things. Ronnie might be a nebulous, turbulent presence, but she was the only one of them equipped with the knowledge and contacts to save it.

Pax remained the only one of Ronnie's children willing to hear her out and help her out, and whilst it hurt quite a lot to do so, it was already starting to heal old wounds. Her oldest sister Alice's resentment of their mother burned on unabated while their brother Tim was hiding in South Africa, his second marriage already failing, his inability to commit almost certainly a throwback to their mother, escaping their father's cold detachment, abandoning them as young children. Maybe that's what made Pax find her own marriage so hard, her need for perfect harmony too perfectionist? In their glory days, Mack had called her his swan, always outwardly calm and serene while her legs kicked frantically beneath the water. Swans mated for life, didn't they?

Mack and Pax Forsyth mated as rarely as giant pandas these days, especially after a row. Instead of making up by making love, they were two repelling magnets, hostility mounting amid domestic norms, her accusation lingering, new enemies who turned their backs at night, digging trenches in the bedclothes. He spent a lot of time with his parents, pretending not to be bothered; she had hushed, tearful phone calls with her friends, cried in the shower, drank too much vodka and cleaned her teeth a lot to hide it.

It was a relief to have a legitimate excuse to back out of the annual Forsyth pilgrimage to Scotland for Hogmanay. The stud desperately needed extra hands, Pax had explained. The puppy needed looking after. She needed time alone to think. Mack didn't put up much of an argument. His parents seemed positively grateful. Last night, they'd all headed up on the sleeper and she'd drunk the rest of the vodka.

It didn't occur to her for a moment that she should question them taking Kes. Her sister-in-law Marianne's family hosted Hogmanay in their big town house in Edinburgh every year. The youngest of Kes's cousins shared his birthday, so getting the boys together was always a special treat. Nothing had changed, as Mack kept pointing out. Just Pax.

Now he dropped a strategically planned bombshell to disprove that.

'Marianne's found Mum and Dad a Victorian villa with views of Arthur's seat,' he told her with relish. 'We're going to see it today.'

'They're moving to Edinburgh?' She tried to hide the delight in her voice.

'Been planning it a while now. They're going to cash in one of Dad's pensions to top up the fund from selling up in the Highlands. It's a tidy sum. They're only grateful they never invested down near us. The market up here's much more buoyant.'

At first Pax took this to be very good news indeed. It was no secret his parents had been regretting the move down from Scotland almost from the moment they'd arrived. Having seen her marriage disintegrating in direct proportion to her in-laws interfering, Pax felt much the same way.

Until Mack added, 'And the plan is for us to come up here with them.'

The spike of adrenaline felt like a heart attack, but Pax quickly talked herself down. She knew him well enough. That was exactly the reaction he wanted. He wanted to frighten her. She dug her nails tight in her palms.

'Did you hear me?' His voice came through the loudspeakers, like a radio play. *Please make this a radio play.*

'I heard.'

'It will be a fresh start, Tishy. Mum and Dad understand we're going through a tough patch; they are being extremely generous by making this offer.'

'How long have you known about it?' She was trying hard not to scream the words. Had they planned this all along, Mack and his parents? Muir and Mairi were never generous. They saw it as a weakness.

'They mentioned it a few weeks ago.' The phone was muffled, and she heard him shout, *'All right, keep your hair on!'* as someone banged on the train toilet door. 'We were going to tell you in Edinburgh, but now you need some space to work through this – crisis, or whatever it is.' The familiar sneer in the voice. 'That changes things completely, doesn't it?'

'How so?' She would have said no whatever had happened. Her roots stretched between here and London, shoots everywhere, closely entwined with others. She and Mack had fallen in love in London. The year after they'd married, living just outside Inverness in another barely habitable restoration project, had been amongst the loneliest of her life.

'Oliver needs stability.'

At the mention of the name, she couldn't speak, the lump in her throat choking her.

Mack knew precisely how much she hated him calling their son that. Like many oldest children, he'd been christened with a traditional family forename, shared with a paternal great-grandfather on whom Mack had doted.

It's *Kes*, she wanted to shout through the suffocating neck-hold. His name is *Kes*.

A white van had parked by the Memorial Hall entrance from which two bull-necked men were unloading disco equipment.

Mack's voice softened winningly. 'The boy loves Scotland.'

Finally the throat-lock released, her voice flat and artificial, the familiar steely calm framing it. 'Don't be ridiculous, Mack. I know this is just you trying to punish me, but it's gone far enough. We have a business to run down here, a home here, and Kes goes to school here. That's his stability.'

'Marianne says she'll have a word with the head at her boys' pre-prep. It's a superb school.' So his sister was in on it too, with her sideways smiles, always acting like a one-woman mouthpiece for the Scottish Tourist Board. The Forsyth clan were quorate. 'We have to put Kes first, wee bird. Think of the benefits.'

Mack started talking in his corporate presentation voice, turning crib notes into unhurried, self-assured conviction. He dropped just enough poison bullet points in amongst the plus points to paralyse her – seen too many messy divorces not to appreciate the stable family, his stay-at-home sister and mother on tap for childcare, outstanding schooling with close cousins. Compare that to her own mother's history of abandonment, her father's tragic end, the mess Pax had made of things after abandoning the Bardswolds for London. 'You'll always be better with Kes and me, Tishy. I *saved* you, remember.'

If there was one thing guaranteed to humiliate her, it was that.

He went on, slick as always, quick to point out that once their portfolio was sold – a small matter of three overspecced luxury barn conversions and a half-finished rectory, all majority-owned by investors and the bank – they'd be wise to cut their losses. The Cotswold exercise had proved a much lower return than anticipated in the current climate. He had good contacts in Scotland, the surveying work guaranteed to supplement restoration.

'What if I don't want to live with your parents? What if I'd rather trap my nipples in a garlic press? I don't want to move to Scotland, Mack. The purpose of the Cotswold exercise was also to be close to *my* family, remember?'

'Nobody's forcing you to come,' he said icily. 'In fact, nobody is inviting you until you straighten yourself out. When I say my parents have invited us to live with them,' he went on with measured relish, 'I mean just Kes and myself for now.' She heard the acid sting in his voice, the same tone he used to tell buyers he didn't like they'd been gazumped. 'You made it perfectly clear on Christmas Day that you no longer want to be a part of this marriage.'

'C'mon, Mack. I was angry. We'd had a lot to drink.'

'Your alcoholism certainly doesn't help.'

'I am no more an alcoholic than you are.'

'Perhaps a trial separation is exactly what we both need. Sort your head out, wee girl – I can't carry you any longer.'

'You've never carried me, Mack. Not even over the threshold.' Stay calm. Stay calm.

'You're a drunk, Tishy. You said it yourself.'

'I can stop any time I like.'

'Do it tonight. Getting sober is a minimum requirement.'

'And you being less of a total arsehole is mine. But you can't do that, can you?'

He rang off and she thumped the dashboard and screamed, making the white van men turn and stare. He was winding her up, she knew it, but she hated him for it. The radio station she had been listening to kicked back in on the speakers, churning out an old ballad that made her catch a sob.

White hot with humiliated anger, Pax messaged her friend Lizzie. *I officially hate him!*

Have you left him yet? she pinged back eagerly.

Not exactly.

Do it, darling. A girl-power salute GIF followed.

Which was easy to say from that happy place of Facebook shop fronts and buzzword answers.

Yet Pax needed Lizzie now; she had to listen to wisdom, however watered down by distance and memes. Lizzie was one of Pax's small and exclusive circle dating back to her single life, mostly childhood friends, not the couple-culture cronies garnered through marriage, children and rugby. They'd been junior riders in the British team a lifetime ago. Lizzie had remained with horses, marrying a professional rider with a wandering eye. Unable to turn a blind one to his flings forever, her marriage had finally fallen apart last year. She was a good sounding board, now in a happy place with a new lover, rebooted self-esteem and strong opinions.

Ditch the bastard! Pax read, emojis lined up alongside her friend's words. *Best thing I ever did.*

But Lizzie didn't have a five-year-old son who adored his dad. She didn't have a business with her husband, debts up to their ears, and puritanical in-laws watching her every move. She hadn't vowed to herself to stick with her marriage no matter what. She didn't owe him like Pax owed Mack.

The puppy in the boot let out an excited yap and Pax looked up as a very muddy Land Rover swung into the memorial hall car park, watching in the rear-view mirror as a broad-shouldered figure stepped out of it, smile as wide as the sky and eyes as blue, a gundog at each heel.

Bay Austen, Compton Magna's unofficial squire.

Frantically mopping the last vestiges of tears, Pax summoned a bristly smile as a gloved hand rapped on the window. She slid it down a fraction and a delicious burst of waxed cotton and Penhaligon's Quercus blew in.

'Darling Pax! Greetings. If your New Year Resolution is to run away from all this bad weather and start a beach bar in Honolulu, thank goodness I'm just in time to join you.'

'Bay.'

Briefly in love as teenagers, now jaw-tighteningly cool with one another, their encounters were never comfortable. Bay, who flirted with everybody like an eager Labrador, still wanted to be forgiven. Pax, who found it too hard to forget, wanted him nowhere near.

Even after more than a decade, being in his presence made all her pulses tighten with that first love hit of lost innocence and exquisite pain. It didn't even help that he'd matured into such a country cliché, perfect bone structure and soulful blue eyes sitting far too exquisitely above the Schoffel fleece collars.

The eyes darkened as they studied her own red-rimmed ones. 'Pax, darling, are you okay?'

'Winter cold. Highly infectious.'

'Bad luck.'

'If you'll excuse me, I'm late.'

'Of course. Catch up properly soon.'

'Yes.' Never. How can one pick up where one left off when over a decade earlier she was so indescribably broken by him?

Starting the engine, she set off at speed, clipping a dog litter bin in her haste to get away, and adding another dent to the car Mack liked to call 'The Fiat Worse than Death' in a bad Geordie accent. Less than five years old and already rusting and battle-scarred, the Italian fake Mini he'd bought her as an apology after writing off her beloved Golf wasn't built to be parked on a flooded building site. Its exhaust, which had been threatening to fall off for weeks, sounded awful, blowing raspberries as she accelerated along Plum Run, rattled through Compton Magna and turned noisily into the stud drive.

Lester was leading dun stallion, Cruisoe, back from his high-hedged field, creased old face lifting like a furled flag in a breeze at the sight of her car. He was a stickler for treating his favourites to the toughest love, and Pax had always been his favourite. In the same way he gave a sharp tug to the chifney bit in his mouth now to remind Cruisoe he had his back, he fixed her with a steely look.

'We were expecting you first thing.'

'Sorry about that. Been a bit under the weather.' Shakes, headaches and tears, the usual morning call. 'Is Mummy around?'

'Mrs Ledwell's already set off.'

'Of course. For, er…?'

'Lunch with friends over Wiltshire way.' His wise old eyes stared, casting light on one of Pax's recent blackouts: a phone conversation she'd only partially pieced together afterwards, remembering trying not to sound drunk, offering to help. She'd worried afterwards she might have dreamed it.

'That's it. She's staying overnight there.'

'Hmm.' He looked disapproving.

'I'm all yours, Lester.'

'Fetch a brush.' The creased face shifted into a warmer welcome. 'And put that puppy in a stable. Not safe wandering round loose. You named it yet?'

'What would you call him, Lester?'

He watched as the deerhound rolled on its back beside Stubbs, gangly and compliant. 'Not for me to say.'

'Landseer maybe? Stubbs and Landseer make a good couple.'

He huffed. 'He the one paints all the dead deer?'

'And lots of dogs. Granny had a sketch of a lurcher in her dressing room.'

'Nothing but trouble, sight hounds.'

'Mummy suggested I stay tonight.' She remembered that much at least. 'Brought a bottle of Laphroaig for old time's sake.' It had been her grandfather's favourite malt. She wondered how soon they could crack it open. Being a keen hunt follower, Lester was probably old-school enthusiastic about daytime drinking.

The creases ironed out more, blackcurrant eyes bright. 'We'll toast the Captain later; work to do first.'

She followed him through the arch as he led Cruisoe back to his stable. From the opposite corner of the quadrangle came a great bellow of protest and a crashing of teeth against grille.

Pax turned to look at the younger stallion her mother had brought to the stud, coal eyes burning in that luminescent pearl-pale face behind his stall bars, mythically fierce and far too terrifying to bribe with a carrot.

'You leave that one!' Lester barked, marching on. 'The Irish lad's welcome to him. Needs fetching from the airport this evening. Best you do it.' He disappeared hurriedly into a foaling box.

At first, Pax didn't understand. Her head was still full of the argument with Mack, the overwhelming need for a drink. She counted the minutes down as they worked their way around the familiar tasks with barrows, buckets, brushes and brawn, grateful for physical work to keep her earthed. *Don't think about Kes.* It wasn't until they'd swept the cobbles of both yards that Lester broke the news that the jet-set pro rider her mother had hired was arriving at Birmingham airport that night. 'I have the flight number written down.'

'Can't he get a cab?'

'Not easy to get a taxi, night like New Year. Pricy, too.'

There was only ten pounds in the petty cash, they discovered. 'Where's Mummy planning to put him?'

'The attic flat, I believe.'

'Has it been cleaned up and aired?'

'To my knowledge, not since your father's day.'

'That was twenty years ago!' Furious that Ronnie never thought anything through beyond the next few hours, she started to march towards the house, the smash of jaw against metal from the grey stallion's stable as she passed it making her turn back to Lester. 'Will you be okay on your own while I try to get the place ready?'

'If you're sure about that.' Lester followed, clearing his throat awkwardly, the same noise he'd make when she was tiny and he was worried for her, his most fearless little jockey.

Pax was touched by his concern, although long numbed to the anxiety she used to feel about the flat that had been home to her parents during their short, unhappy marriage, later becoming her father's refuge to drink and rage. After his death she'd refused to go near it, weeping on Lester's shoulder that it was haunted. Looking back, that seemed silly and self-absorbed.

She jumped as a hind hoof struck out hard against the stable wall beside her. The grey was glaring at them both through his stable bars, ears flat. 'Why does Mummy like hotheads so much, Lester? Men, horses—'

'Daughters?'

She cuffed him playfully with her elbow, startled to find him stiff as a statuette, apologising when he almost fell over. 'I just hope this Luca character keeps his cool and pulls his weight; you can't be expected to do all the heavy work any more.'

'I told Mrs Ledwell that we need a yard helper, not some highfalutin showjumper,' Lester sniffed, always at his most confiding with Pax, who he saw as a kindred spirit. 'Eager youngster, willing to push a barrow in exchange for a few lessons. It's how your grandfather did it.'

'This place needs a professional too,' Pax pointed out, watching the grey weave his head from side to side. 'A cheap local work rider, not James Bond parachuting in with a lunge whip in each hand.'

'You were the best rider this stud ever saw.'

'I was a Pony Clubber,' she dismissed quickly.

'Only one of the children ever tried the Wolf Moon Lap. Even your mother never did that.'

'She had more sense,' Pax scoffed, although a small puff of pride lifted her to hear it.

It was the stuff of family legend – and Pax now thought a ridiculous one – that every year when January's first full moon, the Wolf Moon, was highest in the sky her great-grandfather Major Frank would carry the wind-up gramophone out onto the yard with his beloved Holst's *Planets* on the turntable. Dropping the needle at 'Jupiter, the Bringer of Jollity', he'd mount his favourite hunter and they'd charge around the stud's boundary, a far bigger land holding in his day. If he rode back under the arch before the 'Saturn' brought old age, it would augur a year's good fortune to the stud. This was practically impossible in Pax's experience, although according to Lester, her father had managed it the year she was born. She'd not even come close. Given that Major Frank had also been known for taking pot-shots at his staff and keeping the petty cash in the mouth of the stuffed Barbary lion in his study, she didn't set much store by his business tactics, however profitable the stud's fortunes in those days.

Lester looked at her beadily. 'Moon's full on St Agnes day. We could use a prosperous year.'

'I'll add it to Luca O'Brien's job description, shall I?' she said smoothly before deflecting. 'Alice is convinced the Horsemaker will be all fast-talking blarney and no sticking power. Mummy probably has the hots for him.' She'd said it before she could stop herself, aware how flippant and bitter she sounded.

Lester's lips pursed disapprovingly. 'If you say so.'

'Come on, Lester, we both know she'll end up breaking in the babies and riding everything.' The faded photographs in the tack room of Ronnie Percy hurtling round Badminton and

Burghley in her heyday paid testament to her long tenure as the stud's top jockey, horsebreaker and cover girl. 'She's a control freak just like Grumps.'

It was the perfect pacifier, Lester's face breaking into a rare smile. 'I'll drink to that.'

'Shall we have a quick toot of Laphroaig before I clean the flat?' Pax offered.

His eyes sparkled deep within their creases. 'And you're the Captain's granddaughter sure enough.' But he limped off without taking up her offer.

3

Like many gatherings at Compton Bagot's memorial hall, the village New Year's Eve party had long ago been hijacked by the Turner family from the Orchard estate. Notorious revellers, great clansmen, occasional fighters and indefatigable dancers whose twirling farrucas and flamencos dated back to their Romany days, they knew how to celebrate.

As the unofficial Kate to the family's Prince William, Carly Turner was on show in her best cut-out party frock, painted nails talon-like thanks to sister-in-law Janine, hair up in the tightest face-lift topknot to smooth out the dark hollows around her eyes from staying up all night with teething baby Jackson. Handsome war hero Ash towered and glowered at her side, a wide-shouldered, muscular peacekeeping force, heir apparent to the family chiefdom.

The teenage Turner tribe were already going rogue, trainers squeaking on the polished floor as a dance-off rapidly turned into a fight, from flossing to right crossing, dabs becoming jabs and beatboxing a spitting match.

Carly watched as Ash broke up the fight, admiring his cool and the fact he didn't need to utter a word to command their respect, a jerk of his head alone earning the beta wolf cowers as they sloped away. They all knew Ash could fight better than any Turner. The fact that he'd seen conflict as a soldier was abstract to them, but he'd been one of the family's best bare-knuckle fighters at their age, which in an old travelling line made him a legend.

'You gonna try for King of the Gypsies one day, Ash?' one asked. It was the biggest organised fight of all, tribe alpha against alpha.

'Not he's not!' Carly flared, earning a dirty look from the lad and her husband.

The bare fist bouts had stopped before they'd met, replaced by army boxing and strict discipline. Carly had made him promise not to return to it now his army days were over, which she knew he resented – especially since his old rival Jed still claimed the family fighting crown – but they needed boundaries for the sake of their kids, all under six. She could forgive the occasional marathon *Mortal Kombat* session or lashed all-nighter with his shark pack of single mates so long as he didn't come home with both brows split up and his teeth knocked into his sinuses.

Despite the dance-floor flights and much throwing up of toffee vodka in the ladies loos, the party was barely getting going, having kicked off at six for the younger kids. Carly tried not to yawn, secretly longing to be at home watching soaps on catch-up. It was so early, she'd see the latest episodes as they were broadcast.

'Nothing's going on here for hours,' Ash announced after his second bottled beer. 'Let's head over to Flynn's for a bit.'

Carly gritted her teeth. The shark pit beckoned.

Music thumping, dogs barking and dope smoke rising, nineties rock-star throwback Flynn greeted them at the door of his tiny terraced cottage wearing nothing but a skull and crossbones flag wrapped around his snake-like hips, tattoos and neck chains on show.

'It's an ABC party,' he reminded them.

'What's that?'

'Anything but clothes. Amelia's idea.'

Flynn's latest girlfriend was a teenage university student, the riding-mad daughter of two local doctors, all swishy hair and wide-eyed 'totes!'. Ash and Carly endured her with toothache smiles, uncomfortable in the knowledge that Flynn was sleeping with at least three other clients. Tonight, Amelia had brought a lot of pretty friends, also with swishy hair, excited exclamations and tiny skirts made from sticky tape and bin bags. Carly cast around for any women she knew, but saw none, not in itself unusual. Ash's old gang was a bachelor pack who, like divorced dad of two Flynn, saw sex as recreational sport, their relationships counting down from first chat-up line to pillow-biting revenge porn.

All Ash's usual crew were already there, friends he'd known since schooldays – or bunking-off-school days – none of them embracing the ABC theme, although Ink, the tattooed assassin of the quiet chat-up, was already wearing a pretty blonde on his knee. Meanwhile Roadie, the hulking fridge of music trivia and gross party tricks, was wearing a retro T-shirt featuring a picture of a man with hair like Cameron Diaz.

'Martin Fry – lead singer of ABC, gettit? A… B… C!' He raised a can from his lair by the stereo.

'You both got a hall pass then, yeah?' Flynn gave them beer bottles. He was even talking like a student, Carly realised.

The Turners' three children were sleeping over with their grandmother, a quiet little woman abandoned long ago by Ash's father, her fear of going outside compensated by the sixty-inch television constantly beaming CBeebies, soaps and crime after lights out.

'I'm trying to get Mazur-arty next door to join us.' Flynn picked up his phone to check messages. 'You know, that sweet piece of arse married to the Polish man mountain.'

'You're brave. He's one big bastard.'

'Still in Poland with ze luvink family,' Flynn said, winking. 'Little Mrs M came home early, looking for work. Shame for her to sit alone all night. You go round there and invite her over, Carl. She thinks this party is beneath her.'

'It bloody is.' She eyed the slipping bin bags. One girl had tit-taped CDs to her nipples and thong. 'And don't you dare call a woman a sweet piece of arse again in my presence, Flynn Rix. Not unless you want your plain ordinary man-arse embossed with my trainer treads.' She had no intention of asking the next-door neighbour around, a woman she had no doubt was way too sophisticated for one of Flynn's seedy sessions, where half the room was usually under age or on probation.

To prove her point, with a blast of cold air from an open door, her nemesis arrived, his hooded eyes trailing around the exposed flesh with a piratical smile. Older than the others, battle scarred and aloof, Skully was Ink's big brother, an intermittent member of the group, and the one Carly trusted least. So-called because of the bodysuit of skull tattoos going up to his chin – and because he was rumoured to have broken more skulls than Genghis Khan – he'd been in and out of prison all his adult life, some of it as cellmates with Ash's long-errant dad, Nat. Skully and Ash's close friendship worried Carly. There'd been recent rumours that they were fencing stolen goods, although Ash angrily denied it. Whatever secrets they shared, Sully had a hold over her husband she didn't like.

'Ohmygod! He *so* looks dangerous,' Amelia gushed to a friend nearby, then let out a little squeak as Skully sauntered up to Carly and Ash.

An imperceptible nod passed between the men along with a muttered, 'Brother.' Then Skully bowed to Carly, flashing his gold teeth like a threat. 'Dressed to kill, I see, Carlita.'

'We can test that if you don't call me Carly.'

He forced a laugh. 'You're lucky I like funny women.'

'And you're lucky I like boneheads.' Carly reached across to grab a bin bag before he could reply. 'Skully, love, have you met Flynn's girlfriend, Amelia?'

Grinning, Ash went to fetch more beers while Amelia preened coyly and made introductions to a Sophie, a Chloe and a Figs. Skully looked delighted, especially when Flynn muscled up territorially. If there was one thing the tattooed maverick enjoyed more than winding up his mates' wives, it was chatting up his mates' girlfriends.

'Go next door and ask her over,' Flynn entreated Carly.

'Why?'

'Because, sweetlips, I think you'd really like her. You need a little friend of your own to stop you winding up Ash's.' He dropped his voice. 'It doesn't do to mess with Skully. He'll mess right back atcha.'

Reluctantly shrugging on her coat, Carly found Ash returning from the kitchen, dipping his head beneath the ceiling beam, bottle necks threaded between his fingers.

'Just running next door, okay?'

'No shit.' He glanced unenthusiastically at Skully who was now hypnotising Amelia and her giggly friends with his devil eyes and dirty talk. Ash diverted to join Hardcase who was holed up by the stereo choosing music.

Carly sometimes missed the wild energy of the soldier she'd married, but she was grateful he never sharked, however drunk he got. Ash was no flirt and hated small talk, although Carly still kept a jealous count of the tanned bench-press queens at his gym whose flat abs her husband watched with professional interest. A confirmed Jack the Lad before they'd married – and a little bit after that, if she was honest – his interest in other women rarely flicked beyond *Tomb Raider* and hardcore these days. At home, he could still be a randy sod, but war and fatherhood had changed him, and he lived too deep in his shell to share his mates' brio.

Heading for the door, she felt Skully's eyes on her and turned. He winked nastily. She winked straight back at him, cold-eyed, not caring what Flynn said. He didn't frighten her.

*

'To auld acquaintances!'

Pax held her glass against Lester's, her gaze focussed tightly on the three fingers of malt whisky refracted behind the carved crystal, a fiery golden hit she'd been looking forward to all day. The past last hour had crawled by, feeding the tack room wood burner half a cider apple tree's worth of logs while helping Lester meticulously clean leatherwork for hunting tomorrow. The sun had been over the yardarm for ages, Happy Hours would be coming to an end, New Year's Eve parties already well underway, and at last she had a drink in her hand.

To her frustration, before they could knock back the toast, Lester started reciting a list of family absentees, Laphroaig still aloft. 'The Captain and Mrs Percy, and Major Percy before them – may got rest their souls.' He went on to reel off a register of distant dead relatives, recently departed friends, a couple of favourite horses and a labrador. Mistaking her wide-eyed frustration for alarm, he explained, 'Your grandparents liked to remember those we've lost this time of year.'

Pax thought Lester far too obsessed with death, like many of his age. 'Maybe that tradition can be laid to rest.'

'To Johnny!' he toasted stubbornly.

Pax stared longingly at her glass. 'Yes, to Daddy.'

'Your father was a good man.'

'I know he was.'

'Soul of a poet, heart of a cavalryman.'

'Quite.' Pax drew the glass towards her lips with an ecstatic shudder of anticipation, then realised he was off again, toasting the living as well as the dead now.

'To your brother in Africa and to your sister and her family here. May they have good fortune and good health.'

She felt a beat thud in her temples as Lester took a reedy breath to add more. 'To your mother, who we must help as best we can. To all the little ones who will benefit from the

Percy stud breeding champions again…' He seemed to take pride in pedantically naming all her nieces and nephews. 'And of course, to poor little Oliver, who you miss so much.'

She looked away, the pain instant. 'We call him Kes.'

Lester lowered his glass, voice quiet, 'To Kester too.' The crystal rim touched hers again.

Pax's gaze went sharply across to his face, but his wise eyes had disappeared into their creases as he took a long, appreciative draft of the fine malt.

She knocked hers back in one, temples pounding now. 'As you know, Lester, there's a lot of things we don't talk about in this family. Best left that way.'

With a brisk nod, he admired the whisky left in his glass. 'Attic flat ready for the newcomer, is it?'

Already craving a second measure, Pax let the heat of the malt diffuse through her, grateful for the change of subject at least. 'It'll do.'

Thick with dust and mouse droppings, crammed full of old furniture and reeking of damp, it was a part of the house largely untouched for years. Cleaning it had taken her all the rest of the day.

'Used to have house staff up there when I first worked here.' He set his glass down and went to close the stove flues, stepping carefully over Stubbs and the sleeping puppy. 'Place had status.'

'Another drink?' She grasped the opportunity if Lester was going to wax lyrical.

But he shook his head. 'Roads are going to be foggy later. You'll need your wits.'

Pax watched enviously as he polished off his remaining Laphroaig, gathering the keys and his empty hunting flask from the table.

'Almost forgot.' Reaching in his pocket, he handed her a mobile phone. 'Mrs Ledwell left this behind. Happy New Year.'

'And to you, Lester. May it bring everything you wish for,' she added over-effusively.

He fixed her with a scope-lamp stare she'd almost forgotten. 'I want you back on a horse.'

'We'll see,' she humoured, having no intention of getting back in the saddle.

'Don't let your parents' talent go to waste. Your father rode the Wolf Moon Lap for you, you know that.'

'I'd need all seven planets and Clair de Lune to get round again,' she joked.

'And I would give every star in the sky to see it.' Lester's voice crackled. 'Good night to you.' He limped off, poker-backed.

Retreating to the main house, Pax paced the kitchen, which was the only warm room, the Aga gurgling throatily, its rail festooned in her mother's silk thermals. It was still hours until New Year, the airport run looming between her and one last night in her cups. She was dying for another drink, the almost-full whisky bottle like a golden trophy on the table as she marched around it, fiddle-footed. If she stood still, she thought about Mack threatening to stay in Scotland with Kes and emotion overwhelmed her. She had no desire to dwell on past lives while her son was being taken away from her.

Waking that morning, Pax had looked forward to being here on her own while the year she'd rather forget, and the week she couldn't, slipped away. It would be the first time she'd spent a night in the house where she grew up since her late teens, and the first time she'd ever done so alone. She'd been planning to drink the whisky, listen to loud music and run from room to room, singing at the top of her voice, swan wings flapping and hissing, grateful for her own company, and to be granted a night away from the Mack Shack, from Mack, from marriage, from modern digital communication. But instead she must soberly chauffeur Stud Man or whatever he called himself, probably courteously see New Year in with him too, and she resented him like mad.

Without a drink, Pax was burning up with restless, heart-thumping loneliness.

She knew better than to impinge upon Lester's routine. A creature of deeply entrenched habit, he would remain shut in his cosy cottage watching television after his evening meal of a Fray Bentos pie, then bathing before bed.

Her mother's forgotten phone lay as dormant as her own on the table beside the whisky bottle, the only sounds coming from the shuddering fridge, bubbling flue and the still-nameless puppy, curled up in front of the Aga, having a whisker-twitching dream. She thought jealously of Ronnie partying with friends, merry on half a glass of white, as quick to reel in admirers as she was to cut ties.

Looking at her watch, she was shocked to see barely a few minutes had passed since her toast with Lester.

The hiatus was unsettling, making her mind breed negative thoughts, like bacteria on Petri dishes: a custody battle, her teenage mistakes brought out, her unsuitability as a mother, her family's tragic track record.

At seven thirty on the dot, Pax called Mack's mobile from the house landline to wish Kes artificially bright night-nights, ignoring her husband's hissed, 'Have you got my messages?' before he handed the phone across to their sleepy son. She kept Kes talking too long because her heart hurt, quickly hanging up before his father came back on the line, ignoring Mack's three callbacks, then taking the phone off the hook, pacing all the while. She knew it was childish to avoid talking to the husband she'd lain awake beside just hours earlier, but she was afraid of more one-upmanship and manipulation, of his anger, or, even worse, that stiff-jawed Happy New Year politeness the Forsyths did. She didn't want Mack to have a Happy New Year; she wanted him to get food poisoning.

The clock hands had barely moved.

She lapped her way around the table again, eyeing the bottle, wondering how far down it she'd need to go to kill the grief throbbing in her chest, to still the ever-moving legs. The reception of the old radio on the windowsill was too crackly to endure – how her grandmother had managed four decades of *The Archers Omnibus* with it was beyond belief. It was too cold to settle anywhere else in the house, and she didn't trust the chimneys enough to light a fire. The freezing fog that forecasters had been warning about was already cloaking the Comptons up on their high ridge.

She looked up Luca O'Brien's number on her mother's phone contacts, using the landline to dial it. An automated female voice invited her to speak after the tone.

She matched its robotic, stern depth. 'This is Patricia Forsyth, Ronnie Ledwell's daughter. I shall be collecting you from the airport.' She reeled off her own mobile number. 'I'll hold your name up at Arrivals, but if you miss me for any reason, please call me. Don't call the house – nobody's here.'

Older sister Alice, who had Googled O'Brien extensively, insisted he was a charlatan, unable to hold down a job for long, his departure from the legendary German stud Gestüt Fuchs veiled in secrecy. Their brother Tim knew a wine grower in South Africa whose besotted showjumping wife had spent a fortune on horses at the Irishman's recommendation when he was based there. There was also a strong suspicion that he'd once been Ronnie's lover. None of the three children trusted their mother's judgement.

The old wall clock still insisted it was still far too early to set off for the airport, even allowing for fog. She remembered she had yet to take a set of towels and spare sheets through to the attic flat. The more self-contained Luca was there, the better, she felt.

Contrary to its name, the attic flat ran across three floors, utilizing the maze of old servants' rooms that led off the back staircase beyond the service doors, along with the entire top storey. It had its own small kitchen, sitting room and study, several bedrooms, a vast bathroom that was supposed to be haunted by a giggling housemaid, and lots of little rooms that had once stored laundry and silverware. It was ridiculously big for just one person – her parents and all three siblings had lived there, along with a nanny, before her mother left. It even had its own little courtyard garden, and a roof terrace at the back on which a newly married Ronnie had scandalised her husband by sunbathing naked.

Nowadays, there was little evidence left of her parents' time there together; Pax had been so young when her mother left them that she had no memory of living there before she and her siblings had all moved across to the old nursery in the main house. Her father had stayed on in the flat, drinking himself to oblivion each night, but most traces of Johnny Ledwell had gone. Pax wished her memories of him were sharper. She'd been just eleven when he'd died. Before that day she'd thought he would live forever, not leave her with a decade of fading snapshots.

She'd made Luca O'Brien up the sleigh bed in Johnny's old room, which was at least tidy and had a lavatory next door. Unapologetically masculine, it had been a dressing room once, with a wall of heavy-fronted cupboards still crammed with hunting coats and dinner suits reeking of mothballs, an old-fashioned washstand in one corner, and a big, speckled full-length mirror which she glanced in as she placed the towels on the chest of drawers. Eyes pinched, neck poking scrawnily from her thick jumper, skin pale and dry as a bleach stain, she looked like a tortoise – and at least a decade older than her thirty-one years.

How many times had her father stared into this mirror? Had he seen in it anything that she saw now? It was Alice who had inherited Johnny's dark, fierce good looks; Tim had their mother's blonde perfection. Pax was altogether different, and yet she was the one who sensed a strong bond the others denied: the familial curse.

She unpinned her hair and shook it out, wild liver-chestnut curls that had loosened from clock to bed springs over the years, yet remained defiant, refusing to be tamed. Hers was her paternal grandmother's hair, she'd been told. Johanna

Dwyer had been the fast-riding daughter of Tipperary horse dealers who – if legend was to be believed – had been added as a sweetener to four good hunters and a harness draft, marrying the purchaser to seal the deal. All too briefly a goddess riding astride over Worcestershire hedges and hostess of the best farmers' meets in Kinver, she'd drowned in the River Severn at just twenty-nine, the circumstances of her death shielded in typically gothic Ledwell family secrecy.

Tight-lipped, Johnny would only ever say that his mother had been the bravest of women.

'You have her heart, Patricia,' he'd told Pax when she was about seven, no doubt plastered out of his mind, although she hadn't learned to identify drunkenness until later. 'Kind and fierce. It's a rare thing. You must take good care of it; don't ever let it grow sour.'

Or old? Pax had found herself wondering more than once whether Johanna Ledwell's premature death, like her son's after her, had been of her own making? Was that the curse?

She shuddered. It was so cold up here, she could see her own breath clouding in her reflection.

Looking round at the bleak room, her grandmother's kind heart stirred with a guilty conscience inside her. Luca O'Brien might be used to sub-zero Canadian temperatures, but she couldn't let him freeze to death on his first night.

She fetched the oil heater from her old bedroom in the main house, deciding she could sleep in her mother's room above the warm kitchen. She then locked the doors that linked the annexe to the main house, except the ground-floor one, hiding the keys at the back of a kitchen drawer.

To stop herself gravitating towards the Laphroaig bottle again, she went outside to pick a welcoming spray of rose hips and winter jasmine from the tangled bed by the front steps. The fog was suffocatingly cold now, the gleam from Lester's cottage windows barely visible through its white veils. Having put the flowers in a small jug on the washstand, she went to fetch Luca a few books to read, some ancient stud manuals for amusement, along with *Cold Comfort Farm* and *Wuthering Heights* for irony. He needed a bedside light. She fetched that too, stealing the opposite partner to her mother's bedside table which was one of the few in the house with a working bulb, forced to trail all the way down one set of stairs and up the other because she'd locked the interconnecting doors. Every time she passed the whisky bottle in the kitchen, her jaw tugged for a mouthful.

'You're a drunk, Tishy.' Mack's accusing words taunted her.

She took the back stairs two at a time. She would show him. She would quit drinking at midnight. Damn him blaming the symptoms not the cause.

The bedroom, already warmed by the heater, had taken on a whole new personality. Its reawakened scent hit her like a portal to another lifetime. Her father's smell. Saddle soap, cologne, leather and whisky. Cigarettes, boiling linseed, Hibiscrub and whisky. Coffee, hot horse, wet waxed coat and whisky.

Damn Luca O'Brien for taking her final freedom away. Let him find a cab.

Downstairs again, she sat at the table, reaching out for the malt.

Her mother's phone let out a shrill beep that made Pax jump, her fingers catching the bottle. As it toppled over, she grabbed for it and missed.

Behind her, the puppy had woken and started barking excitedly.

Pax watched helplessly as the bottle rolled away from her to the table's far edge where it teetered like the coach in *The Italian Job*.

'Just bloody smash!' she dared it.

Obligingly it dropped, glass shattering, the distillery reek overpowering.

The puppy whined by the kitchen door.

Snatching him up, grabbing the still-beeping phone too,

Pax went outside, teeth chattering as soon as the cold air hit her, not noticing the puppy doubling back inside to hurriedly relieve himself on the doormat. On the phone screen, an alarm reminder had kicked in: *Text children HNY. Call and check Pax okay.*

It was so unexpected to find that her mother had calendared anything, let alone New Year greetings to loved ones, Pax felt a confused rush of emotion.

She snoozed the message, quashing an ungrateful afterthought that no mother should need reminding to share a celebration with her children. Ronnie was never invited to join in family revels, after all. Excluded from birthdays, christenings, Easter, Christmas, she was isolated and out of the loop. No Service, just like the message read on her phone face.

Back inside, she scraped up the glass with a dustpan and brush and mopped the floor as best she could, but the smell lingered, single malt running in rivulets between the flagstones, soaking through grout holes, washing in a tide beneath the dresser's oak skirting. She opened one of its cupboards, her throat catching to see her grandparents' dusty collection of kitchen 'snifters' still stored in there, the labels yellowed. Blended Scotch and supermarket sherry, knocked back in heavy-bottomed glasses at the farmhouse table, the malts and *fino* served to guests in crystal tumblers in the drawing room.

'One toasts days to remember and drowns nights to forget,' her grandmother Ann had been fond of saying, a Dorothy Parker in tweed and gaberdine, she could outdrink and outthink most men.

If Pax had her Ledwell grandmother's soul, she liked to think she had her Percy grandmother's spirit – and love of spirits. She was nothing like her self-destructive father, she reminded herself, the smell making her gag. Nor was she a guzzler like so many of her friends; no Wine O'Clock, Mummy's Glass, bottle-a-night habit for her. She'd knocked that on the head when the recycling got conspicuous, which is how she knew she could control it. She'd simply been brought up at the hip of an old-fashioned matriarch who rode, dog-walked, stood her ground, fought her corner and outdrank her husband into her seventies. Alice was the same. It was in their DNA.

And like her grandmother, she wasn't afraid of speaking her mind.

Determined and furious, she marched outside with her phone, stumbling through the fog to the far end of the walled garden where a bar of signal was occasionally possible when balancing on the old compost heap, her fingers shaking almost too much to tap the screen. Bingo!

Try to take our son away and I'll make you wish you'd never lived! she texted Mack.

U OK, Pax hun? came the reply

Scrolling up, she realised she'd sent a message to 'Mackenzie's Mummy', added to contacts for a recent party RSVP, an oversharing PTA heavyweight at Kes's school.

The state of the Forsyths' marriage would be all over the mummy mafia before daybreak.

Happy New Year! she typed, then deleted it. That was surely against the trade descriptions act. There was nothing happy about this one.

Bridge was already in a onesie and dressing gown, wood burner glowing, wine poured, cats Barack and Michelle curling around on the windowsill behind her. She'd sent WhatsApp video messages to Aleš and the kids in Poland – the Internet in his family's rural house wasn't good enough to live-stream – and then donned noise-cancelling headphones to wipe out next door's shrill laughter and nineties rock playlist that could penetrate even three feet of sandstone. She was now trying to get to grips with an audiobook she'd lost her place in more than once whilst falling asleep recently. It was a gothic horror recommended by Petra and something extremely unpleasant was about to happen to a couple having adulterous sex in a tapestried bedchamber.

The cats springing off the windowsill behind her, fur on end, made her start and look over her shoulder.

A pale hand was pressed to the glass pane, a mask of a face peering in, black-rimmed eyes huge.

Bridge screamed, which in noise-cancelling headphones was a strange first, like singing underwater.

The mask smiled and the hand waved.

She knew Carly Turner by sight, although they'd barely exchanged more than a few words, which was odd given they had children much the same age. Bridge rarely ventured out with hers in the village, taking them instead into Broadbourne or Chipping Hampton to Tumble Tots, Water Babies and Jo Jingles, to catch up over coffee with NCT friends or to spend time with their cousins and her Polish sister-in-law in Micklecote. Carly, meanwhile, pushed hers miles around the local footpaths in a double buggy and baby backpack, recently accompanied by a scary-looking dog, always stopping for ages in gateways if there were horses there so she and the kids could fuss them. She cut a recognisable figure with her many c-shaped tattoos and slim, road-hardened physique. When Bridge opened the door, she realised Carly was dressed in a clingy, artfully slashed tube of red Lycra that would make anyone bigger than a size six look fat, shoulders inadequately caped in fun fur, her teeth chattering.

Her painted eyes rolled apologetically. 'I've been sent round to invite you to a shit party.'

'Come in, queen, you'll catch your death.'

Carly dived inside gratefully, the cats curling around her ankles like mobile leg-warmers. 'Look at your lovely fire. It's much nicer in here than Flynn's place. All he's got there is home entertainment and recliner sofas.'

'Stay and have a drink,' Bridge offered, grateful for the

company and curious to get some low-down on the bad-boy farrier next door. 'I'm not leaving this house tonight.'

'Don't blame you.' Carly flopped on the harlequin-striped sofa by the wood burner, pulling a big sheepskin cushion onto her knee and gazing around. 'It's amazing.'

Bridge's bold taste and Aleš's love of Polish folk art meant their tiny cottage was a riot of colour: the walls that weren't natural limestone were painted with flowers and patterns like a psychedelic inside-out canal barge; the old wooden shutters were adorned with felt hangings, colourful paper cuttings overlapped on the beams, big raw glazed pots overflowed with riotously bright paper flowers and carved wooden bowls held clutches of painted eggs.

Having loved it at first, Bridge now secretly found herself craving minimalism, the sleek straight lines, walls of light and polished concrete floors of the eco houses her husband's team built for the award-winning architect.

'Picture it full of carrycots, Pampers bags and plastic toys which is more normal,' she said, heading through to the little open-plan kitchen to fetch another glass and glug out some red wine for Carly.

'How old are your little ones?' Carly asked.

'DS is thirteen months and lurches between the furniture just like his dad, and my always-talking DD is three next month. You?'

'Jackson's coming up eight months, Sienna's almost three too, and Ellis will be five in March.' Carly was holding the Merlot out in front of her like a precious orb, and Bridge guiltily wondered whether she drank wine. It was as instinctive to her to pull a cork at six in the evening as it was boil the kettle at six in the morning, but perhaps Carly was more of a cocktail type, or even teetotal. She'd seen her in the village often enough to know that beneath the war paint was a pretty, childlike face whose heavy-lidded insouciance was as artfully applied as tonight's scarlet lipstick. Scrubbed, she could pass for fifteen.

'Can I get you something else instead? Gin and tonic maybe? Tea?'

'This is great.' She took a huge swig, giving herself a red moustache. 'Where's your fella tonight?'

'Enjoying Sylwester in a little village in Malopolska.'

'Isn't he the one that chased Tweety Pie?'

She laughed. 'It's what the Polish call New Year's Eve. They'll all get very drunk and very jolly, and Aleš will cry and promise his mother that we will move back there soon – never! – and then they'll sing and dance, and tomorrow they'll take their hangovers for a forest sled ride to cook sausages over a haybale fire and sing and cry a bit more.'

'Instead you chose to come back here to sit next to that?' Carly jerked her head to indicate the whoops through the limestone, poignantly accompanied by 'Wonderwall.'

'I flew back for a job interview.' Bridge pulled a face. 'Shouldn't have bothered, given Sous fecking Vide thinks Instagram styling is the primary skill of an office administrator. That, and brown-nosing her fecking arse.' It was easier to joke off her disastrous meeting at The Jugged Hare with Carly than the Bags, her steady grey gaze amused and wise. She sensed she couldn't shock Carly, however foul-mouthed she was.

'I'm up for a waitressing job there.' She lifted a well-plucked eyebrow. 'I do shifts at Le Mill, but it's hard getting over there without a car. If it's going to be full of tools, I might forget it.'

'On the other hand, the pay's good. I did my research, and the money's all ethical venture capital: local suppliers, bamboo uniforms, quirky staff perks, no expense spared.'

'Must be minted.'

'With aubergine carpaccio and pickled fecking raisins.'

The Bags would have hooted with obliging laughter, but Carly creased her forehead uncertainly, wary of being taken for a fool.

'Your man's next door, I take it?'

She nodded, eyes staying cynically narrow. 'It's more of a lads' night.'

'Stay here for as long as you like. I was about to watch *Black Panther* on Box Office.'

'Seriously? I love that film. I'll text Ash that I've broken a nail. That'll buy me an hour.' Seeing Bridge's sceptical face, she explained, 'Janine makes out like it's a dark art, and she's so slow at it Turner men think fake nails take longer than heart surgery.' To authenticate her story, Carly took one of her long thumb talons between her teeth and tugged off its fake gel tip, leaving a naked little pad to pat out the text super-fast on her phone screen. About to press send, she pulled a face. 'Then again, the lads might come round here.'

'Tell him we're sharing birth stories.' Bridge winked, reaching for the remote.

'Love it!' The thumb danced once more.

When Pax set off, the white-out on the top of the Comptons' ridge made driving difficult, as Lester had predicted. Even navigating her way to the end of the drive took concentration. She was grateful for the Noddy car's fog lights, Mack's puppy whimpering in the boot of the car.

'It's okay, little one,' she soothed. Remembering that Landseer had gone mad, she'd decided against calling him that. Mack, disinterested, had suggested Rover. Perhaps they should ask Kes to name him. The fog in front of her blurred. *'Stop it!'* she hissed to herself.

As soon as they were on the village lane her phone found a mobile signal and started trilling with incoming messages, the car's dash screen lighting up with a flurry of backlogged notifications. Distracted, she pulled up to read them in a gateway. All were from Mack, each one increasingly desperate for an answer.

He claimed he'd had a change of heart (or a stiff talking-to from his big sister, more likely). He'd been too hasty embracing his parents' plans without discussing them with her first. Of *course* they must talk. They'd work things through. For Kes. For each other.

Pax had motion sickness from the mood swings of marriage break-up, the constant ups and downs, the indecision.

The messages got more demanding and emotional with each successive time stamp. In the last few, he'd added kisses – and *c*s – told her he loved her – and lived for her – and that he mossed, mussed and missed her. If one of them was halfway down a whisky bottle, it wasn't her.

She didn't reply.

Dropping down from the escarpment, she found herself driving just beneath the fog, like an eerie false ceiling. It was just a few feet overhead by the time Pax turned onto the M40, heading towards Birmingham, her radio tuned to rebellious anthems. The rusted exhaust was deafening now. She hoped it would hold out.

At least the noise drowned out the trills of yet more texts arriving from Mack.

He called as she joined the M42, the fog lower now, speed reduction warnings flashing from the electronic boards.

'Where've you *been*?' his slurred voice demanded through the speakers. There was ceilidh music and conversation in the background.

'You know there's no signal at the stud. Is Kes okay?'

'Fine. Fast asleep. Pax, I…' He started to cry.

So unexpected, so unlike him, it made her cry too. She almost side-swiped another car.

'Don't take Kes away from me,' he sobbed.

'*You* want to take him from *me*!' She hid her tears from him, mouth full of marbles.

'YOU want out of the MARRIAGE!'

She made it to the hard shoulder, hazards on, head in her arms on the wheel.

'Mack, it can't go on as it is, can it?'

'Do you shtill love me?' he demanded. He had to have been drinking for hours to ask something like that.

Yellow lights were flashing in her mirrors. She flinched as a shower of grit hit the roof of her car and the salting truck trundled by.

'Are you shtill there?' he asked.

'Yes.'

'And do you? Or washthat "yes" your answer?'

She found she couldn't respond, tears blinding her, only a few ungainly snorts coming out. Damn her honesty. Damn her unflinching honesty.

'I'll make my own mind up, shall I?'

'Let's talk again tomorrow, Mack. When you're sober.' Oh, hollow victory. 'Happy New Year.' There she'd done it. Polite as a Forsyth. Calm as a Ledwell. Tough as a Percy.

'Fuck you!' He hung up.

She drove to the airport in a haze of tears and a plume of exhaust fumes, parking the raspberry-blowing Fiat in the pickup zone and dashing into the arrivals terminal, embarrassed to be late after all the hanging about waiting to set off.

A long row of *delayeds* greeted her on the board.

'Everything's affected by the fog,' she was told by a uniformed official with funky sideburns at the information desk, his accent a sweet Brummy apology. 'Dublin's been out of action all afternoon, now Manchester's grounded everything. Fog wasn't supposed to get here until tomorrow, so it's a ruddy nightmare. Where's he flying from, love?'

'Canada – no, Schiphol.'

The airport worker checked on his computer. 'That's still listed, but you'll have a long wait. It's not left Amsterdam yet. Likely as not, they'll redirect it to London if it does.'

'Which airport?' she asked wearily.

'Can't tell yet. Quicker to wait. They usually lay on a coach. Could be the early hours before he gets here, I'm afraid. Do you live far? Great hair, by the way.'

On red-eyed, bruise-bagged, hollow-cheeked days like this, Pax was ever-grateful for her grandmother's hair. People always loved the hair. It was on a par with a handbag dog.

Damn Luca O'Brien for being late.

'My car's about to die.' She looked around distractedly. It would be midnight in three hours, her last drunken stand of the year – of all time – forfeited. Tonight it mattered. Shameful, desperate tears filled her eyes.

'Boyfriend, is it?' The worker looked at her sympathetically.

'Husband.' She realised too late that she'd misunderstood him, still thinking everyone could see her marriage break-up reflected back from her eyes like a disaster movie. Instead, he saw romance, lovers separated by fog as midnight chimed. It hardly mattered.

'As it's New Year…' he said, reaching under his counter, voice hushed. 'I shouldn't be doing this, but you're too beautiful to be sad and this might cheer you up.' He smiled wider, sideburns stretching, and pulled out a voucher for the airport hotel.

'Complimentary room. Show this to reception and say Dig okayed it.' He signed the back. 'My boyfriend's the manager. He'll make sure you get an upgrade and free drinks at the bar. Make the most of it. Happy New Year.'

Pax took it gratefully. She'd take all the compliments on offer right now.

On the way back to the car, she left a message on Luca O'Brien's number to say where she'd be waiting. At least a hotel room would be a lot warmer and cleaner than the stud, she realised with relief, hoping they took dogs; they could both do with a bath.

*

Carly could hold her drink, but she couldn't hope to keep up with Bridge, who was downing three glasses of wine for her every one, talking horse all over the movie.

'You can put your foot in the stirrup any time, queen. I only started in my twenties.' The self-mocking Belfast lilt hypnotised Carly, full of vim and vigour as she tried to convince her to have a go at riding. 'And I was living in fecking London at the time, can you believe? Could never afford it before then. Used to catch a tube train out to Barnet in designer breeches every Saturday morning, fighting the pervs off – came back stinking of gee-gee a few hours later and they'd come nowhere near me. I've been addicted to it ever since. Vowed I'd buy my own ned as soon as I left the city. Best feeling.'

The first time Carly had encountered Bridge – galloping straight at her through a cornfield on an out-of-control pony, laughing and whooping and apologising all at the same time – she'd hoped they'd be mates. Carly liked rebels, those dangerous souls who dared to live a little bit faster than others. From her trendy silver hair with its pink tips through her geek glasses, paired this evening with a prison-arrow onesie and felt pheasant slippers, Bridge was standout unconventional and a breath of fresh air in the Comptons. Her face had a likeably sharp-nosed, almond-eyed shrewdness, and Carly liked her voice as well, that sardonic flat 'Norn Irish' drawl reminded her of clever comedians on panel shows, and made everything sound ironically amusing. She was clever and grumpy and kind.

The fact she had her own horse deepened the bond, as she told Carly, 'You can have a sit on my wee woolly man any time. I was just like you, loved the creatures since I was a kid, but there's not many grew up on my street ever sat on more than a donkey on the beach.'

Which made it all the more embarrassing to drift off halfway through Bridge telling her all about Craic, only hearing as far as the bit where she'd bought him unpapered and unhandled, fresh off the boat from Ireland for slightly less than it cost to have her hair extensions redone every three months.

Instead, she dreamed about the colt at Compton Bagot stud, Spirit, gold and black like a Versace piece, his white blaze and stockings flashing as he galloped away over the ridge above the Comptons, past the windmill there, disappearing forever.

She awoke with a jerk to find herself covered with a thick red big-knit blanket that smelled comfortingly of woodsmoke, a purring cat on her feet.

'Happy New Year!' From the opposite sofa, Bridge raised her glass and a well-shaped eyebrow, prettily slitted with two shaven tramlines. 'I'm so glad you snore.'

'Shit, did I miss it? Ash will go ape.'

'Don't be daft, you silly cow. It's not even ten. You look done in. Little one teething?'

It was such a relief to be with someone who got it. Turner women rarely shared parenting horrors, at least not with Carly, the closed order around delinquent teens and tantruming toddlers as defensive as owners of dangerous dogs – and they had those on the estate, too.

'You need food, queen. There's nothing of you. No wonder you're knackered. Say, do you fancy nachos and dip? The really lazy sort full of E numbers that comes in a fecking jar. I don't do trendy fermented food unless you count Greek yoghurt that's gone off.'

'Me neither.' She grinned as Bridge sauntered into the kitchen, fielding a call on her mobile. Her hostess catcalled with delight, obviously a close family member, her accent thickening.

Carly checked her own phone. Ash hadn't replied to her text. She sent him another to say she was still girl-talking.

The rock anthem soundtrack and whoops had racked up so much next door that the floor was vibrating, and she shuddered to imagine the state of the swishy-haired students and their Sellotaped fancy dress, especially with Skully in the room. She trusted Ash to just admire the view while he concentrated on getting slowly drunk. Very, very drunk. Not that he betrayed it for a minute. Only Carly recognised the glint of anaesthesia finally clouding the pain, the soporific, seductive Ash she'd learned to live with because the brave soldier had left a part of his soul on the battlefield.

'Sorry about that.' Bridge returned with a tray of jars and foil snack bags and more wine. 'My sister getting the hour difference wrong. She's in Hollywood – works in the film industry.'

She looked so pink-cheeked and proud, Carly forgave her the boast. 'Is she an actress?'

'SFX make-up artist. Mostly TV, but she was in the prosthetics team for *Futureland*. Have you seen it? She had you-know-who in her chair for three hours a day most of last year.'

'You're kidding! I wanted to see that at the cinema, but Ash...' She hesitated. 'We'll get the DVD when it comes out.' They avoided films with long battle scenes or big explosions: his legs and hands starting to jump, face sweaty, eyes fixed.

'I've it downloaded. We can watch a bit if you've got time to break another nail and say we're talking potty training?'

Carly didn't need asking twice.

To Pax's relief the airport hotel accepted small, well-behaved dogs for an extra charge, buying her lie that the deerhound puppy was a Yorkie-poo. 'Oh, sweet! What's his name?'

'Incognito.'

Having found her room – small and corporate with a worryingly empty minibar – she ordered a steak baguette and a large vodka from room service. She wasn't hungry, but needed to legitimise the drink, and she knew the puppy would appreciate the steak. She started to pace again, restlessness kicking in with now-familiar pins and needles and adrenaline.

Her phone rang, a withheld number, and she leapt on it, hoping Luca had landed somewhere. Preferably back in Canada.

'Patricia, this is Marianne,' barked a familiar short-shrift Scottish voice. 'I don't want to discuss what is going on between you and my brother, but we have a bit of a – situation here, and I'm going to need your help.'

'Is it Kes?'

'No, he is perfectly fine, upstairs asleep with the boys. It's Mack. He's rather upset.'

'Oh.'

'The thing is, he's on the garage roof.'

'I see.'

'And he's refusing to come down until he talks to you. Mother is very upset. We all are.'

'I suppose I'd better speak to him.'

'I'll hand you up.'

There was a lot of muffled clanks and she heard Mack's voice demanding, 'Is it her?' before he came loudly on the line, his voice even more whisky- and sob-soaked.

'I'm not fucking coming down until you tell me you fucking love me!'

'For Chrissake, Mack.'

'I can wait here all night!'

'Don't be silly. Just come down.' She tried to picture him up on Marianne's flat double garage roof, accessed by crawling through the bathroom window. It was hardly the Empire State, and Mack wasn't the suicidal sort. She suspected you could throw yourself off it from a hundred different angles and not break a bone, but she didn't want to test it.

'You *worshipped* me once, Tishy!' he wailed.

False gods. Always her weakness.

'There's someone fucking else, isn't there?' he was demanding now.

'There's nobody, Mack.'

'Don't fucking *lie*!'

She laughed hollowly, unable to imagine where she'd get the time and energy for infidelity, let alone the self-confidence. How much simpler would it be to get through this if there *was* an affair, to justify it with a burning new love rather than giving up on a burnt-out one?

'We'll talk when you're back. See a counsellor, maybe.'

'Fuck that! I'm not letting some fucking do-goody nosy parker ask a load of shit about our private life. We'll sort this out now! You say there's nobody else, and I'm prepared to believe you. You love me, I love you. We are man and wife. That's all there is to it.'

'If you say so.' Pacifying, she borrowed Lester's favourite phrase, her thoughts flitting back to the old man's raised glass earlier, toasting Oliver, of whom she and Mack never spoke. Perhaps they should. They'd never sought professional help at the time.

'I fucking know so!' he was raging. 'It's you who doesn't know your own mind, wee bird. You never have. You're fragile. You get all muddled up by your past. Other people exploit that.'

'I'm not muddled up. I've felt this way for a long time. After Oliver was born, I—'

'We've been through all that, Tishy. We're *bigger* than that. We're *us*. You need me.' He was trying to sound cajoling, but it was all muddled with tears and sneers, humiliation rocking his core. 'Don't leave me,' he sobbed. 'Tell me you're not going to leave me?'

Pax closed her eyes, thinking enviously of Lizzie catching her groom-shagging ex-husband in the act, so much easier to legitimately cast off, however painful. It's why Mack wanted to accuse a third party, be it vodka bottle or a lover. How much harder was it when there was no blame, no fault, no moral high ground; when one simply stopped loving? When marriage was drowning you in loneliness, you had to save yourself.

'You're the one who was threatening to leave me and move to Scotland earlier,' she reminded him.

'It's too fucking cold up here.'

'You *are* on a roof, Mack.'

He started to sob again. Long, mournful cries.

'Mack?'

He wept on. She knew that tomorrow he would sharply about-face, sober once more and in need of a whipping boy. He would punish her for this humiliation, the scorpion sting poised. She knew how he worked, and it helped immunise her against kindness, check the compassion that would say all the right things, the pity that would offer him an olive branch in a family tree with their roots entwined deep in dead clay. She had to tip her head up, hold in the tears fiercely, breathe and keep calm.

'Tishy, are you still there?'

Pax, she thought furiously. My name is Pax. It always was. My mother nicknamed me as a baby because I slept so peacefully. Like Kes sleeps peacefully. After she left us all behind, I had trouble sleeping. I still do. We must never do that to Kes. Mummy wasn't allowed to come back for her children. My father and grandfather told her we'd be better off without her. I will *never* let that happen to Kes. Never.

'Still here.'

'Please don't hang up.'

'I won't.' She was Samaritan-calm now.

He sobbed and sniffled. Blew his nose. Sobbed again, reminding her again not to hang up.

She wasn't sure how long her phone battery would last. It was an old handset, and she hadn't brought her charger with her.

'Do you want to talk?' she asked.

'No.'

Fresh sobbing. 'I just need you there... don't say anything... just stay there.'

Minutes cranked past. She looked at her watch. Five minutes. Seven. Ten. Her phone battery was at five per cent. She needed the loo. *Where* was the vodka she'd ordered?

In Scotland, Marianne and the family must have all gone back inside to party on, the concerned voices no longer rising and falling in the background, just wind whistling, distant bass thuds, and Mack's sinal breathing. That grated away her sympathy, a direct reminder of the hours she'd spent lying awake in bed listening to it in its slumber, the snores rising and retreating, her heart hammering, wondering if she'd ever have the guts to end the marriage.

'Don't go,' he reminded her every few minutes.

Twelve. Fifteen.

How long was this standoff going to last? Was he hoping to make her listen to him freeze to death?

There was a quiet knock on the hotel room door. Her reflexes whipcracked, craving the first cold heat of vodka in her mouth. She tried to steal silently across the room to open it, but the puppy started bounding and barking behind her.

A lofty youth in a too-tight uniform stood in the corridor with a tray. 'Hello! I am Radek and I bring you room service this evening.'

Hanging onto the barking puppy's collar, Pax tried to hush him, rolling her eyes at the phone wedged between ear and shoulder, making apologetic gestures. But he was already marching inside, his feet huge, talking loudly in an Eastern European accent about the New Year party going on in the bar. 'You will come down to join guests later, I think. It is big fun night. Oh, sweet puppy.' He put the tray on the desk and stooped down, making 'smoosh' kissy noises as he did so.

'What's going on?' demanded Mack. 'Where are you and who the fuck is that?'

'I'm in an airport hotel,' she explained, which didn't help.

'You're fucking leaving the fucking country?'

'No, Mack.'

But he was too busy raging to listen. The tears and the long, martyred silence were instantly replaced with a barrage of accusations – running away with her lover, bolting just like her mother.

Having finally twigged that she was on the phone and the call was a bit delicate, Radek backed towards the door, but he was having difficulty shaking off the puppy who had hold of his trouser leg with his small, sharp teeth. Hurrying to detach him, Pax felt the phone slip from her shoulder's grip, drop to the carpet. The puppy let go of the hem and picked it up instead, triggering the handsfree speaker, so the shouting seemed to be coming from his mouth.

'You'll never get custody of Kes, you realise? I know about your past, remember? Even the bit you didn't tell the police and social services. *All* of it.' The battery died with an electronic chirrup.

'Happy New Year!' Radek hurried out.

Pax grabbed the vodka. She knew she could call Mack from the hotel phone, try to pacify him, reassure him, entreat him not to rake up the past, but she couldn't face the ranting and paranoia; he was at least half a bottle of Scotch ahead of her and they were getting nowhere. Let him freeze to the roof with his self-pitying tears. He wasn't getting Kes.

In the bathroom to pee, she caught her reflection, registering her hard-heartedness, shocked by it. Had her mother felt this way about her father, or was it different with a lover to share the burden? Should she just find somebody to sleep with to exonerate Mack, like divorcing husbands in the fifties forced to book a prostitute and a hotel for the private detective to photograph, grounds for divorce established.

She thought fleetingly of Bay, her first teenage love, their reunion at her grandfather's funeral coinciding with the dawning realisation that her marriage was beyond repair. Their paths had crossed several times since then, his flirtation an open invitation, his reputation a big BEWARE sign. She'd seen past it all. Now a husband and father, his eyes mirrored hers, a fellow member of the unhappy spouse club, a secret society whose members became evermore apparent to Pax these days. One certainly didn't have to look too closely to see the cracks all over Bay's marriage to his icy Dutch wife. But cracked mirrors brought bad luck. He'd broken her heart twice over fourteen years ago, and revenge on both their houses was not her style.

If Mack thought she was having an affair, he didn't know her at all. But that, surely, was at the decayed roots of it all – his wife had always been ultra-feminine and submissive in his eyes, needing a big, strong man to steer the way. Had Tishy been lying in another man's bed, he'd find this easier to comprehend. Pax, alone and defiant, made no sense to him.

Within minutes, she was pacing frantically again, faster than ever, the restless laps of the marriage breaker. The puppy was now snoring contentedly under the luggage rack, full of steak. She turned on the television, not caring what was showing, just needing its comforting glow. An old Bond movie was halfway through, Sean Connery's brio so reminiscent of Mack's – reassuringly familiar, chauvinist and offering a straightforward solution to problem women. Troublesome Bond girls, those beauties who were too clingy, too bright, or in love with the baddies, simply died.

The vodka had barely touched the sides. When she tried to call room service for another, there was no answer. They were all probably in the bar. She could get free drinks in the bar, she remembered.

Luca O'Brien was arriving soon. She had to limit herself. One more at most. Two if he really was delayed until the early hours.

She ran a bath to stall for time, chin deep in bubbles, eyes closed briefly, until the thought of losing Kes forced her back out with a great tide of splashing water. She had to keep moving.

Pacing around her room again dried her off. She pulled on her jeans and tee. The heating was stifling.

After eleven. She checked her mother's phone, hoping Luca O'Brien had the sense to try that number now hers was useless. Nothing. Bloody man. Bloody men.

It was no good. She'd have to go to the bar. She was stopping at midnight.

4

Accustomed to Aleš demanding silent concentration on movie night, turning on Polish subtitles and rewinding to slo-mo through his favourite bits, Bridge had almost forgotten what it was like to watch a movie with a girlfriend in under two hours, the way it became background noise the better the conversation got, like covering fire, while they got down to the nitty-gritty of putting the world to rights. They'd chatted throughout *Futureland*, polishing off another bottle of red and all the nachos. It reminded her of nights with Bernie, back in the Kilburn days.

Vaguely aware that she was starting to talk very loudly and swear even more than usual, Bridge boasted about her first big job and how high up the management ladder she'd climbed; about the business degree her company had sponsored her to take; about her plans to get her career back on track.

'Sure, will you listen to me mithering on like I'm on *The Apprentice*?' she checked herself, disappointed to find the wine bottle empty again.

'Sir Alan would bloody love you.' Carly took it all in good spirit, not competitive and edgy like the Saddle Bags, those pretty Mexican eyes sleepy, the sweet Wiltshire voice amused as she admitted she'd only ever dogsbodied in dead-end jobs.

'I don't need no CV at a job interview. I just show them the state of my hands.'

Then she had Bridge in stitches describing what it was like to work for her sister-in-law, Janine, who ran her contract cleaning, mobile nail studio and new dog-walking businesses in tandem like a gangland boss. 'She never forgives. A couple of months back, she called a staff meeting to put a hex on this woman from Broadbourne Lane who sacked Fluffy Dusters for not hoovering beneath the beds. We had to burn herbs in candle flames and all sorts.'

'Did it work?' Bridge was agog. *Practical Magic* was another favourite film.

Carly winked. 'According to Janine they've got mice and mould all over the place.'

'Is that like a Romany curse?' Bridge loved the twice annual arrival of the Turner family's many traveller cousins and kin, en route to Stow Horse fair. Aleš, who was paranoid his tools would get nicked, couldn't understand her fascination.

'Nah, she got it off Facebook.'

Most of all they talked about kids, laughed about kids – their little ones that were toddling and crawling, not ones in full-time education like the older Bags. And they talked horse, Carly's great love of them consolidating since moving to the village. Having made friends with local ones over gates and in the studs' fields, her natural affinity was clear. Petra's children's ponies waited at their fence for her every day, and all the Bags were familiar with the extraordinary story of one of the stud's valuable colts, saved by Carly when last year's big autumn storm brought down a tree on him. Gill still called it a miracle.

'Is it true it was your healing hands that stopped Ronnie Percy's best foal from bleeding to death?'

Carly ducked her head modestly. 'I told her your vet friend did most of it, but Ronnie reckons I could use my gift to work with horses. Says she'll help set me up if I lend them a hand over there.'

'Hang on, she's offered you a job?'

'It was a bit vague, if I'm honest. She's got this expert coming over from America or somewhere she says might teach me handling and stuff.'

'The Horsemaker?'

'That's him. I'm not sure. Things is, I want a skill, not a gift.' She looked at her hands with their eight plastic nails, explaining that what she really longed to learn was an old-fashioned country craft like saddlery or blacksmithing. When she'd heard Flynn was looking for an apprentice, Carly had set her heart on farriery. 'But he's a right sexist sod. He wants my Ash to do it and so does Ronnie come to that. She says Healing *is* an old country skill.'

'Yeah, like witchcraft and prostitution.'

Carly laughed, and Bridge was reminded how pretty she was beneath the constant frown and tired eyebags.

'It freaks people out,' she said, looking at her hands again. 'Ronnie's all for it, but other people reckon it's just a con or voodoo or something. My Ash doesn't like it at all.'

Bridge guessed that was the real reason she was doubtful about taking up Ronnie's offer. Carly would take it up like a shot if her husband approved. She felt another spark of connection.

'Janine swears that hex of hers only worked cos of me.' Carly laughed again. 'She keeps getting me to lay hands on Uncle Norm's betting slips.'

'I've a lottery ticket somewhere you can have a go at.' Bridge went to fetch another bottle of wine, although Carly was still nursing the glass she'd refilled an hour ago.

'If it worked liked that I'd lay my hands on our knackered washing machine and a lot else besides.' Carly watched her over the sofa back. 'I'd better just text Ash and let him know we're still nattering.'

It was the third text she'd sent him that night, Bridge noticed, and he was only next door. Everyone around here knew who

Ash Turner was, even if he wasn't seen out much. She'd heard plenty of rumours about the rebel family's war hero, mostly old ones from his ill-gotten youth as village tearaway, but also newer stories from the Cotswold wives who fawned over him at the gym. No wonder Ash's wife wanted to keep herself visible to him, like a radar blipping. He certainly caught the eye on the dipping bars, torso ripped with muscles like cobbles. Not that she'd been looking.

They'd kept off the subject of marriage all evening, but Bridge was insightful enough to guess this was because they both had tricky ones. Who didn't in the Comptons? Even perfect Petra's was a finely balanced house of forgotten Valentine's cards.

Safer to talk career, Bridge's current obsession. Like a terrier with a rope, she found subjects hard to let go, badgering Carly to ask Ronnie Percy what she meant by 'help out'. 'Working with horses would be perfect for you.'

'Doesn't pay much though, does it? I'm best waitressing at the posh pub, I reckon,' Carly said as her fingers clicked on the screen. 'My mum used to love Sous Vide,' she pronounced it 'sows-vied'.

Bridge's lip curled.

The nickname Sous Vide – literal translation 'under vacuum' – was strangely fitting given the way celebrity cook Suzy David sucked up to anyone who would further her career, and shrank away from hard-working commoners like Bridge.

'Suzy David's a sour-faced witch, trust me.' She plonked back down on the sofa beside Carly. 'I can't believe I flew back here to be insulted. In fact, do you remember the words of that hex? We'll cast a fecking spell on her.'

'Don't be daft,' Carly scoffed.

But Bridge was already reaching for her iPad. Too much red wine always made Walsh women brazen. 'It's on Facebook, you say?'

'You can't curse the pub!'

Bridge had never realised there were so many incantations on offer if one had enough coloured candles and ribbons, a well-stocked herb garden and a chalk pentacle. 'It says here tonight's extra potent being New Year. Look at all these spells! This one promises to Bring Forth New Love?'

'I'm fine in that department, thanks.'

She scrolled down. 'Here we go, Get Your Dream Job – all we need's white candles, olive oil and dried basil. Bit like a romantic meal, ha!'

New Year in the Comptons was proving much more enlightening than thigh-slapping her way through incomprehensible folk songs with Aleš's family in Poland, Bridge thought cheerfully as she fell over the cats in the kitchen, forgetting that she hadn't fed them. Within a minute, she'd gathered the ingredients and pulled back the rug to draw a wonky chalk pentacle on the flagstones.

'Trust me, you're getting me out of a tight spot with a kebab van and a potential lawsuit here,' she told Carly, who had reluctantly knelt down beside her. 'Right, we incant this...' She swiped her screen lock code and started reading it out, '*Ancient One of the earth so deep—*'

'You sure about this?' Carly was fighting giggles.

'Too right I am. You and me will be storming up through that glass ceiling this year, girl. *Master of moon and sun, we summon you. Come, come, come!*'

'You're hilarious. You should've been in the village panto,' Carly snorted and started repeating the words, '*Come, come, come!*'

There was a sharp rap on the window and her giggles turned to a shriek. Flynn and the lads were peering in, a muffled cry going up through the glass, 'What are you girls fucking doing?'

'It's a board game!' Bridge waved a dismissive arm. 'Stop spying.'

'We're going to the hall. You coming?'

'We'll follow you there!' Carly looked at Bridge. 'You'll come too, won't you?'

'In a onesie?'

'You can get changed.'

'I'll think about it.' She guessed she probably needed to dance off the wine and nachos – but wishing for a career boost was much more important than finding a frock and heels right now. She tried to picture herself in top-to-toe L. K. Bennett's new season collection, powering past Sous Vide in a Porsche flicking Vs. Anything but a white overall and a kebab van. The candle flame leapt. 'Now repeat this and stir that saucer of oil anti-clockwise three times with your ring finger – where was I? – *We summon you to bring your all-powerful magick, Master, and fuse the union of spirits cast here*. Who writes this shit? There's another three verses. I'll put some music on for atmosphere.'

Wolf Alice filled the cottage with haunting cries, while Bridge took a quick loo break – realising just how pissed she was when she couldn't work out how to undo her onesie and losing another battle with doubled-up laughter – before completing the spell. She defied anyone to say, '*Fill us with your amity, Master! We are receptacles for desire*' without hamming it up like Morgan le Fay.

'Are you sure it was for a dream job?' Carly looked sceptical afterwards. 'What was all that stuff about orgasmic rainbows?'

Refreshing the page, Bridge realised she'd read out the love spell by mistake. Never mind, it was all good fun nonsense. Best say nothing, given Carly's heebie-jeebies about her healing powers. 'Just you fecking wait for the career offers to pour in.'

She felt fantastically liberated and full of mischief, her onesie-night stand hijacked by wine and witchcraft. 'Now let's quickly hex the pub then we can go over to the village hall to dance our tits off; it's got to be almost midnight.'

*

'Your name, Teeshy, it ees like a sneeze, no?'

'Yes, ha ha!' Pax heard her own canned laughter on cue, politely light-hearted.

Being chatted up in a bar full of strangers felt like playing a cameo in a B-movie: woman from out of town perches on bar stool and attracts the attention of a lonesome cowboy at the pool table or, in her case, a short, lascivious Frenchman with over-whitened teeth and extremely hairy wrists. For her last vodka shots as an unhappy, drunken wife, she figured she might as well use Mack's loathsome pet name for her. He thought Tishy was with another man tonight; now she was.

'Teeshy. Pretty, like you.'

She had no idea what her admirer was called; he'd introduced himself as something Gallic and unpronounceable, but he was getting on her nerves with his roaming eyes and uh-hu uh-hu laugh.

Short, swarthily good-looking and dressed expensively, he'd hit on her straight away, reeking of *Joop! Homme* and self-satisfaction, as flirty as Pepé Le Pew. His plans to join old friends in Paris for New Year had been scuppered by the fog, he'd explained. Like her room and bar bill, he was entirely complimentary.

'You have a beautiful smile, Teeshy. Let me buy you another drink.'

'I'll get my own, thanks.' She tried to catch the eye of the barman who was filling flute after flute with cheap fizzy wine in anticipation of the imminent countdown.

The hotel bar was crowded thanks to all the grounded flights – synthetic jazz music piped through ceiling speakers, party spirits roaring, its huge, muted television screen ready to show the New Year fireworks. The countdown clock read seven minutes to twelve. Surrounding Pax were a curious mix of the displaced and the nightshifters taking a short break – couples, families, co-workers – all determined to make the most of things.

The barman was refusing to catch her eye. How many vodkas had she had? Just two, surely. And the one in her room. She must keep count. Maybe make this next one an espresso martini to keep her sharp. It would be her last. She'd sober up with fresh air taking the puppy for a wee break, followed by unadulterated caffeine in privacy upstairs.

Thinking about the deerhound made her jump guiltily. She needed to check him soon. Just one more drink. She waved at the barman, but he'd turned away to serve a crowd of grounded Germans.

Hairy Wrists had moved his bar stool closer, his tailored suit leg pressed against her denim one now.

'Eef you won't let me buy you champagne,' he breathed, instantly summoning the barman for her with no more than a raised finger as though they had concealed earpieces, 'then let me tell you about myself while I work out how to seduce you, Teeshy.'

She laughed her canned laugh again. A bottle of vodka was the most reliable way of getting her horizontal, she wanted to point out. Ordering her martini with relief, she noticed him knock back a flute of fizz in just one mouthful, which struck her as strangely unFrench, as was the wink he gave her. 'You like what you see, no?'

Dark-browed, with a mole like a beauty spot on his upper lip, Hairy Wrists reminded her of a dissolute eighteenth-century vicomte. Probably early forties, his cocky swagger was redeemed by melting laughter-creased brown eyes, the first grey flecks in the black hair lending him gravitas. He worked in industrial development, he told her. Two sons living with his British ex-wife, the divorce recent enough to make him catch himself and look away to regroup. Theirs had been a town and country life. He'd kept the country house. He loved shooting.

He cooked. He played tennis. He had two race horses in training. His greatest love after his children was his Braque du Bourbonnais bitch, Cher Cher.

Had he bothered to ask her about herself, he'd have discovered that they were surprisingly well matched on paper. In a year or two, they could be meeting on a blind date set up by mutual friends, his *amour propre* and diminutive stature a turn-off in sobriety. Would her world ever change that much? It seemed another lifetime.

She felt a warm hand on her leg and looked down to see a gold chronograph watch, its face as complicated as a flight deck, nestled amid her admirer's jungle of arm hair. Six more minutes to get drunk. As she lifted the hand away, his manicured fingers threaded through hers. His white smile flashed wolfishly and he leaned in to her, *Joop! Homme* wafting, breath warm on her ear, his champagne-scented voice exotic. 'Normal rules do not apply on nights like thees, no? Two strangers in strange place. Take off that wedding ring and see how different it makes you feel.' He kissed her fingertips.

A flutter inside, long forgotten. Not for him. For deception.

She snatched her hand away.

'Five minutes to go!' the call went around.

A surge of new arrivals had come into the hotel, wheeling suitcases, some already in the bar, different European languages criss-crossing; a plane must have somehow managed to land or a coach had arrived, mostly uniformed flight staff in transit, along with a few passengers sent to the hotel to await transfers.

The bar staff were racing around with the trays of free fizzy wine.

Hairy Wrists had already lined up flutes in front of them, enough for several friends, his smile even wider.

She held up her hand. 'I gave up wine this year.'

'You tell a Frenchman that!' The uh-hu uh-hu laugh again. '*Why*?'

'I have a drink problem.' There, she'd said it.

On cue, her martini arrived. Pax threw it back in two gulps. She was nowhere near her threshold. There would be no drunken farewell to her spirit friends with just minutes left to drink before sobriety forever.

The warm hand was on her arm now.

'Me also,' he said, and something in his tone made her turn. The soulful brown eyes held hers. 'I was five years sober. I relapsed when my wife walked out on me. *Salut!*' He downed another, then traded it for a full glass which he handed to her. 'I go back to rehab next week. This is, how you say in English, my last drunken dance. Dance with me, no?' His dark, unblinking gaze wouldn't let her go.

She had a running mate. Four minutes to try to hit the wall.

Pax took the flute, fingertips trapped in his for a moment.

'Different rules apply,' he reminded her, dark eyes like GO signs, picking up another for himself.

She thought about Mack on the garage roof accusing her of adultery and, guilty tears rising from nowhere, almost bolted. But she needed this drink, and if Mack thought so little of her, she was doing nothing to worsen his opinion of her by playing the drunken tart.

'*Salut!*' The cheap fizz tasted as blissful as Krug to her impatient tongue.

'Another!' The glasses were replaced with full ones.

Gasping and hiccupping, Pax matched her companion glass for glass, any tears soon sweetened from sad to mirthful. One glass. Two. Three. Four. Five. More were lined up as fast as they emptied them.

They counted up as the rest of the room counted down.

The approving brown eyes watched her, laughter at their edges. A hairy hand went back on her jeans' leg and she didn't immediately move it away this time. The anaesthetic was starting to kick in. Six. Seven. That was over a bottle, even with tiny bar measures. Only the hardcore could go this fast. They were conspirators. She needed more to get there. She needed to get to ten. Ten would make her forget the mess she was leaving behind at midnight.

Eight.

'Ten... nine... eight...' Voices started counting down around them.

Pax and her French stranger stared at one another, picking up two more glasses. In an instant, her mouth was awash with bubbles. Nine.

'... seven... six... five... four...'

They grabbed two more, pitching against each other, competitive and clumsy, sensual too, the drunken conspiracy private, their own bubble. Glass ten.

'... three... two... one! Happy New Year!' the shout went up.

Had midnight come that quickly? The room spun around Pax, satisfyingly fast.

Everyone was kissing everyone else, tens of strangers cast unexpectedly together to wish one another twelve months of joy. And they were kissing too. Only it was the wrong sort of kiss. Tongues, fingers, dizziness, drunkenness, cool champagne still in their mouths. That flutter inside intensifying, a leaping beat now, her naughty secret. She was kissing a stranger in a bar. This was what Mack thought she was doing, so what the hell? The sensation of a new mouth opening to hers, tasting hers. Oh Christ, what was she *doing*?

'Stop!' She pulled away, almost falling over, cannoning into someone behind her.

'Don't be silly.' Hairy Wrists caught her arm to pull her back, smiling knowingly. His laugh had lost its uh-hu uh-hu, his eyes hard and lusty. 'Come here, beautiful.' He sounded different.

'No! I'm sorry. I can't do this.' She shook her head dizzily, fighting to focus.

His body landed back against hers, groin pressed to her thigh, handsome nose level with her mouth. How had she not noticed how *short* he was?

'Pleasegoaway!' Her voice was slurring already, her blood pumping crazy amounts of high-pressure alcohol to trip up her words and pull her off balance, axis upturned as she struggled to shake off his grip.

'Don't be a tease, Teesh.' His voice had thickened, strangely unfamiliar in her drumming ears. His lips slid against hers, stubble grazing her, wiry arms around her, locking her down.

'Let me go!'

'Is this man bothering you?' asked a voice behind her.

'Fuck off, chum,' Hairy Wrists snapped, not sounding himself at all. But he dropped his hold and stepped back to look up at someone taller, lurching as he did so, big eyes troubled and half-focused.

Pax almost fell over, barely able to stand up without a support.

'I'm fine!' she insisted, as much to herself as the concerned stranger behind her, who she tried to reassure by turning to smile at him, but instead executed a bombed pirouette, fleetingly seeing a pair of worried green eyes amid Chewbacca facial hair. Still spinning, on her second circuit now, she realised they belonged to a bearded Viking in a Puffa jacket. 'Fine!' she repeated, rotating on towards Hairy Wrists and managing to stop still, although the room carried on whizzing round.

There was someone standing with the little Frenchman now. Or was she seeing double? No, they were sharing a bear hug.

'There you bloody are!' the second man bellowed, his drunken voice full of plums and silver spoons. 'Happy New Year, Binkers. All bets are off. Mine's scarpered.' He was slapping Hairy Wrists on the back. Then he spotted Pax. 'Fuck me, you got lucky!'

'That's my line,' said Hairy Wrists, honking with laughter.

He didn't sound at all French now.

'*Binkers*?' Pax managed to say it on the third attempt, her vision tunnelling.

'Seb Bink.'

She gaped at him. He was a Gallic romantic. He couldn't be a Binkers.

He was also disappearing down a black tunnel. She swayed, nausea rising. He grabbed her shoulders to steady her. 'Are you okay, Tish?'

'Don't call me that.'

His friend started to laugh, backing away, holding his hands up. 'I'll leave you two lovers together, shall I?'

Pax squinted at 'Binkers' through ten glasses of rapidly circulating wine, vision slewed, swallowing down the rising bile, her brain ever more sluggish. 'You're not French at all, are you?'

'I'm from Worcester.'

She should have seen through it. He wasn't even a good actor. Why hadn't she seen through it? Not that she could see much at all now. If she opened just one eye she could focus on his face. 'Wasthisall some sortof bloody act? Chatting meupforabet?'

'Most of it's true. I've got two kids, I *was* going to a party in Paris; I worked there for years. I have a French dog.'

'What about being fiveyearssober and one lastdance?'

'I'm going to do dry January.'

She glared at him, trying to pinpoint his eyes in his spinning face. 'You lousy liar!'

'C'mon, it's not that bad. We get on, don't we?' He was swaying with her now, eyes glazing, starting to giggle.

'You bastard!' It was herself Pax wanted to shout at. Pax who never lost control, never lost a sense of fairness, who saw through fools and yet suffered them too, perpetually keeping the peace. She was drenched in shame and self-loathing, rapidly losing cognisance as well as balance, her start to the year a self-destructive disaster. She had to get back to her room.

'I do honestly think you're fucking gorgeous,' he was saying in a lazy drawl, eyes crossing. 'Let's start again. Come and sit down with me. We'll order one for *le rue*, shall we?'

'Go to hell, shortarse,' she growled, angry enough to hit him, but far too drunk to try.

'Steady on. I'm not the one wearing a wedding ring, darling.'

She drunkenly made to slap him, but a hand grabbed her wrist to stop her – strong fingered, engraved silver rings, a plethora of knotted leather surfer bracelets around a broad wrist. Not hairy.

The blond, bearded Viking loomed in front of her. Two blond Vikings. Then one. Black Puffa jacket spinning. Eyes the vivid green of sliced kiwi fruit.

'I think you two need some time apart, don't you?' He had an accent she was too drunk to work out.

'Listen, mate, keep your nose out of this.' Binkers looked like he was squaring up for a fight.

'I've got to get back to my room.' Pax started backing away, aware that she was going to throw up any minute. She felt in her pocket for her key card, dog treats, her Visa card and cash spilling out.

The Viking stooped to collect it all, flipping the cardboard key-card wallet over to read the room number. 'I'll make sure you get there okay.'

'*I'll* take her!' Binkers protested, reeling forwards, cannoning into a bar stool and lurching sideways to fall over the back of a leather banquette into a surprised group of revellers.

The Viking was already marching Pax away.

'We can't leave him there!' she protested.

'His friend can sort him out, so he can.'

That didn't sound very Scandinavian. What was it with men and dodgy accents tonight, she thought groggily as he summonsed the lift.

Waiting for it to arrive, she squinted at his profile, which kept doubling, all beard and wild blond curls, part Beowulf, part Lord Flashheart.

'Thisissokind butyoucan leavemehere,' she insisted at the lift's arrival ping, pitching gratefully inside before realising the doors had yet to open and she was head-butting them.

She made it inside on the second attempt.

Pax had no idea which floor her room was on. It was only when she was sliding down beside the buttons, momentarily content to sleep in the lift floor that she realised the Viking had stepped in with her.

'Happy New Year, sweetlips!'

Carly dodged a second Red Bull-flavoured wet kiss from Flynn after 'Auld Lang Syne', her searchlight eyes raking the kaleidoscoping room for her husband.

Ash hadn't come across to the village hall with the others earlier; nobody could remember seeing him for an hour or more. Nor was Skully in evidence. Something didn't feel right – he'd never missed being with her at midnight before, however caned.

The disco kicked in again, glitter ball spinning through ultraviolet darkness, long-haired Flynn dotted with neon tribal marks, teeth and eyes luminous. His leather jeans were so tight he could only dance from the waist up, torso gyrating, shirt open so his neck chains harrowed his hairy chest, the skull and crossbones flag now worn like a scarf.

'The girl next door's *hot* tonight,' he whistled, watching Bridge having a riot on the dance floor, already mosh-pitting to 'I Predict a Riot' with Ink and Hardcase, beer can in hand. 'I wouldn't mind a ride on that Mazur-ati.'

'In your dreams,' Carly scoffed, regretting talking Bridge into the clingy catsuit and hastily applied false eyelashes, Essex facelift ponytail replicating her own – but far sexier with those vintage Raquel Welch cheeks. She looked like a movie femme fatale, the sort who crushed hot henchmen between their thighs.

'Put in a good word for me, yeah?' Flynn shouted in her ear. 'I'm up for a threesome.'

'Shouldn't think you're Aleš's type, Flynn.'

'You know I've always fancied you, sweetlips,' he laughed, eyes still on Bridge, whose pink-tipped silver extensions were swinging like a cheerleader's pom-pom. 'Bet she does, too.'

'Tell that to Ash.' She gave him a withering look, accustomed to the chat-up wind-ups he'd never dream of trying on when six feet of hard-muscled Turner was around. 'Where did all the teenage girls in Sellotape go?'

'Party in Rous Compton.' He pulled a roll-up from behind his ear, trying hard not to look bothered. 'Friends of Amelia's. Skinny dipping, recreational drugs, kedgeree. Not my scene.'

'She dumped you, then?'

'Other way round.' Cigarette in mouth, he closed one eye and squinted at Bridge's gyrating backside. 'I wasn't the one who came dressed in the rubbish bag, yeah?'

Carly knew Flynn's rickety love life well enough to see through the bluff, but she was kind enough to let it go. Ash's mates were big kids in denial that they'd turned thirty, all the bad-lad talk, tattoos and Tinder shags only a blink away from the ruler-flicking, ball-kicking, cider-swigging fronts they'd perfected at thirteen to try to look cool hanging out by the Orchard Estate garages. Underneath it, they were loyal friends and hard workers, happy to settle down and make their home a stone's throw from the place they grew up. Most had never lived outside the county, let alone travelled to war zones like Ash. He was their hard man, the lone wolf who roamed away from the pack, disappearing without warning for hours at a time, as often as not into his own head.

She wondered if he was back at home, lost in one of his

shoot-'em-up console games, music blotting out the gunfire, mad at her for stopping out with Bridge so long. His black moods ambushed them too unpredictably and often for her to ever relax. She checked her phone, the New Year texts and Facebook messages from her old gang of army wives coming thick and fast. Nothing from Ash.

Tucking his roll-up back behind his ear, Flynn swaggered off to dance as the music changed, trying to get Bridge to slut-drop to 'Sexy Chick', both ending up on the floor, roaring with laughter.

The memorial hall had filled up with an after-party crowd, its hardcore of Turners diluted by other village teens – she recognised Petra Gunn's eldest son dancing with one of the vet's toothy daughters – and a few of the old-faithful, like the bearded chair of the Parish Council who always felt obliged to show their faces to sing 'Auld Lang Syne', all nervously still wearing their coats in anticipation of a quick getaway. For now, the Turner teen tribe had turned its attention from fighting to necking, but Carly didn't doubt fists would fly soon, the dance floor seething with grudge matches. At its centre, she could see sister-in-law Janine, a body-stockinged, size 20 missile with three-inch panto-themed nails and a swinging micro bag, giving several arch enemies the evils.

Bridge panted up, one false eyelash missing, the recently applied mascara already sliding off. 'This is the best craic I've had in ages! Flynn's a laugh, isn't he? Will you look at that? Classic!'

Carly observed the farrier head-banging and air-guitaring, back-to-back with Hardcase, to 'You Give Love a Bad Name'. 'Hilarious,' she said flatly.

'Need some fresh air.' Bridge wiped her sweaty face and tightened her ponytail, heading outside, waving at her to follow.

Another hard frost was crystallising, their breath dragon puffs.

'The magic's already working, Carly.' Bridge pulled a familiar-looking roll-up from beneath a bra strap, her sardonic Irish voice laced with mirth. 'You're my lucky charm, I can feel it.'

'You don't say?' Carly wondered again where Ash was. She quashed a fleeting worry that he was helping Skully strip the newly laid lead off the pub's skittle alley. There'd been a lot of bother over Christmas when the church ceiling collapsed at Midnight Mass, its roof lead taken, the finger of blame pointing towards the Orchard Estate. But Ash was no petty thief.

'I'm rethinking my whole outlook.' Bridge was jogging from foot to foot to stay warm. 'You see, I'm usually an all-or-nothing woman. That's been my weakness. But, this time, I figure the orgasmic rainbow owes me. I don't want to overcommit; it's got to be local, low-key and no strings.'

'We're talking about a job here, yeah?'

'Flexible hours!' She felt in her pockets for a light. 'That's what I need. Something I can fit around the kids, like you do, build up speed, plan my empire, earn myself some fun.'

Carly wasn't sure juggling three insecure jobs could be called fun, but if being a lucky charm worked, that was cool by her.

'I heard there's a job going at the village school,' Bridge was saying. 'Office admin. Term-time mornings.'

'Ellis loves that little school.' All the Range Rover mummies she'd heard gossiping about closure rumours at the Nativity play must be wrong if they were recruiting, she realised with relief. 'Sounds good.'

'You think so?' Not waiting for an answer, Bridge went to cadge a light off a nearby clutch of smokers.

Carly hugged herself for warmth. Then she felt another set of arms reach around her from behind, familiar hard-muscle guns.

'Happy New Year, angel,' Ash breathed in her ear.

'And you, bae.' Heart lifting, she tilted her face up to kiss him, loving the demanding warmth of his mouth, the smile waiting there. 'Where've you been?'

'Gave Flynn's friends a lift to their party.'

'You did *what*?' She spun round. 'You've had a skinful.'

'Only a few beers. Anyway, we went across the fields, didn't we? Skully was there, so he had my back.'

'I might have guessed.'

'We charged them a tenner each to hang on tight in the back of the pickup. Minted.' His guarded smile broke cover.

'Christ.' She raked her hair back. 'That's Austen land, Ash. You're lucky you weren't arrested.'

There was a sardonic chuckle close by as Bridge leant in through a swirl of cigarette smoke to murmur, 'Give Bay a truck full of fecking schoolgirls on his land and he'd be the one in danger of arrest. Hello!' She waved at Ash. 'We've not met. Happy New Year.'

'Ash, this is Bridge Mazur,' Carly introduced them, still livid with him taking a risk like that.

She heard him laugh. 'You're Mazur-ati?'

'I love it!' Bridge whooped. 'Can I use that?'

'You work out at my gym.'

'Do I?'

'Does she?' Carly looked up at him over her shoulder, accustomed to her husband noticing nothing and nobody around him, especially when he was on the machines.

'Silver and pink hair, it's like neon,' Bridge told her cheerfully, 'and stops anyone noticing how lazy you are.' She cocked an eyebrow at Ash.

'I've seen you round the village too.'

'That's me. How're youse doing?'

'Bridge, you say?'

'You can burn me or cross me, it's all water under me.'

He laughed again. 'That's good.'

For Ash, usually about as chatty as a rock, this was impressively engaged. Carly's anger allayed somewhat, grateful to her extrovert new friend. 'Bridge was just saying she might be going to work Ellis's school.'

'If they give me the job.'

'They'd be mad not to.' His wolf eyes glinted, pale and amused. 'Place needs livening up. Get old Mrs Bullock shipshape.'

'Too right I fecking will.' She waved her cigarette and tossed her pink-tipped ponytail, looking far from school secretary material. 'Like your wife will at the stud, eh, Ash?'

'What's this?' Ash looked bemused.

'Sure, Carly needs to get her arse over there and take up Ronnie Percy's offer.'

Hearing him sucking his lips, Carly shot Bridge a warning look, but she was looking at Ash, false lashes flapping. 'Don't imagine the Percys offer many the chance to train there. Fecking golden opportunity, I say. That's one classy outfit going on there. Be a total travesty for Carly here not to take them up on it, don't you agree, Ash?' She stepped back, arms outstretched as she struck an assertive pose. With her high ponytail and catsuit, she looked more like a sweetly slewed circus acrobat than a motivational speaker.

Carly braced herself for Ash shutting the line of conversation down. But to her surprise, he laughed again, eyes laser hard in return. 'Yeah, classy outfit.'

Bridge grinned, turning to Carly. 'Told you the magic was working.'

By the time Pax had pitched out of the lift doors onto her floor and navigated the maze of hotel corridors, she'd lost the power of speech and had just the tiniest aperture of tunnel vision left. Like Eurydice returning from the Underworld, she followed the figure that was leading the way. All she cared about was making it into her room to safety. Cannoning off walls, she tried to hold on to what scrap of dignity remained, repeatedly saying, 'Thank you' but it came out 'Phoo'.

A hand held up the key card to a door reader – was it her door? Her hand? She seemed to have lost sense of where any of her limbs were and what they were doing. Suddenly she was very close to the brightly patterned carpet.

She realised she was lying down. She must have passed out. Wet tongue on her face. Seductive, soothing voice. Was he trying to *seduce* her?

'Shh, little fella, you're all right there. Calm down. You're not alone any more.'

The Viking was talking to the puppy, Pax realised, trying to lift her head. She was lying on the floor, halfway through the door, being greeted by the deerhound. The strange not-Swedish voice was addressing her far less sympathetically. 'You okay down there?'

As soon as she moved, the room upended, the contents of her head falling out like a dropped handbag as she crashed around in search of the bathroom. The fragmented montage threw images of a chewed wastepaper bin, chewed mini kettle, chewed shower cap and vanity products, chewed loo seat and then...

The glasses of cheap fizz came out in a reverse countdown, New Year returning. Ten, nine, eight...

She retched and retched.

Seven... six... five... It was counting her down to unconsciousness, the tunnel vision narrowing blissfully.

She felt the hair lifted from her face, that not-very-sympathetic, not-very-Scandinavian voice telling her not to pass out.

'Christ, I'm sorry.' Her sleepy voice echoed around the loo bowl.

'Don't blaspheme. And *stay awake* for pity's sake.'

'Oh no, I'm going to be sick again.'

She thought her stomach would invert. All she wanted to do was sleep.

'You must drink water.' He ordered. *Watter*. Was he Icelandic?

Ignoring him, she curled up beside the puppy on the bathroom floor which was rocking gently, like a ship. 'Thank you. Now go away.'

He took her firmly by both arms and pulled her upright, but she kept her eyes tight shut, terrified of blacking out. She felt a smooth edge on her lips as a plastic beaker was pressed against them, cold water splashing over her chin and onto her shirt.

'Look at me,' he demanded.

She managed to open one eye. Two sharply focussed apple green ones stared back, pale lashed and critical, then four eyes, six, now eight like a spider. Oh God, she was going to pass out again.

'Have you taken anything?'

Was he accusing her of theft?

'Sleeping pills? Drugs? Pills of any sort?'

She shook her head.

'When did you last eat?'

She couldn't remember, the water still running over her lips and tongue, dripping into her throat, for a moment blissfully refreshing and then splashing against reflux.

Vesuvius erupted again, this time without a moment's warning. Unable to turn back to the loo bowl in time, she was violently sick down her front, over the stranger's legs and the puppy. Wine, espresso martini and acid bile dripped everywhere in a thin liquid cocktail, splattered on her chin, wet through her hair. It stank. She was rotten to the core. She started to sob and apologise, fumbling to get away, sliding around in the wet mess like a contestant on a humiliating Saturday night game show involving slime tanks, inflatables and water squirters. She had to find somewhere dry to lie down.

Her good Samaritan was throwing towels over the vomit, talking to her, but she couldn't follow what he was saying.

'Shh!' she interrupted, picking out her words ultra-carefully. 'I... have... to... *sleep*.'

'Drink. Water,' he repeated, moronically slowly. 'Is there anybody I can call?'

Beyond care, desperate to shake him off and rinse away the reek, she clambered into the bath fully clothed and set the shower running, grateful for the sobering icy blast that came first, followed by the warmth, closing her eyes, hoping he'd go away if she ignored him.

Suddenly all she could think about was Kes. Her son, so small and trusting, his parents locked in battle, his mother trying to drown her sorrow one last time and scuppering everything. Mack was right; she'd slid straight back down to ground zero from where he had first picked her up.

Desperate to wash her putrid self-pity, she put her head under the full blast of the shower, reaching blindly for soap, grabbing a damp trouser leg.

A small bottle was pressed in her hand. 'Shower gel.'

She emptied it over her head, her arms leaden, then slipped and slopped around like a dying salmon in the foamy stream.

'Rub it in. Like this.' Her scalp was momentarily raked by the stranger's fingers that foamed it to soft peaks. Then he abandoned her, taking two handfuls of lather to wash the puppy in the sink. 'It's cruel to leave a dog this young alone; no wonder he's chewed everything.'

She wanted to argue her case, but she had no defence, at least none she could say without slurring, and her heart went out to the puppy whose fate she'd made as uncertain as her own. He deserved better. She was mortified, pressing her face in her hands, eyelids burning, the slicing deluge forcing her away from the sleep she craved.

'I gave him to my husband,' she explained, her muffled words drowned by drunkenness and pelting water. 'Then I realised I prefer the dog.' It came out as total gobbledygook, but it hardly mattered.

Rubbing her soapy eyes with the balls of her palms, she realised he was no longer in the bathroom, blearily spotting his shape through the door, puppy wrapped in a white towel now.

The warmth of the water soothed her. It felt safe here in her white enamel boat. Hair rinsed after a fashion, she pushed in the plug to let the bath fill, lying beneath the waterfall, transported back to her tropical honeymoon, floating in the turquoise pool while the monsoon passed overhead and Mack slept in their room, knowing there was no going back.

The taps were abruptly turned off

'Time to get dry, Ophelia,' barked the Viking.

Pax tried to say, 'I'm very grateful, but I wish you'd just go away,' but even to her ears it was more, 'Imgateful wushoo goway.'

He pulled the plug. 'You need to get out of those wet clothes.'

She opened her eyes, squinting hazily up at a lot of facial hair and saying very carefully, 'Haffnothinelstoware.'

'Look in my bag. Leave those jeans in here and I'll wring them out.'

'Why youbeing so kind?'

'I have no choice.'

'Are you the Second Coming?'

'Not quite.' He smiled. It was an amazing smile, bursting from the golden beard like a crop circle in a cornfield, the eyes momentarily bright as sycamore buds. Then it was gone. He unbuckled his vomit-covered trousers, peeling them off to reveal thin, muscular legs and surprisingly garish orange boxers. 'Hurry up; I need to get in that shower.'

The bath had sides slippy as oiled steel and the room kept moving around. No sooner had she wobbled upright than she fell back. He reached down to help her, but she slipped again, almost taking him with her.

'Look away,' she said, scrabbling to pull her own jeans off, which meant she could use them for grip to stand on. As she finally stepped out onto the crumpled towel on the floor, she swayed light-headedly, closing her eyes, fighting back another wave of nausea.

Two hands steadied her before a folded towel was pressed into her arms. 'Well done. Now find dry clothes.'

Pax wasn't sure how she made it into the bedroom, or how she discarded her top, but she realised she was just in her bra and pants by the wardrobe and the Viking was under the shower. She hoped he wasn't a mad rapist, or a third member of Binkers' gang carrying on the bet. She hardly cared. She'd been in much closer scrapes than this and survived. All she needed was sleep.

Making her way across the room to crash straight into bed, she fell over his bag, a stack of clean white T-shirts spilling out. It was a relief to unspring the wet bra and pull one on. What the hell. She wriggled out of her sodden briefs and dragged on what she took to be a pair of joggers. Familiar stitched suede patches settled against her knees, Velcro grazing her ankles. They were breeches.

At the bottom of the bag was a pair of shiny German riding boots.

Eyes drooping, but determined to stay conscious long enough to find his ID, she dug clumsily in the side pockets, locating only a battered paperback and a tube of sugar-free gum. In lieu of toothpaste, she crunched through one and then regretted it, stomach balling up in protest.

A black Puffa was thrown over the back of the chair. She weaved over to it, cannoning off the desk. In a pocket, she found a credit card and cash. She read her own name, Mrs Patricia Forsyth, and started in woozy surprise, forgetting that he'd picked it up when it had fallen from her jeans pocket in the bar. Well, he was welcome to steal her identity; she wasn't going to have it much longer. And he'd be lucky to get anything out of the overdrawn joint account. He'd chosen the wrong victim to target tonight. And while he was washing off her DNA, she had him bang to rights. Not that she felt like calling the police.

No longer able to remember why she was looking through his coat, she put it on, zipped it up like a hooded sleeping bag and climbed into bed, crashing straight out.

PART TWO

5

Pax had been drinking long enough and hard enough to have a striking capacity for recovery. Her body clock jolted her wide awake just after six, albeit totally disoriented, temples crashing and with a mouth like cinder.

Darkness. Small green light glowing on the ceiling. Large building. Distant noises. Closer to, somebody else's breathing. Hotel room. She was wearing riding clothes and a coat that smelled of horse. Her marriage was finally falling apart. Mack wanted Kes to live with him in Scotland. The worst New Year ever.

She groped around for a light switch, knocking over a chewed phone, a dog-eared notepad and a glass of water before locating a row of small metal rectangles and clicking one at random. A dim picture light came on across the room.

Her Good Samaritan – or was he a hustler? – was asleep in the chair with a faded baseball cap tipped down over his eyes and the puppy on his lap. Dressed in frayed jeans, T-shirt and a checked shirt, he resembled a redneck hillbilly dozing on a veranda. All he needed was a guitar across his knee. Or a shotgun. Was he friend or foe?

Most of the previous night remained blacked out, but she could remember a tough, beleaguered kindness. 'I have no choice,' he'd said.

She groped in the pockets of the coat she was wearing, pulling out gum wrappers, flyers, tickets and a passport.

Gianluca Declan Matthew O'Brien, she read. Born in County Kildare thirty-six years ago. The clean-shaven photograph could have been of somebody else.

Groaning, Pax closed her eyes again, more fragments of the night flashing back in a horror strobe. Those awful calls from Mack. Drinking to forget. Abandoning the puppy. Flirting with a stranger in a bar. Kissing a stranger. All her money, her cards on the floor.

Was *he* the stranger she'd kissed? That detail was still in darkness. But one thing made sense: he'd known the moment he saw her dropped credit card who she was; his lift, his boss's daughter, a drunk. Shame curled her toes into the bed sheets.

'Are you awake?' he asked, his voice soft and strangely placeless, a generic Celtic burr, Irish accent polluted from too much travelling.

'Only if you tell me it's all been a bad dream.' She sat up, then realised that was way too ambitious.

'It's not,' he said bluntly, lifting the cap. The smile was unexpected, wide and welcoming, over-bright even. Another flashback. That smile, water, taking her jeans off. Had she got in the *bath* with him?

'Then I'm not awake.' She lay back down, clamping her eyes tight and trying, *trying* to remember more.

Like many season-hardened old countrymen, Lester had an encyclopaedic knowledge of rural folklore, cynical when omens boded well and pessimistic when they didn't. That morning, as he dressed, a barn owl screeched piteously from the roof of the main house. Even in pitch darkness, Lester knew precisely where it had landed, on the overflow pipe that protruded from the dormer ridge of one of the little attic windows. It had perched there just before dawn, day after day, the winter that

Ann Percy died. Old-timers said an owl on one's roof foretold a tragedy.

This was its third morning. He hadn't liked hearing its screech when Ronnie was in the house; he liked it even less with young Pax and the Irish stranger there.

Or were they there? Lester, a light sleeper, hadn't heard a motor outside last night. It was still too dark outside to see whether Pax's little car was parked there. He resented the preoccupation.

It was a Monday Country day, and he refused to countenance negative thoughts when the hunt was meeting in the stud's home vale, with Eynhope Park providing a particularly fine backdrop. The frost and fog would pass and the Fosse and Wolds hounds would sing. Even after so many years, the prospect made him high with anticipation.

The owl shrieked again.

'You go hunting too, my feathered friend,' he said, pulling his checked shirt collar over his jumper neck. 'Best sport for you.'

His own hunting attire was already laid out on the stand: immaculately ironed shirt and stock, cavalry twill breeches, buff waistcoat now on its third lining, and his elderly but serviceable wool coat, well-brushed, replete with a full set of hunt buttons and blue Wolds lapels in honour of his long years' service supporting and following their hounds, one-time amateur whip to the Captain as master and Johnny Ledwell as huntsman. Those were Lester's salad days. The Percy family had led the field, none more fearless and stylish than Ronnie. Then she'd run off, her mother left raising her children, the master, huntsman and whip never really finding their true line again.

Much to the Captain's disappointment, none of his grandchildren had followed their parents' hoof trails across Wolds country with great enthusiasm. Some of the hunt's most legendary Monday runs had once crossed the stud's land, and

Lester had a shrewd suspicion that when the Captain had sold much of that old pasture to a big agricultural holding more than a decade back, the ancient coverts and hedgerows flattened and turned to crop, he'd done so partly from broken-hearted fury. What was the point in maintaining perfect hunt jumps and hedges when Percys no longer led the field? At the time, he'd insisted it was for the good of the stud. After paying off creditors, what was left had bought Cruisoe, the most prolific stallion Compton Magna had ever stood, his great athleticism and distinctive yellow dun colouring passed down to his progeny, winning plaudits across many disciplines, although the Captain was proudest of those who went on to carry the horn. He and Ann had both hunted into their seventies, but as they'd fallen further back in the field, queuing at gateways to avoid jumping the hedges, nobody took their place in the vanguard, just the fading memory of golden-haired Ronnie, whip arm up as she sailed over five feet of birch a length behind the master.

Only Lester still hunted regularly, taking out Ann's hardy, ageing cob, the last in his line from those bred by the Captain's grandmother before the war.

Lester was aware of being the last in his line too, not so much that he was a childless bachelor whose family had long ago been lost to him, but also that he was the last of the Captain's generation at the stud. His lifetime had seen such change, and yet a horse's loyalty was timeless.

Out on the yard just after six, peering through a fog of precipitation and misted cataracts, he realised that Pax's car was still missing. Whilst telling himself it was no great surprise – he had listened to the weather forecasts and reports of travel chaos – it worried him, the owl shriek still echoing in his ears. This Luca character was unknown to all but Ronnie.

He checked round each yard and barn first, as he always did, carrying a flashlight because most of the working lights needed new bulbs, frustrated by his own slowness and the caution with which he had to cross the frosted ground to keep balanced. In the furthest barn, his torch beam caught the little colt they all thought so highly of and he let the light linger to admire him, liking the bold toss of his head as he bustled up in greeting. *Super sort.* He could hear the Captain's voice in his head. *Suit Pax, that one.* Jocelyn had never given up hope of seeing his granddaughter back on a horse. *She has her parents' talent and her grandparents' good sense,* he'd been fond of saying, although they both knew it was her mother, Ronnie, that Pax most took after in the saddle, with that instinctive Percy gift for getting the most out of every horse she rode.

Lester, who had taught Ronnie to ride, had also taught all three of her offspring. None inherited their mother's firecracker nerve. Alice, the oldest, had only ever been a moderate rider, overly impatient and aggressive, her short, top-heavy body not lending itself to elegance and balance. An enthusiastic Pony Club mum these days, she still stewarded at rallies and camp, rode her children's ponies around her husband's family farm during term time to keep them fit, and supported her older son's point-to-point ambitions with fierce determination; but she preferred shooting for sport. Tim was even less interested, a glitz-loving fair-weather dilettante whose natural talent had gone to waste early on, seducing Pax's pony-mad friends and dabbling briefly in polo before devoting himself to the grape as a wine merchant.

It was Pax who had possessed her parents' eye for a stride, and that divine seat which could rebalance itself faster than a finger-click, lower leg never moving, no matter how wild the leap or steep the landing. She'd been bred to hunt. And yet she'd refused to do so almost as soon as she'd graduated from a Shetland's basket chair to a saddle. It was cruel, she'd protested at the grand age of five, red plaits swinging, indomitably, politely stubborn even then. Despite the Captain roaring with laughter and barking, 'She'll change her mind soon enough!' she hadn't altered her opinion over the ensuing twelve years, during which little Pax Ledwell had grown to become one of the most stylish riders Lester had seen, selected absurdly young for British junior teams, tipped to be the next big three-day eventing sensation, the perfect emissary for the stud's young horses. Hers was a different courage to her mother's: not blood-and-guts Percy sportsmanship, but something altogether more cool-headed and analytical that Lester had recognised with an element of concern, that suspension of fear which was almost superhuman. Like her father Johnny...

Then, at seventeen, she'd visited her brother in London one school holiday and never come back to pick up the reins again. Lester still didn't know precisely why, although he sensed it was no coincidence she'd been walking out with young Bay Austen all that summer. At the time, the Captain had brushed it off with talk of academic ambitions, but it struck Lester as most unlikely. She had been ethereal on a horse.

When Pax had taken herself off, Lester had been bereft. It had been like losing Ronnie all over again. Barely eighteen months old when her mother had left, Pax had always been his compensation, the little redhaired Percy cub he'd taken under his wing. Johnny was already too reliant on the bottle to make much of a fist of fatherhood, his emotions buried alive. After his death, Lester and Pax had become even more inseparable, united by their faith in the power of horses to heal grief. Her nature was so different from her siblings, both forthright Percy terriers who snarled to get to the bowl while she hung back through kindness. The most intuitive of all Johnny's children, she'd had a way with nervous mares, and her husky, jazz-singer's voice was beautiful, a choirgirl at school who sang like Nina Simone at home.

Lester had seen very little of her after she decamped to London, fleeting visits when she'd shown no great interest in the horses, always in a hurry, distractedly polite. He'd stored each snippet of news he was told – which was little, Jocelyn and Ann Percy being taciturn, pragmatic sorts – patiently piecing together a picture of a woman quite unlike the girl he'd known, a drifter in a cosmopolitan herd when once she'd galloped a straight line. He'd been even more dumbfounded when she'd married Malcolm 'Mack' Forsyth, a divorced Scot twenty years her senior whom Lester thought very brash. They'd moved to Argyll to start a family, and the Percys had seen even less of Pax until Ann's illness years later, a cancer so aggressive there was barely time to adjust, her youngest granddaughter travelling from one end of the country to the other to visit, toddler on her hip, tears in her big, golden hare's eyes when it turned out the stud's lifeforce was frail and mortal after all.

Lester listened to the owl screeching again. He refused to bow to superstitious nonsense. Death came to them all, and for Ann it had been ignoble but merciful. Full of gin and morphine to kill the pain of the cancer eating at her bones, she'd nodded off in the bath with a cigarette on the go and started a fire, smoke inhalation suffocating her in her sleep. They'd caught the blaze before it spread, and she'd been spared the slow and agonising bedridden death rattle she'd feared most of all.

Soon afterwards Pax surprised them all by uprooting and moving her family and the business she and Mack ran to the Cotswolds, saying she wanted to spend more time with her grandfather. But Jocelyn withdrew himself, deeply antisocial and hard to like by the end. The grandchildren clashed over his care, Alice and Tim ganging up, undermining Pax. Yet the Captain had adored his youngest granddaughter, convinced right up to his death that he'd one day breed the horse to persuade her back in the saddle.

Lester watched the colt flick his head again and trot off on springs.

That's one for Pax, the Captain repeated in his head.

As far as Lester was aware, Pax hadn't ridden since she was a teenager. She'd seemed to lose the passion for horses totally, almost overnight. Even today, she was detached and cerebral around them. Lester found himself disappointed in her, irritated by her ambivalence.

The owl shriek had moved further away, to the spinney beyond the walled garden, making him breathe out with relief.

The bigger stable yard was icy underfoot. He took it very steadily. The cobbles were precarious, and his hips were aching. The doctors said he needed an operation, but he couldn't take time off even if he wanted to.

Grumbling to Stubbs that there would be no hunting if the frost lingered – and none if he didn't get the yard done in time – he set about distributing hay nets and hard feeds.

Ronnie's grey stallion was even more het up than usual, wired by last night's midnight fireworks exploding across the valley from the Austens' farm and by Lester's impatience. The two had built a begrudging respect over the weeks that Beck had lived at the stud, but this was all too easily undermined by displays of temper on either side.

Today, eyes like coal and nostrils two scarlet commas, he struck out at his side wall, bit at the bars and then turned to fire his hind feet at the door.

Lester had quickly learned that Beck was all show: fierce dragon snorting and ear-splitting bellows, teeth bared, neck snaking, hooves lashing out to spark off the flags and rattle the partitions, the door jumping in its hinges. Reaching for the bolts, he ignored him, quashing the instinctive wariness he always felt when handling the horse. Rigidly disciplined in Germany, the stallion had been taught to stand at the back of his stall the moment the door was opened, glaring at the intruder who dared invade his space to attach a head collar, skip out, change nets or refill water. Today, he was particularly ratty, lingering just long enough to nip hard at the old man's shoulder.

'Gerrof, you devil,' Lester muttered, raising a hand. Although a royal wave not a threat, it was enough to send the stallion slamming to the back wall, eyes white-edged, every nerve in his body alert.

Tutting, Lester cursed his arthritic fingers as they struggled to unknot the hay net which Pax had tied far too elaborately the previous afternoon. That girl! She'd forgotten everything he'd taught her. In his peripheral vision – much reduced these days – he could see that the stallion was head-bobbing agitatedly, ears flat back. Warning bells were ringing in Lester's head, his owl shriek tinnitus, but he stilled them, patiently fiddling in the gloom. As he did so, the light from the yard's tungsten floods spilled in, the stable door opening, a soft voice asking, 'Need some help?'

'Get out!' Lester cried, eyes darting to the stallion.

Fast as a cobra, Beck lunged at the open door. In the nick of time, it was slammed shut, his bared teeth clashing against the bars. Then, tossing his great head, he spun to face the man still in his stable. One foreleg struck out and hammered down.

'Get back with you,' Lester muttered softly, lifting his chin, assessing the distance to the door. The horse's head swung sideways, teeth raking against the wall, then dropped low, feet stamping again. Lester kept very still, aware that even a royal wave would provoke attack now. He had seconds at best.

The soft voice spoke at the door, 'Just come here, you big wimp.'

'You are *not* helping,' Lester breathed.

'Who's being a silly bloody clot, eh?'

'Really, madam, I'd rather you – argh!' It happened too fast. The horse swung round to present his rear guns and Lester flattened himself against the wall, eyes tight closed, bracing himself for a body-breaking kick with both iron-shod hind feet.

It didn't come. Instead he heard a soft laugh and slurping. Slowly, he opened his eyes again.

To his amazement, the horse's silver ears were pricked as he nosed the stallion bars, lifting his lip. He'd lost all interest in the man trespassing in his stable.

'Budge up, big boy,' came the soft voice and the stallion stepped back as the door opened again, a blonde head looking around it. 'I'm so bloody sorry. Do you want to come out?'

It was the scruffy, tattooed blonde mother from the estate who Lester was forever catching pushing a buggy full of snotty infants around the tracks. Ronnie had a soft spot for her.

'Carly,' she reminded him.

He nodded, not trusting himself to speak without giving the tremble in his voice away. His heart was still thundering, adrenaline spiking. For a moment he'd thought the owl's omen was coming true. As he brought out the empty hay nets, Carly thrust a sweet bag under his nose.

'Cherry Tangfastics,' she explained, offering him one. 'Me and Ellis save them for lover boy here. He'll do anything for one.' To illustrate, Beck's bristly pink and grey upper lip wobbled through the bars like an anteater's snout.

'That's very good to know.' Lester dusted himself down and glanced at his watch, as much to cover how flustered he was as check the time. He already knew he would never get the yard done in time to set off for the meet if he worked alone. He eyed the girl doubtfully; elfin features, lopsided ponytails, ripped jeans and painted nails. She hardly looked strong enough to lift a bucket. Ronnie's temporary recruits were a motley bunch, press-ganged into volunteering for a few hours at a time until the new manager arrived. He was furious with Pip for letting the side down. For all the pink wellies and chatter, she was as strong as an ox. The two of them had coped perfectly well for months. 'Did Mrs Ledwell ask you to come along?'

She half nodded, half shrugged.

'And your children?'

'Still asleep round at their nan's.'

'You can fill hay nets.'

'Yay!' She did a little victory punch in the air which, despite himself, Lester found rather endearing.

The outdoor bell for the telephone started ringing. Grumbling, but aware that it might be Pax whose continued absence concerned him greatly, he limped into the cottage as quickly as he could. 'Stud.'

'I must speak with Luca O'Brien.' It was man's voice, American possibly, but hard to tell because he was snarling like a bear.

'He's not here, sir.'

'I just spoke with his family in Ireland. They said he's coming straight to you.'

'Have you tried his portable telephone?' Lester suggested.

'He's barred my number.'

'In that case I suggest he might not wish to speak with you. Good day.' He lifted the receiver towards the cradle.

'Wait!' The bellow was so loud he felt duty-bound to ask what the matter was.

'I'll leave him a message,' was hissed. 'What's your name?'

'Lester.'

'Lester, tell O'Brien that if he comes anywhere near my daughter again, I'll shoot him.'

'And your name, sir?'

'He'll know.'

Across the dim hotel room, Luca eyed Pax from beneath the baseball cap, gauging her sobriety and sanity.

She was sitting up, wearing his crumpled clothes, long fingers rubbing her face.

He'd foolishly imagined Ronnie's daughter would be just like her, a pocket-sized dynamo with no off-switch. But she was wired to self-destruct. They looked nothing alike; a head taller than her mother and freckled like an English foxglove, Patricia Forsyth was one of those bony, breedy British types who rattled with neuroses. If she had a battle with her sobriety that was sad – he'd been there recently enough to know its damage – but that was not his problem.

The stud was.

'Are you awake yet?' he asked smoothly.

She felt her wrist for a watch that wasn't there. 'What time is it?'

'Seven.'

She clambered across the bed and sat on its edge, blinking as her head spun. 'I'm so sorry; I didn't introduce myself last night.' Like Ronnie, her voice was throaty and velvet, but several semitones deeper. Her red hair, washed in shower gel and dried on a pillow, was a cloud of dull frizz, her face chalk white.

'I knew well enough who you were.'

'I can explain...' She stood up shakily, having to grab at the borrowed breeches to stop them falling down.

'Save it for later.'

Luca knew very little about the Percy family, but from what little he'd gleaned, Ronnie's three children had wasted no time trying to sell off the once-legendary Cotswold stud after their grandfather died, and Luca's summons here was to prove them wrong by steering it off the rocks and making it profitable again.

If Ronnie's other two children were anything like Pax, those profits were being served on the rocks and knocked back in one.

The puppy wriggled out of his arms and bounded over to her, far more forgiving.

He stood up. 'I want to make tracks. You have a car, I take it?'

'Yes.' She peered at her watch groggily.

'I'll drive,' he said. 'You'll still have way too much alcohol in your system.'

'I can drive.' The treacle-topped voice was practised, like a newsreader reliant on autocue. 'I just need something to eat first. So does that puppy.'

'You'll only throw it up. Liquids are better. You need hydrating. We'll stop for breakfast on the way.' He went into the bathroom, gathering their still-damp jeans which he wrapped in a plastic laundry bag and rammed in his pack along with the rest of her clothes. 'You'll have to tell the hotel about the damage the dog's done.'

She was looking disconsolately round at the chewed flexes, chair legs and soft furnishings. 'I need to make a list.'

'Take photos on your phone. It's quicker.'

'The battery's dead.' She picked up a brace of phones, both screens blacked out. 'So's Mummy's.'

There was something about women of his own generation who still said 'Mummy' that grated on Luca.

'Why do you have your mother's phone?'

'She's staying with friends. She left it behind.'

Now he knew why Ronnie's number had gone to voicemail every time he'd called last night. So much for thinking she'd meet him at the airport, small and indomitable, arms thrown wide, that infectious laugh already coaxing him out of deep hibernation.

Instead, the chalk-faced daughter was standing in front of him. He could smell her hangover, sense the cold sweat and embarrassment. They were the same height, their eyes level. Hers were wide set and rust hazel, the whites bloodshot, nothing like her mother's bright, piercing blue.

'I really am sorry about last night,' she faltered. He noticed how much her hands were shaking, belying the calmness in her voice, nails chewed right down. 'There's absolutely no excuse for behaving as I did.' The apologetic drunk was a lot more buttoned-up when sober, it seemed. 'I'd rather you didn't say anything to my mother. To anybody, really.'

'You could use some help, maybe.'

'It was a one-off. New year, new me and all that.' The soft voice was lullaby reassuring, as if she was reading a bedtime story, although she couldn't look him in the eye for more than a split second at a time. 'I overdid it, that's all.' She held up her hands to underline the point, then grabbed at the slipping breeches. 'I wasn't about to swing from a ceiling beam by my belt – I'm truly fine.'

He tilted his head to look at her, finding the soothing voice hard to read. Then he reached into his bag and pulled out a belt to hand her. 'Try this.'

She looked at it in white-faced horror.

'It's to hold up your trousers,' he said wearily. 'Put it on and I'll drive you home.'

She stooped to pick up her discarded bra and knickers and hurried into the bathroom.

Hoodie over her bobble hat, Dua Lipa singing 'New Rules' in her ears, Carly swallowed yawns as she pushed the muck barrow over the damp cobbles, wrists jiggling like a car's suspension, shoulders balancing like its axis, aware of the old man's eyes on her, berry-black and critical.

After two hours doing exactly as Lester told her, keeping the pace up all the while, not pausing to talk or tea-break as dawn broke, she sensed he was grudgingly impressed. A compliment was hard won. As she wobbled up the plank onto the muck heap, upending the barrow, she heard him bellow behind her, cutting through the electric beat.

'Not there!' he snapped. 'You emptied that far too soon. Look at this heap and tell me what you see.'

She took out an earbud. 'It's a big pile of horse shit.'

'Look again.' He stomped up the plank, proud architect in the grey morning light. 'It's stepped so that it heats up evenly and decomposes more efficiently, you see? Twelve feet high at the back there. It takes months of work to create a muck heap like this, young lady. It is a work of art.'

'An Egyptian pyramid of poo, hey?'

She started wheeling back down but he lifted a hand like a

traffic cop and stopped her, raising a thin smile. 'The last girl we had was next to useless to start with too, but Pip did one thing very important. She *listened*. Now take those things out of your ears.'

She did as she was told, birdsong and crackly opera from a distant radio replacing pop. 'I always play my downloads when I work.'

'Not here.'

He wasn't exactly chatty company, his own choice of dreary classical music droning constantly through the rattly loudspeaker in the feed room which she thought was hypocritical. And he was really slow and stiff. Wheeling beside him was like tailgating a Sunday driver. She wanted to accelerate off but guessed it was bad manners.

'So does Pip still work here?' she asked, needing to know where she stood with Ronnie's staffing plans if she was going to make it a regular thing.

'Not for me to say. I imagine Mr O'Brien will rota casual staff.' It clearly pained him to say it. 'Sweep that bit again, will you? It must be *immaculate*.'

Although told by Ronnie in a burst of enthusiasm that the Horsemaker could teach her a lot, Carly was shrewd enough to work out that it was Lester who held the key to regular work at the stud – nobody would get on the rollcall who didn't meet his exacting standards. She needed to find his right side, and get on it fast. Because this morning, surrounded by doe-eyed mares and bright-eyed young-stock, she'd realised that this was the work she wanted to do, no matter how cold and frosty the weather and her mentor. Spending time with the horses made every moment worth it.

Her favourite, Spirit, was out in a covered barn with his best friend. Now officially a yearling according to her reference book – although Lester insisted sports horses were 'rising' until their real birthdays, unlike racehorses who all shared midnight on December the thirty-first, regardless of the month they were born – Spirit had lost some of his cuteness, but none of his beauty. Herding them along a grass track to their turn-out field with Lester and his small, bearded dog, feeling like a proper wrangler, she whooped with joy to see him streak ahead of the others, pure liquid gold, kicking up his heels and skipping fleet-footed over the mud and ruts while the others waded and tripped.

'He's just the best, isn't he?' she said to Lester.

'You've the making of a good eye.'

They stopped to have breakfast just after eight. Lester retreated into his cottage, his offer of toast declined. Carly's stomach was too knotted with excitement to eat. Taking a mug of tea out to the fields to watch Spirit and take some photos, she found her phone had a bar of reception and called Nan Turner to check she was okay hanging onto the kids a bit longer, and then Ash, just awake, bear-like and not understanding why she wasn't beside him.

'What are you doing there?' he demanded when she explained she was at the stud.

'On-the-job training.'

'It's New Year's bloody Day. What job? Nobody gets a job on New Year's Day.'

'Call it magic.' She thought gratefully back to Bridge's silly spell. 'Ronnie said I could help out any time, remember?'

'For free, maybe. It'll go nowhere. We talked this through, Carl.'

'No, *you* told me what you thought about it, Ash, and now I'm doing it anyway. I have a right to make up my own mind on stuff. Women can do that. Watch the news.'

'Fuck, were you having some sort of feminist meeting with Mazur-ati last night or what?' He laughed sleepily. 'Where are the kids?'

'Still at your mum's. She's happy for you to go around and collect them any time up to eleven. I'm only needed here another couple of hours, the old guy says.'

'I'm going to the gym.'

'Nobody goes to the gym on New Year's Day,' she repeated back.

'Got a lot of beer to sweat off, bae.' He rang off.

Carly growled. He never took anything she did seriously, apart from sex, and not always that. When they'd made love last night, uninhibited and clumsy, she'd glimpsed the man he'd once been, recalled the fearlessness she'd possessed to win him. Lying awake afterwards, her mind made up to come here today, she'd listened to his breathing change as another nightmare started to grip him and guessed he would react like this. He couldn't see that horses were her peace and freedom, the place she went to escape, an armistice he couldn't find. He wasn't mad at her; he just didn't get it.

Watching two deer shoot from field hedge to coppice, she yawned. She hadn't slept much, but she didn't resent the tiredness. It was the best night she could remember in months. Bridge made for addictive company. They'd finally peeled the talkative Belfast mum off the dance floor at close to two and walked her home, declining offers of yet more wine before the door closed. Both Carly and Ash had looked back as they crossed the lane, sharing the joy of seeing her through the window, dancing around her sitting room, pink-tipped ponytail swinging.

They'd made love as soon as they got home, house to themselves, not bothering to turn on the lights or draw the curtains, Ash putting music on his phone and telling her to strip. She'd been happy to oblige, trailing shoes and clothes from front door to bedroom, their laughter catching, still tipsy and not at all sleepy, although he'd pulled her down onto him before she'd got into her stride, and it was over too quickly for her to get much pleasure, his back looming in beside her and his breathing deepening to sleep the moment it was over, the old Ash slipping away.

Lying awake afterwards Carly had recognised how

dissatisfied she felt with her life. She had a new friend who shouted and danced and drank and laughed just for the joy of it. Carly loved Bridge's 'feck it' attitude, the way she targeted what she wanted and went for it. She had almost forgotten what it was like to be that sure of herself – the last time she'd felt like that being the first time she'd set eyes on Ash.

Unable to sleep, she'd taken Bridge's lead and plotted to seize the day. At five forty-five in the morning, still wide awake, she'd decided there was no time like the present. Two and a half life-changing hours later, it was looking like a very good decision indeed.

The orgasmic rainbow owes me... She remembered the spell now with a snort of laughter.

She took a selfie and with Spirit and sent it to the newest number in her phone contacts.

OMG u superstar!! B xx came Bridge's sleepily typed reply, followed by: *Ps) How can you possibly be awake?* Then: *I think I'm still drunk. You up for a coffee later?*

She sent a smile and thumbs up. *I'll have kids with me if okay?*

Beezer cos I miss mine. Come round here. Will be trending jaded from 11. :-o :-p

The nostalgic DAB station Pax's car stereo was tuned to was pumping out themed hits – 'Happy New Year' by Abba, U2 singing 'New Year's Day', 'New Sensation' by INXS – all fighting to be heard over the howling exhaust.

At least the noise drowned out her heaving stomach and throbbing, jackhammer headache. It was also good at covering quiet bleats of fear.

'Steady!' She battled to stay calm as Luca sliced across three lanes of traffic to exit the M42 onto the M40, hands lifting to cover her face.

Unaccustomed to driving on the left for many years, Luca's 'just getting my eye in' had a terrifying blind spot. Horns trailed away behind them.

'Sorry about that,' he said tightly, wincing at the rear-view mirror before accelerating off the slip road, narrowly avoiding a juggernaut. 'Now where'd that big bugger come from?' With his thick beard and long hair, it was like being driven by a recently released hostage. One who had never learned to drive.

Pax kept her fingers across her mouth, voice muffled. 'Can we stop for that breakfast before I throw up?' She wasn't remotely hungry, but the puppy was whimpering, and she longed for solid ground and intravenous caffeine. Plus, her phone was in her bag on the back seat and she needed to charge it, if only to leave a final message for loved ones.

Kes, Kes, Kes. Guilty conscience at its worse in the mornings, and worse still after last night, she wanted to wail, '*What have I DONE?*' but she was with the stranger she'd been sick on – quite possibly her mother's toy boy – and listening to The Carpenters singing 'We've Only Just Begun', so she pointed at the blue sign for the next exit with its reassuring crossed knife and fork, trying not to cry. Even happy songs made her sad.

The services were local ones, not motorway, a labyrinth of roads twisting them around the edge of an industrial park to a retail mecca offering a reassuringly homogenous blend of forecourt and food court, a thin Bank Holiday crowd of hungover travellers stopping for breakfast.

Luca clipped the lead on the puppy. 'I've a call to make. I'll stretch this little guy's legs while I'm about it.'

'He hasn't had all his injections yet,' she warned, still scrabbling to plug her own phone into the car charger.

'What's he called?' He tossed the car keys onto the seat beside her.

'He's not.'

'Not's a lousy name.' With a flash of that startling smile, he strode away.

He uses it like a weapon to keep people at a distance, Pax decided as she went in search of coffee. They weren't so different. She'd used 'Keep Calm and Carry On' as her shield long before the retro poster campaign.

Luca and the puppy were still missing when she returned with a bag weighed down with Coke cans and dog-food pouches, plastic handles digging into her arm, and a hot coffee cup in each hand, what Mack called an 'Irish handshake' when carrying pints in the pub. Her husband had a mildly offensive cliché for every nationality and occasion.

Mack. Like a metronome tick in her head. Mack, Mack, Mack. Kes, Kes, Kes.

Shivering by the bonnet, she drank her own coffee, then Luca's, wondering where the hell he'd taken her dog and if he was still on the phone. It was a seriously long call if so. Weren't they all still in bed in Canada? She knew nothing about the set-up he'd left behind. She must be friendly, find out facts, play detective. Alice would be mad at her for letting the opportunity slip.

At last he reappeared, phone still pressed to his ear, puppy straining to rejoin her, dark eyes gleaming and tail whipping. Handing over the lead, Luca rolled his eyes, mouthing 'Sorry' and then resumed talking quickly into the handset.

She fed the puppy on a disposable plate she'd nabbed from a fast-food outlet, trying not to listen in. It took her a moment to realise that he was speaking Italian, his voice rising and falling far more expressively than it did in his softly spoken mother tongue. As soon as he hung up, he started thumbing a message. She eyed the screen. Was that German?

The puppy didn't like his food, sitting down by the plate and looking up at her apologetically.

Luca was back on the phone, speaking French now, which

he did badly, with a marked Irish accent. They all stood by the bonnet for a while, Pax waiting for him to open the car, but as soon as the call ended, he was back to scrolling and messaging.

'It's cold out here,' she said pointedly.

'Yes.'

'Best get going.'

'Agreed. Just got one more quick call to make.'

She could feel her teeth starting to chatter. 'At least unlock the bloody car.'

'You have the keys,' he pointed out.

Feeling stupid, she felt in her pockets, then looked in the plastic bag, then in through the car windows. Finally, retracing her steps, she found she'd left them on the coffee-shop counter. Crazily jittery and raw, just the smallest of goofs made her want to tantrum.

At least coming back in meant she could slope to the loo. Her reflection looked ghastly. She put on some lipstick and it looked worse, matching her red-rimmed eyes.

Had Mack got as drunk as her last night? He'd sounded so. Had he kissed a stranger? If only she *felt* something. She was so much more jealous of his hold over Kes. That was white heat, white noise jealousy.

Kes. Mack. Kes. Mack.

Back at the car, Luca was conducting a short-tempered call in English – a thick Irish brogue version – turning away as she approached. 'Look, I gotta go. Just tell her to take off the stuff about where I'm working from the social streams, yeah? No, I'm not in trouble, but y'know I don't do all that shit. Thanks.'

He took one look at Pax's pinched, wild-eyed face and insisted on driving again. Her phone came to life as soon as the engine started, a cannon fire of messages queued up, all from Mack. Pax only needed to read a few before confirming that, yes, he'd remained very drunk last night.

The phone rang in her hand as she read through the bitter,

misspelled venom written in the early hours. Mack's avatar was on the incoming call notification, a photograph she'd taken of him with Kes on his shoulders on holiday, both with matching big smiles. She sent the call straight through to voicemail, anger pinching and punching in her throat, angrier still as tears started to slide. How wrong to feel so sorry for him as well as so livid.

Not wanting Luca to see she was crying, she glared out of the side window, trying to blink her salty betrayal onto submission, but they came ever fiercer, soon joined by streaming nostrils and giveaway snorts.

Saying nothing, Luca reached for the glovebox, groping for tissues. The car drifted left, tyres roaring across the white hard-shoulder markings.

'There's nothing in there,' she sobbed, clutching hold of the dash as the car swerved back into lane again. 'Please don't worry. I can sniff.'

The ringtone blasting through the speakers made her jump. Her phone had automatically paired with the Noddy car's Bluetooth. Mack again. She turned it off. Feeling she had to explain, she muttered, 'My husband. It's a bit messy. We're separating.'

'I'm sorry to hear that.'

'It's for the best.' She sniffed and snorted noisily, desperate to deflect, to grapple a comfort blanket of calmness back. 'Tell me about you?'

'What do you want to know?'

'Are you and my mother lovers?'

He almost drove off the road, the defensive smile quick to flash up. 'I've not seen her in years. I'm a horseman. That's what I do.'

Bridge had woken three times already this year, the first at seven o'clock her time, midnight in Los Angeles, Bernie sharing the New Year with her sister on phone screens, one surrounded by beautiful party animals, the other with bloodshot eyes and bed hair. Dozing afterwards, podium dancing with a hunk on a Hollywood sign O, she'd been hooked out of the dream by a message from Carly, a welcoming glow of new friendship. Get-together agreed, she'd drifted off to rejoin the hunk and ride together through the plains. A call from Poland had jerked her awake again, companion galloping off as, gravel-voiced, Aleš complained about his headache before a poor signal cut them off. Waiting for him to call back, Bridge had slipped off to sleep again and into a dream of such erotic splendour that when she awoke an hour later, it felt as though she'd been pleasured all night, wide smile buried in her pillow. She rolled over, body shivering with fuzzy pleasure, reluctant to give up the sensation from the lips that had been on hers and between her legs.

Bridge stretched out in bed, still heavy-headed with a hangover she wore with pride, star-fishing luxuriously as she looked at the time on the bedside clock. Past nine already. She could bring breakfast upstairs, listen to rubbish pop, indulge in a bath. But first she'd close her eyes for another ten minutes. She missed her children and Aleš like vital organs, but there was no denying the lie-ins were bliss. And she had to replay those lips...

One eye opened again, the other scrunched closed. Hang on. If lips had been simultaneously on her mouth *and* erogenous zone, that meant more than one set. Had she been dreaming of group sex? Go, Missus! You might be a married mother of two, but your subconscious can rock some fantasy action.

It was coming back to her now. She'd been on a bench press in a gym, hunk-man approaching to help her lift a heavy weight. She remembered the shape of him, that V from narrow hips to wide shoulders, Lycra shorts full of priapic bulge. Not like her Aleš in football strip with his bearded bulk and buzz cut. Her fantasy figure was clean-shaven, thick-haired, oak-broad and sinewy. He'd started undressing her, telling her she was beautiful. That had been particularly lovely. Aleš had to be coaxed into it these days, sometimes not taking the hint. This man had run his hands up her legs, her miraculously smooth and lean thighs, to bury his fingers in her welcoming wetness, his eyes not leaving hers.

Wolf eyes. All Turners had wolf-pale eyes.

'Oh feck.' She remembered his face and felt a flash of mortified shame. Ash Turner. She'd been dreaming about Ash Turner straight after inviting his wife and children to visit. She sat up quickly, pulling on her dressing gown and shoving her feet in her slippers. She didn't even want to *think* about who the other lips had belonged to.

Good hostess that she was, she'd bake some *języki* biscuits like her Polish sister-in-law had taught her; that would sweeten the bitter aftertaste. First, she needed a cold shower.

'Are all your family in Ireland involved with horses?'

'Pretty much so.'

Luca heard the hiss of a can pull.

Not long into Pax's interrogation about his relationship with her mother, his former employers, the horses he trained and anything else she could fish for, she'd started to gulp diet cola. Getting blood out of a stone was plainly thirsty work. Now on her fourth can, voice ever more painfully husky, she'd moved on to his roots. 'What fields?'

'Same sort of fields as over here,' he said lightly. 'Greener, maybe.'

She didn't catch the joke. 'It's showjumping, isn't it?'

'Pretty much.'

Being grilled made him guard his truths – easier to smile and avoid detail.

'Hunting and dealing as well?'

'That too.'

'So you grew up in the saddle?'

'You too, I imagine.'

'Yep. No choice.'

'Still ride much?'

'Nope.' Her fingers were drumming the door trim, her knees jumping, disliking the role reversal. She jangled with nerves, like a racehorse in the stalls. Yet she had a steely calmness, that brittle Englishness which would not crack however many fissures ran through the walls. It was exhausting to share space with her. He almost preferred her drunk.

She gnawed at a thumbnail. 'Where do you go after this job finishes?'

'Let me unpack first!' he said, laughing easily.

The car was making terrible noises now they'd come off the M40. Looking in the wing mirror as they roared along the Stratford Road, Luca saw sparks and, slamming on the brakes, managed to bring the car to a halt in a pitted field entrance.

The rusted exhaust, full of holes, had dropped from its clips and been dragging along on the tarmac.

'I should have got that fixed,' Pax muttered when they got out to look at it.

'Telling me.'

Reaching underneath to assess the damage, he burned his hand, winced and tucked it under his armpit, tilting his head to look again. 'Sure, that's a sieve under there. I can maybe patch it up to get us home if you've some wire.'

She looked down her long, freckled nose at him. 'Wire?'

'Yeah. There'll be a toolkit in the boot somewhere, am I right?'

'Search me.' She shrugged. 'I'll call the AA, shall I?' She headed back to the passenger's door to reach in for her phone.

A few flakes of snow had started to drift down.

'I have the app,' she explained, tapping away at the screen. No sooner had she switched on the device than it rang. She rejected the call, still tapping and now waving the phone around. 'Patchy data signal.' It rang again. 'Oh, for God's sake!' The voice softened to its honeyed newsreader calm as soon as she answered. 'What is it, Mack? Is it Kes?'

Luca listened to a one-sided call between Pax and her husband, her stern, dry husk of a voice telling him very coolly to go to hell. She'd be murder to be married to, he imagined, all that neurosis upholstered in middle-class chintz. Thank goodness her mother was so different.

He located the small toolkit tucked in with the spare wheel, then dug around in his battered rucksack, locating his folding hoof knife and a pair of spur straps. He gathered up Pax's discarded drink cans from the footwell by the passenger's seat. Pacing around a few yards away, she was demanding that her son came back tomorrow as planned. Luca took his knife and carefully cut into each metal cylinder, removing the ends to create curved sheets of metal. These he wrapped around the holey exhaust to create a shell and then secured it with the straps. All he needed was a couple of twists of wire to attach it to the chassis fixings.

He looked around, but there was nothing in the muddy field entrance. Further along the road was another gateway and he went to investigate. They'd broken down beside a sewage works.

He could see Pax waving her free arm around, hand balled into a fist, landing on the car roof with a thwack. Yet when he made his way back, she sounded no angrier than an irritated teacher telling a small boy to calm down and behave himself.

'Don't be ridiculous, Mack. I'm not going to talk to you about this if you say things like that. Oh, for God's sake, don't start that again. There *is* nobody else.' She caught Luca watching her, glaring at him as though he was the unseen husband. 'I was in a hotel, yes, but I—' Her eyes rolled as she waited out a lot of shouting. 'Is that really what you think I was doing? You know what? You're so wrong. Yes, you are. You want the truth? You do? Well, I picked up a complete stranger and spent the night with him. Isn't that *amazing*?'

Apart from bright spots of colour in her pale cheeks, she gave away no trace of emotion. She could have been telling him she bumped into an old friend in Waitrose. Luca picked up a stream of obscenities from the voice shouting out of her phone.

'You do that,' she said eventually. 'I think lawyers are a very good idea. Yes, I do actually. How clear must I make it that our marriage is over? Do I need to run along Princes Street twirling my bra around over my head singing "I Want to Break Free"?'

Without warning, she hurled her phone over the gateway into the field, turning angrily to face Luca, her pale face livid. For an alarming moment he thought she was going to attack him, but she hissed. 'Do you still need wire?'

'It would help.'

Hands burrowing under her sweater and around her back, she unhooked her bra, small-cupped and conservative cream, and fed it out through a sleeve. Within seconds, she'd sprung out the underwires and handed them to him. 'There.'

'Thank you.' They were still warm. 'Are you going to twirl it around your head and sing now?'

'No.'

His gaze automatically went to her chest where two angry nipples pointed accusingly at him through the thick cable knit of her sweater.

Catching him looking, she tutted under her breath and blew her nose noisily on the bra, then turned on her heel and walked to the front of the car to get back in. He could see her silhouette through the rear windscreen, knees drawn up to her chin, arms round them and shoulders high as she tried hard to hide the fact she was crying again.

He fixed the exhaust back up with the bra wire and tried the engine which, whilst far from a smooth urban purr, was at least sounding less like a tank. Pax had regained her composure and was gazing blankly out to the road ahead.

'You'd better get your phone,' he told her.

'I don't want it.'

'For Christ's sake, at least don't litter the bloody thing!'

She was seriously getting on his nerves now. He climbed over the gate and tracked it down easily enough because it was ringing again. The screen was smashed. It stopped ringing as he carried it back to the car, tossing it on the rear seat.

As soon as they set off the Bluetooth reconnected and another incoming call rang around them.

Cursing under her breath, Pax unbuckled her belt and half-climbed into the back to retrieve it. 'Press the red button on the steering wheel.'

Murderously, Luca pressed the green button.

'Patricia?' a deep Scottish brogue demanded. The husband sounded like Sean Connery. He could do a calm voice too.

'I can't turn it off,' she growled in frustration turning back round with the phone in her hand.

'You're bleeding everywhere,' Luca realised.

'Patricia, what's going on?' demanded the deep voice.

The broken screen had cut her finger, scarlet drips landing on the gear shift. '*Press* the red button,' she hissed.

'Do *not* hang up on me, Patricia,' boomed the voice, 'my son deserves better than this!'

'Respectfully, Muir, this is between me and Mack.'

The blood was dripping down her slim, pale wrist, Luca noticed in alarm.

'That's where you are wrong. *We* are your family. We are your son's family, we are—'

'Watch the tractor!' Pax gasped, grabbing for the wheel. Luca realised, too late, that he was driving straight at an oncoming John Deer.

'Shit!' He pulled the steering wheel hard right. Pax was pulling it hard left.

At the last moment the tractor mounted the verge, taking out most of the hedge as it passed, driver gesticulating wildly. The puppy started barking. Pax slumped back in her seat. There was blood all over the steering wheel.

'You could have killed us!' Luca fumed.

'Who is that?' demanded the deep boom.

'Listen, fella, I'm sorry your marriage is on the rack, so I am, but having spent just a few hours in the company of your lady wife, I have to say it's a fucking miracle it's lasted as long as it has. Now bring the kid home to his mum.' He pressed the red button.

Pax turned to him, eyes wide.

'Stop the car.' It sounded so deathly, he thought she must be about to pass out or throw up again.

But, clambering out, Pax hurled the phone into an industrial wheelie bin on the edge of a village.

Cut hand wrapped in her bra, she reclaimed her seat and fumed quietly beside him. 'That was my father-in-law you were speaking to. I'll thank you not to interfere again.'

'Willingly.'

'You should have let me get the AA.'

'You certainly need their namesake.'

'I've quit drinking.'

'I'll believe that when I see it.'

'You won't be sticking around long enough.'

'I'm staying for six months.'

'So you've signed a contract?' She was fishing again, with a harpoon this time.

'Watertight.' He rolled his eyes sarcastically. Verbal was fine by him. He knew Ronnie was as good as her word.

'The trust hasn't approved it.'

It was snowing thickly now, billowing into the windscreen.

'Pax, can we just make friends?' he sighed.

'Not right now.'

'At least give the dog a name.'

'I already did,' she said stubbornly. 'He's called Knott.'

He laughed, exasperated, watching her face and still looking for Ronnie in it.

'It's a mountain in the Lake District,' she explained. 'Mummy lived in a cottage overlooking it when I was little.'

'Must be a favourite spot.'

She turned on the radio again. The station was still playing New Year tracks, Taylor Swift imploring them to hold on to the memories, making Pax settle back into her seat and close her eyes. 'I never saw it.'

6

The snow, flurrying across from Wales, had turned north before the Cotswolds. Instead, bright sunlight was burning off the frost, warming the scent trail laid for the Fosse and Wolds hounds.

Lester lifted his nose appreciatively as he came out from grooming the liver-chestnut cob, now polished like cherrywood. There were no Percy hunters, ponies or second horses to be readied these days, Lester serving as the singular ambassador for a family who had followed Wolds Hounds for fifteen generations, an honour he took seriously, a way of life he refused to acknowledge was under threat by social change or budget. He would never dream of telling anybody, least of all Ronnie, that he'd paid this season's subscription from his own savings, sparing the diesel whenever he could. He would hack to this meet – it was half an hour across the fields at a good clip.

He went inside to change, Stubbs at his heels.

He'd given the Turner girl the last ten pounds from the petty cash for her trouble. She was a hard worker, if unskilled and unkempt, and whilst prone to littering her possessions about – she'd left her glittery purse in the tack room, her bobble hat by the hay bale and a set of keys on the feed room desk – she was impressively good at tidying up around the yard at speed, not a loose blade of hay in sight. It looked very shipshape when Ronnie's silver sports car powered up the driveway.

Lester, at the dressing-table mirror in his bedroom, tying his stock, looked down from his low casement to watch her park at a rakish angle, the engine roar cutting to dog barks. He almost thrust the pin straight into his windpipe when he spotted she had company, recognising the pelt of peppery black hair emerging from the passenger's side, long denim legs unfolding and battered country boots hitting the cobbles at the same time as a tangle of paws, dogs spilling from all sides.

Lester sighed heavily. Blair Robertson, all Marlboro Man testosterone, a hangover from her Wiltshire years. The wretched man was supposed to get her to call home, not accompany her back in person.

He'd feared this might happen. The Australian event rider had a cool calculator in his handsome head, as good at counting profit as minute markers, and this stud made Ronnie too valuable an asset to leave fallow. Looking at him, Lester found it hard to spot an item of clothing without a sponsor's logo, those embroidery tattoos that professional riders collected with pride. From his Puffa to his underwear, Blair Robertson was a walking billboard for the country elite, an ageing eventing poster boy.

And Lester had inadvertently played matchmaker with its one-time golden girl.

Good mood dissipating, he stomped downstairs and pulled on his boots. Outside, he counted five dogs – two extra terriers and an English pointer.

Ronnie was heaving several saddles out of the boot of the car. 'Happy New Year, Lester! Sorry I'm later than planned. You remember Blair.'

Lester nodded at him, spared formal reacquaintance by the stud's line ringing, the external bell clanging from the clock tower.

'Shall I get that in the cottage, Mrs Ledwell?'

'I'll grab it.' Ronnie was already ahead of him, dumping the saddles on Blair and running in through his front door. 'I'm expecting a call from Tim. Lost my mobile somewhere. Where's Pax?' She vanished inside, not waiting for an answer.

Left alone with Blair Robertson, Lester sucked his teeth and eyed the sky where dark clouds were gathering. 'You told her the Horsemaker's flown in early?'

'Slipped my mind.' He smiled easily. 'In bed, is he?'

'They're not back yet.' Lester scowled.

'Keeping well, I see, Lester.' The Australian's canyon-deep voice always sounded mildly ridiculous amid civilised surroundings.

'As can be expected,' he said tersely, already backing away. 'If you'll excuse me, sir.'

But to his annoyance, Blair followed him into the tack room, yawning widely, no doubt suffering from a late and probably highly seductive night. He dumped the saddles on an empty rack and admired the old photographs of Ronnie sailing over rider-frightener four-star fences in the early eighties. A few newer ones taken by Pip on her phone had been pinned up recently, cheap printer paper curling at the edges, amongst them an early shot of the dun colt Ronnie rated above all the others.

'There's my five-star horse.' Blair tapped it.

'Four,' Lester corrected, the half dozen great three-day events like Badminton, Burghley and Kentucky graded four-star being the toughest in the sport, even watered down from the great endurance feats they'd been in yesteryear.

'New rules, mate. They're adding a star.'

Lester's lip curled. With each generation came the urge to meddle and change things. As they re-emerged into sharp winter sunlight, he wondered where Blair's poor wife was today. An aristocratic beauty in her day, now going senile by all accounts, she'd given up everything for him once: a grand house, title and family. Last year, she'd given up the mad stallion too, which Lester considered a wiser sacrifice.

'His dam's in foal to the same sire this year?'

'If you are referring to the dun colt, that's correct.'

'Exciting prospect. Next you'll have to try her with this guy.' Blair went to see Beck, admiring his ferocious beauty beyond the grilles, his deep rumbling voice doing little to calm the aggressive display.

'That's for Mrs Ledwell to decide,' Lester muttered, adding under his breath, 'Not your bloody place.'

Blair cracked a hoarse laugh and Lester realised he'd been heard. He ground his teeth as he crossed the yard under the man's watchful gaze, hatefully slow and lopsided under the weight of the cob's saddle, its leather-cased sandwich box and hunting flask already attached.

The Australian stood framed in the stable door, a big menacing shadow. 'I'm on my way to lunch in Leicestershire. My most enthusiastic owners have bought each other His and Hers eventers for Christmas that they want me to take away for further education. Ronnie kindly offered me her lorry.'

'Hmm…' Lester knew he had at least two horse boxes of his own.

'Could use a decent run, she reckons. No good lying idle, classy machine like hers.'

Lester marched past him, suspecting the Australian of at least one double entendre.

'We look out for each other, me and Ron.'

'Not my business what you get up to,' he muttered, throwing the saddle up on the cob, refusing to be drawn into it.

'This Horsemaker bloke, Lester,' he squinted over his shoulder where the pack of dogs they'd brought had Stubbs cornered in the tack room, 'd'you know much about him?'

Lester's gnarled fingers slowed over the buckles, sensing common ground. 'Heard he got into a spot of bother a while back.'

'It was more than a spot, Lester. It was a bloody great black hole.'

'Sorry! I left half my clobber here!' exclaimed a breathless voice as, with a squeak of muddy buggy wheel, Carly charged across the yard from the direction of the rear track, pushing two of her brood, the third – a little shaven-haired thug – stomping in her wake carrying a fluffy sabre of some sort, and trailing their evil-looking dog who started barking and dragged him into the tack room to join the pack. 'Get Mum's purse from in there, Ellis!' she shouted as she gathered the keys which she waggled at Lester with a self-mocking expression as he emerged from the cob's stable. 'Had to break into my own house just now.' She grinned.

She'd changed into tight ripped jeans and a boxy fake fur jacket, ankle boots coated in mud. She must have come across the fields, Lester realised, rather admiring her tenacity, although he did wish she'd exert it elsewhere.

Carly was looking at Blair with sleepy-eyed interest. 'We've met, haven't we?'

Clearing his throat brusquely, Lester said, 'Blair is an event rider friend of Mrs Ledwell's, Carly.' He paused, uncertain how to introduce her. He could hardly classify her as a groom, especially dressed like that. She did all sorts of jobs from what she'd said. 'Carly is... a working girl from the village.'

One of her dark, sculpted eyebrows shot up and Lester had a feeling he might have got that wrong.

Blair's craggy face was all smiles. 'Any friends of Lester's is a friend of mine.'

'It's a professional relationship,' Lester muttered, turning back to the stable.

'Wait a sec!' Carly called him back. She sucked her teeth for a moment, twirling the keys around her fingers and glancing at the buggy, where her toddler daughter was tugging at her mother's coat hem mewling to see the horses. 'I wanted to say thank you very much for the job this morning, Mr Lester.'

'You're very efficient.'

She smiled quickly. 'You can't say you didn't get a lot for your tenner, yeah. You'll let Mr O'Brien know what I can do?'

He cleared his throat, aware of Blair's close scrutiny. 'I will.'

'Cool. Is Ronnie back yet?' She looked around hopefully.

'Mrs Ledwell is on the telephone.'

She gathered her hat and crammed it on before shouting for her son. 'Ellis! Pack in winding up them dogs and come back here. We're going round to Bridge's for coffee, so I want best behaviour, yeah?'

'Can we see the horses first?' demanded Ellis, storming out of the tack room, the dog he was trailing now had hackles high, terriers nipping at its legs.

'If you like.' She tousled his hair, eyeing Lester again. 'You don't mind, do you?'

Gesturing tersely to go ahead with her carrot-feeding, Lester hurried back into the stable to fetch out the cob, knowing he'd be late if he tarried any longer.

Outside, Blair was summoning his dog pack with a sharp whistle. He held open the stable door, still watching Carly and her brood heading off in the direction of the turnout paddocks, craggy face amused. 'I'll hand it to you, Lester, you're full of surprises. What d'you get for a tenner these days?'

'Give them an inch they take a mile, her sort. She's a lot to learn.' Lester headed for the mounting block, affronted because he'd paid all the stud could afford.

The Australian held his offside stirrup. 'You keep a close eye on O'Brien, yeah?'

'That goes without saying, Mr Robertson.' He settled in the saddle.

'I'm here if you need me, mate.'

Surprised to find himself grateful for this unlikely alliance, Lester gave a nod, tightened his girth, then checked his watch. Ronnie had been speaking on the phone a long time. And Pax should be back by now. He remembered the owl shrieking on the house roof before dawn, thought about the phone call from the threatening American, and felt the cold press of unease again.

'I need to speak with Mrs Ledwell before I go.'

What are those almond croissanty biscuits called? Bridge messaged her husband in Poland. *When I google Rickylicky I just get a load of weird shit.*

Rogaliki, Aleš messaged back. *I will bring you some home. And licky.* He added a tongue and doughnut emojis, which Bridge was feeling too hungover to find funny.

Need them this morning. Hungry. She added a few smiley emojis with heart eyes to make sweet nothing of her hangover.

He sent a lot of winking ones winging straight back. *I am just hungry for your body.*

Yawning, Bridge matched his winking faces, wrote *Miss your tongue, baby* and raised him some tongue-out winks before flipping screens to google *rogaliki* biscuits.

His reply chimed as she scrolled through the ingredients.

Want it now? He'd sent drooling emojis, plus a peach and an aubergine.

Wondering if they had enough ground almonds in the larder, she distractedly gave him ten kissing emojis and multicoloured love hearts. *It's licking me in my mind.*

Aleš replied before she could navigate back to the recipe screen, his message bubble containing several thumbs-ups, okay hands, phallic-looking aeroplanes and a squinting face with its tongue out. *I am coming, kochanie!*

What did that mean? Bridge looked at it curiously. Had he just self-pleasured? Had they been having emoji phone sex without her realising? She scrolled back up to the doughnut and decided perhaps it had been.

Electing to be kind, she gave him a row of open-mouthed emojis and a *Me too!*

It was only after pressing send that she spotted that her autocorrect had given Me Too a hashtag and made it look like a protest.

In Lester's cottage, tethered to the wall by the tangled phone flex, Ronnie was fielding a call from her furious son-in-law. 'Tishy has taken a stun gun to our marriage, fully intending to cut its throat and bleed it out!'

Sounding like David Tennant playing the fifth act of a Shakespeare tragedy, and demanding to speak with his wife between long self-pitying monologues, he'd been banging on for ten minutes now, mostly self-aggrandised descriptions of what a good husband and father he was, with brief blasts of Othello rage. 'I have done *nothing* to her and she's *destroyed* us!' Getting a sensible word in edgeways was like trying to parallel park a tank in a battlefield.

'You know all about this, didn't you?' Mack was ranting.

'No, I—'

But he was off again, cutting across her to shout that he knew Ronnie was covering for her. She could only imagine at Pax's frustration if this was what she had to deal with behind closed doors. Although mother-and-daughter talks were strictly *verboten* to Ronnie, she'd guessed Pax's marriage was in trouble, unable to find her way across the glacier-filled chasm that still divided them. 'Mack, I've just this moment got back. I'm not even sure where Pax *is*.'

'With her fucking lover, fucking each other probably!'

'*What*?'

'I heard him. Dad *spoke* with him! They're together. Don't deny it. They spent last night in a hotel.'

'Gosh.' Good for Pax.

Cue another unstoppable tirade, extolling how virtuous he'd been – 'there've been plenty of offers, Veronica, many temptations of the flesh laid in my path' – and how Pax had no such qualms given all the marriage vows she'd broken in the last twenty-four hours.

Ronnie turned as the cottage door opened with a blast of cold air. Blair came in, dark eyes questioning. She grimaced, listening as Mack as described his suicidal call to Pax while another man was in her room, and again that morning. 'She *gloated* about it, Veronica.' It didn't sound at all like Pax, but Mack was reeling off times and soundbites. 'She *freely* admitted that she'd picked up a *complete* stranger and *spent the night* with him!' And now he started laying into her character, punching out words. 'She was living like a *slut* when I first met her, so I might have *guessed* she'd revert to *type*. She's not been herself for months. Not since *you* came back on the *scene*.'

'Whoa, or this phone's going down, Mack.' She looked at Blair, who was holding up his hands and backing out. She held out a hand to stop him. 'Are you saying that Pax has left you?'

'At fifteen-eleven on Christmas Day, your daughter said, "This marriage is over". A week later, she rubs her infidelity in my face. Make of that what you will.'

She was still frantically trying to gather fact from vitriol. She'd never once imagined that Pax – so damning of her mother's desertion, so determined to make amends by making her own family sacrosanct – would pull the plug on her marriage, let alone involve another man. It was a red rag to a bully like Mack.

'She'll never see Kes again!' he raged. 'When you see her, tell her I've taken legal advice and she is finished as a mother; Kes needs to be protected from you both!'

'For God's sake, Mack, let's be sensible about this.'

'You're a fine one to talk!' came a piercing interjection and Ronnie realised that Pax's puritanical mother-in-law Mairi was sharing the call on speakerphone. 'You abandoned your wee family. And that's just what your silly girl is doing to hers. The sins of the mothers.'

'This is not about me, Mairi,' Ronnie snapped. Blair was beside her now, a warm hand on her shoulder.

'This all started the moment you came back into her life!' Mairi was still shrilling.

'Pax is a grown woman.' She mouthed *'Where is Pax?'* to Blair. He mimed hands at a car steering wheel, then threw them wide in an aeroplane impersonation, which didn't exactly help.

Meanwhile, the voice in her ear had dropped an octave to a chilling alto. 'Oh, you're not getting out of it that easily, Veronica. Let's talk straight, mother to mother. She will lose that wee bairn as surely as you lost yours if this ends in divorce. I've watched her, and it's no way to raise a child. D'you know how much she drinks? If you ask me, you need to care for your own daughter a wee bit more and worry about the gee-gees less.'

'I'm aware she's been unhappy,' Ronnie said carefully. She'd seen the light draining from behind her daughter's eyes, the glass walls around her thickening, but theirs was such a fragile bond there was no possibility of rushing in to help, the sinner in her glass house unable to cast the first stone.

'She's an alcoholic!' Mack bellowed. 'If you can't see that you're an even lousier mother than I took you for.'

Ronnie could hear Mairi hushing him. She felt a steel blade of fear, cold and familiar, run up through her. The sins of the fathers too. She'd guessed Pax drank too much, but to name it as a disease out loud made it feel far bigger, far more out of control.

She took Blair's hand, square fingered and calloused from riding and breaking horses, his fingers comfortingly familiar between hers as she pulled its weight onto her shoulder and leaned into him.

Ronnie had no great affection for her son-in-law, a man of her own generation, who was at best a well-meaning bully and at worst a judgemental control freak, but she knew silence bred mistrust in a break-up faster than bacteria. 'Come back and talk it through with her, Mack. Your train's booked for tomorrow, isn't it?'

'We'll not be on it unless she agrees to give up whoever that bastard is. I'm willing to make a go of things for the sake of the boy and forget all this happened if she is.'

'That's not up to me to say…' Ronnie hesitated.

'Will you help save this marriage, Veronica?' Mairi demanded.

Ronnie remembered her own escape so vividly. She'd never wanted to go back to Johnny, not for a minute. But if anybody had offered her a way of keeping her children, however duplicitous, she'd have taken it without hesitation.

'I'll help in whatever way I can,' she said.

'In that case I'll call back when you've spoken with her.' Mack hung up without a farewell.

Groaning with frustration, Ronnie turned to press her face gratefully into Blair's chest, his collarbone hard against her forehead.

His arms tightened around her. 'She went to the airport to get your Horsemaker friend.'

'He's supposed to be in Ireland.'

'Diverted in the fog, Lester says.'

'Oh, shit.' She closed her eyes. '*That's* who Mack's accusing her of spending the night with.'

'Fast worker.' Blair looked delighted.

'Don't even joke.' She tried not to let her mind run with the idea, but it had already mugged it, remembering Luca's wild reputation when she'd first known him in Germany, his effortless charm, the girls who hung on his every word, his skill with the most damaged hearts. He'd even tried to seduce her once, a very mannerly Lothario, rebuffed with no lost friendship. But that had been years ago. He'd surely calmed down. And Pax was in no fit state. *Alcoholic…* The word made her shudder afresh.

'No, it's absolutely not possible,' she said, shaking her head sharply. 'Oh, poor Pax. She's going through hell and I land Luca on her.'

'His plane made it onto the runway; I don't think the fog was that bad.'

'I always love your bad jokes in a crisis.' She lifted her face to look up at Blair. 'Goodness, I'm glad you're here.'

'I'm not stopping,' he reminded her, brow creasing regretfully.

'Not even for one night?' She reached up to stroke one of her own blonde hairs from his cheek, the curved bow of his lips ever tempting. Nobody kissed like Blair. But even with adultery, he was an all-or-nothing man.

'You've enough going on here,' he reminded her. The dark eyes glittered.

She dismissed another spike of unease. 'I could use a friend.'

'What about your Horsemaker?' A muscle ticked in his cheek. Much as he loved the idea of Luca tangoing her daughter straight from the arrivals gate to a Travelodge, his jealousy had played with the name too much to believe it either.

'Nobody has an ounce of your…' She lifted her other hand to his hair, letting its peppered weight slide between her fingers, beneath her nails. 'You-ness.'

'Don't,' he scolded gently, jerking back his head and beckoning her outside. 'You'd better put Lester out of his misery. He's waiting out there to speak to you.'

She looked up at the clock; hounds would be moving off from the meet soon. It had to be life or death.

The old stallion man was waiting beneath the clock-tower archway, rigid with impatience, creased face set in deepest disapproval, cob standing four square.

Ronnie smiled up to him. 'You look very smart. Sorry to keep you waiting.'

'I'm concerned about Pax, Mrs L— Ronnie,' he corrected himself with effort, still uncomfortable with first names.

'She's fine,' she insisted brightly. 'She and Luca are on their way, I gather.'

'There was another telephone call for Mr O'Brien earlier.' He cleared his throat. 'An American gentleman, I think. He didn't leave his name, but he was rather angry. He threatened to kill Mr O'Brien, in fact.'

'Goodness, how alarming. Did he say why?'

'Something about his daughter. I thought it best to mention it.'

'Thank you, Lester. We must let you go or you'll miss your sport.' She dismissed him with a nod.

'Jesus,' Blair muttered under his breath as Lester clattered away, 'perhaps I *should* bloody stay.'

'Says the man who escaped one aristocratic father's shotgun by running naked across a parterre full of Japanese tourists,' she reminded him, not betraying the hard thudding of her heart, worrying about Pax again. 'You won the advanced section the next day, as I recall.'

'He'd better ride as well as you say.' He looked at her incredulously.

But Ronnie was watching Lester trot away stiffly, ordering Stubbs back to the yard which the little dog did with his ears back, joining them as his master disappeared behind the walled garden, velvet beagle hat bobbing as he kicked into a canter towards the path up through the orchards to the old drover's track. 'Poor Lester's nose is terribly out of joint over all this.'

'There's more out of joint than just his nose. That man's in a lot of pain.'

'Oh God, you think so too? It's his hips. I keep telling him to see a specialist. He's terrified they'll stop him riding. Lester will die in his boots.'

'Sooner than you think if he doesn't get himself fixed up.'

'Maybe if I offered to pay for his op…' Ronnie rolled a lip anxiously beneath her teeth. Lester's endurance was spectacularly, nobly self-destructive.

'You're broke.'

'I have a credit card.'

'They'll be hunting snowmen in hell before he takes your charity.' He glanced across at the sleet-filled clouds rolling up along the horizon. 'He's that sort.'

'My father called Lester the original iron man.'

'He's rusted.' He reached for her hand and squeezed it in his calloused one. 'I get that you need a rider. I'd just rather you'd chosen a different one.'

Ronnie did too. The one rider she longed to share this place with was standing beside her. She leaned into Blair's side briefly, breathing in his strength, needing her iron men more than ever, especially with her father gone and Pax's marriage unravelling.

Intuitive to her mood as always, he set off across the yard, taking her along with him. 'Show me how that dun colt's looking before I go. See if he can convince me to leave off retirement for another decade.'

Ronnie followed, grateful for the brief diversion and its hidden message: they both knew the colt was their point on the horizon, a shared dream that might just outlive Blair's marriage and her family rifts.

As they approached the field, he swiftly let go of her hand. The dun colt was having a conversation with Carly Turner over the far fence at the far end of the farm track where she'd parked her buggy, the young mum holding up her chubby, pink-cheeked baby to talk to him while her two other children fed carrots to their big, battle-scarred dog.

Like many ageing eventers accustomed to parking up in stately piles each weekend, Blair was an inveterate snob. 'You'll never get rid of that one.'

'Why would I want to?' Ronnie's censorious look won her a brisk nod and crooked smile.

'I swear she was hawking the fork at Lester earlier.'

'The what?'

'Soliciting.'

'Good luck to her if she was.' She waved at Carly, marching onwards. 'You know better than anyone that the greatest talents need to set themselves impossible challenges. Like saving the stud for this chap to stand here.' They both tilted their heads to admire the colt who, shaggy-coated and muddy, looked far from a future superstar. But to their trained eyes, he was pure gold, and one of the reasons Ronnie was determined to turn the family fortunes. He could be the best horse her father had bred in a lifetime.

'I still think you should sell me a leg,' Blair complained. 'It'd pay for an old man's hip.'

'Lester would never stand for emotional blackmail, ha ha.' She ignored his groan with a defiant smile. 'He agrees with me that we're keeping every hair of this one in the Percy family name.' Now within Carly's earshot, she called out to wish her a happy new year.

The young blonde was smilier than Ronnie had ever seen her. 'Lester tell you I helped with the yard work this morning?'

'How marvellous.' She was pulling silly faces at the baby, then looked up as it registered. 'Really? That's so kind.' She'd hoped she might volunteer.

'He paid me,' Carly added quickly.

Ronnie felt her smile stiffen.

'A tenner,' Blair told her, which cheered her up again.

'In that case, we'll have to see if we can offer you something regularly.'

Carly opened her mouth then closed it again.

They all walked back together, Carly carrying her baby while Ronnie pushed the toddler in the buggy and earned a wry look from Blair. Perhaps she was overdoing fostering the young mum a little. But as well as bringing the welcome babble of small children's laughter, Carly did have the makings of a rare, raw talent – that obsession for horses and the workaholic perfectionism, those extraordinary hands – which Ronnie knew her industry ran off, essential to her team. Lester was getting too old, and Luca never stayed anywhere long. Pax, who had possessed so much talent as a teenager, had made it clear there was no going back. Best of all, Carly was keen and cheap.

'It'll be *lots* of fun when Luca's here,' she promised, hoping Lester's curmudgeonly management style hadn't put her off helping again. 'He's generous to a fault and always the life and soul. This village will *adore* him; he even plays a fiddle.' And all the husbands with pretty wives had better watch out, she added silently.

'A fully loaded Celt,' Blair glowered, grumpy once more.

'Oh, I love the Irish!' Carly looked pleased. 'My friend says it's all about the craic.'

'My philosophy entirely.' Ronnie cast Blair a beguiling look, then turned at the sound of a car on the drive, a small, muddy coupé trundling steadily between the poplars, familiar in its Toytown curviness, a flash of red hair visible through the side window. 'Here they are!'

'The Horseman cometh,' muttered Blair in a sardonic undertone.

Ronnie ignored him, the phone call from Mack suddenly playing on a loop in her head again as though she'd just replaced the receiver. *Alcoholic. Picked up a stranger and spent the night with him. She'll lose Kes.*

She grabbed Blair's arm. 'I need you to look after Luca.'

'What?' He snatched it away.

'I have to talk to Pax. Can you make him a coffee and show him around or something? If that really *is* him.' She peered closer. Pax was the one in the passenger seat, a fierce-looking bearded man driving. He was absolutely nothing like she remembered.

'I'm not bloody showing lover boy round,' Blair sounded insulted.

'I'll do it if you like,' Carly offered, unslotting her toddler from the buggy. 'We've got a few minutes.'

'*That's* the Horsemaker?' Blair whistled incongruously as the car turned towards them.

For a moment, Ronnie took the man behind the wheel to be a stranger, her daughter white-faced and murderous alongside. Then the driver smiled, that unforgettable O'Brien weapon of mass destruction, and she felt her heart plummet. It was the only thing she recognised about him. 'Oh Christ, what's happened to Luca?'

Pax cut the radio – 'Holding Back the Years', Simply Red – as Luca steered around potholes and loose dogs in the arrivals yard, Knott barking excitedly in the boot.

'Welcome to Compton Magna Stud. Looks like they've laid on a reception committee.' It was an odd line-up, a babushka doll of surprised faces: her mother and her Australian beefcake lover, alongside a vaguely familiar scraggy-looking blonde with small children hanging off both arms and a leg.

She glanced at Luca; his smile was at full beam as they came to a halt in front of the grand old buildings. With the beard on top, it was an explorer's mask, taking in the tribal ceremony. He kept so much of himself hidden, Pax didn't trust him at all. Only his eyes, green as mint, were giveaway intense, fixed firmly on her mother's pretty features like a castaway spotting a ship.

'Just remember, Mummy's the only one of us happy you're here,' she murmured, realising she sounded like Alice. But she felt like Alice, aggrieved and protective, their childhood home under threat. She'd been denied her one night alone here with her memories. The more her day unravelled, the more she wished she'd been granted its sanctuary. 'I don't think her boyfriend's too keen on you either,' she added, noting Blair's glowering face. Seeing Luca's eyes flicker, processing this, she felt a degree of satisfaction for putting down a marker. If Blair was here at the stud, it was obviously back on.

'Luca!' Her mother was already at the driver's door, charm at full throttle, eyes sparkling. 'I hardly recognised you in your winter coat! Welcome! Good journey?'

Out of the car, Ronnie's small dogs eagerly sniffed Luca's trouser legs and shoes while she introduced him to everyone, circus showman rollcalling her troupe for the benefit of the tired-eyed Irishman: 'my brilliant eventing star friend, Blair', 'my secret-weapon apprentice, Carly' and 'her three ravishing little jockeys in training who are all going to give you a quick guided tour – meet Ellis, Sienna and Jackson – while I have a word with Pax in the house.' Her small, firm hand clamped around her daughter's. 'You two have had quite a night of it with the fog, haven't you? You'll forgive me dragging her off, won't you, Luca?'

'Be my guest.' The O'Brien smile was fixed in place.

Pax looked away, her gaze inadvertently meeting Blair's, sensing his bad temper as he snapped in a gravelly undertone, 'Ron, I'm going to push off.'

'I should get back home too.' Pax took his cue gratefully, needing to pace the Mack Shack and form a plan.

'It's important, Pax,' Ronnie said urgently, her voice lowered so that the others couldn't hear. 'I've spoken with the Forsyths.'

'That's my business!' The last thing she wanted was her mother's involvement.

'If you want to keep Kes, you'll listen to what I have to say.'

Heartbeat spiking at the mention of her son's name, Pax waited with gritted teeth and tightly folded arms while her mother said a brisk farewell to Blair. The formal way they pecked cheeks was at odds with the white-knuckled emotion with which they briefly clasped hands, she realised, struck with reluctant admiration for the self-control with which the two loved one another.

Turning away, she saw that Luca was also watching them. Aware that he was under scrutiny, he glanced across at her. For once he didn't smile.

Luca, tired to his bone marrow, had already forgotten the young woman's name. She seemed to have a lot of children. And tattoos. And disturbingly intense grey eyes, the left bearing two streaks of blue in its iris like clock arms, reading quarter to four.

'What d'you want me to show you first – the mares in foal?' she offered. Her kids looked frozen through, Luca realised. The dog was shivering too. Sleet had started to turn to rain.

Luca fished the deerhound puppy out of the boot. 'A hot drink would be great.'

'There's a kettle in the tack room,' she said, leading the way. 'You come far?'

'Canada.' He couldn't even remember when he'd set out, his sense of time lost; he was beyond exhausted.

'Long way to bring a dog.'

'I picked him up on the way. He's called Knott.'

'Knot as in "tie the" knot?'

'You could say that.' Or untie it in the case of Pax Forsyth's marriage. The bloody woman was unhinged.

'Cute little thing.' The blonde led the way into a big tack room with polished wooden racks, a vaulted roof and a wood burner in one corner. 'That's Pricey.' She indicated the coffin-headed hound, brindle-striped like a tiger, that looked as though it was lovingly but insanely about to eat her children. 'Don't mind the fact she's nutty looking. Heart of gold.'

Luca thought of Pax again. He preferred the dog.

Distracting the older two children with her phone, and the baby with a stainless-steel snaffle that he started gumming at furiously, she set about making coffee at supersonic speed, a pace at which he suspected she did most things. 'Isn't this place amazing?' She pronounced it ''mazing' in a creamy accent. 'Like something out of a telly adaptation. You know, *Downton Abbey*? I love it here. Look at all them old bridles.'

Luca, who had seen a lot of tack rooms, sagged in one of the ancient floral armchairs by the unlit wood-burning stove and looked at her instead. Sleepy hacienda eyes, tattoos, urban clothes and a steel rod of sass belying her Wessex-wench voice, she wasn't at all what he expected of a Ronnie Percy apprentice. The Ronnie he knew, savvy and straight-speaking, had a tight inner circle of contemporaries, generally preferring the company of men.

'What's your name again?'

'Carly. Like Carly Simon. Sang "You're So Vain".' Outside, they could hear a horsebox roaring into life. '*He* probably thinks that song is about him. Sorry if he's an old friend of yours, but he's a grumpy bugger, that Blair.'

'Never met him before.' The man was a legend Luca had long been inspired by. The disappointment of being snubbed was blunted by tiredness. 'Is it always like this here?'

'Dunno. I only started today.'

'So we're both new recruits?'

'Yeah,' she laughed, turning to put the kettle on. 'You're the one everyone's talking about, aren't you? The whisperer.'

'I'm just a horsebreaker.'

'Ronnie says you heal.'

'Does she now?'

'Only I have this thing. With my hands. They get hot and stuff, you know.' She turned back, holding them out like a child showing she'd washed them.

'I know.' It wasn't unusual. His own use of therapeutic hands – a skill that ran in the O'Brien family, useful for de-stressing horses, easing strains and sprains – was no great magic.

'Thing is, not trying to sound weird or nothing but,' she scrunched up her face, 'they feel a bit odd right now. Better

I show you.' She set down the teaspoon she was holding, wiped her fingers on a grubby tea towel and walked up to him, reaching out to take his hands in hers, gold and diamonds glinting on her ring finger.

A hot brand welted his palms. It was as though she'd had them pressed to the scalding kettle.

'What's all that about, then?' she asked matter-of-factly.

Her gaze was earnest, wide eyes a milky grey with smudged mascara and dark bags beneath them. He studied them curiously as the hands burned into his. It was a while before he realised he was holding his breath.

He blew out, forcing a smile. 'Are they feeling any cooler?'

'No different. I'm having a well-weird day, me. Must be the magic working.'

'It's not magic.' He wanted to let go because it hurt, but knew she needed reassuring. 'Nobody knows quite what it is – like divining. It just is. Controlling it's harder.'

'Are your hands hot too?' She laughed, nervously.

'They are now.' Her wedding band was hard beneath the fingers of his right one.

She made to laugh again then stopped uncertainly, and for the briefest moment he saw in through the practical, sardonic front. Immediately, his own hands were pure electric.

She looked at them in surprise, feeling it too. 'What's that?'

'Therapeutic touch.'

'Wow. That's 'mazing.' She looked up at him, eyes widening, black pupils flooding the clock hands.

And from nowhere, inconvenient as hell, and with such a punch it penetrated twenty hours without sleep, Luca felt a familiar pull of attraction. It was a Pavlovian reaction he was trying hard to kick. For some men it was stockings and garters, others a stud in a pierced pink tongue, but for Luca it was a wedding ring. Like a spaniel trained to find drugs in an airport, he could sense out an unhappy marriage.

'Mum, why are you doing that with that man?'

She let go abruptly, returning to the coffee-making, rubbing her forehead with the back of her hand. 'It's a horse thing, Ellis.'

Luca found himself faced by three feet of outraged child brandishing a feather duster.

'It's my 'Splorer Stick,' the boy announced. 'It has super powers, my dad says. He was a soldier and killed lots of bad people. He has big muscles.'

'Nicely to the point,' he breathed, smiling. 'Ellis is a cool name, so it is.'

'My dad's called Ash, like the Pokémon trainer. What's your favourite Pokémon? Mine's Pikachu.'

'Don't bother the man, Ellis. Get back to your game.'

'Charizard,' Luca called out, earning an eyebrow curl of respect over one small bomber-jacketed shoulder. 'I was working in Japan when Pokémon GO was a fad,' he told Carly as she carried a mug across. 'My ex-boss went crazy for it. Kept running round with her mobile between jump-offs.'

'You've worked all over the world, haven't you?' She retreated to the sink.

'Here and there.'

'That's 'mazing.' The black coffee with two sugars he'd asked for turned out to be very milky and sugar-free, and she now wouldn't look him in the eye. He wasn't quite sure what she'd felt when they held hands – maybe, like him, it was as though she'd grabbed a hot grill pan without oven gloves – but it had scared her and he wished it hadn't. He badly needed allies. It was, as she had said, a 'well-weird' day.

'You and your husband live here at the stud?'

'I wish! Close. In the village. He's at college. Wants to be a fitness instructor. Eight years in the army.'

'That's impressive.'

'Yeah, he's the family hero.'

'That's cool.'

'He's lush.' She looked at her watch.

'You gotta be somewhere?'

'Meeting a friend in a bit.' Her fingers drummed the sink. 'I've got a couple more minutes. You want to look around? You can meet Spirit. He's my favourite.'

'It can wait.' He stifled another yawn. 'I just need to find a bed and crash.'

'I only know how to make the horses' beds here.'

'Good for you.'

'Lester taught me today. He's like the main man around here.'

'Not any more.'

She rolled her big, smudged eyes. 'You don't know Lester. I love him already. Tight-fisted bastard, he is, and he thinks a working girl and working mum are the same thing, bless him, but what he doesn't know about horses ain't worth knowing, I reckon. He's gone hunting today. You approve of that, do you?'

The half-closed eyes gave no clues. She had a way of looking askance at you that was challenging as a gangsta moll and disturbingly cute.

Luca, who strongly disapproved of hunting, held his tongue. It didn't do to bandy your opinions about upon arrival. 'That's a great accent. Is it local?'

'Swindon, in Wiltshire. You know it?'

He shook his head.

'It's not that famous. Unless you like roundabouts.'

'Only magic ones.'

'Do you believe in magic, then?'

'I've never seen anything I can't explain yet.' He battled another flurry of yawns

She glanced at her kids, then back, grinning. 'Watch this space, mate. Witchcraft's compulsory round here.'

He closed his eyes, smiling, so beaten up by tiredness and being trapped with the manic redhead that it sounded a very reasonable summary. He'd felt hexed almost from the moment he'd touched down. His hands throbbed warmly.

*

Pax sat at her grandmother's old kitchen table, nursing a glass of water, shoulders hunched defensively, waiting for the lecture to end. The whole room reeked of whisky from the smashed bottle of the previous night, making it almost impossible to convince Ronnie that she wasn't spiralling down the same tunnel her father had.

'He had a disease, Pax. It killed him.'

'I've stopped!' This room was one of the few places Pax ever let herself shout. This was where she'd buried her face in her grandmother's wide shoulders and howled. Ann Percy was never a physically affectionate character – a pat on the back and a 'pull yourself together, there's a girl' was as much as you got – but she loved a good argument, unafraid of raised voices and strong opinions, even the odd teenage tantrum, as long as it was backed up with justification. The heavy-bottomed glasses of kitchen sherry had been slammed down on this table with great passion over bad show judges, ill-mannered hunt followers and rude neighbours on many occasions.

'I've stopped,' she repeated. God, but she wanted a drink. A Bloody Mary to pep her up, with an extra shot of vodka to stop her hands shaking, a cool beer to slake her thirst.

'It's not as simple as that,' Ronnie was saying. 'Addictions aren't. I promised Mack I'd try to help.'

'Help with what, exactly?' Her hangover was staging a fresh wave of hot-cold shivers, sweat springing from her temples. She shrugged off her coat.

'You mustn't make the mistakes I did.'

'I'm nothing like you!'

'I ran away too far too fast; I assumed I could come back for you, but the family closed ranks. That's precisely what the Forsyths will do, given half the chance to keep Kes from you.'

'No, they won't. It's all just threats; Mack will never follow through.'

'That's what *I* thought!'

'*I* won't let it happen.' Pax glared at Ronnie.

Her mother's clear blue gaze lingered, making her squirm.

'What are you wearing?' Ronnie asked suddenly.

She glanced down. A T-shirt with no bra, men's breeches, a belt strangely twisted because it was too big. 'My clothes got wet. I had to change.'

'And those are Luca's?'

She nodded defiantly, hating herself for enjoying the confusion on her mother's face.

'Mack's accusing you of infidelity, you realise? He says you told him you slept with a stranger last night.'

'We slept in the same room.' She shrugged, seventeen again.

Ronnie rubbed her face, stretching the skin around her eyes so they looked briefly startled. 'Did anything happen?'

'None of your business.' That might slow the toy boy's progress down a bit. She and her mother had history on that front.

Ronnie turned away, hugging herself, and Pax felt guilty and sad, her peacemaking solace shredded by peevishness.

'You have to talk to Mack.' Ronnie refused to give up. 'Be open about what you want. Fight the urge to run and hide.'

'He's insanely angry. You heard him.'

'All the more reason to be the rational one, to keep notes and get advice. You're so good at all that.'

'Not right now.'

'I can help.'

'I hardly think so, Mummy.' Then, as if a switch had clicked, the calm returned. She felt it settle over her like a cool, silk sheet.

Ronnie was pacing around even more than Pax had at her restless height, hands raking her thick blonde bob as she thought hard. 'If you really are serious about separating, I think you should move in here.'

'Why ever would I do that?'

'Because it will look better as a home for Kes. You live in a damp caravan, this is a fine Cotswold house. You have support here. We'll help you through recovery.'

'This house is damper than the mobile home – which has three bedrooms, superfast Wi-Fi and decent insulation by the way – *and* I have plenty of support: I have friends; I have Alice. I have stopped drinking.'

She wasn't listening. 'You need a jolly good lawyer. Mine was hopeless. Bunny will know somebody.'

'No, Mummy.' Pax held up her hands, but her voice remained smooth, in control. 'I'm not getting some friend of a friend who hunts with a silk from Lincoln's Inn involved in this.'

Ronnie's protests were cut off by a heavy knock at the front door, which nobody used except salesmen and tourists. At the same time, there was a sharp rap at the back door.

'You take the Jehovah's Witnesses.' Ronnie headed through the back corridor to the vestibule, trailed by her dogs.

Pax made her way to the enormous hallway, hauling aside locks and bolts and cranking the stiff key around.

Carly and her buggy were waiting. 'I'm sorry to bother you, only the new manager has fallen asleep in the tack room. Poor bugger's fit to drop, says he's not slept since Toronto.'

'He's lying,' Pax muttered, remembering him asleep on the hotel chair, her hillbilly guard with no gun.

'That little puppy's with him.'

'Thanks. I'll wake him in a bit.'

'Am I needed tomorrow?'

'For what?'

'Yard work. Only I can change my cleaning shifts if I am.'

'Someone will call you. Does Mummy have your number?'

She nodded, shifting from foot to foot. 'I need minimum wage if it's regular work. Just saying.'

Pax rubbed her forehead tiredly, irritated by her fresh-faced ballsiness. 'I'll pass that on. Anything else? Pension scheme? Private healthcare? Dress-down Fridays?'

'That's all.' She forced a smile, but her jaw was set, the eyes unfriendly. 'See you tomorrow, maybe.'

'I won't be here.'

Pax trailed back through the hall and the breakfast room, dropping down the steps into the kitchen, then freezing on the spot as Penhaligon's Quercus filled her nostrils.

Bay Austen was standing by the Aga, resplendent in red coat, blue eyes dark with concern. 'Darling Pax, I'm afraid there's been an accident.'

'It's Lester…' Ronnie was already pulling on her coat.

7

A pair of hunt supporters had brought Lester's cob back in a muddy trailer being towed by an Isuzu Trooper with a boot full of spaniels. They'd given Bay a lift.

'I didn't see it happen,' he explained to Pax, lounging against the wheel arch in offensively good humour whilst she lowered the ramp. His own horse was standing alongside in the second partition, both fully tacked, steam still rising from their backs.

'We were having a terrific run,' he went on. 'Lester was at the back. All I heard was the cry go up to call an ambulance.'

Pax clambered inside, the high-pitched growl of her mother's sports car still just audible as Ronnie raced away through the village, heading north towards Coventry where Lester had been taken by air ambulance.

'From what I can gather,' Bay's voice continued out of sight as she let down the breech bars, 'a hunt monitor jumped out of a hedge with a camera as the field cantered past; Lester's chap swerved to avoid trampling her and bashed against a tree. The old boy sat it out, but the bump must have cracked a hip. First anyone knew about it was after the hounds checked and we realised Lester had turned grey and was having an asthma attack. Stayed in the saddle throughout. Your grandfather would have been proud. You here alone?' He watched her reverse the cob out.

Guessing Luca must still be asleep in the tack room, Pax was reluctant to involve the puritanical Horsemaker in a crisis so soon after his arrival, still less to introduce him to inveterate gossip, Bay, toxically privileged and pro-bloodsports, who would doubtless spread news far and wide that Ronnie's stud man looked like a long-lost Bee Gee.

'I'll stay until there's news, if you like?'

'Absolutely not.' She led the cob past him. 'Shouldn't you be getting back?'

'I'm not field master today, so I'm all yours.'

Pax felt her indignation smoulder. 'You push off. I'm fine.'

She could hear the ramp going quickly back up behind them, grateful that the supporters would be too keen to get back to their sport to linger for tea and talk.

But Bay was in no hurry, holding open the stable door and watching as she started untacking. 'How's the cold?'

'Much better.'

'You look deathly.'

'Thanks.' All the toxins in Pax's body from months of deep-vein tears, booze and cortisol seemed to be pumping through her heart.

'That husband of yours isn't looking after you properly. You should be tucked up in bed with a hot toddy.'

'Mack's in Scotland.' She heaved at the girth straps, keeping her face turned away, feelings veering wildly between murderous and martyred.

'Apart for New Year?'

'Couldn't be helped.'

'When's he back?'

She paused too long, wondering. Would she have to drive up there to confront him, to fetch Kes home? 'Tomorrow, I think.'

'You think?' He toyed with the word, loading it with playful insinuation.

She nodded, throwing the girth over the saddle, increasingly uncomfortable with the cross-examination, which Bay was predictably turning into adulterous speed dating.

'So you're on your own tonight?'

She blanked this.

'Why don't we catch up later over a drink?'

'Time to go, Bay.' She gave him a weary smile, unbuckling the cob's breastplate.

The hunt supporters were back in their pickup, engine running, checking their phones while they waited for the Wolds' master.

He was scrutinising her face closely now. 'You're not sleeping well.'

'I told you, it's this flu thing.'

'No it's not.' He smacked his lips in thought, making her jump. 'I think you've left old Och Aye the Noo at last.'

'Whoa! Where did that come from?'

'Deny it.'

'It's none of your business.' She pulled the saddle off the cob's back, turning to glare at him and then regretting it. She tried not to blink. How could Bay know? It had to be her mother, spilling home truths after he'd interrupted their awkward confessional. 'For God's sake, don't tell anyone.'

Catching a flash of amused white smile in the stable's darkness, Pax realised she'd just given herself away. Had it just been an educated guess? Bay had been there at her grandfather's funeral, after all, when Pax could barely bring herself to be in the same room as Mack, shuddering with revulsion every time he introduced himself to an old family friend as 'Patricia's better half', or picked fights with her because she refused to guestimate the value of her grandfather's estate. She'd been quietly drunk that day too, their terse war of words in the car home starting the moment they'd reached for their seat belts.

'You always were braver than me.' Bay's face was in shadow, framed in the open door, his hunt coat identical to the one of her father's she'd found in the attic wardrobe the previous afternoon. 'Good luck, beautiful girl.'

For a moment, fourteen years of rattling through life in the wrong direction rolled back, the sadness overwhelming. Pax wanted to bury her face in those blue lapels and weep.

She needed him gone.

'I'll see you off, shall I?' She threw the saddle over the door and hurried past him, a lump in her throat as big as the cob's salt lick.

Back at the Trooper, Bay was all smiles and solicitude again, pausing with his gloved fingers on the door handle to loudly offer the Fosse and Wolds' formal best wishes for Lester's speedy recovery, glancing inside to check the others were still on their phones before adding a whispered postscript, 'Let's have lunch.'

'Why?' She couldn't look higher than his nose. Not so brave now.

'You look like you need a decent meal.' His mouth – the first she had ever kissed – stopped smiling. 'I'll call later.'

'You don't have my number.'

'Actually, I do.' He turned and climbed inside. 'I've made it into my screen saver, look.' He held up a photograph of a familiar-looking kitchen wall. With a wave and a roar of diesel engine, he was gone, trailer rattling.

'Arrogant bastard,' Pax muttered to make herself feel better. She'd forgotten her mobile number was still Sharpied in extra-large letters on the tiles close to the ancient landline phone, along with those of other family members, neighbouring landowners, the vet, plumber and Ladbrokes, all of whom her grandfather had called regularly to shout at. Let him call, she thought with satisfaction. It would ring in a bin somewhere between here and the M42.

As she headed back to the cob's stable to sponge him off and put on a rug, it occurred to Pax that she'd thrown away a lot of control and privacy with the gesture. A call so easily dismissed with a swipe on a mobile screen was public knowledge over an ancient wired line with two inconveniently placed handsets. In a motion sickness powershift, she had an immediate and overwhelming need to know Kes was all right, to explain to Mack as calmly as possible that she'd be staying at the stud for a few days, seek reassurance that he was bringing their son home tomorrow and that they would put his needs first, call a brief truce until they sought something more formal.

Instinctively, she pressed her face into the cob's neck and breathed deeply. That familiar salty, biscotti scent filled her nostrils. Fourteen years rolled back again. Tears briefly wet and soft against a warm, clipped coat, a wall of comforting muscle, the steady crunch of jaw on hay.

Turning quickly away, she picked up the saddle and headed to the tack room.

Luca was indeed still asleep, deathly pale beneath his beard, his cheeks hollow, reminding her again of a prisoner of war, not the golden boy they'd been anticipating. He looked so peaceful, her mother's fallen angel, a man who had seen her at her unforgiveable worst and was consequently hard to like or forgive. The room was refrigerator-cold. Ignoring the small voice telling her to wake him hospitably and show him to a real bed, Pax flicked on the oil heater and shushed the puppy to stay, edging an old wool horse rug over them both and hurrying back to the house.

The landline started ringing as she let herself in and she hurtled down dim corridors to answer it in the kitchen, expecting Mack as she pressed the clunky old cordless house phone to her ear.

But it was Alice, the Cotswold jungle drums working faster than Reuters. 'Just heard what's happened, Mother,' came her sister's customary snappy falsetto, always at its most arch when she thought she was speaking with Ronnie.

'It's me, Lisp – Pax.' Growing up, the Ledwell siblings Alice, Timothy and Patricia had been a Blytonesque trio of Lisp, Moth and Pax, Alice earning Lisp because she couldn't pronounce her 's' words.

'Thank God you're there. Poor Lester. Is it serious? Shall I come round? We've got a shoot going on, but lunch is all made.'

'There's no point rushing here.' She couldn't face the prospect of Alice right now, with her short-fused black-and-white opinions. 'Mummy's ambulance chasing. He didn't fall off, so I'm hoping it's not too bad.'

'Is it really true the antis were behind it? I heard they lay in wait and lynch-mobbed him.'

'Hardly.' She relayed what Bay had told her about the hedge-lurking monitor, then held the receiver away from her ear as Alice spouted furiously about ignorant townies interfering in country traditions.

'Luca O'Brien has arrived,' Pax said to shut her up.

'God, *already*? What's he like?'

'Too early to tell.'

'Which means he's absolutely ghastly. You always like people; I'll come round later. Meanwhile, call as soon as you know more about Lester. Why aren't you in Scotland, by the way?'

'Change of plan.' She felt the approaching sting of exposure. Alice had no idea what was going on in Pax's world. A one-way mirror lay between them through which Pax could see her sister clearly – Queen Victoria in a Joules gilet and layered bob, stalwart Cotswold wife eager to maintain her claim to the stud. Alice just saw herself reflected back. No rancid marriage rotted from the inside out, no tears and tantrums and delirium tremens, no humiliating, unstoppable breakdown with a stranger she now hated for it. Just fierce Percy fortitude.

Alice was name-dropping a tweedy A-list of Bardswolders amongst today's guns on her family farm. Perhaps she should tell all if Bay would be trumpeting her news? But Pax found herself staring at the chair her grandmother had always occupied, imagining Alice's unalloyed horror at her recent behaviour, her insistence that Pax must stick with her marriage at whatever cost for their son's sake, and she let Alice end the call with a cheery, 'Must dash.'

Oh, Kes. Her chest and arms ached with the need to hug him, to breathe in the silken top of his head. She needed to hear his voice.

They'd all be out walking now, the traditional Forsyth yomp up to Arthur's Seat before lunch, Kes on his father's shoulders. She must try to smooth things over a bit, catch a word with her son to reassure him all was well in the world. She was still so jittery that she misdialled Mack's mobile twice, then hung up on his voicemail, furious with herself for getting tearful again.

She headed upstairs to switch on the heater in her father's old bedroom, perching on the end of the bed, discomfort mounting at the prospect of Luca occupying it, the memories of Johnny Ledwell so little stirred in years, now freshly scented with nostalgia and need.

The phone was ringing again. That, at least, was like the old days. It had rung endlessly then. She thundered down to answer it, certain it was Mack his time, the need for diplomacy pressing.

'Lester's fractured his hip.' Ronnie was at her most no-nonsense, calling from a payphone in the hospital. 'He's absolutely livid about it and keeps telling everyone who'll listen that he didn't fall off.'

Pax could imagine his indignity. She moved closer to the window to watch rain fleck the sash's panes.

'At least he gets that hip replaced straightaway, and for free,' Ronnie went on, 'but it's rather more serious than it would have been had he seen a bone man months ago. The fracture goes right down into his femur, poor chap. He'll be in here at least a fortnight, then it's very slow recuperation. The other one needs replacing before it goes the same way too, so he'll not be back in his yard boots for months, and whether he'll ride again is in doubt. Not a word of that to him or anyone else yet, of course. Has Bay gone?' There was an edge to her voice.

'Ages ago.' There was an even sharper edge to Pax's, the mention of his name guaranteeing a frost between them, a quick subject switch essential. 'Lester will need pyjamas and wash things, I take it?'

'Oh, could you put it all together? That would be marvellous. I'll come home as soon as he's moved into a ward, then I can bring it all back here in visiting hours. How's our new arrival?'

'Still catnapping in the tack room.' She had no desire to hurry back.

'That won't do at all. Why not put him in Lester's cottage for now?'

'I've got the attic flat ready.'

'Nonsense. We agreed you and Kes are going to be living in that.'

'We didn't agree anything.' She had a sudden image of herself sprawled on her father's bed, whisky bottle and cigarette in hand, fulfilling the prophecy. 'You can't just give Lester's cottage away, Mummy.'

'He's not going to need it for a bit, though, is he?' It seldom occurred to pragmatic, ever-transient Ronnie that others were more sentimental about their private sanctums. 'Stubbs and that fox need looking after. It's jolly cosy in there, and far easier for keeping an eye on the yard.'

'That's not the point. It's Lester's *home*.'

'I'm perfectly aware of that, but the stairs are totally

impractical. He'll need single-storey living for the foreseeable future. Maybe we can turn the old Stables Flat into a convalescence wing?'

'That has an external staircase and no heating!' The long dormitory beneath the clock tower hadn't been used since before the war.

'You're good at sorting out this sort of thing, Pax. We can offer Stables Flat to Luca instead of the cottage if you like? Although somebody has to look after the bloody fox.'

'*I'll* look after Lester's cottage,' she said in exasperation.

'Good. That's settled.' A purr of laughter. 'You can move your things across today.'

Pax set her jaw, realising her mother had plotted this from the conversation's start. She longed to argue, but for all the Mack Shack boasted high-speed Internet and dry cupboards, she loathed the metal box in which her unhappy marriage had been hermetically sealed for so long. She knew Lester would trust her to look after his cottage more than a stranger. And she could be useful here. With the old stallion man out of action, the stud badly needed her help. For months she'd been filing for the sake of it in the office she and Mack shared, the company overwintering until they sold the barn conversions. Here there were paper piles as high as termite mounds.

Pax thrived on being needed. Her mother was right that the stud was somewhere secure and steeped in Kes's family history, and she had very few alternatives. Her own childhood was close to the surface here, the village familiar and safe, her sister and Lester cornerstones.

The truth that Pax would admit to nobody, not even herself, was how frightened she was that she'd start drinking again if she went back to the Mack Shack. She glanced at cupboards in the kitchen dresser now, knowing Scotch was in there, longing to taste just a mouthful for its burn of confidence. But she wouldn't give Luca O'Brien the satisfaction of seeing her fail.

That was another reason to be here, however uncomfortable the company. She pinched her nails into her palms and headed out to Lester's cottage.

In her hungover greed, Bridge had eaten most of the raw mix for her little *rogaliki* almond biscuits straight from the bowl. This, she realised later, was a blessing. Left in the oven too long, they had cooled to tooth-breaking bullets. Mercifully, her threat to village dentistry barely covered one brightly flowered vintage side plate.

'Hard-core baking, baby!' Ash Turner, all ink and muscle, pumped iron on her kitchen floor.

Bridge ignored the fantasy, stepping over it to get at the utensils drawer. Most dreams vanished with daylight, but hers was following her around. Just as alarmingly, her husband's erotic emoji medleys had been lighting up her phone at regular intervals all morning, aubergines and doughnuts lined up colourfully, *I'm coming, kochanie!* repeated frequently. Fingers flour-covered and timer pinging, she had no time to reply.

'I bet Mary Berry doesn't get hassled like this,' she grumbled at the cats.

Her *kołaczci* – absurdly easy cream-cheese pastry oozing Aldi jam – were a triumph, although Bridge had sampled so many waiting for Carly that they were demoted to a side plate too. Soon, as well as still feeling hungover, missing her babies and twitchy from horny dreams, she felt fat. When Bridge sensed cellulite forming, she was badass.

Fantasy Ash was doing burpies in her sitting room as she set down the plates on the leather-trunk coffee table.

'Stop that!' Bridge shooed him upstairs and checked her reflection in the mirror over the fire. Big blush. Guilty eyes. Biscuit mix on her nose.

At last Carly arrived, cramming a double buggy into Bridge's tiny porch and letting loose three rampaging smalls. She looked happy and muddy, ultra-skinny, her hair in a topknot, cheeks flushed, talking in a rush. It seemed hers had been an enviably action-packed morning compared to Bridge lolling in bed, baking and bingeing and fantasising about Carly's husband.

'He's a taskmaster, that Lester. No backchat. I can't believe I mucked out, like, six horses. Did you ride Craic already?'

'Woke up with a bit of a head.' Bridge felt a cold rash of shame goosebumping her skin as she thought about her forbidden daybreak gym dream.

'You were funny last night. Pick up that biscuit, Ellis!' Carly's children, having taken bites out of the little Polish biscuits and rejected them, were desperate for party rings and custard creams. Only baby Jackson, crawling around the low table trailing a soft book and slipping booties, sucked away appreciatively on a rock-hard *rogaliki*, soothing his aching gums where teeth were breaking through.

Bridge, feeling uncharacteristically humourless, would have liked to ask in what way she'd come across as funny last night, but Carly was again waxing lyrical about her highly active morning, leaning back against the magnet-studded fridge while Bridge made coffee amid a bomb site of baking sheets and spilled flour. Sleepy eyes wide and bright as silver coins for once, Carly described Lester's begrudging acceptance of her help, the joy of handling the horses, and the thrill she'd felt when she went back with her kids to find Ronnie full of praise, then greeting the Horsemaker. 'Like I'm already part of the team. He looks like Jesus or something – all these long golden curls and beard and eyes so green you'd think he was wearing funny lenses.'

'I can't believe you met the Horsemaker.'

'Put his feet up in the tack room and fell asleep as soon as he got there, can you imagine?'

'Bit of a New Age stoner?' Bridge suggested hopefully,

carrying the coffee across to the sofas. Petra's disappointment if he was an acid-dropping soap-dodger might teach her to manage her expectations at last.

'Turners hate New Agers,' Carly flopped down on a cluster of brightly embroidered cushions, 'the sort that bang on about the simple life and buy old gypsy wagons to run vegan patty stalls at music festivals, which is a load easier when Daddy subs you twenty grand a year.' She helped herself to biscuits. 'Luca's not like that. Scared me a bit, if I'm honest.'

'In what way?'

'These *burned*.' She looked at her hands, a *kołaczci* in each. 'They feel it when things are damaged, you know? Animals that are hurt. Diseases that haven't been diagnosed yet. People with secrets.' She popped the biscuits in her mouth.

Thinking guiltily about her Fantasy Ash gym dream, Bridge burned her lips on a gulp of coffee. 'How do they feel now?'

'Like they want to be near horses.' She chewed the little biscuits, one in each cheek like a hamster, smile in between, swallowing. 'You're right, that spell we did is totally 'mazing, like totally. Are you still feeling it?'

Bridge didn't want to think about it. 'That was just the wine talking, Carly.'

But Carly shook her head. 'Something changed last night.'

'The year?' Bridge flicked a finger back to indicate the calendar on the wall behind them.

'Bridges of Ireland?' Carly laughed. 'Nice one.'

'I get one every Christmas. My brother Brendan never lets me down; he thinks it's the funniest joke.'

Eyes now languid and sleepy as they had been last night, Carly yawned and admired January's Peace Bridge in Derry with its colourful backdrop of fireworks. Checking Ellis and Sienna were distracted cracking through the toy pile Bridge had dug out, she whispered, 'I'm knackered. Ash had an anaconda in his pants last night. I didn't sleep a wink.'

'Lucky you.' Bridge forced a bright smile, reluctant to dwell on the contents of Ash's pants any more than she already had.

'Only now he's sour at me for going to the stud first thing. His lot hate Percys even more than New Agers. He went off to the gym this morning with the hump cos I asked him to pick up the kids from his mum's. I swear, those egg-box abs are on account of his bad temper.'

Bridge didn't want to linger on the image that conjured, either. She crammed in a handful of jammy biscuits without thinking, then felt three hundred calories stick to her tongue and the roof of her mouth.

Carly was looking at her very intently. Chewing like a grumpy camel now, Bridge sensed that if it hadn't been for her kids the pretty blonde was in the mood to unload a lot more about her marriage today. Thank God for her kids.

The trio were crashing a lot of plastic Duplo about, buzzcut Ellis ordering his siblings to join in his battle, toddler Sienna mewling a pacifist protest that sounded like 'dun unto', baby Jackson banging a red block against his own head whilst still dribbling on an almond biscuit, all three reminding Bridge that other people's children were never as enchanting as your own and that she still had quite a bad headache.

'Was Ronnie's daughter at the stud?' She cast around for a change of subject, remembering the tearful redhead in the car yesterday, an image she'd found hard to shake afterwards. 'Pax?'

'Snooty cow.' Carly shrugged. 'Her type looks straight through our type, don't they?'

Affronted to be bracketed in the see-through sector, Bridge felt the extra-sweet calories curdle yet more. 'She'll never fecking look through me.'

'Go you!' Carly grinned. 'That's what I like about you. You're like the sun. Nobody throws shade on you.'

Bridge conceded the point, gratefully watching Carly

demolish the biscuits, and they shared indiscreet witchy truths about the villagers they disliked most, from the earnestly dull parish counsellors to the flakily disloyal weekenders, their wrath deliciously vicious.

Soon slipper-stamping with delight as Carly described the worst of the yummy mummies on the school run – 'Don't you dare let that put you off working there: they need you to take them down a peg or two' – Bridge vaguely remembered declaring that she was going to apply for a part-time job at the village school. Surely Carly remembered she was talking to a woman who had once run a team of twenty from a fifth-floor triple-aspect mezzanine office before motherhood and mediocracy had stolen her chutzpah? She'd definitely mentioned it last night. A lot.

'What do I want with a lollipop-lady office job?' she scoffed. 'I'm aiming for the fecking headship!'

'You're hilarious.' Carly gave her a you-wish look.

Bridge tried not to feel affronted, telling herself she was only posing undercover as a village mum while she plotted world domination.

They then spent a brief shift on their knees, gathering Duplo, de-snotting and nappy changing before making a second batch of coffees.

'Can't tell you how glad I am you spared me that lame party last night,' Carly confided as they sank back into the sofas, unleashing her sharp tongue with descriptions of Flynn's posh student girlfriend and her mates and their ABC outfits.

Chippy, observant and mercilessly critical, she brought out the black-humoured cynic in Bridge. 'Face it, we're a lot further through the alphabet than they are. I'm RST – Red Bull, Spanx, Tit-tape.'

'That is so sad!' Carly's sleepy eyes radiated sympathy, and Bridge realised she'd dropped her pearls of wisdom down a bottomless well of Smart Water, G-strings and nipple daisies.

Her phone vibrated on the coffee table with a new message.

'What's wrong with Spanx?' she said as she reached for it.

'I blame those ladies you ride with,' Carly was chiding. 'They're well old school, they are.'

Bridge felt the Saddle Bag bond of allegiance tighten in her sinews. 'You saying *I'm* not a laydee?'

'No, not that. It's just they're not like you.'

'Underneath they are.' She swiped her phone screen to unlock it. 'They're just like us, only…' She faltered, perturbed by another *I'm coming!* accompanied by more aeroplane emojis and smiley tongue-out faces. Was he holding his own again? Where were the kids? His parents' house in Poland had just four rooms with curtains for doors.

'You okay, Bridge?'

'Yes, I…' She read a second message as it chimed through, Aleš declaring *I have rogaliki and big boner, kochanie!* Lots of tongues and doughnuts followed. 'You know when your husband wants phone sex at the most inconvenient times?' she murmured. 'That.' While it wasn't the Anaconda of Orchard Close, it was out there.

'Ash loves all that,' Carly whispered, checking Ellis wasn't listening. 'Do you video call?'

'All the fecking time.' Overdoing the insouciance, Bridge switched her phone off. 'Now *that's* not something a laydee shares with her riding companions.' She feigned an upper-class voice. It was intended to draw Carly in, but she took it too literally again.

'Common as muck, me.' Her sleepy Mexican eyes levelled on the photos on the mantel of Bridge on Craic. 'Flynn says his posh totty are all sex maniacs.'

Eager to keep her sweet, Bridge almost found herself indiscreetly breaking the Bags' golden confidentiality rule and mentioning the Safe Married Crush, ready to confess that hers had long been Flynn. Except suddenly it wasn't, and that fact made her twitchy again. Having a crush on your new friend's husband, however safe and married, was a killer. She had to get rid of it – fast.

Carly was telling her how Flynn's love life had been complicated by his phone automatically saving all the naked selfies his girlfriend sent on WhatsApp. 'Every time he tried to show a client an example of remedial farriery, they got an eyeful of Amelia's snatch in her en-suite mirror.' She'd gamely polished off almost all the biscuits, even crunching her way through the flint-hard almond ones, claiming they were delicious.

'How do you stay so slim?' Bridge asked enviously.

'Not having a second car. Ash says we can't afford one, but I reckon he won't let me have one in case I start to sag and wobble.'

It was the prod Bridge needed. Looking down at her thighs on the sofa, each one wider than both Carly's combined, she knew precisely how to burn off Fantasy Ash.

As soon as Carly was wheeling the buggy back to the estate, Bridge threw her kitbag in the car and drove to Broadbourne, calling in to give Craic a carrot on the way, safe in the knowledge that the real Ash wouldn't be at the gym if he'd worked out there that morning.

Only he *was* still there, seventy kilos of brooding rock-hard testosterone, sweating on a pec deck, wolf eyes on her as soon as she walked in. She kept her gaze averted, avoiding the bench press and hammering twenty minutes on the treadmill with her earphones in, listening to defiant P!nk power anthems before retreating to the showers, aware that his eyes had stayed on her. At least, it felt as though they had. It still felt as though they were still on her in the shower.

Wrapped in a towel in the changing rooms afterwards, hair in wet silver and pink rats' tails, Bridge felt electrified. Perhaps, at last, she was starting to understand the point of this SMC thing.

I am going to ride my husband like he will not believe

when he gets home, she vowed, messaging Aleš with slippery fingers. *I am your Pole dancer, baby, and I can't wait to slide along its length when you get home.* She added flames, tongue, doughnut, aubergine, kissing-heart-eyed faces and a horse (for subliminal effect), along with a row of kisses.

His reply was quick-fire and emoji-free: *Take all your clothes off. Be ready. I am coming, stoneczko! Almost there!*

Again? The man was a right handshake hero, a priapic machine gun in his homeland. No wonder he wanted to move back to Krakow.

My clothes are off, she replied truthfully, closing her eyes and imagining her towel loosening, letting the lust blush steal up her body. Then she shivered with a thrill that caught her like an electric shock. Fantasy Ash had just entered the ladies' changing room.

Turning stiffly in his armchair, eyelids briefly at half-mast in the half-awake half-light, Luca felt the warm weight of the deerhound puppy on his lap. He was in a hotel room near the airport waiting for a lift. No, he was in a snowed-in log cabin by a Canadian lake, waiting for a lover. It was cold; the fire had almost gone out. Was he awake?

He heard a stallion call, that distinctive wild shout. He'd recognise this one anywhere. Long gone now. Cold air conditioning. Staff apartments like igloos, a wall of heat outside by day, but cooler at night. That awful night. Running along the fire escapes at the back of the staff flats, the metal grating booming and rattling like gunfire, the screams ahead both horse and human.

He'd dreamed this scene many, many times since, revisited the great hanger of a barn, the furthest stable isolated, neon lit, sweat-hot, blood spots like scattered rubies on shavings. Each time he returned the angle skewed more, the original cast replaced with newer faces, their behaviour erratic. A redhead shouted at him to go away, barring the stable, telling him he wasn't needed.

The horse never changed: grey coat sweated to gunmetal, dark eyes white-rimmed, nostrils trumpet-flared, cornered and terrified. The bravest, boldest of horses brutalised beyond trust. He called again, ribcage lifting and shuddering.

Luca jerked awake. He had absolutely no idea where he was, just that he was parched. There was a mug of cold tea beside him which he drank gratefully, closing his eyes, lead weights in their lids, mind hollow with exhaustion, trying to get back to his dream. He had to get back to save the horse. Sleep's black blanket cloaked him obligingly. But he was in the wrong place. He was in a hotel room, watching a woman sleep, her skin marble pale in the faintest light. Immune to other people's pain, he had to get out, get back to the horse.

Corridor. Fire doors. Stairs. He was in the bar, surrounded by laughter and drunkenness and flirtation. Smiley Luca, the incorrigible flirt.

The horse whinnied.

'Horse walks into bar,' he heard himself telling a pretty blonde perched on a stool. '"Hey!" says the barman; horse says "Yes please".'

The blonde turned. Ronnie, laughter in her eyes, telling him he's incorrigible and it's a terrible joke, that he can do better.

The horse whinnied.

He jolted up again, awake now, looking around him. A single high, barred window, thick with dust one side and rain-pitted the other, let in thin light. The shapes of saddles on racks and bridles snake-coiled. The familiar smells of leather and oil.

The horse whinnied. He'd know that call anywhere.

Arriving back from the hospital to find the yards deserted, Ronnie tracked Pax down in the stables cottage. She was folding crocheted counterpanes back into the tallboy in the tiny second bedroom, its walls matrixed with faded hunting prints, the brass bed freshly made up.

'Can you believe Lester still uses sheets and blankets? There's not a duvet in the house.'

She'd changed into her own clothes, a dowdy black jumper and jeans at least a size too big. Red hair scraped into a bun and wearing her glasses for once, she looked much younger than her thirty-one years, hers that edge of thinness that all too quickly tipped to fragility. As she led the way next door to gather up Lester's overnight bags from his bedroom, Ronnie could see the bones protruding from her neckline at the top of her spine like little stepping stones.

'How is he?'

'Reliving the accident repeatedly in minute detail.' Ronnie looked round. 'Gosh, I always forget how pretty this room is. I'm glad you're in here.' Triple aspect, its casement windows looked across the driveway paddocks to the south, the stable-yard towers east and the little walled garden west. It streamed with light.

'It's Lester's room,' Pax said firmly. 'I'll be next door with Kes.'

'You can't *both* go in there.'

'It's not for long.' Pax led the way downstairs.

Ronnie said nothing, grabbing the rail to steady herself at the steep oak steps, suspecting it would be many months before the old stallion man made it up here again.

'How's Luca settling in?'

Pax put the bag down and took off her glasses to rub her eyes with the balls of her hands, her lids red from all the crying. 'He's probably still asleep in the tack room.'

'You mean the poor man's flown in early to find us all at such sixes and sevens we've not even shown him to a *bed*?'

'Next time I'll hire a welcome banner and a brass band.'

Ronnie checked herself, remembering she'd no idea what had occurred between them beyond the obvious clothes-swapping and antagonisation. Fierce mother love flared. Luca could be a terrible chancer. 'You shouldn't have been expected to pick him up, given everything you're going through.'

'Nobody else around to do it.'

'I'm entirely to blame. I'm so sorry I wasn't here.'

'Are we talking about last night?' Pax was a ninja at veiled sarcasm, the deep, kind voice softening the blow. 'Or the thirty years before that?' She was equally adept at blocking the comeback. 'Sorry. Uncalled for.'

Fierce mother love deflated a little. Tackling Pax was sometimes like climbing the north face of the Eiger in moon boots. She barely knew her daughter as a woman, wife and mother, disapproval simmering beneath the diplomacy. 'I'll find Luca.'

'Do that,' Pax said, nodding briskly.

Outside, a few icy specks of rain were flicking through low winter sun, a half-formed rainbow fading against the dark clouds. Ronnie hurried across the cobbles and beneath the archway with her dogs at her heels. Then she spotted Luca emerging from the tack room and her heart sank a little, realising the change in him went way beyond all the wild warrior facial hair. The demeanour was tougher, the body harder and the mood far blacker.

Blazing-eyed, hollow-cheeked and defiant, he strode into the yard with his kitbag across his back, like a hired gun into a new outpost. Pale from a harsh Canadian winter, dark bruises beneath his eyes, he was leaner than she remembered, his jaw lost to the coarse curls, shoulders unfeasibly wide above the narrow hips. Gone was the baby-faced, smiling Irish horseman she'd met in Holland, all tight blond ringlets and playful sea-green eyes, seemingly never sobering up or needing sleep, blessed with an infectious laugh that could ignite a room. In less than a decade, he'd jumped a generation.

Now she felt a thud of disappointment, realising too late that she'd called upon him precisely because she needed someone childlike, the fiddle-playing cherubic vagabond who was a shot in the arm and a genius on a horse, whose adorable yen for her had been his reason to ride better, who carried no baggage. Instead, the bags under his eyes alone looked like they'd crossed the Nevada at the gallop strapped to a Western saddle. Had there been a night in the gunslinger's saloon with Pax on the way?

'Luca!' She strode towards him, fierce mother love in its holster. 'So sorry to dash off. What a lousy journey you must have had.'

When he smiled, ten years disappeared in an instant. 'Sure, it's good to see you at the end of it.'

Dropping his bag, he threw out his arms just as Ronnie thrust out her hand to shake. It was like a full-body game of rock, scissors, stone. Ronnie won, receiving a double handshake and another devastating smile as her prize. Although nothing to Blair's knight gauntlets, his hands were satisfyingly calloused, a sign he was still a grafter.

'How awful to abandon you in the tack room!'

'Sure, I've had a decent nap.' His once-merry eyes were tired, darker than she remembered, their sea-green bark weathered. 'Beautiful place you have here. And you're just as beautiful as I remember too.'

Still a flirt, then. Her mother-love trigger finger twitched.

Out came the O'Brien smile.

And *that* hadn't changed a bit.

'You must be hungry.' She wondered what on earth she had in to feed him, hoping it wasn't revenge served cold.

'Only for work.' He stifled a yawn.

'Plenty of that here.'

'It's why I came.' He turned sharply as Cruisoe, the old stallion, bellowed from his corner box. 'That and my undying loyalty.' The smile switched back to her.

Disarmed, Ronnie felt mother love surrendering. Their

party days on the continent were long gone, but he was still young Lochinvar beneath the beard – *so faithful in love, and so dauntless in war* – that all-knowing green gaze excitingly grown-up. No wonder Blair had stomped off in a huff.

'Let's get your bags inside,' she said, turning to lead the way to the house.

With the intuitive rear-view mirrors of a woman under physical scrutiny, Ronnie sensed Luca's eyes on her backside, wishing it didn't feel quite so gratifying. It was her family's livelihood she was laying in his hands, not her ego, she reminded herself. As if in agreement, one of the mares in the far yard let out a shrill squeal to call the shots. Far closer came a stallion's roar, so loud it was like a motorbike starting up.

She spun round, adopting a power stance she hoped was somewhere between board director and Wonder Woman, ready to lay down some ground rules.

But Luca wasn't looking at her at all. He hadn't even followed her. He was standing outside Beck the stallion's stable with his back to her, the blond curls buffeted like sea foam, almost white at its ends.

Man and horse were equally breathtaking, one a war-like musketeer arriving on foreign soil to do battle, the other already armour-plated with anger, his head a dished silver visor in which huge dark eyes and nostrils flared, his perfectly proportioned body rigid with unease, primed to fly or fight at a pin drop.

Ronnie retraced her steps and the stallion stamped in protest, flattening his ears at her as she came to stand beside Luca.

'Bechstein,' he breathed.

'You remember him?'

'I backed him.'

'You did?' It hadn't even occurred to her, but now it felt like kismet. 'How marvellous!'

She should have guessed he'd know the horse. Luca had

been a regular feature in the huge German stud where Beck had spent his early life, breaking hearts and horses, starting off elite youngsters and keeping the trickier competition stallions sweet between stud work and circuit. With many millions of euros of horseflesh under its roof, Gestüt Fuchs was the Harrods of sports horse breeding, its owner an old friend of Henk with whom Ronnie had lived and worked a decade earlier. Visiting the world-famous stallion station every few weeks had been one of life's highlights back then, the horses out of this world. The first time she'd seen Luca in the saddle had been there and Ronnie had been blown away by his skill.

Her memories of Beck from that time were vaguer. Bred in the purple from one of the Fuchs' many prolific showjumping sires, he'd been amongst countless stratospheric home-grown talents with huge price tags, far beyond her own and Henk's wheeler-dealing pockets. Hothoused onto the international circuit by seven, Beck had been sold with an Olympics qualification for megabucks, only to be branded lame before the opening ceremony had even taken place, returning to Germany in disgrace. His grand prix career over – and Fuchs' good name under fire – Beck's retirement to stud was equally quickly mired by a reputation for being unpredictable and tricky. That was when he'd first registered on Ronnie's radar.

Still as a statue, the horse continued staring at Luca, nervous energy radiating from him like static.

She moved beside Luca. 'Still eleven out of ten, isn't he?'

'He's been through the mill, has he not?'

'Ground down to flour. I want you to make the cornfield again, Luca.'

The smile strobed on and off. Then he tilted his head to look at the stallion again, sucking his lower lip doubtfully.

'You're here to help find out if he's still got what it takes,' she said, secretly wondering whether Luca still had it in him either. He looked like he'd blown in from three months' jungle survival, and yet, as he approached, Beck, rather than slamming his teeth against the bars as usual, watched him intently, lowered his muzzle to sniff at Luca's hand and then curled up his lip. It reminded Ronnie of Luca's uniqueness, of how unrushed he was, of that stillness he carried deep within.

'He recognises you,' she said softly, amazed.

The Horsemaker rested his open palm against Beck's forehead now, a gesture the horse would have never tolerated from her or Lester.

'Where d'you find him?'

'Long story.' She moved closer.

'He retired injured.' Luca's hand ran the length of Beck's face.

'He's sound now.'

'Fuchs is a bastard!' The harshness in his voice startled her, as it did Beck, who let out a warning roar, his whole chest shuddering, his lip curling again. The stallion snaked to the back of his stall and glared at the Horsemaker with white-rimmed eyes.

Ronnie felt her pride tested, conscious that the first Compton horse he'd met was its controversial new mutineer, her nemesis. Beck was dark-flanked with stable stains, his bedding a mess because he box-walked. His 'toys' – snack balls, licks and mirrors lovingly provided by his previous owner – were battered and tooth-marked. Ronnie had rarely encountered a horse more indignant and disorientated, but she knew also that he was exactly the sort of challenge Luca relished.

He said nothing, cheek muscles taut above the beard. He looked wretched.

She needed Luca to see what she did in Beck, however dismal a picture he made in his stable, tucked up and tail whipping.

She glanced at her watch: past twelve. 'Let's get him in the lunge pen before lunch and you'll see he's no more lame than I am. The hunt'll be long gone by now.'

He threw her the big lifeline smile. 'Sure.'

They put the horse in a chifney bit and double led him,

a technique she'd perfected with Lester that just about kept control whilst running the gauntlet with him rearing and plunging across the yard and as far as small paddock to the circular fenced area, where Beck exploded into a fly-bucking, rolling breakdance routine.

Trying to look disapproving, arms crossed, head tilted critically to the side, Luca let out an involuntary laugh as they watched the sheer energy of him charging round at liberty. 'I never thought I'd see him alive again.'

'He certainly has bit of a death wish.' Ronnie winced as Beck bucked, smacking his hind feet against the metal fencing which rattled and hummed, sending him into a careering frenzy.

'God gave that one springs on his springs,' Luca whistled. 'I'd forgotten how he moves.'

Ronnie watched his face in delight, seeing the old Luca merriness light up in it.

Some horses stole your heart, even a tough old pro like Luca who rode ten a day. Ronnie recognised it because Beck had stolen hers, too.

They watched him spin and plunge, Luca shaking his head, big smile conflicted. 'He was a nightmare to breed from, you know that?'

'Some of the best ones are. He's not sired many, but those he has are all first class. He's going to father lots more now,' Ronnie predicted confidently. 'My plan is to have a full stud book come March.'

Hearing a dog yap she spotted Pax over the wall of the stable cottage garden and beckoned her down across the paddock to join them.

'Pax is brilliantly organised, so she'll keep the bookings in order,' she told Luca, familiar with her daughter's OCD need to file. She beckoned Pax more impatiently, her own mother's firm voice in her head, demanding they all sacrifice ego. The stud needed to rally its troops, and this was all it had. Reluctantly,

Pax let herself through the garden gate and started making her way down towards them.

'I do the selling and marketing side. I need you to focus on straightening out this chap's bad attitude, Luca.' She watched Beck trumpet his authority, the ultimate cage fighter. 'He's a total rapist. If he's going to cover naturally – which he's only ever done once to my knowledge, by accident not design – he must be a lot safer to handle and better mannered. And if we're flogging straws of semen fresh from the dummy or deep freeze, he needs to be as reliable as a student going into a cubicle with a pot and a porn mag.'

'I've missed the ladylike way you talk.' The green eyes sparkled, a flash of the old Luca again. 'I've missed everything aboutcha, Ron.'

'It's been a long time.'

'You've not changed a bit.'

Pax joined them with a self-conscious cough, paler than ever, watching Beck still rodeoing around like his tail was on fire. 'I know that feeling.'

'Don't we all?' Luca offered a conciliatory laugh.

'How soon until you horse-make this one, Luca?'

His smile grew fixed.

'He'll be back in work within the week.' Ronnie was determined to keep the mood up. 'His mind's too busy to stand idle. And we want Luca to get his leg over something truly classy while he's here, don't we, Pax?'

Crossing her arms, Pax rolled her tongue round her teeth and said nothing, much as she had years ago at school when Ronnie had flirted with the headmaster on sports days. Those long drives to far-flung boarding schools for formal events when her children were teenagers had sometimes been her only way of maintaining contact, her letters unanswered, her rebellion as hard-wired as the stallion now in front of them.

Beck sprang forwards into his floating trot once more. He

was addictive to watch. Ronnie remembered Paul Fuchs telling her that he was the most photogenic horse he'd ever stood.

'We'll have to get you back in the saddle too,' she told Pax, certain the endorphins would do her good.

'No you won't.'

'Nonsense. There'll be plenty to ride out once Luca's backed a few, plus poor Lester's little string will need to be kept going.'

Pax shot her a don't-go-there look from a lifetime ago. That tall, quiet teenager who had ridden so exquisitely, shyness inevitably shaken off when she was on a horse, and positively ebullient at high speed across country.

'I'm happy enough riding everything,' Luca offered easily. 'It's what you pay me for.'

'Luca saves the day,' muttered Pax, crossing her arms tighter and watching Beck spin a hundred and eighty degrees as fast as a polo pony.

For the first time it occurred to Ronnie that her daughter might have lost her nerve. She'd seen it happen enough times, especially when women had children, their mortality bound so tightly to motherhood. Riding might have kept Ronnie sane when her marriage ended, but her daughter was a much more urban fox. And yet, as every horse-mad, husband-hating Cotswold wife knew, horses were the perfect antidote to an unhappy home life.

'Pax will be living on-site,' she told Luca now, ignoring Pax's mutters about it only being for a few days. 'Which makes us the Compton Magna Stud team.'

'God help us all,' Pax sighed, then added to Luca, 'That wasn't blaspheming, by the way. It was a prayer.'

Luca's fixed smile hardened beneath all the wild-man blond fur.

Ronnie felt another thud of disappointment, sensing the friction between them.

The phone began ringing, the bell peeling out across the yard.

'That's probably Mack.' Pax stayed rooted to the spot for a moment, jaw clenched, then sprinted like a hare back up the hill.

'Her husband.' Ronnie turned to Luca, wondering how much he knew.

But he'd already wandered off to stand by the round pen, reaching up to hold its perimeter fencing with his fingers, forehead lowered against the chain link.

Within seconds, the stallion stopped circling and turned to him, head high. Saying nothing, Luca kept staring at the ground, Ronnie watching in surprise as the horse lowered his nose and stepped towards him almost without hesitation. Snorting in deep, inquisitive breaths, moments later his muzzle was against the wire mesh.

'You're not wrong about him remembering.' Luca spoke quietly.

'That's wonderful!'

'Maybe.' He straightened up and the horse spun away; Luca watched him circle and turn back, ears flicking. 'Ronnie, there's something I need to tell you about him. Something—'

'Luca!' The shout from behind sent the grey spinning away. 'Call for you!'

Pax was almost back down the hill, looking even more bad-tempered. 'The phone's in the cottage kitchen. Don't talk too long.'

'Who is it?' he asked suspiciously.

'She wouldn't say.'

Ronnie noticed his eyes tighten. Then, with an apologetic smile, he loped away.

'Posh foreign.' Pax stepped alongside her mother, puppy bounding around them. 'My guess is forties, married for money, stalkerish, names her horses after designer-jewellery brands.'

'Did she make any death threats?'

'Not to me.' Pax looked at her inquiringly.

'Lester seemed to think he took one earlier but I'm sure it was just one of his muddles.' She sighed. 'Pax, I appreciate Luca might come across as a bit louche. He's a wandering minstrel with lots of pins in his map – and he's certainly clocked up some air miles since I last saw him – but he's *very* good at what he does. Try to be nice to him.'

'Fuck off.' She turned and walked away.

8

'Luca O'Brien speaking.'

'At last, Gianluca!' The woman's voice, all too familiar, was sternly irritated. 'You do lead us a merry dance. You are lucky he likes you so much.'

'Aren't I just?' His heart was beating in his throat now.

'He would like to speak with you, if you will hold.'

'Holding is what I'll do.'

Music played at the other end, like a customer service line, a jaunty Mozart concerto.

'His Highness will speak with you now.'

However many years he'd been receiving these calls, Luca had never quite got used to hearing that.

'My boy! I am so angry with you!'

Thinking about Beck, Luca felt the first splash of panic.

He closed his eyes with relief when he heard laughter. 'You are like a son to me as you know, Luca, but *such* an errant one! You are the eagle who never lands, merely perches. Now that I know where you are, I shall look forward to our next visit to England immensely. Tell me, are you near Ascot? Quite my favourite British racecourse; you must be my guest there in June.'

'I'm honoured, Your Highness.' He had a brief, ludicrous image of himself in a morning suit and top hat. 'Unfortunately, I may be working on the continent again by then.'

'As you wish.' The receiver was covered so that orders could be barked. His attention returned. 'You are keeping well, I trust? Are you in need of anything? You only have to ask, you know that.'

Another phrase Luca always found deeply uncomfortable.

'Thank you, but no, sir.' He edged as far as the cord would stretch to look out of the window at Beck. 'I'm grand.'

'You are my most honourable servant.'

Pacing the pen's perimeter, Beck let out a flurry of barrel kicks, the metal frame shaking. Luca retreated back behind the kitchen wall.

'It is your New Year, I believe,' the prince was saying. '*Kul am wa antum bi-khair*.'

'And Happy New Year to you and to all your family, sir.'

Luca had only worked for the prince briefly, a majestic and magnanimous man with a hundred horses, twelve daughters, five homes, three wives and just one, much-adored, son. To have saved the life of that precious only son, as Luca now knew to his cost, was to be bound in perpetuity.

Granted a status somewhere between courtier and adopted child, Luca had spent the past six years cherished and protected like all of the family's most valuable assets, be they people, horses or money. The prince's office kept tabs when he changed yards so that he could call, a fatherly gesture which also served to remind Luca who was in control – both reassuring and unsettling. His patron paid absolutely no heed to time zones, weekends, holidays or start dates, loathed mobile phones ('walkie-talkie calculators for the young'), and wasn't averse to giving a yard owner hell if he thought they weren't treating Luca well enough. For a long time, he'd tried to procure the Horsemaker lucrative jobs and even set him up with his own yard, but he now understood the nature of Luca's free-ranging spirit, his urge to go where he was needed, not wanted. 'Like Nanny McPhee!' the prince often exclaimed. He watched a lot of kids' movies because he was a big, obstinate one himself.

It should have been the greatest of privileges to have such patronage, tied by honour for one heroic, life-saving act. But if the son whose life you'd saved hated you more than any man alive, it felt more like living under close surveillance.

'I was speaking about you with Prince Mishaal only last week.'

Luca's sinews tightened in reflex at the name.

'He is very happy that you are in England. It is his new wife's favourite country. They are regular visitors, and indeed Mishaal is coming to London this month to buy a football team, I believe.'

Not good news.

'You will not recognise him, I think. He has changed a great deal.'

Luca pitied the poor wife, no doubt chosen by Mishaal's family for her great patience and tolerance, just as his horses were.

'Endurance races are his passion now, you know?'

'Oh, yes?' He could hear Beck bellowing again, furious at being left alone, and quashed an illogical urge to slam the phone down in case the call was being recorded and they recognised the whinny.

'It is all he talks about,' the prince went on, 'racing across deserts like a dust storm, racing through forests, racing over mountains. Beautiful horses, like Al Khamsa. He is very successful, but his people are not trustworthy, not wise. He needs a horseman with your backbone, Luca. They want him to win at all costs and that is not God's way, is it?'

Luca knew precisely who wanted to win at all costs. Mishaal was a far more serious character than his father, devoted to his sport and deeply competitive, but lacking the talent and mindset, he'd always tried to buy his way to the showjumping podium. It came as no surprise to Luca that he would try the same approach in another discipline.

'He obviously commands great loyalty,' Luca said carefully.

The roaring laugh. 'You always think so positively, Luca! We have a saying: *be wary of your enemy once and your friend a thousand times because a double-crossing friend knows more about what harms you.*'

'You sound like my father,' said Luca.

'Luca, I *am* your father!' He laughed with great hiccupping whoops this time, the *Star Wars* joke a favourite. They had always got on well, the older prince's robustly silly sense of humour rewarding the fiddle-playing, trick-riding horseman with a regular audience during his employ, his wives and twelve dancing princesses delighting in their father's *faris*.

'Your family are well, I think.' The prince – who had a long-standing love of the Irish, stemming from forty years of owning and breeding race horses – hadn't confined his largesse to just one O'Brien. Luca's brothers all benefitted from his sponsorship and connections, all volunteered without his knowledge, the pet leash tight. 'You are happy with your new position, Luca?'

'Yes, sir.'

'And what are the horses like there? Is there one I would like to buy?' Picking up a horse wherever Luca went, like souvenirs, was another generosity Luca was trying to wean his indulgent, likeable, infuriating benefactor out of.

'Not this time,' he said firmly, although he had only met one of them so far. But that was a horse the royal family must never know was here.

'I have told Mishaal to contact you,' the Prince said, his voice hardening. 'Do as he asks, Luca. It's extremely important.'

Perhaps they already knew.

Leaving the stallion stamping around his turn-out pen, shouting for mares like a caliphate for his harem, Ronnie tracked Pax down on the yard, putting out lunchtime feeds, wild red hair slipping out of its clip. There were huge dark smudges under her eyes.

'I shouldn't have spoken to you like that,' she said, turning back from dropping a bucket over a half-door, not looking her mother in the eye. 'I'm angry about everything right now.'

Ronnie nodded, heart going out to her. 'Let me help. You look done in.'

'I need to keep busy.' Pax grabbed a shavings fork, letting herself into Beck's empty box to skip it out.

'Of course.' She still remembered the zero-gravity confusion of her own marriage coming to an abrupt end. Seeing Pax stirred memories of the same whirlwind shock of anger, its guilt and fear still vivid almost thirty years later. Those awful phone calls, like flurries of gunfire. The power play and panic.

Pax was a whirling dervish, dropping bedding everywhere, her head constantly turning in the direction of the cottage.

'Do you think he's off the phone yet?' she asked eventually.

'Depends if his married stalker is threatening to tell her husband,' Ronnie suggested, but Pax's dark humour fell flat repeated back.

'Your expert field, not mine.' Pax squinted at the cottage. 'You need a second landline.' She glanced at her watch. 'It's two hours since Mack called.'

'I thought you didn't want to talk to him?'

'I don't. But he told you he'd ring back, didn't he? He's not answering his phone. What if something's happened to Kes?'

'It's New Year's Day, they're doing family things.' Like us, she thought wryly as she gathered two brooms and handing one across. 'Kes will be fine. Missing you, but fine.'

'Are you sure?'

'Sherbet.' It was an old Percy saying, one Anne had coined from a gambling-mad Irish gardener, an abbreviation of 'sure bet'. Seeing Pax's half-smile of recognition as they swept cobbles side by side, Ronnie felt better. Was it terrible of her to admit that she was grateful for this rare time together, however awful the crisis? Its intimacy was a little foundation stone.

'Maybe I should call him again?' Pax fretted. 'He has no idea my mobile's dead. There are bound to be voicemails and messages I can't access.'

'He knows you're here and he has this number.' Ronnie spotted the cob's bridle abandoned on a hook and picked it up. 'Let him cool off.'

'Really?' Pax followed her into the tack room. 'No, I definitely should call.'

'Pax, when your father and I separated, I did exactly this, and it's—'

'I am *not* you! I will never be like you! I can't lose Kes. I can't! Shit!' She turned away, mopping tears with her sleeve, batting away the hand Ronnie tried to put on her back, talking through gritted teeth. 'I j-just need to use a phone. And I need to *stop bloody crying*.'

Ronnie stepped back. Pax was right; the situations were very different. She'd run away with a lover on a madcap whim, light-hearted and impetuous, believing that she'd be reunited with her children within days. Having grown up in the lengthening shadow of its consequences, Pax had clung on to marriage until her fingers bled.

'Luca must have finished that call. Let's check, shall we?' She found herself caught between talking to the toddler she'd left behind and the grown woman so like her younger self.

'You go on ahead.' Pax mopped her eyes with her sleeves. 'I don't want him to see me like this.'

Even thirty years after being married to an alcoholic, Ronnie sensed straight away that Pax had spotted a drink. Johnny had hidden bottles in hunting boots, feed bins, gutters and every coat pocket going by the end.

Her eyes alighted on the hunting flask, still in its leather holder buckled to the cob's saddle. She fished it out with a casual, 'I'll just take this back.'

Pax cleared her throat as Ronnie hurried out, tipping the contents in a planter as soon as she was through the arch.

In Lester's cottage, Luca had just rung off, turning to smile as she came in. 'Sorry about that. An old friend.' His eyes were that little bit too intense, thinking fast behind the mask. 'Then I took the liberty of ringing home. My auld ma's been passing the number here round a bit freely, I'm sorry to say; I hope you've not been bothered by calls?'

'Just a few. Lester's bound to have written them down somewhere.' She looked around, her eyes settling uneasily on a bottle of plum gin abandoned on the dresser, where Lester must have filled his flask earlier. 'You're a popular man.'

'Accident insurance scammers, I'll bet.'

'They must think you're particularly liable to personal injuries.'

'Sure, I'm a horse rider.'

Ronnie laughed, vaguely remembering him juggling love and work between Holland, France and Germany, his appeal to married women getting him into trouble more than once. Now he'd gone global, he needed his own switchboard. No wonder his mobile was out of credit.

He was gazing around Lester's museum-piece hallway, peering at the fox heads and old showing photographs hung in regimented grids above the dado rail. 'Sweet old cottage. Lester's the auld fella you told me about, is he not? Where's he today?'

'You don't know about the accident!' she exclaimed in horror, telling him about the stallion man's fractured hip. 'It means lots more work for us all, I'm afraid. Lester's such a one-man army, I'm frankly not sure how we'll cope without him. He'll be off a while.'

'Lucky I'm here.' Luca raised a wry eyebrow.

'You'll be doing two jobs,' she said, to make sure he was in no doubt. 'The Horsemaker can't lord it over everyone in his riding boots here, I'm afraid. You'll shovel shit with the rest of us.'

'That's not a problem. The harder I work, the harder I play.' The smile widened. 'Unless it's the fiddle; breaks the strings.'

'I hope you have it with you?'

'Ah now.' His tilted his head. 'Sometimes all the strings break. I was going to pick up another at home in Ireland.'

Reading a coded message in green eyes that had once been so open, Ronnie crossed her arms and adopted her no-nonsense power pose. Whereas he'd always been full of naughty tricks, now it seemed he'd graduated. The court jester could play serious drama; the cherub had manned up. Yet his manner remained gentle, the quiet man with the heart-melting talent.

'Thank you for agreeing to come here, Luca.'

'Sure, it's good to see you.' He put his hands on her shoulders. Worried he was about to try to hug her again, Ronnie stiffened with British ironing-board resistance, reaching up to hold his fingers like dungaree straps. The Percys had thrived for centuries with a no-hugs policy.

'Your poor body clock must be in ruins.' She could feel a chunky Claddagh band on one of his fingers, its crowned heart battered from long hours holding ropes and reins.

Ronnie realised what had changed him so much since she'd last seen him: somebody had broken wandering minstrel Luca O'Brien's heart.

'Lunch!' She patted his hands kindly. 'Or would you rather to go to bed for a bit?'

They could hear the dogs barking and growling outside the door, Pax calling them back.

'Only reason to go to bed in daytime, is if you have company, so it is.' New Luca might have sadder eyes than before, but the flirty patter was still there, a classic male on the rebound. He was looking at her, but Ronnie sensed he was seeing her through a lens blurred by self-absorption.

'Or flu,' she said briskly.

There was a sharp bark as Stubbs bustled in censoriously, followed by Pax carrying the wide-eyed deerhound puppy, her pale face determined, tears dried. 'Ah, good, the phone's free. Your heelers are cougars, Mummy.'

Stepping back, Ronnie brushed Luca's hands off her shoulders, but not before she caught Pax's sideways glance.

'They won't leave Knott alone,' Pax complained as Ronnie's younger black-and-tan bitch rushed inside, the old one lumbering in her wake. Both barked shrilly up at the wriggling puppy, tails gyrating.

'Maternal urges,' Ronnie sympathised, aware that her dogs weren't the only ones plagued by them. 'I'll put them in a stable, then we'll all have lunch.' She edged towards the half-empty plum gin bottle.

'There no food whatsoever in the house,' Pax pointed out, glancing at the phone, desperate for them to be gone. 'I'm going home to fetch some clothes soon. I'll bring back eggs and cheese, and I think there's half a gammon left.'

'I'm vegan.' Luca brought out the big guns' smile. 'Sorry, I know it's a pain in the arse.'

'That'll be all the fibre,' muttered Pax.

'How fantastically disciplined,' Ronnie said quickly. So much for fond memories of him in nothing but swimmers and an apron barbecuing rows of fat bratwurst by the Fuchs' pool while she, Henk and a bunch of grooms smoked dope in the sun. She tried to remember what vegans ate apart from lentil dahl and chickpeas. 'When I take Lester his things, I'll try to find a supermarket that opens on New Year's Day and we'll all have a big high tea later.' Picking up the plum gin, she slipped it nonchalantly under her arm, hoping the others wouldn't notice. 'I'll show you to the attic flat, Luca.'

'Do you want some ice with that, Mummy?' Pax asked lightly, setting Knott down in his bed, shooing the heelers away. Stubbs was glaring at them all from under the table, horrified by the invasion. 'Watch your toes in the attic bathroom, Luca.' Pax straightened up and marched to the door to hold it open for them. 'I laid mousetraps.' She smiled.

'There are mice?'

'No, I just get pleasure from other people's pain.' She was standing outside, holding her arm out like a hotel doorman seeing off guests.

'You'll want to unpack, I'm sure.' Ronnie hurried ahead of Luca, eager to park him, worried about leaving Pax too long in her brittle state. When she quick-fired sarcasm, it was a sure sign she was counting down to a big anger bang.

Luca had paused beneath the cottage porch, trapping Pax outside. 'Sure, a walk will do me good. I'd like to take a gander round the place. The sun's coming out.'

'Let's all go together,' Ronnie suggested.

Pax was looking straight at the gin bottle under her arm. 'I should call Mack.'

Equally certain she shouldn't, Ronnie pressed her case. 'Leave that a bit longer. You always love seeing the broodmares. Let's take Luca round, get some fresh air. You know the set-up here as well as I do.'

'It's been years since I played a part here.'

'Longer still for me.'

'Yes, remind me. How many decades ago was it you ran off and abandoned us all?'

Ronnie glanced at Luca, who had stooped down to make a fuss of her dogs, politely pretending not to hear.

'Well, I am *not* abandoning Kes.' Tension was radiating off Pax like white heat, calm voice at odds with wild eyes. 'Which is why I need to speak to his father to work out some details.' She looked away, encroaching tide of tears turned back by furious willpower.

Three centuries of Percys not hugging were nothing to Ronnie's burning need to wrap her arms around her daughter at that moment, but she knew that to do that would infuriate and upset Pax more. 'A walk round will help to clear your head, take your mind off things.'

'I don't *want* my mind off things. I *want* to think about Kes and about Mack and his family and how we're going to make this work. I *want* my head full of all the ways to ensure none of us hurts any more than we have to. I don't want to take my mind off any of it, because it's important. You took your mind off Daddy so long he drank himself to death.'

'Whoa! That's a bit harsh.' Luca stood up.

'*You* keep out of this!' Pax snarled.

'Yes, best keep out of this, Luca,' Ronnie said quickly. 'I'll show you round.'

'Good idea,' growled Pax, pushing back through the porch and hurriedly closing the door.

Luca blew out through his lips. He'd noticed the plum gin under Ronnie's arm too, she realised as his green eyes levelled with hers, secrets reflected between them.

'Just putting this in the car for Lester.'

Hangover lifted, Bridge felt refreshingly pukka as she drove home from the gym, Fantasy Ash bound and gagged in her car boot. Having willingly sacrificed her JOMO New Year's Eve to red wine, girl talk and owning the village hall mosh pit, she'd decided she would make the most of her last night without Aleš and the kids: scented candles, comfort pasta, charcoal mask and serious job-hunting. Plans for a career swerve were fresh in her head. Her tiny, tidy house was waiting for her. Fantasy Ash could stay trussed up in the boot. He'd just clutter the place up, and she had some serious Zen me-time planned.

Singing along to Anne-Marie, she banked the car up on the pavement outside the cottage, not caring how wonkily because Aleš wasn't here to see her lousy parking.

The cottage felt chilly and lifeless without the family, both cats out hunting. Bridge pulled on the chunky home-knitted sweater from Aunt Broda that Aleš teased looked like a poo emoji. She lit the wood burner, scraped her hair up into a tight bun secured with a popsock, selected a Rebel Girl playlist on Spotify and neatened every surface to OCD satisfaction before opening her laptop at the little crackle-glaze table.

Her freshly edited CV, carefully tweaked for Suzy David, looked exquisite on the page.

'Fuck truffle caviar and gingko nuts.' She deleted it, cracked her knuckles and typed:

PLAN A: Get high-flying HR position and flick SD two fingers No openings atm.

PLAN B: Start own business and flick SD one finger No start-up capital atm.

PLAN C: Apply for part-time job at school and do not flick fingers.

'Just Heads, Shoulders, Knees and Toes,' she muttered, about to cross that one out before remembering that during her drunken midnight rethink – now rethought – Ash had said something very sexy about how much she'd liven the place up. Not that she'd let herself imagine livening it up in a very short suit and heels, locking up alone after a parents' evening, Mr Turner running in late, all sweaty from his gym. Oh no. There were safeguarding considerations to factor in here. Not to mention Carly and the kids.

'Stay in the car,' she growled.

Twenty minutes into Googling through situations vacant, Bridge was increasingly depressed by the lack of anything new. Meanwhile, Fantasy Ash was kicking hell out of her boot outside, demanding to come in. It was a lousy time of year to look for work, she reflected, weakening, listening to his army boots pummelling against her spare wheel. No HR department worth their salt would advertise until everyone had their feet back under their desks in January, or in her case, their Uggs under a small plastic table at a soft-play centre.

Fantasy Ash sprang the car boot.

She leaned back and stretched luxuriously, allowing herself a quick dreamscape in which he kicked open her front door, dressed in full paramilitary garb, to 'rescue' her from domestic servitude. Off came the flak jacket – witness dog tags, tattoos, hard muscles, narrow hips and big boots – off came the khaki vest. Oh, those egg-box abs. Carly hadn't been wrong.

Don't think about Carly.

'Come here, gorgeous,' growled Fantasy Ash.

Reaching for her phone, Bridge changed Spotify to Arctic Monkeys' 'Do I Wanna Know', pulled out the popsock bun and shook loose her hair. She closed her eyes and licked her lips. 'You'll have to come and get me.'

There was a sudden blast of cold air and Bridge's eyes snapped open in shock as she heard the front door crashing open against the upcycled umbrella stand. *'Kocham Cię na zawsze!'*

Beard, gargantuan shoulders, duffel coat, Christmas jumper.

Her husband, so huge he had to duck to come in. Biscuits box in one hand, vodka in the other, brows lowered.

'Why d'you park car so badly?' he roared. Then burst into laughter at Bridge's shocked face. 'I brought you your biscuits, *kochanie*. I told you I was coming, yes? *Zdejmij majtki*. Take your clothes off.'

Like any good horseman, Luca studied teeth closely, human as well as equine.

His own were a part of his language; he smiled a lot, something he'd done unconsciously since his first gummy grin. He smiled more than he spoke. Obama-smiling, his last boss had called it, a surly Canadian showjumper who hadn't smiled since last standing on the Olympic podium in the nineties. It was a natural pacifier, a communication that was subservient in packs and dominant in herds; you could tell a lot about a human the way they used their teeth. Pax Forsyth bared hers like a wildcat, for all the purring voice; he had yet to see her smile.

Ronnie's teeth were small, even and naturally palest vanilla, not the artificial glacial white dentists added. She had a gold crown that glinted when she threw her mouth open to laugh. He looked out for it now as she chattered easily on the whistle-stop tour of Compton Magna Stud, starting by walking the fields while there was a break in the rain, striding along at breakneck speed and making Luca laugh a lot – she seemed intent to do so as often as possible – as she filled him in on local geography and history. Heels warmed by her two little black-and-tan dogs trotting in their wake, Ronnie made no mention of the exchange he'd just witnessed between mother and daughter. Instead, she explained how the stud fitted into the old-school Bardswolds with its long-established families, big hunting fields, eventing-mad landowners and nosy villagers.

'Nothing changes around here when it comes to horses – new money on the flat, old money over jumps, amateurs dabble in whatever's trending, and if you breed sports horses, you either need a second job or a criminal masterplan. I have neither, but I do have better blood and turf than most.'

He couldn't fault the pastureland bouncing underfoot, which even a punishing winter had been unable to muddy more than superficially. Fenced with fine old park railing interspersed with thick hedges and post and rail, it was in enviably good nick, and Ronnie bounded over it like a foundation mare.

Seduced by the endless hazy green striated horizon, grateful for the peace of the place, Luca half listened as she pointed out the farm's practical details in between sweeping views and statements. 'We once had four hundred acres, but most of the land's been sold – that's a bridleway all along there, three miles of off-road at your hoof tips – here's the bore hole – we don't cut our own hay any more, so the sward's rough as a reed bed – you can see four counties from here – there's no arena but the turf's so good we've never needed one – over there is Eyngate Park where the political Percys lived – this is where the stud's best stallion is buried, see this plaque? – look down there and you'll see the standing stones on Church Meadow, known as the White Witches, and that's the village green off to the right. All weekender cottages there now, but there's still a roaring local social scene. They will all love you. We need to find you a fiddle.'

Luca didn't want to think about his violin, splintered to firewood four thousand miles away.

'There's bound to be one. It's so devilishly dull in winter, we all fiddle a bit.' She let out that tiger-growl laugh he'd never forgotten. The way she kept stopping to cross her arms and strike a power pose was unspeakably sexy.

She was the perfect feather pillow for a weary head, a tireless hedonist with old-fashioned manners. Ronnie knew how to find a good horse with her eyes closed, which made her irresistible. He and other male riders at Gestüt Fuchs had all made fools of themselves trying to chat her up. She'd run rings round them, much to the amusement of her Dutch lover, Henk.

She hadn't changed: an explosion of ageless positivity, and still just as blasé. The 'sweet little stud in need of your magic touch' was clearly riven with a big family feud, decrepitude in plain sight, the drunken daughter and frail old retainer like balls and chains around her legs. Beneath this bouncy welcome tour, there was the breathless relief of a Sister Maria let loose from the convent. Having always taken Ronnie to be as much a nomad as himself, he wondered what or who was keeping her captive. The brooding Australian was an obvious suspect.

A big part of the answer came to him as they stood at the top boundary, overhung with skeletal ancient oaks, looking down at the secret valley in which the village nestled, a ridiculously pretty cliché of Englishness. Like Ronnie, it was pretending nothing was wrong in the world, and it was doing a convincing job, from its golden stone walls hugging each picture-perfect house and field to the smoke trails rising from its ornate chimney pots into a cold, cloudless blue sky, the dark rain chugging north to bother Shakespeare country, a rainbow cast in its wake. Luca half expected unicorns to come galloping beneath its arch, trumpeting the crock of gold.

'What do you think?' she asked, breathless from walking uphill fast.

'You sell it well.' He laughed, loving it, however archaic and arcadian. Luca wasn't in search of a crock of gold, but something much less tangible, a free spirit he'd shared in younger years. The free spirit who had always cheered him up, who believed utterly in a talent. A spirit he'd always been a little bit in love with. One who, for all her plucky imperialism, could look him in the eye with a wise blue gaze and see straight to the truth.

When Ronnie had first invited him to come and work at the stud, he'd imagined that it would be just like this: an old-fashioned fairy-tale setting. What he hadn't foreseen was the curse at its heart.

Below them, he could see Beck trotting round the big sand pen, calmer now he wasn't under scrutiny, and as beautiful as any myth. The shock of seeing him again had been like the explosion of smoke that brought the genie from the lamp. He was still blinking and taking it in. Be careful what you wish for; a fairy tale could fast become a pantomime or worse.

He wished Ronnie would stop behaving like a thigh-slapping principal boy.

'Let's march on.' She launched her way back down the hill, hurrying him. 'Pax will think we've done a runner.'

As he strode in her wake, hands plunged deep in his pockets, Luca was willing to forgive her all the jolly hockey sticks chivvying, accentuated here in her family home. Compared with Pax's company, she was sunshine after a storm. And she was right to be worried about her daughter. *He* was worried about her daughter, her shadow across the fairy tale, Maleficent in her cottage.

He needed his cavalry. Ronnie's next tour stop was what he'd been waiting for.

'Come and meet the Compton Magna herd,' she said, holding open a gate. 'You must tell me *exactly* what you think.'

Growing up the middle of five brothers had taught Luca that sparing his words got him further and kept the peace. While a personality like Ronnie's made everyone that she met feel like the only one in the room, Luca always observed a group as a whole. He was exactly the same around horses; quiet and watchful, aware of the dynamics between the personalities as much as the individuals. It's what made him so good at studwork and breaking in, at conquering so-called 'untrainable' horses.

He said nothing as she led him down to look at the in-foal mares out in the fields.

The visiting mares that were being looked after until they foaled were uninspiring types – a few cobs and stringy ex-racers, and a warmblood showjumper common enough to pull a gun carriage. The home-owned mares were much higher spec, but they were no spring chickens – the four top foundation mares, all heavy with foals, had a combined age of seventy-six.

In his last years at the helm, Jocelyn Percy had retained too many youngstock and hadn't brought in new lines. Where the Percy family had once bred a much-admired mixture of thoroughbreds with enough blood to race and chase, the stud's progeny was now more utilitarian; working hunters and entry-level eventers. The best youngstock had already been snapped up by Blair Robertson, it seemed; few of those remaining stood out – one buckskin colt was exceptional, and there were some nice full-blood three-year-old National Hunt stores – but the rest were mediocre.

'That dun colt will win Badminton one day.' Ronnie was ever-positive as she marched him onwards, blonde fringe swinging.

Luca doubted the Compton Magna Stud would survive long enough to see it; it was unlikely to make it through another eighteen months, patently on its knees financially, brought there by a long era of Ronnie's die-hard father selling off assets just to keep it running, with no thought to modernisation or improving the bloodline. Frozen in time like a museum, it was understaffed and poorly managed. Whilst it had possibly the best and most undervalued stallion in Europe charging around in its lowest paddock – his shouts ringing around the valley like a singing bell – it had none of the equipment required to stand him.

'This is the covering barn.' Ronnie showed him into a dingy broad-span with broken Yorkshire boarding and a potholed floor covered in straw and droppings. 'It doubles up as a kindergarten through winter.'

The grand limestone stable yards were beautiful by comparison, like a *Downton Abbey* backdrop. Accustomed to huge state-of-the-art facilities, Luca thought the once-grand Victorian stud was as quaintly impractical as an antique doll's house. The date 1839 was stamped over one of the stable-yard arches.

'How long's your family run this place?' he asked Ronnie.

'They built it,' she said simply, leading him to a big corner box where the stud's long-standing – and last-standing – stallion, Cruisoe, bobbed his handsome head over the V grille, bellyaching for food and attention.

Seven parts thoroughbred speed and stamina to an eighth cool-headed, no-nonsense draft, Cruisoe was Irish sports-horse aristocracy with the noble good looks of an Old Masters' painting, coloured in by an excited child – his body bright gold, his mane, tail and points black. He was an extremely class act, but his pedigree was out of favour and, at twenty-one, he was pensionable. He was also carrying far too much condition, his legs filled and his over-crested neck hard as a stone bridge, eye-bulges hinting at early Cushing's Disease.

'He's got quite a following for show-hunter breeding.'

Ronnie rubbed the old horse's greying forehead and he leaned into her hand appreciatively. 'Lester dotes on him. We think he's got a few years in him yet.'

Again, Luca said nothing.

'You can see how much I need your Midas touch, Luca.' Ronnie stepped back and looked up at the verdigris cupola topping the dome above the central archway, its weathervane horse galloping east. 'I *have* to make some money out of this place this year. That means handling, backing, breaking and tarting up everything we can sell, and pimping that old Irish golden boy. Not to mention working out what the hell we do to transform Jekyll over here into Hyde.'

Crossing the smaller second yard, as pretty as a miniature Oxford collage quad, Luca found a head collar and the chifney thrust in his hand, the round pen ahead. In it stood the horse that until today he'd thought he would never meet again.

'It usually takes me and Lester an hour. Let's see if you can do it any quicker.'

'He's hardly been out here forty minutes.'

'Longer than that and he starts kicking it apart, believe me.'

Luca could believe it. That horse could bring down a city if he chose to. His heart thudded hollow in his chest, the lump in his throat hard as bone knuckle, relief at knowing Beck was alive and safe was tempered by the danger this reunion put them both in.

Pax was a Pink Panther of clothes collection, slipping in and out of the Mack Shack unnoticed in little more than twenty minutes of minimalist packing. Not that there was anybody to see her on New Year's Day: no builders – they'd been off for months anyway because Mack hadn't paid them – and no neighbours, the closest a field away either side.

Knott followed her round, yawning and trying to settle down to sleep whenever she stood still for a few moments, then wearily waking and tracking her down when she moved on. She moved on a lot, flitting from station to station, extracting, folding, neatening what was left behind.

Throughout, she tried to imagine she was wearing blinkers, going straight to the drawers and cupboards containing the things she needed, not letting herself look around the fibreglass and metal caravan that had been home for two years. It had been left immaculately tidy as always, Pax's natural propensity for mess rigidly controlled during her marriage. She'd been the last to leave the building; there were no surprises here. Holding herself together was made easier because Kes was tidied away too, his toys out of sight as usual, his room door shut. She wouldn't let herself go in there.

She took some washing out of the dryer and put it away, emptied the tiny countertop dishwasher and took down the cards and minimalist Christmas decorations, one to recycling, the other boxed back in the shipping container on the drive. She had to talk herself out of going outside to cut a winter spray to put on the coffee table. She wanted to leave it perfect, no room for error.

An outsider looking in might have seen a perfectly normal-looking domestic scene, but Pax wasn't remotely calm in her head: a thrash metal anthem was playing on a loop, her chest so full of beating heart it felt as though it was going to burst open her rib cage like saloon doors. She wanted to kick or break everything of Mack's that she saw.

She took a little food, mostly things with the shortest sell-by dates and the fruit nobody else would eat, leaving the lion's share for Mack's return. When. If. *When.*

He hadn't picked up any of her calls. Anger and paranoia curdling, she resisted an almost overwhelming urge to take his new golf clubs and beat up his precious sports' bike.

Instead, forensically efficient, she extracted all the hidden vodka bottles, empty and full, and buried them as deeply in the skip on the drive as she could. Her throat burned throughout, tears boiling unwept behind her sinuses. It felt like burying a family pet, the dog she'd hugged through her marriage.

Finally, she gathered up her laptop – not that it would be much use at the stud farm. She knew she should take advantage of the shack's speedy Internet to look up all sorts of things first, but she could only think of one: she looked up the number for a divorce lawyer.

'*Sloneczko, moje szczęście, kocjane*... you are on fire!' groaned Aleš ecstatically.

Smiling, Bridge closed her eyes, partly because it felt so good, and partly because she never really liked the sight of her husband's orgasm face, which seemed to transport him elsewhere, this other-wordly Aleš whose all-consuming pleasure was all his own. Hers was always a mutual thing, even if she was helping it along, a duet he liked to share, to watch, to help play its final note. His was a trumpet solo, his eyes losing focus from hers, thoughts retreating into pure sensation. For that split second of his carnal firework show, Bridge felt as though he was inside himself, not her, and she could be anyone.

They had spent the last hour making love all over the ground floor of the cottage – on the floor, the sofa, against the fridge and, briefly, on the crackle-glaze table until the legs started to give way. Upcycled furniture lay toppled and upended everywhere, the brightly coloured cushions and throws scattered far and wide, along with biscuits, fallen Christmas cards and their abandoned clothes. Aunt Broda's poo emoji jumper was in the kitchen sink, Aleš's beanie was hanging from the wood-burner handle. His booming voice was telling her he loved his little kitten, little flower, little frog (when Aleš whispered sweet nothings, the whole village heard – he had no volume control). It had been clumsy, irrepressible, New Year reunion sex. Fantasy Ash, shut in the cellar throughout, had not been invited to join in. It was her husband's red, eye-bulging face above its big beard she'd been with to the end, even if she couldn't bring herself to look at it.

'I can't believe that was the first time we've made love all this year, baby,' she sighed as he pulled on his pants and headed into the bathroom.

'Huh?' He brought out a loo roll and threw it to her.

'Romantic!' She caught it and unrolled some to clean herself up.

'This *is* the first day of the year.' Aleš often missed her ironic jokes, especially after sex. 'I made flight change especially.'

Bridge was just as guilty of abandoning thoughts. It had taken an hour from her husband coming home – and five minutes after he'd come – for her to sit up in shock now and ask, 'Where are the kids?'

Luca followed Ronnie down from the yard to flat pasture where Beck was prowling the round pen, a white lion in his cage.

'Where d'you find him?'

'Sold through a little West Country auction ring, can you believe? No papers of course. Must have changed hands a dozen or more times before that. His provenance had long gone – came with a replacement passport with the name Beckham – but my auctioneer friend spotted that he was branded and entire, so did some microchip detective work and called me. Astonishing he still had his bollocks on, isn't it?'

Luca said nothing, thinking the horse lucky to still be alive at all.

As they approached the pen, Beck began to charge around again, snorting wildly, a fast-moving blur kicking up sand.

'He's his own worst enemy, poor chap,' Ronnie sighed as they waited for the wall of death circles to slow enough for Luca to go in. 'We've tried turning him out on grass, but he panics and breaks every fence. He's not been ridden in over a year. I refuse to give up on him; he's a grandson of Heraldik and elite graded, which as you know is to sports breeding what a newly discovered, signed Picasso was to the art world.'

'I bet you're popular.'

'He won't mount the dummy and he tries to savage his mares. I can't stand him at stud until we sort that out. That's why I need you on his case straight away. If we can get his name out there by March, there's a chance we'll have a full book. I've done a bit of word of mouth, but I can hardly spread the word far if he's going to try to kill all his wives.'

He felt hollow with relief. That meant few people knew the horse was here. He could get him across to Ireland, maybe. If he persuaded Ronnie he'd never be safe to breed from, she might buy into the idea. 'You need a better temperament if you want eventers.'

'Two of his sons were BuCha finalists last year…' she said, shooting him a wise look.

Making the final of BuCha – or Bundeschampionate, Germany's showcase for young event horses – was the Holy Grail.

'My mares all have temperaments sweet enough for two. Look at him!' She threw up her arms and he floated in circles like a swan. 'He's utter class. He had the best grading scores in his year by a mile; his sire's frozen semen still commands four figures a squirt; his half-brother's five-star. He cost more than a Cheltenham town house at the sales as a weanling and sold for more than a Chelsea one before the London Olympics.'

Luca knew all this, of course. He'd been thrown in as part of the deal, the travelling Nanny McPhee tasked with keeping the notoriously tricky horse sweet while his new rider formed a bond. Instead, the boy and the stallion had almost killed one another. Had it not been for Luca's intervention, one of them would undoubtedly be dead.

'What was it you were going to tell me about him earlier?' asked Ronnie. 'The phone call interrupted us.' The wise blue gaze that saw straight to his truth was tight on his face now.

Luca looked away, briefly reliving that awful night: running from the apartment block to the stables, hearing the screams from Bechstein and then the young prince. Racing along the corridor, blood on the shavings, splintered wood, the smell of fear and sweat rising like mustard gas. He could never describe the hell of it, even supposing he hadn't pledged his silence, the prince's loyal courtier, the door to a gilded shark cage always open if he needed it.

'He was about the trickiest horses I ever rode,' he said truthfully. 'Not just sharp – flying daggers coming from all directions. Get unbalanced and he'd have you eating sawdust before you knew what hit you. Sure, he's brilliant. He was fearless once. But he's always been unstable; it was like riding uranium.'

It had been criminally irresponsible to sell a horse like Beck to a young and inexperienced rider, however many millions Paul Fuchs had pocketed from an indulgent Arab royal whose son wanted to play at being an international showjumper. Somebody should have spoken up.

Luca should have screamed dissent to the air-conditioned indoor school rooftop when he'd seen the boy failing, day after day. Instead, he'd buried his head in sand, Scotch and sin, far away from a love affair that had gone wrong, treating his job in the Middle East as heartbreak in exile. He'd relied on his riding instinct to get him through, that innate connection with Beck that he'd always taken for granted and ultimately abused. To his eternal shame, Luca had rather enjoyed the boy's humiliation and his own breezy ability to get back on and show him how it was done. *Look what money can't buy you, kid.*

In the intervening years he'd found it easiest to see Mishaal as a pantomime baddy in Italian breeches and diamanté-crusted hard hat, a modern cliché of a moneyed sporting villain: spoilt, petulant, egotistical and vain, his limited talents as a rider outweighed by his father's limitless purse, his ambition all-encompassing. Better by far to have chosen motor racing or yachts. Cars and boats had no sentience.

Yet his conscience knew the young prince was a more complicated figure than that. Mishaal genuinely loved horses, his warrior steeds. The only son after a dozen daughters in a rigidly patriarchal family, his duty was to bring honour. Starved of affection, sent away to a strict English boarding school at eight, he was a far more serious character than his father: edgy, obsessive, not good at making human attachments. He'd seen the Olympics as the ultimate crusade. Poor coaching and over-spoiling were undoubtedly partly to blame for his bad riding, but more so the overwhelming expectation. If Luca had been on the ball, he'd have realised that the young prince would crack long before the toughest of his warrior horses.

That breaking point had come on the eve of a competition to which his father had invited tens of grandees, eager to show off his brilliant son, losing not an option on the horse he'd paid millions for. Unwilling to admit fear or failure, the young prince had bribed his most corruptible groom to lame Beck, determined not only that he would never have to ride him again, but that nobody would. The plan had been simple; feed doped with sedative, one hard crack of a steel bar across a tendon. But the groom, also frightened of the stallion, had backed out at the last minute, agreeing only to keep watch. To protect himself, he'd hidden his phone in the eaves of the stable, recording the unwitting prince who had set about the task himself, armed with a taser and enough dope to knock out an elephant. Neither of them counted on Beck's instinct for survival.

The red mist of Mishaal's humiliation had lent him ferocious cruelty. Unable to watch the horse struggling to escape the rain of electric shocks, the stable-hand had quickly fled. By the time Luca arrived on the scene, Beck had his attacker cornered. The sound of steel shoe cracking against bone had been like gunfire.

Luca still had no idea how he'd pulled Mishaal out from beneath crashing hooves and teeth without getting struck, the unconscious prince's face smashed and bloodied. His head injury had looked horrific, Luca fearing that even if the boy lasted the night, he would be permanently brain-damaged.

He hadn't accounted for the legendary toughness of the family, descendants of Islamic warriors who had crossed deserts bearing far worse injuries. Regaining consciousness en route to hospital, Mishaal was immediately calling for the horse's destruction, his father in agreement, the order made to the veterinary team to do it that night.

Watching Beck charging around now, Luca still remembered the war that had raged inside him six years earlier when he'd waited with the horse, trying to calm him, sending up every prayer he knew.

The luck of the Irish didn't often shine on Luca, but it had that night. As Beck hammered the walls in a wild-eyed, shaking muck-sweat, guessing his fate, the phone belonging to the stable-hand had been dislodged from its hidey-hole and landed at Luca's feet, its camera still recording.

Later that night, offered any price he wanted to name in exchange for surrendering the phone and pledging his silence, he'd asked for Beck to be spared.

Livid to find himself overruled by his father, Mishaal had suffered the humiliation of seeing the horse's safe return to Germany, the Horsemaker rewarded for saving his life by sparing the very thing that had tried to end it. 'You have made an enemy of me!' he'd screamed at Luca when he'd visited him in hospital to take his leave. 'It is written in the Qur'an and in your Bible – an eye for an eye.'

To this day, Mishaal's father, the royal prince, had made no more mention of the stallion or of what had really happened. It was rewritten as heroic myth: 'You saved my only son's life, Luca. I will repay your loyalty as any father would. You will stay under my protection always.'

An eye for an eye.

The stallion's big, dark eyes shone brighter than ever as he switched direction, turning on his haunches, sending a large sand clot rattling against the metal wall. Years in the wilderness had lost him none of his élan.

It wasn't supposed to be like this, Luca reflected angrily. The horse was supposed to be protected too, the door of his gilded cage kept shut. At Fuchs, with its Fort Knox security and army of incorruptible staff, he'd been safe.

When Beck had been flown home to Europe after less than two months in the Middle East, a hastily fabricated buy-back story had been concocted to cover embarrassment and maintain honour all round, the royal family's vet supplying X-rays and a report confirming that Bechstein had a severe meniscal injury which meant his jumping career was over. The horse would retire to Gestüt Fuchs to stand at stud; he would never be sold or compete again. It was Beck's death pardon. The official line – that horse and rider had been injured entirely separately, one getting cast in his stable, the other in a high-speed car crash – ennobled a far less palatable truth.

Nobody involved in Beck's ignominious return wanted the deal to be public knowledge, because doing so risked the full story coming out. There had never been an insurance claim; the enormity of the sums involved meant the vet's report would need to be verified to get a payout, and that couldn't happen. The Arabs had lost millions of euros in the eight weeks they'd owned the horse. What Mishaal had lost was beyond price.

'Paul Fuchs should never have sold him on again.' He felt his sinews tighten. His former boss, former friend, had double-crossed him spectacularly.

'That was my fault,' Ronnie confessed as the husky, infectious voice launched into a story so typically old school Veronica Percy that it was deserving of clinking glasses, sponsors' tents, tweed and tannoys. 'I was at the Gestüt Fuchs' stallions parade when this grey chap came out and wowed us all, breaking loose from his handler, cavorting around, jumping clean out of the arena and buggering off to gallop around for an hour, refusing to be caught. I'd never seen anything move like it. I absolutely fell in love with him. The Fuchs team were in despair because the horse was such a nightmare to handle. We were told he'd been retired to stud injured, but he certainly wasn't lame that day.'

Luca played with the head-collar clip, quietly incandescent. He was only a nightmare because they'd stopped handling him as he'd taught them. They should never have paraded him. Gestüt Fuchs was the only place Beck felt safe by the end. He'd known it all his life, its institutionalised enormity and rigid routine calming him like pink noise.

'I told Paul about one we stood here in the seventies, Golden Orb,' Ronnie went on cheerfully, 'a Derby trials winner who'd bust a tendon and had become such a rapist in his Newmarket stud at coverings that my father got him dirt cheap. The only way to keep him sane was to keep him busy, so Daddy stuffed him full of bute and did everything with him: hacking, hunting, jumping, you name it, even broke him to harness. He pulled the village float. And, bingo, he was fabulous to his mares. Give him just one day off and he'd beat them up again.'

It was Ronnie who had suggested Paul Fuchs put Beck back in work to settle the horse into his stud duties. 'I'm surprised they didn't ask you to do it, Luca.'

'I'm not,' he muttered, looking across at her, flashing a fast smile when she frowned. After he'd brought Beck back from the Middle East, Paul had never hired him again. It was, they had both agreed, for the best. When someone wanted you both dead, it was safest not to stand together too often. 'Go on.'

'Paul sent me a thank you message a few months later, a video of the horse looking a million dollars, popping one sixty at home then shagging the dummy like Valentino. I'd moved back to England by then and I forwarded the message to Henk, who shared the video on social media, the swine. It went viral – priapic horses are up there with cute cats on YouTube, I gather – and before you know it, a Lottery winner from Yorkshire, who was on a massive spending spree to fill her new bespoke stables, had asked "how much?". Henk brokered the deal. Beck only had half a dozen foals on the ground at that point and none of them stood out, so Fuchs figured they had nothing to lose selling him. The woman didn't even go over to Germany to see him. Henk got the impression she had a professional rider lined up, but apparently not. You can imagine the rest.'

Luca should have guessed that Paul Fuchs would sell anything for the right price. Working in Brazil at the time, it was weeks before he'd heard of Beck leaving Gestüt Fuchs, his sense of betrayal overwhelming, torn apart imagining that Mishaal was somehow behind it, buying his revenge. If there was one living creature in existence that Prince Mishaal hated more than Luca O'Brien, it was Beck. He carried the scars of their battle to this day, a constant reminder of the horse that had stolen his looks and the vision in one eye.

'Shame he missed a pop at the Olympics.' Ronnie tilted her head cheerfully, sounding as though he'd missed out on a local hunter trial. 'Meniscal injuries are notoriously tricky to diagnose, aren't they?'

Especially ones that are entirely fictional, Luca thought bitterly, imagining Paul's delight when the offer came in. As it turned out, Mishaal seemed to have had nothing to do with it, his father as double-crossed by the wily German dealer as Luca had been. The prince had said nothing, making Luca question for the first time whether he was being protected or gagged under the beadily indulgent gaze of his royal patron.

By breaking his word, Paul might have severed any future chance of selling to one of the richest horse-loving Arab states, but it had been a calculated risk, and it had apparently paid off richly. Beck had netted him a very fat profit not once, but twice.

But away from the German stud, Becks was an open target. If Mishaal had gone after him at that point – and Luca had no way of knowing – it was the stallion's volatility that had spared him, changing yards constantly, soon harder to trace than a stolen sports car. Having terrified his Lotto-winning owners and hospitalised at least one dealer, Beck had been sold on multiple times in the UK, Ronnie explained, swiftly disappearing under the radar, and getting madder and badder until an auctioneer friend who knew that she had an eye for a bargain tipped her off that there was something classy coming to his sales ring.

'By then his progeny were starting to make seriously big names for themselves in Germany, so I was lucky nobody else spotted him. I wanted to give him to Daddy to stop this place going under, a peace offering, but the stubborn old bugger wouldn't touch anything with warmblood in. He went to a friend instead, but that didn't work out...' She paused, watching the horse, her face momentarily sad. 'He's my bad penny. Or should that be Deutschmark?'

'Euro.'

She brightened. 'He's worth a lot more than one of those. Paul doesn't know I've found him yet, but he'd buy him back like a shot if he did. I very nearly drove Beck over there before I decided to stay here and try to make a go of it.'

Luca didn't hesitate. 'Take him back there, Ronnie.'

'That's no longer an option.'

'I'll take him,' he offered. 'I'll do it this week, bring you back something younger and easier to stand at stud here.'

'Whoa!' She held up her hands. 'Much as they'd like this chap back now that he's turned out to be the father of gold-plated superstars, we need him here. *That*,' she told Luca determinedly, finger pointing into the pen, 'is our future.'

'Like fuck he is.'

'Sharpen up, Luca.' The blue eyes hardened, and he got a glimpse of what happened when the jolly hockey sticks were split over her knee, splintered ends brandished. 'I didn't invite you here to load my only bloody chance of making money straight in a lorry to head off on a road trip.' She crossed her arms, watching him closely. 'What do you know that you're not telling me?'

He weighed this up, already backtracking, smiling his way out of confrontation. Telling Ronnie the truth meant revealing his complicity in selling a brilliant young horse down the river. Telling her meant revealing how close Beck had come to killing a man. Telling her meant revealing that his loyalty had been bought and still was. His *silence* had been bought, he reminded himself.

He held her gaze steadily. 'His brain's fried.'

The returning smile was defiant. 'You're the one who always says no horse is born bad.'

'Some are born cowards.' He knew it wasn't strictly true of Beck, but it was simpler put like that.

'If I didn't know better, I'd say you were the one who could be accused of cowardice.'

Maybe she was right, thought Luca, the prince's call still fresh in his head. *Do as Mishaal asks.* A remote, bodyguarded figure who Luca occasionally glimpsed in newspapers or racing pages, the scarred playboy prince had a reputation for cruelty, but he'd never pursued his threat. It was his father who had asked him to contact Luca. He'd talked of endurance racing and birds of prey, not old scores. The Horsemaker might be tracked by the prince's team like a tagged child, but Beck wasn't.

It was still possible they didn't know the stallion was here. Their world of skyscrapers, sand and turf was a far cry from muddy event riders in lorry parks; Ronnie's drumming up interest by word of mouth alone would never reach them, the stud's digital footprint still lighter than a hummingbird's. If he couldn't get Becks to safety, he had no choice but to stay and protect him. They'd both made the same enemy six years ago.

Every instinct in Luca wanted to help this horse. He looked at him again, unable forget that riding him had been amongst the most exhilarating experiences of his life. Luca knew the principle of deserving a second chance as well as any man. This was his own second chance too. That unspoilt, darkly dappled youngster that Luca could have ridden into battle, jumping cirrus in the sky all the way, might be a ghost of what he had been, but Beck was still the horse that had haunted his waking thoughts and deepest dreams more than any other.

'Let's try it,' he said quickly, before he could think on it too much, the plan forming as fast as he could say it. 'On one condition.'

'Which is?'

'Stand him here just one season then sell him back to Fuchs.' He held up his hand when Ronnie started to protest. 'Visiting mares by invitation only, a restricted number.'

'Why limit my profit?'

'It's more lucrative. Next year you can cherry-pick his first generation to retain as your foundation line. That's your long-term investment while your quick profit comes from selling him afterwards.'

Ronnie look at him shrewdly. 'For a gifted man who doesn't say a lot, you make sense when the gift of the gab takes you. Keep talking.'

'With his bloodline and progeny, we both know you can persuade Paul to pay big money for him, especially once we get him looking as good as he did in that video.' He nodded at Beck who was steaming with sweat, eyes wild, unclipped coat filthy, churning a groove in the sand as deep as a mill furrow.

'What are you thinking? Half a million?'

It took him a moment to realise she wasn't joking.

'You're the boss.'

'Don't forget it.' The infectious laugh came deep from her throat, eyes Lapis. 'Half a mill would leave me plenty of loose change to bring back a smart young stallion or two to stand here next year, keep us ticking over while we wait it out for Beck's babies to be old enough to breed from. You're quite brilliant, Luca. I love a plan. We sell the golden goose, but only after we keep lots of golden goose eggs to hatch.'

In the round pen, Beck was still running for his life. He'd run until he dropped if he had to. He would never surrender. He was that sort of horse. Does he know he's in danger too? Luca wondered.

'Of course, all this depends on whether we can turn him round or not.' Ronnie grimaced, crossing her arms and adopting her power pose, which Luca was finding increasingly beguiling. 'We'll set a deadline. I can't afford to be a sanctuary, and I need you breaking and schooling on youngsters and overseeing Cruisoe servicing his mares. If Beck doesn't buck up his ideas in time, I'll cut my losses and offer him straight to Paul.'

Luca ran his tongue across his teeth. If ever he had an incentive to fail, that was it. But this was Beck he reminded himself. This was Ronnie.

'Now catch my horse,' she ordered brusquely, tilting her head, wise blue eyes gleaming.

Beck, who had slithered to a halt to watch them, shot off across the pen when Luca let himself in. He walked a few steps towards him and the stallion reared up, a white tower looming overhead, threatening to strike out.

With a soft burr of the tongue, Luca raised his arms and the horse dropped back down. He swung the head collar, calling for him to get going and Beck tossed his head furiously and charged off in a breakneck circle.

'He can do that all day,' Ronnie said, watching from the other side of the metal gate. 'Lester gets terribly dizzy. He thinks we're feeding him too much.'

Luca moved further into the circle and the stallion flew between them faster than a roulette ball spinning on its wheel. 'He's completely lost trust.'

Quietly clicking and whistling to attract Beck's attention, he turned to look at Ronnie through the metalwork, ignoring the horse when he spun round and started to career in the opposite direction.

'He needs a good role model,' he told her, clicking quietly again. '*Here, lad, tsh tsh.* Let's give your old Irish stallion a new next-door neighbour to talk to.' He whistled once more. 'We'll move him into the stable beside Cruisoe.'

'Are you mad?' Ronnie was indignant. 'Beck attacks other horses. Put him next to another stallion and he jumps out even with the grille. I've seen him barrel it clean off the door at the last yard.'

'Isolating stallions is the worst thing you can do to them. Now you and I need to be quiet,' he hushed her as the grey went down through the gears to a floaty trot before stopping dead with a hydra shake of his head.

He was staring at Luca, snorting suspiciously, ready to go up again, brutality on a hair trigger. The once-familiar bond between them was a spectre, shape-shifting and indistinct.

Luca waited, his own eyes staying on Ronnie.

The horse stamped an indignant foot.

Still he waited.

Beck bellowed.

Luca gave Ronnie the ghost of a wink.

Slowly, suspiciously, serpent head tossing, Beck moved closer. They'd done this before, he and Luca.

He waited until he could feel his breath on his shoulder. Only then did he use his voice again, low and soothing, reassuring him that he was in a safe place, that Luca had his back now, that he wouldn't let him out of his sight again.

He then turned and swiftly clipped on the head collar.

As Beck dropped his head in surprise, Luca sent a silent apology, knowing he'd just taken a circus trick shortcut. To regain a horse's trust took infinitely longer, but it was the quick fixes that pleased the crowds. And he wanted to please.

'I always forget how easy you make it look.' She was thrilled, holding the gate open for them, beaming as they passed. 'I could watch you all day.'

He turned, remembering how gratifying her blue-sky enthusiasm was, the intimacy with which she praised. *Touché*, Mrs Ledwell.

Growing up, Luca's school friends had resentfully ribbed him about the fact that working with difficult horses attracted some girls faster than any number of hours of bench-pressing, a fireman's uniform and a bottle of baby oil. His four brothers all took regular advantage of this, especially showjumper Donal who was knee-high to a stable door with a face like a fruit bat, yet always had girlfriends who looked like models. Their father, a bandy-legged, balder fruit bat, had used his horse skills to woo their beautiful mother. In Germany, whenever Ronnie had visited Gestüt Fuchs, Luca had often outridden everyone else entirely for her benefit.

'Let's get this house move underway!' She overtook them as they walked back to the yard, hurrying ahead to start making up a bed in the stable beside Cruisoe.

Ignoring Beck performing a snorting sideways dance beside him, Luca yawned as he admired her perfect apple-shaped backside. Still up there in his top three. She'd always been far too classy for a rogue like Henk, who everyone knew was a deviant. He doubted Blair Robertson was much better.

Taking advantage of his distraction, the stallion caught him a nip on the arm, so staple-gun sharp that he couldn't breathe for a moment.

'You're right,' he agreed under his breath, shaking the rope in reproof. 'Work comes first.'

There was no hot water washdown, he discovered, resorting to an old-fashioned sponge before putting Beck back in his old stable, rugged up to dry off while he helped Ronnie haul straw bales into the horse's new quarters to break up and bank up, listening as she recounted the stallion's unruliness. 'He jumped straight out of one of the stallion paddocks and took off across the village just before Christmas. Climbed on a mare out hacking. It was awful. Lucky not to get sued.'

Learning that Beck was only ever turned out in solitary confinement, usually in early mornings before the mares went out – the opposite end of the day to Cruisoe who watched the sun go down – Luca insisted both stallions needed their own fields all day.

Ronnie shook her head vehemently. 'They'll kill each other.'

'If there's lots to eat, plus plenty of thorn hedge and electric wire between them, they'll be fine. And Beck needs a companion. Something small and fearless. He's scared of his own shadow.'

'A sacrificial goat?'

'A pony would be better.'

'"Companions are for ladies" my father used to say.' She laughed. 'If Lester gets wind of all this, he'll have the nurses pushing his hospital bed here from Coventry Hospital to put a stop to it.'

From what little he'd gleaned of the elderly, broken-hipped hunting devotee, Luca suspected he'd be hitching the bed to a towbar and driving it straight back.

As he'd predicted, the two new next-door neighbours had a brief bout of furious stallion bellyaching and snorting, like neighbours well versed in bin and parking disputes, then settled to their hay nets to regroup, both quietly pleased to have something new to think about.

'I think we'll turn him round, don't you?' Ronnie was in her power pose. 'You're exactly what he needs. We'll have him right in no time. How long are you thinking it will take?' she asked, gathering up rugs, ever impatient. 'When's our deadline?'

Luca suspected it could take months. He thought about her offer to take him straight to Germany if he couldn't do it. 'We'll know by Valentine's Day.'

'I'll love you by then if that's true.' She laughed.

'I'll hold you to that.'

9

'C'mon, *kochanie*, you love having me all to yourself.'

'You've abandoned our babies in a foreign country!'

'In my *homeland*, Bridge.'

Shocked that Aleš had left their children in Poland without consulting her, Bridge was determined to get an apology from him. Flavia and Zak would be flying home with his brother's family tomorrow, and even though she knew they'd be perfectly safe, and they loved their *wujek* and *ciocia*, and that it was lovely to have just made carefree love all over the house, she still wanted a sorry. Just a little one.

The argument, which had been going in circles so long she was feeling dizzy, was typical of the Mazurs. Feeling aggrieved about something – usually justifiably – Bridge would buzz and needle and rag until big, patient Aleš conceded with a grand romantic gesture. Or exploded. It was a calculated gamble.

'They need Mummy or Daddy there.'

Her martyrdom was slightly blunted when he started pulling dirty laundry from his suitcase mid-argument and sorting it out.

'They're so tiny,' she wailed as the sea of rugby shirts rose.

'*You* left them,' he pointed out matter-of-factly, separating lights from darks. For a mountainous and masculine man, Aleš was refreshingly domesticated. Friends always assumed Bridge had house-trained him, but he'd come fully loaded from the start, with added stain-remover and fabric conditioner.

'I came back early for a job interview! You just wanted a booty call.'

'But you did not get job,' he said as he loaded the machine. 'I did get booty call.'

'What's that supposed to mean?' Bridge felt uncharacteristically tearful, which she guiltily acknowledged could be as much about the job as the kids, who utterly adored being in Poland with all the family. 'I can't believe our babies are thousands of miles away right now.'

'I could only get one stand-by ticket. I had to be with you, *moja kochana*.' He pulled off his shirt. It was a very Fantasy Ash move, only marred by Aleš studying the washing instructions on the label.

'We were apart *one* night.' The fight had gone out of her argument as she tilted her head and, squinting, visualised the dog tags swinging against the six pack. 'Just one night.'

'How crazy is that? I missed you so much.' He cast her a smile over one big shoulder, and she found herself wondering if he wouldn't suit a tattoo there, something Maori perhaps, or a Roman armour sleeve like the one she'd seen at the gym. On the pec dec. A man with wolf eyes.

Loosening the knot on her dressing gown, Bridge levered herself up onto the washing machine so she could wrap her legs around him. 'You crazy big Pole.'

'Hey, what is this?' He had a sock in each hand.

She slid her hands around his neck and pulled him closer. 'Do you think you can go again?'

Ash was out of the cellar.

Mack *still* wasn't answering his phone. Ringing from the stable cottage, Pax wished she'd emailed him while she had the chance in the Mack Shack, craving the cool calm of written words compared to the improvised chaos of speaking after the tone: *I think it's best if I stay at the stud for a few days. I have collected some of my things. Can we talk about Kes ASAP? Pax*. Not: 'Mack, it's me again. We need to – that is, I'm going to – be quiet, Stubbs! – my phone died and I'm now at the stud, I mean don't call my phone, call here. Kes can stay here. I'm staying here. He can be with you too. We need to work out days. Can you call me when you get this?'

Her laptop sat uselessly on the table behind her, a reminder that her late grandparents and Lester had barricaded themselves into their generation, firmly attached to a world where one wrote letters, even to near neighbours, and stayed married at all costs. Ronnie, who sprang from a mobile-free, guilt-free era of baby boomers that left notes on mantelpieces and deserted marriages as casually as popping out to the shops, was equally unbothered by the stud's prehistoric isolation, treating it as a digital detox; she was happy camping here like a gypsy, a temporary curator, her bags barely unpacked. For Pax, doing without Wi-Fi and alcohol simultaneously was a double cold turkey which, so soon after Christmas, was already choking her. Her thrash metal headache was pounding now, the urge to kick things making her leg muscles twitch constantly.

Cutting off Mack's droning outgoing message by hooking the receiver angrily back on its wall holster in the kitchen, she pulled up the little blind above the sink, so stiff it was like raising a portcullis. Behind it was a tiny casement window that looked out into the main stable yard. Her mother was talking to Luca outside Cruisoe's corner box. Why was she standing like a badass bouncer?

Pax turned away, eyes skirting the ugly oak-trimmed melamine cupboards, already knowing what her unconscious mind was seeking out. Having thought she'd never want to drink again just hours earlier, the tug at the back of her mouth was getting too persistent to ignore. She tried Mack's line again, an activity to stop herself searching for booze as much as anything else, shuddering with revulsion at his nasal outgoing message, the Scoooootish vowels soooo irritating. Normality had turned to demonisation so quickly. She wondered if she'd be able to bring herself to like him again one day, and if he could bring himself to forgive her for all this, to accept this was a good thing, releasing two escape capsules before the big, burning impact. He'd never forgiven his ex-wife for deserting him and taking the children beyond reach… Oh shit, not more tears. Oh, Kes. When would the thrum of adrenaline washing constantly around her body *stop*?

'God, I need a drink,' she told Knott. Luca would probably tell her she just needed God. If only he could turn water into wine…

As Pax picked up the receiver to dial Mack's number again, it occurred to her that her multiple call attempts would come up on his phone's log. She'd worked too hard at self-control to let him power-play missed calls. She rang Lizzie instead, grateful to be able to cry on the shoulder of someone who understood and was prepared to listen as she unloaded the horror of the past twenty-four hours. Playing down her drunken awfulness at the hotel, she wept and growled with frustration about Mack's current stand-off.

'They always do the into-my-cave after the he-man shouty control thing,' Lizzie reassured, annoyingly eager to move onto the subject of Luca O'Brien. 'So, is the Horsemaker good-looking?'

'If you're a Chewbacca fetishist. And into priests.'

'He's a *priest*?'

'He's a moralising veggie which is close enough. Mummy's predictably all over him already. I caught them in a clinch, earlier. He must be twenty years younger than her.'

'Ew.'

Pax peered out of the sink window, wondering if 'clinch' was a bit misleading; they'd looked more like they were about to Morris dance. But there was been something about the way Luca looked at Ronnie, the way so many men looked at her mother, that put a fist in the hollow between her ribs.

Luca was letting himself out of the stable beside Cruisoe's, carrying a wicking rug. He looked exhausted. She suddenly felt incredibly bad for not helping out. He'd flown all night, slept on a chair, and he was out there while she skulked in here pressing redial.

Taking the rug from him, Ronnie now strode across the yard with a toss of her blonde hair. Luca watched her backside the whole way. Pax stopped feeling bad about not helping.

'Bay was here this morning,' she told Lizzie, moving away to open the cupboards within reach. Row upon row of Fray Bentos tins faced her. Lester liked to buy in bulk.

Lizzie was satisfyingly outraged. 'That bastard! What did he want? Whatever it was, I hope you told him to get lost.'

'I was very polite,' she said, bursting into tears again.

'Stay brave, kid,' Lizzie soothed. 'Remember, the best thing you ever did was breaking it off with Bay. You should have literally broken it off and pickled it. Saved a lot of women a lot of heartache.'

Pax dug her fingernail into the flex. 'I not sure I can stay here, Libs. I'll go mad and commit matricide, then I'll never get Kes.' Why oh why wouldn't the tears *stop?*

'Come to us. We'll downward dog together in front of Nicholas Sparks' movies.'

'I love your sweet heart, but I'm—' She nearly leapt out of her skin as she spotted her mother's blue eyes peering in through the window, and just for an unguarded moment she saw the exhaustion and despair in them. Spotting Pax, they crystallised into focus and sparkled. If Luca O'Brien used his smile as a weapon, it was a popgun compared to Ronnie's façade. She'd spent half a decade turning and galloping the moment things got too emotional.

'I'm going to unmask my mother,' she finished.

★

Throughout her early life, and again in recent weeks, Ronnie had checked her reflection in Lester's little kitchen window, conveniently located between rug and feed rooms, its glass kept immaculately clean despite the fact he hadn't, to her knowledge, raised its dark brown blind in forty years, the glazed lean-to on the cottage's garden side flooding in light enough. It made the perfect mirror for a quick check-over, and today she wanted to flick her hair, pinch her cheeks and roll her lips beneath her teeth to redden them.

Instead, she was staring at her younger self, at all the tears soaked into pillows and stables, never once shed in front of her mother.

What? Pax mouthed furiously, not waiting for an answer as she turned away to pace back and forth. Tethered to the wall by the phone cord, she resembled a chained dog.

Watching her grab a tea towel to mop her tears, Stubbs trotting loyally after her, Ronnie felt her heart fold into itself, tighter and tighter, powerless to help.

Pax was glaring at her again. *Stop spying on me.*

I'm sorry, Ronnie mouthed back. *I wasn't spying I was—*

The blind came down abruptly and she found herself staring at her own fifty-something face, weather-beaten from hours in the saddle, starting to bag a little at the jowls and chin, her eyes strangely incandescent. To her shock, they bore great glistening tears. She swiped them, rolled her teeth over her lips, pinched her cheeks and strode back to Luca who was watching the grey stallion again, arms tightly crossed and broad shoulders hunched.

There were lots of jobs still to do on the yard but they would have to wait. She wondered again how they would survive without Lester.

'I must go back to the hospital and you must have a rest,' she told Luca over-brightly, beckoning him to follow, aware that the poor man was on his knees with fatigue. 'I'll quickly show where you're staying – it's a bit of a labyrinth, but the outlook's pretty. You'll have the run of the house and use of the car,' she briefed him as she marched off the yard. 'I don't eat supper as a rule, but I'm happy to count you into soup at lunchtime and breakfast after the yard's done. Or you can self-cater. It's up to you. Use the main kitchen whenever you like – yours is very basic – and you can have friends round any time as long as they don't frighten the horses. Pip, the housekeeper, might reappear at some point and will probably try to mother you, shag you or both. Again, up to you. UK calls only from the phone, I'm afraid. There's mobile reception up the lane. All your liabilities are your own. I can only afford you long enough to get the foals down and the mares covered again. And please don't forget,' she paused in the rear courtyard, glancing up at the top row of dormers, 'to be nice to Pax. She's going through a bloody tough time.' She turned to him.

He looked unimpressed behind the gentleman-explorer's beard. 'And you're not?'

'I'm just plain bloody tough.' She indicated the long glass vestibule that formed the rear entrance of the house and doubled as a boot room. 'Your flat is through there, the door straight ahead here. It's all unlocked.' Amid a sudden din of barking, the gate creaked behind them.

Dressed in an ancient shredded Barbour, yard boots and an ugly woolly hat, Pax was holding out Lester's overnight bag. Her swollen red eyes were as fierce as before, emotional Armageddon barely in check. At her feet, Stubbs was defending Knott from the heeler bitches.

'I'll do the yard while you're visiting Lester,' she said, not looking at them. 'Bring everything in and tidy up.'

'Are you sure?'

'I told you, I need to keep busy.'

'I'll help,' offered Luca.

'I don't need your help.'

Oh dear, she really was spoiling for a fight, thought Ronnie, taking Lester's bag and, as an afterthought, gathering up Stubbs. 'I'll try to be back as quickly as I can.'

'Take as long as you need.' Pax pocketed her glasses and rubbed her face, raking her fingers up through her hair and retying her bun so tightly her red eyes tilted up at the edges.

Ronnie's heart turned again. Oh, the pure, unrelenting hell of a marriage ending. 'The broodmares need bringing in first.'

'Fine.'

'I'm really very grateful, Pax, and I—'

'I want to do it.' Her big hare eyes warned her off sentimentality like all good Percys. 'It *helps* to help. Send Lester my love.'

'I will,' Ronnie said and smiled, turning away. 'I'm just showing Luca up to his – oh.' He'd swung out of the gate and was loping across the arrivals yard. Under the first archway, he paused and waited.

'Tell him I don't need him,' muttered Pax. 'He's shattered.'

'So are you.' Ronnie wondered at the endurance marathon going on between them. 'I don't think you have a choice.'

As she drove away, glancing in her rear-view mirror, Ronnie saw them trudging up towards the turnouts together with head collars, and sent up a little prayer that her daughter made peace as usual, quashing the worry that Pax was in the sort of frenetic, angry mindset that made her more likely to start a stampede or push a new manager in a water trough.

At the bottom of the driveway, a mud-caked Land Rover was turning in, its lights flashing hello. Gritting her teeth, Ronnie barred its way with her car.

The window buzzed down, a plume of aftershave rushing out. Bay had changed into casual clothes, hair wet from the shower. He glowed with good health, winter suntan – and bad intentions. 'Thought I'd check how it's all going, lend a hand if you need one.'

'It's fine. Now be a good boy and bugger off.'

'Come on, Ron. I'm being neighbourly. Is Pax still here? She's not answering her phone.' When Ronnie gave no more than a withering look, he leaned out of his car window further, voice conspiratorial. 'Is it true she's given Och Aye the Noo his marching orders?'

'None of your bloody business.' Surely Lester hadn't said anything? Even delirious with pain, he was usually the soul of discretion.

'I'll come back tomorrow, shall I?'

'Go home, Bay.'

He gave her a mock hangdog look, but he did as she asked, reversing around and shooting off again with a wave from the open window.

'*Kochanie*, I am not sure I can hold this position.'

'Just – oooh, grrrgh – try a bit – ahhh – longer.'

'I have a little back pain and cramp.'

'Nothing to what – eaughh – I'm feeling, Aleš. Oh, Jaysus, that's good! How about if I do...'

'*Zajebisty*!'

'... this?'

'Oh, yes. *Zajebisty*! Oh yes. Oh yes.'

They were up against the front door, rattling it on its hinges, the ultimate knee-trembler. Bridge's ankles were on Aleš's huge shoulders, his shins wedged against the old wood-planking, forehead against the lintel, one big hand supporting her buttocks while the other was splayed across the little peep-window, knuckles in her shoulder blade. Both were secretly getting off like wildfire on the fact dog walkers, motorists and cyclists were passing just a foot or two away from their pounding, sweaty coupling. That and the fact it was the coolest spot in the room with the log burner at full blast, and they appreciated the draught they'd complained about all winter, no longer muffled with upholstered sausages and thick drapes, but whistling around two finely balanced, semi-naked bodies.

'Oh, oh, oh!' Bridge wailed joyfully as Aleš turned her round so that his back was to the door now, blotting out the little glass pane, head crammed at an angle, shoulders as wide as the entrance porch. This way, she could hold onto the rail for the door curtain, lean right back and...

'Ooooooooooooooh.'

It was sensational.

'I am coming!' Aleš warned.

'Not before me,' she panted as the electric shocks tickled and that whoosh of well-being flooded up inside her. Happy, happy homecoming. So rarely had they come together, at exactly the same time, it was like getting married again. Take that, Fantasy Ash. I love my husband!

'Something strange is between my legs!' Aleš wailed in a strangled voice.

'Telling me!' she groaned and shuddered appreciatively. 'Ten inches of it's inside me.'

'Aghhhhhh!'

With fairground-ride giddiness, Bridge felt herself free-falling several inches through the air as Aleš almost dropped her.

'*Kurwa*! Arghhh!'

'What's wrong?' She clung on, still half-coming, heart hammering as her body went into meltdown.

'Something against my balls. Feel it, quick. Like it bugger me! *Kurwa*!' He shrugged her legs urgently off his shoulders and pulled them round his waist. In moments of high excitement, Aleš's kinkier demands were often lost in translation – and he could be quite kinky – so Bridge tried to ride this, body still crackling and fizzing like popping candy, doing what he wanted and reaching around to finger his balls and anus.

They closed around a tightly rolled pamphlet. 'What the...?'

Aleš groaned as she swiftly removed it before taking a look. *The Compton Villages Parish Magazine, January Edition* ran with the headline Church Tower Under Risk of Collapse After Lead Theft Reveals Deathwatch Beetle. Brian Hicks and his wife Chris distributed the little booklet around all the local houses on the first of each month without fail, rolling it up neatly to post it through the Mazurs' letterbox.

'I think you've just been buggered by the Chairman of the Parish Council, my darling,' Bridge told him, feeling his tower subside in sympathy with the beetle-infested church. 'Would you like a cup of tea and an almond biscuit to get over the shock?'

Thinks happy thoughts, think happy thoughts! Pax could feel it, the tumour of rage multiplying ferociously, dividing and multiplying again like cells. She was holding a hose to wash mud off hooves as the herd came in from the fields, but longed to drench Luca in its icy water instead.

'You've missed that near hind,' he told her, passing behind with Margaret, the sourest-faced of the broodmares who looked almost as pissed off as Pax felt.

'The girls never usually get their legs hosed,' she said.

'They do now.'

Think happy thoughts! She pressed the hose trigger hard, the water pressure so high it snaked out of her frozen fingers, drenching her own leg, not doe-eyed Barbara's.

'Best check her frogs when you pick her feet out, yes?' Luca passed behind her again, heading off to grab Shirley from the tie-ring.

'Do you speak to my mother like she's some half-witted pony-clubber?'

He looked back at her in surprise. 'I speak to her like she knows what she's doing.'

'*I* know what I'm doing.'

'So you'll have seen that mare looks a bit footsore.'

'Of course I saw.' She hadn't noticed. *Think happy thoughts. Think happy thoughts. At least you're not in Scotland with Mack.*

'Must have been tough going back home, so it must,' he said out of nowhere.

Pax hesitated, furious that he was being so personal. Watching somebody throw up, slither around a bath in their underwear and sleep in your clothes might give you a right to ask after their mental health, but not *now* and not *here*.

'Yes, mustn't it,' she replied eventually. He didn't interrogate her further, which was good because she'd have waterboarded him with the hose.

At the end of a mixed ward full of oxygen-masked geriatrics, Lester was pale and composed, horrified that Ronnie hadn't thought to bring him a supply of Fray Bentos pies or this week's *Horse & Hound*, and the pyjama tops were striped, the bottoms checked. 'I always fold them in matched pairs in the drawer. It's a system. It makes no sense to muddle them.'

'I'll bring the right ones tomorrow,' she promised, deciding not to remind him that he'd in all likelihood remain bottomless in a hospital gown until his op. At least the sight of Stubbs smuggled in a Bag for Life soothed him – although he was snobbishly irked it was an Aldi one.

'Operation's on Thursday. I'll be up again in no time,' he assured her, white with fear. 'Didn't even fall off.'

'I know, Lester. You owe nothing to the Tumblers Club.'

He looked relieved to be believed, giving her a wily look. 'The Australian gone home, has he?'

'Hours ago,' she sighed. Blair was another wrinkle that needed smoothing.

'That's a shame. Useful to have someone around the place who knows what they're doing while I'm laid up.'

'We have Luca now.'

'Never hurts to have experience on side. Not a lot that Robertson fellow doesn't know about horses.'

'Lester, are you encouraging me to see more of Blair?'

He stared her out beadily.

'I'll give him a call, shall I?'

'If you say so.'

Ronnie wondered if they'd overdone the opiates. She tested the theory. 'Lester, I hope it's all right, but while you're in here I've found you a house-sitter.'

'Very good.' He sagged back against the pillows, frail and pale.

'It's easier to look after Stubbs and Laurence that way.'

He had his eyes closed now. 'I won't tolerate curried food, pipe smoke or lavender bags. Your mother was a devil for slipping a pomander on a doorknob when I wasn't looking.'

'I think you're safe with Pax.'

His eyes snapped open. 'Please don't tell me you put her in my cottage?'

'I thought you'd be pleased. She's coming back to live at the stud.'

A hand gripped hers tightly. 'Get rid of the letters.'

Rather than hurl the parish magazine into the wood burner as revenge for being rimmed by it in a kinky threesome, Aleš had been – rather disturbingly, Bridge thought – engrossed in it for the ensuing half hour while she guzzled *rogaliki* biscuits and enjoyed the afterglow. Both freshly showered and jogger-clad, they sprawled on a sofa each, Bridge scrolling her phone while Aleš read twenty curled A5 pages of prayers, psalms and church services.

'There are many poems from the little church school here.' He smiled indulgently. 'It is very sweet to see.'

Bridge was touched that he took an interest. Their kids were still a way off school, and they'd already agreed they favoured the bigger, better-funded school in Broadbourne where their Polish cousins went.

'Good place to work, yes? Safe place? Little part-time job is nice idea.'

She eyed him warily.

'I read list earlier when you lie there.' He nodded towards the table where her notes about job applications had been crumpled under their lovemaking. 'It says something about job at school?'

'It's just one left-field idea I'm toying with,' she muttered. 'I'm not taking it too seriously if—' She stopped herself. 'Are you saying that you were studying my job ideas list while we were having *sex*?'

'It was in my eyeline.'

'Remind me to leave *How To Be a Woman* out next time.'

'That would be strange.' He looked at her levelly, sarcasm lost on him as usual.

'I'm looking for something a bit more challenging, work-wise, Aleš.'

'You have a home to look after.'

Bridge gritted her teeth. They mustn't argue after this much sex. Not on their only night alone together. Her body was still rippling with the pleasure of it all.

Closing her eyes to count to ten, she was alarmed to find Fantasy Ash waiting there in the darkness, emerging through the gloom of a deserted schoolyard, asking if he was too late for parents' evening. Oh, those hard, tortured silver eyes.

'D'you think you might be ready to go again later?' she said, turning turning to Aleš, but he'd fallen asleep with his mouth open.

*

Hazy grey twilight had thickened into darkness around the stud's stable yards, their cobbled quadrangles golden islands in the tungstens, the surrounding fields black seas through which Pax and Luca navigated, torches bobbing.

By the time they'd brought in half a dozen big-bellied broodmares and herded youngstock back into barns, Luca was dead on his feet. Pax hadn't uttered anything beyond snipes and monosyllables, crosser than ever because she kept disappearing to try calling her husband from the landline, only to storm back out less than a minute later. Luca waited each time, increasingly impatient. It seemed hubby was now playing the silent stand-off. It was all tactics and gameplay, ending relationships, he reflected sorely on his own rifts. Horses were far easier.

He checked on the bellyaching stallions – the new neighbours engaged in straightforward out-shouting each other, interspersed with deep, appreciative inhaling and lip-curling – then tracked down Pax in the feed room, pouring hot water over quick-soak sugar beet and sobbing silently into the steam, trying to hide it as soon as she realised he was there, pulling on brittle British politeness like a uniform. 'Almost done!'

Luca felt too tired for sympathy. But she was Ronnie's daughter and she was in distress, and he could no more leave her suffering than he could any animal.

'I'll finish this off.' He put his hand on her shoulder, its bones hard as pebbles in his palm. 'You look done in.'

A memory flashed, her soaked through in the hotel bathroom, body thin as a greyhound's.

'Everything's mixed up...' Her deep voice trembled.

'We all lose our way sometimes, life gets mixed up,' he reassured her gently. 'Go and lie down. Let me take over here.'

'I said the *feeds* are all mixed up,' she explained, teeth gritted, turning back to the buckets and picking up the stirring spatula. 'Why don't *you* go and lie down?'

'I don't want to lie down.'

'Neither do I.'

The stallions bellowed.

'I'd rather carry on with this alone, if that's all right.' The polite brittleness was cracking.

'Ronnie left me in charge.'

'I didn't hear her say that.'

'I'm the manager now.'

'That's a matter of opinion.'

'D'you have a problem with it?'

'This place will never make money again.'

'I don't agree.'

'That's because my mother is paying you to agree with her.'

Luca's irritation needed little needling. The long journey, missing the chance to see his family, the heartache he'd left behind in Canada, the shitty welcome, the call he always dreaded, all crowned by finding Beck here was all under his skin like splinters. 'Ah, get over yourself.'

Very tired people should never argue in Luca's experience, but as Pax turned to face him he felt an unassailable urge to shake her out of her rigid, neurotic politeness and point out that there were more important things at stake here than her self-obsessed marriage misery. He'd just landed Compton Magna with a whole heap of problems. She didn't even know the start of it.

'You're not *my* boss,' Pax fumed, 'so bog off while I trot on.'

'Fuck off yourself, calling me a bogtrotter!'

'I didn't call you a bloody bogtrotter, I said BOG OFF, Mack!'

'Now it's Mick, is it? What sort of Irish-hating racist are you?'

'I said *Mack*. It's my husband's name. Shit! I'm going mad – sorry.' She held up an open palm, politely compelled to take the sting out of the exchange, although the murderous base note still gave her hostility away. 'Be grateful I didn't call you Mummy.'

'Heaven forbid,' he muttered. 'No girl over the age of ten should call her mother that.'

'Why not?' Pax glared at him. 'Does it remind you that Ronnie's old enough to be yours?'

'Hardly.'

'She's grandmother to six.'

'I'm sure she loves them all.' He stared her out, unblinking, but the thought wasn't one he wanted to dwell on.

'You have no idea at all about our family, do you?' Her voice was climbing again.

'It's not my business to know. It's dysfunctional horses I sort out, not marriages.'

'What are you insinuating?' Higher still.

He sighed, softening his approach. 'Crying into the feeds just makes their oats salty.' He held out his hand for the food scoop she was still brandishing. 'Let me take over here.'

She crossed it tightly in her arms, the words fired out staccato. 'I know it might not look like it to you, but I'm trying very hard to keep what's going on in my personal life separate from Mummy and this stud; I suggest you do the same and we'll be just fine.'

'My personal life has nothing to do with anyone here.'

'C'mon, Luca, you took this job for Mummy. That's personal.'

'I've not landed five minutes!' She had some serious trust issues with Ronnie, he'd started to realise. No matter that she was right. He'd never been able to resist her mother's charm. 'How come you're so jealous of her?'

She tutted the question away. 'And what about all the calls? The woman I answered today, who refused to give her name? Don't tell me she's another grandmother you're keen on? Poor Lester's had to field messages for days. He even took a death threat this morning.'

'What death threat?' Ice shot through his blood.

'I don't know. Do you get many?'

'Of course not.' He pictured Mishaal, his twisted scarred face, then forced the image away.

'You really shouldn't have come here, Luca. Everyone says we should sell this bloody place,' Pax raged on, eyes wild, the façade truly cracking now. 'I thought Mummy should be given the chance at turning it round because it's what Grumps wanted, but she's blowing the budget on you. This is our family's future and you're just breezing in like some fucking gigolo.'

'You don't know me.'

'I don't like you or trust you, either.'

'Me and your husband both. Or is it all men you hate?'

'You bastard!' She hurled the feed scoop at him. Her aim was surprisingly good and it whacked him over the eye.

'You bitch!'

'Bastard!'

Luca's jazz hands went up, accompanied by a piano-key smile. 'Hey, you need to calm down.'

'And you need to leave my marriage out of this! This is *not* about that! This is about hundreds of years of family history, Percy history, which I can't stand back and let my mother screw up on some nostalgic shag-fest. All your pompous, moralising shit is so fucking phoney! You just saw pound signs and cheap thrills. Even Mummy called you "louche". I can't believe you had the nerve to question *me* about *my* lifestyle choices!'

Then she started shouting, real proper hysterical shouting, glass-shattering and vicious. Luca had no idea somebody so classy and British was capable of such foul language, such total fury. It would be impressive if it weren't so relentless – and violent.

She called him Mack twice, Scottish once – and a bastard so many times he lost count. He stopped trying to shout back after a while, but he was stripped of sympathy, watching her in horror. He'd never seen emotion this raw.

And then it struck him far harder than any of her words. I'm the husband substitute, he realised in shock. She's fighting her battle with Mack through me because he won't talk to her. No wonder he's lying low, poor bastard. She'd annihilate him.

The next moment a mixing spatula glanced off his ear. It hurt. Really hurt.

'Stop that, you mad fucking cow!'

'Don't you dare speak to my sister like that!' roared a regal voice from the door.

Small, fierce and unafraid of violence, Pax's saviour stormed inside and almost upended Luca with a sharp elbow as she marched past.

Sobbing, the redhead rushed into her arms. 'Make him go away, Lisp!'

'Gladly.' Luca held up his arms and backed out of the feed room.

All in all, it wasn't his greatest first day in a job.

On the yard, the stallions were screaming at each other again.

Blood beating through his arteries like club music, he went to check on them, but the nervous energy coursing off him made Beck fly to the back of his stable to stare fearfully at him, huge black eyes awaiting punishment. Luca stepped away, finding it impossible to calm down. He knew he should go back and apologise – the woman was obviously in bits. He could hear the little deerhound puppy howling in the stables cottage.

She also had a young dog she was lousy at looking after.

As Luca went to let Knott out, the stud's phone started ringing again, that plaintive shrill bell that he was already learning to hate. He expected Pax to sprint past him to answer it, but it rang on and on as he opened the door and the puppy burst out to cavort around him. Through the gloom he could see the hall was full of chewed paper, several puddles and a small poo neatly deposited on a shoebox lid. The phone was still ringing and the paper trail led on into the small kitchen.

Luca plucked up the phone receiver, longing to drop it straight back down again, but aware that it appeared to be the only line of communication and it could be an emergency – Ronnie in crisis, or Pax's son taken ill... He held it to his mouth.

'Yes?'

'Is Pax there?' Deep, dull Scottish voice.

'I can go and see.' He didn't relish the prospect.

'Wait! Who are you?'

'Luca. Is this Mack?'

There was a long silence.

'I'll go and see if I can find her, shall I?' he asked, starting to wonder if the man at the other end had hung up, watching Pax's puppy trotting towards him, crumpled paper in mouth.

'No,' Mack said tightly. 'Just give me a moment.'

Luca unravelled some of the tightly curled phone cord, an elaborate dance that led him back almost to the hallway again. He could see the puppy's path of destruction, which had started with a low dresser shelf of several shoeboxes, some still neatly stacked, two upended, neat A5 sheets fanned around the largest one.

He could hear Mack breathing heavily at the other end of the line. What was he doing? It sounded like a dirty phone call.

Knott had followed him to the hall, shredding his piece of paper as he went.

Luca took what was left of it from his mouth and turned back to smooth it on the small, much-oiled expanse of wooden countertop between sink and hob. It was a letter in faded blue fountain pen on old-fashioned watermarked paper, the handwriting distinctively round. *Dear Piggy,* he read. *Please destroy this the moment you have read it like all the others. I know you will. And thank goodness for you.*

It was a love letter, he realised.

We are so alike, you and I, so wretched in our wretched honour. I was supposed to be coppicing this morning but I sat up on the old wall by the fattest elm and watched you ride for a whole hour, unable to tear my eyes away. It was the most beautiful sight, outshining every grace of nature, the copper beeches bowing as you passed, the grass beneath you sighing. I imagined you saw me. Did you? It was as though you were riding for me.

'Would you mind giving her a message, Luke?'

He jumped guiltily, pushing the letter away. 'Sure.'

More heavy breathing.

'Will you tell her that I know you two have been fucking for months, and that I will fucking come over there and kill you if you lay one fucking finger on her again. Got that?' The call ended.

Luca's palm splayed on the tattered paper. Today just got better and better.

He carefully refolded the chewed letter and went to pick up the rest, tidying them into the shoeboxes as best he could – he had to throw out the soiled lid – and cramming them into the dresser. He then tracked down a pile old *Daily Express* newspapers, neatly stacked by the fireplace, which he used to cover the wet patches on the quarry tiles, all the time girding himself to return to the feed room. Straightening up, the yawn that racked through him almost split his jaw.

Fuck it. Let them sort it out between them. He was going to bed. Wherever that was. From now on, he would be utterly professional. He would not flirt with the boss or fight with her children. He would stay in Compton Magna long enough to help Beck, and for Ronnie. He would have absolutely nothing more to do with Pax Forsyth beyond rigid professional politeness.

'What are you doing in here?' She burst in, all red hair and bobble hat, like Where's Wally.

'Yes, what are you doing in here?' The small, fierce sister was behind her, fists tight at her sides.

Great.

'I answered the phone.'

'There's one in the house you can use,' snapped the sister. Then, remembering her manners, she thrust out a hand. 'Alice Petty.'

'Luca O'Brien,' he said, shaking it and finding his fingers gripped and released as though shut in a car door. 'And I've not actually been in the house yet.'

'Was it Mack?' Pax was demanding. She couldn't look him in the eye, he noticed.

'Yes.'

'Why on earth didn't you come and get me? Is he still there?' Pulling her hat off, she hurried towards the wall phone.

'He told me not to get you. He asked me to give you a message.'

She spun around, looking intently at his left shoulder.

'It's a bit personal…' He glanced at the other sister, uncertain whether Pax would want her to hear it, however ludicrous. It might be a truth once removed, another man, an illicit love affair. She was a beautiful woman. There was all too often someone else involved; he should know.

'Alice, why not go over to the house and put the kettle on?' Pax suggested.

'Are you sure?' Alice eyed Luca fiercely.

'Absolutely.' Pax's eyes flickered guiltily towards Luca, and he realised that he might have known her less than twenty-four hours, but he almost certainly knew more of her inner life than her sister, from her decimated marriage to her drink problem.

She waited for Alice to go, staring at his ear now. Her voice shook. 'So what did he say?'

He repeated it word for word, including all three fuckings.

'Can you say that again?'

He did so, without the fuckings this time.

When she started to snort, he thought she was crying, and wearily went in search of some kitchen roll. She let out a weird half-wail, leaning against the countertop, which she slammed with her palm.

Luca hoped she wasn't about to get violent again. He'd just about had enough.

Cautiously, he edged beside her and offered the hunks of tissue across. She howled, banging the surface again.

He put a reassuring hand on her back. It shook beneath the thick coat fabric.

And he realised she was laughing. Was totally overcome with laughter. Breathless, she turned to face him, pressing her hands to her cheeks and slapping them to pull herself together. Her eyes gleamed. 'Oh God, this is so cruel, and I can't bear it that I'm laughing at him, I really can't, except...'

She was off again, her head bashing against her arm as she doubled over, dislodged hairclip releasing a sea of red curls. And there was something so infectiously liberated about her sheer joy, so unselfconscious, that Luca couldn't help smiling. It was like watching Beck earlier, the first few moments the stallion had been let loose in the round pen, when he'd turned himself inside out kicking up his heels and rolling before he'd frightened himself again.

'I'm sorry.' She struggled to regain her breath, wiping her eyes with the kitchen roll as the laugher finally abated enough to talk. 'And I'm so, so sorry that I shouted at you, and I know you won't forgive me, particularly as we really don't like each other very much and you almost certainly want to go to bed with my mother, which means I'm probably never going to like you, so you're quite the wrong person to share this with, but we have been through a lot today, you and me, so I might as well to tell you.' She took more deep gulps of breath, like a marathon runner who'd just burst through the tapes. 'I've just realised something.' The smile widened, golden gaze bright as harvest moons. 'I've just realised I'm free. I'm actually *free*. Thank you! I could kiss you.'

Her eyes gleamed, looking straight into his now, effervescent with happiness.

Luca swallowed, recognition dawning. He'd seen just that look on another face, on another continent. A face of someone he'd loved very much. He hoped Pax could hold on to her freedom. 'It must feel amazing.'

'It's like coming up to the surface after nearly drowning at the bottom of the ocean.' Her deep voice was still breathless. 'And I know my head will go back under the water many times, and that I have to swim against the current, really swim hard, and that I might drown again if I'm not careful, especially if I open a vodka bottle,' she gave him an apologetic look, 'but I've taken my first big gulp of air. Beautiful, sweet, fresh air. That's what it feels like.' She smiled, and it wasn't a teeth-bearing grimace. It lit up her face like a full moon, pale and pearl bright.

He nodded and smiled back. '*That* good?'

Their faces were too close. Their hands were almost touching. The smiles dropped away and he realised, too late, that he could picture himself as the stranger she'd kissed in the bar, the cheap quick thrill of it burning blood to his groin.

'I promise, Mack's totally incapable of killing anybody.' She looked down at their fingers, nail tips dark with molasses. 'Unless you count boring them to death about golf. If he caught us *soixante-neuf* on that sofa right now, he'd probably just tell you about the sixty-nine he once scored round Royal Dornoch.'

Luca laughed, but wished she hadn't planted the image. 'I'll watch my back.'

'Two death threats in one day, Luca.' She looked up brightly. 'That's just selfish.'

'Comes with being louche.'

He wondered for a moment if she was about to add a third. *Fuck this job up and I'll kill you.* She was so hard to read, the black humour counterpoint to the childlike realisation that she was free. Again, he was aware that, by circumstance, he'd witnessed something nobody else in her life would.

'I'd better introduce you to Alice,' she said, not moving.

'That would be grand.' He didn't move either.

She looked down at their hands again, head tilting, studying his rings: scuffed Claddagh, signet, eternity. 'We can show you where the flat is.'

He could feel the soft weight of her extraordinary hair brush against his cheek. It still smelled of last night's hotel shampoo. 'Thanks.'

'I still don't like you very much if it helps,' she said, turning briskly away, snatching up the crumpled kitchen roll to put in the bin.

It did.

PART THREE

10

The Bags were trotting at speed in their ongoing quest to burn off post-Christmas bulges, swerving around a clutch of oncoming runners with heads down and earphones in.

'Morning!' the riders greeted brightly.

The quartet weren't the only ones pounding along the local tracks and lanes on a January detox campaign. Almost a week into the new year, the Cotswold fitness tribe had regrouped – creased jogging bottoms, cycling shorts, leotards and trainers had been pulled out of the backs of wardrobes; iPod playlists filled heads with motivational beats; the recycling bins showed a noticeable drop in wine bottles.

This morning, with the local children starting back at school, the village was positively thrumming with recalibrated Fitbits. Spotting another kitbag on a passing car's passenger seat, Bridge sensed the Broadbourne gym might at least be too busy for mutual ogling with Ash Turner, the past week a gauntlet-run of sweaty eye-meets in mirrors.

'How's the job hunt going, Bridge?' Gill called over her shoulder.

'Sure, I'm taking my time to find the right fit.'

'To fit round coffee shopping and the running machine, you mean?' said Petra, and Gill laughed, making Bridge smart, especially when Gill added, 'Oh, to be a yummy mummy!'

'I am *not* a yummy mummy – which incidentally is TOTALLY last decade. I'm a flexi-tasking mammie seeking lifestyle balance.'

'You'll land your dream job, Ms "Chartered Institute of Logistics and Transport Office Manager of the Year 2015",' Petra pep-talked.

Bridge knew it had been a mistake to ask a novelist to look through her CV – which now contained fifteen adverbs and a lot of semi-colons.

Craic barged sideways past a desiccating Norwegian Fir dumped on the pavement outside Duck Pond Cottage ahead of Twelfth Night, its needles still sparkling with foil strands.

'Ride him forwards, love!' Mo urged.

'I never fecking look back, me.' Bridge maintained her sangfroid, stomach secretly churning.

What neither Petra nor Gill knew was that, later today, Bridge had an interview for the role of part-time office administrator at the village primary school. She'd sworn Mo to secrecy, anxious that she might be as overqualified for this as she'd been overeager for the last. For Job Interview Reloaded, Bridge would have to keep a cool professional head. Her mistake had been trying to run back up the career ladder instead of taking it one naughty step at a time.

As they trotted on up the short, sloped drag of Back Lane, she glanced across at her empty cottage, long since de-Christmassed, the blood-rush of relief to be outside in the fresh air wiping out the twitch of guilt that she'd dumped the kids with her sister-in-law.

'Sous Vide fired her first team of builders, apparently.' Petra pointed her whip at the village pub as they turned left. 'I hear they're so behind, the big opening might have to be candlelit. You had a lucky escape there.'

'Sure, I told Zuckerberg and Musk as much when they were fighting over my payroll skills.' Bridge held on tight as Craic took the scenic route in protest at the loud sound of power drills coming from The Jugged Hare.

The Bags made their way through the open gate to the set-aside field that ran alongside the Plumb Run orchards between Compton Magna and Bagot, and Bridge was grateful for the fast canter around the big strip of headland there, the wind loud in her ears, conversation impossible as she enjoyed Craic's thundering attempt to catch the bigger and faster horses ahead.

Not telling the Bags about the interview conflicted her. She felt a degree of shame she couldn't explain. It wasn't snobbery, she told herself, even though the job would be a significant step down professionally. The Bags would think no differently of her whether she ran the office of Unilever or Compton Magna C of E Primary. The problem was more that Bridge was, totally unexpectedly, nervous as hell. None of her friends or family knew how much her disastrous Suzy David interview had dashed her confidence; she might have turned it into a dine-off-it comedy experience, but it was one she threw up in secret afterwards.

The only person she'd told this to was Carly, their fledgling friendship another secret she was keeping from the Bags.

Go for it! Carly had messaged first thing, adding, *Unleash hell!* She was a big *Gladiator* fan, her life a Roman battle in domestic miniature. Carly understood how Bridge was feeling, that fulfilment was measured out in smaller scoops when life had shrunk into isolation behind the front door of a testy marriage and tiny children. And Carly was a pro at brushing away her own disappointment, claiming to be unbothered that she'd heard nothing back from Ronnie Ledwell at the stud. 'I don't work for nothing. Strength and honour, Bridge. I love doing it, but I'm not doing it for love.'

Bridge felt the weight of their enchanted New Year pact all the heavier. If only she'd cast the right spell. They needed jobs, not new love and orgasmic rainbows.

Conscience at her heels, she kicked Craic on, overtaking a surprised-looking Petra. She just hoped Carly didn't plan vengeance in this life and the next if she ever discovered her husband's starring role in the purple patch that had pepped up the Mazurs' sex life gloriously of late. Since Aleš's return from Krakow, Fantasy Ash had never been far from the master bedroom in the little cottage on Back Lane.

They'd made love every night, and twice on Sunday, a lusty record not seen since becoming parents. Now putty in his wife's hands, Aleš enthusiastically supported her quest to abandon her family for employment, loudly insisting that she need look no further than the village primary school and quoting one of his mother's favourite sayings: 'He who chases two rabbits catches none!' Despite going at it like rabbits all week, Bridge feared another Babcia Mazur adage was more accurate: *Jak sobie pościelesz, tak się wyśpisz* – you made your bed, now lie in it.

Aleš's customary post-Christmas homesickness for Krakow had been all too quickly joined by martyrdom now that he was back to working long hours on site, which meant more bear roars and backache snores. Last night's lovemaking had been noticeably one-sided. Half-awake afterwards, twisting the bedclothes between hot, guilty dreams about the village's war hero and nightmares about school headmistress Auriol 'Battleaxe' Bullock, Bridge had found herself making a pact with her inner devil – get this job and she would redraw the pentacle on the sitting room floor and kill Fantasy Ash.

Luca's bathroom had no shower, just an ancient tap mixer over its peach-coloured bath with perished rubber grips that kept blowing off, the water pressure intense this high up in the house, its temperature never more than lukewarm. Having managed a perfunctory wash before it turned ice-cold, then dragged on his riding gear, he pounded back down the rear stairs, munching on a stale breakfast muffin and swigging cold instant coffee as he went. Ronnie never seemed to need to stop to eat, mealtimes something she waited out for other people's sake, impatient to get on.

This morning, she wanted Luca to ride Beck. He'd argued that the horse wasn't ready, certain they'd have serious protests as soon as they left his comfort zone. Worked in hand, the grey stallion hadn't put a hoof wrong all week, already calmer on the yard and in the round pen, the stud's herd more familiar. Luca trusted his bravery, but it was asking the world of him to trust a man on his back again.

He hoped Ronnie would stick to her word and hold back at least another month from any public announcements about the stallion standing. For now, it felt as though the rest of the world was outside this place's bubble time warp, and Mishaal with it, but he had no way of knowing how long for. Whenever Luca's mobile phone was in signal, it registered multiple missed calls, although that wasn't unusual. His outgoing voicemail message remained deliberately vague. The stud's landline rang rarely, and almost inevitably for Pax. The debris of her exploding marriage was everywhere – the phone arguments, comings and goings, hastily wiped tears, and Ronnie's perpetual distraction.

As he hurried outside, the familiar klaxon was sounding again. Spotting Pax hurtling under the first stable arch, grey puppy and the old man's dog in her wake, he hung back in the courtyard behind the main house, watching the long legs sprinting across the arrivals yard in just a few deerlike bounds before she disappeared into the cottage.

The klaxon stopped with a rattling ping.

Hearing a growl behind him, he realised one of Ronnie's dogs had his boot heel in her teeth, eyes playful and white-rimmed, backside gyrating. The other, older one appeared a moment later and laid into his other boot.

He waited for Ronnie to follow. When she didn't appear, he headed back inside, small dogs growling at each foot.

She was in the kitchen, coat half on, phone pressed to her ear, blue eyes brimming. Hushing the dogs furiously, she hung up. He'd never seen Ronnie blush before, as unexpected as a wink in a royal portrait.

'Pax must have picked it up at the same time.' She adopted an indignant power pose. 'That *ghastly* man is so pompous. You know he—' She stopped herself. 'NOYB. Sorry.'

'Go on if it helps.' He was growing accustomed to life in the eye of Pax's marital storm.

'Mack's using his parents to—' She stopped herself again. 'No, it's not fair to involve you, Luca. Let's take that handsome chap of mine for a hack, shall we? Blow off the cobwebs.' She whisked past him, dogs trotting behind like ladies in waiting.

The Saddle Bags had pulled up at the opposite end of the set-aside field, where a second gate opened onto a grass track that led back past the old manor's garden walls to the Plum Run, Mo dismounting to undo the twine tying it shut, puffing heavily from her gallop.

'That'll have got your blood up for your interview, Bridge, love!' She beamed as Bridge passed.

Bridge big-eyed back: *What fecking interview?*

Thankfully Gill was in full flow, grumbling that Compton Magna Manor – just visible beyond its high honey stone walls beside them – was still lying empty a year after going on the market because no buyer was willing to pay several millions for a mouldering, impractical piece of history. 'Madly overpriced, with no land, listed up to its medieval oak-framed eaves – you'd think it would be perfect for some foolish celeb or banker.'

'Don't forget it's haunted,' Mo panted cheerfully as she wrestled the gate over thistles. 'The Woman Bricked Up in The Walls howls all night, every night, between Hunter's Moon and Frost Moon, they say.'

'I know how she feels,' Petra groaned, also breathless from the canter. 'Cabin fever is pure hell. I don't know how I'll survive the next few weeks, trying to keep the Gunns fully loaded while I stay locked in the garden shed.'

Petra wrote a historical trilogy a year, customarily retreating from village life between deadlines. The chestnut mare was having her shoes off later today and would be taking a sabbatical with her pony pals so that her mistress could devote herself to the second instalment of a Civil War epic.

'You need a mother's help,' Bridge said, an idea forming.

'Mum lives near Leeds.'

'Not your own mother's help, *a* Mother's Help. A Girl Friday who tidies the teenagers' pits and mucks out the horses, maybe does some school runs so you can work uninterrupted a couple of days a week.'

'That sounds heaven, but we can't afford it.'

Behind them, Mo clanged the gate shut, still chatting to Gill about village ghosts.

'A few hours a week is cheaper than you think,' Bridge told Petra, a chalk pentacle forming in her mind. 'Imagine writing uninterrupted, without worrying about changing the beds or washing skips full of sports kits. Imagine someone there to order the heating oil if it's low and make packed lunches, walk the dog and take over driving hundreds of miles taxiing Charlie and the children around?'

'Far too ruddy self-indulgent.' She was doing her chippy northerner thing.

'C'mon, Petra, you're trying to fit a full-time job around four children with no concessions.' Mo kicked alongside while Gill walked out ahead. 'Mo! Tell Petra she needs a Mother's Help.'

'Bloody good idea,' panted their red-faced friend. 'Especially with another little one on the way.'

'Whaaat?' Bridge gaped at her. Petra already had four and had to be mid-forties.

Petra pointed down at her chestnut mare. 'Gill scanned her yesterday: baby on board.'

'She's in foal,' Mo clarified.

'Why am I always the last to know these things?' demanded Bridge. 'Are you going to sue?'

When the notoriously hormonal mare had come unseasonally into season just before Christmas, Ronnie's hot-headed stallion had found her irresistible, the resulting public display of affection one the village would take a long time to forget.

'You're kidding!' Petra patted her mare's neck. 'It's equi-yoga and wellness all the way for my girl. This foal is going to be worth a fortune.'

'In that case you can definitely afford a Mother's Help.' Bridge refused to be deflected. 'Like Mo says, you need one.'

'Charlie already accuses me of being lazy.' Petra's apology smiled over her shoulder.

'Bollocks to that!' Bridge stood up in her stirrups. 'Charlie's never here; you say yourself that he treats the London flat like an Airbnb. You're an amazing cook, you manage the household budget, keep that huge garden under control, look after all your neddies, plus a delinquent dog and God knows how many chickens and even find time to listen to your mother calling to discuss *The Archers* for hours on end – don't deny it, you always fecking complain – *and* you've been hoodwinked into sitting on every charitable committee within a ten-mile radius.'

Mo backed her up: 'and lending a sympathetic ear to friends near and far.'

'Only because I nick your best stories for books,' Petra joked, but Bridge could see she was buying into it.

'How can you be expected to keep on top of it all whilst working flat out? You need help at home – you deserve help, you can't live without help.'

Petra's big brown eyes softened. 'Are you asking me for a job, Bridge?'

'Not me!' Bridge prickled with offended pride. 'I want you to give Carly Turner a job. Author's assistant, groom, domestic goddess, PA, occasional healer.'

'Oh, I like Carly. The house is ten times cleaner since she joined Janine's team.'

'So cut out the middleman!' she said triumphantly.

'Doesn't do to cross Janine...' Mo sucked in air through her teeth and tutted.

'Rubbish,' Bridge dismissed airily. 'Carly's been looking for something new for ages, Janine knows that. She does extra bits and bobs for you already, doesn't she, Petra?'

'Well, she's holding the ponies for Flynn today.'

'There you go!'

Mo chuckled. 'You sure you don't want to be a Girl Friday yourself, Bridge? We all know you'd love to hold something for Flynn.'

'As long as she can still be Aleš's girl Sundays through to Thursdays,' Petra laughed.

Already crabby, Bridge snapped, 'I'm my own fecking woman, thanks.' She ignored the phone in her pocket sounding off with her husband's custom message notification, a power drill that had once seemed funny, but now set her teeth on edge.

Carly's day had got off to a bad start, lack of sleep and an unwanted guest conspiring to fray her temper. Last night, while she'd been bathing the kids, Ash had shouted upstairs that he was off out with Skully, the door banging before she could reply. He'd come back in the early hours, his dead weight crashing into bed beside her, sleeping through every alarm a few hours later, even the Green Day track on Carly's phone that normally had him springing up as if under air attack.

Getting a fractious Ellis organised for his first day back at school, she'd found Skully asleep on their sofa, equally out for the count despite Pricey, the bull lurcher, clambering up to join him and Ellis prodding him with his 'Splorer Stick.

Now, having walked Ellis to school, left the other two with their nan and rushed back to the house to drop off Pricey ahead of her cleaning shift, Carly found Ash banging about in the kitchen looking for carbs and Skully still out cold.

'Where d'you two get to last night?' Keeping her tone light, she tidied up the kitchen surfaces as he covered them with breadcrumbs. However mad she was with Ash, she'd learned to always test his mood.

'Out Micklecote Way.' He was all yawns and seductively drowsy eyes, still puffy with sleep. 'Seeing a man about some labouring work.'

'Not till that late.' She fetched him a plate and knife, voice raised to be heard over the boiling kettle.

'We went to the Old Swan afterwards, then to some caravan up the other side of Drover's Woods with mates of Skull's. Played Fortnite. I messaged you, bae.'

She checked her phone now, last night's messages from him all bearing the same time stamp. 'At two in the morning?'

'There can't have been any reception up there.' He yawned again, pulling every jar out of the cupboard in search of the peanut butter.

She relented a little, realising his messages must have all been queued until they set off home. She put the jars back, then reached for teabags to put in mugs.

'You at college today?' She didn't like the idea of leaving Skully in her house while she cleaned Petra Gunn's house.

'Starts next week,' he was deep in the fridge now, 'if I go back.'

'You're thinking of giving it up?'

'Too many fitness trainers round here already.' Straightening up, he managed a crooked smile over the door, eyes heavy-lidded. 'I can earn cash now.'

'You've got to think long-term though, haven't you? Have a trade.'

'I trade these.' He held up his hands then slapped his biceps. 'Skully's got the contacts.'

'Is packing in college his idea?'

'Mine.' He swung the door shut and pulled her into a kiss that tasted of orange juice, only breaking away when his toast popped.

'I don't want you to pack it in, Ash. Not without a safety net.' Making the tea, she took a mug through to Skully, dumping it on the coffee table and shaking one skull-covered arm.

'Mm?' He didn't open his eyes. The reek of stale cigarette smoke, sweat and booze made her step back.

'I want you the fuck off my sofa and out of my house by the time I get back, understood?' she whispered.

'You sound just like the wife. Can't remember which one.' A big, broken-toothed grin broke out, his eyes still shut.

Carly could hear Janine's engine pull up outside, then a short toot of the horn, her little cleaning van fully loaded for a morning's waxing and bleaching.

Hurrying back to the kitchen, she found Ash applying peanut butter as thickly as mortar.

'Flynn'll be at Petra's later,' she told him. 'I can talk to him some more about the farrier idea, if you like? About you apprenticing?' She ignored another beep from Janine's horn, more insistent this time.

'I've told you, Flynn's a mate.' He scratched his fingers through his hair and she noticed the joints were red and scraped. 'You don't work for mates.'

'What's Skully, then?' she asked him, reaching for his hand, not dropping his gaze.

The horn outside beeped long and hard.

Her palms folded warm and firm round bruised knuckles, and she saw a muscle in his cheek jump in pain as he regarded her levelly, the sleepy sweetness gone, silver eyes armoured.

'*He* works for *me*. Now stop asking questions.' Kissing her on the forehead and pulling his hands from hers, he turned away to bite into his toast.

Janine was beeping furiously.

'At least let me talk to Flynn, Ash.'

'It's a free country. Talk to anyone you like.'

Carly grabbed her coat and bag, muttering. 'Just not you, eh?'

The Bags waited at the fork by the Green for the bus to drop a couple of pensioners at the stop before it edged its way cautiously past them with a hiss of air brakes that sent Craic bounding into reverse. The bus had an advert for a slimming club on the back.

'I'm going to get so fat, stuck at my desk,' Petra grumbled. 'This time, I'm digging out the *30 Day Shred* DVD Charlie gave me.'

'*OHM*!' The Bags' combined chant might sound to an outsider like a mounted Buddhist meditation, but OHM stood for Off-putting Husband Moment, from fat-shaming gifts to cutting their toenails in bed.

Petra laughed. 'It's the most exhausting sixty minutes imaginable, and I've only watched it once, lying on the sofa with a glass of wine.'

'You need one of them personal trainers,' suggested Mo. 'Why not try Ash Turner? He'd make you a good Roundhead for your book, all silent and brooding. Bet you wouldn't say no to a few burpees with him in your plotting shed.'

'Only if it's free.' Petra laughed. 'Maybe they'll do me a BOGOF if I hire husband and wife together?'

'He's not qualified yet,' said Bridge proprietorially.

'Petra could be his guinea pig,' Mo suggested.

'The Turners already have two guinea pigs, named Claudia

and Tess.' Bridge didn't want her fantasy stolen, and certainly not by Petra who was already casting her that milky-eyed, knowing look.

'How come you know so much about our village war hero and his pets, Bridge?'

She was spared answering as Craic sprang sideways, a small group of cyclists in lurid Lycra whizzing past, breathing hard. Also taking exception, Petra's mare skittered across the lane.

'Bloody mamils,' hissed Gill as the riders regrouped, her husband's cycling obsession having lent her a deep resentment of all road-hogging, shaven-legged men in knee-length stretch fabric. When the others looked blank, she explained, 'Middle-Aged Men In Lycra.'

The Bags loved their acronyms, especially Gill.

'What does that make us, love?' laughed Mo. 'Middle-Aged Birds In Breeches?'

'Speak for yourself,' snapped Bridge. 'I vote slits: sexy ladies in the saddle. Let's all rock Viv Albertine!'

'Is she in the Comptons WI?' asked Gill.

'We're Bags and always will be,' Petra reassured them. 'Bad Arse Gallopers.'

Exchanging smiles, they rose and fell happily in their saddles with togetherness and horsiness. It felt bewitchingly spring-like, the Gulf Stream blowing them along with unseasonal warmth, sunlight piercing the chugging clouds in a thousand places like a laser show.

Trotting alongside the Green, they were briefly distracted by the sight of the sexy new husband from Well Cottage out jogging, but their smiles froze at the sight of a Cossack moustache of Christmas growth.

'He looks like a 118 man,' Petra said disappointedly.

The Bags were great authorities on male facial hair.

Bridge's new-found sexual enthusiasm was already waning in the wake of Aleš's stubborn refusal to shave his, a subject on which vet Gill was more than sympathetic as they compared hirsute husbands, dodging more dog walkers and runners.

Gill's short, cycling-mad husband Paul was a long-term fan of face fur. 'I can't stand the way he scratches at it, like a nail brush. The sound sets my teeth on edge.'

'But at least Paul's is aerodynamically stubbly,' Bridge pointed out, waving a car past with a thank-you salute. 'It's a dusting. Aleš's Balbo's like a living creature.'

'What is a Balbo?'

'Robert Downey Junior,' said Petra, trotting alongside.

'Don't you start that old celeb thing again,' Bridge warned. 'I have to sleep with this man.'

'Johnny Depp.' Petra stuck out her tongue.

'Still not doing it.'

'Now I'm rather fond of a Shakespearean beard,' Gill said as they dropped back to a walk and funnelled from the Plum Run into Church Lane, the lychgate end double-parked with white vans and a scaffolding lorry, men in hard hats standing in the graveyard looking up at the tower.

'Aleš grooms that fecking thing on his face like a pet. It has its own personality. I've forgotten what his chin looks like, but I know sticky ribs weren't off the menu, and it felt better between the thighs.'

'I love a man with a beard down there,' Petra giggled. 'It's retro *Joy of Sex*.'

'Not if he likes you to be shaved smooth as a baby's arse, trust me. That's like setting a Schnauzer on an oven-ready chicken.' Bridge shifted uncomfortably in the saddle.

'Really, ladies!' Gill's eyes bulged. 'Someone might hear. This is the village conservation area.'

'*So* sorry – Labrador with a guinea fowl,' Bridge corrected in a hoity-toity voice, and Petra started snorting with laughter.

Hushing them, Gill stole an anxious look at the ornate

greenhouse recently constructed in the garden of The Old Alms Houses. It was steamed up, a figure silhouetted inside.

'What are you all gossiping about?' Mo had caught up breathlessly on the cob.

'Heritage glasshouses,' Petra said kindly. 'Kit Donne's a convert since Ronnie replaced his – look.'

'Lovely cold frames.' Mo admired it. 'And those finials are ever so classy.'

'Think the Bardswold Bolter pops in to see his seeds sprout?' Bridge gave Petra a leading look.

'She'll be far too busy with her Horsemaker,' she sighed.

The unexpectedly feral-looking Luca O'Brien had been spotted twice at a distance on Bag hacks, although frustratingly it seemed not even Petra had managed to get an introduction yet.

'He's far too young for her,' Gill scoffed.

'What is a big, wild beard like Luca O'Brien's called, Bridge?' asked Mo.

'A fecking mess?'

'A yeard,' Petra insisted excitedly, clearly entertaining another retro *Joy of Sex* moment. 'I can't believe I'm going into hiding just as *the* most exciting man arrives in this village,' she groaned. 'Charlie's in a permanently foul mood now he's back in chambers; I need a new crush to keep me company.'

Bridge guessed the Gunn marriage was uncocked again. On the surface, Petra's festivities might have seemed an enviably M&S Christmas advert affair, but the Bags all knew one another's home truths well enough to see that beneath all the tinsel and Tartan Stag sheets, Charlie and Petra Gunn wore emotional mittens and bobble hats. There was nothing lonelier than close confinement with a cold shoulder and the other cheek turned. It was no secret that Petra escaped into the plots of her racy bodice-rippers to compensate. She'd killed off the character inspired by Bay at the end of the last book.

'I'm going to make the Horsemaker one of Prince Rupert's cavaliers.'

'How can you write it if you haven't even met your new leading man?' Gill pointed out.

'I'll use my imagination. It's what I do for a living.'

'Wait! Can you hear what I can hear?' Mo gasped excitedly.

Hooves thundered in the distance.

'It's fate!'

They all stood in their stirrups and peered past the church yews and pollarded poplars and beyond the drystone wall at the far end of the lane where the church meadows swept up to the standing stones. There, two riders were silhouetted romantically on the brow of the hill, sexily slender and well-balanced.

'That's Monique Austen and her groom,' Petra identified, the Bags all slumping back in their saddles disappointedly, suspecting that Bay's dressage-loving wife – who rarely left the luxury of her arena – was out scouting for the new arrival too.

'Let's ride past the stud,' Gill insisted, waving them into action. 'Mohammed is going to the mountain. Trot on!'

'Bagsy me ride up the mountain first!' Petra was already in trot.

'Then tie the mountain up and have your wicked way with him,' muttered Bridge, wishing she'd applied some more Sudocrem to her beard-ravaged privates as Craic bounded in pursuit. At least scouting for the Horsemaker took her mind off her job interview.

'It took *eight* messages to get you to ring me back, Pax!' Alice complained.

'Sorry, Lisp,' she whispered, 'you know the signal here. You could have tried the landline.' Her sister loathed calling that in case she got their mother.

'Where are you?' Alice was demanding. 'You sound like a spy.'

'Up in the stables tower. There are bat droppings everywhere, plus a pair of binoculars and a notebook. I think Pip Edwards used it as her lair.'

'Is she still AWOL? You must tell me *everything* that's been happening. How's Luca O'Brien settling in?'

'He keeps himself to himself.' Pax was grateful for it. For six days, they had successfully avoided looking one another in the eye, being alone in the same space or addressing more than half a dozen words to the other.

'Not strong and silent like Lester, surely?' Alice sounded surprised.

'Less of his mettle.' Whereas the stud's old stallion man wasn't afraid to stand up to their mother, the new arrival did as Ronnie said, smiling all the while.

'Well, the old boy does now have titanium hips,' her sister said drily. 'I thought Mother's golden boy was all brass neck when I saw him, shouting the odds.'

Pax didn't want to dwell on the feed-room argument Alice had interrupted. She'd said some unforgiveable things.

'He's just snappy, like all lapdogs.' She picked up the binoculars and trained them across the yard where Luca had Beck cross-tied in a standing stall, bandaging his stamping, cow-kicking legs. He was already under Ronnie's cosh, just as Pax would be if she didn't take daily evasive action. One of the reasons for sneaking up here to call Alice was to avoid being legged-up onto Lester's cob to ride out. 'He's clearly besotted with Mummy.' She knew it shouldn't bother her as much as it did.

'Men always swoon at Mother's feet,' Alice scorned.

The stallion let out a bellow as Ronnie led out her retired eventer, Dickon, with a clatter of iron on cobble. A scrawny thoroughbred the colour of a scuffed oak floor, Dickon was as laid-back and kind as Beck was explosive and combative.

'Is it mutual?' Alice was asking.

'Shh, I'm listening.' She craned forwards. 'The new stallion's not been ridden in years and Mummy has just said, "Don't be so wet, once around the woods is just what he needs." Luca might be about to join Lester in an orthopaedic ward.'

'Good.'

'Wiser to wait until this place is in better shape first. Wish broken bones on Mack instead.'

'Don't tell me you're still giving him the cold shoulder?' Alice lectured. 'That must have been quite a tiff.'

'*On the Twelfth Day of Christmas, my True Love gave to me, grounds for a Decree Nisi,*' she sang flatly, binoculars still raised, watching the stallion humping his back as a saddle was lowered onto it.

'It's nice-*eye*,' her sister corrected. 'Is that what Mack's been giving someone else. Or is that the glad eye?'

'Nobody gives the glad eye any more, Lisp, they sext. And there's nobody else involved in this, unless you count his bloody parents.'

Alice was having difficulty grasping the gravity of Pax's marital problems. 'Don't tell me doughty Muir and Mairi still bear a grudge because you refused to wear the Forsyth sash at the Royal Caledonian Ball?'

'They want him to seek sole custody of Kes.' Her throat caught. She was grateful to Knott who came to lean hard against her side.

Now Alice was taking her more seriously. 'Tell them to bugger right off!'

'It's not that simple.' Kes adored Granddad and Nana Forsyth – who he'd recently taken to calling 'Grandforce' and 'Nanaforce' like superheroes – and Pax had no desire to poison that bond. All this was affecting him deeply. And while she found it maddening that her in-laws were policing the five-year-old with strident overkill, she realised they represented much-needed stability. Added to which, Pax's personal history made treading on eggshells the only way forwards. 'I don't want a fight, Lisp.'

'We're an old military family, we all fight. Good idea to set up temporary base camp at the stud. You sit pretty and keep an eye on Mummy until she pushes off.'

'Mack's parents insist Kes being here is a health and safety risk,' Pax told Alice. 'The trouble is, he's totally unafraid of horses. The moment my back's turned he's in with the yearlings or cosying up to a mare in foal. But he's stayed with me in the cottage just one night since coming back from Scotland.'

In what appeared to be a well-planned coup, Muir and Mairi had called round first thing the following morning to offer to 'take our wee man to his favourite wildlife park' while Pax helped on the yard. Twelve hours later, after leaving a stack of panicked messages and driving back and forth between the Comptons, their locked bungalow and a deserted Mack Shack, Pax finally received a call to say Kes had enjoyed a wonderful day and was fast asleep in their box room, so best he stayed there. It had established a pattern; another Forsyth family jaunt took place the next day. Today's outing was on a steam train. They were maxing out the Tesco vouchers.

'For God's sake don't let Mother put Kes on a pony,' said Alice. 'We'll never get rid of her if she thinks he's the next family protégé. When does he go back to pre-prep? That'll square things up.'

'Next week, in theory, but Mack's told them Kes isn't returning.' He and the headmaster were exchanging increasingly angry emails, with Pax caught between, loyalties torn. While Kes had yet to settle happily in the tough, old-fashioned little school at which Reception pupils were hardened off with cross-country runs and choir practice, Mack's proposal was far worse. 'The Forsyths are already packing to go back to Scotland, saying he'll be educated there.'

'Apply for whatever emergency hearing one does to get a custody ruling in these situations.' Alice was straight to the practical solution. 'Tell them Mack wallops you if you have to; everyone knows he's a thug; I'll back you up.'

Pax watched the puppy curled up warmly against her, innocent in sleep, his slim grey-whiskered face folded in his huge paws.

'Mack's never hit me, Lisp.' Bullies like her husband broke spirits, not bones, all too often shrouded in I'm-doing-this-for-your-own-good morality. 'It won't come to that,' she said, closing her eyes and praying. 'It's typical hot air, like telling me I'm fired from the business. Our life and our work are still here. Mack can bang on all he likes about Scottish divorce laws making it hard for me to bleed him dry; right now, all I'm asking for is a simple separation agreement naming our son's primary residency with me.'

'At the stud?'

Hearing the self-interest loaded in the question, Pax waited for its sting to soften. 'Not for long. I'll rent somewhere. I'm looking at new schools this week, seeing one today in fact.' She sounded a lot calmer than she felt, the panic that bubbled up around Mack's threats never far from the surface. 'The village primary school here.'

'Good God, Pax!' Alice sounded shocked at last. 'I had no idea it had come to that. You're off the juice, I take it?'

Again, Pax let indignation subside. Outside, her mother had mounted Dickon and was clattering around impatiently while Luca tried to find a girth long enough to fit the stallion.

'High and dry,' she told her sister through gritted teeth. Without Kes at home, the only way she'd maintained it was going to bed at teatime to read gripping thrillers, sweating through the need for Scotch, battling to focus on whodunnit and why she cared.

'Well, I hope your solicitor's good.'

'She is.' Straight-talking, refreshingly upbeat and also a mother – her daughter went to the village school – Helen Beadle worked from her attic office with such tenacity that

Mack, predictably, had sneeringly dubbed her Hell On Call. 'She's more softly-softly than *his* grand inquisitor, and her track record's good in disputes over children.' It was on Helen's advice that Pax hadn't kicked up a fuss about Kes's day trips and sleepovers with his grandparents. 'She says Mack's doing himself no favours, freezing the joint bank cards and changing locks. My clothes were dumped in bin bags at the end of the drive here yesterday – Mummy's horse spooked at them and almost went under the postman's van. Then, apparently last night, Mack put a rant up on Facebook accusing me of everything from bankrupting the company to shagging his best plasterer.' Social media was the deep, dark woods to Pax – ironically, Mack was the one who'd talked her out of it, claiming it was full of predatory paedophiles and lifestyle envy – but friends had told her, and it stung like a wasp swarm. That he'd later deleted it was no comfort. 'It could be worse, apparently. Revenge porn or suchlike.'

'Good God, is that a thing? Please tell me you haven't...'

'I don't think pictures of me sunbathing in a bikini in Cornwall count.' For once, Pax was grateful for their unadventurous, uncatalogued sex life.

'If you ask me, it all boils down to money. Supposing Mack has divorce in his sights, he'll be after maximum return on his eight years; bad PR devalues your stakehold. There's the stud to think about now, Pax. He's an acquisitive sod, let's face it.'

'He's in bits, Lisp.' Pax was shocked. '*I'm* the one calling time on our marriage.'

'Don't you *dare* feel guilty,' Alice snapped. 'You're telling me he wants to take your son away from you.'

'Well, he won't get him!' She'd barely slept more than three hours strung together all week, more weight dropping off, anger chasing blame around in circles as she paced the cottage's small rooms. She'd never imagined it would all happen as quickly as this, but Mack had always been knee-jerk. Often without the knee.

'That's the spirit!' Alice applauded. 'Mack's just hiding behind his parents like most big girls' blouses.'

Grateful for the rallying cry – even if it did sound more Blyton than 'Fight Song' – Pax caught sight of her mother lounging in the saddle like Nancy Astor, urging Luca to hurry up as he put a bridle on the leg-lashing, sweated-up Beck. Witnessing Luca's predictably compliant smile, she felt a fresh spike of exasperation. 'Mack's an entire clothes rail of blouses, Lisp. He's even accusing me of sleeping with Luca O'Brien. I'm more likely to run over the man. All bloody men in fact!' She let out an angry growl then ducked as Ronnie looked up.

Her sister snorted on the phone. 'Of course, the quickest way to get rid of him is to out-ride him. Men hate that that.'

'Buy a motorbike, you mean?' She had a vision of herself in full leathers snarling past Mack's sports' bike at 100 mph on the Fosse Hills.

'No, out-ride this Horsemaker-on-the-make. You can do his job, darling. Make him redundant.'

There was a furious clatter of hooves on cobbles and she peered out to watch Beck prancing across the yard to be mounted at last, her stomach tightening involuntarily. He looked half wild.

Pax had to hand it to O'Brien, he was up in the saddle before the stallion knew what was happening.

'Nothing ever stood in your way when you rode for the stud,' Alice pep-talked.

She watched Luca sit out a couple of huge bucks and ride out through the arch after her mother. With his helmet brim low as a visor and Puffa zipped up over his chin, he looked like a black knight.

'I'll pick my own battles, Lisp.'

Her first was with the muck heap, descending into chaos in Lester's absence. If she couldn't roar back to the Mack Shack to drive the tractor over her shit of a husband, the next best thing was flattening his namesake.

'I'd lay money on you and Mack being back together again by Valentine's Day,' Alice predicted. 'And you'll see off Luca before that.'

Bridge sang 'Holding Out For A Hero' in a flat, sardonic undertone as the Bags trotted up the bridle path beside the stud like guardsmen, all heads looking left across its paddocks to the stable yard.

'Movement nine o'clock!' Gill held up her hand and they all pulled up to look.

A tall figure was driving a tractor with a bucket on the front, reshaping the muck heap into steps. The red hair was unmistakeably Pax Forsyth's.

'Our lady of the manure,' Bridge muttered, remembering Carly saying the woman had looked straight through her.

'Now she's your classic Demelza Poldark,' Mo sighed.

'I prefer my fictional heroines buxom,' Petra dismissed.

'Good technique on that hydraulic lift,' Gill admired. 'She must be helping out while Old Lester's laid off.'

'Thought I'd seen that Noddy car of hers in the village a lot lately,' said Mo.

'Still making calls to her Chipping Norton-set lover from lay-bys, then?' Bridge scoffed.

'Why don't I know about this?' Petra was agog.

But the Bags were distracted by Mo letting out an excited squawk as, in the far distance, two riders crossed the track, heading towards the woods on the hill's brow.

'That's him!' Gill pointed out a flash of blond beard that looked fittingly Royalist.

'Be still my beating heart,' Petra breathed.

Bridge had to admit there was a certain nobility about the Horsemaker's upright stature and the way he remained so still while his horse, a magnificently wild-looking grey, bounded along on springs. Riding three lengths behind, neat as a jump jockey, Ronnie's distinctive petite frame was crouched low over a wiry bay.

'They're using Sansom Estate headland to cut across to Poacher's Woods,' said Gill. 'That can't be Ronnie's warmblood stallion he's riding, can it?'

'We can go up to the ridge, loop around and meet them on circular track.' Mo had her blood up. 'That's no stallion, Gill love.'

'I *am* a vet.'

'Bet you two shepherd's pies and a game casserole.'

'Raise you a vaccination and a box of bute.'

'You're on!'

Off they cantered, hammering along the deep tyre ruts, splashing through puddles and kicking up stones, the view spreading out in all directions the higher they climbed.

'Isn't this a bit sad act, hunting the poor man down like stalkers?' Bridge shouted at Petra as they set off after Gill's ground-eating gelding, Mo falling behind already.

'You know Gill loves the thrill of the chase,' Petra called back.

At that moment, Craic took exception to something in the hedge and kinked sideways, cannoning off Petra's mare and stumbling down on his knees. Pitched forwards, Bridge was then smacked firmly on the chin as he scrambled up, her lip caught in her teeth. She could taste blood.

'Great.' She wiped it with the back of her hand. 'Just what I need before an interview.' Lisping at Mrs Bullock through red foam.

'You have a job interview?' Petra demanded.

Bridge tried to close the question down with a non-committal hum, grateful for Mo reappearing between them on her cob, less so when she shrieked, 'Oh my good lord, what happened? There's blood!'

'It's just a nick.' Bridge felt her lip with her fingertips, and realised it was bleeding quite a lot.

The three riders set off again, Craic pogoing fretfully from rut to rut, impossible to get back into a canter.

'Try lowering your hands and softening your contact, Bridge,' Petra suggested kindly. 'What job interview?'

Bridge, who found being told how to ride by Petra only slightly less irritating than being quizzed by Petra about her employment status, sucked her sore lip, which already felt the size of a wrasse's, glowering at Craic's grey ears. 'It's just a fecking job, okay?'

Mo tutted. 'You want to watch your lip, Bridge.'

'I'll fecking swear if I want to!'

'Your *sore* lip.' She smiled kindly. 'It's going ever so swollen.'

Bridge reached up and touched it in alarm. Still bleeding, it did feel very odd.

Craic had planted again, head shooting up. A rustling from the trees beside them made him shoot sideways. Then he gave a loud, alarmed snort as Gill came thundering back down the track.

'There you are!' she hissed urgently, turning at speed like a polo player. 'You owe me three suppers, Mo, it's definitely the stallion. I just spotted them from the ridge. They're still at the far side of the woods, keeping off the main tracks. I think we need to clear off.'

Picking up the urgency, Craic needed no more invitation, setting off at full tilt.

'Oh feck,' muttered Bridge, realising she had no brakes whatsoever. And they were heading straight for the woods.

Sitting on Beck felt phenomenal. Luca had forgotten the feeling of exaggerated, quick-thinking movement, a rocket engine one could only hope to control by building co-operation and confidence. He'd ridden thousands of horses in his lifetime, and only a very few of them possessed anything close to this purity of power.

'I could watch you ride all day, Luca.' Ronnie had been buttering him up from the moment they rode off the yard to keep him onside. 'Didn't I tell you he'd settle?'

'Sure, he's happy enough.'

He'd quickly learnt that as a boss Ronnie had fixed ideas about things, along with a short temper, impetuosity and a boundless enthusiasm. With no riding arena at the stud and the fields midwinter-slippery, her method was the old-fashioned one of getting on a raw horse and riding straight out at a brisk trot, sticking to hedged tracks and woodland so he had too much to think about to want to turn tail or escape into open country. Beck was unfit and unshod which also made him less inclined to bolt for home.

Despite his protests, in his heart, Luca had wanted to ride the horse again as much as she wanted him to.

On his toes and eager to go forwards, Beck remained amazingly light in the hand, all his disciplined German training still at Luca's fingertips. Stiffer, admittedly, and understandably tense, but less argumentative than Luca had anticipated given all the bad riding he'd endured. It would be self-aggrandisement to imagine Beck remembered his rider after all these years, but Luca sensed he recognised the technique, the quietness of seat and contact.

But Luca was all too aware that he was sitting on a ticking bomb, and Ronnie's unswerving belief in them both made him uncomfortable, as did any interest in Beck's past.

'Did you ride him much in Germany?' She was still admiring them.

'For four or five years on and off.'

'Oh, I wish I'd seen that. I bet it was arena porn. No wonder he sold for so much.'

Upbeat and chatty, Ronnie was no fool, aware of the secrecy surrounding Beck's sale to the Middle East and his inglorious return, that hurried, dust-storm cover-up. The deal to spare him the bullet made each answer Luca gave feel like a step along a ship's plank. Luca knew his silence could be the only thing keeping Beck safe.

'Ever jump him?'

'At home, setting him up for big competitions, you know. This one got pretty uptight on tour.'

'Like Keith Moon?'

'Who's Keith Moon?'

'The Who's Keith, yes.' She laughed and he looked at her curiously, growing accustomed to the private jokes that she dangled half a generation out of reach, cat to mouse. But Luca was no mouse, as those who mistook quietness for timidity knew to their cost.

'The horse was unpredictable, explosive. Ruled out of home teams.'

'Thank goodness he's such a survivor. He spent some time as a field ornament before coming here, so perhaps he's had time to clear his head. My friend Blair bought him for his wife...' She paused, looking away so he couldn't see her face. 'Verity's an absolute darling, a brilliant horsewoman in her day, but she's very ill now, and, in hindsight, already was then. I did him a terrible disservice agreeing to it.' It was unclear whether she meant Beck or Blair.

A pheasant flapped squawking out of the undergrowth so close that even old Dickon shied back, but Beck – already so overwhelmed by everything that each muscle was hinged tight – merely turned an ear.

'He's a donkey,' Ronnie teased.

'Give him time,' muttered Luca. History had taught him that a horse as sharp as Beck wouldn't tolerate shock and awe tactics long. His father Malachy, a horse dealer all his life, was fond of the old saying: *You can tell a gelding, but discuss with a stallion*. This felt dangerously like dictating terms. But Ronnie was the boss, and history had also taught Luca you underestimated her at your peril. The old saying ended, *and you ask a mare*.

'What makes you so sure this horse can turn the stud's fortunes?'

'*We* are going to turn them, Luca. All of us.' The blue gaze held steady.

Hers was a Charge of the Light Brigade hot-headedness which refused to countenance failure. With the stud's fortunes clearly galloping into cannons, Luca needed to address her battle plan: from what he could tell, she seemed to be fighting both for her family and against them. He needed to find a way to penetrate her antique varnished Englishness. But oh, what an oil painting he'd landed in. Looking across hibernating fields, curled around a sleeping goldmine, it was hard to imagine the war being waged here.

'May I ask you something?'

'How formal.' Ronnie gave him a knowing smile. 'Which must mean you're going to ask something awkward, wayward, bedward, or all three.'

'That would be far too forward, so it would.' Luca spun, his timing lousy, the stallion tensing, sensing his rider's disquiet, the imperceptible bond breaking.

'Oh *do* be forward. Say what you're bloody thinking.' Her eyes glittered beneath the hat peak, catching the flirtation and playing with it. The cat once more.

'Ever thought about selling up?'

The glitter disappeared. 'Why would I?'

'Your kids want that, don't they?'

'Pax doesn't.'

'But she doesn't want to run it.'

'Doesn't she?'

He didn't want to talk about Pax, muttering vaguely, 'She's enough on her plate.'

'She never has enough on her plate! She hardly bloody eats.' The good-humoured despair in her tone masked deeper feelings, regret so close to the surface, it was impossible to hold her gaze without feeling sucked in. 'She used to love the stud, the land, the horses. Daddy had her lined up to be his successor. Entirely my fault it didn't happen. I let her down so badly.'

'When you left?'

'When I came back.' She sighed. 'Do you think we should sell it, Luca?'

Beneath him, Beck was balling up, back shorter and tighter, ready to spring. Pax's words rang in his ears again: *You have absolutely no idea about our family!*

He shook his head, tossing the question away with a smile. 'Forget I asked.'

'At my age, that's entirely probable.' She dangled one of her flirtatious, age-gap hooks, sharing the smile.

'Sure, age means nothing; it's how grown-up you are that counts.'

'Oh, I do like that. Now I want no more mention of selling anything but horses. We *must* sell horses, Luca.'

Relieved, he suggested instead that he start educating the thoroughbred three-year-olds, eager to get going on those bred at the stud with the class to make her money fast. 'They look plenty ready.' The comforting simplicity of breaking young horses was a much-needed one.

With a dismissive wave of the hand, Ronnie explained that she'd entered them all in the Doncaster sales later that month. 'They're Oak Hill's last crop, so Lester thinks we'll get a decent price, even at this time of year, and it's fewer for you to break in.'

'Cancel the entries. I'll make you more money from them.'

'It's a quick turnaround – and cashflow is a little tight.'

'Why d'you ask me here, Ron, if it's not to do what I'm best at?'

'We have some nice youngsters earmarked for you to start.'

Luca said nothing, although his body stiffened imperceptibly with displeasure, and the stallion snatched at the bit and shied at a shadow.

'I just wish we could get Pax back in the saddle,' Ronnie was lamenting. 'I can just see her towing little Kes round the lanes on a lead rein, can't you? Wouldn't that be heaven?'

Luca was thinking the opposite, when a switch tripped beneath him.

He felt Beck spring-load long before he heard anything. He seemed to grow six inches, the crabbing trot exaggerating to passage, his whinnying bellow feeling like sitting on the main amp in the O2 Arena during a rock guitar solo.

Then they heard the hoofbeats.

Moments later, three women came flying along the track on horseback as though riding a racing finish, one on a hairy grey pony, its white eyes bulging, another kicking along a huge bay as she tried to head off the first. Not far behind them, the third woman on a chestnut was shouting at them both to pull up.

Beck was already up on his hind legs, slamming back down and trying to pull the reins out of Luca's hands as he plunged sideways, head shaking.

'Put him behind me!' Ronnie rode off the track to make space for the galloping lunatics.

But Beck had no intention of letting them pass. Whinnying again, he lunged forwards.

Luca knew in an instant that all communication had gone, sitting through a twisting, turning series of explosive bucks. He might as well be on a tiger's back.

With another screaming bellow, Beck reared up again, striking out at the approaching horses in warning as he did so. The woman on the bolting grey let out a shriek and both pony and rider disappeared into the trees.

The bay pulled up sharply ten metres away.

The chestnut mare at the rear had other ideas. Letting out a squeal of recognition, she tossed her head and flattened her ears indignantly. Moments later, she was throwing her own series of twisting bronco disco moves that deposited her rider on the track.

'I'm fine!' the woman gasped and sprang up with a nervous laugh.

Pitching himself against the stallion's neck as he reared again, Luca fought for balance. The chestnut mare was still trotting towards them, ears flat back, furious at such a machismo display.

'Get that horse caught!' Luca shouted, startled by her behaviour, the kamikaze bravery of a pissed-off alpha mare. Her owner was equally foolhardy, running in pursuit, face beaming.

'Don't worry,' she shouted cheerily at Luca. 'They've already shagged.'

But as the mare drew closer, skipping this way and that, the whites of her eyes glinted with malice and her rear end pivoted around ready to deliver a sharp reminder of girl power.

Luca hauled Beck away just in time to miss two hard-rammed, metal-rimmed hind hooves punching through the air towards them.

At this, the stallion landed back on all fours and every one of his vertebra seemed flex and click like knuckles as his back bunched up and his head flew down.

'Oh shit!' Luca could guess what was about to happen.

11

Bridge had parted company with Craic whilst travelling at speed, thanks to a low tree branch swiping her into a holly bush like a golf ball into the rough. The pain was up there with the third hour of labour, and she was mortally offended the little sod didn't wait for her, tanking back off instead in the direction of his cob friend who was still trotting through the trees to catch up with them.

As she scrabbled out of the bush, her skin ribboned with cuts, Bridge heard Petra scream further along the track.

Limping to her aid and battling through the veil of skeletal tree branches, she could just make out the big grey horse Luca O'Brien was riding going bananas.

'Holy feck!' She stumbled closer. Scrambling out on the track, she found herself near Gill on her high horse.

'*That* is why I said we go the opposite way.' Gill was frozen with disapproval.

'How can he sit on that?'

The grey stallion was putting on a rodeo display, head between its knees, twisting around in gravity-defying leaps, dodges and lunges while the mare flicked her back legs at him in a short, bad-tempered barrage.

Like a centaur fused with his equine half, Luca followed each stomach-churning rotation, moving with the furious horse. Beck was up on his hind legs again now, almost vertical, then spinning and bronco-ing again, a blur of twisting tonnage, seemingly determined to shake off both his female assailant and his rider, head snaking out, his teeth sinking deep into the mare's red neck.

Squealing in outrage, Petra's mare backed away.

The stallion charged at her, his course only diverted by his rider's seemingly superhuman strength, turning his head like a stunt horse.

Now, instead of sitting passively, Luca kicked him forwards, starting to circle in bounds and leaps at first, urging him onwards, fingers moving like a pianist on the reins, his hands speaking to the horse's mouth, telling him to listen, to get busy, to get to work, his body so perfectly weighted that the stallion had no choice but to stay beneath this light-seated counterbalance of a man who knew exactly where they were going. There was ten metres at most between the lines of trees, but after three jagged loops, his circle started to look symmetrical, the horse's head coming down, his ears flicking back and forth, and within a few more dizzying rounds his black-eyed concentration matched his black-coated rider's, only a letter box of handsome face visible between hat and collar.

'Bloody hell.' Mo panted up to Gill and Bridge, leading Craic. 'You'll not see the likes of that every day.'

'You will on YouTube from now on.' Bridge was videoing it excitedly on her phone. 'This is so going viral. What a fecking brilliant rider.'

'Never seen a mare attacking like that,' Mo clarified. 'Look at Ronnie's face!'

Standing up in her stirrups with Lawrence of Arabia eyes, she was shouting at Petra to 'bloody well catch that bloody mad mare!'

'She's nuts, that one,' Bridge agreed.

'She's got the hots for him,' Gill said drily.

'Are we talking about Ronnie here?' queried Mo.

'The horse of course! Classic wild instinct.'

'*That* was flirting? Talk about treat 'em mean.'

'I used to flick boys I fancied in class with my ruler,' sighed Mo.

'Do you think she was telling him off for getting her up the duff?' suggested Bridge.

'Breaking the news, maybe,' Gill conceded. 'She's a very strong-willed mare.'

'It's like *Jeremy Kyle*,' chuckled Mo.

Looking grudgingly impressed, the chestnut was trotting back towards her friends with Petra in hot pursuit. Behind them Ronnie dropped her reins and clapped as Luca rode back to her, her big blue eyes bright as speedwells. The Bags distinctly heard her purr, 'Let's get out of here.'

Swinging his head to watch his redheaded attacker retreat, the stallion stopped four square and bellowed before the Horsemaker turned him quickly away.

'He fancies her back,' Gill huffed. 'Brazen!'

'Their foal's going to be beautiful.' Mo patted her hot cheeks.

'I meant Ronnie, this time.'

The Bags' collective jaws then dropped to see the Horsemaker touch his fingers to his wool-muffled lips and hold them up.

'Is he blowing a kiss?' Bridge whispered, angling round for a better view.

'Saluting her with one, I think.'

'He's like a medieval knight,' Mo sighed dreamily.

'Now *that*,' breathed Gill, watching them ride off, 'is flirting.'

Walking back towards them, having caught the mare, Petra fanned her face. 'What a nightmare! No need for ambulances, thank goodness, although you're looking a bit *Kill Bill* there, Bridge.'

The other two women turned to her with a collective gasp.

'God alive,' Gill leant closer, 'what broke your fall? Edward Scissorhands?'

Looking down, Bridge realised there was blood all over her yellow high viz. 'Is it that bad?'

'You might need a bit of extra make-up for your interview, love.' Mo tried to sound reassuring.

Gill was less so. 'You have an *interview* with a face like that?'

'No make-up will cover that,' Petra predicted.

Bridge felt her face, gashed lip swollen like a wasped plum now, great bramble slices on her nose, cheek and forehead. Hurriedly switching her mobile phone's camera to selfie, she let out an anguished cry. Something from a horror film was staring back, skin lacerated with blood-jewelled strings of scratches, lower lip distorted into an obscene trout pout.

As they remounted and headed back along the track, desperation rose in Bridge. 'There must be something I can do? Gill. You're a vet. What can I use?'

'A paper bag?' Petra suggested.

'Well, there's fibrin sealants, I suppose – wound glue – which might close it all up neatly enough to put foundation on, but I wouldn't advise it.'

'I'll take it!'

'I can't let you have any, it's completely unethical.'

'Sod that, I'm a fecking mate.'

'The veterinary one has blue dye in it. Go to the minor injuries unit in Broadbourne.'

'There's no time. We waited four hours last time we were there and *still* got sent to Warwick Hospital. And that was just for a towel rail burn.'

'Apparently, if you rub cocaine into wounds, it's like ET's finger,' Petra said informatively. 'Instant healing.'

'No kidding? And where would I get cocaine round here – Great Compton Village Store?'

'Surely a rock-and-roll woman like you has a stash?'

'You need Lee Welch,' Mo told Bridge.

'Who?' One ear was bleeding too, she realised. She was lacerated.

'Skully, they call him. Can't miss him. Covered in tattoos.'

'Forgive me, Mo, but tattooing my face to hide this is way too extreme.'

'He's the local dealer; he'll get you sorted.'

'Bridge is *not* buying cocaine,' Gill squawked. 'I'm shocked at you, Mo.'

'I was talking about the wound glue, love. A lot of the travelling crowd Skully mixes with won't go to doctors. They call him the Medicine Cabinet on account of the fact he's nicked that much from dispensaries he's better stocked than Lloyds. My bet's that wound stuff gets used by all the bare-knuckle boys.'

'Bare-knuckle fighting?' Petra was agog. 'Round here?'

'There's a lot of honour in it for gypsy families.' Mo gave them all a wise look. 'Big money too. Turners been doing it for years. Skully patches them up afterwards like a regular cosmetic surgeon.'

Gill was peering closely at Bridge's face. 'It looks worse than it is. That lip's going to keep bleeding on and off when you talk or eat, but the rest will all scab over very quickly.'

'What's Skully's number?' Bridge demanded.

None of them had it.

'Okay, we all know this job's going to be high flying and cancelling isn't an option,' volunteered Petra. 'So tell them you had a bad day doing voluntary work clearing brambles from landmines.'

'In the Cotswolds?'

'Canals, then.'

'Or tell the interviewer the truth, maybe?' Gill suggested.

Bridge couldn't shake the mental image of herself rolling up at the school to meet Auriol 'Battleaxe' Bullock with blood splattered over her best white interview shirt, looking like she'd just been mugged by someone wielding a bike chain. If she cancelled this close to the interview, she'd never get a recall. Illogically, she now wanted this job more than life.

'You know her, Mo,' she mopped up more blood as it dropped on her tabard, 'your kids go there. Will she buy into the heroic horse fall thing, d'you think?'

Mo pulled an apologetic face. 'Mrs Bullock's more of a cat person.'

'You could say your cat did it?' said Gill. 'I've had colleagues look worse after a routine worming.'

'Hang on! Mrs Bullock, you say?' Petra had just sussed it. 'My tennis club friend's chair of Maggers' PTA and says the woman's totally batshit amazing. They all adore her, but Helen's convinced the governors are in collusion with the LEA to close the place because it's safeguarding chaos. The children love it there. It just needs legitimising. Bridge, you are magnificent. I might have guessed you'd seek something like this, a quirky challenge out of altruism rather than financial reward.' Her dark, wide-set eyes looked genuinely enchanted.

'Yeah, I'm woke like that.' Bridge sat up taller.

'What a super thing to want to do,' agreed Gill.

'That's what I've been telling her.' Mo looked pleased, pink face beaming.

Bridge wanted to cry. 'Anyone have a paper bag?'

'God, those women!' Ronnie growled as she and Luca rode home. 'If they can't control their bloody horses they shouldn't be allowed on bridleways. Petra's a chum, but a very daft one. I'll call her out about this later.'

'It was Beck that overreacted.' The eyes behind the smile were fixed. 'He did the same thing in a warm-up arena once. Almost killed his rider too.'

'That chestnut mare's the one he escaped to before Christmas. Comes into season all through winter, apparently. Total menace.'

'She's violent, dominant, a natural running mate. She's attracted to him.'

'In the wild, maybe. As I keep reminding you, this is the Cotswolds.'

'You're saying being sex mad and cycling all year round isn't normal here?'

'Put like that...' She laughed, grateful for his easy forgiveness. Even at her most tenacious, Ronnie had the sense to know when she'd misjudged a situation, and today was one such. Luca was right: if Beck needed to work to keep his mind happy, it must be reintroduced slowly. Manageability around mares was non-negotiable.

'You still think I'm mad standing him at stud, don't you?' She looked at him.

'I think it's dangerous,' he said, his face guarded.

'The bloodline's flawless.'

'There's bad blood, sure enough, but it's not in his veins.' He ran a hand along the curved crest of Beck's neck, its silver mane as glossy and even as a fifties curtain fringe.

'In his past?'

'Horses are no different from us – some find it easier to forgive than others. Beck's just not the forgiving sort; all that instinct, too much mishandling.' He zipped his padded collars higher. 'We need to worry about what he does now, not then.'

She held his eye, both unsmiling now, mutually aware he knew more about the horse than he was letting on. Lester had said as much, dropping dark hints left, right and centre like Miss Marple in a hospital gown, dosed up on hunt gossip and Dick Francis.

They rode on in silence for a while, low sun dancing through the bare tree branches swaying and rattling around them.

The stallion let out a furious, spine-shaking whinny, calling to his distant herd at the stud.

'Was it you he almost killed in the collecting ring?' It occurred to Ronnie with a jolt of horror.

Luca shook his head.

'Who then?'

He took too long to answer, with a deliberately nonchalant shrug. 'Young lad with all the gear and no idea; they never got on. He's as tough on his riders as he is on his mares, this one.'

'You wouldn't think it to look at him.'

The stallion, hopelessly unfit and exhausted from his tantrum, was soft-eyed once more, ears flicking back each time his rider spoke, telling Ronnie about a boss he'd worked for who made him ride her horses in for two hours before she'd get on. They really did look splendid together, reminiscent of the glossy picture plates from her parents' coffee table bible about the horse in portraiture which she'd pored over in lonely adolescence: George Washington on Blueskin, Napoleon crossing the Alps – truthful alongside the ruthless – Van Dyck's King Charles I and V – one monarch as arrogant as the other was moral. All the horses grey. All beautiful. None more so than Beck with the scarf-masked ninja on his back, soothing him all the while.

'He likes you a lot more than most, I think.'

'I'm easy to like.' The smile crossed between them again, Luca's mouth buried beneath his coat collars and scarf, but creasing the corner of the green eyes.

Ronnie wasn't so sure it was as easy as it had once been. He had more layers to him these days, and not just winter padding; it made him harder to read, shaded in with subterfuge and a lot more anti-social.

She thought back to the impish, flirtatious young man in Germany. That Luca never stressed or needed sleep, riding like Bellerophon into battle. He'd followed her round like a puppy, fiddling late into the night while they all drank and made merry. Now he bore the scarred signs of a romantic fugitive: over-working all day, holed up silently in the attic flat like a legionnaire setting up camp by night. So like Pax, who went to bed at toddler time if the dark windows of the stables cottage were anything to go by.

At least the stud's unofficial curfew was saving electricity, she reflected bleakly. They were all tucked up with lights off by nine.

Her own solitary bedtime ritual, a prolonged indulgence of bathing and reading, music and radio, sprang from many long years as a mistress. Family, guests and men got terribly in the way of it, although she missed them like mad when they weren't around, a contradiction she'd never matched up.

Blair remained incommunicado in Wiltshire, still in possession of her horsebox. Somewhat against her better judgement, she'd succumbed to impulse with several bright and breezy texts, the most recent of which said, *Bring my box back!* with five smiley faces. The returning silence spoke volumes. Blair had admittedly never been a big texter, but still…

Ronnie got more chat from Lester than any of them right now. Bored in hospital and obsessed with the minutiae of institutionalised care and his recovery, he was as talkative as she'd ever known him. He'd also discovered the Internet thanks to a neighbouring patient with an iPad. The old stallion man's enthusiastic online research into sports horse bloodlines had thrown up all sorts of information he was eager to share with her.

'Lester googled Beck's breeding,' she told Luca, noting the way his eyes sharpened. 'He's new to search engines, so he read an awful lot about German pianos before he found anything interesting. He did show me a piece about him being sold before the London Olympics.' She and Lester had almost fainted when he'd read out the price rumoured to have been paid for the horse. 'Did you ever meet him, this crown prince who bought him?'

'He's just an ordinary prince, I think. There are seven thousand of them out there.'

'Cuts down on kissing frogs, I guess.'

'Especially with polygamy.' The smile flashed over his zip tag.

Ronnie caught it like a yawn. Oh, that smile! So full of

after-hours promise. He might be getting early nights, but she had a shrewd suspicion he wasn't sleeping much. After her own nightly analgesia of bath, Bowie and reading, she'd sent up more than one prayer that he'd smile at someone his own age. Flirting with him was far too easy.

'I do think wives should be taken one at a time, don't you?' she joked now. 'Even if they're not one's own.'

He didn't answer, eyes still sharp.

Was she married, Ronnie wondered, this woman who had left a crack in the playboy's heart? She let it go for now. Experience had taught her that it served little purpose to dredge up a bad past with men or horses. Better to motivate them to succeed, these creatures of need and greed. With confidence, they focussed unswervingly forwards.

They'd reached the gate from the bridleway to the stud's rear farm track. Stretching down from the saddle to enter the bolt code, she caught Luca watching her backside.

'We must introduce you to some of the local set,' she said as she waved him through, Beck calling to the herd again. 'I can't hog you all to myself.'

'I'm good, thanks.'

'Pax needs to get out too,' she said as she turned Dickon to close the gate, realising too late it sounded like she was setting them up. Over her shoulder, the luminous green gaze had dimmed.

'Like I say, I'm good thanks. I'm sure Pax would rather be spared my company.'

'What is it with you two?' she grumbled. 'I know she's impossibly stressed and it's not always easy to know how to handle it, but if you talked to her occasionally it might stop me wanting to fall on my pitchfork.'

'I work with horses, Ronnie; I don't do backchat.'

'I've seen dozens of downtrodden girl grooms blossom under your friendship, remember?'

He gave a gruff laugh. 'Never worked with you, did it?'

'I was already in full bloom.'

'You're a whole bloody rose garden.' The eyes creased again.

'Watch out for the thorns, Luca.'

They were riding back onto the yard now, hooves clattering loudly on cobbles, Cruisoe and Beck shouting angry greetings at each other. She looked around for Pax whose car was still there, but there was no sign of her.

'I'll be out for the next couple of hours,' she called to Luca as she jumped off. 'Lester's new ward has all-day visiting, so I'm nipping in this morning. That way, I'm here when Pax brings Kes back. She might need moral support.' Running up her stirrups, she forgot her vow of discretion. 'I hope you'll be all right holding the fort? Keep an eye out for Pax? Remember to be nice?'

When she turned, she found he'd already disappeared into Beck's stable. She led Dickon across to look over the door, watching him untack. 'Petra has a Shetland that might suit this chap as a companion. I'll ask. After what happened today, she owes us one.'

He took off the bridle, the stallion springing to the back of the box to hug against the wall. 'I'd rather she lent us her mare.'

'You're not serious? There'd be a bloodbath.'

'I disagree. She'd be good for him. I've seen it done before on yards, pairing a bolshy mare and stallion off-season. Sure, it's tricky to start with, but the results can be spectacular.'

'I'll ask for the Shetland.' Ronnie had never heard of anything so ridiculous. 'Perhaps Kes can learn to ride him? Now be nice to Pax, Luca, or I'll make you give pony lessons.'

Carly liked cleaning the Gunns' house which was full of books, quirky *objets d'art*, family photos and high-tech gadgetry. The latter inevitably kept Janine distracted, usually a blessing, but today Carly wanted to quiz her about Skully and his hold over Ash.

As usual, Janine was taking a very long time to clean the kids' playroom, a Tardis of consoles, screens, surround sound and interactive smart technology. 'All the static makes for tricky dusting,' she excused.

When Carly marched in with a mop and bucket to tackle the floor, she spotted her sister-in-law's phone docked to download the Gunns' latest music and movie collections, Janine's meticulous console-button cleaning having 'accidentally' switched on the Nintendo, on which she was now 'accidentally' playing.

'What is it Skully does to make his living?' Carly asked, sluicing Dettox.

'Matter of debate,' Janine deflected, eyes on the ninety-inch curved screen where a cartoon redhead wearing unfeasibly large trainers was covering opponents in colourful goo, in a game of superannuated digital paintball.

Knowing the best way to engage her was in combat, Carly picked up a second controller and joined in. Years of close proximity to Ash playing snipers and felons had lent her a cruel assassin skill, a dragon tattoo away from psychopath. Janine's little redhead was splatted in seconds.

'Why d'you do that?' Janine squirted the screen with Mr Muscle bad-temperedly.

'You were telling me about Skully?'

'I wasn't, but if I was, I'd be telling you not to ask.' She whisked off to dust a punchbag.

Carly mopped her back against the wall, boxing her in with two leather sagbags and a triangular floor cushion. 'Why not?'

'Just trust me on this,' Janine sighed, spider's leg eyelashes chorus kicking. Then seeing Carly's killer face, she relented. 'He's harmless. Good man to have in your corner.'

Carly stared her down. 'What does he want with Ash?'

'What's anyone want with Ash?'

'You tell me.'

'A piece of him.'

'He'll get a piece of my mind first,' Carly fumed, letting Janine dart away to feather-duster the light fittings.

'Skully's got his knuckledusters in a lot of pies,' she relented. 'But it's mostly protection work, I think. Bodyguards, doormen.'

Carly's phone vibrated in her pocket before she could corner her with the mop again to demand to know more. Reading the incoming message, she let the mop handle drop. 'So what would someone like Bridge Mazur want Skully's number for?'

'Contract killing,' Janine breathed. 'Everyone in the village knows that big Pole of hers throws his weight round. One call to Skully and he disappears – like that!' She snapped her fingers, long talons flashing.

Janine deadpanned so well, Carly took a moment to see through it.

'Either that or she wants his inky body.' Janine gave her a who-cares? look.

Sucking her teeth, Carly mirrored it back. She knew when there were secrets being kept from her. But whose? Bridge might be a new friend she'd only met for coffee twice, but they messaged non-stop and she'd never come across as someone who would want to make the acquaintance of a local villain known best for fighting, fencing and fleecing.

Everything OK? she messaged Bridge.

A big smile emoji and a thumbs up came back. *Looking to price some turfing.*

Not in January, thought Carly. Not unless she was burying a body in the garden. She stepped outside to call Ash. 'Skully still with you?'

'Long gone.' She could tell he was fibbing.

'I need his number, then.'

'Why?'

'Favour for a friend.'

'Who?'

She felt a fresh layer of misgivings settle. 'Bridge.'

'What's she want?'

'Usual reason someone would want Skully.' It was a familiar game, shadow boxing around a bluff, pretending to know more than she did, hoping he'd let something slip.

But the only thing slipping was Ash's finger across the screen button, cancelling the call with a quick 'okay.' A few seconds later, he sent through a vCard for Skully which Carly forwarded to Bridge with the warning: *Don't leave him alone in your house.*

'Helloooo!'

Carly pocketed her phone and Janine went into dusting overdrive as Petra burst in, dressed in mud-stained breeches, carrying mugs of coffee for them.

'Forgive me! I went straight from my ride to the plotting shed. Had to get some ideas down. Everything all right, ladies?' she asked distractedly, hurrying towards the stairs, then swinging back. 'Carly, I need to talk to you about something later. Are you still staying on to help?'

'As long as you're okay for me to fetch my kids first? Their nan has the chiropodist coming.'

'Mum's got bunions the size of wine gums,' Janine elaborated.

'How lovely…' Petra wasn't listening, gazing instead at the huge multicoloured chandelier they dreaded dusting, a gift from her publisher in her heyday. 'I have got *the* most sensational hero for the new book,' she breathed. 'I can't wait to lock myself in a room with him.'

'Bit of a Christian Grey, is he?' Janine asked eagerly.

'*Much* sexier.' She pulled out her phone to show them. 'My hacking buddy just WhatsApped this.'

'Oh!' Carly baulked at the sight of Bridge with a fat lip.

'Sorry, that's the selfie she took after a disagreement with the love of her life. Check this one out.' A clip of a rider on a bronco-ing white horse started playing.

Carly pretended to watch, her mind racing, her hands immediately throbbing. Bridge had told Carly that Aleš didn't want her to go back to work, that she had a job interview today; their rows were legendary and Aleš was huge and scary-looking.

As soon as she was alone, she called Ash. 'This thing with Bridge wanting Skully's number, maybe you should check it out?'

'Don't worry, bae. Whatever it is, he's not going to be interested. See you later, yeah.'

'Wait!' She stopped him ringing off this time. 'I think her other half might have clocked her.'

'That's their business.'

She thought back to Bridge, the frustrated stay-at-home-mum in a onesie, casting a spell to break them both free from closing the front door on dreams and ambitions. It's not like that was really going to happen. Carly still had a bottle of bleach in one hand, a bucket in the other and a husband in a bad headspace. When Bridge had told her that she had an interview at the school, she'd just as quickly dismissed it as 'low grade enough to preserve Aleš's ego'. Nothing changed round here.

'Walk on by, why don't you?' she told Ash. 'Look the other way. It's not like you're serving queen and country any more. Just yourself.' She rang off angrily.

Having examined her face in the bathroom mirror at length – the cut on her fat lip was a blackened mess around proud flesh, the scratches across her cheeks and forehead pure horror film – Bridge knew that even if she dropped today's job interview, Aleš would take one look at her and bar her from riding again. It had to be worth getting a ballpark price from Skully the Medicine Cabinet, at least.

His phone was answered within a ring, the reception making it difficult to be understood, his evasive manner more so. 'You've got the wrong number, love,' he laughed when she'd asked if he had surgical-grade fibrin sealants.

Bridge explained again, seriously doubting the wisdom of this. 'Like you'd use after a fight, you know? To close a wound.'

'What d'you say your name was?'

'Bridge Mazur.'

'Never heard of you.'

'Please, Skully. I really need your help. I live in the village. In Bagot. I'm a friend of Carly Turner.'

'Hang on.' The phone was muffled, a conversation going on his end, a bark of angrily exchanged words, then he came back to her. 'You Flynn's neighbour, yeah?'

'That's right.'

'Been in a fight, have you?'

'You could say that.'

The phone was muffled again, another exchange, quieter and more urgent this time.

'You at home?'

'That's right, but I need to go out in a couple of hours. It's really important I don't draw attention to the cuts.'

'Wait there.' He rang off.

Immediately regretting the call, worrying she'd plunged herself into an underworld racket that could leave her scarred for life, Bridge took a quick shower before pulling on joggers and a fleece, hair turbaned in a towel ready to style later. Her face looked even worse scrubbed clean. If ever there was a day she needed her sister's magical make-up skills it was now. She took a selfie and sent it to Bernie. *Help! Urgent advice. Job interview in 2 hrs.* Checking the clock, she remembered it was the middle of the night in LA.

WTF? Bernie had predictably not yet gone to bed.

Disagreement with a tree. Someone's suggested surgical glue? FaceTime me NOW.

The video call was still ringing through when there was a knock on the door and a tall, big-shouldered shadow moved behind the small glass square.

'I've changed my mind!' she called through the letter box, finding herself talking to a denim crotch, fly buttons excitingly bulging. 'Sorry to waste your time.'

'Open the door.' The voice was husky, local and familiar.

She pulled it open on the chain to find Ash Turner, hoodie up, silver eyes darting from her face to the shadowed room behind her.

'Delivery service.' He held up a small tube of liquid. 'You alone?'

'Skully sent you?'

'The wife thought you might be in a spot of bother.' His pale grey eyes ran expertly across her face and then, brows lowering, he looked past her into the shadows of the house. 'He's gone, has he?'

'Who?'

'Your other half.'

'He didn't do this!'

He obviously didn't believe her. 'Kids here?'

'At my sister-in-law's.'

'You going to let me in?'

She could hear her sister's voice coming from the phone on the table, demanding to know why she was looking at the beamed ceiling. 'Bridge! Hello! Don't tell me you've fecking fainted?'

'Tell me what I owe and you can just give me the stuff.' She told Ash.

'You'll make a right mess of that pretty face if I do. It's like superglue. You need me to do it.'

'And you'll do a better job, will you?'

'See any scars?' He lowered his face closer through the gap. Silver eyes level with hers, his skin bronze smooth. He smelled of soap. Thump, thump, thump went her shameful heart.

Bad, bad spell.

'You'd better come in.'

*

Having taken out her latent aggression first on the muck heap and then the rug room's neat, towering columns of ancient jute – why did Lester never throw anything out? – Pax had lost track of time. While she'd marked those to be burned, she'd heard returning hooves, her mother's clear bell of a voice – 'Be nice to Pax, Luca, or I'll make you teach pony lessons!' – and later a car driving away. Trying not to let her pride corrode her calmness, she was reminded why solitude suited her, far from the steam of winter horse breath, sweet-scented muzzles and the shifting percussion of tens of legs through straw. Because horses brought comfort, and comfort made her feelings come alive, and she didn't want to feel anything. Feelings hurt right now, from the sting of false friendship to the acid attack of a wronged husband.

'*Bloody, bloody, bloody man!*' She caught herself hissing in time to her rug-folding and stopped.

Feelings were dangerous today, catching her at her most premenstrual, volatile and vulnerable. Because as well as making Pax lose control so that she shouted and cried and forgot to be kind, feelings brought with them the familiar soul-soaked need for a drink, her reflex comfort, even this early. They drank *caffè correcto* at daybreak in Italy, beer with breakfast in Belgium, raised Pimm's glasses to toast the first on course at Badminton, so why not here? Her grandfather had always argued that the sun was over the yardarm somewhere in the world, hip flask brimming before dawn autumn hunting. Pax's first drink had been at a meet, cherry brandy or blackberry whisky or some such sweetness that had given her the pluck to tackle hedges the grown-ups quailed at. By the time she was competing in Young Riders' teams, she was well-accustomed to downing a vodka miniature in the back of the horsebox before each phase: the first to relax one's dressage, the second to get the eye in showjumping, and the third made one fearless across country. They'd all done it, even Lizzie who got legless on a flute of Buck's Fizz. But Pax was the one who couldn't stop, who had ridden her dreams off a cliff.

Returning here so many years later, with liberation from a deeply stale marriage, came a sharp clarity of thought that was migraine-harsh at times. Talking to Alice had stirred a hornets' nest of memories. There were too many long-buried regrets at the stud, the desire to seek the pure white simplicity of a fresh start overwhelming. Horses were in her past. Putting her foot back in the stirrup, as her mother advocated, would just mean riding into trouble again. She wasn't sure how much longer she could bear it here.

The sooner she and Mack thrashed out some practical arrangements the better. Solicitor Helen was reassuringly on that case, although her firm advice was to stay put. It was she who had quietly recommended the village school as 'the Bardswolds best-kept secret'. On paper, Compton Magna C of E Primary was perfect: sweet and much-loved, its classes smaller than any independent pre-prep in the area, a big emphasis on play. Pax had booked an appointment to look around it that afternoon, but as the time drew closer, she found herself dismissing it, telling herself that it was too uncomfortably close to her mother's reach, that it wouldn't be able to cope with Kes's aggressive anxiety, that Mack would no more allow it than she would let Kes attend school in Scotland. Antisocial belligerence gripped her. She could stay hiding here instead of going. Or have a drink.

I'm out of my marriage, I can do what I bloody well like, she thought rebelliously, which wasn't strictly true, but it made her feel momentarily elated. Whilst still never quite matching the giddy high of liberation she'd felt in Lester's cottage kitchen on New Year's Day, the daily doses of random euphoria were a much-needed Yang to the guilty, fearful Yin. She'd experienced happy headrushes doing the most prosaic of tasks from brushing her teeth to making a cup of tea, daily rituals that she now performed with an occasional jolt of recognition: I'm free. For all the hell she faced dismantling and rebuilding her own and Kes's lives, she was finally free.

Getting up from his temporary Witney rug bed with a squeaky yawn and a back-kick stretch, Knott trotted to the door and looked back at her over his shoulder. The bright, innocent expectation in his dark eyes reminded Pax of Kes – the young expected their seniors to know exactly what they needed. She pictured her son on his first day in Reception just a few months earlier, swamped by his old-fashioned oversized uniform, trusting and excited as he put his hand in hers, the mother who'd already known in her heart that it was the wrong place to send him, that the draconian discipline Mack favoured would terrify him, that he deserved so much better than this prescriptive childhood born of a terminally ill marriage.

Despite her twenty-five-year head start, Pax still craved wise elders of her own who knew what she needed. In childhood, that had been her grandparents and Lester, always so decisive and capable. Later it had been Tim, the dashing big brother all grown-up in his London flat. Never her parents. Pax had no experience of close parenting until becoming one herself, and by then she'd turned gratefully to Mack as her wise voice in all things, already a father twice over. For most of her adult life, it was Mack who told her what she wanted and needed, what to do. Without him, she felt rudderless, uncertain if she trusted her own judgement, the wild elation flip-sided with a sense of being utterly lost. At her lowest, she wanted to phone him and ask him what to do.

Knott whined again.

'You're right,' she told him. 'He won't pull the wool over our eyes any longer. I *will* see this school.'

Emerging from the dusty mildew of vintage horseware and breathing fresh air gratefully, she noticed her mother's car missing and felt a tick of guilt.

Lester.

Pax hadn't been to visit him yet. Somehow the intimacy of living among his possessions made it hard to face the reality of seeing him out of context, the layers of neat order, leather and tweed stripped down to cotton pyjamas and reading glasses. It was easier to imagine things as they had been years ago, when he'd been fast on his feet, always in control, and as reassuring to have around as Dr Who or Robin Hood. He was the wise elder she had outgrown.

In turn, Lester saw in her a legacy she could never match up to. He saw her mother flying around Badminton, her father leading hounds and riding hell for leather around the Wolf Moon Lap. He still saw what she could have been, not who she was.

Knott shadowed her heels with his grey ears inside out as they crossed through the brightly sunlit stable yard and beneath the arch. The wind had picked up with bitter breath and Pax cursed the lack of a hairclip, red tresses buffeting like seaweed. It badly needed a wash. If she was quick, she'd have time for a shower.

A horn beeped, a familiar horsebox making its way up the drive. Her heart plunged like a pond pump into cold, muddy waters, simultaneously sinking and pounding. Her mother's lover, Blair Robertson had borrowed it, she remembered. Now he was returning it, and she was the only one around. She could hear the quad bike in the far distance; Luca delivering hay to the field feeders.

Pax hardly knew the Australian rider, apart from watching him hold up medals and trophies on television, but his legendary volatility made fielding him alone an unwelcome prospect, especially given that the only previous occasion they had met – apart from the fleeting, bad-tempered greeting on the day she'd arrived with Luca – was at her grandfather's funeral. Quick to defend Ronnie against her children's hostility, he'd ended up hurling insults at them over the coffin.

Handsome as a polo player, Blair had been Lizzie's eventing pin-up when they'd competed as juniors together. Pax, a devotee of Blair's great rival Hugo Beauchamp at the time, had spent long hours arguing her man was the better rider. How fiercely they'd defended their idols, claiming ownership of these married older men. Given her mother's track record, Pax should have guessed Ronnie would end up bedding at least one of them.

Not that Blair was showing any signs of leaving his wealthy wife. For all Alice's dark warnings that he was eyeing up the stud as a base, Pax knew their mother's on-off lover was a business ally they couldn't afford to lose.

Smoothing her mad hair, Pax waited while Blair parked in the yard with a hiss of brakes, the smell of cigarette smoke curling from the cab as the door opened and he jumped out, all swagger and animated brows, a craggy cliché of brawn, the wide smile disarmingly friendly.

'How y'doing?' He kissed her cheeks, stubble cuffing her skin, her red curls whipping his face. 'Brought your mum's wagon back. She here?'

'Not right now.'

His lips drew back with a click of regret. 'Just my luck.'

'She's visiting Lester in hospital.'

'Old boy's doing great, I hear.'

No doubt her mother updated him in seductively furtive calls.

'He's on the mend.' She glanced down at her watch, hoping Blair had arranged transport home.

'I would have called, but…' The sentence was briefly suspended in a smile no less white than Luca's charm defensive, but considerably more lopsided and ironic. 'I like the element of surprise.'

'Is a folding bicycle your next one?'

'Come again?'

Pax's hair was all over her face again as she struggled to

hold it down, inadvertently spitting out strands as she spoke. 'I'm running late and can't give you a lift anywhere, I'm afraid.'

'And there was me expecting bed for the night and home-cooked grub.' Gravel-voiced with sarcastic amusement, he reached back into the cab for a brace of wine bottles. 'Here – peace offering; I was warned you're a chippy cow.'

'By whom?' she bristled, crossing her arms and trying to shake the hair off her face.

'The chippy cow you inherited it off.' The big grin flashed up again; he and Luca should really have a smile-off. 'It's all right, I'm not hanging about. I'm needed in Wiltshire at four. Do you want a tail bandage?'

Her hair was up her nose now and fanning around her head like helicopter blades. Damn this wind. She edged towards the cottage. He followed, still holding out the wine bottles like two guns.

'Luca might drive you to the station if we can find him,' she offered, glancing over her shoulder in time to see the smile harden.

'I've a lift coming, thanks.' He squinted into the wind. 'Your neighbour's just bought a Percy horse off me.'

Surprised, Pax pulled her hair back with her hands. 'Why not buy direct from us?'

'This little mare's one of the four-year-olds I took home last autumn,' he said, placing the wine on the cottage doorstep like milk bottles, dropping the lorry keys alongside. 'He says his wife fell in love with her in the field. Amazing place they've got. Huge bloody arena.' His eyes trailed past the crumbling Cotswold walls to the stud's soggy paddocks and round pen. 'Sort of place your Irish horsebreaker fella's more used to, I reckon.'

His tan, deep even in midwinter, emphasised the whites of his eyes, dark lashes as long as his temper was short, irises the same deep pewter grey as Knott who he now stooped to greet. He was just Ronnie's type, ultra-masculine and uncompromising.

Alice dismissed Blair as a gruff chancer living off the

patronage of rich older women but Pax, who had witnessed his heroic talent as a sportsman closer-up over many more years, wanted to like him for Ronnie's sake.

He straightened up, grey eyes crinkling against the sun and wind. 'Tell Ronnie thank you,' he paused for a beat, 'and that I'm sorry to miss her, yeah?'

As throwaway and gruff as the words were, Pax sensed their weight, her heart thudding. To love with such self-restraint must be terribly hard. Who was she to judge infidelity? She'd wished herself in love again a thousand times since marrying.

'Of course.' She reached for the door handle, torn between the polite obligation to invite him in to wait for his lift and the overwhelming desire to be alone with her thoughts. Over the wind, they could just hear the quad bike in the distance.

'Is that the new guy?' Blair's head turned to listen.

'Why not go and say hello while you're here?' she suggested overeagerly. 'He'd love that!'

Blair's expression darkened, the smile a degree colder. 'Yeah, why not?'

He trudged off.

Turning quickly back to the cottage, she stopped short as she saw the bottles of wine on the step. Two grenades attached to the trip-wire between her, a shower and much-needed hairbrush.

Just leave them out here, she told herself firmly. If you take them in, you'll be tempted.

But the thought of a glass of wine, right now, just one small glass, kept her rooted to the spot, staring straight at the enemy. Sweet fruit. Temptation.

'Tell me what to do?' she whispered, seeking her grandparents, her father, Lester, Tim, Blair, *anybody's* voice that knew what she had to do.

Still she stared, felt her tongue soften and curl as it imagined the red wine's kiss, her quickfire heart sinking deeper in its cold water, devoid of guilt. One quick drink to steady the nerves. She started to reach down to pick them up, and then it came to her, like a chorus in her head, as certain as a favourite piece of music. She knew precisely what she must do.

Turning tail, she fled back under the arch. Blair was already at the far end of the second yard, not noticing her diving away to the right and sprinting across the cobbles.

Lester's cob looked up in surprise when she pulled open his door. Much neglected in the past week, he whickered with pleasure at the company. His neck was just as she remembered it: hard, soft, stubbly, velvety, warm, sweet, salty, solid, everything familiar. The comfort of horses. Feelings overwhelmed her, choked her, stole all sense from her except one. She was safe here. She was safe right here.

Luca was heaving a bale onto the quad bike rack when he heard the engine stop. He looked up to find Blair Robertson leaning against the seat, the whites of his eyes and teeth bared in his handsome leathery face, nose broken by fist fights as often as horse falls..

'How you doing, mate?' He thrust out a hand, voice like a lion growl. 'Sorry we didn't get to meet properly when you arrived.'

Smiling warily, Luca shook it firmly but found his fingers crushed, the Claddagh taking another dent.

'Settling in okay?'

'I'm good, thanks.'

'Yeah, I know you're good.' He laughed gruffly. 'We have plenty of people in common, you and me. You've got a lot of admirers, mate.'

Still smiling, Luca sensed an exception.

'I had a ring round when Ron said you were coming here. She's always lousy at chasing up references.'

'Fine by me.' He waited.

'You sure as hell have pissed off the Flying Maple Leaf.' Blair clicked his tongue, drawing in a pointed breath.

'Seems so.' His old boss in Canada had even called the stud here to say that he'd shoot him if he ever came back.

'Says you let him down badly, that you were like a son to him then threw it all back in his face.'

'I worked my full contract. Didn't miss a day.'

'Christ alone knows how you stuck it out, mate. The man's a fucking sadist.'

Luca looked at the craggy face in surprise.

'You had an affair with Maple Leaf's daughter, yeah?'

Luca sucked his teeth. More than that. A decade more than that. 'Yup.'

'Mate, I wouldn't ride one of that man's horses without his written permission, let alone a member of his family. How come you're even still *alive*?'

'I ride too well to kill.'

With a soft laugh, Blair clicked his tongue again, his eyes hardening. 'Not if you let Ronnie down, you don't.' He thrust his hand out again.

'Understood.' The Claddagh took another pasting.

'I'm glad we've talked.' Blair turned away, squinting at the blackening horizon, gaze scanning the fields. 'I didn't think I'd like you, mate, but I've never heard old Maple Leaf so mad. Made my day. Worked for the crazy bastard myself when I was just starting out. Takes a brave man to defy him.'

Luca smiled despite himself.

'You still hung up on the girl, mate?'

The truth was still somewhere in between, hung out to dry, a slow crucifixion.

'You could say that.' It was as close to it as he could venture. And it satisfied Blair, who slapped him on the back then set off towards a wind-scudded field in which a group of woolly youngsters were huddled together by the feeder, one golden deserter charging up and down the far fence showing off to the older horses in the neighbouring field.

'Now come and tell me how I get Ronnie to sell me a leg of this little colt!'

'I don't even remember your name,' Pax whispered gratefully, a moustache nuzzling her neck, 'but I think I love you. Thank you. I must go.'

Lester's cob stood stoically for a farewell hug, far too well-mannered to search her pockets for treats, although unable to resist ramming his cheekbones against her arms for a thorough face rub, hay slobber scatter-gunning.

Hurrying out, Knott stumbling sleepy-eyed after her from his straw nest, Pax knew she'd be late if she didn't leap straight in her car like Daisy Duke. She'd just have to brazen out the mad-haired, hay-scattered, red-eyed look as part of the act. As she sprinted across the yard, the two stallions trumpeted her along in stereo, and she felt infinitely cheered. The comfort of horses. It was almost better than vodka. Almost.

She could hear another engine approaching along the stud's long drive, too throatily diesel to be her mother's. Please let it just be the postman, she prayed as she ran underneath the arch, hit by the full force of the wind. Let loose again, her red curls spiralled up, whipping round overhead like a lasso which she scraped sideways to watch a Land Rover Defender snarling its way into the arrival yard far too fast, Bay Austen at the wheel.

The comfort of horses bolted away. It was too late to run inside and hide. Engine cutting, he jumped out, all expensive tweed and turned-up collars. 'Pax!'

Why did her stomach hollow so instantly? 'Hello, Bay.'

Unlike Blair's affably grating greeting, Bay was a smiling, smooth-shaven charm assassin, armed with a welcoming kiss that could stop a weaker heart. Placing a manicured hand on her arm, his mouth swooped straight to her cheek, far too close to her lips, claiming back a decade in a breath. He smelled of expensive aftershave and predatory freedom. She curled away, belly folding itself inside out.

'Who is this darling creature?' He stooped to greet Knott who was shivering against her shins.

'If you're here to see Ronnie, she's out.'

'Hardly.' He was up again. 'That bloody woman's been guarding this place like Rapunzel's mother all week, stopping me coming to see you.' He tilted his head, looking at her flying tresses, reaching out to touch them. 'I used to love climbing up that hair.'

'I've got to be somewhere.' Pax jerked away and gathered it into a bunch to twist tightly under her collar again, feeling a rare rush of gratitude to her mother for keeping him away. 'If you'll excuse my rudeness.' She set off towards the cottage.

'No, I won't,' he said, following. 'You're being rude. At least offer me a drink.' He stooped to pick up the wine from the doorstep. 'Blair brought these, no doubt. Gnarly Dudes. How apt. Where *is* old Mr Tight-arse?'

'Sit Tight,' she corrected.

'Bloody fleeced me.'

'*You're* the one who bought the horse?' She was astonished.

'Had to be quite the detective to track her down.'

'I'm surprised Monique fell for anything of ours.' She knew Bay's wife only by icy reputation. 'Isn't she a dressage purist?'

'Purist being a polite way of saying total snob.' Bay laughed unapologetically. 'Eventing is her groom's thing, whose boyfriend insists that mare is the next Headley Britannia. Monique's mentoring them both.'

'And you're their sponsor?'

'Only way to stop her staff from walking out is to buy them presents every time she makes them cry. Now invite me in and we'll find some wine glasses.' He looked at her, the blue conceit of his eyes taking her aback. Their youthful virtue was long gone, sold to the devil for acreage and adultery.

Oh, for the warm, slaking juice of good red wine. The taste was already a ghost in her mouth, its energy coursing through her, galvanising her to tell Bay exactly what she still thought of him, that he would never hurt her again, that he was dead to her. She longed to grab the bottle from him, twist the lid off and neck it right back on the step.

'Pax.' Misreading the fevered look in her eyes, he stepped towards her, gaze unwavering. Her hair was out of control again, finding its own wind funnel to whip his collars and shoulders like Medusa's snakes. And then he was in amongst the red serpents, his face almost against hers, his voice in her ear. 'I have never stopped regretting what I did to you, you do know that, don't you?'

'Let's please forget it ever happened.'

'How can I? It was entirely my fault, and I ruined everything.'

'It's forgotten.'

'Forgiven?'

She pulled away, heart thumping in her throat. Her gaze fell to the bottles in his hands. His signet ring glittered on his little finger. She'd worn it on a gold neck chain that long summer they'd been together, running it across her lips each night in bed, a small engraved game bird and an inscription of the Austen family motto inside.

'*Dum Spiro Spero*,' she said, remembering.

' "While I Breathe, I Hope".' His gaze didn't leave hers. 'I've never given up hope you'll come back to me, Pax.'

She wanted to hear him say it again. Every word again and again and again. Only better. Louder. Shouty and broken. With tears and sobs and snot and real, deep pain like she'd felt fourteen unlucky years ago. The sort of on-your-knees pain that sent a life racketing in the wrong direction like an Exocet missile. The sort of pain that still hurt today when she looked at him.

'Dum Spiro Spero,' he repeated.

'You'll be holding your breath in hell,' she said gently.

'Rather a contradiction in terms, don't you think?'

'Don't bloody patronise me!' She pushed him away. The puppy, cowering, started to bark underfoot.

'I always loved that temper of yours.'

'Get lost!'

'We'd have fucked sensationally after every row.'

'Something you'll never know.'

'Oh, I think we will.'

'You are so fucking shallow!' Her hand flew out with all the instinctive, venomous rage of her teenage self, her slap deflected easily by his arm, her rings scratching across the glass of the bottle he was still holding.

He caught her fingers against its neck, admiring the big sapphire overlapping its neighbouring gold band, both now too loose. 'Still wearing Mack's ice and a slice, I see.'

'What's it to you?' Snatching her hand away, she folded its fingers into a fist, the rings a little knuckleduster ready to knock a tooth or two of his smile out.

'I want to see you happy, Pax.' The arrogance had vanished. 'Back in the day, we discovered love together, and that means a lot.'

'Cut that out.'

'I did.' He patted his knuckles against his chest, wine bottle swinging. 'I cut it straight out of here to give to you, but you'd gone.'

She rolled her eyes. 'You always were a self-dramatist.'

'And you still care…' He moved closer again, voice low. 'Which is why you're angry.'

'No,' she kept hers as calm as she could muster, 'that is because you're a bastard, Bay.'

His eyes glittered, fine lines at their edges now and on the forehead above, like music staves. Happy music always played in Bay's head, Pax remembered – Fats Waller or Louis Armstrong – old-fashioned and jazzy, ready to get the party going. He'd made her entirely happy once. Its simplicity was intoxicating.

Tell me what to do, Bay, the voice in her head pleaded before she could stop it. *Tell me what will make me happy again. Please just tell me.*

She could feel the heat of his body as he lowered his mouth to her ear again. 'This bastard isn't ever going to give up on us, you know.' She felt his fingers thread through hers, raising her ringless right hand to kiss, blue eyes watching her over it with such old-school intensity she wanted to laugh. Yet it caught in her throat because her heart hurt. It literally *hurt.*

Tell me what to do! I'm begging you.

'For God's sake stop looking at me like that, Pax.'

Hearing voices and laughter, Pax sprang back as Blair and Luca appeared from the arch together, long strides matching, lopsided and mile-wide smiles lined up for comparison, one set in stubble, the other a white-blond beard, both surprisingly genuine.

'Here come Russell Crowe and Gandalf.' Bay propped a bottle under his arm and straightened his collars, eyes flicking across to meet hers, conveying an urgent farewell.

'Give the lady her wine back!' Blair called with gravelly amusement.

'Everything okay here?' Luca's voice, soft and light by contrast.

'Marvellous! Two old friends getting reacquainted,' Bay said smoothly, still looking at Pax as he handed her the bottles, mouthing, *meet me*. 'We go back a long way.'

Pax gave a barely perceptible shake of the head, turning away.

Eager to get going, Blair was already striding towards Bay's

Land Rover. 'I'm going back a long way – back home, so we'd better make tracks.'

But Bay – whose manners had always been immaculate – was now shaking Luca's hand to introduce himself. 'Your reputation precedes you. I do hope we'll see you riding out with the Wolds soon.'

Hugging the wine tightly, Pax counted the seconds until she could be alone with it. One small glass, she promised herself afresh. A dressage measure; just to take the edge off.

12

Ash must have been a good soldier, thought Bridge. Talking her through each stage of tidying up her messed-up face with minimal fuss, he was thorough, unhurried and no-nonsense, doing everything by the book from antiseptic swabs to rubber gloves. Not many men looked as unremittingly macho in disposable latex, at least not on their hands.

Any doubts she harboured about the dangers of receiving unqualified medical treatment – and there were a great many she was too hypnotised to voice – were eclipsed by the sheer presence of the man, as reassuringly in command as a comic strip superhero. Bridge found the combination of trust and fear A-Class, the high making her banter too sharply.

'My face is in your hands, Mr Turner. You do fillers and eyebrow tattooing too?'

Unsmiling, Ash clearly took his task too seriously for jokes. He'd made her wash her wounds first, scrubbing his own hands at the sink alongside her, field hospital coming to Cotswold cottage. Then he'd carefully cleaned the remaining clotted blood away from her forehead and lip, deliberately exposing the deepest cuts and abrasions, which stung like hell. He treated each with antiseptic, deft and precise. Finally, working quickly, he neatly swabbed and glued, barking at her to stay still.

'It gloody hurts!' she complained, mouth wedged open by his thumb which, despite the supreme pain and expediency of the situation, still felt regrettably erotic. 'Ouch!'

'Don't be a wimp,' he gave her a stern sideways look.

'Ig goo say arly is omming ere?' She sounded like a dentist's patient having a filling, but he was obviously practised at interpreting bashed mouths.

'She's working up at the Gunns' place. She'll call you later.'

'Eaning iv Ganine?'

'And helping with the neds.'

'At's goog.'

Bridge focussed hard on the thought of Carly. Carly was kind. Carly was her friend. Carly had somehow figured out that her need for Skully's services were greater than turfing and had sent her husband in as medic. Her hands must be hot. She needed Carly. She'd be gentler than Ash for a start.

'Ucking *ouch*!'

'Chin up, beautiful. I've taken worse myself enough times.' His accent, pure Comptons, all Cotswold marl and folklore, did nothing to dispel the squirming shame of pain combined with lusty crush.

They were in the bathroom, which had the best light, still steamed up from her shower. In common with most of the old cottages on Back Lane, it was downstairs in a lean-to extension built off the kitchen. Perching on the bath rim, Bridge was uncomfortably aware that she and Aleš had enjoyed sex in it late last night, lube and intimate toy just out of sight behind the shower curtain.

'You ight a lot then?' She remembered Mo's dark talk of high-grade gypsy bouts. 'Are-uckle?'

He didn't answer, eyes close to her skin, focussing on his task. He smelled of menthol shampoo and gum, undercut with the sort of testosterone that was lethal around married women.

'Uz arly ot ind that you ight?'

'You're not to talk to Carly about fighting.' The silver eyes fixing hers were gun barrels. Then they moved back to their task, and she could relax, studying his brows at close range, perfectly shaped in a way no man-salon could emulate. There was a bell-bar piercing in one, a thin scar through another. Aleš, who had brawled throughout his teens and twenties, had eyebrows scarred like tyre tracks. Maybe Ash landed more punches than he took.

'Is are-uckle ighting hard?' she persisted, captivated by the alien world of gypsies slugging it out in secret.

'I don't fight.' Ash didn't blink. 'I *train*.'

She pulled her chin back so he was forced to let go. 'And mule drugs.'

The silver guns held her hostage. 'You want me to finish this or what?'

She shut up, wincing as he took hold of her chin again, patching up her shredded lip.

He focussed on his work, head tilting, thick black curls flopping over one steely eye. 'As soon as Skully figured your old man's the big Polish bastard, he was happy enough for me to do the honours. He's crap at this anyway. Thanks to him, Jed looks like Thanos. You're too pretty to deserve that.'

As if having him in her house with his thumb in her mouth wasn't disturbing enough, being called pretty tipped the scale. Bridge stared fixedly at the mouldy air vent to dispel the thrill.

'I don't get you.' He reached back for another cotton wool bud, dipping it in antiseptic. 'If your old man didn't do this, why hide it?'

'Egoz gy horse did it. And gy old gan has it in for gy horse.'

The gun barrels levelled on her again. 'He has a point. Useless buggers, horses.'

She glared back, antiseptic stinging like mad.

He raised one perfect pierced brow. 'You going for a job at the school today, Carl says?'

'Gat goo.'

'That too,' Ash translated, bemused. 'You'll walk it, scar-face.'

'Ost gy onfidence,' she admitted, appalled to find herself welling up.

'Everyone knows Mrs Bollock's a lush,' he stage whispered. 'Needs someone to tell her what day it is.' He pressed a latex finger to her throbbing lip to hold it together while the liquid dried.

'You're kidding?'

'Keep your mouth shut.'

'I'm not telling anyonc.'

'I mean,' he looked at her through his lashes, and she almost fell back into the bath, his sex appeal intravenous, 'keep your mouth shut while this dries.'

Lifting his finger, he blew on her lips, as practical as nail-artist sister Janine drying acetate. Bridge's head, heart and pelvis spun like a trio of glitter balls.

Stop thinking it, Bridge! He's forbidden fruit.

Beyond the obscured glass window, one of the neighbours' dogs was barking to be let in, an unfamiliar yapping. It wasn't any of Flynn's pack of terriers, who always travelled with him in the back of his farrier's pickup. He'd be taking Petra's mare's shoes off now, she remembered. Carly was holding the Gunn kids' ponies.

Ash's thumb was still on her lip, his eyes on her face, and she felt a pulse start throbbing somewhere it wasn't allowed.

Stop it, Bridge! You're mother to two beautiful children. You and your loyal husband made love in this very bathroom last night. Talk to him about his wife.

'Carly says you might be training to be a farrier?'

'Keep your mouth still.'

'Talk to me about it, then.'

He sucked his teeth. 'Not much to say. I prefer training in the gym. End of.'

'To be a fitness instructor or for bare-knuckle fighting?'

'Stop talking.'

She nudged her eyebrows encouragingly.

'Sign up to be my first customer, if you like. You could do with a workout.'

She rolled her eyes.

'Shoeing neds is back-breaking. Flynn don't smell great, neither.'

Ash, by contrast, smelled fantastic, all that mint and testosterone seeing off her bathroom's ageing reed diffuser. She sniffed appreciatively.

He tilted his head back to admire his handiwork. 'You'll do. You can talk now.'

Belligerently, Bridge said nothing.

'You're a funny one.' The corners of his lips curled just slightly – or it could be a trick of the light. His face had a mask-like quality, as though his feelings were buried deeper than an arms dump. 'C'mon, say something so I can see this lip move.'

'Like what?'

'Whatever uses it. F words are good.'

'You want me to talk dirty?'

'Consonants that make your smackers pop: B, P, F, M, W.' He pronounced them phonetically, his lip movements exaggerated.

'All right, Henry Higgins,' she laughed. 'Body perfect farriers make women horny.'

'That a fact?' He was giving her that look again, the one that made all her forbidden bits prickle.

'Too right it's a fecking fact. Look at myths right back through history from the Iron Age, and you'll find the blacksmith's always bang there at the centre; bang, bang, bang on his anvil, the big hero, seeing off the devil, shoeing the gods' horses or making kings' magical swords. Why do you think we strike while the iron's hot and go at it hammer and tongs? I don't want to ride roughshod over your plans, Ash, or see you with too many irons in the fire, but let's cut to the quick, farriers were the first mortal celebrities and superheroes – still are round here. Great arses, big trucks, cute dogs, all fire and sparks and wads of cash. If you want your average Cotswold wife at your feet offering you riches, forget being a personal trainer, shoe her fecking horse. Your wife's not wrong. Even your name's fecking perfect, Ash. You could make a killing round here, the war hero in the leather apron. Shame you can't see it.'

'Okay, you can stop talking now.' He gave a quick smile and a dismissive nod.

'Sure?' She felt she was just getting into her stride.

'It's holding fine. You always that gobby? Should have glued your lips together.'

'You can fuck off.' Feeling her face grow hot, realising she must have banged on wildly, Bridge reached up to her mouth with tentative fingers. Whilst still trout-pout swollen, it was remarkably smooth.

'Kissable...' Ash admired his handiwork with the detachment of a tattooist who's just inked MUM on a bicep.

'Thank you *so* much,' she said with feeling. 'That's amazing. How much do I owe you?'

'Let's say it's a favour I'll call back in.'

'Any time.'

'I'd better get going.' As he stood up, the shower curtain shifted and, with a clatter, Aleš's favourite sex toy was knocked into the bath, a shiny purple anal plug.

Ash raised his perfect pierced eyebrow once more.

'Rubber duck.' Bridge brazened it out, springing up to lead the way out through the bathroom door.

He followed.

Racing through the cottage as though it was on fire, her libido flapping and buzzing like a trapped aviary in her jogging trousers, Bridge now found her fantasy figure all too bloody real. *And* she was blushing, that wretched giveaway face-stain of hers. She needed make-up on and she needed it fast.

'I'll show you out.'

'You do that.' He overtook her at a leisurely walk, turning in the door, his bulk barring her from the latch. 'Put antiseptic on it every day.'

She nodded. 'Thanks again!'

'And don't go kissing anyone.' He reached up to test the patched-lip with his thumb. It rested there too long, his eyes almost crossing as they watched its tip tracing the moist delineation between dry pout and wet mouth.

Without thinking, she sucked it. The sexual rush was fantastic.

The thumb was removed.

'If you ever do that again,' he said very slowly, 'I can't promise I'll be this good.'

After he'd gone, pickup engine snarling away towards Broadbourne, she leant against the back of the door, breathing deeply. Bloody, muddled-up spell.

'Bridge!'

She looked around in shock. A ghost?

'Get over here! I can here you fecking panting.'

Bernie was still on FaceTime.

'I've had a shower and a run since you answered this call, you cow. Show me your face.'

She held up her phone.

'Where d'they fecking go?' Bernie demanded in shock. 'You looked like you'd been bitch-slapped by Wolverine half an hour ago.'

'That man's a magician. Shit, Bernie, tell me to get a job at a nice wee school and behave myself and never do the bad, bad thing.'

'Don't do the bad thing.' Her mirror image looked grainily bemused on screen.

'Thanks.' Cutting the call, Bridge fanned her face with the phone, not sure she could trust herself.

*

Cheeks bulging and cake crumbs on his chin, Lester looked uncharacteristically shifty when Ronnie swept into his ward of four, weighed down with magazines, Fray Bentos tins in the Bag for Life, Stubbs gyrating in an old holdall slung over her shoulder, his nose already threading through the broken zip and beneath her arm.

'Can't stay long,' she said, plonking herself down on the chair.

Lester nodded. 'Of course not, with the Australian visiting.'

She gave him a sharp, suspicious smile and watched him pick a chocolate chip from his pyjamas. 'If you're talking about Blair, I've not seen him since New Year.'

She'd missed him. She missed him.

'Sold the Austens that rangy filly out of our Master Imp mare. Nice sort.'

'How extraordinary.'

'Drove her up today.'

'Are you sure?' Ronnie wondered if Lester's new-found Googling skills had been on overdrive.

Aware that he had her full attention, he tilted his head, deflecting. 'Pax keeping well?'

'Much better,' she said briskly, wishing she believed it.

He admired the front covers of *The Field* and *Country Life* before setting them aside. 'Not got her on a horse yet, I'll wager. Too busy worrying about her boy. Hardest on children, divorce.' He gave her a penetrating look.

She gave him one back. 'Not if the marriage is dead.'

The bedclothes rustled crossly. 'Still, sensible looking into the village school for him.'

'Is she?' Ronnie was astonished.

'Headmistress there is a rare sort, I'm told. Not the most discreet, but strong on old-fashioned values. Very fond of parkin. They have actors' and lawyers' children there.'

Ronnie hadn't thought him interested in anything in the village unconnected to four legs. This new-found, garrulous

Lester was a revelation, not unconnected to epic amounts of recent anaesthesia and analgesia.

There was an unfamiliar Tupperware tub on his bedside table, lid bulging beneath its baked contents. 'Lester, has Pip been here?'

He sucked his teeth, reaching a hand out to Stubbs' head, the creases on his face folding in defensively. 'Hear the Irish lad's been on the stallion this morning.'

'Good grief, the spies *are* out. Tell me, has Pip got a new job? With MI5 maybe?'

'Useless with a shavings fork, that woman.' His tongue probed his cheeks for the last cake traces. 'The Turner girl's a harder worker. Better not leave it any longer to snap her up. There's others have their sights on her.'

She narrowed her eyes. 'How do you know all this?'

'Hard workers get noticed in a village.'

'Well, Carly hasn't come back to help us.'

'Have you asked her?'

'Pax insists we can't afford anyone else.'

'Pay her my wage; I'm no good to you while I'm in here.'

'Don't be ridiculous, Lester.'

'Irish fellow's not one of those as picks up a broom for the love of it.'

'You'd be surprised. And we have Pax too.'

'She'll run.'

'Of course she won't.'

'Just like her mother, that one.' He gave the bedsheets a fractious tug. 'Did you deal with the letters?'

Ronnie started guiltily. Those confounded letters. 'I will, I promise.'

He glared at her.

'Pax is way too distracted to nose around your cottage, Lester.'

'Give the Turner girl a job. You need time to sort your family out.' He reached out his old-fashioned pocket diary and dictated a telephone number which she obligingly fed into her phone.

'Call her, then.' Lester looked so old and frail in his striped pyjamas, she couldn't bring herself to argue the point.

'We can't afford more staff.' She lifted the phone to her ear, grateful for Carly's monotone announcing she couldn't answer her phone. 'Voicemail. I'll text her later.' Relieved, she offered the ultimate pacifier to take his mind off it. 'Will you teach young Kes to ride when you come home? I don't think Luca's terribly keen.'

The creases unfolded in delight. 'We'll make a guardsman of him like his great-grandfather. Have the little man fit to gallop into battle in no time.'

'Just rising to the trot will be fine, Lester. Let's spare him any more conflict.'

'Can't stay!' Carly hurried into her mother-in-law's maisonette, a grotto of tropical warmth day or night behind its drawn curtains, television and gas fire glowing. Having cut across the fields and abandoned her muddy boots at the door, her socks gave her static shocks on the cheap carpet as she scooped up Jackson and Sienna. 'We're going to see the ponies!'

Sienna shrieked with joy. Jackson bawled, cleaving back to his grandmother and Twirlywoos.

Nan had her ice pack and peppermint oil out, a sure sign that she had one of her migraines.

'Thanks a million for minding them.' Carly ignored the phone ringing in her back pocket. 'You still okay for tomorrow, Nan? Janine wants me double shifts again.'

Ash's mother was a meek little character who rarely looked anyone over the age of ten in the eye, but she gave Carly the full benefit of her rare, unexpectedly heart-melting brown gaze, lashes still long as a Jersey cow, pain riven through their dark centres. 'You're a good girl, you are, Carly.'

'Thanks.'

'My Ash is lucky to have you.'

'Thanks.'

Nan Turner always made Carly feel awkward. The kids adored her, but there was a tragic air about her that Carly felt deep in her bones.

She'd been duskily pretty once, from a big fairground family, a tiny Edith Piaf of the candyfloss stall. Unlikely framed photographs of her in a pinny with big eighties hair scattered the house. Long held prisoner by her agoraphobia and passivity, she reminded Carly of a zoo animal who no longer has an ounce of fight left. She had a quiet fear that Ash would become like that one day if the nightmares and boozing kept him hostage long enough.

'His dad is a bad lot, you know.' It was one of Nan's stock phrases, along with 'Wipe your Feet' and 'Your face will stay like that if the wind changes'.

'Ash is nothing like Nat.' His dad remained an inveterate traveller rogue, sweet-talking his way along old gypsy routes in a traditional wagon, with a girlfriend half his age following in the rusty transit van crammed with carved mushrooms, fenced goods and lurchers.

'You make sure he stays that way, yes?' Nan urged, looking tearful. 'I always knew when Ash was being bad as a nipper. I felt it here.' She patted her temples and winced.

'Don't worry, I'm on it.' Carly rubbed her fingertips against her own sweaty palms, stupidly hot again, even though she knew that the old bird was just being overdramatic. Nan watched a *lot* of soaps.

She sprinted back out with the kids strapped in the double buggy, wishing she had time to call on Bridge and check she was okay after the weird texts, but she was already running late. Powering back to Upper Bagot Farmhouse by lane along Plum Run to avoid the buggy getting stuck, wind slapping her face like an angry handbag, she took the call that had been buzzing against her bum for the last ten minutes. It was Ash, shouting over his rumbling truck engine.

'Your friend looked a bit like the kid in *The Exorcist* after a crucifix face-slash session, but she'll live! Might even get that job.'

'You checked on her!' she cried gratefully. 'Was Aleš there?'

'She fell off her horse!'

Carly felt an idiot. When Petra had said Bridge had come to blows with the love of her life, she hadn't thought of Craic for a minute. 'So why did she call Skully?'

Ash's signal was breaking up.

'Ash?'

'I've been thinking on… farrier apprenticeship… more, yeah?'

'You mean it?' she shouted back over the wind.

'Worth… conversation.' He sounded very upbeat.

She air-punched. 'What changed your mind?'

'Full of nags, this village.' His laugh broke up.

She could see across the paddock to their farrier friend's big van parked on Petra's stable yard. 'I get him to call you.'

The signal came back, his voice overbearing in her ear. 'Tell him we'll talk.'

'Love you, bae.' She punched the code into Petra's electric gates. 'Catch you later.'

As she waited for the gates to open, she scrolled her other missed calls. The most recent was a mobile number. Dropping to her haunches to pick up one of Jackson's boots, she pressed Return Call. It went straight to voicemail: *It's Ronnie, leave me a message!*

Carly felt like an Alka Seltzer dropped in water. *Ronnie Percy had called her.*

Hesitating, uncertain what to say, she found the phone snatched out of her grip by Sienna in the buggy, eager to get back to her favourite game.

'Pou!' she screamed into the phone.

'Give that back.'

The gates were closing. She hurriedly pushed on through, at the same time trying to grab back the phone which her daughter was gripping tightly, demanding to nurture a small, brown, unfortunately named blob.

'Pou! Pou! Poooooooou! Want POU!'

The call was still open when Carly wrestled it back. What was the number for rerecording? She jabbed at 3 on the keypad just as two hands grabbed her from behind and Flynn growled his customary greeting, 'Run away with me this minute to have my babies, sweetlips,' making her jump. Her screen now read *Call Ended.*

It had taken Ronnie almost an hour to take her leave from Lester while he listed every overall show champion triumph the stud had achieved during his long tenure, so engrossed he hadn't even noticed her making several calls and taking a power nap. Now she was trying to navigate her way back through from the Hathaway wing the hospital to the car park exit, a labyrinthine maze that had taken her past the Macmillan volunteers twice and accidentally into Phlebology and X-ray, her feet squeak-squeaking along furlongs of polished floors.

An incoming text from Blair cheered her somewhat. The message simply read, *You?*

Good. You? she replied on the move, matching his brevity.

The reply came straight back. *All good.*

Not trusting Lester's rumour-mongering or her heart ringing the changes like out-of-time church bells, Ronnie asked, *Where's my horsebox?*

Up yours.

Up yours too!

It's up at your place.

She laughed, hearing his dust-dry voice. Then she felt sad. *Sorry. Misunderstood.*

Missed you, Ron.

God but I miss you too, she replied before realising that he was probably just saying she hadn't been there when he'd dropped by. A pragmatist like Blair didn't engage in anything as metrosexual as emotional texts. He was much more direct. She'd just given herself away.

Want me to turn back?

She paused in the stairwell, breathing hard, her longing bone deep. She'd sworn to give him up for her children's sakes, to respect his marriage even if his poor, sick wife had almost no memory of it any more. Yet she missed his company like oxygen. Blair was a crosspatch, sexist and a cultural wasteland, but he could make her laugh and make the world stand still just by looking at her, seeing straight through to her base metal.

Keep going. Rx she typed, removing the kiss and pressing Send before she could change her mind.

Feeling sadder than ever, she sat down on the stairs and hugged her knees.

Her phone beeped with a voicemail. Hoping it was Blair breaking the alarm glass, she leapt on it with indecent haste. Then she listened to it again. Twice. Then she started to laugh, her mood lifting.

Perhaps Lester was right after all. Carly Turner could prove extremely refreshing to have around.

Bridge was amazed how good she looked. Amazed. No way could scar-face become this fresh-faced unless witchcraft was involved. That, or highly illegal practices. Or just plain lust.

Even the swollen lip looked pretty after she'd meticulously painted her face. Her eyes danced knowingly back at her from the mirror.

You. Have. A. Big. Fat. Crush, they told her.

On. Your. Friend's. Husband, shouted a shameful twinkle in one.

He fancies you back, her dark pupils sang in response.

Bad as it felt, it was making her glow. No man should make anyone feel this good.

Bridge sent a rare selfie to Aleš. It was midday – Polish lunchtime – which meant he was eating his sandwiches and surfing his familiar 4G round route like a kid on a bike: Twitter, Santander savings account, YouTube, porn, Instagram, Reddit.

The message was to the point. *On way. Take your clothes off.*

He was home from the new eco-build in five minutes, cock springing from his flies as fast as he could unbutton them, recent full-on maritals making him priapic with readiness. Match fit, they'd been practising a lot. 'Beautiful wife, I want you around this now!'

'I have a job interview in half an hour.' Bridge backed away, jazz hands flapping because her nail varnish was still drying.

'It's okay, we just do oral sex.' Aleš's pupils darkened, loving the little lady act. 'You look so hot.'

'Absolutely not!' Her lower lip throbbed. 'No oral.'

'Boob wank?'

Bridge's bra was new and had cost fifty quid. And just saying 'boob wank' was a *Real Wives* giveaway. 'You go down on me,' she suggested, brightening at the prospect of closing her eyes and fantasising tattoos, dog tags and...

'I just eat chilli wrap.' He sucked his lips.

Lunchtime sex was a rare negotiation, especially when they were pushed for time. Aleš flying back from Poland on New Year's Day to upend the furniture had been spontaneous, uncontrollable. This felt more like arguing in a Pret a Manger queue.

'Vanilla?' Aleš offered, making her feel 'meh' again because it wasn't a word they usually used. *Missionary* if they were being technical, *you go on top* was her trying to sell the idea, most often when she was half-asleep and they fumbled their way towards it in the dead of night.

But this was daylight. Upstairs, their bed had eight alternative interview outfits spread out across it. Both cats were curled on top last time Bridge had looked. Aleš was very pernickety about banishing them during coitus. She didn't want to evict them, let alone start hanging up clothes.

'Why vanilla?' She weaved towards him. 'Why not pistachio?'

He looked briefly intrigued. 'I like vanilla.'

'Strawberry?'

'Vanilla.' His top came off with Baltic aplomb.

'Rum and raisin.'

'Vanilla.' He stepped out of his trousers.

'Mint choc chip.'

'Actually, that *is* a sex act, *kochanie*.'

'Is it up our street?' She was briefly thrilled.

'Something with toothpaste and anal.' He looked hopeful.

'Ew. How do you *know* these things?'

'I have a mind that cannot forget. Let's vanilla,' he indicated at his watch. He was fully naked and at full mast while she was still in the first interview suit she'd tried on. 'I have quantity surveyor coming in half an hour. You have job to get.'

And in that moment, Bridge felt the love that fired each cell in her body. Aleš remembered every birthday in the family, just as he remembered how many sugars every casual labourer who worked with them liked in their tea, the names of wives, and the sweet spots on her body however vanilla the sex.

She felt plugged into the mains. She reached for him: warm satin skin, her thumb circling faster as he hardened beneath her touch, anticipation bubbling between her legs. 'Hands only. And if you want to touch any part of me, you're washing yours first, Chilli-Wrap Man.'

'Vanilla for dessert.' He reversed her towards the sofa.

'If I get this job,' she told him, 'there's no ice-cream flavour beyond reach.'

'Ash know you're here?' Flynn asked Carly as she hung onto a nippy pony who didn't want his feet trimmed, her hood battering the side of her head in the wind.

'Course.'

'That chip on his shoulder turned blue, has it?'

'Meaning?'

'You fraternising with the village pelf, the wallets.' His brows hiked, tossing the rock hair, rasp aloft. 'Not like a Turner.'

'You'd be surprised.' Ash never objected to her doing extra little jobs for Petra, whose generosity meant the Turners were dressed in designer cast-offs, had a huge kids' DVD collection and more books than they knew what to do with. It helped that Petra didn't mind Carly bringing her children along. In the tack room behind her, Jackson was snoozing in the buggy. Sienna had curled up in a quilted horse rug with a spaniel watching *Peppa Pig* on Carly's smartphone while Pou slept off an exhausting session jumping around on lily pads.

'She's been good to me and Ash, Petra has,' she told Flynn.

Pink from the shower, she'd disappeared back into her Plotting Shed an hour earlier, telling Carly to help herself to coffee from the high-tech machine with the real espresso scoops while she was 'throwing a quick proposal together. But don't go before we have that chat!' Her life, like her house, was impossibly glamorous.

'Thought Ash didn't like you playing with gee-gees?' Flynn was clipping a hoof with his big pincers. The pony was relaxing now, leaning hard against Carly while her reassuring hand ran along his neck and withers, fingers raking in and out of his mane.

'He'll have to get used to it if he's going to be farrier with you.'

'No kidding?' He looked up, eyes crinkled with amusement.

'Straight up. Says he'll talk to you.' She wasn't sure she believed it herself yet; she mustn't overplay it.

'What about his college course?'

'Up for discussion.' She scratched the pony's forehead and rubbed behind his ears.

'It's not just about having arms like Popeye,' he warned her.

'I can see that.'

'Hey, feel this.' He lowered the pony's leg back to the ground and offered her a bicep. 'Nothing on Ash's gym humps, granted, but there's more skill in lifting a neddy's leg than swinging at a punchbag. It's not one night of fighting glory. Takes a lot of commitment, farriery.'

'Ash isn't afraid of that.' New Year, new start Carly hoped. Fewer nights on the lash, fewer late-night poker sessions in Flynn's cottage. She was banking on the two men both growing up if their livelihoods depended on each other. Flynn's daughter was in the same class as Ellis. For all his swagger and flirtation, Carly knew him to be an old-fashioned soul and a hard grafter. Ash thought a lot of him and his family. She was determined to make this idea work. 'You know Ash is a good man, Flynn. A good dad.'

'With a good wife.' He curled his rasp around the Shetland's little hoof as perfectly as Janine shaped a nail.

As Carly watched him, fascinated by the process, her excitement built. She knew Ash could do this. She curled her fingers distractedly through the thick mane, then around the little furry flame ears, imagining hammer on anvil, regular income, horses.

'How d'you bloody do that?'

She realised Flynn was looking up at her, equally fascinated as the Shetland leaned against her even more heavily, soporific, almost asleep. 'That little bugger usually never lets up kicking out.'

'Dunno. I just do.'

'You're definitely on the team.'

She waved the compliment away, secretly euphoric. She was going to stand up to Janine and the Turners and make this happen. Bridge's New Year spell was going to come true for them all.

Her phone lit up with a message.

Regrettably, I can't have babies or run away. I can, however, offer you weekend work and some midweek mornings if you'd like some? Call me. Ronnie.

She reread it.

'Bloody hell, Ronnie Percy just offered me a job,' she breathed, fireworks and fanfares in her head.

'Sick.' Flynn didn't even look up. 'Ask her what she's paying – Percys still think slavery's legal.'

When do I start? she messaged Ronnie back.

As she pressed send, Petra burst out of her Plotting Shed and hurried towards them, waving a sheet of A4. 'Carly, I've been thinking something over. I'd like to offer you a job. I've bullet pointed a two-page brief, but I can write it in more detail if you want.' She thrust the pages at her.

Carly took them. 'What job exactly?'

'How much do you want per hour to be me?'

'Now *that's* an offer you'd be mad to refuse,' Flynn said grinning, dodging a kick from the Shetland.

Alone on the yard, the wind now Wizard of Oz high, Luca was a solo yachtsman skippering a boat in need of a crew. Usually it wouldn't bother him; he'd circumnavigated the world alone enough times to appreciate solitude, the ever-changing surf of horses his sea, the call of the siren his downfall. Yet today he couldn't shake the sense that he'd sailed straight past a perfect storm.

He was stopped in his tracks every few minutes by his whipcrack conscience, like the snap of a sail that drew his eyes to the same place each time, the same small window, a porthole beyond which some unseen ballast shifted inside him, a loyalty he hadn't yet fathomed. It frustrated him. He had no reason to concern himself with Pax's whereabouts, and yet he did. It was his curse since arriving to have her always on his radar.

Be kind to Pax. Ronnie had asked it.

Watched by a concerned Beck and Cruisoe, Luca criss-crossed the biggest yard, small practical tasks rendered increasingly long-winded as the pressure grew in his head.

The whip cracked again. He looked across at the stable cottage.

He couldn't shake the look on Pax's face earlier, the first colour he'd seen in her cheeks. Not hard to spot the cause. Luca was disappointed in her, guessing Mr Blue Eyes the posh-boy neighbour was something to do with her marriage coming apart.

He wanted to push it all out of his mind, but he couldn't. Since Posh Boy had left, Pax had gone to ground. She usually worked on the yard like an addict. They both did. It was their therapy. And Ronnie had said something about her collecting her son, hadn't she?

Be kind to Pax.

Eventually, he jogged beneath the arch to the front of the stables cottage to knock on the door. When there was no answer, he turned back and played ship's head beneath the little porch for a moment, telling himself that this was absolutely none of his business, and that he didn't want it to be.

Be kind to Pax.

And where are you, Ronnie?

You have absolutely no idea about this family!

Tell me, Pax.

Still he remained rooted, the same compulsion to play sentry as the one which had kept watch from the chair in her hotel room a week earlier. He felt in his pockets, pulling out the leaflet he'd picked up in town a few days earlier, raided from a display by the chemist's pharmacy counter. If he posted it through the door, he guessed she'd take terrible offence. He folded it back up. He could hear music – a kitschy Latin Jazz – and had a brief involuntary mental image of Pax as a fifties housewife slewed on gin, head in the oven.

As he went to knock again, the door opened, leaving him like a Chinese lucky cat offering an awkward power salute. She was buttoning up her coat, surprised to find him there. Her hair was a mess, her swollen-lidded eyes wild behind their unflattering glasses. It was obvious she'd been sobbing for a long, long time. And drinking. He could smell it on her. Her car keys were in her hand.

She looked at him, disconcerted. 'You forgot your smile, Luca.'

'May I come in?' *Be kind to her, Luca.* If Pax wanted to pickle herself on his watch, fine. But she would do so without getting behind the wheel.

'I'm running an hour late.'

An hour in which she'd consumed both Blair's bottles of wine judging by the glazed expression.

'This won't take a minute.'

She looked poised to tell him to go to hell, but then she let out a cry and turned abruptly back inside, rattling through the cottage to fetch her handbag. 'Oh God, where's my bloody phone?'

Pushing the door closed behind him, Luca followed. 'You threw it in a skip.'

'I have a new one.' She started pulling open drawers and

cupboards at random. It was, inexplicably, in the fridge. She lobbed it in her bag. The big headlamp gaze turned to him, daring him to comment. 'What is it you want, Luca?' She was brittle with self-control, no trace of any tears now.

'I'm not sure you should be driving.'

'Says the man who's scarier behind the wheel than Mr Magoo. You don't have worry, I'm perfectly safe to drive, Luca.'

'I'm sorry, but I don't agree.'

Her jaw set, a thousand freckles framing a determined chin dimple. She plunged back through the kitchen, returning with the two unopened bottles of Barossa Valley shiraz. 'Take them, although they're wasted on you and Mummy. You two really should start up the Compton chapter of the Temperance Society. She took one of the neighbour's keys away in the pub car park to stop him driving not long ago. He wasn't even over the limit, for the record.'

He could smell the sweet hit of her breath. Was it port? Cassis? She must have raided the old boy's larder. 'Let me drive you. I could use the practice.'

'Don't be ridiculous. You're needed here. I only have to stick my head in to the village school then pick up Kes from his grandparents.' The deep voice wasn't remotely slurred, but there was a wilful agitation that told Luca to trust his instinct. She was saying something about her in-laws taking her son out for the day. 'They're on a sodding steam train. I've told them if they're not back with him when I get there, I'm going to stop the train by waving big red knickers. Now where did I leave those keys?'

She started looking for the car keys she'd put down when searching for her phone. 'Oh come *on*, Pax, think!' She stood still and swung round. Her eyes, red-rimmed and unfocussed, darting from object to object.

Luca followed them, tracking their guilty trail for the telltale shadow of a vodka bottle behind the toaster or rum in the bread bin, but there was nothing, just a plastic bottle of blackcurrant squash by the kettle and a pink-stained mug. He crossed the room, pretending to look for the keys too.

'Hot Ribena.' Pax picked up the mug and thrust it under his nose. 'When we were kids, Lester used to make up a flask of "hot bina" to drink out hunting. It's a habitual comforter. Did Mummy ask you to nanny me? Don't answer that. Of course she did. I heard her.' Her face lit up at the sight of her keys by the sink, dumping the mug there to retrieve them. She clicked her fingers for Stubbs to get in his basket, the grey puppy shadowing her as usual as she turned back to face Luca, frostily polite. 'Please just get on with what you're doing on the yard, Luca, and trust me when I tell you that I can drive.'

'I apologise if I've misjudged the situation.' Still certain she was covering, he noticed the anxious threading of the keyring from finger to finger, clumsily letting go so they dropped on the quarry tiled floor with a clatter that made the puppy streak away. Her hands were shaking too much to pick them up on the first attempt. Stooping over them, a sob wracked through her, furiously swallowed back down and masked with a cough.

'I'm sorry too.' She looked up at him, then quickly away. 'It's been a tough morning. I've just spent the past hour staring at that wine, willing myself not to open it, so you weren't entirely wrong.'

Luca crouched beside her. He rarely gave anything much away about himself, least of all to someone he wasn't sure he could trust, but he knew no other way to appeal for the truth than by offering it. 'Pax, I've been where you are; I'm still there, if I'm honest.'

She stared across at him, unblinking. For a moment, he felt a collision of compassion. The look in her eyes he'd seen earlier was back, that emotional whirlwind. Then it was averted just as swiftly.

'Oh, I don't think so.' She stood up briskly.

Luca stood too, catching her arm. 'It's easier to overcome it with help.'

'Thank you for your concern, but I'm not about to wallow in self-pity. I must go.' As she brushed past him, he caught another waft of liqueur sweetness.

'How come it was a tough morning?' He followed.

'Not now, Luca.' She was at the door.

'You and Bay Austen looked pretty intense earlier.'

Her hand faltered on the latch. 'That's absolutely not your concern.'

'With respect, it is if you're drunk at the wheel.'

'I am not *drunk*!' She turned back, eyes huge.

'Seeing Bay upset you.'

She crossed her arms, saying nothing.

'I've been where you are,' he reminded her.

'Upset with Bay?' she mocked him, cried-out hare's eyes glowing golden. 'And there was me thinking it was Mummy who pulled your strings.'

'Let's leave your mother out of this, shall we?'

'The thing is, Luca,' she leaned back against the door, scuffing a foot on the sisal mat, 'my mother *is* right in the middle of it all. So is Bay, if you must know. He caused it, our rift.'

'Go on.'

She was staring across at an old framed photograph, that blue flame heat back, and it spilled out in a quiet, rushed undertone. 'Austen and Percy children always played together; we were like cousins. Mummy pushed off when I was tiny, so she was never much part of that. Bay was closer to my brother and sister at first; he's five years older than me and I just remember him winning everything at Pony Club and being a menace at sleepovers. I was eleven when Daddy died, in a hell of hormones and grief. Bay was terribly sweet about it, coming here of his own volition and singling me out. He was about to take GCSEs, all floppy hair and loud waistcoats. Afterwards, I was sent away to boarding school and we wrote a few times, but we barely saw each other again until the summer he came back from university to learn the ropes as a gentleman farmer. By then, the curtain hair and waistcoats had gone and he was quite the best-looking man I'd ever seen. I was in my first year of A levels and competing for the stud every weekend. We really fell for each other. Three months in, I was hopelessly in love and Bay said it often enough for me to think he was too.'

Luca sensed the point coming, its romanticised prologue seeking to sweeten something soul-destroying.

'Then Bay slept with my mother.'

Luca hadn't seen *that* coming. She gave him a curiously apologetic smile.

'Such a stupid phrase, isn't it? Sleep didn't come into it at all. I suppose I've always just thought of it like that because I was seventeen and wanted to wake up and find it was all a dream.'

'That's a hard betrayal to take.'

'Isn't it just?' She threw up her palms, car keys jangling, playing it too lightly, soft laugh contradicting the pain in her eyes. 'How do you forgive two people you love doing that to you?'

'I don't suppose you can.'

'I certainly couldn't at the time. It made no difference that they hadn't met since he was tiny, that they pleaded a moment of mad mutual attraction, a no-names' once-off. It's all it takes, ultimately, isn't it? You can wipe out everything in a night. One fuck. One night.'

'What did you do?'

'I left home. Life was a bit messy for a while. Fast forward fourteen years – a lot of which I've spent in a marriage which I realised very early on was the worst rebound ever – and Bay desperately wants to say sorry, which I know I should be grown-up about, in the same way I've tried to patch it up with Mummy – it's ancient history, after all – but d'you know, I really don't think I *can* forgive him.'

'Then don't.' Luca had disliked the man on instinct, and

what he'd witnessed hadn't looked like much of an apology. 'Tell him to jump off a cliff.'

Her eyes sharpened, surprised. 'Not many cliffs round here.'

'Offer to drive him to one. Just not today,' he added quickly. 'Not until you've had the strong coffee I'm about to make you, and something to eat. You look like you never eat.'

'That's what Bay said.' The hall clock chimed a quarter. Her face resumed its panicked look. 'Jesus, I am *so* late! I've phoned the Head twice with a lie about a flat tyre. Christ!' She turned to the front door then spun back again. 'Sorry. Blasphemy. Oh God, and I'm being so ungrateful as well. You're a kind man, Luca, even if you're only doing this for my mother's sake, and to avoid teaching pony lessons.' She'd overhead Ronnie say it, he realised in horror. 'It was very noble to say that you've been where I am, even if we both know it's not true.'

Luca stiffened. He could smell the alcohol again. He took in the compass points of her face, from high cheeks to dimpled chin to furrowed forehead, her mother's beauty dusted with fiery cayenne and soured by too many twists of melancholy.

'The night I arrived here,' he told her, 'I'd downed one whisky after another on a seven-hour flight from Toronto then chucked it all up at Schiphol. The six months before that, I'd barely been sober. If I'd walked into that hotel an hour earlier, I'd probably have got drunk with you. I owe you my sobriety right now. You are where I was – and seeing it close up is what's stopping me going there again. I can't watch you do it again either.'

The amber eyes scorched afresh. 'I'm not doing it again.'

A looped slideshow played too fast in Luca's head whenever he remembered that night: her kissing a stranger, throwing up, wet skin, her total raw despair, his own need to comfort.

'I'm not doing any of it again, Luca,' she repeated carefully, letting herself out.

The cold wind caught her unawares. Gasping, she lurched off the step.

He followed, sprinting past to put himself between her and the car. 'Let me help you, Pax.'

'Cut out the therapishtact.' She stopped, aware that she'd just slurred. She held up her hands. 'My teeth are chattering, okay?'

'Let's go to AA. Or you can talk to an addiction counsellor. If you won't talk to me, talk to someone else.'

'I told you, I'm fine!' She tried to push past him, stumbling as the puppy threaded in front of her, losing her balance and flailing to avoid stepping on him, a strange high-stepping dance that pitched her into the cobbles.

Luca caught her before she hit her head, shocked by how much she was shaking, toxic with adrenaline. He steadied her for a moment as they crouched by her car, then she shrugged him away with a muttered 'thanks', pressing her forehead to the polished metal door, mortified.

'What did the Ribenas have in them?' he demanded.

'Plum gin.' She put her face in her hands. 'Lester has enough stored under the stairs to hospitalise a rugby club.'

'How much have you had?'

'Only a splash, but the man makes it navy strength.' She looked at him through her fingers. 'You'd think a closet alcoholic could hold her booze, but I had *one* lousy glass and look at me.'

'When did you last eat?'

'I can't remember.'

'There's your answer. That and the fact your measure was probably a half-pint mug.'

'I'm so sorry.' She buried her face in her arms. 'Christ, I'm a terrible mother.'

'Let's cancel the school, shall we?'

'God, no! I'm bloody doing this!' she shouted into her sleeves.

'Then I'm driving you,' he told her wearily, standing up again. 'And don't blaspheme.'

'Were you once ordained or something?' Her voice was still muffled.

'I'm no priest, Pax, I told you that.'

'So the altar boy has an alter ego?' Her face lifted, incredulous. 'Luca the lush who gets the plum gin vibe.'

'I get all of it, Pax,' he said, holding out a hand to help her up.

'And if I don't want your help?'

'That's no longer an option.'

13

The sliding glass screen in the front reception area of Compton Magna's small primary school was still polka-dotted by the nervous fingerprints of parents signing in late pupils that morning. Manning it, head teacher Auriol Bullock was moist with anticipation beneath her ruffle-necked Boden. An inch of white creeping into her burgundy bob, eyes outlined twice in kohl like a circle around a misspelling, crimson lipstick bleeding into old smoker's creases, Auriol bore the ghost of the glamour that had won her two handsome husbands, a leading role in the Broadbourne Amateur Dramatic Society and an Ofsted 'Good' twice running ('Outstanding for Parent Satisfaction', boasted a banner on the school gates). A stickler for correct uniform, manners and posture – and for being greeted with a bright 'Good day, Mrs Bullock!' by all – Auriol possessed unexpected theatrical panache as well as an allergy to paperwork.

She was intensely proud of Compton Magna C of E Primary School – or 'Maggers' as she referred to it when emailing former colleagues – which had gifted her merriment in widowhood. Her little barn conversion in nearby Greater Compton was a haven after the sociable cathedral city years with her choirmaster late husband, and with both adult sons in the army, Auriol was a self-styled grandmother-in-waiting, early retirement beckoning.

This role, a step down from her previous headship, was easing her gently into a quieter life, grateful that she had fewer of the little buggers' names to remember in such a small school. Her memory had become increasingly unreliable throughout her fifties and faced with a long list of Mias, Ellies, Rubies, Ethans and Freddies, Auriol regularly blanked. Even worse was trying to recall what their confounded parents called themselves, which should have made it rather useful that there were so many here with one surname. Yet even thinking the name Turner made Auriol's left eye twitch involuntarily.

The village school had been on the brink of closure when she'd taken over the headship four years earlier, and whilst it still struggled with numbers – draughty Victorian classrooms in an Internet dead-zone were no rival to the high-tech, architect-designed Cotswold learning hubs in Broadbourne and Chipping Hampton – Maggers now boasted old-fashioned boaters-and-slates discipline and modern wrap-around care. Being just inside the catchment for Warwickshire's best grammar schools meant it was ripe territory for those who wanted a Cotswold postcode whilst still looking to save money by getting their little Edies and Axls through the Eleven Plus. Under her leadership, 'Maggers' offered extra tuition from the get-go, plus breakfast clubs and high tea for the convenience of busy commuter parents, lots of externally sourced educational after-school clubs that parents paid through the nose for, and ever-more lavish play facilities funded by a PTA with more high flyers sitting on it than Alan Sugar's boardroom. Its divorce lawyer Chair was a volunteer-enlisting legend, on occasion also discreetly steering new parents in the school's direction. And today, Mrs Beadle might just have landed Auriol with a very fine feather for Maggers' cap.

Annual budget stripped bare, Auriol had, by necessity, become adept at enticing parents with deep pockets, the redistribution of wealth starting at her school gates. Old money always attracted new in Auriol's experience, and where a hand-stitched country boot led, the well-heeled followed. She glanced out of the glass door again, eyeing the lane for movement. Where was the blasted woman? Among social influencers, blue blood was gold dust.

A devotee of the *Observer*'s glossy style magazines, Auriol had a sharp eye for trends, her latest mission to recreate Soho Farmhouse's Teeny Camp and Barn to satisfy the influx of hipster parents emigrating from London. And whilst she couldn't deny that almost a quarter of her register shared the surname Turner, she liked to think her little school was gaining a name for being select, cosmopolitan and just a little bit boho. On its register were the children of an artist, the head of a charity and an actress who had appeared in *The Archers*; one of the parent governors had written speeches for Blair, another was in a same-sex relationship with the Birmingham Symph's lead cellist, and of course Mrs Beadle, the PTA's Lord Kitchener, had personally overseen three celebrity divorces and lifted the Bardswold MP's super-injunction. Auriol's roll-call even had a glamorously high ethnicity thanks to the two large families who now ran the old coaching inns on the Fosse Way as Indian and Thai restaurants. As credentials went, socially diverse Compton Magna was up there with champagne-socialist Islington. Only with more Turners and less funding. Attracting liberal-thinking, philanthropic parents was a priority, especially if they had enough land for a forest school.

As such, it had been a thrilling start to spring term to receive a call from a bass-voiced, noble-sounding mother who said she was considering Maggers for her son on the advice of Helen Beadle. Auriol's spies – AKA dinner lady Mrs Rogers and cleaner Janine – told her the family was village royalty, which meant that this mummy was either a leftie, broke or that the son had special needs – quite possibly all three – causes which Auriol joyfully championed for her inclusive little learning ark.

Spotting a figure on the path at last, she straightened her hair and glanced up at the clock. She rarely forgave poor punctuality, but she was making an exception for this much-delayed appointment, and craned eagerly round the smeary glass panel to admire an expensively cut suit in fur-collared tweed, racily matched with geek glasses, air-brushed matte make-up, a spectacular trout pout, and the defiant jewellery punkery of the modern aristo.

Beaming, she buzzed the visitor through the door, greeting her with a vigorous hand shake. Oh bother, she'd forgotten the woman's name and her notes were in her office. 'Welcome! I'm Mrs Bullock. No time to lose, let's sign the book and go straight round, shall we?'

She peered beadily over the tweed shoulder as the visitor wrote her name in a small, neat hand, but without her glasses it was impossible to decipher.

'We'll do a quick tour first!' She ushered her through the inner security door. 'Let me take you straight to the newly refurbished IT suite. Feel free to ask questions as we go.' A soliloquist of guided tours, she then kept up a non-stop patter which brokered no interruptions, spoken in her best matriarchal stage voice, warm and anecdotal with just a smattering of hard-sell statistics, fingers trailing along the more impressive equipment bought by the PTA, from sensory wall to digital boards.

Auriol's well-rehearsed, whistle-stop route around the school was faster than ever by necessity. Not only was she conducting a job interview imminently – the wretched Governors insisted that her 'it's-all-in-my-head' approach to admin needed outside help – but there were very few windows of opportunity in which the school's four classrooms were anything less than chaotic bedlam. By luck, today's delayed circuit timed out between the messy miscreants from Reception starting art and the Year Five thugs heading outside for sport, its finale coinciding with Class Two's music lesson in which Barnaby Nairsmith – who had been hothoused through his trumpet grades by ambitious parents – was treating them all to his Grade Three pieces.

Her visitor looked impressed, even though Harry Unwin, sporting noise-cancelling earphones, wouldn't stop banging the cymbals in close proximity.

'He's on the spectrum,' Auriol explained in hushed tones, sweeping her hurriedly away before Harry could start on the bongos. 'We *love* our special children here. Now tell me *all* about your son!' She ushered her into her office and then did a U-turn as she heard the door buzzer going. 'Sorry – there's nobody in the front office, so I'll have to go down let them in. Job interviewee. A friendly little school like this is nothing without its multi-tasking Head!'

As soon as Auriol saw the woman waiting behind the sliding glass screen, she knew she wouldn't be offering her the position of office administrator. Thin and scruffy with dreadful dreadlocky red hair, she'd made no great effort. She looked half-asleep. She was totally the wrong type, but one must go through due procedure.

'Take a seat,' she ordered snippily, cranking open an inch-wide gap. 'I'm just meeting a prospective parent. I'll be with you shortly.' She snapped it shut again, almost taking the woman's freckled nose off.

Upstairs, the classy fur-collared mother – whose name Auriol still couldn't remember – was gazing out of the window, no doubt admiring her family's extensive acreage. Standing beside her, Auriol wondered whether to casually mention the need for a forest school.

'So there's more than one applicant here today, is there?' the mother asked jealously. Her pronounced lower lip – it had to be cosmetically enhanced – was affecting her speech, the drawling vowels sounding almost foreign.

Auriol was thrilled that the mother might imagine places at this school were as hotly contested as her son's alma mater (the name of which she'd also forgotten, but she knew it was one of the Cotswold preps parents put their children's names down for at birth).

'Oh lots!' she lied gushily. '*Everyone* wants to be a part of Maggers. I'm practically turning parents away. Remind me, Mrs – um...' She groped for her glasses to look at her computer screen, but the school logo had long since kicked in over her calendar meaning she'd have to look up the password in her diary again. 'Your son is how old?'

'Just over a year.'

'Nothing like getting the name down early! But I thought you said...' She copied MYP455WoRD laboriously from diary to keyboard. Aha! 'Kester is five?'

'Kester Forsyth probably is five.' The woman turned back from the window, eyebrows raised, the pierced one glinting. '*His* mother's just leaving the building.'

Auriol looked from Mrs P. Forsyth's details on her screen to the plump-lipped usurper. The pendant on her necklace bore a big sparkly B.

'Is this what they call a Specsavers' moment?' she asked in a small voice.

'It's what they call your lucky day that I'm here, Mrs Bullock.'

For the first time, Auriol realised that what she'd taken as a Chelsea drawl was an Irish accent. 'And who are you?'

'Bridget Mazur, your job applicant.' She offered her hand and shook the Head's firmly. 'Hire me now and you won't muddle up your appointments again. My synchronised diaries are things of beauty.'

'Get her back in here, Mrs Mazur, and the job's yours.'

'I'm not authorised to do that.'

'You are now.'

The phone on her desk rang with perfect theatricality. Auriol plucked it up, using her sing-song receptionist voice. 'Compton Magna Primary School, how may I help?'

'Auriol Bullock,' droned the caller. Bound to be a sales rep.

'One moment, please.' She covered the receiver and mouthed *very important call*, waving the usurper outside to catch her runaway mother then, settling back and reaching for the biscuit drawer, she switched her tone to dragon. 'Mrs Bullock speaking.'

Moments later, a packet of M&S shortbreads went flying. Ofsted would be inspecting Maggers the following morning. All thoughts of social influencers and forest school forgotten, she rang Mrs Beadle. 'It's a Code Red, repeat Code Red! We need to get the PTA booze out of the kitchen and COSHH to assess the barbecue gas.'

Unlike most head teachers, Auriol thrived on drama, always relishing the buzz of an inspection, like discovering a few minutes before curtain-up that a critic is in the theatre. Clicking her knuckles, she started making a list, top of which was *Hire Mrs Thing as Secretary* and *Get Hair Done*.

Pax hadn't appreciated how spaced-out on plum gin and lack of sleep she was until gripped by an overwhelming desire to throw the guitar tuition flyers on the reception desk at Auriol Bullock and tell her to fuck off for being so offhand. Lester, old school when it came to competitive hip flasks, clearly dosed his mix with pure ethanol. The dressage measure had ridden roughshod over her straight thinking.

Now safely outside, gulping cool air, she regretted not taking Luca's advice to eat something, or at least drink coffee. Her mouth tasted of toothpaste, still undercut with a burn of bile from making herself throw up before she'd come out. But he didn't know about that.

Pax could hear him speaking Italian on his phone in the Noddy car. Her stomach squirmed and churned all the more. Reluctant to share confined space with the multi-lingual Puritan again so soon, she was now battling an urge to run away across the village green. Half a mile of his driving had already made her car sick. She was mortified by his hairy humanity in close proximity.

Take charge, she told herself furiously. You're not the child here. Your son is.

When she wrenched open the passenger door, he looked up from his phone in surprise mid-call, finger sliding across the mic hole. 'That was quick.'

'I'm not sending my son here.'

She threw her bag inside, looking back as a voice shouted from the pathway, 'Wait!'

A silver-and-pink-haired woman in glasses was running towards her.

'I'm so, *so* sorry, Mrs Forsyth,' she swung through the gate, 'Mrs Bollock – I mean Bullock – is snowed under with appointments today.'

'She was incredibly offhand.'

'Entirely my fault! I mistook you for the – um – the nit lady. Total jobsworth; evil with a comb. But the kids love her!' she added, flustered, hurrying across the car park, wincing as she turned a high heel.

'I've changed my mind. I'm not coming in. Sorry.'

'You are *so* going to regret this.' The pink-tipped woman wasn't giving up. 'Sure, it's a great little school. At least have a look round. I make a cracking cup of coffee – and we give away free pens. I'm Bridge…' She gazed imploringly across the car roof. Inside, Luca was talking on the phone in Italian again.

Pax eyed the pink-haired woman, who looked endearingly bonkers, like a dark-hearted Alice from *Vicar of Dibley*, with a huge, fuchsia-painted lower lip.

'Bring your husband in this time, why doncha?' She'd leant down to wave at Luca through the window where he was still jabbering in Italian. She resurfaced, pink-faced. 'Only that's not your husband, that's the Horsemaker.'

'How d'you know Luca?'

'Long story, so it is!' Brash and direct, her accent was shot through with Belfast good humour that was comfortingly familiar, a reminder of a friend Pax had known years ago, a teenage bond in extremis. 'Are you coming back or what?'

'What did you say your name was again?' Pax asked her.

'I'm Ms Mazur.' She held out her hand to shake over the car roof. 'Shit, that sounds like one of He-Man's enemies, doesn't it? Mesmerising Mezmasur. I didn't just say shit, did I?'

'It's fine, Mezmasur.' Pax shook it, finding a smile creeping through her scowl. 'I'm too mesmerised to notice.'

And the strangest thing was, she did feel pleasantly hypnotised by Bridge Mazur, by this warm glow of déjà vu. Pax could taste the memory of that old friendship in her mouth like lime and salt, feel the rush of her blood pumping faster. Seventeen again, rebellious and courageous. The first friend she'd made after she'd run away to London had been a girl from Belfast, with the same grey almond eyes as this woman. Over cheap weed and tequila, she'd restored Pax's sense of humour.

'Truth is, I don't actually work here yet,' Bridge confessed in a whisper. 'This is my job interview and if you come back in with me, I'll get it.'

'Do you really want that woman as a boss?'

'I really do. Please help me out. You don't have to send your wee lad here, just humour Mrs Bollock for five minutes.'

'Bullock.'

'That's her name now.' *Noi* she pronounced it, a once-familiar riff. 'She's a livewire; original Minerva McGonagall, so she is. Devoted to this place.'

Pax looked up at the Victorian school's red-brick face, the two inverted V gables glowing like chunks of Toblerone, its gingerbread too sweet to be soured by the fierce headmistress. Kes was extremely fond of sharp-tongued women if his affection for both grandmothers was anything to go by, and at least it spared her being trapped in a car with Luca again. She could pay it lip service then leave.

Luca was still yabbering on the phone.

'Okay, I'll take a quick look,' she said, joining Bridge who hurried her back up the path, signalling to a first-floor window, then pointing towards the classrooms. Pax spotted

Mrs Bullock with a phone receiver pressed to one side of her glossy blonde bob making frantic hand gestures and miming a throat being cut.

'The Head is preparing to teach Class Four about the French Revolution,' Bridge said smoothly. 'She'll catch us up.'

As soon as Bridge began guiding Pax Forsyth round the same lap of the school that she'd recently taken, she could hazard a guess why Mrs Bullock had made throat-cutting gestures from her window. The classrooms, a bastion of calm discipline minutes earlier, had descended into pandemonium, rulers, exercise books and Sharpies flying, the wall of sound painful. The small boy in headphones from Class Three, now in possession of bongos, was lost in a Hendrix-like trance. In another classroom a cookery lesson was taking place beneath a fog of flour and icing sugar. Outside, a herd of ten-year-olds in red sweatshirts appeared to be trying to bury each other in mud.

'Lovely age to be!' Bridge shouted over the din, guessing it was a far cry from the hushed, cloistered seats of learning the family was accustomed to.

She stole another look at Pax, quietly relieved to find that she wasn't nearly so hot at close quarters – the pale marble skin, dotted with freckles, was waxy, there was a spot on her chin, hair was unwashed, eyes bloodshot – although her voice was pure honey. 'Do your children come here?'

'Not yet, but friends' kids do. One has a little boy who started here last year and she reckons it's given him bags of confidence, stopped him being so aggressive. He was a right thug, apparently.'

'I blame the fathers,' Pax muttered.

'Me too usually, but this one's dad's pretty cool,' she sighed. The bare-fist fighter with the bare-faced cheek, and hands of a surgeon. 'So's his mum, come to that.' She pulled herself together. 'Total angel. Terrific with horses. A natural, everyone says.'

Pax was looking at her curiously. She really stared, Bridge noticed, her big, fawn eyes not looking through her as Carly described, but instead seeming to see into her thoughts, that shameful medley of sex toys, skin glue, Ash's finger in her mouth and lust leaping to her groin. Her sore lip throbbed.

'So this is a lovely learning environment as you can see!' She tried to think educationally worthy thoughts, but instead found herself imagining Fantasy Ash was taking the PE class outside, all steamy clouds of breath and muscly football legs. 'You can just see how much fun all the little ones have, whilst still benefitting from first-class teaching.' She marched Pax across a covered courtyard so she could look in on the deserted school hall set with lunch tables. 'And we feed them too!' she improvised badly. 'Nutritionally balanced superfood, not any old shi – sh – she— shish kebab, you know?'

Pax was staring at her intently again. 'Have we met before?'

'Sure, I don't think so.' Bridge hoped she couldn't pick her out of a line-up of riders in bobble-topped helmets who might have gawped at her weeping in her car a week earlier. She recrossed the courtyard at a wobbly high-heeled jog, starting to feel out of her depth. 'It's Reception your wee man's going to be in, is it not?'

'That's right.' Pax paused to admiring a sensory wall. 'Kes never stops; he's got no off button.'

'I'll bet there's plenty here like that.' Bridge led the way back along a corridor lined with small, brightly coloured coats on pegs, abandoned backpacks and wellies, pausing as she tried to remember which classroom Reception was.

'His current school tries to run his batteries flat with rugby,' Pax was saying, 'French vocabulary and choir practice. He's *five*.' She picked up a brace of fallen Mini Rodini coats to hang on neighbouring empty pegs labelled *Ignatius MacMaster* and *Inigo MacMaster*.

'Pair of iMacs,' Bridge registered breathlessly.

Pax tilted her head, eyes lingering on the labels. Then she

looked away with a low, amused hiccup Bridge caught like a sneeze.

Without warning, infectious laughter seized them both, a silent, rib-pinching intimacy they didn't know what to do with. They turned in opposite directions to bring it under control.

'Ssstop,' the honeyed voice whispered, a slight slur to it that made Bridge think of those drawling voices from *Made in Chelsea*. Too posh to talk proper, her mum would say.

A small boy hurtled past on the way to the loo, breaking into a walk as he drew level with them, nodding a polite head, then pelting on.

'This place,' Bridge confessed in an urgent whisper, 'it makes you believe that not all's wrong in the world, you know? Even though this is like the weirdest interview ever, and the Head's barking mad – and don't worry, I know you're never going to send your kid here – I still want this job. It matters. That gut thing's going on, you know?' She tapped her belly. It was busy, butterflies galore, although in fairness most had been airborne since Ash had told her he couldn't be trusted around her. 'Crazy, is it not?'

'I know exactly that gut thing.' The eyes intensified, curious.

Bridge had heard so much about Pax Forsyth from the Bags and Carly, it had never occurred to her that she might like her. There was something about her which made her an instant confidante, that dangerous edge women recognise in one another, the ballet dance along blades.

'Intuition and indigestion feel different, don't they?' Bridge whispered.

'I can never work it out.'

'You're a horsewoman. Stand up in your stirrups and gallop; you never want it to end, do you? It's just the same thing standing in your heels, knowing exactly what you want.'

'I'm not that person.'

'Sure, you are,' Bridge insisted, infused with such certainty she rocked back on her own heels. 'We all are. The only thing that stops any of us is not believing it.'

The freckled face coloured, eyes bright, listening to the babble in the classrooms, the loud, amused voice of the teachers, the shared laughter and chatter. They looked at each other in a brief, unguarded moment, skirted by pegs at hip height, and friendship clicked.

'I have the gut thing today, too,' Pax said incredulously.

'Trust it,' Bridge urged, although looking at her, she did worry Pax might be feeling a bit dyspeptic. She looked as if she was going hot and cold, her cheeks red-stained now, dizziness in her eyes.

'I shouldn't trust myself with anything today.' She turned to look at the art on the walls, hallucinogenic interpretations of Van Gogh's *Starry Night*.

When they finally located Reception's classroom, the children that Bridge had seen lined up in clean smocks half an hour earlier had mutated into sand-crusted, paint-splattered Picassos, devoting their creative talents to brightly coloured grainy masterpieces. Despite big plastic smocks, paint dripped from hands and faces, and their form teacher had a Frida Kahlo-monobrow paint smudge.

'We're experimenting with texture,' the teacher announced cheerfully, stepping back as a small boy charged past trailing red sand. 'Walk, Ellis Turner! Picasso walked! Matisse walked. Turners *walk*.'

'That's my friend's boy,' Bridge told Pax as Ellis apologised and went into an exaggerated tiptoe creep to his easel, making his classmates laugh.

'He's sweet.'

'Anxious little fella, but he holds it all in. They do, boys, don't they? You have to turn their lives upside down to let it drop out sometimes.'

'Do you really think so?' The all-seeing gaze was sharing her headspace again.

'Sure! Why not?' Bridge focussed hard on all things positive. 'Works on men, too.'

Pax looked down, red cheeks now tinged with purple, and for the first time Bridge thought to question why Mr Pax wasn't here.

They could still hear blood-curdling war cries coming from the playing fields, just audible over the bongos and science lesson shrieks in neighbouring classrooms and the excited artists clattering and splatting around them. Bridge watched Pax's gaze follow the colourful little group, the way her natural warmth bubbled up through the polite restraint when a little girl came and tugged at her sleeve, demanding, 'Who are you?'

'Kes's mummy.' She was on her haunches straight away, the girl playing with her amazing hair.

'Who is Kes?'

'I hope you'll meet him soon.'

Dropping down beside them, Bridge high-fived the girl, who giggled.

They watched her skip away, the friendship clicking again.

Back out in the corridor by the coat pegs, Bridge couldn't contain her excited astonishment. 'You're going to bring Kester here?'

'I'd like him to try it for a day. I'm standing up in my stirrups like you said.'

Bridge wanted to hug her. They paused by the iMacs again. 'Sure, it's a bit of a madhouse.'

'Kes needs noise and chaos,' Pax had kind creases at the edges of her eyes, 'not cricket whites and oak-panelled corridors carved with war heroes' names.'

'Too fecking right!' Bridge laughed without thinking, then clamped her hand over her mouth. 'Shit, sorry, I swear I've got Tourette's syndrome. I blame my foul-mouthed da.'

'I inherited Debrett's syndrome which is far worse.'

'No titles here. Everyone's equal, comrade.'

'Which is why I'd like Kes to try it out.' Pax pulled a phone from her pocket and started to type a message with a deft thumb. 'Thank you *so* much for showing me around, comrade, you've helped enormously.'

'I did nothing.' Bridge shrugged, delighted. *Apart from ignoring every professional jobsworth tick-box red tape bureaucratic guideline I know.* Education rocked.

'Oh, you did,' Pax insisted, thumb still typing. 'How's your stomach feeling?'

'Fierce. Yours?'

'Better.' She sent her message, head tilted, scrutinising Bridge's face again. 'You really do remind me of someone.'

'Anyone famous?' She hoped it would be Lady Gaga or Pink.

'Friend from years back. We shared a house in London. Can we see the Head now?'

'Yes, of course. I'm sure Mrs Bullock will have finished her Very Important Call by now.' *If I'm lucky, she might even remember to interview me.* 'Would you like to come this way, Mrs Forsyth?'

'Mezmasur.'

Upstairs, Auriol Bullock had repainted her red cross-hatched lips to cover up after a comforting sugar binge, telltale biscuit crumbs in her ruffle neck, the phone still hot and covered in face powder from being pressed to her ear. Beckoning them in, she flipped over a piece of paper covered in handwritten notes and tucked it under a box file. 'Tell me, how did you find our little slice of paradise, Mrs…?'

'Mrs *Forsyth* has some good news for you,' Bridge said helpfully.

Auriol's eyes bulged ecstatically from their painted rims when Pax asked how soon Kes could try out a day at the school.

'Like yoga swamis, we pride ourselves in our flexibility here at Maggers.'

'I've got to speak to Kester's father first.' Pax glanced at her phone screen again. 'I've messaged him, and if he agrees, Kes can try it out next week if that's all right?'

'Absolutely! I'll need you to fill in a form.' Pulling down a big box file marked New Student Primary Admissions, she opened it to reveal some old copies of *The Educator* magazine and half a bottle of Courvoisier. 'Ah! Just need to print some new ones off.' She groped for her glasses, stooping over the computer. 'Oh bother, it's locked. Where's that password again?'

Bridge discreetly pushed her diary towards her. After Auriol made several failed attempts inputting the password, she did that for her too.

'Thank you, Ms Mazur. In fact, could you stay and take Mrs Forsyth's details too?'

'You'll need my CRB and DBS checks verified along with making a formal job offer and receiving acceptance before I can process data,' Bridge reeled off. Her wretched swollen lip was giving her an ever-worsening lisp. 'I shouldn't be showing prospective parents around unaccompanied either.'

Mrs B drew her closer, whispering, 'If you want this job, consider yourself screened and working,' then aloud, 'Do use my desk and perhaps Mrs Forsyth would like a coffee?' She gesticulated towards an old-fashioned filter machine puttering toxically in the corner. 'I'm just popping out to check on the little people and have a quick word with my staff. Back in five!' As she left, Bridge distinctly heard a hissed *yesssss* from the corridor.

'I think I just got the job,' she told Pax, in a shocked undertone.

'Congratulations.'

'That's batshit, that is. This day is so turning out to be fecking weird. Like I'm drunk or something, you know?'

Pax smiled awkwardly. 'I might have that coffee.'

The coffee, which had evaporated its way to bitter caramel, tasted vile.

'We'll have a pod machine, plus Rooibos and peppermint tea on offer by half-term,' Bridge promised, adding a slick of UHT milk from a plastic capsule into the cup before handing it across. 'And frothed, filtered milk.'

'It's honestly delicious.' Pax gulped some, fielding an incoming message on her phone and frowning, thumb firing off an immediate reply, then glancing out of the window at her car, in which, Bridge remembered, Luca O'Brien was sitting like Parker awaiting Lady Penelope. Intriguing.

'This won't take long.' Behind Mrs Bullock's screensaver, she found an open Google search for chiropodists in Chipping Hampton. The computer's files were a predictable bomb site, but she tracked down what she needed quickly enough, pulling up the official-looking form. 'Can I start with your son's full birth name?'

'Oliver Alexander Jocelyn Forsyth.' The deep voice tightened.

'Not Kester?' Bridge looked up in surprise.

'Names were never my husband's strong point. He registered the birth.' Pax had a sweet laugh, but her eyes betrayed her, that flash of honesty women recognised in each other. Bad things had happened.

'I'll put Kester as his given name, then,' Bridge whizzed on kindly, her sensors on high alert. 'What's his date of birth?'

It was two years and a day earlier than Bridge's chunky monkey Flavia's, her beautiful girl whose father had wanted to call her Jakub even after the three-month scan revealed that their firstborn was unlikely to ever score for Arsenal's premiership male team. Aleš's obvious disappointment that she wasn't a son still maddened Bridge, one of her husband's shortcomings that she stewed over in the early hours, woken by his snoring and unable to get back to sleep.

'Address?'

'That's rather complicated. Kes's father and I only separated last week so we've not entirely sorted the living arrangements out yet.' Pax's eyes gleamed – was that tears or elation? – and

Bridge had to bite back a 'fecking hell'. It made complete sense. The lay-by phone calls; being at the stud so often; the change of school; the electricity coming off her that was strangely uplifting, almost redemptive.

'Changing his school is terribly bad timing, I know, but...'

'We've a Walsh family saying: "There's no such thing as bad timing, just timing. And the clock's ticking",' Bridge had carefully edited out two feckings.

'I like that.' Pax made a valiant attempt at a bright smile. 'Thank you.'

Fearing her professionalism was already so highly compromised that her Chartered Institute of Logistics and Transport Office Manager of the Year 2015 would be stripped from her bedroom mantelpiece, she resisted the urge to draw her chair closer in sisterly support and ask how they were all coping, ears wagging.

Typing in two different addresses for Kester's parents, Bridge sensed that today's bureaucratic form-filling in a small village school office was Pax Forsyth's Magna Carta. For all her careful, politic answers, hers was plainly a war-torn motherhood. And with every answer, she seemed to grow brighter, bolder, to claim ownership of a boy she'd only seen through the refracted lens of an unhappy marriage, her son's five years on an open file: religion, ethnicity, disabilities, behavioural issues. Bridge, who had handled personal data throughout her career, felt like she was gathering something far more intimate than facts: pieces of a relationship that was being liberated. Pax's independence was so new, it was as though she had to remind herself every few minutes that she was in control of her life, her ever-lifting mood catching as they covered meal preference ('he'll eat whatever the school serves and finish off everyone else's') and image permission ('you can try, but it'll be blurred because he won't stand still').

'Mode of transport to school: private car, car share, taxi, bicycle, bus, walking?'

'Is there a plane and tank option?' she laughed. 'Kes travels everywhere in an imaginary one or the other. Put walk, although we'll have a screaming match about it.'

Bridge found it hard to imagine jazz-voiced Pax shouting at anyone. 'Does Kes have a nut allergy?'

'Only if they have broccoli attached.' Pax was looking out of the window. Following her gaze, Bridge saw the blond, bearded Horsemaker – a tousle-haired Zeus – now out of the little car, pacing around impatiently.

She was dying to know what was going on there. Just wait until the Bags heard about it.

'Won't keep you much longer,' she promised, typing the stud's address again in the Emergency Contact section. 'It's a beautiful place you have there; I've always admired it from a distance.' Lay it on, Bridge. 'It must be amazing inside.'

'Come over and I'll show you around if you like,' Pax offered obligingly.

'I might just take you up on that!' That would put Petra's nose thoroughly out of joint, she thought, saving the file and locating the printer which was spewing out hard copies. 'That's us done if you'll just sign it here. I'm free to come to yours any time.'

'Perhaps you could bring along the friend and her boy who's in Reception?' Pax suggested, signing with an exaggerated, swirly P and F. 'One afternoon next week after pickup if you like? It would be lovely for Kes to meet one of his classmates before he tries a day here.' She stood up and shrugged on her coat.

'It's a date! I'll walk you to your car.' On a roll and now hopeful of an introduction to the Horsemaker. Today was turning out to be vintage.

'Don't come out in the cold.' Pax turned with a firm handshake in the little front reception. 'Thank you, Mesmazur. You live up to your magical name.'

Glowing happily, lip throbbing gently, Bridge bounded

back upstairs to write her own contract, texting Aleš first, *Got the job!* He replied instantly with a row of smiley faces and aubergines.

Pax felt supercharged, zinging with strong coffee and rare high spirits. Today's 'I'm free' headrush was hardcore, wired to the mains, Luca yet again uncomfortably close witness to it.

'I'm probably completely mad,' she laughed as they set off. 'I think the Head has early onset dementia, the new secretary's plans for world domination start with the filing cabinet, and the children are all feral, but it feels right.'

'Where am I going?' He was driving too fast, eager to get on.

Pax longed to send him back to the stud but couldn't face the fight. She might not yet be legal to drive. She probably wasn't in the best state to make life-changing decisions for her son or face her in-laws either, but she was too ebullient to care. 'Follow the signs to Broadbourne. I'll text to make sure they're back.' She started to type the message, adding, 'I'm really so grateful for this.'

'The place certainly cheered you up.'

The soft voice had a sanctimonious edge she let pass, unable to contain her enthusiasm. 'That little school, for all its chaos, is just the sort of positive environment Kes needs. The schools I went to were just like the one he hates, and I hated them too, especially when we got older and were sent away to board. I was always bullied: about my mother, my hair, my deep voice, my big feet, you name it. I was miles from home and lonely, and I loathed all the one-upmanship and toadying. I remember swearing that my own children would be state educated, but when it came to Kes, Mack overruled me and my grandfather backed him up.'

Pax felt in control for the first time in months. She'd even made a new friend. 'He needs to learn to be a kid again, you know? Like that grey beast of Mummy's needs to remember how to be a horse. And I need to relearn how to be...' She hesitated, realising saying *a woman* might be misconstrued.

'Sober?'

Again, she let his moralising wash over her. 'If you want, I can lock all the bottles of plum gin in the tack room safe and give you the key when we get back, Luca. I'm not screwing this up for Kes. He'll suit that little school, I know it.'

She could almost feel her feathers lifting from depression's oil slick, her urge to fly towards blue sky overwhelming.

'So you're planning on sticking around at the stud, then?' he asked, eyes fixed on the road.

'Don't worry, Father O'Brien, I'll keep out of your way.'

'I don't want you to do that.' He looked across at her. 'I want you to come with me to an Alcoholics Anonymous meeting.'

'Take a right turn here.' She didn't want to think about it. 'Why are we stopping?'

He pulled into a passing place and cut the engine, silencing the booming bass from the stereo as he turned to her, the smile gone. 'I know you think I'm a pain in the arse, but I won't let this drop.'

'Fine! I'll go to one.' She wouldn't.

'You won't.'

'Did you?'

'A couple of times, before I left Canada.'

'Mack had a friend who went through Gamblers Anonymous. He had go and ask forgiveness from everyone he'd hurt through betting, like a door-to-door salesman.'

'That's not until step nine or ten.'

'How many are there?'

'Twelve.'

'Isn't it a bit excessive? I just want to cut down.'

'Your husband is almost certainly going to accuse you of alcohol dependence in order to get custody of your son, am I right?'

She nodded, getting his point, the phone in her hand a loaded gun of texts from Mack, quick to disavow her of the idea their son would try out Compton Magna's primary school, starting with *You must accept that he's coming to live in Scotland* and most recently *NOT HAPPENING!* Just reading them made her hands clench in need of two big vodkas, one to drink and the other to throw in his face. She was determined to prove him wrong, although praying for God's absolution from Absolut with Luca O'Brien was surely a step too far.

'Luca, I really appreciate what you're trying to do, but there's no way I can stand up in front of a room of strangers and say, "My name is Patricia Forsyth and I'm an alcoholic. Here is my story..." It's like asking me to take my clothes off.' Then she remembered she'd done just that in front of Luca whilst drunk. The car suddenly felt very small and her face very hot.

'You can just listen. I didn't tell anyone *my* story.'

'Is it that bad?'

He didn't answer and it occurred to her that Luca might not be telling her the whole truth, that as a self-confessed drunk he knew all the same cover-ups she did. 'How do I know you've really stopped?'

'Because I've not had a drink in a fortnight?'

'You could still be boozing on the sly too; I could be trapped with the Keith Moon of County Kildare here.'

'I'm not,' he snapped. 'Is this Keith Moon fella a family friend or something?'

She was surprised at his sharpness. 'He was The Who's drummer.'

He looked blank.

'You know the song "My Generation"?' Pax sang a few lines, stopping before the bit about hoping to die before growing old in case he used it as leverage. 'My brother wanted it played at our father's funeral, but the grandparents put the boot in, insisting on "Abide With Me". He drove a Rolls Royce into a swimming pool.'

'Your father?'

'Keith Moon. He walked away afterwards. Daddy slammed a Subaru Forester into a horse chestnut on the A46. Not so lucky.' She read a reply from Muir, who inevitably texted as though writing a telegram: *Disembark train 14.45 hrs. ETA bungalow 15.00 hrs. Be advised fish lunch. M&MF.*

That's much later than agreed, she replied. *Can you drop Kes off at the stud on your way home?*

Negative. K can stay overnight with us if preferred. M&MF

'Piss off,' she told the phone, good mood evaporating as she typed: *Will be there 3 p.m. sharp. Be advised, NOT happy about this.*

'We might as well go back, Luca,' she said distractedly. 'They're running late.'

She wanted to scream and kick the footwell. They'd be calling Mack now, she guessed. He would log the exchange in his meticulously kept records. Records that would undoubtedly catalogue the many, many times she'd drunk a whole bottle of wine to herself in an evening, sometimes two, not to mention the swigs from the cooking wine box in between, the vodka bottles he'd found hidden behind the recipe books, miniatures in her knicker drawer. The evidence was all there against her. She needed her own to prove that she was changing all that.

Luca hadn't started the car. He was waiting.

'Okay, I'll go with you to a meeting next week.' She had to work hard not to add 'you bastard' as prickles of irritation returned like a plague of ants, adding instead, 'On one condition.'

'Which is?'

'You tell your story. Right now. To me.' That would see the engine started and get them back home in five minutes, she predicted.

The smile was back. 'I can't do that.'

'Why not? Afraid I'll tell?'

'It's not that.' He glanced across at her warily.

'You don't have to talk about yourself to a room of strangers. Just me.'

He brandished the smile again, overpowering in the small space.

She mirrored it, fed up with all the hush and myth surrounding the Horsemaker, with strange incoming calls and multilingual outgoing ones, their International Man of Mystery in breeches. Was he even a drinker at all?

'What's stopping you?'

'You just want to shame me, Pax.'

She laughed, looking away, hating the truth bared. 'You think I'm that cruel?'

'I think you're that pissed off with me.'

'It's them, not you.' She shook her phone, as if little voodoo dolls of the Forsyths would rattle around inside and break a few bones. 'And I *do* want to know your story.' As she said it, she realised it was true. She'd never met anyone who had openly admitted to sharing the same problem. 'It might help. I won't shame you, I promise. We have time. The Grand-Forces' train is barely pulling out of Cheltenham.'

The smile fought her off. 'You really think it'll help?'

'Yes.' Curiosity catching hold, Pax pushed harder. 'Tell me how you reached your plum gin moment?'

In the back seat, Knott stood up to stretch and curl back down again. The car rocked as a gust of wind caught it.

Pax turned her phone to airplane mode. There was something strange happening inside the Noddy car, a shift in atmosphere she couldn't place, but it made her nerve ends tingle, her resolve deepen. She was known in the family for her ability to get blood from a stone, as well as her patience. She crossed her arms and settled back. This was a stand-off.

Luca stared out at the road. 'You're a stubborn woman.'

'Yip.' The car rocked again in the wind. 'When did it start?'

'A while back. I've always liked a few jars with the lads, you know? I was no lightweight.'

'What changed?'

'Oh, the usual. Unlucky in love.'

'Get dumped, get drunk?'

'Her dad had other plans for her and warned me off, but yeah, same end result.'

'How old were you?'

'Late twenties. I took a job out in the Middle East afterwards. Muslim country, but we all drank more than a night on the lash back home. Hard liquor, none of your Beamish and lager. I got my taste for Scotch there, I guess. I was downing a hell of a lot more by the time I came back.' He threw a glance at her, eyes intense.

'Go on.'

'Things had gone badly out there. They didn't get much better when the fella who'd warned me off his daughter offered me my old job back in Canada. I figured I'd got over it enough, and I wanted to stay out of Europe. Grand yard, he has, middle of nowhere. He can out-drink anyone and still jump off fastest against the clock. I kind of carried on in that fashion.'

'Nothing to do with the daughter?'

'She married someone else.' His eyes flashed. 'They moved away.'

'This is where you were working before you came here?'

He nodded. 'I went back most years. Your man there breeds horses like you've never seen, cool-headed as fighter pilots and scopey as hell, not like your tough hot bloods here. It's a big old place – a thousand hectares, near enough – easy to find your own headspace. Never as many stars in the sky as there.' Smiling, he looked away again.

The Irish brogue lent him a natural storyteller's voice, his enthusiasm bewitching.

'There's a fifty-acre lake in the woods with a log cabin the family use for fishing trips. We'd drive up there to work on our functioning alcoholism. It's probably thanks to him training me up that I eventually got so I could drink a bottle of liquor a night and still ride ten the next day.'

'You should be dead.'

'It was only in the last few months it got that bad. Winters there are harsh. The man's a showjumping legend, but he's a hard bastard with people, especially his family. Five Olympics his horses have competed in, one for each of his marriages.'

'A difficult character, then?'

'No more than many. I've worked with him a decade on and off; we understand each other. They treat me like family when I stay, and he protected me from some bad stuff going down after the job in the Middle East. But I went against his wishes, let him down.'

Pax remembered the call before he'd arrived, the death threat that had so shocked poor Lester and amused Ronnie.

'What happened to the daughter who got married? The one who's the reason you started drinking in the first place?'

He studied the road ahead. 'She had an affair.'

'With you?'

'It's over now. I drank way too much; I had to break the habit. That's my story.'

'That's barely an elevator pitch!' Pax complained. 'If it took you from highballs on the pontoon to suicide in a saddle, that's some love affair. I know what it takes to drink, remember? What changed?'

There was a long pause. Pax waited, sensing its energy crackle.

'I found out one of her kids is mine.'

She turned, open-mouthed.

'Her daughter, *our* daughter,' he corrected. 'She's six.'

Pax tried to imagine the shock of discovering he'd fathered a child older than Kes was now, a fully loaded little person, features shaped by genetics, character formed, loyalty forged to the parents who had raised her. 'What's her name?'

'Dizzy.'

'It's a sweet name.'

'Opening a bottle alone to toast my shock entry into fatherhood wasn't my finest hour.'

'It's a lot to take in.' No wonder he didn't want to tell it to a meeting room of scraping chairs and strangers. 'You never suspected?'

'They'd moved to the States by the time Dizzy was born; I was back in Europe. It was ten months after the wedding, so everyone always assumed she was a honeymoon baby.'

'The affair happened when she'd just married?'

The smile flashed uncomfortably. 'The wedding marquee was being taken down the day I arrived back there after drinking myself stupid in the Middle East,' he explained. 'Her dad's a cruel bastard. He wanted me to get the message loud and clear that his princess was taken.'

Pax envisaged the princess, wholesome in checked-shirt and jeans, ponytail swinging, perched on white post and rails. 'What's she like?'

She waited out a long pause.

'Fierce, funny, fearless.' Green eyes met hers. 'She'd been the original wild child. It drove the boss mad, even though we all knew she was a daddy's girl at heart. I was a part of her rebellion. She married another hard-bastard showjumper like her dad, a protégé of his.'

A car swept by with a swish of displaced air.

'And you flew back in to find the wedding tent still up?'

The green eyes held hers. 'They were living at the farm while they were waiting for their new yard to be built in Vermont. She used to come and talk to me, cry on my shoulder. Said that her husband was cold, all ego, useless in bed, that she'd never wanted to go through with it. I was still more than a bit in love with her, so you can guess the rest.' A finger tapped fast on the wheel.

Pax wanted to grab it and still it.

But the metronome cranked up to allegro. 'It was crazy

exciting. I suppose we both got off on all the secrecy. We decided to make a run for it, planned a fresh start in Ireland together; I bought the tickets, drank vodka in my coffee, rum in my Coke, fantasising myself as Hemingway. When she couldn't stop chucking up every morning, I thought it was nerves; I threw up plenty myself, knowing her dad would kill us both if he found out what we planned. Then, the day we were due to fly, she told me she couldn't go through with it. There was no talking her round. Said she wanted to make her marriage work. My first experience drinking myself stupid long-haul. Not my last.'

'She didn't tell you she was pregnant?' Pax felt a crash of empathy for the new young wife, forced to choose between safety and freedom, her first life-changing decision as a mother.

'I had no idea.'

'How long before you went back?'

'A couple of years. The old man wasn't letting me go and, if I'm honest, I needed the money. There's not many bosses who don't care if you ride drunk or sober as long as you ride well. I could go months without a drop, but then I'd just go off on one, y'know?' His gaze stayed fixed on hers.

'My habit's more of a daily dose.'

Luca nodded. 'You mould your life round it, don't you? I'd started taking jobs for that rather than the horses, places where hard-drinking was a part of the culture: big Dutch and German barns full of Slovak workers with their vodka, the South African dipsos, macho Brazilians lunchtime drinking. My Canadian friend was by far the worst for running a bar through the day, from Bloody Mary breakfast to triple measure nightcap; I went back there every year after that.'

'Did you ever see her?'

'Never saw, never asked. Her dad's not the sort to talk about family. There are pictures of horses on walls there, not grandchildren. But then last summer I flew in and she was living back home.'

'She left her husband?' Another rush of empathy.

'Oh, she'll never do that. He was there too, backslapping me like I'm a long-lost brother, saying the yard in Vermont cost too much to run so they'd brought his horses back over the St Lawrence to set up with her dad. Then he introduced me to their three kids: two little dark-haired, dark-eyed boys, the spit of their parents, and a girl with curly blonde hair and green eyes.'

'Dizzy.'

'She shakes your hand like a president and rides a fence like a deer. Pure O'Brien.'

'Oh God, that must have been agony for you.'

'Don't blaspheme. It was. It is.'

'What did you do?'

He glared at the windscreen, smile flashing like gunfire. 'I said nothing, did nothing. Drank. Went out on the lash with the boss. Drank some more on my own.'

'But you knew Dizzy was definitely yours?'

'Do two bays breed a palomino? Her mother was in a bad way, saying she'd never let herself believe it, that her husband was a devoted dad who lived for his kids even if the marriage was lousy and she suspected him of being unfaithful. She bought a home paternity test kit and sent off swabs from my mouth and Dizzy's, just so there was no doubt. Maybe she wanted it to be his, a miracle to make the marriage sparkle again. Back it came five days later telling us what we already knew. I'm Dizzy's natural father. She couldn't stop crying. Our love affair started again that night.' He raked his fingers through his hair, eyes wincing self-critically.

'I knew it was a mistake, but she thought so little of herself, I couldn't hurt her. She was right about her husband's infidelity. I'd been along on her dad's boys' only nights, playing poker for hours in the back room of this big old bar in Ottawa he liked, the sort with more hostesses than decent whiskys, y'know? While dad stayed in the game, husband threw in his hand to get straight on it, buying himself a private dance or two, and the rest. Wanted me as wingman, but I was having none of it. The drinks cost too much for a start.' He cast her a sideways smile, and Pax got a brief hint of the easy-going hellraiser who was happy to party with the devil all night as long as the bar was free.

'What about Dizzy?'

'I wanted the truth out in the open, but her mother insisted that the kids were too tiny, that she needed more time. Every time I made to leave, she'd win me back round, beg me to stay longer. She'd sneak to my apartment over the garages in the dead of night with a bottle of President to mix Raymond Massey cocktails – that woman could drink me under the table, always has – and we'd argue until dawn. She likes arguing, picking fights. It's her opera, her theatre. I was her audience.'

'Do you still love her?'

'What sort of a question's that?'

'An honest one.'

'She made me feel consequential, you know?'

She looked at him curiously. That bloody smile was in the way again. Without thinking, she reached up a hand to mask it from her line of vision like a spotlight. He jerked his head away violently.

'Sorry,' she said, recoiling.

'Have you heard enough now?' He was cornered and angry, veins high in his neck, pupils flooded. He looked, she realised, like her mother's grey stallion.

'Yes.' Pax looked away, ashamed.

But her head worked on, shocked to find itself thinking back to the night in the hotel airport, to her own drowning, out-of-control unhappiness. Comfort and care were instincts to Luca, even when it was the last place in the world he wanted to be. Pissed or sober, he gave comfort; in extremis, in transit, in loco, he put others' needs first. He'd be the medic on the front line, saving lives as mortars rained down.

'Actually, no.' She turned back. 'Tell me, did she hit you?'

The smile sent the eyes darting away for cover, fingers rubbing his chin. 'Is that another honest question?'

'Yes.'

'Sometimes, she hit me.' She could feel the mortification rippling off him.

'And you hit her?'

'Never.'

Pax rubbed her face. 'Sorry.'

'Why are you sorry?'

'It can't be an easy thing to admit to.'

'Sure, I work with horses, Pax. I've been kicked, bitten and trampled by plenty who've lost all trust in humans. I don't blame the horse, I blame the person who hurt them in the first place.'

'Horses don't drink a bottle of Scotch a night to blot it out.'

'Fair point.'

No matter how awful her marriage had become, how much he'd goaded her, Pax had never once got close to hitting Mack. His self-control was pure steel, the mental pain he inflicted dosed in metronome blows. In a passionate love affair, by contrast, sex and violence sometimes had a dangerously thin line between them. She remembered trying to slap Bay earlier that day and her hand burned in her lap.

'It wasn't all bad. I'd never stayed past September before. Autumn in Canada was my compensation, all golden trees and blue sky, pretending nothing was wrong. I used to go to the lake cabin after work, watch the moon on the water, play the fiddle, drink myself numb. Ronnie's invitation to come here was heaven sent.'

'How did they react?'

'I'd agreed to stay to the end of the year, so there was no point starting fires on ice. It's a long siege out there in winter – you can't imagine how cold it gets. The snow just falls and falls. I had the job of ploughing clear the track to the lake. I'd stay up there some nights, sitting by the fire in the cabin trying to compose a letter telling her I was leaving. I was drinking so much I'd blank for hours, find pages I'd written I had no memory of. One night she drove up there after the family had gone to bed and told me she wanted us to run away to Ireland again, only this time she promised she wouldn't change her mind.'

'And the children?'

'She insisted we'd come back when things had cooled down, spend summers in Canada, make it work. She said they belonged on the farm, that their father and grandparents would look after them better than we could.'

Pax felt the punch of recognition to her throat, her voice winded. 'Just like my mother.'

'When I said I didn't see a future for us any more, she went full-scale banjax and said she'd tell her dad I'd pushed myself on her the summer she'd got married and that Dizzy was the result.'

'That's awful!'

'No worse than Mack's threats, I'll bet.'

Pax chewed her lip, knowing Mack had no need to lie about her shabby past, and that his discretion was something she could no longer rely upon. She shivered. Without the engine running, the car was turning into an ice box.

'We'd a filthy row,' Luca went on. 'We'd both had a skinful by then. She knows stuff about me that could get me into a lot of hot water. When you drink and argue, you get to the stage where there's nothing you won't threaten, don't you? She held my fiddle over the fire saying she'd burn it if I didn't change my mind. It was my great-grandpa's; I'd lugged it so many times round the world I'd lost count.'

'She burned it, didn't she?'

He rubbed his mouth, stopping the nervous smile, that all-consuming twitch that charmed all comers. 'After she did it, she let me go without another word. When an Irishman says enough, he means enough.' Raking his hair with his fingers, rings glittering, he looked away. 'So I flew here, drinking all the while. First person I met was a fellow lush who threw up all over me, told me I wasn't wanted and shouted a lot. Suicidal secret habit she's got going on there. If helping her stop takes boring her with a load of old heartache I've never told another soul, so be it.' He turned to her, offering his hand. 'My name is Luca and I have an alcohol problem.'

She shook it, surprised it felt so warm. Hers was freezing. 'I'm Patricia and I owe you an apology. You totally get the plum gin vibe. I'm sorry I misjudged you.'

Thinking back to washing up Christmas lunch a fortnight earlier, she realised it made no difference if it was Taylor slinging Martinis at Burton in Beverly Hills or a despairing Cotswold wife waving a Dishmatic at her husband – drinking made break-ups toxic.

'And I'm sorry I was so awful when you arrived.' She held his gaze.

'It pulled my head out of my arse.'

'The first reaction I always aim for.'

His mouth twisted a smile away and he dipped his head. 'Will you let me help you now?' When he looked up, it didn't feel like criticism any more, but friendship.

She nodded, watching as he reached into his coat and drew out a tightly folded piece of paper. 'They meet every Thursday.'

She pocketed it without looking. 'Thanks.'

'You know, talking about it helped me too.'

She nodded. 'You need to get her out of your system as well as the alcohol.'

'When you asked if I still love her, the honest answer is no. It got way too poisonous and it turned us into bad people, all the goodness rotted out. But falling out of love with somebody feels like such a sin, especially if you know you share a child. You look around for someone else to take the fall with you, don't you?'

Pax thought about her mother to whom Luca had been drawn for her *carpe diem* optimism. 'A lover?'

'Or a drinking buddy.'

'Or a priest to take confession.'

'I stopped doing all that years ago. I sit in cars with complicated women instead.'

'This isn't your first time?' She feigned innocent shock.

Half smiling, he looked away and they fell silent as they sat side by side in the confined space, staring out of the windscreen. Not lovers or drinking buddies. Something far more intimate. The car suddenly felt very small again.

'Am I supposed to give out Hail Marys and Our Fathers now?'

'Just directions.'

She jumped as the engine started.

'It's nearly three. We'd better pick your lad up.'

14

Ronnie was baffled to find the stud deserted like the *Marie Celeste*, no response to her shouts as she marched round under the watchful eye of maternal mares and surprisingly companionable-looking stallions. The yards were immaculate but unmanned.

She started emptying the car boot, crammed full of credit card-bought groceries to indulge her grandson, tempt her daughter to eat, and explore the wonderful world of soya protein for Luca. Determined to pull family and team together, she sensed the place to start was around the kitchen table in the shadow of her mother. Picking out a Kinder egg, she thought ruefully of her plan to enlist her grandson's help to unpack the shopping – 'There's something for you in one of these bags!' – while Pax and Luca, talking horse, nursed steaming mugs of tea, bonding over the big box of biscuits she now rammed on a larder shelf. If an army marched on its stomach, it needed to stick around the mess long enough to eat.

Where are you? she texted Luca, then huffed as the No Service warning flashed up on her phone.

Had they argued again?

She went back outside to try to find some signal.

The sight of her horsebox compounded her disappointment. How could she miss Blair's visit? So typical of him to blow in and out like a storm. The lorry cab, which had been left open with the keys in the ignition, still smelled of him. Climbing in, she curled her feet up onto the seat beneath her, dogs settling alongside as she looked out from her high vantage point across the raised paddocks to the village and vale, never failing to love the view, yet wishing she shared it more often with company that had two legs rather than four. Preferably two familiar, rock-hard hairy ones with high tech metal plates holding one femur and one ankle bone together and a small, faded tattoo of a wallaby on the left buttock dating back to 1986.

Whose court was the ball in? The divorce court if they risked it again, she feared.

A year ago, she and Blair had been together at competitions as owner and rider, discreet dinner party guests amongst Wiltshire allies and utterly zip-mouthed beyond it, love a manageable balancing act in which Verity's dignity and well-being were always first priority.

By the time Ronnie inherited the stud in trust, their affair had become an open a secret in eventing circles, and Verity's family were increasingly gunning for Blair. Ronnie's profile was suddenly so high, the affair felt too risky.

Then there was his jealousy, which was tiresome.

The yard phone started ringing. She hurried back in to grab the kitchen receiver.

'Compton Magna Stud,' she shouted through a hailstorm of interference, the line terrible.

'I wish to speak with Luca O'Brien.' It was one of the politely exotic, silken-voiced calls Lester got so excited about.

Talking into the snow of crackles, Ronnie explained that he was unavailable, silently adding *possibly abducted by aliens*. 'Can I take a message?'

'Please confirm his current cellphone number?'

Ronnie had no intention of giving it out without credentials; besides which, she'd left her phone in the lorry. 'May I ask your name?'

The answer was swift, incomprehensibly Arabic, and almost definitely prefaced with the word Prince. 'And with who am *I* speaking?'

'Veronica Ledwell. Call me Ronnie.' She adopted her honeyed, husky sales voice.

'One moment, please.'

Just an ordinary prince, she remembered Luca saying. *There are seven thousand out there.*

Ronnie waited, picking up the pile of post she'd collected from the box at the end of the drive and flicking through the envelopes. Bills, bills and more bills. She cast them aside unopened, receiver crackling in her ear.

'Hello?' What was she supposed to call him, she wondered: highness, majesty? 'Still there?'

'I am Googling you. Please be patient.'

The cheek! He'd have no luck with her. 'Our website is under development I'm afraid.'

'There is adequate information here. You breed horses, Mrs Ledwell. I buy horses.'

'What serendipity.' She glanced at the bills. 'You must visit.'

'Indeed, but I wish to speak with Luca first.'

Ronnie felt a frisson of expectation as Luca grew in stature, his enigmatic absence less vexing.

'I'll get just his number. Wait there.' She went back out to fetch her phone and look it up. This time, clambering into the lorry cab, she spotted that Blair had left a bulky envelope propped up against the dash, defiantly old school, the *Ron* in his scratchy handwriting making her reach out to pick it up so that she could trace the letters, hearing his deep growl of a voice. Inside was a CD, Bowie's *Station to Station*, a rare boxed set. She turned it over and saw that he'd circled 'Golden Years', which made her smile. More scratchy writing beside it. *Open the box*. Inside was a golden chain with a delicate leaf pendant on it. Looking closer, Ronnie realised it was an olive branch, some of the leaves picked out in diamonds.

'Now that's made this a whole lot harder,' she told her dogs, switching on the engine and slotting in the CD, skipping to the second track and then settling back to text thank you.

When a short and deliciously flirty exchange was cut short by her signal dropping out, she listened to 'Word on a Wing', feet up on the dash, vaguely recalling that Bowie claimed not to remember making the album at all. How she'd adored the Thin White Duke. A teenager at the time, she'd dreamed of marrying her own nobleman, naughty Bunter Worcester maybe or even Prince Charles.

Just an ordinary prince.

'Shit!' She scrabbled out of the cab and ran back to the house to snatch up the phone from the kitchen table. He must surely have rung off. To cheer herself up, she said 'Your Highness?' in her best creepy courtier voice.

She almost dropped the receiver when he replied smoothly, 'I am still here.'

'Goodness, I'm so sorry. Bit of an emergency. Loose… er… horse.' Morals.

'I am a patient man.'

'Here you go.' She read Luca's number out, adding, 'I really am most—'

But the patient prince had already rung off, leaving Ronnie listening to nothing but crackle.

Luca drove in near silence along a maze of country lanes edged with stone walls, hedges and woods, Pax's voice low and monotone as she gave directions.

He wished he felt better about what he'd just told her. He'd not said that much in one heartfelt conversation in years, possibly ever. It had felt awkwardly one-sided. And he'd cheated by leaving a big chunk of the story out.

Pax was much tougher and more insightful than he'd appreciated, the tears and fragility hiding formidable, rebellious resolve. And she kept pulling out surprises, not all of them welcome.

She reached into the back seat as they dropped down a hill to a pretty, sprawling village, pulling out a sparkly pink woolly hat with an oversized fluffy bobble on top. 'I need you to wear this.'

'You're kidding me, right?'

'Mack's convinced I'm having an affair. If he thinks I've brought lover boy with me to pick up our son, he'll go ape. This way, if one of them spots you sitting in the car, you'll look like a girlfriend.'

'Get away! I'll look like a pervert.'

'Please, Luca. It's just a hat.'

Pulling over by a Neighbourhood Watch sign, he put it on. 'Satisfied?'

'The beard's a bit Conchita Wurst. You'll need to keep your head turned away.' He felt her nervous energy building, the anxiety associated with seeing her husband.

He caught his reflection in the rear-view mirror and blew himself a kiss. 'Sexy.' He looked ridiculous.

'Actually, you do look strangely hot,' she muttered.

As they set off again, she flipped down the visor to look in the mirror, only to flip it straight back up with a groan. 'Oh God, they'll probably photograph my face as evidence of daytime drinking.'

'You look fine. Now don't bite your nails. Or blaspheme.'

'Flatterer.' She looked at him, half smiling, only the whites of her eyes revealing how nervous she was. 'You must hate watching reality TV. There's a compulsory ohmygod every ten seconds.'

'I don't watch television,' he said truthfully.

'I'm starting to love your weirdness. Especially in that hat.'

Her dry, throwaway humour took a bit of getting used to, the effusiveness undercut with sarcasm. The word 'love' lingered, although it shouldn't have.

They were at the far side of the village where ugly bungalows with incongruous names like Little Nooks and La Cabana hid, squat and double-glazed, behind laurel hedges.

'It's on the left here. That's Mack's motorbike, so he's here.' He could almost hear her pulses spike straight to three figures. 'Go past the house a bit. Park up there on the left.'

Luca stopped the car out of sight from the large, neat white bungalow, the Italian rust bucket tucked against its garden's freshly trimmed holly hedge. Above them, a To Let sign was holding firm in the wind. Pax had found a hairband in a pocket and was scraping her hair up into it.

In the rear-view mirror, he could see the yellow of a wasp-waisted sports' bike snarling alongside a very clean Honda Jazz on a neatly raked gravel drive. 'That's some horsepower.'

'Mack's Christmas present to himself. Probably why he wasn't interested in a puppy.'

'Don't tell me – Mack is short for Middle-Aged Crisis?'

She double-took, a rare laugh breaking cover. 'A dog's for life, not mid-life.' She pulled the door open, cold air snapping in, lifting the petrol receipts in the central caddy so they flew round the car like spells. And as she glanced back over her shoulder, the magic of the car's closed intimacy, the good humour, seemed to swirl around them and then just as quickly it was sucked outside.

'I have to talk to Mack about schools. I'll try to be quick.'

He glanced at the dash clock.

'You need to be back at the stud, I know. It's crazy you chauffeuring me here like this.' Slam. Magic over.

Luca cursed under his breath. Having just bared his soul, he was now sitting in a rusty car like a transvestite getaway driver, and she was still making him feel like an annoying stranger.

Be kind to her. Ronnie's voice was again in his head.

Ronnie hadn't asked for this, he reminded himself. This was Luca O'Brien doing what he always did, completely over-playing it.

His phone rang. Expecting a call back from an Italian cousin, desperate for the music of another language, he answered it without looking. 'Pronto, Matteo.'

'Luca, this is Mishaal.'

He wouldn't have recognised the voice. Deeper. Less domineering, more in control.

'Mishaal.' He drew his jaw up, swallowing slowly. 'How y'doing?'

'You are in England, my father tells me.'

'That's right.'

'As am I. We will meet.'

His manner of speaking hadn't changed. Far more businesslike than his flamboyant father, Mishaal had always possessed a robotic quality. It made him difficult to read.

'Might be tricky,' Luca managed to say, his mind back in that stable: Beck facing destruction having fought for his life; the death-row pardon; the curse from the hospital bed, Mishaal quietly awaiting payback time. He couldn't think fast enough to get out of this.

'There's a matter of importance I wish to discuss,' said Mishaal, his monotone steely.

'How long are you here?' Luca checked the rear-view mirror, jumpy as a getaway driver. He wondered where exactly Mishaal was.

'I fly in one week and do not return until June.'

'Sure, summer's much better for me.' Luca would be gone by then, as would Beck; he'd make sure of it. 'I've only just started this job, you see, and it's full-on.'

'I have spoken with your employer and she has kindly invited me to visit. It is a part of the country I should like to see more of.'

Luca kicked into the car's footwell. He'd been naïve imagining Mishaal wouldn't know precisely where he was.

'We must meet face to face, Luca,' he was saying. 'When

are you available? Outside work hours, of course. This cannot wait any longer than necessary.'

Stay cool, Luca reminded himself. He's a dutiful son making contact because his father ordered him to, the old prince convinced that Mishaal and the Horsemaker should build bridges, that Luca would help him win endurance races. They have no idea Beck is here. Bluff. A week passes very quickly. 'I don't have my diary with me.'

'Then let us speak again when you do.' With a sharp beep, the call was ended. A moment later a vCard was texted through with multiple numbers, emails and even an IBAN code. Maybe he wants to blackmail me? Luca wondered illogically, blood thrumming in his ears. Was there a price for what he'd lost? *'It is written in the Qur'an and in your Bible: an eye for an eye!'*

He thumped the steering wheel, glaring out at the lane. Pax was right. It was craziness being parked up here like a cabbie when he should be looking after the horses. He started the engine, for a moment not caring if he drove off and left her here. The radio burst into life: Jess Glynn singing 'Don't Be So Hard On Yourself'.

Knott, who had been asleep on the back seat, scrambled his way over the central console and came to sit in Luca's lap, licking his chin. Luca stroked him distractedly, listening to the song. Every word of it could be about Pax. Or him. He cut the engine.

As he did, he could hear a man's raised voice out of sight behind the car, a familiar soundtrack from the stud in the past week. He'd only ever seen Mack from a distance – not hard to spot his thick-set bulk and the way he used it to put his wife in reverse, Ginger Rogers dancing backwards around the cobbles – but his voice carried like a dictator at a rally.

Catching movement in his mirrors, he turned to see Pax's little boy standing by the yellow motorbike, carrying an oversized cuddly rabbit and a toy steam engine. Stocky, round-cheeked and glossily brunette, he took after his father. Yet it was his mother's haunted, soulful eyes that peered out from beneath the heavy fringe. Out of sight, Mack's voice shouted and raged, Pax's urgent attempts to quieten him unheeded.

Luca watched as the boy set down his toys and picked up a handful of gravel, pushing it into the exhaust of the big bike, followed by another, then a third. The fourth handful was hurled at the shiny yellow paintwork. As he turned for a fifth, he caught sight of Luca watching him and promptly disappeared.

Luca's phone rang again. It was Ronnie, the line so bad it sounded as though she was grinding coffee. 'Where in hell are you? I've been shouting my head off on the yard, didn't you hear?'

'I'll be there in a minute,' he promised as the coffee grinder scattered its contents down the line, her response inaudible.

At last Pax wrenched the back door open, helping Kes into his booster seat, her tone predictably hypnotic with soothing reassurances. 'Now, have we got everything? You have Rab the rabbit, yes? Right. Remember Luca, Granny's stud manager? Say hello!'

The boy said nothing, staring fixedly at Luca's hat.

She buckled up her seatbelt beside Luca, lowering her voice 'Sorry you had to wait so long. Hide your face and *drive*.'

As they headed back to the stud, Pax got out her phone and fired off several messages, reading through her inbox, not noticing that the car's intelligent dash screen was keeping tabs, eagerly offering to read aloud an incoming email from *Helen Beadle, Solicitor*. Another message – *Mack Mob* – made her grit her teeth, hand and phone banging back into her lap, face turned to the window as she took a couple of deep breaths.

After a pause, she addressed Kes brightly. 'Daddy's had a think and changed his mind about you trying the new school next week after all, which is good, isn't it?'

'He said it was a rubbish school.'

'It's small and fun.'

'Oliver doesn't want me to go to a rubbish school.'

'Let's not talk about Oliver.'

'Oliver says—'

'I said *no* talk of Oliver!'

Luca turned in surprise at her sudden sharpness. But she was already smooth-talking again, reassuring. 'This isn't about Oliver, darling, this is about Kes.'

'*I* don't want to go.'

'You have to go to school, Kes.'

'Don't!'

'We can walk there from Gronny's house, with Knott.'

He clung to the puppy beside him. Big ploppy tears edged onto his lower lashes. 'Daddy didn't say goodbye.'

She reached round to grip his hand, her phone slipping from her knee into the brake well. 'He sends lots of love and says he's sorry he shouted and that he didn't give you a big hug, but he'll give you twice as many hugs when he sees you to make up for it.'

Catching sight of her glowing screen as he changed gear, Luca could see the incoming message just read: *Solicitor says school try out OK. Fuck you.*

Ronnie let her dogs run in the highest field, her phone coming back into signal with a flurry of texts – no more from Blair, she noticed sadly – and a voice mail from Petra, her dog-walking friend. 'Ronnie, I can't apologise enough for what happened in the woods earlier. My mare was totally out of order. Can you possibly call me back? I need to pick your brain.'

Petra answered her phone in one ring. 'Thank God! What could a horny seventeenth-century cavalier get up to with Lord Goring's wife in a stable that doesn't involve doggy or knee tremblers? I had too many of those in the last book.'

'You're back at work already?'

'I have a new Girl Friday who refuses to go home until I've

written my synopsis. She's going to revolutionise my life.' Her merry voice deepened to a growl as she teased, 'The *same* Girl Friday who's your new weekend groom, I hear.'

'Carly?' Lester was as sharp as a tack, she realised.

'Right clever, aren't we?' Petra played up her Yorkshire accent. 'Now you have to help. I've a new anti-hero with an insatiable sex drive.'

Ronnie – who had been rather indiscreet about her wicked past over some of their dog walks – was Petra's unofficial sex-scene consultant. 'What happened to Father Willy, the lusty priest?'

'I killed him off. He was far too corrupt. Seán O'Shaughnessy is a brilliant horseman and mercenary, fresh from the Catholic revolt, who travels to England at the height of the civil war, tasked by the Royalists to assassinate Black Tom, our heroic head of the New Model Army.'

'Right.'

'He lives for his cause, his horse and the lonely wives of his roguish commanders. You're *just* the person I need to talk to for details of windswept couplings and haystack coitus.'

'It's been far too long to remember any al fresco risky business,' she said vaguely, far preferring a bed these days.

'Still, I bet you had a bonk more recently than me. Charlie does dry January, which means absolutely no sex. Even Gill gets an annual roll on Burns Night because it's Paul's birthday.'

Ronnie didn't want to think about recent bonks, the memory of Blair's touch fading far too fast.

'I'm furious with Gill,' she raged instead. 'It was downright irresponsible coming through those woods.'

'Bridge's pony had bolted again.'

'Is Bridge the one with pink hair who can't ride for toffee?'

'In fairness, I fall off my evil mare more often.'

'Because your mare *is* evil. Luca thinks she and Beck are star-crossed.'

'Really?' She sounded terribly pleased. 'Maybe Beck's the

Petruchio to her Katherine Minola? Shall we marry them off? Being a mum should calm her down, Gill says. Oh, I don't think I've told you she's in foal yet, have I?'

'Good grief!' Ronnie was thrilled, not least to have such undisputable proof of her stallion's fertility after so many years off stud duties. She guessed Luca would be all for reading the banns, but she was in a position to overrule that. Watching *The Taming of the Shrew*, she'd always thought the bully Petruchio should have stayed shacked up with his manservant. 'My grey chap needs a Grumio, not a wife.'

'Isn't Luca his groomio, ha ha?'

'Your Shetland's not doing a lot at the moment is he?'

When Petra heard what Ronnie was asking, she laughed. 'He's an absolute devil, you do know that? He'll corrupt that stallion completely. He thinks he's Goliath. And he is *very* special.'

'We'll take tremendous care of him.'

'And he'll get ridden, you say?'

'Kes is super keen.' He would be as soon as she told him.

'He'd love that. He misses having a special person. I tell you what, he's all yours if you give me some good sex.'

Ronnie racked her mind, thinking back to the heady days of the late seventies before marriage, Aids and a replacement hip. 'Okay, this happened in a horsebox rather than a stable, but you could adapt it: wrists tied to the hay rack by leather reins, mouth silenced with bandage tape. *The* biggest cock I'd ever seen in my life.'

'Hmm, I can't see Sean O'Shaughnessy tying a woman up.'

'I wasn't the one tied up.'

'I don't want Sean gimped.'

'This man won Badminton the next day. He's a national treasure. Still commentates today.'

'Just no.'

'All right; how about your lovers climb up into the stable eaves. He lies along the big tie beam holding the ones to either side for balance while she straddles him, riding on top, stockinged legs dangling back down into the stall. It's thrillingly mid-air – very *Greatest Showman* – and the horse can stay in the scene throughout.'

'God, you're a genius. You actually *did* that?'

'A neighbour. When I lived in Cumbria, I was throwing a drinks party and popped out to check the horses. Went in to straighten a rug, looked up and saw her in her finest cocktail dress going at it with the local poultry farmer. A bronze turkey was left on my doorstep every Christmas after that.'

'I love you!' Petra rang off.

Spotting Pax's silly Italian car come whining up the drive, Ronnie hurried back down to the yard. As her dogs rushed ahead, barking their heads off, she realised Luca was at the wheel in a fetching pink hat. That was a turn-up for the books.

But far better than that was the small, dark-haired person on the back seat clutching a tartan rabbit. '*Keeeeeeeesteeeeer*!' she hurtled under the archway. He waved back furiously as the car came to a halt.

'Where have you lot been?' Ronnie demanded.

'Sorry!' Luca was already out of the driver's door, whipping off the hat.

'All my fault.' Pax spilled out the other side and hurried back to open Kes's door.

Ronnie's mood brightened further, noting that both looked interestingly furtive, opening their mouths to explain at the same time:

'I offered to—'

'I asked Luca to—'

'Oh, it really doesn't matter.' She waved it away, scooping up Kes in a hug instead. 'Now, tell Gronny *all* about your day.'

'Want to see the horses!' Kes shouted.

'You are so right. Horses are much better boring old news.'

'And dogs!' Kes loved her two Lancashire Heelers, although the older bitch, who thought children unnecessarily bothersome, pulled nasty faces at him that made Pax overreact protectively. Lots of things made Pax overreact these days.

She was fussing now, saying that Kes should change, and that he needed food and orientation. 'And there's lots to do on the yard, Mummy.'

'I want to see the horses with Gronny!' Kes shouted again, beaming at Ronnie.

'We'll all go together!' Ronnie offered.

'Someone has to stay and help Luca.' Pax was doing her martyred, jaw-set face, big eyes sorrowful with a touch of passive aggression. Ronnie knew that she was meant to offer to take that on. But if she did, Kes wouldn't see the horses.

'We'll be back before you know it!' She hurried him away before his mother could protest more.

Time with Kes would never make up for her absence from his mother's life, but she saw some sort of redemption in him nonetheless. The fact they adored each other was a very good start.

Ronnie longed to make a better fist of being a grandparent than she had a parent. Having married Johnny at just nineteen and borne their children by twenty-five, glamorous grannydom was always on the cards. Her dismay at becoming a grandmother for the first time had been a result of her total exclusion from the process, not her young age. Alice was adamant she should play no role in her three children's lives. Now lanky teenagers, they barely knew Ronnie. Equally, Tim's ex-patriot life had made it difficult for her to see his two children more than a handful of times, and divorce had taken them even further out of reach, her sixth grandchild currently on the way from his second wife who she'd met just once, at her own father's funeral.

With Kes came Ronnie's first opportunity to be involved, and she was determined to embrace and enjoy it. He was about the same age Tim had been when her marriage had ended, but Kes was nothing like the boisterous blond dynamo she'd kissed goodnight that heart-breaking March night, her plan to leave his father and take the children with her about to backfire horribly.

While her own son had always been a typical Percy, even at five – witty, mischievous and sporty, his generation still one of *Swallows and Amazons*, Kes was a solitary, defiant little character, fiercely stubborn and clever enough to carve tantrums and demands into a fine art. His bull-necked father might claim the Forsyth genes dominant, but Ronnie suspected Kes owed his brooding good looks less to Mack's black-browed Gaelic colouring and more to his grandfather, Johnny Ledwell; the affinity with horses surely stemmed from there.

'Here he is.' She led Kes into the barn where Spirit, the dun colt, strutted across to them eagerly, nipping rivals out of the way, eyes gleaming with mischief and self-belief. That was the look she wanted to see on her grandson's face. Everyone loved Spirit, knowing he was going to be something special one day. He knew it himself.

'Lift me up, Gronny!'

She heaved him onto the second rail so he and Spirit could cuff noses, his little fingers sinking into the colt's mane, scratching and grooming while the young horse flexed his neck ecstatically.

'When can I ride him?' asked Kes.

'Not for a few years. You'll have to let Gronny's friend win Badminton on him first. I've promised he can. Then he's your ride, and you can both represent the country in... 2032,' she calculated. 'You'll be eighteen and he'll be fourteen. "The Olympic gold medal for the Individual Three Day Event goes to Kester Forsyth riding Compton Spirit for Great Britain!"

'I'm Oliver Alexander Jocelyn Forsyth,' he reminded her.

'Isn't it funny how we end up with different names? My Great-uncle Cedric was christened Cornelius Winchelsea Pitt-Dacre, imagine that? I far preferred Cedric, just as I love Kester.' Ronnie hadn't been invited to the christening and wasn't quite sure the origin of the nickname, although she vaguely remembered her mother grumbling in a long-ago letter that Jocelyn had only been added at the last minute to stop the poor child bearing the initials OAF.

'I'm named after my brother,' he said now.

'Your brother?' She steadied him as he stretched to rub chubby fingers through the colt's forehead whirl, his touch instinctive.

'The one who was born dead. Nanaforce says he's an angel in heaven, but it's not true. He's *here*,' he whispered dramatically, putting a finger to his mouth.

'Here?'

He nodded. 'Only *I* can see him. Oliver does really naughty things, Gronny. He likes playing tricks on people.'

'Does Mummy know this?'

'She says I mustn't talk about Oliver. You won't tell her, will you?'

'No, but it's always best to be honest, Kes, not keep secrets. They can hurt terribly, secrets.'

Ronnie watched unseeing as Spirit nibbled at her cuff, remembering the letters hidden in Lester's cottage with a pinch of conscience. Too many family secrets.

Pax had never told her she'd lost a baby before Kes – such a devastating event, and another reminder of Ronnie's failure to be there at the moments in life when a mother was needed most of all.

'Oliver gets me into trouble,' Kes was saying. 'Like hiding all of Granaidh's reading glasses at Christmas so he couldn't do his sodco.'

'Sudoku,' she corrected, holding him close.

'Today he put stones in Daddy's motorbike.'

'Good for him,' she said before she could stop herself, forced to add a 'that was very, *very* naughty, though.'

'Why did Oliver die inside Mummy's tummy, Gronny?'

'Sometimes these things just happen.' She tightened her

arms round him, that awkward but heartfelt Percy hug, heart thudding with pity. 'Nature can be very cruel. But it's also very kind. It gave us you, and who couldn't love it for that? And for Spirit?'

She took him on a hunt for wild teasels, but he soon got distracted, charging into the woodland on the stud's top boundary to pretend to shoot invisible enemies while Ronnie tried not to imagine how different things would be had his older brother survived for him to play with.

Absorbing the shock, she was again reminded that so much of Pax's life was totally lost to her. After the terrible, regrettable mess she'd left behind between Pax and Bay, mother and daughter had barely spoken for years, so many olive branches rejected that she had her own grove.

Piecing together a partial picture of her children's progress from rare, formal correspondence with her mother Ann, Ronnie had worked out that running away to London had propelled her youngest daughter into a druggy trust-fund set who partied through winter and rattled between festivals in summer. Pax's grandparents – along with Tim, whose London flat often doubled as her refuge – had spent years bailing her out of trouble and calling in favours to set her up with jobs and internships through friends of friends, none of which she held down for more than a week, rejecting stuffy art galleries, estate agencies, banking, insurance, until eventually she'd temped in a big heritage architect's office and met Mack Forsyth.

A father of two, almost twenty years Pax's senior, Mack had still been living with his first wife at the time as far as she could work out, which should by rights have horrified Pax's stuffily strait-laced, forsaking-all-others grandparents. Nevertheless, when Pax's age-gap relationship very quickly became serious enough for divorce papers to be served and a sapphire ring shown off, the Percys hailed Mack as a Very Good Thing. He'd totally transformed his new fiancée, Ann had reported in a letter to Ronnie, breaking the news before the formal announcement appeared in the *Telegraph*. The dreadlocks and friendship bracelets had gone, chignons and pearls in their place, and an engagement party was hosted at the stud, a small ceremony in Ayrshire following just weeks later, the first Percy daughter not to marry in St Mary's church for three centuries. Her rebel daughter.

Had there been a bump? Ronnie wondered now.

Not invited to either celebration, she'd sent good wishes and an over-expensive gift, receiving a polite thank-you letter from Pax in return. That had been their last contact for years. Pax the peacekeeper, who had once forgiven her so much, had become a total stranger after marrying. She hadn't even had an address for her.

The thought that she might have struggled through the loss of a baby made her ache with remorse for not trying harder. Instead, Ronnie had decamped to Holland, determined to pull herself together after a run of bad, black-dog years. Living in exile with wild and wonderful Henk, her ageing parents increasingly insular and anti-social, she'd become detached, keeping the tiny, outdated photographs of her children folded in the back of her diary because they hurt too much to look at.

Their rapprochement had only started when Ann died, and even then it had been a tiptoe dance of grandmother's footsteps until this crisis had thrown them all together: emails, stilted calls, a few meetings with Kes, awkward lunches when Tim was in the country. There were still so many secrets between them, and so much hurt and distrust from Pax. A family tree through which secrets grew like ivy.

The letters, she remembered again with a cold spasm of fear. She had to get rid of the letters.

She and Kes started back down towards the yard. It was getting dark, the lights glowing from the bays and half-doors. She could see Luca hard at it again, Pax helping him, the one wearing the pink hat now. Ronnie had noticed how well they worked well together from day one, both fast and efficient.

They barely communicated – were positively frosty to each other if she was honest – and yet everything got done without fuss. If it was a stand-off, it was a productive one, both equally eager to be finished and part ways.

Coming back onto the yard now, she sensed a shift in atmosphere. They were talking together, both stooped over a piece of paper. Ronnie hoped it wasn't another bill.

'We've been collecting teasels!' she shouted from the opposite end of the stable yard. 'And Kes has found an owl pellet with a shrew's skull in it!'

Looking up, eyes huge, Pax shoved the piece of paper in her back pocket and missed, sending it billowing across the cobbles. She and Luca went running after it, comical in their twists and turns as it changed direction, swept up, down and around in the wind.

Shrieking with laughter and dashing to join in the game, Kes employed the Percy cricket catch to grab it from under their noses, looking at it and proudly reading, 'A… A.'

He turned back to thrust it at Ronnie. 'What does the rest say, Gronny?'

Glancing at it, Ronnie resisted an urge to kiss it. 'Boring grown-up stuff,' she said as Pax hurried up, and Ronnie told her, 'I don't think he read the rest.'

'It's okay, Kes can only read the alphabet and words of one syllable.' She stooped to pick him up, quickly mouthing *thank you*.

Ronnie brightened. 'One syllable, hey, Kester the Genius? There are many Percys who never get beyond that at fifty, let alone five! I'm one of them without my specs.'

Ronnie turned as Luca appeared beside her and handed the flyer to him. Dear, kind Luca, whose smile gave nothing away. 'Get her on a horse again and I might just give you your weight in gold,' she said quietly, then called across at her giggling grandson, 'Kes is going to start riding, aren't you, darling?'

Pax's protests that he was too young were drowned out by her son's banshee cry of delight as he scrabbled down to charge around the yard pretending to gallop.

'Born to ride!' Ronnie realised that she sounded like her own mother.

Pax's voice was brittle. 'I suppose it'll really piss off Mack, at least there's that.'

Letting this pass, Ronnie watched as Kes charged up to Luca to butt him like a goat, which he took with an exaggerated 'oof!', pretending to reel backwards, then clicking him on as he cantered away again.

Breaking the good news about the tough-thug Shetland who would soon be Beck's sidekick, she sensed she didn't have Pax and Luca's entire attention. Both were looking at everything but one another.

She changed tack. 'I'm hiring a weekend girl on the yard so you can both have more time off.' Vague nods greeted this.

'Who?' Pax asked eventually.

'Carly Turner.'

Pax and Luca both spoke at the same time again: 'She'll be—'

'Expensive,' finished Pax as Luca said, 'Good.'

They glanced at each other with an energy that made Ronnie step back.

'You know we can't afford it, Mummy,' Pax insisted.

'We can if we sell some horses.' Watching Pax racing after Kes, she told Luca about his mysterious royal caller.

That got him standing to attention, in as far as he ever did, languid leanness shifting from one foot to another, smile rearranging itself. 'Yeah, he rang me after.'

'Old friend?'

'He's a time-waster.' He clicked his tongue in his cheek, watching Pax as she rejoined them with Kes, whose cuddly rabbit was covered in teasels, burrs and now hay.

'Who's a time-waster?' Pax asked.

'Luca's Arab friend – sorry, Arab *acquaintance*.'

'AA!' Kes identified proudly, grabbing Ronny's hand.

'Well done, Kes.' Pax gave her mother guilty eyes above a frozen smile, then glanced at Luca.

That same electric look passed between them again, Ronnie noticed. A precarious intimacy, alien to them both.

'So who is your Arab acquaintance?' Pax asked him.

'Just a guy I worked with once.'

'A prince,' Ronnie deadpanned.

'Really?' Pax looked bemused.

'You know a *real* prince?' Kes could do big-eyes just like his mum. 'Like Eric or Naveen?'

'Sure, it's nothing,' Luca smiled.

'Does he have a magic sword? Or a magic carpet?' Kes made hand swoops whilst doing imaginary flying.

'No, just a magic da.'

'Like my daddy?'

Pax's face developed its rigidly kind look. 'Like Daddy, yes.'

An ordinary prince. Ronnie thought back to Luca talking about the run-up to the London Olympics. 'Does this mean you're still in touch with the royal family who bought Beck, Luca?'

'Kind of.'

Ronnie's business head now had *stud fees* on a loop, knowing there were huge performance horse programmes taking off over there, semen straws flying east first class at tens of thousands a pop. 'Do they breed?'

'Not sure.'

'I can get Blair to check if you like. He has a lot of contacts. He coached in the UEA and Saudi and knows—'

'Excuse me!' A rabbit was thrust up between them all. 'Rab and Oliver say grown-ups are reeeeaaaally boring.' Kes made a fart noise. 'Can we play with the hosepipe, Gronny?'

'What a good idea,' Ronnie took his hand, quashing the need for Blair's grown-upness more than ever.

*

Pax tried not to let a sense of *Schadenfreude* take over when her son doused her mother from head to foot in cold water. It wasn't that she didn't want them to get on, but she found Ronnie's all-consuming desire to be super-granny overwhelming sometimes. All that love-at-first-sight mutual adoration still felt too new to trust, like everything in the last few weeks.

When Ronnie disappeared into the main house to change and dry off, she tried to persuade Kes in to the warmth of the cottage, but he clung to the yard, thin moon sliding up the night sky overhead now, horse silhouettes moving in a magic pool of golden light.

Waiting for him to finish loudly counting the saddles for Luca in the tack room before he locked it, she read a few of the messages that had come through while her phone had a signal: her solicitor Helen confirming their next meeting; one of the pre-prep mums who didn't realise Kes wouldn't be returning this term; *Lunch tomorrow? Bx* from an unfamiliar mobile number that she swiped past with a brief heartbeat rush to find a more welcome one from livewire Bridge Mazur. *I got this number from your parental data sheet. Hope okay? (Probably get fired before I officially start.) Grand to meet you earlier. Let me know when best to bring my friend and her boy over. Looking forward. :-]*

She smiled, messaging straight back with a couple of dates, going outside to wave her phone around to try to send it on its way, then proudly listening to Kes counting past thirty inside, his voice schoolroom sing-song, Luca's bouncy encouragement possessing the same effortless spontaneity she'd noticed in others from big Irish families.

Was she mad to want to move him to such a little school? she wondered. Mack was right that a school like his pre-prep had huge resources to give its pupils educational advantage.

Self-doubt gripped her, the all too familiar comedown, a headache already knocking.

'Me and Luca are best friends!' Kes appeared beside her, hot breath pluming.

'That's nice.' She watched the Irishman pull the door closed to lock it. In her hand, her phone let out an irritated buzz to tell her it had no signal and could not send.

It was only when she looked down to tick the Send Later? box that she realised she'd replied in error to Bay's message, not Bridge's. How awful if he'd received *That would be lovely! Let's make it soon! Tues/Weds? xx* The unsent message was easy enough to delete. Harder was the pounding in her chest and the recklessness with which her mind imagined what might happen if she left it there. Catching Luca looking at her curiously, she pocketed the phone. 'Thank you for everything today.'

'Don't mention it.' They watched Kes charging off to say goodnight to Beck and Cruisoe.

'I think you got out of teaching pony lessons.'

He said nothing, his eyes shifting away, a rare streak of colour in each cheek, the smile firmly in place.

Realising that was a mean, headachy dig, she reached out to pat his arm and wish him goodnight. His hand covered hers.

It's funny how the most everyday moments sometimes had such significance, she thought a moment later, the unexpected heat of his hand catching her by surprise again. And she knew in that moment, with a capsizing heart-lurch, that their friendship mattered now. It was something she needed.

'Goodnight.' He set off unsmiling, and she knew he felt the same way.

Kes, stomping on cobbles as though they would pop like bubble wrap, big-stepped towards her. 'Can Luca and Gronny eat supper with us?'

'Not tonight.'

He tilted his head. 'Why not?'

'I want you all to myself.' She glanced at Luca's retreating silhouette

'Oliver says you are a boring smelly-pants!'

She thought Oliver had a point, but she knew better than to acknowledge her son's imaginary friend. 'Let's get you something to eat.'

'I've come to read Kes a bedtime story and give you a present!' Ronnie told Pax brightly from the doorstep of Lester's cottage, feeling as welcome as a Jehovah's Witness, and uncomfortably duplicitous.

'He's had a story.' Dressed in just a towelling gown, Pax had coated her hair in some sort of conditioner that made her look like a bird in an oil slick.

'An embarrassment of riches, then.' Ronnie wasn't giving up easily, holding up a foxed copy of Beatrix Potter. 'He told me earlier he'd never heard *The Tale of Mrs Tiggy-Winkle*.'

There was a gurgling of pipes from above. 'I'm just topping up the bath. Hang on.' Pax dashed upstairs to stop the tap. Nipping inside and closing the door to shut out the cold, Ronnie found herself standing right next to the big dresser in which Lester had told her he kept private correspondence.

She glared at it reluctantly. The letters.

Pax was back down before she'd even located the right cupboard. 'Another night, maybe? He's almost asleep.' They could both hear Kes playing loudly with his toy car, making vrooming noises overhead. 'All this is still so new. Best not overstimulate him.'

'Of course. These are for you.' She handed across a large plastic bag from the Bardswolds' one remaining old-fashioned saddlery shop and knew, the moment Pax registered the horse head logo emblazoned on it with a frozen smile, that she had judged it wrong. 'Just a few practical things to wear around the yard.'

Pax pulled out a pair of charcoal designer breeches, riding socks, thermal layers and gloves, then a padded gilet and short coat. 'These are riding clothes, Mummy.'

'Work clothes. They're dual purpose.'

'You can't afford all this.'

'You'd be amazed what Nectar points can buy these days.'

'It's terribly kind of you. At least you stopped short of the hat and boots.'

'They're still in the car. Call it an early birthday present.'

'Thank you,' Pax said, rigidly courteous.

'While I'm here,' Ronnie tried to sound airily casual, 'Lester asked me to pick up a few things.'

'Be my guest.' Pax sat down on the bottom stair to make a fuss of Ronnie's little heelers who had muscled inside too.

'Don't let your bath get cold.'

'It's fine.' She looked up. 'What things, exactly?'

'I'll make you a cup of tea while you're in the bath, shall I?'

'I don't want a cup of tea.' Pax cocked her head. 'Is something bothering you, Mummy? Is this about what Kes told you?'

'About what?'

'His brother.'

Wrong-footed, Ronnie hesitated, unaccustomed to such directness. She'd forgotten how swiftly truth came out of the mouths of infants.

'He says he told you about Oliver?'

She perched beside Pax on the step, voice low so that Kes couldn't possibly hear. 'He told me he died.'

'That's right: Oliver, the baby we lost.'

'I'm so sorry,' Ronnie reached out for her hand, but it was snatched away.

'It was a long time ago.' Pax chewed at her thumbnail, staring hard at the wood of the newel. 'Now Kes has decided Oliver's his imaginary friend, it's hard to avoid the subject.' She stood up, moving away from the stairs to the gloom of the passageway. 'He'd be nearly ten now.'

'Oliver was stillborn?'

The pause stretched, vrooming noises above, the tick of Lester's old wall clock marking the silence. Wait, Ronnie told herself. Wait. She'll say it. Pain comes out.

'The cord had got stuck around his neck, they said. I had no idea until it was too late.' A light switch by the kitchen door was under close scrutiny, her hypnotic voice covering emotion. 'I was three days overdue and when my midwife came to talk about inducing labour, she couldn't find a heartbeat. They rushed me in for a caesarean, but he was already dead. He was the perfect little person when I held him: his fingers, his ears, hair like mine.'

They both stared at the light switch. Wait, Ronnie, wait.

'They let you have a funeral when a baby's stillborn, but not a christening. We'd chosen his names way back when the scan showed he was a boy – Oliver because we both liked it; Alexander from the Forsyth side, Jocelyn from ours.'

'I can't imagine how devastating it must have been.'

'We were offered grief counselling, but Mack said it would only keep dredging pain up. He wanted to try for another baby straight away, blot out what had happened, but it didn't work like that. I blamed myself, still do. How could I have not known my baby was being strangled inside me? When I told Mack that's how I felt, he didn't deny it. He thought it was my fault too.'

'That's so wrong!'

Pax headed into the dark kitchen, crossing to the little Rayburn, leaning against the range for warmth, prayer hands to her nose. 'It took five years to conceive Kes, eight rounds of IVF.' Her fingers thrummed together. 'It almost finished us; perhaps it should have. It has now.' She walked to the fridge, reached out for the handle, then changed her mind and walked back again.

She wants a drink, Ronnie realised, almost offering to find her one before remembering.

'Kes was our Band Aid, five years too late.' Pax was back at the Rayburn. 'Mack was adamant about christening him Oliver, our second son given the same names as that little headstone, like a replicant. It's not uncommon apparently, but I hated the idea. I should have fought it more. I was just too grateful that he was healthy, and too ashamed that it was taking me so long to love him when I'd held his lifeless namesake in my arms and just loved, you know, just *loved*. For a child so wanted, it took me forever to bond. I love him more than life now.' She glanced up at the ceiling. 'Even if I feel like I don't deserve him a lot of the time.'

'Oh, Pax, I wish I'd known all this.'

'Why? We never spoke; we were living in the Borders, you were in Germany. Alice knew, and she was kind, but there's not much one can say, is there?'

There was a great deal, Ronnie thought, she and Pax needed to say, but not right now. She could see how much the effort of talking about it had already cost her. 'I like the name Kester; it's Lester one removed.'

Pax slowly clapped. 'You're the first to get that.' She smiled briefly, glancing round the little hallway then back to her mother, both acknowledging the man who had been so important in their parallel childhoods. 'I've never once called him Oliver. Mack and his parents tried Olly for a bit, but it never stuck. He's Kes.'

'But he thinks of his brother Oliver as his alter ego?'

She nodded. 'Mack hates it, and I try to discourage it, but the truth is I don't mind that much.'

'Because it brings Oliver to life,' Ronnie guessed.

Pax's eyes brightened, surprised at being understood.

Ronnie couldn't resist reaching out a hand. This time, Pax let it rest on her arm.

'I'm so glad you're here,' Ronnie said with feeling, alarmed to find a lump in her throat as big as a tennis ball.

'Talking is good,' Pax acknowledged with a half laugh,

withdrawing. 'Much as it pains me to admit, Luca was right about that.'

'I'm glad you two are making friends.'

'You ordered him to be nice to me which is quite a different thing. Now he's glued to me like a buddy programme. But he *is* right about talking. There are donkeys with no hind legs everywhere that man's been.' Pax did her walk to the fridge door handle and back again, pausing to straighten a picture of a bowler-hatted rider on a shiny show cob and say, 'Sorry, Lester.' They could both quietly imagine his horror at such intimate conversations taking place on his quarry tiles.

'He'd be jolly chuffed to know Kes was named in his honour.' Ronnie watched Pax opening and closing the glass cupboard now, without taking one out. 'Les and Kes has a wonderful music hall ring about it, don't you think?'

'It was Lester's shoulder I cried on after losing Oliver.'

Ronnie masked her surprise. Lester was many things, but a good listener?

'I came here for a few days not long after it happened. Mack didn't know what to do with me because I couldn't stop crying. Neither did Granny or Grumps, but Lester was very kind.'

'Oh, he *is* kind.' She could imagine him polite, poker-backed and dutiful while the older Percys hid away.

'He told me something about Daddy, something he said nobody else knew.'

Ronnie stiffened.

'He said my grandmother, Johanna, had a baby after Daddy who died at just a few days old; apparently she never got over it. Maybe that's why she drowned herself.'

Ronnie had to forcibly stop herself snapping that Lester hadn't known Johanna, they none of them had, and that Johnny had never breathed a word of it to her. Lester had always been a terrible myth-monger. And yet he'd also had Johnny's confidence, letters passing between the two men for years despite barely a word spoken.

She'd never seen the letters, but she could guess at their contents. Her late husband and Lester had been more than close, although any physical relationship was short-lived. Rigidly self-disciplined, they had behaved with total propriety to ensure nobody knew of the alliance, her own suspicions unspoken until long after Johnny's death. Raised in an era when homosexuality was illegal and belonging to a society from which its discovery would have ostracised them as surely as her open adultery did her, the two men had coexisted in deep denial for years.

Lester would no more speak of it now than he would cut off an arm, but he trusted Ronnie to set aside personal feelings, find these letters and store them safely. She knew she must spare Pax the awfulness of discovering the truth about her father by accidentally stumbling upon them, but the fact that she was still covering up for Johnny years later infuriated Ronnie, to still be the one who had been judged, whose infidelity had broken a family apart. It maddened her yet more that Lester had painted a gothic tragedy when nobody really knew the truth of Johnny's poor dead mother. It was criminally irresponsible to suggest to a young, grieving Pax that the grandmother she so closely resembled had topped herself after losing her own newborn.

'Lester has his own theories on many things,' was all she could say, her relentless need to jolly up and move on already at full gallop. 'He finds it terribly hard to call me by my first name, have you noticed?' She edged along the range rail as Pax returned to press her hands to its warmth. 'He starts saying "Mrs Ledwell" then stops and changes it. I've been "Mrs Le— Ronnie" for months.'

The haunted eyes flickered with amusement.

Ronnie tried to hold her gaze. 'You should visit him, Pax.'

'I'll wait till he's stronger.'

She's worried that Lester will judge her because her marriage has failed like mine, thought Ronnie. 'I know he seems old-fashioned, but he's a lot more forgiving than you think, Pax. He's seen a lot.'

Pax leaned back against the rail beside her mother, tilting her head closer. 'I remember when I was a little girl, one of the mares had a stillborn foal out in the top pasture. I'd tagged along with Daddy and Lester to check over the herd, and there she was, standing over this lifeless bundle she'd just licked clean, protecting him, nudging him. It was the first time I'd seen anything like that. I can't have been much older than Kes, six or seven maybe. Daddy wanted to call the kennel man, but Lester insisted we should leave them together for a few hours, "field grief", he called it. She stayed with her foal all morning, grazing alongside him – just long enough for a soul to leave, Lester said – then quietly moved on. I thought about that day a lot after we lost Oliver; I used to close my eyes and imagine I was a mare, galloping away from all that pain, all that feeling. I galloped for miles, for years; I still do. I close my eyes and I gallop.'

Ronnie covered her hand on the rail. Pax let it rest there as, without speaking, both women closed their eyes. And as the grass, hedges and clouds flew past in Ronnie's head, she sensed how terribly alike they were.

'When things got really bad with Mack – not the recent stuff, but before, when we were trying for Kes and he got so high-handed, I found I couldn't do it at all, couldn't close my eyes and ride away from it in my imagination.'

'How do you mean "high-handed"?'

'He's always been a bit of a control freak, but he took conception so seriously, reading my temperature every day, checking my weight, making me take all sorts of supplements, wear loose clothes, do certain exercises, eat only certain food. He knew more about my cycle than I did by the end. He wouldn't let me discuss trying to get pregnant with my girlfriends, wanted baby-making to be this intimate, private thing, but I felt like a lab rat. And every month I was a failure because I bled.'

Ronnie's own blood boiled at this. 'Was it Mack who stopped you making any contact with me?'

'Alice was pretty set against it too,' Pax hedged. Then she nodded, confessing, 'Mack said you were a bad influence. I never told him about Bay,' she added quickly, looking away. 'I was in a bit of a bad place when we met.'

'I heard your London friends were pretty wild.'

The hand beneath hers slid away. 'My bath will be cold.' She headed towards the stairs.

'Run another later.'

'You should go.' She said it so kindly, it was a can't-turn-down invitation.

'I'll let myself out.'

Pax kissed her mother goodnight at the bottom of the stairs. 'Let's not talk about this again.'

'If that's what you want.'

'I've talked enough. Kes needs to believe there was love between his parents, just as I did.'

'I loved your father very much once.'

'And now you love Blair Robertson.'

Ronnie step back in surprise. 'Pax, I really don't—'

'I think you two need each other more than you realise. Please call him.' With a bright, defensive smile she must have picked up from Luca, Pax headed upstairs.

Guiltily and furtively, Ronnie hurried to the dresser and opened the bottom left-hand cupboard. A Horace Batten boot-box tied up with old horse-rug fillet strings, he'd said. You couldn't miss it.

But the box wasn't there.

Ronnie felt a sudden angry ache for Lester. He was needed here, guarding the secrets, demanding protocol. This was all wrong.

She could hear the tap running in the bathroom, the radio on, volume low. *The Archers*' theme tune was playing through, an anthem that took her straight back to childhood, her mother cooking at the Aga, stepping over the dogs, sherry schooner and cigarette on the go, recounting every visitor to the stud that day. Pax's childhood too. Mirror images.

Maybe nothing much had changed.

Heading through the courtyard to the back door of the main house, Ronnie could smell onions frying and saw Luca moving about in the main kitchen, drinking his funny green tea, freshly showered, all golden hair and big shoulders. Soon enough Pax would realise that he came straight out of the jar ready-mixed with concentrated goodness. Perhaps she had already.

Zipping her duvet coat tighter, she took her mobile up to the tower above the far arch. The wind had dropped, stars thrown out in a wintry canopy, Orion overseeing them all, reminding her of Johnny again, her original huntsman.

'I'm so mad at you for not calling first,' she told Blair.

'I called *on* you.' He was on hands-free; she could hear the sat nav telling him to turn right. 'We hate phones, you and me.'

'Rubbish. You were texting mistresses when mobiles were the size of shoeboxes. You just feel guilty because you pin-hooked my mare. Please tell me Bay paid far too much for her.'

'A fortune; I owe you commission.'

'Good. I'm broke. How soon can I have it?'

'Give me two hours.'

It was that simple.

15

Exhausted from his first day back at school, Ellis fell asleep midway through the storybook Carly was reading to him, his 'Splorer Stick under one arm, Pricey the lurcher stretched out beside him. Next door, she could hear Ash still telling one of the three little pigs that he would huff and puff and blow their house down, his voice animated, the good mood sticking. Yawning, she stretched the cricks out of her shoulders as she padded though to join him, remembering Flynn telling her that all farriers had bad backs. Cleaners suffered the same fate.

Ash's back was a wide triangle of well-honed, massaged perfection, its landmines of tension and jumping nerves down to poor sleep rather than occupational hazards nowadays. He could still fight a war, but he lost the battle with insomnia night after night.

She ran her hands along its familiar rock face, warm as granite baked by the sun, moving on to kiss Jackson, standing up in his cot with his hands braced on the rail like a tourist on a hotel balcony, laying him back down. Sienna was sleepy-eyed in her toddler bed, snuffly with a cold that moistened her top lip. Carly carefully kissed around it.

She tried not to think back on that wet, snotty slick when Ash cornered her on the landing straight afterwards with a demanding kiss of his own, already primed for action. 'You owe me one, bae.'

Since when was sex a debt, she wondered, her stomach rumbling. 'Let's wait for the kids to settle. We need to eat.'

Some nights, seduction came easily, a passive sacrifice to her body loving his, but tonight Carly felt uneasy. Her brain was too busy downloading the day to feel horny just yet. Two new jobs. She wanted to share her good news on social media, to take a boost from the likes, to know Ash was really okay about it all.

'It's exciting, Ash,' she told him over tea, his food disappearing a fast as hers went cold. 'They give me choices.'

'Yeah,' he fed her a chip, 'like whether to tidy up after someone else's kids or shovel shit. How mad was Janine when you told her?'

'Not done it yet.'

'Good luck with that.'

'I know this might not seem much, but it's all about potential. Like Bridge says about that little job at the school.'

'She'll eat that place and spit it out, I reckon.'

'She's not that bad.'

'For a ball-breaker.' He was already wiping the gravy from his plate with a slice of bread. 'It's okay, I like her.'

'She makes me laugh.'

'Bit over the top, but yeah, she's pretty lit.'

'Pretty, too.'

His eyes levelled with hers, amused. 'Fancy her, do you?'

'*You* do, you mean,' she teased, knowing he did.

'Not my type.'

She gave him a mock-disbelieving look. 'Go on, admit it, you'd love a threesome.'

He laughed. 'I'm digging my own grave whatever I say.' He ripped off another hunk of bread, then looked at her from an angle as he chewed it, eyes sparkling. 'Are you serious?'

'Gotcha!' She knew she'd been right. 'You fancy the arse off her.'

'Not half as much as I fancy my wife. And I'm not sharing you with anyone, bae.'

As they ate, Carly could feel the old chemistry kicking in, his gaze on her body. He could always do this to her, muting conversations before they were started, feeding her lines from his lips and food from his fork, making her laugh with no more than a lift of his eyebrow. Strong and silent even when he was joking around, Ash really was in an exceptionally good mood.

In bed, long before their bedtime, he was more attentive than he'd been in months, taking charge, not with the usual nod to foreplay but a full-scale heads-down focus on her pleasure, all the more squirmily delicious as he told her to stay still and enjoy, his fingers and tongue finding every one of her hot spots.

Downstairs, Pricey was barking to be let out. 'I'd better go.' Carly slid off the bed and reached for Ash's T-shirt to cover up and go down.

A frost was hardening. Pricey took a long time to find the right spot in the garden to do her business, tiptoeing around out of sight. Shivering with cold as she waited by the back door, Carly heard a yell above and turned, listening for sounds of one of Ash's nightmares, instead making out tinny movie music and tyre-squeal soundtrack.

By the time she started back upstairs, Jackson was kicking off with telltale snivels as the head cold woke him, hot and tearful, his nose streaming. His nappy needed changing. Sienna woke too, red-faced and snuffly. Calpol administered, lullabies sung, she rejoined Ash.

He was awake and watching a movie on the iPad, some smash-'em-up action franchise with four battered beefcakes and a token babe. Face blue-lit, he looked up with a slow smile as she crossed the room. 'You're beautiful, you know that?'

She struck a *Tank Girl* pose. 'Even though I'm not wearing leather biker gear with a Kalashnikov in each hand?' She nodded at the little screen, in which the babe was dispensing with baddies, cleavage pert throughout.

'Come here.' He threw it aside and pulled back the covers.

As soon as she climbed on, he was straight to action with barely a spit on his thumb to prepare her, fast and silent, the abandoned tablet lighting the room with unwatched, flickering action bouncing off the walls as though they were underwater. Rounds of gunshots rang out. Pump, pump, pump. A helicopter took off. He turned her over to get deeper. Carly held her breath to stop herself drowning, arm across her face, torn between animal delight and guilt at enjoying it so much, fingertips on fire.

Shouts on the little screen, calling for backup, another screech of wheels, a rumble of caterpillar tracks and boom of incendiary fire.

She could feel Ash starting to go soft.

Grabbing the iPad, he fumbled turning it off, a music app starting instead; Drake, all grinding, beating hip hop heart. It should have helped, but it didn't.

Carly did all she could, angling her hips, moaning encouragement, reaching down to coax his ever-flagging cock back to life. Nothing made a difference.

It wasn't the first time. Sometimes Ash was apologetic, sometimes angry, or sometimes silent as now, rolling away uncommunicatively, cursing under his breath then muttering a terse, 'Let's forget it' as he picked the tablet back up.

Carly knew from experience that he loathed being consoled with platitudes or being told it didn't matter, that to reassure him was worsening the blow.

Instead, she lay awake, knowing she could no more say anything than she could sleep. Eventually, she opened her book to read, one Bridge had lent her which she hadn't had time to start until now. An hour later, she was still reading, wondering at how women like Bridge and this author with her white-streaked hair and street cred could be so confident in their own minds, so upbeat and flippant about the things that had shaped them from schooldays to bullies to family to menstruation. All

Carly remembered was following friends into womanhood in a rush, like cramming through a door, only to find Ash holding it open on the other side.

Ash's breathing deepened to sleep. She flicked more pages, feeling both stupidly naïve and a part of wider new friendship, a tribe of Bridges, women who said it like it was and thought differently to her mother and schoolfriends, to the army wives she'd known, to her.

Ash's nightmares started kicking in early that night, barely an hour after he'd fallen asleep. It wasn't yet ten.

She laid a hand on his arm, but he was already deep down in his subconscious, mumbling 'Do not move!' It wasn't directed at her. It was his soldiering voice. Then, 'You are safe. *La ta khaf. La ta khaf!*'

His nightmares, which often started with a moan then a shout, were quick to escalate, an arm flying out so fast Carly had to duck, his stop-start breath-quickening, then a silent terror that was a precursor to the screaming which always made her blood run cold, frightened the kids and forced her to wonder at what it was he'd seen that he could never unsee.

Scrabbling round onto her knees, she tried to shake him awake to try to stop it, breathing in his ear. 'There's no war, Ash. You're home.'

'Home!' He thrashed the other way, still asleep. 'Can't lose this fight.'

'There is no fight here.'

'Honour fight,' he murmured, coming up through layers of memories and distortion. '*Jihadi.*'

'You're out of the army, Ash,' Carly reassured him. Then he said it again and she realised her mistake.

'Jed and me. Burns Night. Big fight on Burns Night.' He sat up, rubbing his face groggily. 'Gotta beat the bastard.'

'What fight?'

Removing the heels of his palms from sleepy, reddened eyes,

he looked surprised to find her sitting beside him, her bedside lamp still on, the feminist book raised in one hand like a court witness with a Bible.

'What fight?' she repeated quietly.

'King of the gypsies.'

She closed her eyes and groaned. A big fight between traveller men, bare-fisted and brutal, the Turners traditionally used it to settle a family dispute (and make a lot of money on the side).

'I have to do it. It's family honour, Carl.'

'What about *this* family, *our* family?' She slammed the book down to emphasise the point.

He picked it up, eager for distraction, looking at the cover. 'What's with Lily Munster?'

She snatched it back. 'It's frank, funny feminism.' That's how Bridge had described it to her, with an added 'fecking' before feminism.

'Is it now?' He looked amused, which she guessed was the point. His nightmare was abating, the veins on his neck already coming down, the sweat drying.

'I don't want you to fight, Ash,' she said plainly.

'We're grown-ups, bae. I don't much like you reading frank funny feminists, but I'm not going to stop you.'

'It's hardly the same thing!'

'Yeah, well, I've changed my mind about Bridge.' He rolled away again, presenting a big, tattooed shoulder. 'You can tell her to steer the fuck clear of me. And my wife.'

'She may be the face *której nie mogę zapomnieć…*' Charles Aznavour had nothing on Aleš, who had gone to the Polish supermarket in Broadbourne after work – via the pub with his brother – and returned in full voice, singing his way through the soundtracks from Richard Curtis movies while he prepared a congratulatory meal to celebrate Bridge's new job.

Aleš was a famously slow, messy, entertaining cook. To Bridge, who was only staying awake thanks to a handful of caffeine pills washed down with a bottle of Bull's Blood, it seemed hours after starting with 'Gimme Some Loving', an onion and a chopping knife in the kitchen – toasting her throughout with refilled glasses of *Żubrówka*: 'My clever career wife!' – that he finally danced to the table with a pot of *bigos*, singing 'Love Is All Around'. There, lifting pot lid and vodka glass simultaneously, he announced through the rising steam, 'My gift to you, *kochanie*!'

Grateful for his signature dish of porky sauerkraut, she quashed the suspicion that he'd be far less effusive if she'd just landed Head of Human Resources at Jaguar Land Rover. He didn't even mind when she broke it to him that she'd been asked to go in tomorrow. 'It's their Ofsted inspection.'

'Of course you must go; *moja bratowa* will look after the children. Eat!'

To her shame, Bridge then found two mouthfuls of Poland's favourite pork stew totally filled her up, indigestion threatening. Her body clock was long past its optimum supper time.

Aleš's appetite had no such limits. He had seconds, then thirds.

Knackered, with a lip that hurt – a lot – Bridge had to concentrate hard to stop her eyelids drooping while he talked about his stew, Poland, football and himself for ninety-five per cent of the time, her new job for five. 'You think you'll like it, yes?'

'I already love it.' Her new job paid a fraction of the Sous Vide glamour job, had a status a stratosphere lower, but Kismet had led her to it. She was needed from the get-go, her phone's note app already chock-full of school inspection requirements grabbed online. It wasn't about the money. She was Médecins Sans Frontières landing in a warzone. The biggest difficulty was going to be coming home and casting off the flak jacket.

'There's something different about you tonight, I don't know what.' Aleš tilted his head. 'You change your hair?'

'Employment changes a woman.'

It surprised her that Aleš hadn't noticed the swollen lower lip straight away, although she'd made sure she kept her trademark red gloss topped up at all times to hide it, wine glass raised to her mouth whenever it wore a bit thin, regularly escaping to a mirror to reapply, ashamed of her vanity. Now she checked her reflection in the microwave's black glass. Quite sexy from certain angles, but unnaturally huge. Did she look hot? Hot enough for Ash Turner to fancy her? Stop that!

Aleš sang her upstairs with a husky reprise of 'Love Is All Around', slapping her backside playfully all the way up the narrow treads, hushing past their children's doors, then bursting into their own room, so low-ceilinged that he hit his head on both door frame and ceiling light, a sure sign that he was stocious. 'I want those big lips around my *chuja*.'

Bridge licked her sore lips, tasting paprika, Malbec and pain. Her husband's sudden and inconvenient interest in a blow job was doubtless not unconnected to the huge, glistening pout. But the thought was eye-watering. Every nerve ending there pounded.

'I'm cream-crackered, lover,' she lisped, diving into the bathroom to clean her teeth and tone down her make-up, keeping the scars covered.

You should tell him the truth, her reflection admonished.

He'll make me get rid of Craic.

You just like secrets. They empower you. She closed her eyes, briefly reliving the blind, foolish moment she'd taken Ash Turner's thumb into her mouth, the sheer thrill of it.

Back out again and Aleš was lying back in just his checked underpants, his cock protruding hopefully from the gap, listing left. 'Hey, *kochanie*, you eat my beautiful food, now I give you dessert…' In Aleš's mind, cooking was as seductive a piece of foreplay as hours of toe nibbling or massaging.

Stifling a yawn, she waved a dismissive hand. 'We need a night off. I've got to be at the school first thing.'

'Just kiss it quickly, eh?' He invited her closer to his crotch with open palms like a shopping channel presenter showing off a Lightning Deal, as if she might not be able to navigate her way there without this helpful gesture.

Bridge summoned her sleeping libido back to life with the emergency button, allowing herself another flashback of Ash's thumb in her mouth and silver eyes on hers.

'I'll ride you if you like.' Not giving him the chance to negotiate, she climbed aboard, swiftly removing the boxers from around his listing *chuja*, which hardened gratifyingly fast.

For a few brief minutes they both revelled in the thrill, then it went rapidly downhill.

Offended that Bridge was facing his toes – 'What is with reverse cowgirl?'...' 'What's with you fecking knowing it's called that?' – Aleš spun her round to face him like he was rotating a king post, then grunted crabbily when she leaned so far back all he could see was her twin peaks.

Staring up at the ceiling, she wasn't thinking of England. Or Ireland. She was thinking of the Orchard Estate. To Bridge it felt briefly electrifying.

But Aleš ruined it by sitting up and tipping her back, looming over her, his huge torso eclipsing the light, grumpy because she refused to kiss him or his hairy body, fearing her lip would split open again. Her libido jumped ship totally when he called her a *lafirynda* for coming to bed still in make-up, which she mistook furiously to mean whore, although Aleš explained in flagrante that this was more of a jokey 'old trollop'.

They broke apart to regroup, gathering intimacy back around them like bedsheets. Aleš's double standards astounded Bridge: shaming the wife whose sore mouth he was now repeatedly trying to guide down to his groin. But her own duplicity was surely worse? To prove her point, tired and ruthless, she remounted to ride him home as fast as she could, a galloping finish whipped along by Fantasy Ash who she closed her eyes to join one last time.

'*Moje szczęście!*' Aleš cried as he came. *My happiness.*

Not mine, thought Bridge sadly, kissing his forehead with her sore lips and hopping off to pull on her gown.

'I think I just heard one of the kids awake,' she said and escaped to the landing, pressing her hot face against the cool wall outside their door, touching her throbbing lip.

Both children were fast asleep. In the bedroom she could hear Aleš already snoring.

Bridge stole downstairs, gathering her powers. It smelled of *bigos* and blown-out candles. She relit them. Plain white, but they would have to do she thought as she carried them across to the sitting room, balancing them on the repaired crackle-glaze table and shouldering the coffee table chest and sofas to the walls, then peeling back the rug.

The chalk pentacle was still almost perfectly preserved on the flagstones. She set the candles in its centre along with a recently washed bowl and summonsed her search engine – Incognito Window – to navigate her way to a spell that would send Fantasy Ash packing.

With limited witchy resources at her disposal – white candles, household herbs, some gift-wrap ribbons – it was like searching for a recipe using store-cupboard standbys the day before the online groceries order arrived. She found just one that might suit her needs – *Ye Olde Spell to Lift a Curse.* It was very straightforward, a Jamie fifteen-minute meal of a spell. It would have to do.

She set to work, sprinkling a bit of dried lavender and thyme over her candle flame, saying a few lines, dripping wax into the bowl and spitting on it, feeling increasingly stupid for doing this, not to mention tired and cold; and she was now inconveniently hungry. Her phone, running low on battery, died as she incanted the final line, which felt a bit spooky. Then a dark shadow fell across her flickering pentacle.

'What are you doing, *kochanie*?'

She looked up at Aleš, huge, blinky-eyed and naked.

'Hi!' Not thinking, she blew out the candle. It plunged them into total darkness. 'Shit!'

'I get light switch.' There was a crash as Aleš fell over the sofa which wasn't where it was supposed to be. 'Oof!' and the coffee table got him next.

Bridge managed to fumble the bowl, candle and ribbon out of the way before the lights went on full blast, making them both blink.

'Almost ruined my surprise!' she game-faced, indicating her chalk pentacle, and wondering what on earth she was going to say to explain it away.

'Huh?' Aleš was at post-midnight, post-two-bottles-of-red monosyllabic which helped. As long as it sounded vaguely feasible, there was a chance he would swallow any explanation for the sake of getting back to bed. Pavement art?

'Parquet!' It came to her in a flash.

'Eh?'

'I always loved parquet. You know, the wood block flooring? So I thought I'd map out my ideal pattern. Plan a treat for the house when my first pay cheque comes in. What do you think?'

She braced herself. Poor, Bridge. Very poor. This is a flagstone floor in a grade two listed cottage. You hate parquet. He will damn you as a witch and have you dunked.

He chuckled, squatting down to admire the chalk shape. 'I thought just same thing when we moved in here. I like this design! I have man who does very good parquet. I call him.' He took her hand. 'Now come to bed: I am horny again.'

She gaped at him.

'Joke!' he grinned, breaking another yawn and lifting her hand to kiss it.

Bridge felt his whiskers thread beneath her nails, always marvelling at how small her fingers looked in his. And she realised the spell had worked. Fantasy Ash was no longer with her.

'No joke, Aleš, but I *do* actually feel quite horny...'

★

It had gone midnight, but Ronnie couldn't sleep, the solid wall of warmth alongside so rare that a part of her wanted to savour every moment, to wear its comfort through the night. The paradoxical part always found it disquieting to share her bed, this invasion of heat and shape and noise.

Blair's breathing was deep and hoarse, like a tide on shingle, but he didn't snore. Rare in a man over fifty she'd found, as was his body: lean, strong and demanding, even in sleep where he took up much of the mattress, an arm thrown out across her, leg bent, knee against her thighs. Her own body, folded neatly around his sharp edges, felt soporific as it always did after sex, still restfully aroused, affection amplified so that she wanted to bottle it, this essence of loving and being loved physically and in mind.

To miss somebody's presence as much as she had his meant making love was never a ritual of lust and habit; it was a reunion they couldn't take for granted, that might end in a moment. It never mattered when or where they found each other so long as they could revisit their shared, private space. On the competition circuit, the lines had blurred but remained distinct, two seasoned gypsies who never unpacked.

Now Blair was in her home. He was staying the night. The sudden shift to a new foothold both frightened and excited her.

Ronnie's childhood memories were tucked in every corner of this house, her marriage had played out here, the loss of both her parents. Her daughter and grandson were sleeping in a cottage across the courtyard, Blair's car parked amongst the family ones.

She could hear an owl shrieking outside, then a fox bark. Another noise, less familiar, the faint bang like a door – a horse perhaps? Unaccustomed to being awake at this hour, Ronnie drank in its nocturnal strangeness, the rise and fall of

Blair's chest and her own in simpatico. Just one night together to savour.

He stirred, head lifting to study the luminous hands of his watch before it turned to her, eyes gleaming in the near darkness. He'd always napped like a cat.

Drawing her closer, he grumbled that she'd put on pyjamas. His fingers slid beneath the top, their tips tracing up her ribcage.

'I was cold.'

'I can keep you warm…' He followed his fingers with his lips, the familiar low growl of his voice a never-ending aphrodisiac. 'You want to go again?'

'We're not teenagers,' she laughed, not sure that she did, her state of contentment now deeply bedded in.

'In horse years we are,' he reminded her, head reappearing opposite hers, smile wide. 'I can still ride round Badminton twice in a day.'

'I can't…' She smiled through the darkness because her body was telling her otherwise, alert and back into action, desire's drawstring tightening inside her. It had been left too long without him and demanded more.

They made leisurely, sleepy love this time, breaking off to get the fire going, and again when Blair went to the bathroom to pee and Ronnie nipped downstairs to silence her dogs who were barking at nothing, egged on by Blair's pack, fetching a bottle of water while she was there.

Awash with San Pellegrino and tiredness, they lazily slipped into a favourite place, tightly slotted, face to face, knowing how and when to make the other come. Ronnie was trying to hide hiccups, making him laugh, his mirth shaking through her to speed her up deliciously. The dogs were barking again. Something clattered outside. The dog fox was still shouting its hoarse cry. It didn't matter. They were there, letting out delighted groans, relieved they'd made it, still riding round twice and adoring one another all the more for it.

Then they heard thudding above them as feet hurriedly crossed the attic landing to the back stairs.

'Oh God we've woken Luca,' Ronnie whispered into Blair's hot skin.

They both looked up as something clattered outside again, louder this time.

A moment later, the dog cacophony stilled, then started up in earnest as the back door banged.

'Is someone out there?' Ronnie was alert now, adrenaline pumping.

Blair peeled away and went to check at the window, silhouetted suddenly as the yard lights went on. He squinted into the bright light. 'It's bloody misty – I can only just see him. Hang on there *is* somebody else – on the other side of the wall. He's onto it.'

Ronnie hurriedly joined him, peering out through the mist to a triangle of light cast across Lester's cottage garden and recognising the furry hat with earflaps and padded coat. 'It's Pax. Why is she up?'

'You want me to go and check?' Blair's teeth were already chattering as the draughts from the old sash window bit into the freshly post-coital heat of his naked body.

Ronnie folded her arms around him and watched Luca cross the yard to knock on the wall doorway to the garden, Pax opening it and beckoning him quickly in. From the way they huddled together talking, her daughter's arm pointing to the big hutch by the back door and then the raised vegetable beds, she suspected there was no need for reinforcements. Perhaps the energy she'd sensed between them earlier was as sleepless as her own.

'They're fine.' At least it had stopped her hiccups. 'Come and warm me up again. The fire's almost out.' Taking his hand, she led him back to bed.

'My fire's never out, you know that, Ron.' Blair landed beside her like a lion on a rock, wide awake again, pulling the covers right over them for warmth and kissing her shoulder.

'You can't possibly ride round a third time, surely?'

'Let's walk the course and find out, shall we?'

'I've lost Laurence,' Pax told Luca in a low voice through the thick scarf that covered her face from the nose down, shining her torch around the garden.

'Who's Laurence?' he asked, alarmed, wondering if there was a man lurking in the bushes.

'Shh. Lester's fox cub. He's a bit of a wimp.' The torch beam swung around the garden. 'I let him out for a play as usual, only there's a big dog fox barking in the spinney and he took fright and scarpered somewhere. He's got to be in here.' She sounded calm, tired and fed up. Definitely sober, Luca deduced, remembering that her boy was asleep in the cottage.

She'd stomped into the corner illuminated by the yard lights and was peering into a bushy shrub. Wearing her coat and wellies over pyjamas, big mane tucked up in a furry hat and glasses propped on a cold red nose just above the high scarf, she looked strangely androgynous and alien.

The L-shaped garden was enclosed by walls on all sides, two formed by the cottage at right angles to the high yard wall, the others made of well-laid Cotswold drystone capped with vertical topstones at chest height. It was unlikely the young fox could scale those, certainly not if he was terrified of what might be out there.

'He's normally close by,' Pax explained as he helped her hunt through the borders, looking for the reflection of eyes in torchlight. 'He likes digging in the veg beds. We've started to make friends, or so I thought.'

'You always let this fox out in the middle of the night?' Luca was incredulous.

'I wake up every night at one like I'm alarmed. I'd only lie awake, overthinking, if I stayed in bed, and foxes are nocturnal so he's happier playing at this time. Just twenty minutes or so.

I let him out at dusk and dawn most days too when the chooks are in, although I need to be careful around the dogs. Knott loves playing with him, but Stubbs would finish him off in a breath.'

Luca glanced across at the cottage where he'd spotted the bearded head of the fox terrier glaring at them through the cat flap.

'Laurence is only young,' Pax was saying, rooting through a clump of scraggy foliage. 'My guess is Lester will release him back into the wild when he's old enough, after the season closes.'

The yard's work lights only lit about a third of the garden, the rest of it monotone in the low gleam of the bulkhead light by the back door, shadows pooled in the corners. There were a multitude of places to hide, old-established herbaceous borders packed tight with shrubs and perennials, a greenhouse, woodstore, compost heap and chicken run as well as the shed.

'Have you tried bribing him?' Luca asked, stifling a yawn.

She flashed her torch across the grass lawn to reveal a trail of dogfood kibble and white cubes. 'Feta. His favourite. There's some bacon lardons and peanuts in there too. I'm keeping the balsamic glaze as an emergency measure only.'

'How long have you been out here?'

'About an hour,' she checked her watch with a flash of torchlight on drawn back glove, 'and a bit.'

'You must be frozen through.'

'Two layers of thermals,' she reassured him, then noticed it was Luca who was shivering. 'You go back to bed. I'll find him. He always comes eventually.'

'I want to help.'

'Then at least have a hat.' Before he could argue, she took off the big fur trapper's one – revealing the pink bobble hat underneath it – and put it on Luca's head, straight over his hoodie, his second coronation of the day.

'There.' She stepped back and tilted her head to admire him

before quickly spinning around, trying to hide her laughter as she pointed the shaking torch around the wood store. Two reflected eyes gleamed back. 'Aha!'

But it was just a fat black rat that gave them a hard stare before disappearing behind the logs with a flick of its tail.

The fur hat was incredibly warm, and he was grateful for it. He started to think straight.

'Turn the torch off,' he suggested, indicating for her to step into the shadows with him. 'Let's just stay still and see what happens.'

'I've tried that.'

'Try it again. Humour me.' He swallowed back another yawn. The hat smelled of something scented. Lavender maybe, or lime. It was nice.

She stood beside him. 'This won't—'

'Shh.'

There was a low whine from the cat flap. An owl hooted.

'He won't—'

'Shh.'

The scent was stronger now she was close beside him, heady and citrussy. Out of the corner of his eye he saw her turn her head to glance up to a window in the house, guessed that was where Kes was sleeping. The owl hooted again. Their breath condensed in baby dragon clouds by their faces as they waited. He felt her arm accidentally brush his. All at once he was plugged into the mains.

They waited a long time. Electricity pulsed through him.

She shifted impatiently, breathing. 'You know Blair Robertson's here?'

'Yes,' he breathed back.

'Is that okay with you?'

'Why shouldn't it—'

'There!' She flicked her torch back on.

The fox was behind the chicken run, eyes gleaming through the honeycomb pattern of wire. He looked far from frightened.

He was gazing at the little coop in which Lester's laying bantams were roosting.

'Little sod. They're all wile and instinct,' Pax said admiringly, moving forwards to call for him, reaching down for some feta to throw within sniffing distance. Laurence the fox seemed to weigh up his options, pale eyes unblinking – all-night stake-out versus Greek mezze – and then slunk round to eat the scrap before trotting forwards to eat more from her hand. She scooped him up calmly, the young fox surprisingly trusting as she delivered him back to his big hutch where he began tucking into a bowl of dog food.

'Thank you.' She turned back to Luca, ducking her head with a polite grimace. 'Again.'

He braced himself for a sarcastic remark about pony lessons, but it didn't come.

'Pax, I'm not being nice to you because Ronnie asked me to. It's because…' The reasons were too conflicted to explain, the hour too late.

'It's because you're nice?' she suggested.

'Yes. That.' He gave up.

She smiled, stepping forwards and reaching up to his face. 'Goodnight, Luca.'

For a ridiculous moment he thought she was going to take his bearded cheeks in her hands, the volts ramping up. Instead, she gripped the flaps of his trapper hat and lifted it off his head, cramming it back on her own and turning away in a waft of lime and lavender.

'Goodnight, Pax.'

PART FOUR

16

Shocked emojis greeted Gill's Monday morning revelation to The Saddle Bags' WhatsApp group that she'd spotted Blair Robertson driving away from the stud at first light: *it was either him or Gary Lineker.*

Unimpressed, Bridge sent a 'meh' face, although she was ashamed to catch herself Googling both men afterwards to check out the comparison. She maintained a dignified silence through the two-day debate that followed, phone buzzing non-stop as the Bags argued whether or not footballers were sexy, photographs traded like Top Trumps, mostly of ageing pundits with fake tans, the general consensus being not, although they were all very taken with a vintage shot of George Best posing naked on a silk sofa, Miss World 1977 in his lap.

Enough! She interjected on Tuesday evening. *You know the rules, ladies. NO retro pin-ups, sexism, exploitation or excessive body hair.* To which she'd added a photo of Princess Leia in a gold bikini kissing a Wookie and a row of namaste emoji.

But the conversation refused to die. By the following morning Mo had shared a picture of a sexy Chelsea forward who she was always telling Bridge looked like Aleš. *That's his Balbo. Deny it!*

More goatee than GoT, she pinged back distractedly over breakfast, bracing herself for another facial hair debate.

Instead, she received a rain-soaked selfie of Mo and Gill setting out on a hack captioned *Lightweight!*

If only they knew how heavy her heart was.

Some of us have jobs to go to! Bridge drew beards on their picture and shared it back before setting off for Compton Magna Primary school – lazily taking the car, telling herself she should be relieved to let the duo brave the icy, needle-sharp rain that had driven in from the east.

As another morning crawled by trapped in Auriol's office bringing order to chaos, Bridge reminded herself that the pay-off would be to blast across a field on Craic entirely self-funded. She wasn't officially on the payroll until the beginning of February, but her quick-thinking boss – recognising that Bridge was a shaman of the spreadsheet who had saved her skin through the Ofsted inspection – had insisted upon 'on-the-job-training' to keep the office manned. She'd even found enough in the budget for an 'emergency stipend' (which given it was cash-in-hand and largely made up of old pound coins, Bridge suspected was not entirely LEA approved).

This week, riding felt like an indulgence while her work/home and bank balance found new levels. She relished her new pet challenge, even if organising Auriol felt like herding cats and her marriage was in the doghouse.

Several humdinging rows with Aleš had meant no lovemaking for four days. There was no Fantasy Ash any more to cheer her along, just typing callouses. When Aleš had set off for work that morning he'd left her with his VAT return to file instead of a kiss. All a stark reminder that you must be careful what you wished for. Her and her big witch mouth. Literally, she kept catching herself sucking her misshaped lip. A 'pastie lip' her dad would call it, although Bridge's latest diet meant no pastry was allowed near it.

She returned home for a cottage cheese lunch at the folding picnic table, her sitting room unrecognisable as the cosy nest of a week ago, the familiar, squishy sofas in Aleš's lock-up, stacks of flooring materials in their place. Last Friday – reeling from two days' chaotic 'on-the-job training' in the midst of Compton Magna Primary School's inspection – Bridge had come home to find her sitting room stripped bare, Aleš laying chipboard over her beloved flagstones in preparation for parquet she didn't want, using her bad-spell pentacle as a design, his dedication absolute, his temper darkening daily.

Yesterday's quarrel meant he had already abandoned the project. Bridge blamed black magic and too much lip.

A message from Pax lifted her spirits: *See you around 3.30. Kes and I are making a cake. Don't forget to bring your friend.*

On your marks, get set – bake! She sent a row of smiley faces, then texted Carly: *Still up for later?* When a thumbs up came back, she quashed disappointment.

Bridge knew it was selfish to want to keep her playdate visit to the stud all to herself and yet a lifetime of chameleon friendships meant she sensed a mismatch. Carly was very black and white, lacking the molten, volcanic emotion which had drawn Bridge so instinctively to Pax, a woman who had stuck her head above the married-with-kids parapet to admit what all the rest of them struggled to say. She was a freedom fighter, whereas Carly was in for the long siege.

Her phone buzzed – Petra joining in the Bags' WhatsApp chat at last. *Keep the footballers coming, ladies! Need inspiration. Beards mandatory… I have Cavaliers nostril-deep in muff here.*

Raising a dry chuckle as she imagined Gill's shocked face reading it, Bridge was tempted to interject with *I've told Aleš my lady garden is going wild if he doesn't shave his,* but discarded the idea because it was only half the story and she didn't trust them not to guess the rest.

She yawned. Last night's row – another corker – had been a game of two halves, the first of which had been Aleš's discovery of naked George Best on her phone's gallery, along with Lineker in his underpants and Ginola all silver-foxed up in a tight polo neck. He was now convinced she had a kink for ageing soccer stars. Served him right for snooping, Bridge thought as her phone lit up with laughing-crying faces from Mo.

The second half of the Mazurs' domestic meltdown had been far closer to the bone, sparked by Aleš suggesting that they should start looking around for somewhere bigger to live now that she was earning too. A plot on which he could build his family a home with enough rooms for more babies – one more, maybe two. All they needed was a bit of land. No, not for Craic; he'd laughed when she suggested it. Chickens, maybe. She wouldn't have time for horse riding. It was a full-time project planning and creating their dream home to grow old in together.

'I will lay parquet in all the rooms for my darling wife!' he'd announced with the theatricality of W. B. Yeats saying he would lay his dreams at her feet.

At this, Bridge had bridled. 'I don't like fecking parquet!'

'But you ask me for engineered flooring, *kochanie*.' Aleš had looked hurt. 'I just got best rate on European Bordeaux oak in Midlands.'

'I don't know what I was thinking. I like the flagstones. I like this cottage. I don't *want* parquet!' she'd wailed, knowing that what she meant was *I don't want more babies and I don't want to grow old*.

With a bright chirrup, a calendar reminder appeared on her phone: *PICK UP KIDS*. Guilt cold-splashed her face.

Gratefully abandoning Aleš's VAT return, she drove to Broadbourne where her sister-in-law pressed her with strong black coffee and showed off the latest high-tech gadgetry Aleš's brother had installed throughout the house he'd built for his ever-expanding family. 'I just say "Alexa, turn on light" and it turn on light!'

'Queen, I just say "Aleš, turn on the light". Same difference, and no spyware is sharing my private conversations with marketeers.'

Driving home, her indignation mounted as she wondered whether Aleš had told his sister-in-law about the row, and that was why she'd been so keen to showcase her house.

Flynn's pickup was parked in her husband's cherished spot outside the cottages, his dog barking from the open back canopy which housed shelves of different sized horseshoes and a gas forge to heat and shape them.

He came out of his front door, shrugging on a coat as she unlocked hers. They exchanged neighbourly hellos, Zac on her hip and Flavia toddling alongside. Reaching back for the folded buggy, Bridge discreetly admired his rock god looks as he closed the pickup's tailgate, grateful to have her Safe Married Crush back in play.

'See you at the wassail later, maybe?' he called over the roof as he climbed in.

'Yeah, maybe.' She'd forgotten it was the village's annual knees-up to wish for a good harvest, staged in the orchard just after dusk. Aleš loved it, throwing himself into the singing and cider-drinking because it reminded him of celebrations at home in Poland.

When she got inside she found he'd messaged her phone with a sticker of a bear throwing love hearts around. No aubergines in sight.

Bridge looked at the chaotic mess he'd left downstairs, had a brief vision of herself trapped in a newbuild with endless VAT returns, a slalom of highchairs and smart speakers that listened to her every 'feck', and decided not to reply just yet.

'Take another picture, Mummy!' Kes hugged his new BBF again, striking a pose. 'Gronny!'

Pax waited as he waved his grandmother back into shot from the end of the lead rope, then captured them on her phone, grateful that poor Internet and a bad marriage meant she'd always shunned Instagram, the picture of privileged indulgence briefly flashing on screen. If Kes had thought Ronnie was the best thing ever before the Shetland arrived, now that she'd found him a pony to ride on, that love was unconditional and carved in stone.

The Shetland *was* adorable, she had to admit. Berry-eyed, bargy and infinitely bribable, he was a grey-and-mud force of nature, bursting with greed and small-man syndrome. It was obvious that he lived for food, attention and, above all, hero-worship, instantly luxuriating in the love of a five-year-old boy. As soon as he and Kes body-slammed, nuzzled, mutually scratched and hung out, it was also clear that this was going to be all-out devotion.

'A match made in heaven!' Ronnie concluded, posing with Kes and the Shetland for her writer friend from the village who had led the pony across the fields, and who was dressed incredibly glamorously for the task, Pax thought. 'Aren't they just adorable?'

Pax remained cautious, aware that the pony had another job to do, and uncertain the threesome would prove a safe one, her worries compounded when the yard's trickiest stallion was introduced to his new companion on the cobbled yard.

To begin with, it was picture perfect as they touched noses, Ronnie's friend taking more pictures before waving a cheery farewell to head back across the fields.

Then, with an ear-piercing squeal, the Shetland flattened his tiny tufty ears and swung his head to nip Beck on the shoulder. Pax drew Kes into the safety of an empty stable as Beck flew straight up on his hind legs, landing back on the cobbles with a fierce roar, shaking and striking out at the unimpressed hairy Gael, who skipped round and cracked a double-barrel kick against his cannons. Luca only just hung on as the stallion ran backwards and went up on his hind legs again, eyes white-rimmed, convinced the interloper had to be a big cat in disguise.

'Let's put them out together for a bit!' Ronnie ordered, marching the Shetland towards the side arch.

Pax heard Luca objecting that it was too soon, but Ronnie took no notice.

'What's that thing, Mummy?' Kes pointed at Beck's huge erection flapping around beneath his belly as he was led dancing past.

'His willy,' she said, catching Luca glancing across at her and wishing she'd used a more technical term.

'Does he need a wee-wee? Can we go and watch?' He was already scrabbling back out through the door. Pax followed, praying she wouldn't have to explain away attempted sodomy on a Shetland.

But Beck was far too frightened for rape and pillage. Huge and light-footed, skin quivering, eyes bulging, the grey was soon backing around the smallest of the high-hedged stallion paddocks while the hairy new arrival charged about looking for something to eat.

Hanging back, Pax watched Luca and Ronnie lean companionably over the gate to monitor the get-together, Kes rammed low between them, face pressed against the rails, demanding, 'When can I ride him, Gronny? What's his name?'

'Oh rats, I forget. A Scottish island, I think. Rum? Mull?'

'Bute?' Pax suggested, and Luca glanced back over his shoulder, humouring the bad joke with a familiar show of teeth. Bute was also a common anti-inflammatory used for horses. She raised an apologetic eyebrow.

'Muck?' he suggested.

'Coll,' she countered, guessing he wouldn't get it.

'Beck and Coll.' He got it straight away, green eyes amused.

'Just how I like my men!' Ronnie ruffled Kes's hair, hooking him closer as he gazed adoringly up at her. 'And you'll ride Coll at the weekend, little man, although dear old Lester isn't home to teach you yet, so you'll have to put up with Gronny towing you around while Mummy holds you on. I wonder where the hunt's meeting on Saturday?'

'Absolutely not!' Pax stepped forward to cover Kes's ears, her mock-furious face to her mother met with a defiant cheer.

'If he's as like his grandfather as I think, he'll hunt.'

'He's nothing like Daddy.' She gathered her son up into a protective hug at her hip.

'Your grandfather was the best horseman and huntsman this county ever saw,' Ronnie told Kes.

Hiding her annoyance, Pax said nothing, watching Beck and the Shetland, at opposite ends of the paddock, one gazing in bewilderment as the other munched into the hedge. It wasn't the first time her mother had acknowledged Johnny Ledwell's talents that week, making a big point of giving her late husband a positive PR spin. It was doubtless her way of trying to compensate for a permanently busy landline and clandestine after-dark visits. Not content with seducing married sporting heroes and making five-year-old boys love her, Ronnie was flirting with the memory of the husband she had abandoned, dusting off Pax's father's tarnished, Scotch-sodden memory and putting it on the Percy trophy shelf. She'd been especially zealous since visiting the hospital earlier that day.

'Lester in good spirits?' Pax asked cautiously. According to Alice, the stud's old retainer had his finger surprisingly on the pulse, making it more than likely he'd heard the fresh Blair rumours.

'Exceedingly.' Ronnie gave nothing away. 'He was eager to know if we've got your foot in the stirrup again yet.' Her sharp blue eyes offered no mercy, looking to Luca for backup.

'I could certainly use the extra help when you do,' he obliged. 'I hear you're an incredible horsewoman. I bet you'd back the babies far better than I could.'

'Hardly,' she scoffed.

But Ronnie was on a roll. 'Now that Kes is on the Compton Magna riding squad, I told Lester you're raring to go, which perked him up no end. He might even forgive you not visiting him if he sees you back on a horse.'

Pax had forgotten how manipulative she could be. Dreading Lester's reaction to her marriage ending, certain of his disapproval, she'd still not visited.

'He was talking about the Wolf Moon Lap. Do you remember it? Probably before your time.'

'I remember it,' Pax muttered. She turned to watch Beck again, edging along the hedge and calling to the Shetland, who ignored him, only his bottom now visible, poking from the hazel as he laid into it searching for old cobnuts.

'It was one of my grandfather's traditions, long abandoned,' Ronnie told Luca. 'Major Frank Percy was a great believer in setting personal challenges. It quite terrorised my poor father growing up, although he became an extremely good pundit because Frank would give him one shilling to gamble in the flat season and one over jumps and no pocket money in between.'

'Sounds quite a character.'

'They both were. They did so love their racing. Which reminds me, I'm out this evening, meeting up with an old friend after Newbury races. You two will be fine if I'm not back until tomorrow, won't you? Probably dying to get rid of me.' She winked.

'Sure we will,' he said smoothly.

What friend? Pax wanted to ask but held it in check because her mother would only offer a vague 'you don't know them' and they both disliked lying. The conceit they constructed around Blair was laughable, and yet somehow necessary.

The Blair affair made Pax uncomfortable, aware she was complicit and her siblings disapproved as much as Lester did, but there was no denying the mood at the stud had lifted. Ronnie was recharged, the inner glow so bright she was like a moving brazier, irresistibly warming. Awkwardly, it had also put Ronnie in Cupid overdrive. As subtle as Mrs Bennet, she'd spent all week making her excuses to 'leave you two to get on with it' the moment Pax and Luca were within ten metres' radius of one another, Kes or no Kes. Luca tolerated it far more genially that Pax who had to bite her tongue hard, as now, to maintain her customary cool.

'There'll be lots of opportunities coming up for you gorgeous creatures to have the run of the place without me getting in the way,' she announced, running through a series of upcoming nights away that undoubtedly coincided with Blair's work diary. 'I'll be absent quite a few weekends when Kes is with his father, so I'm relying on you to make sure Pax doesn't mope, Luca.'

'I'm too busy working to mope.' Pax found Luca catching her eye, holding it.

'On which, I'm not going to argue about the cost again, Pax; I'm getting in that girl, Carly whatnot at weekends. I've already called her to say so. You and Luca both deserve a Sunday lie-in.'

Pax let the doubling-up of the lie-ins pass, aware of Luca's steel toe laying into a cobble. Tired arms joggling Kes as her mother started briefing them on all the things they must make sure to do tonight while she was gone, Pax guessed Luca must be troubled by Blair. He obviously had a pretty big thing about Ronnie. But his reaction was typically to smile it all quietly away.

'We've it all covered, Ron. You'll be back tomorrow, yes?' he checked, his eyes back on Beck as he tossed his head and stamped to try to get the Shetland's attention.

'Of course! And I haven't forgotten I'm babysitting for you two.' Ronnie made it sound like they were co-parents going on a date night.

'It's not important,' Pax dismissed quickly, dreading the AA meeting.

'It *is* important,' he said but didn't look at her.

'We're looking forward to our cowboy sleepover, aren't we, Kes?' Ronnie insisted, lifting Kes back across into her arms to swing him around.

'Yeeeeeeeeehaaaaa!' Kes squealed delightedly.

Still at the gate, Luca's focus was entirely on Beck, the horse's body language laden with warning signals as his forelegs slammed down, pawing at the ground, ears flattened to his head, aggression uncoiling at the little interloper like a flamethrower.

'We need to get them out of there!' Pax reached for the gate latch without thinking.

He put out a hand to stop her. 'Let's find out if this is going to work or not.'

'You said it was too soon.'

'Maybe I was wrong.' The green gaze remained fixed on the field where Beck was snaking his neck and baring his teeth. 'Look.'

It was little Coll who had the stallion cornered, planting two small hind hooves squarely in his big white chest with a furious karate cry squeal. Beck looked confounded. Ears flattened, he went to attack. Coll double-barrelled him again without hesitation. This time, the stallion dropped his head sheepishly, feigning an elaborate need to scratch his nose on his knee. They were soon mooching around side by side, tugging at grass tufts.

Pax whistled, looking across at Luca. 'That's it?'

'Sometimes there's no such thing as too soon.'

When he returned her gaze, for once unsmiling, Pax felt a sharp jolt and turned away, bursting with a strange, unfamiliar shame as real as pain. She'd been fighting it all week. It disoriented her. Was it pity? Empathy? Please let it not be desire.

Ambling back to the gate, looking very pleased with himself, the Shetland thrust his nose through the bars in the hope of a carrot. Behind him, Beck hung back chivalrously, still pretending to snatch at the grass.

'There'll be no more trouble between them.' Luca turned to Ronnie as she brought Kes back to pat his clever pony, smile billboard wide.

'If only it was so simple with humans!'

'Maybe it is.' Luca caught Pax's eye again, and again she felt a stitch catch beneath her ribs.

'I *love* Coll!' Kes shrieked, clambering up the gate rails to pat and hug him. 'He's the best *ever* pony. And I love you, Gronny. You are the best person in the world ever, ever, *ever*.'

Avoiding everyone's gaze, especially small self-satisfied Coll's, Pax told herself she must be grateful that a pony's fierce lust for life was cheering her son up, however tightly her teeth were gritted at such obvious emotional bribery.

A loud shrieking made her turn. It was coming from Lester's cottage.

'Is that the phone?' asked Ronnie hopefully.

'Oh hell!' Pax recognised the sound. 'Smoke alarm.' She sprinted back to find the scones she'd forgotten about were charred to black lava. The baking tray burnt her fingers through the thin tea towel as she pulled it out of the oven, dropping it on the quarry tiles, eyes smarting. 'Ouch!'

The frustration and jealousy she felt around her mother and Kes hijacked her as she let out a sob, dropping to her haunches and wrapping her head in her arms.

'Everything all right?' Luca appeared through the black fumes with an old CO_2 extinguisher, just a yellow helmet and a hose short of heroic. 'Your mother thought you might need this?'

'Fine!' Pax sprang back up and flapped the towel at the screeching alarm. 'I've never been able to bake.'

'When you're perfect in every other way, who needs cake?'

She rolled her eyes. 'Flatter me, why don't you?'

'Why not?'

'Because you're being creepy.'

'*Creepy?*' he laughed.

It was the wrong word, but it was out there before she could think of a better one. Trying to cheer her up seemed to be one of his new missions but if he wanted to make her feel good about herself, he kept laying it on too thick. 'Creepy' sounded like she was accusing him of being a perv, not overdoing the mood-lifting.

Once the alarm had been quietened, he studied the black remains. 'You're right, you're shit at baking.'

She laughed, relieved. 'Creep.'

'Cake wrecker.'

Illogically, Pax now had an urge to salvage her reputation by pointing out that she could throw together an asparagus soufflé and rack of lamb in her sleep, just not bake. Knowing such boasts would hardly impress a vegan, she kept quiet.

On the way out, he fixed on one of the photographs on Lester's wall. 'This is you, isn't it?'

It was herself at three or four on a fat Dartmoor pony.

'She was called Mouse and pure evil. She once bit my brother so hard he fainted. And I know what you're doing, by the way.'

'Good. My first pony was called Banjax, a little Vanner stallion who teased the mares. Da wouldn't let me have a saddle until I could jump him over every field wall on our farm bareback. Look at you, all prim and pretty. Is that your auld fella holding the lead rein? Good-looking man.'

'That's Lester!' she laughed, remembering her grandmother saying he'd once been a village heartthrob.

Pax pointed to the noble figure of her father on a hunter surrounded by hounds in a neighbouring frame. 'That's Daddy.'

'He looks kind.' He sounded surprised.

'He was, especially to his horses. He far preferred them to people.'

'I've met enough who do in our business.' His eyes trailed the other pictures. 'This him too?'

'Yes, with Grumps and Granny at Eyngate Hall. The hunt always meets there on New Year's Day. That's Alice in a basket saddle with Mummy leading. Tim was only a baby. She's pregnant with me, can you see? It must have been the year Daddy rode the Wolf Moon Lap.'

'What *is* this Wolf Moon Lap?'

She told him about her eccentric great-grandfather's annual challenge. 'After he died, so much of the stud's land had to be sold to cover inheritance tax and other debts that the Wolf Moon Lap became little more than a ten-furlong circuit you could get round in less time than it took to play a pop song, so Grumps redrew it to include a loop around Compton windmill, making it the same length Frank would have galloped. He never made it back before Saturn kicked in. He used to say if any Compton horse did, it would make our fortune.'

'What a fantastic challenge!'

His enthusiasm took her by surprise. 'I told Lester we should add it to your job description.'

'Sure, I'd have a go, wouldn't you?' His eyebrows shot up beneath the blond curls.

Amused, Pax looked away, taken by surprise by sharp tug of conscience. *I would give every star in the sky to see it.*

'Sure, horses are in your blood. It's why your boy loves that wee pony out there,' said Luca.

'Here we go.' Pax gave him a wise look. 'Kes has to live in a real world. I was far too cossetted.' She eyed the little figure in the photograph with her toes and nose up, wanting to warn her to break free sooner. 'Up to the age of ten or eleven, I thought everybody had ponies. Look at me here…' She moved across a few squares and tapped herself at fifteen flying across country, red ponytail like sea-spray, face of the Virgin Mary. 'I was like one of those characters from vintage pony books, brought up here with hunting-mad grandparents, educated in living museums as far from civilisation as school fees could buy, riding every free moment. It might as well have been the fifties. Immersive doesn't begin to describe it.'

'No wonder Bay took advantage of you.'

'He didn't,' she said quickly. 'I was still wrestling with my conscience whether to let him near my bra clasp when he slept with Mummy.'

'I wish I'd known you then.' His eyes glittered as he studied the photograph.

'I was only interested in horses.'

'So was I.'

Eager to stop talking about herself, she headed towards the door again. 'Would you have galloped up the drive on your Vanner cob to overthrow the status quo?'

'I'm not much of an overthrower.'

'More underhand then?' Looking out through the upper-door panes she could just make out Kes and her mother still hanging over the gate to the stallion paddock, nose to nose.

'Call it a quiet rebellion. We'll get you back on a horse.'

'Don't be so sure.' When she turned back, his smile was in its usual spot.

'Ronnie thinks you've lost your nerve.'

'She can think what she likes.' Zipping up her coat, Pax held the door open.

'You're so funny when you talk about her; your eyes pop.'

'They do not.'

'Do.'

She rolled her eyes.

'There you go.'

'Right.' She waved him out.

In Lester's walled cottage garden, Luca stopped to admire the view across to the stallion paddock. 'Your mother wants your happiness more than anything, you know that.'

Pax sucked her teeth. 'She'll leave again. It's what she does. Runs away into the sunset.'

'Not from this place; she's always wanted to come back here.'

'C'mon, Luca, she's been eyeing the door since the day she arrived. As soon as the stud is heading in the right direction, she'll leave. That's why she likes me being here.'

'You don't want to take it on?'

'I can barely see past my nose right now.'

'It's a beautiful nose.'

'You're being creepy again.' Realising how close he was standing, her pulses bolted. Her nose suddenly felt Pinocchio enormous, her lies laid bare.

'I'm being honest.' He sighed, stepping back, hands held up.

'Did Mummy put you up to this?'

'Will you quit being so paranoid?'

'If you quit flirting.'

'I'm so not flirting! You're right, you were seriously cossetted if you think this is flirting. I can flirt. This is not it.'

'But you do know my mother is trying to make us do just that?'

'Of course I do.'

'I wish she'd lay off. It's just not fair on Kes.' Pax looked across at the little figure by the gate, her heart thumping like a marching army. 'Mummy doesn't understand how much he needs balance and consistency, a sense of normality, not ponies and hero figures. He thinks you're his new best friend.'

'I think he's mine. He reminds me of my nephews.'

Pax rolled her eyes. Yet it occurred to her that Kes hadn't mentioned Oliver in days.

'Let him make believe he's a cowboy with that hoofed furball as his sidekick for a little bit, hey?' Luca said kindly. 'He's five; he's a boy; it's normal. This place is a very big part of his world.'

'My father used to call it a walled fortress of horse and hound.' Pax let her gaze trail up along the yard's golden stone sides again. She never failed to be thrown by its scale, by its emptiness without its familiar cornerstones: her grandparents gone, Lester sidelined. Her father's tenure might have been the briefest, but his shadow fell longest of them all.

Luca was still looking across the fields from which they could hear much chatter, giggling and bossy pony squeals. 'We need to separate those two before they grow so attached they make trouble.'

'It's far too late for that,' she sighed. 'Mummy's convinced Kes that he'll be the first rider to compete in all three equestrian disciplines at the Olympics with wife and teammate Princess Charlotte at his side.' She unlatched the door through the wall to the yard and held it open for him.

'I was talking about Beck and the pony.' He ducked through it, adding, 'I love it that you're funny. It's sexy.'

Flustered, Pax found herself noticing his backside for the first time. It was a seriously well-made backside. She looked determinedly away and marched through after him. Forgetting to duck for the stone lintel, she clouted herself hard on the forehead, reeling sideways and tripping over a boot scraper before falling against Laurence the fox's cage. 'Ooofuck!'

A split second later, Luca had her shoulders gripped in his hands. 'Pax? You okay?'

For a moment, his hand was on her cheek, like a lover's. She couldn't stop looking at his mouth. Why was she looking at his mouth?

'You okay?'

She looked up. His pupils were huge. Surely hers were the ones that should be dilated after a knock on the head? Then again, they probably were.

He was the one looking at her mouth now. 'Pax, you know I think you're the most—'

'I'm fine,' she said carefully. 'Stop being creepy.'

Laurence backed her up from the cage behind her, snapping his jaws and making huffing and snarling noises as he paced from side to side, glaring at Luca through the wire, his spine arched up.

Pax let Luca help her up, noticing how quick he was to step away afterwards and hold open the door in the wall, her three-figure heartbeat in her throat as they walked back to the field in silence.

*

Having been unable to persuade Flavia and Zak to settle for their overdue afternoon naps, Bridge battled to finish Aleš's VAT return amid sticky fingers, tearful tumbles and screaming bumps. The figures were still way out, HMRC's online submission page warning her that it didn't add up. Sod it, she'd balance it with a few made-up additions. This time it uploaded and she hurried upstairs to repaint her face with fifties eyeliner slicks and a bright pout.

She overdid it, rushing because she needed to get Flavia and Zak ready to go out too, one currently applying glittery green eyeshadow at her side, the other coasting around the bed with a heavy nappy drooping to his creased, pudgy knees.

Tired and fractious from playing with their cousins, Flavia and Zak didn't want to go out again, mewling as she changed them from the jogger combos to corduroy and fleece newly bought from the overpriced boutique in Chipping Hampton, ashamed that she'd shopped especially: Bridge, the rebel, dressing her children in Hackett and Joules in her quest to have friends as rah as Petra's.

She checked WhatsApp again and stared in shock at a message from Petra featuring a photograph of her evil Shetland pony looking like mini-me alongside the stud's big white stallion. It was captioned: *Ronnie has stolen my man! Let the bromance begin...*

Competitive streak stoked, Bridge tapped: *Hee! Cute! I'll say hello when I'm having tea there with Pax this afternoon. *Mummy playdate alert**

Furious with herself – the asterisks were stooping low – she heard a wail and turned in time to see Flavia upend an entire pot of bronzing powder over her brother's head.

Her phone buzzed again, a private message from Mo, another from Petra.

You okay, love? asked one; the other just said *Chin up*.

They might not always see past the painted face, but the Bags were straight onto humblebragging.

Kes was so besotted with Coll that when they brought the pony and his big scaredy-cat friend in from the field, he didn't want to leave the Shetland's side, glued to Ronnie and Luca too, firing questions about horses. Distractedly hurrying back and forth to Lester's cottage, trying to bake something for her visitors without burning it, Pax didn't realise at first that Ronnie had disappeared to make one of her long calls, leaving the Irishman to play babysitter as well as run the yard.

'Sorry!' she said every time she reclaimed Kes, only to find he'd sloped back a few minutes later.

'Sure, it's no bother.'

'I'm Loo Car's assistant manager!' Kes announced, making Luca laugh.

Pax had noticed the easy way the duo rubbed along from day one, another strand to her complex jealousy. Knock-knock jokes had flown back and forth between them in the past week, along with silly voices and at one point she was certain she'd heard Luca singing. They brought out good qualities in each other; Kes was less physically aggressive and more focussed around Luca, and, like the sun coming out after days of dark skies, Pax had seen far more of O'Brien the jester, Luca's reserve drawn out by Kes's determined thirst for knowledge and laughter.

'Luca grew up in a big pack,' Ronnie was quick to point out when she reappeared with a reddened phone-call ear to find Pax in a flour-covered pinny, spying on them picking out pony hooves. 'Super with kids.'

Unlike me, Pax reflected anxiously. Parenting was something she always felt pressurised to get right, like exams, a systemised process some people had the knack for, while others like her had to work very hard at it. Being passionate about one's subject wasn't enough. She loved Kes fiercely, but as Mack

– who had often made her feel incapable as a mother – was fond of saying, 'parenting is so much more than just loving'. She was too passive, he'd told her, too childlike herself, an orphan to maternal instinct.

'Kes needs normality,' she said it again, thinking hopefully about the little village school, about the bright-eyed children she'd seen covered in paint like at Holi festival.

'We both know there's no such thing. His father's an utter shit, mind you.'

'Isn't he just?' Mack was now only communicating through his parents and solicitors.

'I meant Luca's father. Total crook. Makes Johnny seem saintly.'

'But you keep telling me Daddy *was* a good man. He was just a drunk one.'

'It's a bit more complicated than that.' Ronnie's eyes stayed fixed on Kes.

'How so?'

'He had his secrets, like we all do.'

'I don't want to know.' Pax felt her throat tighten. 'Whatever it is, it died with him.'

'I thought you might say that.'

Sensing her mother was about to launch into one of her positive-spin spiels about the misunderstood brilliance of Johnny Ledwell again, Pax fished out her kitchen timer. 'I must check my scones.'

'I'll do it!' To her surprise, Ronnie marched off towards Lester's cottage. Not for the first time that week, Pax was reminded how much of a bossy stranger she remained at times, how fractured their bond. That must never happen to her relationship with Kes, she vowed as she went to help him sort through the pile of tack Coll had come with.

Five minutes later, when her kitchen timer went off, she realised she could smell burning.

'Not the scones again!' She belted inside to find more

char-black pucks pluming smoke in Lester's Rayburn. On cue, the smoke alarm went off. Tears welled in her eyes once again, furious at herself for entrusting the task while she daydreamed. 'Mummy, where are you?'

A cough behind made her jump. 'Unforgivably distracted,' Ronnie said briskly, stepping out of the hallway. 'I was looking for something.'

While her mother balanced on a kitchen chair trying the wrestle the battery from the alarm, Pax carried her fuming baking tray outside. Eyes smarting, she checked her watch. There was no time to cook more. Bridge and her little tribe would be here soon. At least she'd managed some rock-hard fork biscuits that looked like cowpats and a lopsided Victoria sponge that had sunk soggily in the middle.

The cottage was silent again. Ronnie watched her from the door. 'I can run to the farm shop quickly, if you like?'

'Honestly, it's fine.' Wishing she'd done that in the first place, Pax stomped back onto the yard where Kes was badgering Luca again. 'Come here, Kes!'

He ignored her.

'Here!'

Nothing.

Kes was trying to make Luca laugh by holding the Shetland's mane up to his face like a moustache and beard.

Beside her, Ronnie smiled. 'Aren't they just the pair? Mowgli and Baloo.'

'Hardly. HERE, Kes!' Her jolly call voice was shrill and unfamiliar now. 'Luca has a job to do, darling. Let's leave him to get on with it while you help me whip cream to fill the cake.'

'Sure, it's no bother,' Luca said cheerily, and she watched in despair as Kes bounded back, realising she was growling under her breath.

Ronnie sighed alongside. 'If we find you a Shetland companion, will you stop feeling so sour, I wonder?'

'I'm *not* sour.' Pax regrouped, cocking her head. 'Shouldn't you be setting off soon?'

'Not for an hour or so. Just got time to get you on a horse and round the Poacher's loop before we lose the light. Luca can mind Kes. I want to talk to you about your father.'

'You forget I have friends coming.' Pax said a silent prayer of thanks to pushy Bridge, whose visit she'd been looking forward to with almost indecent excitement as well as bad baking. Her need for a village mum gang was great, no longer barred by Mack's disapproval of her having her own friends.

Without warning, a thousand firework sparks exploded again. *I'm free*, she remembered with a burst of delight, the customary high turning her black mood upside down.

By the time Kes thundered up, towing an apologetic Luca by the coat sleeve, she was beaming, arms wide as her son rammed into her legs with a killer hug tackle. 'Mummy, I love you! Loo Car just told the best joke. Tell her, Loo Car, pleeeeeease.'

Luca cleared his throat awkwardly, eyes rolling at Pax. 'Knock knock...'

It was the eye-roll that did it. Was it deliberate? It shouldn't have been funny, but it was. Stupidly funny.

'Who's...? Pax's laughter morphed into giggles liked a hiccups.

He waited.

'Wh—?' She waved the question away, chest in a vice.

'Knock knock,' Luca repeated, green gaze on her contorted, teary face. He rolled his eyes again.

Pax was incapable of speech, body shaking with laughter.

Ronnie stepped in. 'Who's there?'

'Idy Dap,' Luca said awkwardly.

'Idy Dap Who?' Ronnie asked obligingly and then, as Kes, Pax and finally Luca dissolved into a heap of snorting weeping, laughter, she held out her arms in confusion. 'I don't get it. Am I missing something? What's funny about Idy Dap Who?'

The more she said it the harder they laughed, clinging onto

each other, chests aching. Straightening up, eyes meeting, Luca and Pax were smiling so much their faces hurt.

Sometimes there's no such thing as too soon she recalled his words with a jolt, identifying that long-lost feeling at last. It was something that had been far more dangerous and forbidden through her barren marriage than pity, empathy or even desire. More precious even than male friendship, into which she'd so gratefully boxed him. It was having someone who understood her.

Getting the punchline at last and starting to laugh, Ronnie bellowed, '"*I did a poo*". Is that it?'

And they all collapsed into giggles again.

When she took Kes back to the cottage, the back door was open. A rubble trail of black crumbs led from garden through the kitchen and past upside-down cooling racks on the floor to the dog beds. These were covered with telltale cake and biscuit crumbs. The soggy-bottomed Victoria sponge was a memory, the cow-pat biscuits wolfed. Even two trays of black scones on the back step had been demolished.

Watching Pax take in the scene from beneath the table, Stubbs and Knott thumped nervous tails.

'Mummy, please don't cry.' Kes gripped her hand.

'I'm not crying.' Why did the giggles keep resurfacing? 'I think we'd better clear this up and have a quick wash, don't you?'

'Knock knock.'

'Who's there?'

'Olive.'

'Olive who?'

'I love you too!' he beamed and she hugged him tighter than ever. He smelled very strongly of Shetland.

Carly worked with absolutes: I will be there, we will do this, this is what is happening. The vague time-keeping of village life maddened her; the 'whenever suits you', 'we'll be around this week', 'sometime tomorrow morning' fluidity left her lost at sea.

Accepting a job with Ronnie Percy fitted into that fluid category. They'd vaguely agreed Carly would help out on the yard some weekends – but she'd heard nothing more. Whereas writer Petra was surprisingly timetabled, Ronnie had yet to reply to a text, didn't answer her phone and was never on the yard when Carly called in. She was starting to think she'd imagined the job offer, and she felt awkward about Bridge inviting her along today – especially given she hadn't found Pax Forsyth too friendly the previous time.

Pushing their buggies around the village green towards the stud, flecks of rain spitting sideways at them, Carly listened as Bridge chattered too fast and loud about how great her new job was going to be, how mad Aleš was driving her, and how funny and down-to-earth Pax was.

'She's got her head screwed on, that one, which is why her wee lad's trying the school tomorrow. Honest to God, but it's a little gem, so it is. I told Aleš that's where I want ours to go. He can laugh all he likes, it's something special.'

'Ellis likes it there.' She watched him running ahead of them, rattling his 'Splorer Stick against the trunks of the wintering horse chestnuts.

'That's what I told Pax. She can't wait for him to meet Kester.'

Carly thought it a weird name, like a character from a BBC costume drama. 'Ash wasn't happy about it. Says they're a bad lot at the stud. Stuck-up.'

'Pax isn't stuck-up, queen. She's roughed it. A woman can tell.'

'Ash says there's history between Percys and Turners.'

'Turners hold a grudge against most folk round here, don't they?'

'I guess. They're all bad-tempered buggers, especially the men. Better watch their backs. Ash is psyching himself up for a fight.'

'With the Percy family?'

'No, his own.' She felt the familiar tug of worry.

'A bare-knuckle contest?'

'You know about that?' She looked at Bridge in surprise.

'I've heard rumours.'

'Yeah, well I've told him no way,' Carly said darkly.

'Think he'll take any notice?'

'Do they ever? It's all fists and honour with men, isn't it?'

Bridge made a harrumphing noise. Beneath the thick make-up, that bee-stung mouth was still more Joe Louis than Angelina Jolie, Carly had noticed. She'd yet to get to the bottom of why she'd wanted Skully's number the day she'd fallen off her horse, although she'd heard Bridge complain that her husband thought of Craic like a love rival.

'Everything all right at home with you now, is it?' she asked casually.

'Fierce. I don't know where you get the idea Aleš lamps me about. I'd fecking deck him first.'

Carly sucked her teeth uncertainly. Her hands had started buzzing hotly on the buggy handles, sensing something in pain or distress, but she didn't know Bridge well enough yet to pry.

'Mother of God, will you look at this place?' Bridge said when they rolled into the stud's first big stable yard. 'It's like Blenheim Palace. Let's dander under the arch. Is that Ronnie?'

A small figure in a huge squishy coat and bobbled beany hat was letting herself out of a stable, blue eyes taking in the young mums and toddlers invasion with delight.

'Carly!' She strode across beaming, quilted horse rug over one shoulder. 'Just the person! Your ears must be burning. When can you start? Saturday too soon?'

'Fine by me.' Carly admired her hat, which had the biggest and fluffiest pom-pom she'd seen. In person, Ronnie always reminded her of a posh Kylie, far less intimidating than she was barking on the phone.

'Wonderful!' She stooped to greet the occupants of the buggy, both equally entranced by the pom-pom. 'I don't suppose you can spare a few mins now? I'm not here on Saturday, and it'll save Luca's valuable time if you're already up to speed.'

'We're both here for the grand tour.' Bridge stepped forward, looking eagerly at Carly who realised too late she was expected to introduce her. 'Pax invited us.'

'Oh, she's still baking I think,' Ronnie said brightly, straightening up. 'We've got time to go through the basics. *Luca!*'

'Yeah, great,' came the Belfast drawl, 'but the thing is, queen, we've got the kids—'

'You'll look after them, won't you?' Ronnie cut off a now shocked-looking Bridge. 'I recognise you from the village. What beautiful children you have. Have you been skiing, little chap?' she asked Zak, his face weirdly bronzed now that Carly looked at him. He let out hiccupy giggles as small dogs crowded round the buggies, the two matching black and tans and Lester's wire-haired terrier with his Tom Jones beard full of crumbs.

'Where's your big lurcher?' Ronnie turned to Carly again.

'At home with Ash. Mrs Bullock says she frightens some of the mums.' Poor Pricey – another scar-faced female – had been banned from school pickup.

'As does Battleaxe Bullock herself, I gather.' Ronnie whistled hers closer. 'Do bring her here when you work; there are kennels if she's a bother. We're thrilled you can help cover weekends. The pay's not much as you know, but we can throw in lots of lessons.'

'I don't want lessons.' Ash hated the idea, and Carly only had to look at Bridge's lip to remind herself why. She preferred equine company from the ground. 'I don't want to ride.'

'Heal, Carly!' Ronnie was already striding away with the rug.

'Did she just say that?' whispered Bridge, still in shock. 'Like you're a dog?'

'*H-e-a-l-ing* lessons, not riding lessons!' Ronnie continued shouting over her shoulder as she marched out through the archway. 'I've already told Luca he must harness that gift of yours. He'll talk you through the weekend routine when I can find him. *Luca!*'

'Do you think she expects me to go with her?' Carly asked Bridge, looking around for Ellis, whose red nylon book bag was abandoned nearby.

'You stay put,' Bridge scowled. 'I'm with Ash on this. Talk about stuck-up. *And* she was rude about Mrs B.'

'I *want* this job,' Carly reminded her in an undertone.

Ronnie was still bellowing in the adjacent yard. '*Luca!* Come and give this pretty girl your number and talk to her about Saturday. Where *is* he?' She marched out of sight.

Carly and Bridge waited awkwardly for a moment, Jackson letting out squawks of protest as the dogs raced away after their mistress.

'Get off that, Ellis!' Carly spotted him balancing precariously on the stone mounting block steps.

Their wait stretched on, Jackson's nappy now full judging by the smell.

'Does Pax even know we're here?' asked Carly.

Bridge looked around. 'I don't know which bit she lives in. This cake had better be worth it or I'm fecking right off.' She winked to reassure Carly it was a joke, their senses of humour not always on the same page.

'Maybe it's a complicated recipe?'

'Hello?' a soft voice called, and they turned as an arched door in the wall at the far side of the yard opened with a rusty creak and Pax emerged, cramming a hat over hair still wet from the shower, small boy and grey puppy hiding behind her long legs. 'You poor things, I didn't know you were here! Welcome!'

Carly had forgotten how beautiful she was, tall and model thin, her waxy, translucent skin foxed with freckles. She felt her hands throb more, suddenly hot as coals.

'Hello, who are you?' Pax laughed as she was brought up short by Ellis with his feather duster racing across to stand to attention at her knees and gaze up, enthralled and too tongue-tied to speak. 'It's Ellis, isn't it?'

'Hey, Pax!' Bridge was already belting across with her buggy like a yummy mummy eager to score a favourite seat at a pavement café. 'This is the lad you saw at Maggers last week.'

Maggers? Carly's lip curled. Why was Bridge suddenly sounding like Miranda Hart?

'And you know Carly.' She beckoned her to follow.

Watching Carly push her buggy over the cobbles, Pax's yellow eyes glowed like hurricane lamps. 'Oh goodness, *you're* Ellis's mum?'

She nodded defensively. Her hands were pure electricity now, driven by a thousand needles. 'Say hello, Ellis.'

Ellis scuffed his toes shyly, still gazing up at the beautiful freckled face.

'Hello.' Pax's wide golden gaze softened as she stooped down, arms outstretched to introduce Kes. 'I hope you two will be friends.'

She thinks she's the Duchess of Cambridge, Carly thought irritably, the cold rain pips like sharp gravel against her skin as she reluctantly acknowledged just how much she resented Pax her privilege, her family support, Bridge's girl crush and her beautifully mannered son who was introducing himself to the still-mute Ellis and asking if he'd like to meet his pony.

'You two are going to be in the same class tomorrow,' Pax was telling the boys.

In school not life, thought Carly, saying, 'Show your manners, Ellis, say hello!'

'This is my 'Splorer Stick.' Ellis showed off the manky feather duster he was illogically attached to, and Carly felt a rare flash of mortification, especially when Kes held out a classic one-eyed vintage bunny and introduced 'Rab C. Nesbitt' in a posh sing-song voice.

'His father named him,' Pax muttered at Bridge who snorted with laughter.

Excluded because she didn't understand the reference, Carly wondered why someone like Pax would want to send her son to the village school.

Her hands were on fire.

'I'm afraid I burnt the cakes like King Alfred then the dogs ate the rest,' Pax was apologising. 'I'm truly sorry.' The deep voice was hypnotic enough to be forgiven anything. To Carly's ear, it was ridiculously plummy. She added, 'I think I've enough egg and flour left to make drop scones with lashings of honey after our walk round.'

'Eggs on toast is fine for Ellis.'

'Say, how about we eat out?' Bridge suggested, her strong accent turning all the 'ows' into 'ighs', and Carly noticed Pax looked politely baffled.

'Norn Irish for "how about we eat out",' she translated helpfully.

'I heard what she said,' Pax pointed out in her deep, over-kind voice, 'I just was wondering where?'

Carly felt squashed.

'They're wassailing in the old orchard at dusk,' Bridge was explaining. 'There's always loads of bacon sarnies and mulled cider on offer. Why don't we all go after you show us round here? Your lot'll be there, won't they, Carl?'

'If it's not raining.' Carly shrugged, still smarting at being corrected. The Turners were big on wassailing, a tradition of blessing the cider apple trees each new year. She'd never understood the appeal and the cider punch was always lethal.

'They still do the wassail?' Pax was wide-eyed. 'I thought that stopped years ago. It used to lead to anarchy.'

'Sure, it's now a fun village tradition, very family friendly with a big bonfire and *buckets* of grog,' Bridge laughed. 'Everyone gets rat-arsed on cider, but they do a Health and Safety assessment first so it's all good. Shall we go?'

'I'm not sure it's—' Pax started.

'Course we will!' Bridge had already made the decision. 'Hear that, Carl? We're having a hooley! Did I not say this woman's one of us?'

Carly caught Pax's eye and knew for certain she wasn't.

Calling her son with the weird name back, Pax turned to look across the yard and then her face developed a fixed expression. Following her gaze, Carly watched Luca O'Brien stride up, all leather boots and smiles, black Puffa over a green farmer's overall. Eyes bright as nocellara olives, he looked a million times better than the exhausted traveller she'd met on New Year's Day.

'Carly, how are ya?' The deep Irish accent was double cream in contrast to Bridge's sharp lemon Belfast lilt. He handed over his number on a piece of paper. 'Best to text on that number with the bad signal here. It's this coming weekend you're starting, yeah?'

'I can do seven till midday. This is my friend Bridge.' She made sure she got her manners right this time.

'How're you doin'?' He nodded at Bridge and the children, his smile disarming.

'Better for meeting you.' Bridge gave him comedy lash-bats over her glasses. 'How are you settling in?'

'Sure, it's a pretty place.'

'Come wassailing later. We're all going. Beezer cheap cider.'

He looked to Pax, Carly noticed. Was he seeking permission?

Arms tightly crossed, Pax flashed her big hazel eyes back at him. He shrugged, still smiling. 'I might. I've the yard to finish, mind.'

'Carly's going to help you,' Bridge said brightly. 'Work experience.'

Carly gaped at her.

'We'll look after all the kids, won't we, Pax?'

Pax was gaping at Bridge too now.

Carly heaved Jackson from his harness. 'This one's nappy needs changing first, but if you'd like to do it, Bridge...?' She held him out.

'Wet wipe allergy.' Bridge held up her hands, eyes glittering, enjoying the backchat. 'I'm sure Luca can hang on for five.'

'Sure,' he smiled and Carly was reminded how kind his face was.

'Use the cottage.' Pax pointed her towards the arched gateway. 'It's unlocked. Kes and Ellis can play in the hay store.'

With a grateful war cry, Kes raced off again to an open bay side of the stable yard where several big round bales were stacked for netting up, Ellis and his duster in hot pursuit.

'Come and find me when you're ready.' Luca raised a black coat arm, loping off in the direction Ronnie had taken earlier.

'We will!' Bridge called, steely eyes rolling from Pax to Carly, voice hushed. 'Oh my fecking God, is he *hot* or what? That's a *lot* of testosterone right there.' She returned to her buggy to hoik Flavia out, sending her in after the boys, then turned back for Sienna, catching herself, eyes cast up to heaven to mouth 'sorry' before turning to Pax and Carly. 'Sorry. Language. I've a Belfast docker's mouth, so I have.'

'It's nothing compared to the language these walls have heard; horsemen are far worse,' Pax laughed, which made Carly like her a bit more.

She picked up her changing bag to carry inside with Jackson, using her teeth to pull her gloves off scorching fingers as she went, no longer convinced their healing heat was for Bridge.

The cottage smelled of burnt cake, polished leather and dog, a big mantel clock creaking uneven ticks as Carly laid Jackson out on his changing mat on a threadbare woven rug. There were antlers and stuffed fox masks on the walls and lots of hunting paraphernalia lying around, incongruously counterbalanced by brightly coloured toys underfoot. Jackson mewled for a large remote-controlled car nearby.

Leaving him crab-crawling towards it, she bagged up the soiled nappy and took it through the kitchen and out to a dustbin she'd spotted on the way in, stopping in amazement as she realised that what she'd taken to be a ferret in a hutch was a fox, fast asleep; it was the same colour as Pax's hair. Carly was transfixed by its caged closeness.

A gurgling wail of fury brought her back to the present and she dashed inside to find Jackson had pushed the toy car into the hallway, losing it under a bowed Welsh dresser, small grabby fingers now pulling out the contents of a big box stored there, which he was rapidly emptying.

'You little – oh!' As she dropped down to tidy the mess, she realised they were letters, a lot of them ripped and creased. Surely Jackson couldn't have done so much damage in so little time? She raked them out of the way, reaching under the dresser for the car to distract him again.

The letters, many in small fragments, were written in beautiful old-fashioned ink handwriting on thick paper, something she'd never seen. Nobody wrote letters any more, she realised. At least not to her. Ash had written a few when he was deployed in Iraq, but by the Afghanistan tour it was all email and Skype. He wasn't a great wordsmith, unlike this correspondent in whose flowing lines she could already spot phrases like 'the moonlight silvers our tears' and 'a thousand nights for one with you'. Two different hands, she realised, one rounded blue ink copperplate, the other black and spidery, both sides of a secret conversation.

Jackson was chewing on one. She tried to pull it away and he wailed furiously.

'Give that back to me, you—'

'Everything all right?' The plummy voice.

Carly was straight on the defensive. 'I was taking his nappy to the bin. He pulled them out.'

'Oh dear.' Pax stooped beside her to help clear them. 'Lester's going to be furious with me. He keeps all sorts of old – oh!'

'Everything all right?' Carly watched her study a shred of paper, the luminous eyes stretched wide.

Pax didn't respond or move, breath stilled as she read. Whatever was in the letters was a bone-deep shock.

Carly's hands were raw with the heat that was now stealing up her body. 'These were already ripped like this when Jackson found them!' she flashed.

Pax had turned her face away. 'Please would you mind leaving me alone?'

'It's not his fault.'

'I'd like you to go right now.'

17

The kids had been playing in the hay a long time; Kes's eyes were turning mouse red, Ellis's 'Splorer Stick was coated with seeds, and both girls were runny-nosed with cold, their baby brothers growly and restless. The light was fading. Ronnie had just clattered off down the drive on a horse with a cheery goodbye, stirrups showjumper short, no high-vis on whatsoever.

Bridge hadn't been able of get much out of Carly beyond a gruff summary that Pax had got the hump over some old letters and had been very rude.

'We should go and check she's okay,' she said after Pax had failed to reappear for ten minutes.

'Be my guest.' Carly was perched high in the hay to get a signal, adding filters and stickers to the pictures she'd just taken of her kids to post onto her Facebook and Instagram feeds.

'Did you see who the letters were from?'

'No idea.' Easily offended, accustomed to having a million things to do, Carly wasn't one for hanging around. 'Perhaps I should be helping Luca out like Ronnie suggested.'

'She might be really upset.'

'Still bloody rude when you've got guests,' Carly complained, taking a picture of Bridge in the gloom to add to her news story. 'I thought we were all getting a guided tour and going wassocking.'

'Wassailing. Don't tag me on that. Aleš doesn't know I'm here.'

'What's it to him if you are?'

'I like to maintain an air of mystery.' After last night's row, Bridge wanted the possessive sod to stew. She'd turned off her own phone and needed her timelines to stay clean too. Unlike Carly and her personal propaganda army, Bridge kept family life off screen. On principle, she and Aleš never posted pictures of their children, home, each other or their food. Instead, Bridge curated dark-humoured video funnies, GIFs and memes, spreading lovehearts and scream-faces wherever she went, while Aleš shared pictures of plant machinery and roof trusses. Both secretly checked one another's feeds and friends on a regular basis.

'I could murder for a cup of tea,' Carly said, shivering. 'You know, I might as well be helping Luca out right now.'

'Go ahead, why doncha? I'll knock for Pax and follow with the kids in a bit.'

Carly was gone faster than smoke. The moment she did, Jackson started bawling, setting Zak off.

Lacking her usual breezy cool, Bridge hovered by the cottage gate with a heavyweight screamer on each hip. She bellowed at the older boys to get away from a lethal-looking rusty chaff-cutter; Sienna was draping Flavia with binder twine.

The door in the wall opened before she knocked. Bridge recognised the signs: bloodshot eyes, red-tinged nose, dry and swollen upper lip. 'Sorry, sorry, sorry! You poor things. That was so rude of me.'

'Is it the ex?' Bridge secretly relished the prospect of some insider dirt.

'No, nothing like that.'

The smile surprised her, the deep voice hypnotising, the gather-up-all organisation effortless, Jackson lifted and muted with a nose-rub within seconds.

'Do you want a cup of tea and a chat?'

'Really, it's all fine. Let me show you round before it gets dark. Let's go, everyone!'

She was a Boudicca of self-control, Bridge realised with grudging admiration, watching the children gathering like eager Von Trapps and wishing Carly was still there.

Luca was grateful he didn't need to tell Carly anything twice. It was clear her reactions were lightning quick: mind, hands and hair-trigger sharp tongue.

'Muck out, turn out, pick out, skip out,' she rapped coolly, 'tie-up, rug-up, mix-up, fill-up. Not necessarily in that order. Have I missed one?'

He grinned, shaking his head. He was looking forward to having her on the yard. She reminded him of an acerbic German groom he'd worked alongside years ago who could muck out a stable in four minutes, liked horses far more than people and ran back-to-back marathons for fun.

'Let's get this yard swept and we'll put the kettle on. Give that here...' She took the yard brush from him, making short work of clearing hay and stray wood shavings from the cobbles. 'That Pax isn't much of a one for offering guests a cup of tea, is she? She's got the right hump with me.'

'How so?'

When she explained that her baby had dug out some old letters from under a cupboard he felt uneasy, realising they must be the ones he'd stuffed there after the puppy had shredded them. He tried to remember what he'd read in them, the love letters written in two old-fashioned hands.

'Pax on the yard much at weekends, is she?' Carly asked leadingly, clearly hoping not.

'We all muck in, depending what needs doing. Sure, we're all pretty new here, and the work's always there if you look for it.' He thought back to the previous weekend. While Ronnie had vanished like a shot the moment Blair rolled up, Pax had taken her mind off Kes being with his father by undertaking a gargantuan sort-out of the tack room, unearthing all manner of museum pieces. There had been no shortage of tea that day, swigged while boggling at kinky-looking vintage bits and leatherwork. Worried she wasn't eating, he'd also made her falafels for lunch which he later spotted in Laurence the fox's cage.

'I'm not one for backchat if that's okay,' Carly was saying. 'I like to get my head down and work. You okay with me wearing earphones, yeah?'

'If it's what you want.'

'I listen to audiobooks and podcasts mostly,' she told him, eyes fierce, keen to be taken seriously. 'I like learning things. At the moment I'm listening to a book called *Everyday Sexism* that Bridge recommended.' The side of her mouth curled up. 'And Beyoncé.'

Luca sensed she took no prisoners. In that, she reminded him of Pax. But whilst Carly seemed to want to like the horses more, she handled them awkwardly, manoeuvring one heavily pregnant mare out of her stable like a pallet trolley.

'You'll get used to it,' he assured her, distracted by a waspish buzzing against his hip as, finding signal briefly, his phone started vibrating.

He had four missed calls, its screen told him, all Unknown Number. There had been many in recent days, the frequency increasing in the past forty-eight hours, but no voice messages. Was it Mishaal?

The prince's London visit was helpfully all over the sports pages, the devoted fans of his newly acquired football club thrilled by the millions being sunk into their team, less so by the family's cut-throat reputation for humanitarian crime and corruption. Luca had been perpetually on edge this week, counting down the days until Beck's royal nemesis was safely back in the bosom of his family in the Middle East. Knowing Mishaal was in the same country made Luca very jumpy indeed, no matter how often he reminded himself that a man who travelled with such a rigidly fixed itinerary wasn't about to slip out to the Cotswolds at the whim of his father. He had done his duty and called. They would both be relieved to leave it there.

By Luca's calculation, there were just one or two more days before the prince and his caravan court departed until summer. Almost there. While the unknown calls to his phone were almost certainly ambulance chasers and sales scams – Mishaal had the landline number here, after all, kept under constant siege by Ronnie – he still preferred to ignore them until he knew for certain the prince had left the UK.

'What next?'

He jumped when he realised Carly was beside him again. Mind still on Mishaal, he showed her where they pressure-hosed the feed buckets and barrows.

'What exactly *is* my hour rate again?' she asked between blasts.

'That you'd have to ask Ronnie.' Who had yet to pay *him* anything, but he remained too loyal to share that information just yet.

'I've given up two other weekend jobs for this.'

Luca was grateful to hear a child's voice yell beyond the walled yard and then a familiar husky catch of laughter amid talk: Pax.

His ear was already tuned for it, able to pick it out in an instant.

'I need a contract,' Carly insisted.

'It's just casual weekend work.' Even Luca didn't have a contract.

'Where I come from, we don't do casual – work, dress or sex.' The lip curled prettily again. 'Once bitten and all that. Working for Bay Austen taught me that.'

'Yes?' He realised Pax and her entourage were moving further away. Then he registered who Carly was talking about, his blood quickening angrily. 'Bay Austen, you say?'

'That man screws everyone,' Carly said bitterly. 'I wasn't the first.'

'He took advantage of you?' Surprised at her frankness, Luca was appalled.

'Promised me I could stay on at the farm shop and be first in line for a good job when they open the café there, instead of which I was put on a zero-hours contract with no hours.'

'I see. That's bad.'

A snort of rare laughter. 'Did you think I meant he'd booty called me? I'm married with three kids. End of. My old man's going to be a farrier soon.'

'Good on him.' Her fierce expression twisted his belly instinctively, unwanted and tight as a stitch, remembering that familiar tug of attraction he'd felt towards her when they'd first met. Unhappy wives were his forte, and his fool heart had hit the ground running, the race on to fix on someone to rescue like an over-zealous knight, unaware that his affections had already been ambushed.

He listened for the others as he hurried Carly around the yards, finishing up the day's work, intermittently catching sight of Pax and her pink-haired friend herding children in the distance.

'You got kids?' Carly caught him by surprise as she watched him add more bedding to Beck's stable, already box-walked to a grooved track. She hummed a tune that made the horse turn from his customary shadow statue at the back of the stable, ears pricked.

'Not with me. So you like Beyoncé?' he diverted clumsily, recognising the tune she was humming.

'She's okay, but my favourite music to work to is film tracks. You can't beat *Gladiator*.' She held open the door for him.

'True enough.'

'Or *Last of the Mohicans*. You know it?' Carly started humming, 'Dum ditty dum ditty dum ditty dum ditty da da da. Dum ditty…'

'Stop dumming.' He'd played it in Canada until his fingers were too numb to hold down the strings.

'Am I that bad?'

'At dumming, yes. At yard work you're top-notch there for a beginner.'

'And you'll teach me healing?' She scratched Beck's nose through the stallion grille.

'You don't learn it, Carly. You feel it. What you're doing right there, you have no idea how exceptional that is; he'd have anyone else's fingers off.'

She grinned. 'Ronnie reckons I'll earn a fortune from these hands. They're on bloody fire again today. Feel.'

He flinched as they landed on him like red-hot brands, a palm on each forearm, grey eyes cool by contrast.

'Why's that happening, then?' she asked, removing them.

'They'll tell you when they're ready.' He turned away, fires sparking in his own palms, incubated in work gloves. He glanced across the yard to the white head of Beck watching him through the stallion grilles. How do you heal a rift like that between a horse and the abuse he'd suffered at the hands of a man?

'Come this way and I'll show you the observation tower.' Pax's husky voice sounded like a harbour bell, closer now, that deep vibrato she only used when she was sitting on a suitcase of unhappiness. How did you heal hers?

When she and Bridge finally trundled buggies noisily across the cobbles, he knew straight away something was wrong. She knew he saw it, determinedly avoiding his gaze.

Bridge hailed them noisily, gratefully handing the yawning toddler on her hip across to Carly and chuckling. 'You two ready to wassail close to the wind? It's started already. The parish committee are very hot on hurdy-gurdies. Listen.'

They could all hear the wheezing of a medieval instrument in the distance.

'We thought we'd go and stake a good spot by the bonfire,' she said, elbowing Luca. 'You're coming too. No arguments. Carly has helped you finish the yard specially. Just so we're clear, it's all old baldy men dancing with handkerchiefs and weird Wicca Man rituals but we need a bacon butty and cider right now more that we need fecking oxygen, do we not?'

He watched Pax's face, freckles crowding as she frowned, not wanting a chaperone. He could guess why. They both knew that rolling down to a cider-fest wasn't a wise idea, even surrounded by a small army of children. He wasn't feeling too safe himself.

'Sure.'

From the top of the stud's drive, it was possible to see down into the little walled orchard opposite the Green, one of the few remnants of the Comptons' cider-producing heritage. As a small child, Pax had imagined its trees to be courtly dancers, skirts trimmed with blossom lace in spring, embroidered green tassels in summer and red fruit in autumn, then in winter as twisted and gnarled black skeletons. Today those skeletons had been joined by a few hunched figures in woolly hats. A thin plume of smoke rose up from one corner, cast sulphur yellow by a horizon-low winter sun that was striping everything gold as it sank amid fast-dispersing clouds.

Ahead of Pax, Luca's black Puffa jacket was like a tiger's back as they set off for the wassail, Bridge hurrying to keep up alongside him.

'I warn you, compared to back home the music's always totally fecking shite, even if the grog's sensational,' she said.

Instinctively, Pax glanced at Kes, imagining him parroting 'fecking shite' back at his father, and then she decided it served Mack right if he did. She liked the way Bridge spoke exactly as she found. Carly's barbed tongue was more circumspect, letting off her own buggy brake with a huff, eyes sliding past Pax without looking at her. 'We could always go to yours if it's crap, Bridge,' she called. 'I'm dying for a cup of tea and a biscuit.'

Walking alongside, Pax let the sarcasm wash over her. Her mind was far too busy, thoughts churning like a curdling sauce. *Keep thinking about something else.*

'Looks like we're in for a starry night,' she predicted brightly.

'I'm sorry about them letters,' Carly muttered, not sounding it.

'Forget about it.'

'It wasn't Jackson's fault.'

'I said forget it. Honestly.'

'Were they important?'

Unable to answer, Pax knew Carly's chippiness was because she couldn't possibly understand how devastating the discovery of Lester's box of letters was. It rewrote her childhood. *Keep thinking about something else.*

'Don't our boys get on well?'

'Ellis gets on with everyone.'

Pax doubted that. 'I'm so grateful you brought him.'

Watching Kes charging about with Ellis, happier than she'd seen him in weeks, Pax could forgive Carly her sullenness. The two boys were lost to a five-year-old world that lifted them above the rest of the party, an instant, loyal bond where worlds, real and imaginary, coincided joyfully, far from the paranoia of adulthood with its hormones, heartbreak and hubris. And its hooch.

God, but she longed for a drink.

Her father was the first one who had taken her wassailing, she remembered. He'd probably only done because he wanted to get pissed too. Had Lester been there?

Keep thinking about something else.

She focussed on Carly, forcing a smile. She was a beautiful woman, her high cheeks and grey-denim eyes like her son's, both with angular, boyish bodies, fierce walk once again marching forwards, broody looks cast sideway at Pax who admired her uncompromising indifference, a marked contrast to her loud-mouthed friend. Bridge was adorably entertaining, but Carly had steel spun through her.

Ahead of them, the phone in Luca's pocket started ringing. He silenced it and it started again.

'Demanding girlfriend?' laughed Bridge.

'Something like that.'

He glanced back over his shoulder, brows low as he studied Pax's face, then the neon smile switching on for Carly. He seemed very taken with Carly, she'd noticed with a heat-rash feeling in her skin that annoyed her, a misplaced possessiveness.

Confusingly, when she'd looked through the letters and realised the truth, cold with shock, the person Pax had instinctively wanted to tell was Luca. But talking wouldn't help keep the family secret.

Keep thinking about something else.

She needed a drink. She was boring herself with this need, this weakness, this *thinking*. She must stop thinking.

In her pocket, her own phone had started buzzing furiously, a full signal flooding her inboxes. She ignored it, not wanting Mack's vitriol to touch her.

'Mummy – look!' Kes was balancing along the low stretch of drystone wall by the gate entrance, Ellis behind him. She hadn't seen him so happy in months.

I love him. I can't bear how much I love him. She clapped overhead, grateful for laughter bursting through before tears dared, feeling her rings slip off as she did so, the 'ice and a slice' as Bay had called them, too loose on bone-thin fingers to hold on.

They landed silently amid the leafy mulch alongside the tarmac, and she had an overwhelming urge to let them lie there. Her mother had left her rings in the bathroom the day she ran – one Pax's flame-haired grandmother's emerald engagement ring, the other a gold band battered from hard riding – equally untreasured. An abandoned marriage, like hers. Her father and Lester. The shock.

Keep thinking about something else.

'You dropped something.' Carly had turned back again and was watching her.

'It's nothing,' she dismissed.

Carly put on the buggy brake and hurried to look, pulling off her mittens and dropping to her haunches to feel through the wet leaves. 'Here!' She unearthed the wedding band. A moment later she was holding up the engagement ring.

Pax felt ridiculous for wanting to leave them there, her cheeks flaming, quickly checking the other two hadn't noticed. 'Thanks.'

'You should be wearing gloves in this cold.' Carly straightened up, reaching out for her hand to put them in it.

They both gasped. The rings were almost too hot to touch.

'It's you!' Carly sounded incredulous, glancing up at her in shock, still holding on.

'What's me?' Pax was baffled.

Carly was looking down at their hands again, muttering, 'They would tell me, he said. I might have bloody guessed. Of *all* people.' She let out an irritated little sigh.

'What?' Pax persisted. Luca was looking back.

'*What we do in life echoes in eternity*.'

'Is that Shakespeare?' Pax humoured her, wondering if she was entirely sane.

'Maximus Decimus Meridius. Listen, Pax,' Carly rubbed Pax's hands as she would one of the children, 'I'm sorry about the letters, really I am.'

'It's fine, really. Not your fault. They were just there.'

Keep thinking about something else.

Trying to take her hands back, she found she couldn't. It felt discourteous, like breaking a spell. Warmth was steeling up her arms.

'I know I'm just staff and all that,' Carly was talking again, her voice hushed and fast, 'but I hope we can get on. Bridge reckons you're not as stuck-up as all that and you're going through a tough time, and I want you to know,' she grimaced, plucked brows furled as she looked up into Pax's eyes, 'that I've got your back.'

'My back?'

'Yeah. In your corner, watching out for you. *Strength and honour.* You understand what I'm saying?'

Pax looked at her pretty, earnest face, not really understanding at all. Warmth was flooding through her now. It was oddly comforting, like drinking brandy. Having always sensed hostility fizzling off Carly, it was also a revelation.

'I hope we can be friends too,' she said with feeling.

'Really?' Carly looked surprised.

'Yes. I admire you. You're kind and fierce.' As she said it, repeating the words her father had used to describe her as a child, she realised they weren't so very different at all. 'And you love horses. Dream combination.'

Carly seemed to grow taller, shaking her hair back. 'Yeah, and our boys get on.'

'There's that too.'

'*Strength and honour.*' One warm little hand fist-bumped against hers.

'Strength and honour.'

'Now don't lose these again, you hear? Flog them instead.' With a knowing grin, Carly took the rings from Pax's hand and put them back on her finger, the strangest of driveway weddings to seal an unexpected friendship.

'Thank you. I will.' She reached in her pockets and pulled out her gloves with an apologetic shrug. She hardly needed them any more. She was glowing.

They hurried to catch up the other two who had stopped to wait near the bottom of the drive, deep in conversation.

Luca gave Pax a curious look, but she looked away, uncomfortable under scrutiny. He probably thought they'd been swigging WKD Blue stashed in the nappy changing bag.

'Don't let me drink more than a couple,' Bridge was saying as they set off again, closing in on the antiquated racket coming from the orchard. 'The first year we moved here, after they'd sung the wassailing bit, Aleš thought it was folk free-for-all and started on a load of traditional Polish songs. Couldn't shut him up. My man can drink, but that cider's a killer. I was hallucinating for days.'

Her machine-gun delivery helped Pax, covering fire for her shell shock. Round and round the carousel spun. Her father and Lester. It had to be a bad dream.

Keep thinking about something else. Don't think about it.

When they arrived in the orchard, the woolly hatted half dozen gathered there grumbled that nobody knew what was happening. The bonfire was smoking like a Korean factory, the wassailers hadn't arrived and the temperature was plummeting fast as the last strains of light faded in the sky, the few remaining clouds clearing away to herald a frost.

'Where are the bacon butties?' Bridge demanded hysterically. 'The drink?' She cocked her head back at the others. 'Badly organised as usual. Thank God I have Yoyo bars.' She delved in her handbag.

Taking in the scene, Pax realised her distorted childhood memories had fooled her, the streaked winter sunset, ribboned apple trees and small children less rose-tinted in real life. Tattered summer fête bunting had been strung loosely between branches, fading fairy lights flickered on dwindling battery power. One of the village faithful had revved up an old kettle barbecue, on top of which rashers of bacon lay autopsy-flaccid alongside a great cauldron of tepid spiced cider. On the two memorial benches, a hotchpotch scratch band was being led by the rapturous hurdy-gurdy devotee who was turning the handle on his wheezing, twanging discord accompanied by two of the primary school's Year Sixes on recorders, a long-haired teenager on a guitar and an over-enthusiastic Auriol Bullock on an Irish bodhran.

'Jeez, it's worse than fecking ever,' Bridge hissed. 'Sorry, Luca. It's not exactly the Fleadh.'

His phone was ringing again. He swiped left without even glancing at the screen.

'Can you not turn that thing to silent if you don't want to talk to her?' She tilted her head to take in the medieval music. 'On second thoughts, keep it on. It sounds better than this.'

'If one of them played in tune it would be a start.' He looked around uneasily.

Pax wondered if the calls were from his ex in Canada, uncomfortable with how bothered the thought made her.

'We can always try to borrow you a violin,' she said without thinking.

'Don't tell me you play the fiddle?' Bridge was impressed.

'In that case I'm right on it!' Carly's sardonic voice was sweetened with the West Country cream of a mission. 'Grandpa Norm's got at least three and "Swallowtail Gig" is the only tune he knows; he plays it every Christmas and birthday. I'll text Janine.'

'You're all right.' Luca flashed his most defensive big smile, holding a hand up.

'It's no bother.' Carly's thumbs were already flying over the screen. A moment later, she was reading out a reply scattered with emojis. 'They've already set out. Janine's sending one of the kids back for it. Norm loves the wassail. He'll be made up there's a fiddler.'

As they all moved across the orchard, Luca fell in step beside Pax with a quiet, 'Thanks for that.'

'I'd like to hear you play.'

'Has something happened?'

Don't think about it. 'It's nothing.'

'You look upset. I'm worried about you.'

Their jaws hardly moved, aware of Bridge and Carly navigating buggies in front of them, hailing village friends.

'I'm fine.' Again she wondered if he'd come along to police her drinking.

'Liar.' His phone rang again. As before he didn't look at it, simply cancelling the call.

'Who *is* that?'

'Don't change the subject. Tell me what's going on?'

'It's an old village ritual, Luca,' she said loudly, deliberately misunderstanding. 'It dates back to the Anglo-Saxons.'

'Aleš thinks it's devil worship,' Bridge laughed, turning around.

'It's an English apple-growing tradition,' Pax explained. *Don't think. Talk.* 'A procession comes to bless the orchards and ask for a good harvest next autumn by putting cider-soaked toast in the tree branches. There's a king and queen, usually village teenagers, who lead the songs and light the big bonfire.'

'Were you ever queen?' Bridge asked.

'Years ago.' *Don't think.*

'Who was your king?'

'I forget.' *Don't think.* Pax felt the memory pinch painfully, looking across the apple treetops to the dark silhouettes of the horse chestnuts on the green, the same arboreal audience that had witnessed her night as consort to a long-gone doctor's son who she'd kicked when he'd tried to French kiss her behind the cider tent, even though he'd looked like Billy from *Neighbours* and it had given her butterflies. She couldn't have been more than eleven because her father had still been alive. Not that he'd come to watch that year. She'd relayed it all afterwards, exaggerating the beauty and high drama, missing out the tongue-kissing thing.

She sensed Luca's eyes on her. The sides of her mouth were palpitating with the need for alcohol now. She looked around for Kes to stabilise her, spotting him with Ellis clambering over the drystone walls. Breathe, Pax. You love him.

'My hacking buddies' son and daughter are this year's king and queen,' Bridge was telling them. 'Their mums keep trying to set them up, but you can't force your kids to love each other, can you, Luca?'

'Terrible idea.'

Pax realised Luca was standing too close. It made her want to reach for his hand. She crossed her arms and watched Carly rolling back as Bridge rattled on.

'My mam spent years trying to force me and my sister Bernie on the Dooley brothers because she thought their dad being an accountant gave them good prospects. One's in prison for GBH and the other's living as a woman now. Oh, a soul could die of fecking thirst round here. You're buying the first round, are you not, Luca?' Her eyes batted mock-coquettishly.

'Sure.' Pax could see the easy smile lighting up in the gathering darkness.

'I'll help,' offered Carly, abandoning her buggy to Bridge, Jackson asleep in it, Sienna toddling between the trees with Flavia in a shrieking game of peekaboo. 'Keep an eye will you, Bridge?'

'Everywhere I look, I see triangles,' Bridge sighed, leaning into Pax for warmth. 'Must be the fecking bunting. You okay, queen?'

'I'm good.' Pax looked at the bunting, only seeing her father's handwriting proclaiming love. He'd been so terribly in love. More than she'd known in her own lifetime.

Keep thinking about something else. Don't think about it.

'That Luca fancies the arse off you,' Bridge whispered. 'Doesn't take his eyes off you.'

Reluctant to explain that he was here to stop her drinking sly apple brandies while in charge of her five-year-old, Pax said nothing. Her thoughts were being ransacked, memories shredded. Was the love between Johnny and Lester the reason her mother had run away? Had she known about it before her own ill-fated love affair?

Don't think about it.

'Here comes the Clodfather. Wassail must be about to get going,' Bridge announced cheerfully as the Comptons' unofficial Vito Corleone, 'Social' Norm Turner, was charioteered in amid a swarm of family heavyweights, his huge tombstone torso swathed in blankets, arm raised in greeting, oxygen tanks to either side of his wheelchair like jet packs.

'Does he really still rule the roost round here?' asked Pax. Even her grandfather had been wary of Norm.

'Put it this way, if he doesn't like someone in the village, they don't stay long,' Bridge breathed. 'Luca had better fecking fiddle well.'

They watched in fascination as, on the other side of the paddock, Carly introduced Luca to the hard-muscled, silver-eyed mob headed up by her sister-in-law Janine at the handlebars of the wheelchair, a bulldog in long black hair extensions, nail art glittering. She was giving Luca a thorough cross-examination by the look of it. His eyes flitted back across the field to where Pax and Bridge were standing.

'What's the story between you two?' Bridge persisted.

'There's no story.'

'Like feck there's not. I have a nose for desire. Grab him while you can. There's others will if you don't.'

'I only walked out of my marriage a fortnight ago,' Pax whispered, shocked by Bridge's directness.

'Which means you've been looking around for ages.' Bridge was unapologetic. 'C'mon, *I'd* barely unpacked my honeymoon bikini. We all do it; I've friends who make a hobby of it. They're all knocking on, mind you.'

Pax shook her head. Whilst it was true that she'd desired men other than Mack for a very long time, they were all abstract facsimiles, her natural default forged a long time ago, her type hardwired. And it wasn't Luca's blond-lashed, smiling kindness, surely? 'Kes is my priority.'

Bridge watched the boys playing. 'He's lovely manners, your wee man; Auriol will lap him up.'

'I hope he likes it.'

'They all like it there.'

'How's the job going?'

'Org*as*mic,' Bridge thrilled. 'It's better than sex, and I've not even officially start—'

'*There* you are!' A sharp Scottish descant rang out behind them, making Pax's blood fast-flow dizzily. 'Where's my wee soldier? *Kes!*'

The Elnessed white helmet of her mother-in-law emerged through the darkness, stooping to greet Kes as he hurtled in from the left and slammed himself into his grandmother's arms.

'Nanaforce! Have you come to watch the weaselling?'

'No, wee man. Go play a minute while I talk to your mammy.' Mairi straightened up, propelling Kes away before turning to address Pax in a hushed hiss, 'Is it wise to bring the child to see blood sports? I thought they were all illegal these days. Are there dogs?' She looked nervous.

'Weasel hounds!' Bridge laughed, then saw Pax's face and coughed, stepping away.

'What an unexpected surprise, Mairi.' Pax forced herself to stay calm.

'Indeed.' Mairi waved her arm and a tall shadow materialised, Muir Forsyth joining his wife, stone sentries in padded gaberdine.

'Tishy…' He nodded politely.

'Call me Pax.'

They looked at her blankly. Pax had been repeatedly saying it for the past fortnight, but she might as well have asked them to call her Derek.

'You know why we're here.'

'Er, no.'

Bridge was still hovering nearby, tactfully pretending to admire some of the tattered bunting.

'We went up to the house but there was nobody there.' Mairi's hiss grew more accusatory.

'You should have called. Is everything okay?'

'We're here to pick Kes up, my dear.' Muir was playing good cop, all condescending smiles and rigid manners.

'Don't want to go!' Kes wriggled away from Mairi and velcroed himself to Pax whose arms flew around him.

'There must be some mistake.'

'It's Mack's midweek access night if you've forgotten.' Muir tilted his head, scrutinising his daughter-in-law's face like a kindly psychiatrist with a sectioned patient.

'You've got the wrong week, I'm afraid.' Pax clenched her jaw so hard it almost cracked her teeth, aware of Kes shrinking tighter against her legs. 'Alternate Wednesdays. It was agreed last Friday.'

'Indeed so, Tish dear. Starting this week.'

'*Next* week,' Pax corrected, longing to see them wither away like garlic-pelted vampires.

'Don't want to go!' Kes bleated again, gripping onto his mother's legs.

Pax hugged him closer. 'You don't have to, Kes. *Next* week you're spending your fun Wednesday night with Daddy, Nanaforce and Grandforce as well as having a lovely weekend with them to look forward to before that.' Damn her throat tightening, that giveaway wobble. 'I'm sorry you've had a wasted journey. We're all so muddled at the changes, it's an easy mistake, but of course Kes is with me tonight; he's spending the day at the village school tomorrow. With his new friend Ellis.' She played it as lightly as she could manage, aware that Ellis and his feather duster were standing nearby, waiting and watching with extraordinary silver eyes.

But Grandforce and Nanaforce wouldn't be defeated.

'Mack will bring him into school *and* collect him tomorrow,' Muir said firmly, kindliness under threat from murderous eyes. 'You can come and pick him up afterwards, Tishy. Handover is at 4.30 p.m. as stipulated. It's a legal matter, so we suggest you honour it.'

'We've got you scampi and chips for tea tonight,' Mairi told Kes brightly; his favourite. 'With Smarties ice cream to follow.' Also a firm winner. 'And when Daddy comes home from work he's bringing that electric doggy you wanted, from *Paw Police*.' Hat-trick.

'*Paw Patrol!*' Kes shrieked rapturously, letting go of his mother and crossing back over the divide to those open arms.

Fearing her child had been won with two courses of processed food and a toy so expensive that Mack had squarely rejected it as a Christmas one, Pax started to splinter. Wrong-footed, furious at the low blow – they'd be offering Irn Bru and a guinea pig next – she demanded to know where Mack was. 'He and I need to talk about this.'

'He's still in the office, poor man.' Mairi sighed sadly. 'He's been putting in such long hours. Twice as much work to do since you walked out, of course.'

Pax had her teeth gritted so tight her jaw started cramping. She knew Mack well enough to guess he was only there to avoid his parents and flit between active windows on his five daisy-chained monitors, indulging in the belief that surfing live news streams and sports footage counted as work.

She called his numbers. He didn't pick up. Still she kept her voice low and calm. 'Mairi, Muir, let's go back to the house. We can sort this out there.'

'No need, dear,' Mairi countered, artificially bright for Kes's benefit. 'Best we head off before you get yourself upset. We've the car in the gateway over there, and we don't need to fetch anything for Kes seeing as he's got Rab C. We've all that he needs at home, haven't we, Kes?'

'*Paw Patrol!*' Kes roared excitedly.

'I have the email on my phone, I can double check the dates.' Pax scrolled the messages furiously, but was unable to find it. 'Hang on, I'll call my solicitor.'

'Dinnae fuss, lass.' Muir was a standing stone of granite stubbornness beside her. 'The bairn wants to come home with us.' His voice, tinged with aggression was just like Mack's. 'It's time you faced the facts.'

'Face this fact: it's the wrong day.' She pressed the phone to her ear, dismayed that Kes had a tight hold of Nanaforce's hand, eager to be off to meet his *Paw Patrol* icon. A few paces away, standing on one leg and holding his duster like a Maasai warrior, Ellis watched them, his silver-eyed face impassive.

Poke them in the eye with it! Pax wanted to beg as a recorded voice greeted her and she hurried to find a better signal to leave a message and ring round the other numbers she had for solicitor Helen Beadle. When they all went to voicemail, she started tapping out a frantic text instead. From the corner of her eye, she was eternally grateful to see Bridge launch herself into the fray, keeping the Ms talking. Neither Forsyth being by nature chatty, and both increasingly cold and fractious, it was a doomed mission. Their expressions darkened when Carly and Luca reappeared through the darkness, carrying a brace of brimming polystyrene beakers each.

'It's made from Turner cider, so it's bloody lethal!' Carly warned loudly. 'Luca just made everyone laugh their heads off pretending he and Pax don't – oh, hi.' She spotted the elderly gatecrashers.

'These are Kes's grandparents!' Pax's predictive text was going rogue, her fingers shaking too much to hit the right letters, her son rechristened 'Ken' in her haste.

She could hear Bridge introducing her in-laws in her Belfast brogue. 'Murr and Merry, this is Luca and Carly.'

Mairi's reply was drowned out by the hurdy-gurdy hotting up. Still typing, Pax edged closer and walked straight into a tree's cage of branches, poking herself in the eye, phone flying from her hands.

'We're all Pax's bezzies,' Bridge was exaggerating on the other side of the tree before stage-whispering to the others. 'There's been a bit of a mix-up over dates!'

Pax dropped to her knees and searched around in the dark grass, grateful to find her text still beaming from her phone screen in badly typed readiness.

'What are you doing down there, Tishy?' Muir demanded from beyond the canopy of branches.

'With you in a tick!' She waved at them, closing one streaming eye anxiously to see Luca offering up his beakers to the Forsyths, violin case under one arm like a mafioso.

'Can I tempt you to a mulled cider?'

They both stepped back as one and Muir held up a Puritanical hand. 'Certainly not.'

Backing up to get one signal bar, Pax could see she had mistyped so many words, the message looked Dutch. Through the tree branches, somebody said 'Sláinte! She heard Carly's creamy voice ask, 'Have you ever been to a wassail, Murray?'

'Feck, but I need this.' Bridge was soon making slurping noises as she knocked back her steaming cider cup.

Through her one good eye Pax could see her in-laws now backed up against a stone wall, looking mutinous. As she pressed 'send', she felt a little gloved hand slip into hers. Kes's eyes brimmed up at her.

'I want to go, Mummy.'

'It's not the right night, darling.'

'Oliver wants to go too.' He tugged at her hand.

'Oliver's not here, Kes.'

'He is!' Wrenching away, he ran back to his Grandforces.

Pax followed, covering her streaming eye with her hand, tripping again.

Muir muttered something at his wife, questioning her sobriety.

'You heard the boy, Tishy.' Mairi was impatient. 'He wants to go with us.' She gripped Kes tightly to her. 'He needs his father.'

Muir's amen was worthy of a pulpit. 'A drunken night out's no place for a bairn his age.'

'It's not even five o'clock.'

'And the alcohol flowing!' Mairi shuddered.

No matter how many episodes you cry side by side through *Call the Midwife*, to have married a mother's son was to make a secret enemy of her, Pax realised forlornly. Especially if you are the second person to do it.

'We'll bring him back here tomorrow to try the wee village school as agreed,' Muir reassured her unenthusiastically.

'And Daddy has other schools lined up to try next week!' Mairi told Kes. 'Much better schools, with special things like swimming pools and pets!'

His wet eyes glimmered.

In the shadows, Ellis scuffed away, trailing his 'Splorer Stick.

Pax could hear the Wassailing procession making its way along the lane beside the Green at last, braziers crackling.

She crouched in front of Kes, heart thumping, voice at its most reassuring, 'What do you want to do, Kes?'

'I want to go, Mummy!' His voice caught with sobs, tears starting to stream, overwhelmed by it all.

She hugged him tightly.

'Enough,' she sighed hoarsely, kissing his woolly-hatted head and wet cheeks. 'Of course you can go back with the Grandforces, Kes. Good plan! Mummy will see you tomorrow after school and can't wait to hear all about it.' Releasing him, she ignored teeth-sucking intakes of breath beside her from

Bridge and Carly and cupped his face. 'I will miss you more than the sun.'

'I will miss you more than the galaxy.'

'More than infinity.'

'More than infinity and – beyond!'

They hugged again, squeezing hard. They were safe with routines, already growing accustomed to painful goodbyes. Pax's heart thumped against his through the winter layers, her painful eye streaming while the other held determinedly on to its tears.

'Come along, Kes,' Mairi said briskly. 'Let's leave Mummy with her… friends.'

Still Kes clung to Pax. 'Come home, Mummy,' he said in a small voice. 'Please let's go home.'

Throat tightening so much she could hardly speak, heart ablaze, Pax had never felt so torn and alone. *This is home now.* 'I can't, my darling.'

'Because you don't love Daddy any more?'

'We both love *you* so, so much. Now you enjoy that new toy, wake up with a smile, look out for Ellis at school tomorrow, and remember I'm with you every step of the way.' Her voice was catching, razor blades flailing in her throat. '*Every* step.'

'Okay. See you tomorrow, Mummy!' He turned to gambol away, quicker to recover, a happy survivalist. His normal; her living hell.

'Don't wave him off, Tishy.' Muir stepped in front of her. 'It'll only upset the poor bairn. You enjoy your wee celebration.' He turned and set off, raising his arm in farewell.

'And you can go to hell,' she breathed to herself.

'I heard that!'

It would be logged in the Big Book of Bad Mummy.

Pax pressed a heel of her hand to her sore eye again, glancing at the others with her good one, unable to speak, the blood roaring through her head so loudly she thought it might burst from her ears. She wanted to be somewhere else fast. Somewhere else, alone with a drink.

'That was brutal,' Bridge whistled.

'I'm sorry you had to witness it.' She managed to sound a lot more normal than she felt, grateful that Bridge's brand of sympathy was Teflon-coated as she received a pat on the back guaranteed to cure hiccups or dislodge a sweet from a windpipe.

'Let's get you another drink, queen. You need your mind taking off it.'

'Looks like the wassailers are almost here.' Carly's creamy voice was distracted as blazing fireballs on sticks appeared on the Bagot footpath at the far side of the orchard, Morris bells ringing. 'You still okay to play, Luca?'

'Sure, we'll catch you both up.' Luca's face was in darkness, his phone ringing again. He still had a cup in each hand, Pax realised.

She turned at the sound of car doors slamming beyond the orchard wall as Mack's parents prepared to set off, and she fought an almost overwhelming urge to run after them. Watching the headlights of the Forsyths' car blazing away, her wave was lost to the dark along with her stricken face. Thank you, darkness. She tipped up her chin, just one thought thundering in her head like hooves: *Do not cry; you must not cry; I refuse to cry.* But all too soon the chasing field of bad thoughts surged past. *How soon until I can get back inside Lester's cottage for a drink? I need a drink, deserve a drink, I must have a drink now. The plum gin is still there. But so are the letters. The bloody, bloody letters. Think about something else. Kes. Oh, Kes. Do not cry. Don't think about any of it. I need a drink. No. No. No!*

'Breathe, Pax.'

Pax realised Luca was standing very close, his warmth eclipsing her personal space, his eyes on her face in the near dark. She didn't mind for once, grateful that she had to behave around Luca.

'I'm fine.'

'You want this?' He offered a cup to her, the tang of cider ramped up with a hit of apple brandy and cinnamon.

She stared back at him through the gloom, open-mouthed. 'Is this a test? Because your timing is pretty harsh.'

'You'd fail.'

'I will *not* fail!' *Do not have that drink,* she instructed herself. *Another drink, maybe, definitely. Later. In private. And a cry. And a text rant at Mack.*

'Pax, we both know you're going to get banjaxed tonight.' Luca withdrew the cup, voice a kind earworm of Irish brogue. 'Better I keep you company than you do it alone.' He still had the violin case under one arm, she noticed, like a novelty clutch bag.

'I'm *fine.*' She closed her watering, tree-poked eye again, not prepared to acknowledge the truth out loud. *I'll get home soon. Get plum gin.* 'Arguing would have made it worse. Kes wanted to go with them.'

He said nothing.

She could see the glow of the procession drawing closer along the footpath, the flaming torches ritualistic and pagan. 'You heard him say it.'

'Sure I heard him.' He stepped back, looking up at the sky, a scattering of stars out on show now the clouds had chugged off. 'I want to go, Pax.'

'Be my guest.'

'I. Want. To. Go,' he repeated carefully.

'Be. My. Guest!' she snapped back.

'Don't you see?' His voice had a break of empathy in it. 'I don't want to leave *you* here, just leave this place. With you. I want to go.'

'What you want to do is frankly your—' She stopped, a knife between every rib. *I want to go, Mummy.* Kes hadn't said that he wanted to go with his grandparents at all. She'd been the one to jump to that conclusion, flustered by their certainty, by imaginary Oliver.

She covered her face, reliving his tears and confusion. He had even begged her to come too. Overwhelmed, overtired, overstimulated Kes. It was past his teatime. It was cold. There were lots of strangers here. Her humiliation folded in and in, a paper spill ready to burn. 'I'm the worst mother.'

She felt dizzy and sick, ready to run, yet grateful that Luca was a wall in front of her.

'You're a bloody good mother,' he insisted. 'You love your son more than the world. Now toughen up and love yourself.' For a moment his forehead was almost resting against hers as he tipped his head to be heard over the approaching crowd, a waterfall of curls ticking her brow. 'Right this minute, you want to run home and drink until you're numb.'

'You're wrong,' she lied. *I'll be home soon. There's plum gin.*

'I have a drink right here.' He stepped back.

'I'm *fine*.' She'd never felt this deep a craving.

'I'll go first, shall I?'

Taking her hands from her face, she saw the cup was at his lips.

'Stop that!'

Luca offered her the other, eyes unblinking. 'On the count of three?'

'What are you *doing*?' She made to knock the raised cup out of his hand, but he whipped it away too fast.

'I'm coming with you on this bender whether you like it or not.'

'Get a grip.'

'One: I've not played the violin sober in years for a start. Two: *I* need a drink. Three…' Luca shut the argument down, draining the cup while Pax watched, bewildered.

'Why do that?'

He proffered the second cup. 'You're not drinking alone tonight, Pax. And if anything's going to stop you, it's seeing me langers. I'm a seriously annoying drunk.'

'You're seriously annoying.' She glared at him, his face, just visible in the lantern and firelight spilling from the other end of the orchard, a flickering mask. 'I *do* know what you're playing at here, Luca.'

'And what is that?'

'Making a moral sacrifice to prove a point.' She waved an accusing arm, anger bated. The wassail procession was finally in the orchard proper and whooping its way towards its first tree. Even in the dark far corner, she now had to shout to be heard. 'You're playing truth or dare, aren't you?'

'And which will it be?'

'You already know my truth!' As she shouted it, the wassailers hushed to listen to the chair of the parish council make his welcoming introduction, Pax's 'know my truth!' carrying evangelically across the orchard.

'Which is?' Luca asked quietly.

God, he was milking this.

'I'm a secret drinker,' she hissed obligingly. 'We're good at secrets in my family; my entire childhood was built on one, as it turns out. Mine is bottles of vodka in the tea-towel drawer.' She paused to breathe, determined not to cry or to let her voice climb scales, pushing the letters and Kes's departure from her mind. 'This stupid drinking game is just one of your holier-than-thou gestures.'

He crossed himself, which she didn't find funny.

'You think if *you* drink it'll shame me out of it, but I refuse to have you on my conscience.' Pax felt another flash of anger at his martyrdom. 'You can end up legless in a ditch for all I care, playing dirges on that violin. Because, when it comes down to it, you can't stop me drinking any more than I can stop you.'

Across the field, cups were being filled from a ceremonial jug, a few *huzzahs* raised, the parish chair still droning on about the tradition of tree blessing.

He said nothing for a long time, then, 'Thanks for the explanation. And there was me thinking we might simply get fluthered one last time before Step One.'

'This isn't like you, Luca.'

'That's the thing. It's very like me. The old me you've never met. I thought it was time I introduced him. I don't think you'll like him overmuch. And I warn you, he'll serenade you from the ditch later. Any requests?'

She crossed her arms. 'Please stop this.'

'You said it yourself, Pax,' his voice stayed soft, unhurried, 'you can't make me stop any more than I can you. Although this stuff is awful enough to do it.' He tossed the contents of the second cup in the grass, looking up with a smile that glinted in the half-light.

Pax felt a rush of relief, in desperate need of strong, principled Luca. Then she watched, dismayed, as he flipped open the violin case and pulled out a quarter-size bottle of whisky from a compartment alongside the bow. 'No self-respecting fiddler travels without poitín.'

Pax wanted to turn and walk away, but her legs refused to move. 'Luca, don't.'

'I forgot you prefer spirits.' He poured a measure, offering it to her. 'Save you running home.'

She hardly dared breathe, her need was so great. Damn him for knowing. 'What's got into you?'

The smile flashed and faded. 'You, Pax.'

Surprise kept her rooted to the spot.

For a moment Pax let the frisson quiver through her, assumptions jettisoned, feeling strangely high. But then she fell just as fast, and kept falling, into deep, dark self-doubt. This absolutely couldn't happen. Nobody had seen her so raw as Luca had. She was a woman who had thrown away her marriage, carried family secrets, pushed her son away – and now she'd even driven her kind, patient minder to drink. She couldn't take him under with her while the storm was still raging in her broken life, its whirlpools like black holes. They could never be trusted together drunk. One of them had to stay on dry land.

'No way.' She took the cup from him, raised it in a toast and poured its contents out onto the grass.

'Good girl.'

'That's what you wanted?'

He nodded, turning the bottle in his hand so it caught glints of flame light. 'Forgive me.'

'You're only trying to help.'

'Not for that.'

Realising what he meant, she looked down, heat spots in her cheeks. She had enough on her plate without being told she was in his head. He was in hers, too. It was getting way too crowded.

His phone started ringing. He ignored it, holding the whisky bottle like a grenade, free hand raking his hair so it stood up in strange spiral peaks.

Yet she still couldn't move. She wanted to tell him how much his friendship meant, but she worried she'd give too much away and his phone was still ringing. No sooner had it stopped than it started again.

'Why not just answer? Whoever it is isn't going to stop until you do.'

'Maybe I need to be drunk first.' He took a swig from the bottle.

It's not me on his mind, Pax realised with a thud of recognition; it's whoever is making that call. It should have been a relief but wasn't.

'Is it her? Dizzy's mother?'

'No.'

Across the orchard, the crowd launched into a song:

'Here's to thee, old apple tree,
That blooms well, bears well.'

'I've not been to... ...est, Pax.' It was hard to hear him over the din. His face was in darkness again, just the glow of firelight eclipsing his gold hair like a corona, and a glimmer of the bottle as it went to his lips again.

'Not been what?'

'Hats full, caps full,
Three bushel bags full,'

The dancers drew closer and they could hear the crackle of the flames.

'Honest.'

It shocked her. She'd started trusting him implicitly. 'About what?'

Rubbing his face then raking back his hair in his hands, he seemed to change his mind. 'Forget it. It's best you're not involved.'

'An' all under one tree.
Hurrah! Hurrah!'

Cheers went up amid much bell-jingling and tub-thumping, the hurdy-gurdy in overdrive.

In Luca's pocket, his phone was in full cry once more. When somebody calls that often, Pax reasoned, they are very obsessed indeed.

'Are you in danger?'

Ignoring the question, he watched through the trees as the wassail king and queen, in rival elaborate leafy evergreen headdresses, soaked toast slices in the ceremonial flagon of cider and wedged them in the branches. 'That's just weird so it is.'

'Luca you *have* to tell me about this. Are you in danger?'

He ducked his head with a dry laugh. 'Catch me in that ditch later and I'll tell you all my secrets. I'll probably tell you I love you too, but I say that to everybody when I'm blootered.'

The wassailers were singing and dancing round the trees nearest them now, bringing the braziers closer, light spilling into their dark corner of the orchard, burnishing trunks and casting golden shapes through the branches. The whites of Luca's eyes flashed, and his face was gilded in light for a moment, hollow-cheeked, lashes like gold veils, a sun god out after hours.

Attraction cut through Pax without warning, a reckless urgent need to kiss and be kissed. To be loved by Luca, however briefly, even Bacchanalian in a ditch.

'I'm not a nice drunk, Pax,' he repeated. 'I'm selfish and I'm greedy and I'm horny. Please don't trust me.'

Touching her face with his hand in apology, he turned and walked away.

Cheek on fire, Pax stared into the darkness after him, wondering why she suddenly couldn't breathe.

Her own phone lit up with a call, vibrating furiously in her hand. Helen. She had to move to the far wall to be sure of enough reception to take it.

'Sorry – been with a client. It *is* your week for Wednesday nights, I've checked,' Helen's warm, firm voice insisted. 'You absolutely don't have to let Kes go with them. They're bullying you. I'll take this up.'

'Thanks,' she said quietly, ringing off and closing her eyes, allowing herself one silent sob, violent as a mule kick, shame burning. *I want to go, Mummy.* She'd got it wrong. She always got it wrong. She was too weak, too passive, too fair. Kes came first, above everything, always, and yet she'd politely let him go.

The revellers were moving back towards the other end of the orchard, singing another wassail song, *Love and joy come to you* repeating every few lines.

She didn't want to rejoin the others. She wanted to go home just as Kes had.

Pax was fed up with being polite. She'd been a polite daughter, polite lover, polite wife and mother, polite drunk. Her good manners were the reason her son was with the Forsyths again tonight. The same well-bred silence that surrounded other family secrets would keep the contents of the letters safe too. It meant graciously acknowledging that she was still too much of a displaced wife to step away from its shadow without a customary period of mourning: three weeks ago, she'd been renewing the family's Amazon Prime subscription and planning their summer holiday in Crete; everything was still in joint names, Mack hadn't a clue how to sort the recycling and most of their friends didn't even know they'd separated yet. Wasn't it just common courtesy to continue ignoring the worst-timed bit of human chemistry fate had ever offered her? Being polite meant pretending Luca's words didn't make a difference, that his compassion wasn't one part comfort to two parts bad-timing.

The last thing Pax needed right now was mutual attraction. A fortnight was an intake of breath compared to a marriage.

She held her hands to her cheek where he'd touched it. She'd dropped her gloves somewhere trying to call Helen. Her fingers were cold, the loose rings rattling. She carefully pulled them off and slotted them onto her middle finger where they now fitted perfectly. It seemed apt; she was giving her marriage the finger after all. She gestured in the dark, not at all politely, and felt better. *Strength and honour.*

Thinking about it, Pax hadn't been very polite to Luca at all when they'd met, which was at least something. He'd arrived with a crush on her mother, hardwired kindness, suicidal driving and a puritanical streak. She'd seen no evidence to suggest he'd changed. Apart from those looks, *that* feeling, the deep feral pulse which beat louder. What was it Bridge had said? *He fancies the arse off you.* Mesmazur would have no qualms about leaving now without saying goodbye to anyone so that she could go home, slam the door and enjoy very rude thoughts in private.

Pax set off across the dark, hillocky orchard like a fell runner, aiming for the stile that led to the stud's wooded boundary through which a half moon was rising to point her way. She dodged trunks and branches, ducking and swerving. Almost there, she tripped over a tree root. In three big, unbalanced steps, she was on her knees and head-butting the hawthorn hedge. Trying to sit up, she rolled backwards and downwards like Alice.

Love and joy come to you! sang the wassailers.

Bad eye smarting, Pax looked up, furious with herself that whilst she rarely ever took a spill drunk, she was flat on her back for the second time in an hour. Did falling in love earn its name because it started this way? she wondered fatuously. Directly above, she could see the distinctive W of Cassiopeia and remembered her grandfather once telling her that Cassiopeia and Cepheus were the only husband-and-wife constellation in all the night sky, the very epitome of growing old together.

'Are you okay?' Luca was stooping over her, catching his breath from running. 'Don't try to move. Did you hit your head?'

Slow down, heart. 'Can you see the birds too?'

'What birds?' He crouched over her. She could smell the sweetness of the cider on him, the peat of whisky undercutting it. Her mouth watered.

'The ones flying round singing Disney songs.'

'Seriously?' Then he made a *ha* noise. 'Are you rolling your eyes? It's too dark to see down there. You know you're in a ditch?' There was an ironic tone she didn't recognise. He put out a hand to help her up.

'Just warming it up for you.' She scrambled out without him, almost treading on the violin abandoned on the bank.

Luca picked it up, plucking a couple of strings. 'I came to find you to apologise,' he said, 'for all the rubbish I said earlier.'

She looked at him, wondering whether he was referring to confessing dishonesty or drunken love. Maybe they amounted to the same thing.

The big bonfire had just been lit, the smell of burning apple logs drifting in smoke through frosting air, golden light spilling far enough to illuminate the orchard clearly.

'Hey, Paddy, we need music!' demanded an unseen voice across the field.

Ignoring it, Luca tilted his head, able to see her face now. 'You've hurt your poor eye.'

'It's not painful,' she lied.

He put his hand on her face, unexpectedly warm. 'Let me look, angel.' He brushed his thumb lightly across her cheekbone and over her brow.

She'd never heard Luca call anyone angel before. She wanted to clamp her arms around herself to stop everything fluttering inside so much, giving her away. How *warm* were his fingers?

'Close your eye a minute.'

She felt the heat of his thumb crossing her lid, yet it didn't seem to touch her. It should have made her flinch, but it didn't. Was it her imagination or did the eye feel less angry? He did it again, more slowly. It felt amazing. That warmth.

This is the gift her mother had talked about, Pax realised. The same gift Carly possessed, untamed and untrained, the reason her touch had felt so odd. But Luca was assured and controlled, the energy focussed into a single movement.

'There…' He wiped the tears away with a light stroke of his little finger and stepped back. 'See if that feels better.'

She opened them in astonishment. 'How did you do that?'

'Hey, Paddy!' the voice shouted again, a long shadow falling towards them. 'Horsemaker! You're on.'

'Let's make a run for it,' he whispered.

'You have to go,' she urged. 'If the Turners fetch you a fiddle, you play.'

'Then stay and listen.' He lifted the violin to his chest and plucked a few blues slides like a guitarist. It was a neat trick. The smile told her she was safe, she was adored, she would have the time of her life.

'I'm not ready for the old Luca.' Remembering his warning, she wished she didn't fancy his alter ego so much.

'You coming, bro?' The shadow was closing in.

'You sure you're all right?' The Luca she knew was back all too briefly.

'Maybe a touch of amnesia.' She pulled some twigs from her hair. 'D'you know, I can't remember anything you said this evening at all. Not a word.'

'That a fact?' The O'Brien smile lit up the shadows, a mask she couldn't lift.

'All gone.'

'Bet you forget this too.' The kiss was the sweetest, briefest taste of adventure.

He was irresistible drunk.

Pax vaulted over the stile and bolted for home.

18

It had been an underwhelming wassail in Bridge's eyes, the bacon butties a particular let-down. 'Since when did two wet rashers laid to rest in unbuttered medium-white sliced call itself anything other than an obscene profit margin conjured from Lidl basics?' she'd complained to the chef, adding 'with no fecking ketchup.' The spiced cider was admittedly spectacular this year, but she'd only allowed herself two thimblefuls with the children to look after. Carly was in a strange mood, currently sulking because Luca kept vanishing with a sacred Turner fiddle.

'I championed him,' she moaned, sounding like Cheryl let down by an *X Factor* boy band. 'It's my neck on the line.'

'In fairness, you've never heard him play, queen. He could be shite.'

'I'm going to look for him. You're okay keeping an eye on Jackson and Sienna, yeah?'

Watching her go, Bridge's lip curled. She'd spent most of the past hour as glorified babysitter, trending the two-buggies-and-an-empty-cider-beaker look. While the braziers blazed and the Morris men pranced, her eyes had stayed trained on the opposite end of the orchard, where for a long time a couple had been silhouetted under one of the oldest apple trees in excitingly close proximity. Now they'd gone.

Bridge felt very let down by Pax. Whilst there was no denying she and Luca had a smokingly sexy vibe going on, Bridge had nobody to talk to, unless you counted Auriol Bullock, immaculate in M&S camel hair, trilby hat and high spirits, trying to hide the fact she was smashed on cider punch. Bridge supposed she would have to get used to work encroaching on her social life now.

'I've lent my bodhran to that ver' attractive young man,' Auriol, heavy-lidded, pointed out Monique Austen's handsome groom beating out a rhythm.

'Baron.'

'Is he?' She looked delighted. 'I wonder if he has children of school age?'

'No, the Irish drum is pronounced "baron".'

'I'll stick with bo-de-ron, thank you,' she said with crisp headmistress starch and just the slightest lurch to the left.

Auriol was waiting for a lift home from the hurdy-gurdy player, still only part through telling his potted history of medieval instruments to a glazed Mr Well Cottage (sideburns more Liam Gallagher than George Best, Bridge noted). None of the other Bags had been there to witness Bridge roll in with the Horsemaker and Pax, not that they'd hung out any longer than washing in a winter downpour.

She was feeling so neglected she'd even switched on her phone and texted Aleš to let him know where she was. He hadn't yet replied. To add to her FOMO she had PMT, period pains tugging. Her lip throbbed again and her eyes itched. She wanted to be make-up free in the sagbag in Flavia and Zak's room, hot wheat bag pressed to her belly, bingeing Julia Donaldson with them.

'Who is this violinist we're waiting for, Mrs Mazur?' asked Auriol, every sibilant subtly slurred.

'The Horsemaker.' Bridge hammed up her own accent. 'Many meet him but nobody knows him. The Don Quixote of the Comptons. They say he rides horses' very souls.'

'Is he any good at racing tips?' Auriol looked impressed.

'It's a safe bet he'll be racing away from here if he doesn't pick his bow up soon.' Bridge glanced at the biggest group of Turners, a broiling tattooed mass styled by Sports Direct.

'I used to have a great many beaus,' Auriol sighed, pulling a hip flask from her pocket and offering it across.

Bridge took a swig purely out of professional duty – Amaretto, delicious – then perked up as a bearded blond figure stepped forward from the dark Turner massive, eyes lively, fiddle already at his chin.

'Here he is!' she told Auriol.

'Beowulf!' The headmistress shivered ecstatically, paying attention now.

With a polite nod from Luca to the little crowd around him, the bow danced on the strings.

'Oh my lord,' Bridge gasped.

Beside her, Auriol closed her eyes blissfully.

When Luca played the fiddle, the village fell in love as one. The Lord of the Dance had arrived, his fingers racing across the strings like galloping thoroughbred legs, the bow whipping them on faster and faster as, picking up Zak, Bridge started to dance.

Lucky, lucky Pax. Where was she?

Crossing the bigger yard with a bottle of plum gin under both arms and one in each hand, Pax stopped and listened, skin prickling. The music being carried up from the village orchard had changed timbre, its tempo heartbeat fast.

Flanked by Knott and Stubbs, she hurried out to the arrivals yard, crossing beneath the carriage circle cedar and putting down the bottles, clambered up onto the stone wall beside the drive to sit and listen. She looked down on the glow in the village orchard and hugged her knees.

It was exquisite.

She touched her lips, reliving the kiss in her mind for the hundredth time. A very chaste kiss. And yet it had dropped a depth charge inside her that wouldn't stop detonating.

What was it Bridge had said last week: *There's no such thing as bad timing, just timing, and the clock's ticking.*

On, the fiddle sang. Kes would love hearing it, thought Pax, the hard pinch of missing him in her chest. But it was already well past his bedtime, she reminded herself. Kes's musical tastes so far peaked at Tractor Ted's 'Muck Spreading'. He could hear Luca play another time. If the Forsyths hadn't swept him away, she'd be weeping quietly into the plum gin right now, agonising about her father's secret. Instead, she'd shared her second wassail kiss in a lifetime. While the first had been too soon, the second made her feel like she was waking up after a hundred years asleep in a glass cage.

There's no such thing as bad timing, just timing.

Pressing her hot cheeks to her denim knees, Pax let the music sink beneath her skin, briefly casting her mind back to the boy she'd kicked all those years ago, then to Luca again, to the soft pad of his lips, the taste of him. Had he felt the same headrush? She was a virgin again, like Madonna had told her she'd feel. She'd hardly evolved at all, in fact: the clown fall clumsiness wasn't great; her baking would never win a man's heart; calling him creepy could be improved upon, and then there was driving him to drink. But on the plus side, she no longer kicked.

What felt like a stitch pinched at her sides, a heartburn balling towards her throat. Her eyes prickled. She thumped her chest as her breathing caught. It abated, then came back with a quivering reflux. It felt like hiccups at first. When holding her breath didn't work, she thumped again, harder, to stop it interrupting her listening. But her body kept its regular jolt, spasms closer together, the cheeks of her face tightening, her eyes watering. Was she having a fit? She pressed her forehead to her knees. *Breathe.* Luca's voice in her head.

The reel skipped on, ever faster, twisting joyfully. Having

scrabbled up onto the wall, Knott licked her chin. Stubbs was rabbiting unsupportively in the field in front of her.

Still Pax struggled to breathe. The stitch worsened. The music was in her toes, torso, head, radiating out. She touched her eye, recalling the warmth of Luca's fingers. If her heart was packing up, it was as noble a moment as any. Her ribs rattled. Again, she convulsed all over, replaying his kiss and her promise to forget everything.

It was happening again, she realised with an explosion of glee. A high like no other, a concentrated joy that flushed out all the misery. As unexpected and welcome as that evening in the cottage kitchen when Mack had mistaken Luca for her lover and she'd realised she was finally free. She was laughing. High end, Grade A laughter. And this time, it was more than liberation; more than sensing she'd made it through the wilderness or could one day love someone new.

This time she was laughing at herself. She'd missed that feeling so much.

Climbing off the wall, she started to dance. Turning circles, stamping, throwing up her new ring finger, she danced across the turning circle, back beneath the cedar tree, and across to Lester's cottage garden to let out Laurence the fox.

The Turners were all looking in the same direction for once. Social Norm's oxygen mask was steamed up excitedly, Janine's talons held her iPhone aloft, live-streaming on Facebook.

Carly just watched, open-mouthed.

Luca's fingertips were almost too fast to see, perfectly pitched, stampeding, each bow stroke cutting into Carly's heart because talent always hurt when it belonged to somebody modest. First the 'Swallowtail Gig' for Social Norm. Quicker and quicker, notes soaring as cleanly as curlew cries.

Even Ash, freshly arrived with his rowdy lad army, stopped

to listen on his way to the cider bar. 'Better than the usual bollocks. Who is it?'

'The new guy from the yard, the Horsemaker.'

At this, he looked less impressed, turning to mutter something with Flynn, both men clearing throats with laughter before swaggering off.

Carly ignored them, bewitched as Luca launched straight into another Irish gig, Turner feet stamping around her, all the family whooping. Grandpa Norm was wiping a tear. To this cliquey, tight-knit tribe, fellow nomad Luca was one of them. To Carly, he was from another world, his pure focus something she'd never seen before. She knew he'd had a few drinks, that there was tension between him and Pax, that he'd not wanted to perform at all. Yet he was lost in his music. She envied him that release, the self-control to use his gifts sparingly. She must learn everything he could teach her. Maybe, with his help, she could even heal Ash who rejoined her now, hard-muscled arm swinging around her like a fairground safety bar, proprietorial kiss on her head. Carly sensed the hum that ran through him like high-voltage power lines these days, a silent signal that she was in for a bumpy ride if he drank too much. He was spoiling for a fight. Carly didn't want the bout with Jed to go ahead, but she sensed his need to discharge the pent-up energy. The safety catch was off, the hours of punching leather bags and crunching bench presses awaiting pay-off. If a fly dared land on him tonight, he'd right-hook it into space.

'So he's your new boss?'

'I'm covering his days off mostly,' she said, shrugging, deliberately indifferent, turning to watch a small group of revellers jigging around nearby, Bridge among them.

Catching her looking, Bridge gave a double thumbs up, adding a high kick and a pelvic thrust for effect.

Ash was still fixed on Luca. 'He should be a professional.'

'He is,' Carly said. 'A horse professional.'

Ash's expression darkened yet more.

Jig over, applause loud, Luca tried to take a polite bow and leave, but they bayed for more, shouting and whistling, bribing him with drink and refusing to let him hand the violin back. Smiling, his next piece was all too familiar. Carly recognised it from the first three notes, burning into her soul. As a ripple of 'What is it? I know this!' spread through the crowd, she sensed it was for her; she'd told him it was a leitmotif, and Luca played it so passionately that they all stopped to listen, some clapping along, others dancing, lit by bonfire flames and strings of fairy lights.

'*Last of the Mohicans*!' Ash and his lads were congratulating one another for identifying the film, ignoring Hardcase the music trivia expert arguing that it wasn't the film's main theme. 'You don't hear this until halfway through the movie. It's called "The Kiss".'

Drifting away from them, Carly checked on the kids again – two fast asleep in the buggy, the third still charging round with his cousins – then she stood alongside Bridge, hugging herself tightly, both watching Luca play.

'He can stay.' Bridge was breathless from dancing. 'As my grandma used to say: "If music's the food of love, there's no aphrodisiac like an Irish fiddler".'

'Did she really say that?'

'Of course not. We're a totally unmusical family. Uncle Pat plays the spoons, but it's two bits of cutlery clacking together at the end of the day. This man's fingers are pure sex appeal on a G-string.' She lowered her voice. 'But someone should tell him he only needs to lose that beard and the village wives would be on their *knees*.'

'Maybe that's why he *has* the beard?' Carly grinned, grateful for Bridge's dryness.

She ruined it. 'You wouldn't say no, admit it.'

'I'm going to pretend I didn't hear that.' Carly was mortified she might have given that impression.

But Bridge, a stranger to discretion, was in waspish mood. 'C'mon, queen, you've been like a cat with two fecking tails this afternoon, *and* on heat.'

'Take that back!' Carly snapped, glancing around to check that Ash was still talking film trivia out of earshot.

'It's all right, your man Luca's besotted with Pax, so he's no heed of it.'

'You're so wrong, Bridge.'

'They're star-crossed, trust me.'

'Wrong about me! How can you imagine I think that way?'

'Crazy, isn't it? What would the woman married to the sexiest man in the village want mooning after Ronan Keating over there?'

'Like you mooning over Ash, you mean?' Carly felt mean as soon as she'd said it. Most of her friends in the garrison had fancied Ash. She'd never minded.

Bridge's eyes narrowed, chin lifting. On the familiar music danced, fast and furious. She tapped her foot in time defiantly. 'Was it that fecking obvious?'

'You said it, he's the sexiest man in the village.'

'In my defence, I was under the influence of some *very* black magic at the time.'

Reading this as a typically cynical Bridge joke, Carly laughed. 'Yeah, it's called a boring marriage.'

'Whose are you calling a boring marriage?' Bridge flashed.

'Easy, tiger! You're always complaining that Aleš is getting on your nerves and—'

'I am not!' Bridge was quickly at her testiest. 'My husband is a charming man who can build things and sing and cook and shag, all at the same time on occasion. And I'll have you know he's a fantastic lover. With a huge dick.'

'Talking about me again, girls?' laughed a voice behind them as Flynn sauntered across carrying a handful of brimming cups, Ash scowling behind him flanked by Hardcase and Ink.

Flynn made a flirtatious beeline for Bridge. 'Glad you came, hotlips. Mr Mazurati letting you play outside on your own again this evening?'

'I've got the kids with me,' she muttered, still looking irked, 'and Mrs Bullock.'

'Greetings!' Behind her, Auriol raised a cup of cider. 'Isn't this jolly?'

'All right, Bridge?' Ash handed her a cup.

'Good, yeah. Beezer,' she muttered, not looking at him, and Carly felt sad, knowing that Bridge wouldn't be her over-the-top party-girl self with him again. Ash needed lightness. Listening to the final strains of *Last of the Mohicans*, she wished she'd told Luca she liked a score for a more upbeat movie in which nobody stepped off a cliff – like *The Muppets*.

When it came to an end to whoops and cheers, again Luca wasn't allowed to put down his bow, plied with more drinks as the Turners shouted out requests for favourites: old jigs and reels from the Turners, 'Come on Eileen' and 'Cotton Eye Joe' from others, and from the lads' corner Sex Pistols and Prodigy tracks.

'Friggin' in the Riggin'!'

'Stop it, Hardcase,' Carly hissed, watching Luca settling the fiddle beneath his chin. He was very pale; his eyes seemed miles away.

He fixed the crowd with his killer smile. 'This really is my last song. I hope you enjoy it. It's called "Dick Gossip's".' He launched into a lively tune.

Flynn spluttered his drink everywhere. 'Legend! He must have been listening in to your conversation, ladies. *Dick Gossip's*. Love it.'

Carly hoped it would at least cheer up Bridge.

But she was still glum-faced. 'It's a well-known Irish reel.'

'Remind me, is "Friggin' in the Riggin" from *HMS Pinafore*?' Auriol asked Hardcase, the two soon nose to nose talking music.

'Word is Paddy there's jumping both the mother and daughter,' Flynn told Carly as they watched Luca's bow moving ever faster.

'Whose word?' Carly scoffed.

'I was shoeing horses up the hunt kennels last week and the head girl there swears there's a threesome going on in a yard in this village…'

'Better watch yourself, Carly,' muttered Bridge.

'It's all happening, she says: fast riding and boozing, a cougar, a marriage on the rocks.'

'Now who's the dick gossip?' Bridge ribbed him.

'It's not like those two at the stud don't have form,' Flynn pointed out. 'Everyone in the hunt knows Bay Austen's already been there.'

'You don't want to listen to banter,' Carly dismissed.

'Actually, rumours in established hierarchies like work places and rural communities are ninety-five per cent accurate according to research,' Bridge offered helpfully. 'I learned it on an HR course.'

'That's it.' Ash drained his cup. 'You're not working there, Carly.'

'Bridge didn't mean it, did you? Take it back, Bridge.'

'Will not.' Her stubborn face reminded Carly of Sienna refusing to eat vegetables.

'You're only saying it because I hurt your feelings.'

'Am *not*.'

The violin was getting faster and faster.

'Bridge,' she implored.

'What if it's true?' Her eyes gleamed, mood lifted by the wind-up. 'Before you know it, you'll find yourself stripped naked and strapped to the saddle rack by a pair of stirrup leathers.'

'Can I buy tickets?' asked Flynn.

On the reel flew: dum-da-da-da-da-da, dum-da-da-da-da-da, dum-da-da-da-da-da…

Carly felt her heartbeat match it, indignant and livid. 'Take that back, Bridge, or we'll tell Ash the real reason you're mad at me, shall we?'

'Tell me what?' Ash glanced round.

'Bridge?' Carly demanded, not caring.

Bridge stared back wide-eyed, like a cat facing a vacuum cleaner nozzle. 'Can you not take a fecking joke?' she blasted. 'I'm only ruminating on a bit of idle talk here, and you can't deny the statistics or the fact that Pax has a hold over golden boy over there that my eyes tell me makes him very hot under the collar, and my eyes don't lie.' Talking as fast as the fiddle bow, she was refusing to back down on principle. 'So don't you drag me into your jealous imaginings about your husband – who, incidentally, only ever showed me kindness when he spent ages patching up my face without even demanding so much as a cup of coffee – and don't you threaten me with anything, Carly Turner.' Then, as unexpected as the Queen throwing a V-sign, Bridge welled up, turning quickly away to hide it.

'WHO is UPSETTING my WIFE?' demanded a hundred-decibel war cry behind them. Man-mountain Aleš towered over them all in a donkey jacket and woolly hat.

'Carly, apparently.' Flynn held up his hands and stepped back.

'HOW?' demanded Aleš, who only had two volume settings, loud and deafening.

'Oi!' Ash stormed forwards, all squared shoulders and clenched fists. 'Don't you raise your voice at my wife like that.'

'Whoa,' Carly tried to soothe him. 'They're my ears, bae.'

Aleš jerked up his chin dismissively at Ash and turned to his own wife, booming voice tender, 'What is it that has upset you, *kochanie*?'

'Already forgotten.' Bridge mopped her eyes on her sleeve, glancing at Carly, repentant. They both knew their husbands would fight at the slightest provocation.

'An incident involving Mr and Mrs Turner, I believe,' Auriol prompted as kindly as she would the parents of two Year Threes snivelling in her office. 'Something about coffee – or was it group sex?'

'That's bollocks,' Bridge scoffed, then went pale as it occurred to her that she was addressing her new boss, commonly nicknamed Bollocks.

Thankfully, Auriol was too spellbound by the testosterone levels pumping between Ash and Aleš to notice.

'What upset my wife?' the Polish builder was demanding as he squared up to Ash. He was far taller and larger, but his body was soft, his eyes kind. It was like a brown bear goading a panther.

'No idea.' Ash pulled back his chin, head tipped, face insolent.

'Start thinking fast.'

'Or what?'

'You don't want to know.'

'Try me.'

'You really want to find out?'

They were straight into action movie dialect, Carly realised, stepping in beside Bridge who was telling them to pack it in, or at least take it elsewhere.

'There are kids here,' Bridge hissed.

Luca was still reeling a wild accompaniment nearby, the crowd around him clapping in time, the handsome stand-in bodhran player thundering in time.

'You'd better watch yourself, mate.'

'Watch YOU make a FOOL OF YOURSELF, you mean.'

'Move this somewhere quieter!' Carly backed up Bridge, pointing at the furthest end of the orchard behind the younger trees, amazed to see the two men doing as they were told, walking sideways like huge, fierce crabs so they could keep goading each other.

Hurriedly calling over Turner teens to keep an eye on the children, Carly followed with Bridge.

'You don't want to cross me, mate,' Ash was snarling.

'Says who?'

'The last one to cross me.'

'Cross *me* and you won't be talking for a long time.'

Grabbing Carly's hand, Bridge breathed, 'It's like a bad fecking episode of *EastEnders*.'

'I was thinking *Terminator*.'

'How do we stop them?'

'I've no idea.'

In a clearing, their husbands were ratcheting up the rhetoric, two fighting cocks pecking and scratching their way towards an inevitable feather-flying death match. A small crowd including Auriol had come across with them to follow the action.

'You'll regret this.'

'Not as much as you.'

'I don't think so.'

'Dream on.'

Bridge held Carly's hand tighter. 'Where do they *learn* that shit?'

'They're almost there,' she realised anxiously. 'Ash will throw a punch soon.'

'Do they even know what they're arguing about?'

'Us.'

'Sorry.'

'Me too.'

They hugged tightly. At that moment, Ash got the green light he'd been looking for all week as his adversary pulled off his woolly hat, crossed his huge arms and demanded, 'You want to FIGHT?'

As they drew back fists, an upright figure in a camel-hair coat stepped between them. 'Now, now, boys, we're not the Very Angry Ladybird, are we?'

'Oh shit!' Carly rushed forwards.

But Bridge was quicker. Realising her new boss was about to get crushed, she hurled herself through the air to rugby tackle Auriol to safety. Brushing her down afterwards, she turned back to pull in Carly beside her. 'Ladies, we need to be more strategic. I'll go first. I did Taekwondo for ten years.'

The husbands were in a body lock, each trying to wrestle the other to the ground, both grunting and swearing furiously.

'*Stop now or I'm going to kick you!*' Bridge threatened.

'Scary stuff,' Flynn chuckled behind them.

She growled furiously, lowering her centre of balance, adopting a martial art pose.

'Keep out of this, *kochanie*.' Aleš landed a fist in Ash's ribs.

'I won't warn you again!'

'Fuck off, darling,' Ash dismissed, cracking his elbow into Aleš's eye socket.

'Ew!' Bridge and Carly looked away, unable to watch.

There was a loud whack as Aleš head-butted Ash.

Carly looked again, catching Ash uppercut the Pole's big bearded chin with an audible crack.

'I will fucking kill you!'

'Right, that's it. Heeaagh!' Bridge spun, one leg high as a ballet dancer, heel smacking hard across the back of her husband's neck. He went down like a felled tree. Swinging again, she angled her foot at the critical last moment to clout Ash on the jaw.

'Fuck! That hurt!' He reached up and stroked it.

'Ow!' She was hopping around on one leg. 'Are you made of fecking steel or what? I think I might have broken it.' She sank to the ground to examine her heel.

Carly hurried to Bridge's side. 'You okay?'

'It's nothing, queen,' she said, grimacing, tears in her eyes. 'Have they stopped?'

'They will.'

Aleš was lumbering back up again, looking like an enraged rhino, Ash eyeing him, ready to pounce.

Carly stormed between them. 'Will you both STOP. THIS. NOW. Or you're not getting fed or fucked for a month, understand?'

'Touché!' Bridge rallied, hopping back up. 'No food, no sex and I'll raise you no laundry or childcare.'

'Oh, bravo!' Auriol cheered from the sidelines.

Behind Carly, Flynn muttered, 'What's so unusual in that?'

Ash and Aleš turned away from each other, arms up, conceding an angry, resentful ceasefire, trying to look like it was all a joke.

'Now shake fecking hands!' shouted Bridge, and to both women's amazement they did.

'Us too,' she muttered sheepishly to Carly, holding hers out. 'I'm truly sorry, queen. When I get a cob on, there's no fecking stopping me.'

'That kick was bloody brilliant.' Carly hugged her again. 'I can't believe Aleš went straight down like that.'

'He had to.' Bridge winked, stooping to pick up her husband's discarded woolly hat. 'Ash would have made him look a much bigger fecking mug than I just did.'

'You mean he…?' She started to laugh, realising the big man had staged the fall like a footballer.

'That was quite marvellous!' Auriol hurried forwards. 'Would you both be interested in running some female empowerment and self-defence workshops together for my Year Six girls?'

'And there was me thinking you were going to fire me for public affray before I even started.' Bridge looked hugely relieved.

'Quite the opposite,' Auriol insisted. 'You are the jewel in Maggers' crown, Ms Mazur.'

'Does that mean we can have the coffee pod machine after all?'

Leaving them to it, Carly made her way to Ash who gave her a suspicious look, still simmering just below boiling point.

'Don't try that number on me again,' he warned.

'This isn't your fight, bae, you know that. Keep your powder dry, hey?'

He set his jaw, looking sideways at her, wise enough to let it rest when physical and sexual starvation were threatened this close to a family bout.

She looked sideways back. 'You're a dark horse. Army first-aid training came in useful, then?'

His eyebrows curled questioningly, then he remembered. 'Yeah, your mate was in a bit of a mess that day.'

'My hero.' She reached up to his face and he responded with a long, hard kiss.

Something still bothered Carly. 'So why'd she want Skully's number?'

'Turf,' he said smoothly, nodding in the direction of Bridge who was walloping Aleš with his woolly hat. 'Ask her yourself.'

Carly let it go. She also needed to keep her powder dry if, as she suspected, Skully dealt his in small packages. She'd see him off eventually.

Ash's brows had lowered, his expression darkening. 'I'm still not happy about you working for Percys.'

'It's just a few hours at weekends. There *are* no Percys there any more, Ash. The family name died out. Turners rule this village, remember?'

'*Riverdance* boy is coming nowhere near you.'

'That story's so fake. Luca's soft as a puppy. You'll like him. Total non-threat. I'll introduce you.' Carly knew she was laying it on a bit thick. What she would never admit to a soul was the seed of truth in Bridge's accusation. There was something about Luca she couldn't quite shake from her head.

But when they walked back, the wassail singers had launched into another folk anthem, hurdy-gurdy player spinning enthusiastically. Carly scanned the orchard. Luca had long gone.

⋆

'If he knocks we'll open it. Otherwise silence, understood?'

Dogs to either side, Pax sat with her back against the wall in Lester's cottage hallway, feeling the sisal doormat scratching through the cotton of her pyjama bottoms, raking her hair back with her fingers.

'There's no such thing as bad timing, just timing,' she whispered. 'And the clock's ticking.'

She was, she realised, behaving slightly – very – madly. Feeling increasingly as if she'd lost her mind tonight along with her heart and quite a lot of dignity, she didn't trust herself. It was uncomfortably like being drunk. The toughest night for staying sober had left her breathless, unable to sit still, her thoughts in a vortex. Nothing settled her. She'd let Laurence play, later walked round the yard with the dogs, tried to watch television and then read. She was just killing time, she'd realised. She must *stop killing time*. So she'd put on some washing and started Sellotaping the love letters back together for Lester, working forensically. She treated it as a jigsaw puzzle she must solve, not reading more than the sentences she was matching up at a time, not prying into the story that was a part of a private past, and yet in her own way becoming familiar with it. Having it in her hands made her feel better about things, accepting the simple truth of her father's greatest love and its concealment, the reactionary prejudice in this corner of country life not so very different even today. *There's no such thing as bad timing, just timing.*

Feeling cold, she'd gone upstairs to fetch another layer, pulling a heavy jumper from a drawer to find the breeches that her mother had bought her tucked beneath it. Through the little casement window, bright as an apple slice was the waxing half-moon, a week away from its full wolf face. It had made her think of Lester, still carrying his lost love.

I would give every star in the sky to see it.

That's when she'd heard singing, drawing the curtain and killing the lights before taking up her position by the front door.

She closed her eyes as she recognised 'My Langan Love'.

'Her welcome, like her love for me,' sang Luca,
Is from her heart within;'
He pitched left.
'Her warm kiss is felicity
That knows no taint of sin.'
He pitched right.
'And, when I stir my foot to go,
Tis leaving love and light'
Centre line, change of leg at X.
'To feel the wind of longing blow
From out the dark of night.'

Luca might be having difficulty waking in a straight line, but compared to his hard-drinking heyday he was barely over the yardarm. And to his monumental relief he'd found he could stop, hold his hand up and walk away from the offers to make a night of it, promises that his drinks would be free, his supper sung for. He wanted to whoop, to stand on a fence rail and shout to the valley, 'Look at me, I am calling it a night and it's early evening!'

From the first drop to now, his greatest fear had been that of gathering momentum like a meteor, the out-of-control drinking that always ended in unconsciousness. The drinks had kept coming when he played, still pressed on him after he'd decided he'd had enough. It had made him feel feather light and intoxicatingly exhilarated again, his fingers only able to remember their way through the tunes at top speed when his head was spinning too fast to think. That he had turned and walked away afterwards without a second glance almost shocked him.

He didn't end up in a ditch. Nor did he try to serenade Pax's dark, curtained cottage windows. He'd handed the violin back for a start, and she'd made it clear enough that she had no desire for his half-cut company. The memory of opening his eyes from a kiss that had nourished his soul only to see her racing off across a field wasn't a great one.

He went to check on Beck and the other horses, realising from the amount of hay in nets and the fresh water with no strands it that she'd already been round.

He turned back to look at the cottage. He wanted to know she was okay, but he could feel himself swaying a bit now that he was standing still.

Beck watched him, the insomniac who missed nothing. His neighbours were asleep, old Cruisoe curled up in deep shavings with his gold and black legs tucked underneath him, the little Shetland flat out, his big stomach like a fluffy white snow mound in straw.

Luca's phone found the signal sweet spot with a buzz and he checked how many times the Unknown Number had called. Twenty. Still no messages. His battery was on its last gasp.

He went back to feed Beck a mint. 'Have you been involved in an accident that wasn't your fault?' He impersonated a recorded telemarketing voice. 'Sure I haff.' He tried a German accent with a vague recognition that he must be wasted to wisecrack at a horse. 'Can I haff ze compensation if some Scheisskerl tried to taser me und lame me for life? Shut up, Luca.' He marched out onto the yard, slapped his arms and face to try to sober up, to shake the menacing vision of a black-windowed car sliding up the drive, Mishaal stepping out, bringing with him a white-coated vet with a lethal injection, a brace of heavies with sledgehammers and his new bride with a shotgun for good measure.

He rubbed his face. 'One more day and he'll be thousands of miles away. It's all cool.'

He headed unsteadily towards the house.

'Wouldn't be able to walk along the white lines on the road tonight officer, no.'

It took all his willpower not to knock on the cottage door.

Pax must have gone to bed. It was still early, but there was no light on. That had to be a big, lonely bed. They could talk. No funny business, she was too fragile. He liked talking to Pax. He could tell her about Mishaal.

'Fuck, no.' He forced himself to walk on, knowing that more than anything he just wanted to kiss her again.

Then he turned back, reeling round further than he intended. He *had* to see Pax. Recrossing the yard, he stood on her doorstep, taking a few deep breaths to steady his nerves and spinning head. There was a low, gruff bark from just inside as Stubbs identified a prowler.

About to knock, Luca stopped himself. Was that what Pax would think he was too? Luca prowling around in his cups? It was how he was behaving. He held a position of trust here, had a job to do, must stop thinking about himself. This matters a whole load more than you feeling thirsty, he reminded himself. He heard his Canadian former boss yelling in his head, 'Keep your bloody pants on, boy.'

Stubbs barked louder, there was movement in the hallway beyond the door.

Had he said that aloud? In a Canadian accent?

He turned and hurried away.

Lined up outside the back door to the main house were four wooden boxes crammed with bottles of plum gin. There was a note:

Thank you for keeping my sobriety. I'm sorry you lost yours a little.

Pax.

He carried it upstairs, tucked it under his pillow and stared up into the beamed eaves of his attic room, wondering if he'd ever sleep. A half-moon was brightening his row of little casement windows and throwing shadow blades across the ceiling.

The drink was his sedative, a lullaby of heavy-headed breaths seeing him into slumber curled beside the imaginary warmth of a woman until the early hours, when he woke from a fitful dream in which Mishaal was hunting down Beck, a great circus whip in his hand that he cracked overhead as he ripped through the stud's fields on a black Arab horse in tasselled Bedouin finery.

Luca took a moment to adjust, to tell himself it was a dream. The moon-shadow daggers on the ceiling had moved and were pointing at him now.

Then he realised he could hear hooves hurtling out in one of the fields, an urgent shout. Nothing was turned out overnight. Did they have an intruder? His first thought was Beck.

He stumbled out of bed, pulling on jeans, hurrying to the window, his heart full throttle.

A horse and rider were thundering around the biggest of the hay fields.

The moonlight was at half strength, but he recognised them straight away: the horse compact and short-coupled with a hogged neck like a truss arch, its rider standing in her stirrups and punching the air, a stream of wild red mane flying behind her.

Heartbeat slowly returning to normal, he watched as she cantered the willing little cob in huge loops, skirting along the treeline, then back out across the field, a teardrop to turn back on herself, a showman's gallop alongside the rail and then back to trot to bring the horse slowly down, raining huge pats on his neck before pulling up and slumping forwards to hug him. Even at this distance, Luca could feel the sheer unfettered joy.

Tonight, he was jealous of a horse.

PART FIVE

19

Pax was accustomed to Luca not saying much first thing, but this morning he was beyond taciturn, earphones in, eyes averted. He had to be seriously hungover, she guessed.

Having barely slept, stiffly bow-legged from her late-night ride, she wasn't feeling too sociable either, grateful they'd established a routine early on, working a stable yard apart most of the morning shift. At the first opportunity, she took Knott and Stubbs and up to the top field to call and see how Kes was doing.

'Compton Magna Primary School.' Bridge's phone voice was so ultra-assured – like a Radio Four news announcer – that Pax didn't recognise her.

'This is Kes Forsyth's mum.'

'Pax, queen!' The professionalism was short-lived. 'How are ya? Don't blame you taking off last night. That was fierce. Such a shame the little fella's not well today. Have you called to rearrange?'

'Not well?'

'His granny rang not five minutes ago. Touch of tummy wobbles, she says. We can try for Friday instead if that suits you?'

Thanking her, Pax phoned the Forsyths, finally tracking Mairi down on her mobile. Pax could hear a car engine.

'How is he? Are you taking him to the doctor?'

'He's feeling fine now, thank you, Tish. He'd just got a wee chill from standing about in that cold orchard. In fact, he's so much better we thought we'd treat him to Sea Life Centre.'

'Is Mack with you?'

'He's working of course, poor man. We might be late back, so Kes can stay another—'

Pax gritted her teeth. 'I'll pick him up at four thirty on the dot.'

Despite a rare, uninterrupted blue sky and bright winter sun, her spirits were lowering by the minute. Last night's high felt as though it had happened in a parallel life.

She found herself wanting to tell Luca what he'd done, to share the thrill of it, the resurrection, but she held it back, already feeling too guilty, the squirm of self-loathing eating through her. Secret drinker. Secret rider. Secrets keeper.

She retreated to the main house to work through calls that needed returning and cheques that needed writing, praying they wouldn't bounce. At least the antiquated way the stud paid for everything bought them enough time for the deposits from new bookings for Cruisoe coverings to clear. There were precious few of those.

The booking diary was an old-fashioned leather-bound tome and not a diary as such, its entries dating back many years, Lester's neat handwriting cataloguing generations of visiting mares. That same handwriting in the letters which had been interleaved with her father's.

She slammed the book shut and watched through the big, twelve-paned window as Luca rode past on the old point-to-pointer they couldn't sell because it hadn't raced in years, leading an unbroken three-year-old out to nanny around the village for experience. She'd done it herself a hundred times a lifetime ago, that parallel life she'd all too briefly ridden through last night.

Back out on the yard, safe in the knowledge he'd be gone a

while, she made a beeline for Lester's cob, burying her face in his solid neck and focussing on breathing. In out, in out. Deep lungfuls of that sweet, addictive comfort.

'Shall we tack him up for you?'

She swung round in alarm to see her mother beaming over the door at her, fresh from a night of sin. She looked radiant.

Did she know about Pax riding? But the smile was unwitting.

'No thanks.' She gave the cob a perfunctory pat, hoping Ronnie would think she was just checking him over. 'Good night?'

'Better than yours by the look of it. Come and see Lester. I'm driving over there now.'

'I can't. I have lots to do.'

'Nonsense. We'll take Stubbs. I've found a trolley suitcase he fits in perfectly. Is he in the cottage?' She was across the yard to the wall door before Pax could stop her, calling over her shoulder, 'Luca's riding out, I take it?'

Pax followed slowly, pulling off her boots at the back door, knowing exactly what her mother would have just stumbled across. Why hadn't she put them away? Half-sellotaped letters were spread out on the table in Lester's cottage.

Ronnie pressed her hands to her cheeks. 'You found them then?'

Pax stood in the doorway uncertainly.

'He wanted me to hide them.'

She crossed the room, fighting an urge to do as Lester wanted and stuff them all back in the box. 'How long have you known?'

'Longer than I realised. Self-denial is an incredibly powerful thing. Lester was worried you'd come across them. He wanted me to put them in safekeeping, but I couldn't find the ruddy box, and now—'

'I'm glad I know.'

'Is it terribly selfish to say I am too? It's not an easy thing to carry alone.'

As they stood close together, looking down at the jigsaw of crumpled paper and heartfelt words, Pax felt an extraordinary flood of relief. Something deeper surfaced alongside it, a belief she'd stayed true to through all their years of estrangement, however bad things got: they shared the same capacity to forgive. Her mother – tough and kind and courageous, never giving up on her children – had kept Johnny Ledwell's secret unswervingly.

'I can't imagine how hard it must have been, living that lie.'

'For all of us. There were happy times, and many of them, but I do so wish they could start afresh today when so much has changed.' Ronnie turned to smile up at her sadly. 'The curse of being my age is to want to go back and live one's life again with the benefit of hindsight. Appreciating how good something is in the moment is so much harder than looking back at it afterwards.'

Pax looked at her tough, upbeat mother whose life had been so filled with regret and rejection, and felt a fierce pride at her endurance, and at her homecoming.

'Does Lester talk about Daddy?'

'God, no. Our elephant must stay in the room like a taxidermist's *chef d'oeuvre*.'

They leaned closer for a moment, an embrace within reach that neither knew quite how to make.

'I can't face him, Mummy.'

'You'll have to some time.'

'I need to ride the Wolf Moon Lap first.'

Ronnie looked astonished. 'Why?'

'I have to be able to look him the eye.' It was hard to explain to a pragmatist like Ronnie why gut instinct told her Lester expected no less, that this would heal her as surely as hospital was healing him. Grapes and magazines were all very well, but family honour needed a greater power to restore it. He'd made it clear what he expected her to do.

Of all the people in Pax's life, Lester had always seen deepest inside her and pushed her into making the right decisions, her mentalist. She'd craved his approval since early childhood, a surrogate father to her drunken one, a step-parent in heart and soul as it turned out. It was Lester who had travelled with her to competitions, coached her, bolstered her, torn strips off her for getting it wrong and praised her for getting it right; he'd comforted her when her father died even though his own hidden grief must have been soul-destroying. She'd broken his heart when she'd turned her back on it all, but he had never censured her, had remained a constant in her life to whom she'd returned whenever she needed grounding and no-nonsense sympathy. Throughout, he had waited for her to ride again, patient as can be, certain in his belief that she would.

Ronnie was right that self-denial was a powerful force. Pax had always known it wasn't her marriage ending that would disappoint Lester if she visited – it was that she had come back to live at the stud and not got on a horse.

'We'll start now! Get you in training.' So easy for Ronnie to say, the get-going toughie who picked herself up and dusted herself down after every big fall, getting straight back on again.

'I can't,' she said stubbornly.

'You've lost your nerve, haven't you?' Her mother's blue eyes creased with sympathy.

Pax couldn't look at her, the memory of last night's ride still vivid in every muscle. My secret. My secret. Mine.

She must not let it out yet, however dishonourable it made her feel to keep it to herself. If she shared it, she'd never let herself go there again.

'Oh poor Pax,' Ronnie sighed.

She shook her head, her need to be truthful overwhelming. 'It's not that. After what happened with Bay, I suppose I denied myself the thing I loved most. I had to punish myself.'

'But why? I was the one who deserved punishment.'

'I wasn't good enough. I was always in your shadow. The pictures all over the tack room: Badminton at eighteen, Olympic selection at nineteen.'

'I never went.'

'I know, but to Grumps, you were his superstar. Every class I won, you'd won it first. Every horse I broke would have been just your type. I was poor compensation.'

'And then I came back and unwittingly stole the first boy you fell in love with.' Ronnie's eyes had lost their sparkle, her face etched with remorse.

'I never wanted to get on a horse again.'

'Even now?'

Pax thought about the restless, belly-deep need she always felt around horses. The galloping she'd done in her imagination, the hooves in her ears through her listless marriage; horses galloped alongside every car she drove, every train she took, every nightmare from which she ran away to wakefulness. They were the percussion to her life, the stampede that told her there was something better over the horizon. They'd stayed with her no matter how far removed she'd become from the little red-haired girl in the photographs on Lester's walls, no matter how hard she'd tried to disassociate herself from her, to punish her for never being good enough.

Bulimia had come first, long before leaving the stud: public self-denial, private gorging, that oh-so-secret solace, then the purge of forcing the comfort straight back out, acid and loathsome. For a brief while, drugs fast-tracked her to a secret headspace, offered a release. Later alcohol, her hand over the glass at dinner parties before excusing herself to her host's downstairs loo to neck vodka straight from the bottle hidden in her handbag. Now moonlit riding, trying to get a reckless kick replicating the heroines of the pony books she'd read as a child: *By day, Patricia was a frilly Pollyanna cossetted amongst nannies and governesses, by night Pax and her pony owned the moors*. Who was she kidding?

Ronnie stepped closer, a hand on her arm. 'What's stopping you doing it now, Pax?'

'I'm frightened it might feel like coming home.'

At that moment, she realised she was already there.

On a narrow, sunken section of lane, Luca was being heeled by the rattling diesel of a Land Rover, the barking dogs inside causing the skittish youngster he was leading to jump up the bank while his mount stayed determinedly on the tarmac. Disconcerted, he found himself leading a horse with its hooves at head height. Even more alarmingly, the Land Rover was now trying to squeeze past before they reached a passing place.

Battling to keep the younger horse calm and close without it breaking loose or jumping back down on top of him, Luca raised an arm in warning, calling, 'Wait!'

Still the Land Rover edged onwards, drawing level, passenger window lowering. In the seat, a rumpled brunette with smudged red lipstick. Stretching across her, Bay Austen was in cashmere and Schoffel, a trace of the same lipstick on his lower lip.

'Luke, isn't it? Keep meaning to pop in and see how you're doing?'

'Just grand.' He hung onto the plunging youngster.

'Give my regards to the girls! Tell Pax we'll do that lunch soon.' As he rumbled off, the youngster sprang off the bank like a deer, clean over Luca's head, landing remarkably sure-footedly on the lane to trot amiably alongside again.

Encounter with Bay cast aside, he grinned widely. 'Now *you're* going to be right up my street.'

Trotting up the stud's driveway, he moved the horses aside as Ronnie rattled towards him in her sports car, buzzing down the window. 'I'm off to see Lester. What do you think of that young one? Make a nice sort for Pax, I thought?'

He smiled, saying nothing, heart twisting. He'd train any horse on the yard to be well-mannered for Pax if asked, even Coll the Shetland.

Ronnie put the car in gear. 'Back after lunch!'

Nodding, he set off again, the youngster pogoing alongside him once more as the sports car snarled away.

Pax was back in the main house, seated at her grandfather's desk which looked out over the driveway and front paddocks. He saw her framed in the big-paned window as he passed, pretending not to notice him, the awkwardness of the day not yet waning. They had to shake it off before tonight, which was going to be tough enough for Pax without this overhanging it. He raised his arm and waved, smiling when she looked up. The same moment, his phone buzzed in his pocket before ringing its way noisily into action, making him jump, now dreading each Unknown call. Sensing his disquiet, both horses spooked in opposite directions, leaving Luca somewhere in between, balancing on one stirrup like a Cossack, somehow grappling them back, but not before a considerable loss of dignity.

When he turned to smile it off, Pax was at the window, muffled call asking if he was all right, Knott appearing beside her, paws up on the sill. The movement just made the horses shy again, banging together now and kicking out, the old point-to-pointer spinning away beneath him. Not concentrating, eyes still on Pax, Luca fell right off this time, landing on his feet, somehow holding onto both.

He quickly turned to the window to bow with exaggerated chivalry.

Eyes brimming with amusement, Pax returned to her paperwork.

It was a start.

When Ronnie came back in a blaze of headlights, supermarket pizzas and biscuit treats for Kes sliding off the back seat, it was far later than she'd intended, a long call to Blair having diverted her in Aldi's car park, then again halfway home. The affair was at fever pitch again. Although she'd always suspected that time apart might create extra frisson between them when they reunited, she'd underestimated how much. She was missing him a ridiculous amount when they were apart.

Pax was about to set off to fetch Kes, that deep soothing voice surprising Ronnie with, 'If they aren't back, I am going to eviscerate Muir with his skean dhu.'

She drove off looking murderous.

'Oh dear.'

Ronnie collared Luca. 'Please make sure Pax has some fun tonight.'

'It's not really that sort of gig, y'know?'

She gave him a wise look. 'May I suggest something very straightforward which I think will cheer her up enormously?'

When Luca heard what she had in mind, his face lit up with that amazing smile. 'I've been meaning to do that since I got here.'

'And there were HUGE turtles that went RIGHT over my head and Grandforce said that they have existed for two hundred million YEARS which is even longer than him…'

Steering the Noddy car back up the stud's long driveway, Pax checked the dash clock, grateful to see she'd have time to settle Kes before she had to go out again. Mercifully her evisceration threats had been entirely unnecessary, the Forsyths ready and waiting with their grandson clutching a plush stingray while their son clutched a solicitor's email.

'My chap suggests we draw up a calendar.' Mack had tried to maintain a pompous higher ground. 'Save any more,' he'd cleared his throat, 'mistakes.'

Helen Beadle's unequivocal and cross reaction to the wassail seizure seemed to have finally brought some semblance of cooperation. Walking them to the car, Mack had also admitted with tight-jawed reluctance that the 'Scotland Plan' was going to be delayed on his part by some interest in the barn conversions, the business being less dead in the water than he'd imagined.

'So I'll be here for mediation,' he assured her with an attempt at a conciliatory smile.

She turned into the arrivals yard, parking alongside the rusted Subaru that had once belonged to her grandfather.

A chisel-jawed man was talking to her mother in the glow of the first archway, good-looking enough to make her double take.

She peered at him, vaguely recognising the beanie and Puffa jacket. 'Who's that?'

'Silly Mummy!' Kes was already unbuckling his seat belt. 'It's Luca. I'm going to show him my turtle.'

Pax stared, astonished, pulses fizzing like Sodastreams.

The beard had gone.

Returning from a two-hour marathon in Evesham's Tesco superstore, Bridge gritted her teeth in the passenger seat beside her husband, listening to *The Wheels On The Bus* playlist as their children gradually re-entered Earth's atmosphere from cosmic tantrum to sleepy trance in the booster seats behind them.

Aleš always insisted on shopping with them, despite never grasping that there was a time limit attached to taking small children into supermarkets which didn't allow for him to choose individual onions with slow perfectionism, haggle with the man at the fresh fish counter, or linger lovingly by the Polish food section remembering a recipe his grandmother used to cook. By the time they'd reached the tills with a double-toddler-seat trolley stacked to chin height, everyone within a fifty-metre radius longed for ear defenders. She was only prepared to forgive him because he'd put in chocolates, pink champagne and fillet steak, still on his absolute best behaviour after last night.

'And if we buy a plot to build a house it will *definitely* be big enough to keep Craic there?' she confirmed for the umpteenth time, holding her phone out to record it for posterity this time.

'I guarantee it, *kochanie*.'

She smiled, kissing her fingers and reaching across to place them lovingly on his bristly head. Much as Bridge despised male violence, her husband's aborted fight with Ash Turner had provided fantastic domestic leverage, as well as being strangely stimulating. Two men sparring over her honour had given her a secret frisson. The sex had been spectacular afterwards, the Mazurs back in full cry.

As they drove up the sunken lane towards the Comptons, another car came towards them.

'He is closer to passing space.' Aleš drove on bullishly, forcing the other car to swiftly reverse, even though Bridge knew it would have been much easier for them to go back to a nearby gateway. Aleš always followed too closely, radiator to radiator, intimidating drivers into zig-zagging into the verges.

This one was far better than most, and as they stalked it at close range, Bridge recognised Pax's little Noddy car. She'd turned away to look out of the rear window, but there was no mistaking that mane of red hair. There was a passenger sitting beside her, his face dipping in and out of shadow as they bounced over the potholes. Hugely handsome, all high cheeks and square chin. Some women had all the luck.

Bridge leant forwards, peering closer.

'Oh my fecking life!' she breathed, reaching straight for her phone as the Noddy car swung into the recess in the bank and they flashed past, already WhatsApping the Saddle Bags.

*

The Chipping Hampton Friends Meeting House was tricky to find, impossible to park near and challenging to access. Keen to protect its inscrutability, a Bardswolds Alcoholics Anonymous meeting was harder to track down than the VIP rooms of a London private members' club. And like a private members club, many of the participants knew each other on the outside. When Pax and Luca finally located the room, ten minutes late, Pax peered through its small glass panel. Her eyes widened, already recognising a startling number: an architect she'd worked with, a friend's nanny, a banker with a lisp she'd met at a dinner party recently, someone she'd been at prep school with and a comedian turned children's author who had bought one of the farmhouses that she and Mack had renovated. Which in a group of fewer than twenty made it less of an anonymous gathering, more of a reunion.

'You ready?' Luca whispered, looking more than a little tense himself.

She nodded.

Only a few looked round as they sidled their way into the second row of the small circle of seats. Most were focussed on a thin-haired man in a crumpled suit telling the group how he'd relapsed over New Year, staying up late to binge drink a bottle of Drambuie, the leftover amaretto from the tiramisu and several craft gin miniatures. 'I nearly stopped at the quince, but I was at rock bottom.'

Pax stole another look at Luca, almost unrecognisable without his beard, his anonymity guaranteed tonight at least. Several other women in the circle were sneaking peeks at him too, she noticed. He was really quite hard not to look at.

Scrutinised by the friend's nanny, Pax was grateful for the oversized knitted slouch hat that covered her trademark hair, scarf wound high over her coat, her glasses further cover. Now she was in the room, she also spotted one of the semi-retired teachers from Kes's old school and the ears of the blonde woman with the tight bun sitting directly in front of her also looked suspiciously familiar, one fringed with multiple high piercings.

Okay? Luca mouthed, reaching across to squeeze her hand.

Pax nodded, her hand now feeling as though it had been massaged in Deep Heat. She'd picked up a leaflet from her chair which she flipped through now, half-listening as the man in the creased suit moved on through cooking sherry and Advocaat to 'a bottle of perry cider somebody brought to a barbecue about three summers ago which reminded me that I had friends once. I've driven them all away through my alcohol dependence.' Pax looked up as he caught a sob and a caring-looking man in a Fair Isle tank top – who, she realised, must be the group leader – asked him to tell everyone how he felt about that. He still had his office swipe card on a lanyard around his neck and for some reason it made her want to run away, this reminder of the lab-rat lives outside this room which drove them all to unscrew the tops of vodka bottles. That wasn't a tribe she could sit easily amongst.

'It makes me even more grateful to have God in my life,' Perry Cider man said.

Pax deliberately didn't look at Luca. The leaflet in her hands reminded her why she'd always worried that this would not be for her. The recovery message was positive, supportive and self-affirming, but there was no denying the evangelical sway of it all. From ten commandments to twelve steps was just a hop.

Flicking a page, she could almost hear 'hallelujah!' with descant, strings and cassocks.

She glanced across at Luca again. He was reading his leaflet too, forehead creased just as doubtfully. Catching her looking at him, he gave her the ghost of a wink.

Too much from the all-new, clean-shaven, drop-dead-gorgeous Luca. She looked away, pink-cheeked. He believes in God she reminded herself. This works for him. My devilish thoughts have no place here.

She was starting to feel the familiar tight-chested panic of needing to be somewhere else. Urgently.

Perry Cider man had fallen silent and Pax joined in the muted applause, wondering if she could stick it out, especially when Fair Isle man asked if anybody else wanted to share their stories? He seemed to be looking straight at her. 'I think you're ready, am I right?'

She shrank lower.

But it was the blonde woman sitting immediately in front of them who spoke, and as soon as she did, Pax knew why her ears had looked familiar.

'My name is Monique and I am an alcoholic, okay. This is my story.' She looked around with her bulging, ice-blue eyes.

Pax put a hand up to shield her face, looking to Luca in a panic mouthing *Bay's wife!*

He pulled an uncomprehending face.

Monique's voice – Dutch accent ironic and monotone, accustomed to shouting across arenas – echoed around the room with a jeroboam more self-belief than Perry Cider man. 'So I'm married to a man who can't keep his dick in his pants, okay. He has many affairs. We both do. It's nothing new. He liked it that I am bisexual when we married, now he is less happy because my lovers are both boys.' She laughed ironically.

There was a creaking of plastic chairs as everyone sat up to listen.

Is she in the right group? Pax wondered.

'We both drink a lot,' Monique went on. 'I mean *a lot*. Stiff gins at six, chin-chin, with supper is maybe three bottles of wine, more afterwards, then brandy. More when we eat with his parents, more still if we eat out, which we do a lot. He classifies himself as a heavy drinker, I classify myself as dependent. On alcohol. And on him.'

Maybe she was in the right group. Pax could feel her face flaming. Luca was looking at her questioningly. She mouthed *I know her.* This time he understood with a quick nod. Then he studied at Monique's profile curiously, eyebrows shooting up as he turned back to Pax and mouthed *I know her too.*

Monique played to a rapt audience. 'My husband is like a puppy, always, but he is also very much a one-person dog. Nobody matches up to the one that broke his heart. She was his first love. Ah, sooo sweet!' The bitterness of her sarcasm sucked air from the room.

Pax couldn't look at Luca. Her face was blazing now, the tight chest suffocating.

'Our marriage was always on an understanding: I get a nice life, good horses, I must hostess well and always look great, we have beautiful children and once or twice a year we have drunk sex, you know? Mostly it's better with other people, like my boys. But they are threatening to leave.'

Pax remembered Bay mentioning Monique's groom and his boyfriend, the reason he'd bought the Compton-bred mare back from Blair. 'Only way to stop her staff from walking out is to buy them presents every time she makes them cry.'

'But now I have a problem.' She licked her lips. 'I need a drink before breakfast, okay, to stop my hands shaking. I have to drink maybe two, three shots before I get on a horse. My husband has been fucking our nanny, which I do not like. Our children love her, and that's a messy thing, a painful thing. Now he no longer wants her, and he is doing everything to avoid her until I agree to fire her, but I cannot look after them alone.

'I lost my driving licence last week…' She stopped again, another sharp breath. 'That's so bad for me.' Her voice was getting lower, thicker with emotion. 'My husband was very nice about it. He's always nice. It makes me sad sometimes because he wants to be loved very much. But he is not a caring man and I am not a good wife. I am forty, so why do I sweat and why do I shake and why do I think about drink all the time and why I am scared…'

Pax slipped from her chair and fled for the door. Her chest was in a vice.

*

Ronnie and Kes had a sofa, a roaring fire, a dog on each lap, a Stetson and feathered war bonnets on their respective heads, and *Toy Story* on the DVD player. It was well past his bedtime, they'd eaten their body weight in popcorn and Pink Panther biscuits and it was – according to Kes – the Best Night Ever.

Then a voice called 'hello!' from the kitchen.

In a big rural house like that at the stud, the old custom of friends and neighbours walking in through the back door still held true. It rarely ever happened because the late Captain had gone off friends in his decrepitude, Ronnie hadn't had the time or inclination to make many locally, and they had few near neighbours. To walk in after dark was a liberty preserved for only those oldest and dearest friends one knew intimately. Ronnie supposed Bay loosely fitted one of those three categories.

'We're in the snug!'

Tucked to one side between the breakfast and sitting room, the little tapestry-lined nook was close enough to the Aga to be warmer than the cavernous reception rooms – toastier still with the fire going – and was regrettably easy for a gate crasher to navigate.

'Darling Ronnie! Gorgeous feathers, Minnehaha.' Bay shouldered the doorway. Handsomely doing as handsome does, his hair flopped over his eye and he had a shirt tail poking out from the hem of his sweater. 'Forgive the intrusion. Lost a gundog across your fields. Bitch on heat. In the car now, thought I'd pop in and see how you are.'

'Bay. This is Kester Forsyth, my grandson and Pax's son.'

'Splendid to meet you.' Bay shook Kester's hand, glancing at the screen. 'Are you a Woody or a Buzz man?'

'I like the dinosaur,' Kes said, craning to see the screen round him.

'And your children, Bay?' Ronnie asked pointedly.

'At home with our nanny,' Bay told her, watching Buzz

trigger his wrist laser. 'Monique's at one of her charity things.'

Ronnie wondered whether one should make a point of turning off the film and being hospitable as her mother would have been. She decided not. Times moved on. This was her night with her grandson.

Bay was helping himself to popcorn. 'Pax not around?'

'Mummy's gone out with Luca,' said Kes, not taking his eyes from the screen.

Bay gave Ronnie a shock-horror look which she ignored, riled by his hypocrisy. Rogue males always started circling when a pretty wife broke free from the pack, she'd found.

'They're at a health class.'

'Good for them.' Like a moth drawn to the light, his attention was also now rapt as Woody tried to convince Buzz he was a toy. He reached for more popcorn. Soon he was groping his way to the spare sofa. 'Bloody good film, this.'

'Not there!' Kes looked round in alarm.

Bay sprang back up, peering down at it. 'What is it, guinea pig or hamster or something?'

'Oliver's sitting there. You can sit over there.'

'Can I offer you a drink, Bay?' Ronnie asked wearily.

'Marvellous idea! Now this is a *really* good bit, Kes...'

Luca found Pax pacing tight circles outside the Friends Meeting House fire exit, anxious and nail-chewing. 'She didn't see me, did she? Knowing I was there would make it so much worse.'

'No, of course not. Who is she?'

'Bay's wife. Monique. Christ.'

'Don't blaspheme.' He raked back his hair. 'Are you sure that's his wife?'

'Of course I'm sure, why?'

'Only I saw him in a car earlier with...' He grimaced, remembering the rumpled brunette with the smudged lipstick.

'Let me guess, another woman?'

'You're rolling your eyes.'

Pax started circling again, the same crazy box-walking she'd done when he'd first met her. 'It could be me, talking back there. If I'd married him, I mean. Not that I'd have a bisexual threesome with two men, or drink vodka before breakfast – I've never done that, have you? – just that she's so unhappy and we should all be happy, shouldn't we? We've only got one bloody life. In another version, reader, I married him. And maybe we'd have been good together. Maybe it's all my fault that he's not happy and she's not happy and *I'm* not happy. I loved him so much and I went completely off the rails afterwards, I mean completely!'

'Pax stop. *Breathe.*' He took her shoulders, square and delicate as a carved lectern.

She leant against him, steadying herself, heartbeat fast against his chest. Then she looked up, her eyes intoxicating, that wild hare wariness. 'Sorry.'

'Don't apologise.' He knew the way her vulnerability darted out of sight all too quickly, that calm sea surface she pulled across it. He longed to keep it uncovered, to find out where the storm raged. 'Let me buy you a drink. There's a pub across the square there.'

'A drink?'

'Non-alcoholic. You're a secret drinker, remember? And if we can't help each other to stay sober in a pub, God help us.'

'Is that blasphemy or a prayer?' She half smiled, her gaze trailing round his face, still unfamiliar with its contours, lingering on his mouth then back to his eyes.

Luca wanted to kiss her very badly indeed. But to overwhelm her with his hot-headed instinct right now would be to frighten her into silence, and she needed to learn to heal, to start to draw some of the venom of self-blame from the wound.

So instead he took her hand, warm and slim-fingered, and turned to walk her towards the pub. Pax didn't budge, digging her heels in. When he turned, the hare eyes had lost some of their guardedness, warmth infusing them.

'Jesus, but I'm glad I met you, Luca O'Brien.' She pulled him back towards her and kissed him before he could tell her off.

Bay was wearing the Stetson and polishing off an ancient Talisker Ronnie had unearthed from the drinks cupboard, a fresh batch of popcorn on the go. They were now watching *Toy Story* 2, sporadically breaking off to sing 'You Got a Friend In Me'.

'I should go in a minute,' he told Ronnie, words he'd been repeating like a quarter chime since arriving, along with 'bloody good film, this'.

'It is *very* late for Kes,' Ronnie chided, getting up to answer the phone which had started ringing in the kitchen.

'I'm not tired! You promised me a cowboy sleepover, Gronny.'

Raising her hands, she went next door to pick up the handset, grateful to hear Blair's voice, even crackly with interference on a bad line.

'How's it going, beautiful?'

'I have two to babysit,' she sighed, hearing shrieks and hoots next door, followed by the 'You Got a Friend In Me' refrain. 'Talk to me like a grown-up, Blair.'

'My pleasure,' he growled. 'I've missed you.'

'I've missed you more.'

Which, Ronnie realised as they carried on in much the same vein, wasn't very grown-up at all. But she wouldn't change what they had for the world.

On a leather sofa by a pub fire, drunk on no more than mutual affection and honesty, Pax and Luca made a pact to start out on the road to recovery together with their own rules and no need to involve God, who they agreed was happy to keep a close eye on Luca and turn a blind one to Pax's agnosticism.

And even though she knew he'd be gone by harvest, she felt stronger than she'd thought possible, not wanting to live in anything more than the here and now. All she had to do was think back to the wind on her face as she galloped, to his lips on hers like a first kiss, to her lioness determination to stand up to the Forsyths' bullying and give Kes her best self. Her sober self. Her shiny and new self. Anything was possible just so long as she concentrated on putting one foot in front of the other.

'I'll be here for you every step of the way,' Luca told her, his smile so different without the beard, no longer a defensive shield, but a force field with her inside it, with the best of company.

'Not Twelve Steps.' She pulled the leaflet from her pocket and held it up.

He took it and ripped it in two, their fingers touching, setting off a charge deep inside her. 'We'll make up our own twelve.'

'One – admit you have a problem.' She got lost looking into his eyes.

'I am a drunk,' he said quietly.

'I am too.'

Neither of them looked away and he leaned closer. 'Seek help for your problem is Step Two.'

'Help me.' She broke the eye-hold first, swallowing the sting of shame on her tongue, looking at his unfamiliar chin, transfixed by the new shelf of his jawline. She wanted to run her finger along it. But it was Luca who reached up, touching her cheek and tracing a line to her own chin, gently tilting it so that she was looking at him again.

'I'll help you.' He held her eye.

They said nothing for a long time. Looking at each other was lovely.

'Three,' she whispered eventually, 'we must trust each other.'

He made a fist and she followed, knuckles dovetailing together. 'Four, admit our weaknesses.'

'I lick the butter knife and leave lights on.'

'Shame on you. Five,' his hand slipped warmly over hers, 'don't be ashamed to talk about what's happened to you.' She pulled a face and he smiled because he knew it was a hard one for her.

'*I* was Five,' she pointed out mulishly, deflecting.

'You have to take this seriously, Pax.'

'I am taking it seriously!'

'Take Six and Seven then.' He let go of her hand and put his up in mock surrender.

'Six,' she thought about it for a long time, 'ask each other's advice.'

She waited for a quickfire comeback. When he didn't say anything, she removed her glasses, pulled her slouch hat down over her face and then put then on again, a move guaranteed to reduce Kes to prolonged giggling hysterics. 'Tell me, Luca, does this suit me?'

'You're still not taking it seriously,' he sighed.

'I am.' She kept the hat and glasses on, voice muffled. 'I'm asking your advice.'

He didn't answer, and she suddenly started to panic that he'd walked out in a huff, leaving her at a pub table with glasses over a woolly face mask.

She was about to reach up and snatch it off when she felt his fingers brush her neck as he removed them, her hair tumbling everywhere. '*That* suits you. You're beautiful, you know that?'

He studied her face, red tendrils everywhere like medusa.

'So are you... Seven: point out each other's strengths.'

'Eight. Ah yes, Eight.' He sat back, rubbing his mouth. 'In AA that's the one where we list all the people we've hurt, harmed or wronged through our drinking.'

'And Nine is tracking them down to tell them we're sorry, yes?'

'Up to you. Start with someone you love and trust, maybe, and work out from there.'

She picked up her glass, watched the bubbles rise, looked at him over it. 'I'm sorry, Luca. I was hell when we met. I passed out on you, threw up on you and DT-ed alongside you. I hated you for seeing me like that.'

'It was one of the most amazing nights of my life.' He held her eye again. On and on. Then he smiled, the big sugar-rush smile that started in his eyes and burst out across his face. 'Ten: forgive yourself and love yourself, because no matter how many times you hear it, *you* have to be able to believe it, Pax. Keeping things bottled up shatters self-esteem.'

'That's Ten *and* Eleven, surely?' She looked away uncomfortably.

Her phone buzzed on the table. He stretched across to mute it and turn it over. 'No distractions.' His hand had been inching towards hers on the sofa back, now the warm tips of his fingers ran to and fro across her nails. 'You know, I don't know anything about your marriage to Mack: how you met, how you got wed, what went wrong.'

Her anxiety spiked instantly, making it hard to breathe. She tried to mask, watching his fingers, hypnotised by the rings on them. 'You don't really want to know about it, do you?'

'You have to start getting used to the fact I want to know *everything* about you, Pax. I will never bore of hearing about you. As I keep telling you: talking helps.'

'There's really not that much to tell.'

He laughed softly. 'You are breaking Steps One, Two and Three there, possibly Four, definitely Five; Six and Seven less so, quite probably Eight and Nine, you're decimating Ten and Eleven, and as for Twelve…' He puffed out his cheeks and grimaced. 'Blown it.'

'What is Twelve?"

'Let's get to that after you tell me about being married to Mack.'

*

'Darling, I have to get back to Kes,' Ronnie told Blair, leaning from the kitchen into the breakfast room passage, just able to make out the glow of the screen.

'Get rid of Austen.' Blair was extremely suspicious of Bay.

'I think he's laying siege until Pax gets back. Either that or he wants to buy more land off me.' She lowered her voice. 'I've heard rumours that his marriage is finally coming unstuck.' Lester had turned into a positive goldmine of scurrilous tittle-tattle.

'Definitely tell him to sling his hook in that case.'

'While he's here, I have him where I can see him. He's the last thing Pax needs.'

She'd rarely confided much of home to Blair in the past, but now their strings had tightened through rapprochement, and she valued his advice. In the past week, their calls had been getting longer, often hours at a time. She'd happily live with him in her ear. His unguarded humour and blunt, matter-of-fact approach to relationships was her touchstone.

'Ron, you've got to let her life happen. It's not yours to put right. If she's going to royally fuck it up, she'll go ahead and do it.'

'What if she's even better at that bit than I was?'

'You turned out all right in the end.'

'You say the most romantic things.'

It was hard to tell if the interference on the line had worsened or his deep, gravelly voice was more emotional than usual. 'We found each other, didn't we?'

'We did,' she smiled, knowing they were both incredibly better for it.

'Tell me about your relationship with alcohol?' Luca guessed he might only have one crack at this before Pax clammed up and joked it off, too self-protective to see how much it would help her to share it.

'You make it sound like we've dated, married, separated.'

'Didn't you? It was with you all the way, I'm guessing, starting when – fifteen, sixteen?'

'Put like that... Yes, I got sloshed as a teenager like most of my friends; I just wasn't as good at stopping as them.'

'But you could stop?'

'No choice. I had no money, especially after I left home.'

'It was after you married you developed a problem?'

'Yes, no. I mean, I was far more out of control before then. I was a disaster.'

'Tell me.'

'You really don't want to know all that boring rubbish about me, do you?' She looked round awkwardly.

The bar was all but empty, just two tourists chattering in Italian and scrolling their phones and, by the fire, Luca and Pax curled up on an oversized oxblood chesterfield that clashed beautifully with her hair. Knees drawn up, she asked every few sentences if Luca really wanted to hear this because it was terribly dull.

'Yes I do. Stop asking that.'

She told him reluctantly, her voice lower than ever. And as she spoke, Luca learned a history to Pax he'd never imagined, one that started to make sense of the secrecy and need for control, the desperation to appease. Having dropped out of school at seventeen to join her brother in London, she'd holed up in his student digs, initially acting as a glorified housekeeper, but soon falling in with a party set that eclipsed his student crowd: the club DJs and Chelsea-toff drug-pushers, trustafarians and art students.

Boyfriends had been easy to come by. 'The hair did all the work,' she explained self-effacingly, 'especially with arty types who get off on the Pre-Raphaelite thing. The quieter I was, the better; it just added to my brooding muse. And I *was* quiet. I was just heartbroken. I thought I'd never be happy again, which made me the perfect artist's companion. We'd sink bottles of tequila and absinthe, fantasising we were latter-day bohemians. I took any tab or toke I was offered because it helped me forget Bay.'

He watched her lips move as she explained that her brother's crowd soon seemed too square and rah, so she'd moved out, landing in a squat with a boyfriend who sold vintage records. Luca adored the way her mouth curled when she spoke, the open-heartedness with which she couldn't help speaking.

'It was full of musicians and street artists and performance poets, lovely people.' Her eyes warmed up at the memory. 'I thought I knew what I was doing, but I was a mess underneath, and there were a lot of drugs. We were raided regularly. Granny and Grumps had no idea, thank God. I couldn't hold down work or a relationship longer than a few weeks. Then a distant cousin got me a job temping at a swanky architecture firm. Mack was the in-house structural engineer there.'

She'd pulled the hair back from her face and was twisting it tightly into the crook of her neck, her fingers white-knuckled.

'I'd caught my boyfriend in bed with someone else, things were really awkward at the squat. The architect's office had a shower and even a gym. One day after work, I hid in the ladies until everyone had gone home and then slept on the sofa in the directors' suite. I felt safe and warm for the first time in months, so I did it again the next night, and all that week.

'Mack rumbled me when he stayed late after work one evening. He could have had me fired on the spot, but instead he took me under his wing. He explained that his marriage was breaking up, so he understood what it felt like to be a bit lonely and lost. He invited me to be his lodger, rent-free. This bit's quite boring – shall I skip past it?'

'No, I want to hear it. You were his lodger…'

He sensed her discomfort but could no more let it drop than when asking a horse like Beck to explore new pasture, aware his every urge was to bolt back to the stable.

She picked at a cushion, looked up at him with the big hare eyes then away at the fire. 'He let me have a room in his house – his wife had left, taking the kids. It was so sad, their toys everywhere. I'd come back to the stud or stay with friends at the weekends when he had them to stay. He cooked amazing meals and told me all about architecture and history. He nicknamed me his pet tramp.'

Luca winced. *Grooming you, Pax. He was grooming you.* 'Go on.'

'I thought he was the kindest person I'd ever met. It was down to him that the firm spotted my potential and offered to sponsor me through college so I could get qualified. I loved the restorations they did. At home with Mack, I just read and read. He had hundreds of books about architecture, I was like Belle in *Beauty and the Beast*.'

'And Mack was the beast?' he asked carefully, realising that Pax had unwittingly gifted herself to a Svengali.

'Not to me, not at first. I mean yes, he had a pretty fierce reputation at work, and his wife was slinging all sorts of allegations about unreasonable behaviour and bullying, but he was sweet to me. He hardly drank and never at home, he ate healthily, worked out and soon I was doing all that too. He changed my life completely.'

'By controlling it completely for years.'

'Not back then.' She looked angry, needing to believe it.

Luca checked himself. 'When did you become a couple?'

'Not for almost a year. I was trying to get him Internet dating, can you imagine? I wrote his profile for him on Match dot com – Good-looking, sporty Scot late thirties, into travel, architecture and fine dining WLTM slim, independent female twenty-five to thirty-five. I had no idea he felt that way about me.'

'How old were you?'

'Nineteen.'

He tried not to wince. 'So how did you get together?'

'One weekend when he had his kids there, I went to a party with some friends and saw my ex there. I ended up going back to the squat with him. I texted Mack to let him know I was staying on there a few more nights – it was one of my college weeks, and the squat was only a tube stop away from my class. He went berserk, turning up on campus, then trying to get me fired at work, accusing me of taking drugs. When I went back to have it out with him and remind him that my life was my own, he told me he was in love with me. Just straight up. "I love you." You can guess the rest. Blah-di-blah-di-blah.' The cushion edge was being shredded now.

'No I can't. He told you he loved you, and did you feel the same way?'

She rested her left hand on the table and looked at her fingers, long and fragile, their tips drumming like hooves, the rings her husband had given her on her middle one now. 'No man had ever said that to me, not even Bay. After him, all my boyfriends had been...' She looked at the fingers as they stampeded, and he could guess what she was trying to say. He'd been there enough years himself. Throwaway physical relationships that felt good at the time but left you empty.

'They never lasted,' she said carefully. 'I was staggered, flattered, moved. I cried. Mack said he'd always look after me. Then he took me to bed.'

Luca didn't want to think about it. There's nothing like a middle-aged man with a new plaything, he reflected bleakly.

On the table the hooves had stopped galloping, the stampede sliding to a halt on a canyon edge. He saw she was dashing a tear away, jaw set, determined not to cry.

'It was the worst night of my life.'

'Did he hurt you?'

'No, nothing like that.' She shook her head. 'It's just that... I mean, I didn't think I was all that experienced and he'd been married for years, but that's when I realised... Do you really want to hear this?'

'Only if you want to tell me.'

The Italian tourists had gone, the bar unmanned. An old Coldplay track played over the speakers. Luca could see her mind working, sensed the unhappiness attached to what came next, truth's tipping point trying to keep balance.

'The sex was just awful,' she whispered. 'I remember lying in bed afterwards in shock, thinking *is that it*?' She looked up at him, red bands of mortification streaking her cheeks.

'Why did you stay with him?'

'Because I thought it would get better. Because being young and naïve I thought I could teach him a thing or two. He loved me and I thought I would grow to love him back because I couldn't love Bay any more, and I'd only ever loved Bay. I stayed because I felt sorry for him. And I stayed because…' She put her hand across her mouth, looking away, tears threatening again. She shook them away, forced an ironic smile. 'Because our son Oliver was conceived that night. He died, he was stillborn…' She held up her hand, cutting off his next question. 'And please don't say "I'm so sorry".' She second-guessed sympathy now.

Luca could only imagine the pain it must have caused.

She was staring at the fire. 'By then I was Mrs Forsyth. I'd walked into it willingly, even if it didn't take long to realise that the sex was never going to get any better, and that my husband was a lot more controlling than other people's. He didn't like me behaving indecorously or spending time away from him or having my own friends. But slowly, over the years, I started making secret friends: Stolichnaya, Absolut, Glen's, Tamova.'

As she stared into the fire, her expression changed to one of incredulity. Luca waited, watched, knew that first taste of redemption as well as he knew the blissful slake of Scotch burning his tongue. She had got there. She'd mined the past to find its seam, just as he had sitting together in a car in a lay-by, believing he was lecturing her on how to avoid the path to ruin.

He took her hand, running his thumb across her knuckles. 'My poor angel.'

'The one thing I was absolutely determined about was that I didn't want to desert my marriage like Mummy had.' Her fingers threaded through his. 'Only now I have.'

'And here we are.' He turned her rings in his fingers, wishing their still being there didn't bother him so much.

She looked at them too. 'Don't let go.'

She drew her hand back, slowly easing the finger out from the gold hoops, before looking up at him. It seemed ridiculous that it felt so intimate, the heat rising between them. Luca hooked the two rings on the end of his forefinger and handed them to her, and she smiled, dropping them in her bag without a second glance.

She laughed as he held up his own hands, the rings a hotchpotch of love tokens and souvenirs, the Claddagh a gift from his ex in Canada that he'd hurled across more than one room. One by one, Pax took them off his fingers. Again they both caught their breath, glancing furtively around as though they'd stripped each other half-naked and might be caught at any moment. Then, putting their hands together, unadorned fingers briefly intertwined, they formed fists so they could dovetail their knuckles again.

'Step Three,' she repeated. 'Trust.'

'We've got to Five,' he pointed out as their eyes locked together, brimming with gladness.

'Remind me, what is Step Twelve?'

'I think it's going to feel a bit like this…' And he kissed her.

20

Ronnie finally coaxed an exhausted Kes to bed, which he would be sharing with her when she came up a little later. But the novelty of it was giving him another energy spike and he wouldn't settle. Every time she tried to creep out of the room, he thought up another excuse.

'Gronny, I think there's a spider…'

'Gronny, can I have a glass of water?'

'Gronny, my tummy hurts.'

Trotting in and out, Ronnie hoped her uninvited guest would wake up and let himself out eventually. Having fallen asleep stretched out on the sofa with all four dogs on him, Bay was still downstairs. She hadn't had the heart to wake him for the dogs' sakes.

'Gronny, I've dropped Rab C. and can't find him!'

'Gronny, when will Mummy be back?' He was behind the curtains looking out of the window.

As she settled him into bed again, she heard an engine outside and guessed it must be Bay's car leaving. Phew. His company wasn't something she felt entirely comfortable with. It wasn't that she feared Bay's seductive reputation – hers was far worse and they'd already chalked that adventure up to bitter experience – it was that she feared that he was going to pour out his anguished soul to her. Given he was shallow as a puddle, this would probably take all of five minutes, but she didn't want to test it. He was still very sweet on Pax.

His engine really was *very* loud. He needed to get it looked at.

'Night, night, little cowboy.' She backed out of the room, inching the door almost closed.

'Gronny…'

She looked up in despair, peeking in. 'Yes?'

He was behind the curtains again. 'Why is a helicopter landing in the front field?'

Luca was laying waste to everything on the Chipping Hampton pub tapas menu that came with a *v* beside it.

Watching him, getting used to the beauty of his new-found face, Pax found a smile impossible to shake. They were going to take this so slowly, they'd agreed. Kes came first. And their sobriety. Trust took a long time. She'd already entrusted him with her biggest secrets. She'd never felt an instinctive draw towards anybody as strongly as she did now.

She drank in the sight of him tucking back sweet potato fries, olives, garlic mushrooms and cauliflower bonbons, telling her he'd originally quit eating meat as a bet with one of his brothers, who still owed him a hundred euros. 'He thought I'd never stick it, and it's true I'd never starve for the sake of a lump of cheese, but it helps keep the weight off. We're all porpoises in my family, which is tough when you ride horses for a living.'

She loved the way he described the big, boisterous O'Brien tribe in Ireland, his eternal restlessness growing up, the healing skills his father had wanted to exploit to pass off lame horses as sound and make his chasers race faster. 'Sure, he's a terrible crook, but he's not a bad man. He knows no better, like the fella in Canada I worked for. They're all the same under the skin. Horsemen.'

'Not like Horsemakers?'

He smiled at her over a plate of miniature stuffed peppers, offering her one. 'We need to feed you up.'

She wasn't remotely hungry, but she ate one to make him happy. It was delicious. She ate two more and polished off the sweet potatoes, sharing horror stories of her grandfather, the Captain, another old-fashioned horseman of questionable ethics and unflinching principle.

Then she told him about her father and Lester.

With each secret she shed, she saw a clearer picture of everything, like an oil canvas being revealed by a restorer after years of grime, over-painting and varnish. The colours were brighter, cheering and healing.

Unable to stop herself, she told him about riding the cob the previous night.

'I watched you,' he admitted, taking her hand, both their fingers bearing pale stripes where rings had been.

'You spied on me?'

'I heard hooves, thought you were a loose horse.' He sucked his teeth, looking away to pull up a smile. 'You looked great.'

'I'm far too rusty really to take on the Wolf Moon Lap. I've absolutely no hope of doing it in the time.'

'Does it matter? If you cross under the arch while Jupiter's playing, it'd be good luck, yes? But that doesn't mean it's bad luck if you don't.'

'I suppose not,' she conceded. 'I just don't want to disappoint Lester. The full moon's only a week away.'

'Sure, he'll be made up. He wants you to ride it again, not set a record. Had anybody told you you're a perfectionist?'

'Many, many times,' she laughed.

'Nothing in life is perfect, Pax. It's the imperfections that make things meaningful. Maybe I'll ride it with you.'

Her heart was in her throat, bursting with happiness.

'You,' she kissed him, '*are* perfect.'

While Luca went to the bar for more drinks, she turned over

her phone to check her messages in case Kes wasn't settling. Her screen was striped with missed calls from the stud. Trying not to panic, she called back, but there was no answer. She hurriedly dialled voicemail.

Her mother had left a message from the stud's crackly line sounding breathless and excited to say that a friend of Luca's had just turned up and could they come back as soon as possible? It was rather urgent, she stressed.

It took so little to undermine her, for her imagination to run riot.

He'd kept his phone switched off all night, she'd noticed. She'd foolishly thought he'd done it so they could focus on their conversation, but now she thought back to all the unanswered calls the previous evening, to his jumpiness. He'd even told her that he hadn't been entirely honest. She'd overlooked it because he'd kissed her and she'd run home to gallop around a field for real because galloping in her head no longer soothed her.

She watched him saunter back towards their sofa now, all smiles and blond curls. He was so close to perfect, so nearly utterly perfect. Trust him, Pax. Tiny steps.

'A friend of yours has turned up at the stud. Someone called Michele?'

All the colour drained from his face.

'Are you a racing man, Your Highness? Point-to-pointing's my passion.'

'My father has a few horses in training, yes.'

'We've two out campaigning this season, how about you?'

'In your country, about five hundred.'

'Marvellous. More tea?'

Thank heaven for Bay, thought Ronnie. His natural loquacity had kept their unexpected guests going, and she was having a tough time with Kes.

'Gronny!' he called from the stairs turn again. 'Gronneeeeeee!'

Making her apologies, she hurried out. She was rapidly going off being a hands-on-grandparent. 'What is it, darling?'

'I did a poo!'

'Ha ha, yes very funny. Knock knock, I—'

'No, I really did a poo, Gronny, and I can't make it go down the loo. When I put the brush in, the handle came off.'

'Excuse me, Mrs Ledwell?'

Ronnie jumped as she realised the prince's wife had followed her out, a pretty western woman in an embroidered abaya that couldn't disguise her pregnancy bump.

'May I use your…?'

'Of course.' Oh, God, Kes had just incapacitated the one bathroom in service, and the only functioning downstairs lavatory was off the back lobby, a pink enamel antique with cobwebs festooned on its windowpanes and a novelty light pull. Her grandfather – who had once sold hunters to Arab playboys – was probably in there, haunting it in horror. 'Let me show you.'

'Gronneeeeee!'

'Don't worry about it, Kes. Gronny will pop up and deal with that in a minute. You take Rab C. back to bed.'

'It's the best bed ever.' Big yawn. 'Love you, Gronny!'

'Love you too!' She bowed her head apologetically at her guest as he trotted off. 'This way, your high—'

'Call me Atiya.' The princess smiled with a very unregal wink.

'Pretty name.' Ronnie led the way.

'Isn't it? My husband gave it to me when we married. It means Gift of Allah.'

'How charming. I really am most sorry we're not terribly hospitable. Had we known…'

'It's we who should be apologising. Mishaal's a *very* determined man, and he insisted we must come here before we fly home. The plane can wait on the tarmac at Heathrow for as long as it takes, but it is very rude of us to take up your time like this.'

'Not at all. Here you go!' Ronnie reached in and tugged the Eiffel Tower light pull. It was just as bad as she'd feared: freezing cold, it smelled of cheap air freshener and mould – thank goodness not wee – and had Kes's booster step in front of it, an abandoned Minion on the windowsill.

But Princess Atiya was looking at the framed photographs that tiled the walls with such wide-eyed delight, Ronnie could have just led her into Santa's grotto. 'OMG! You *know* these people?'

'Back in the day, yes.' Ronnie followed her gaze around the little room, a Hall of Fame for latter-day Compton Magna horses that had gone on to the most successful competition careers: showing, point-to-point, jumping and horse trials. Amongst them was an elite scattering of four-star eventers. Her royal guest was studying these closely, spotting Britain's hunkiest Olympic eventing pin-up aboard one, his much-loved wife on another. 'Those two were my absolute heroes as a girl. Look at these! There's Ginny and there's Lucinda, and Hugo again here. It's like a *Who's Who*. You still breed horses like this?'

'It's our stock-in-trade.'

'I know it's an imposition this late in the evening, but I would love to see them.'

'Not a problem!' Ronnie backed out, now delighted by the power of her downstairs loo. *Thank you, Grandpa*, she mouthed as the door closed, just in case he was in there, before hurrying back to check on the prince who Bay was trying to convince to try pheasant shooting.

'We've some marvellous drives just across the valley here.'

Resplendent in his white throbe and shemagh headdress, the prince had a rather sinister scar, like Blofeld, running across one eye. He'd been wearing dark aviator glasses to cover it when he arrived, but due the extreme dimness of the house's light bulbs, he'd dispensed with these, his one seeing eye all-knowing.

His bodyguard stood cross-armed behind their sofa. It

looked like a scene from a James Bond movie, apart from the open *Toy Story* DVD cases and abandoned Mini Boden hoodie. Ronnie would have liked to have taken her guests to the drawing room in which Major Frank had entertained Prince Aly Khan, but when she'd put her head in it earlier it had been so cold she'd seen her breath, and one of the dogs had disembowelled a rat on the Persian rug.

The prince was looking at a chunky blue and gold chronograph watch. 'Luca will be back shortly?'

'Expecting him any minute!' Ronnie had heard nothing, which wasn't entirely surprising because she'd run the cordless phone battery down talking to Blair. 'Bay, I wonder if you'd mind keeping an ear out for Kes if I show Princess Atiya around the yard? She's eager to have a quick look. Perhaps Your Highness would like to come too?'

For the first time since arriving, the prince smiled, showing very expensive white teeth. 'I would like that very much.'

In the neighbouring kitchen, the phone's battery had re-charged enough to make a half-hearted attempt at ringing. 'That'll be them!'

'Whatever you do,' Luca's voice breathed urgently, 'don't let him anywhere near the horses!'

'Why didn't you tell me the truth?' Pax growled furiously.

'Can you drive any faster?'

'Not up this hill.' She was hammering the Noddy car as hard as she dared, the climb from Chipping Hampton up into the Comptons a horsepower-sapping drag of hairpin bends.

'He'll have the horse destroyed if he sees him. Worse, maybe. He wants to hurt him.' Luca was mad at himself for complacently believing Mishaal had left the country. Madder still for not telling Pax, keeper of so many secrets that she had shared with him, now deeply hurt that he'd kept this one to himself.

'Kes is there.' She negotiated a tight left with a squeal of tyres. 'If he's in danger or sees anything that—'

'He isn't, he won't.'

'You don't know that!'

He couldn't argue.

They crossed the Fosse Way and were charging along the straight chestnut-lined avenue at last, passing the Austens' farm on their left, a mini Daylesford peppered with discreet heritage-tone signs offering game cookery, country crafts and pottery courses, then up the slow climb to the outskirts of the village, the verges banking up to tunnel them, then opening out on the crest of the hill, where they could both see across to the stud, its yard lights glowing like a football pitch, in front of which sat the silhouette of a helicopter like a giant wasp, its pilot still sitting inside.

'Oh shit.'

Pax careered up the driveway, raking the car to a halt beside the yard entrance so that Luca could spill out. As soon as he was through the arch, he spotted the four figures gathered outside Beck's stable. He ran like his heels were on fire, not caring if he got a prison sentence for punching a member of an elite royal family to the ground. 'Stoooooooooooooooop!'

Mishaal turned in surprise, his pregnant wife frozen beside him, feeding the Shetland a carrot.

Luca put the brakes on hard, feet sliding across the cobbles like ski moguls before tripping his way to a halt a few feet from the prince. He was looking apprehensive. 'Luca, my old friend!'

Friend?

He gaze automatically went to Beck's half-door. It was in darkness, no insomniac white face or pink nose. A bulky shadow of a henchman stood in front of it. His heart slammed.

'Luca, we've been calling and calling!' With a shimmer of gold embroidery, half-eaten carrot brandished like a light sabre, Mishaal's wife rushed forward. 'How wonderful to see you!'

He recognised the big, naughty blue eyes. So like Ronnie's,

but without the wisdom. Still brimming with an appetite for fun and fortune, they were set in a pretty face with a surface so smoothed by chemicals it had no expression. And the huck of laughter was unmistakable.

'Signe?'

'I am Princess Atiya now,' she said graciously.

'Good on ya.' Luca's gaze flicked to the stable door again. Darkness. Heart slamming harder.

'Luca!' Ronnie bustled between them, the original and authentic blue eyes fixed on his like emergency lights. 'About bloody—'

'MUMMY!' There was a banshee wail from the archway. 'WHERE IS KES?'

'If you'll excuse me, Your Highnesses?' Ronnie marched off towards Pax.

Luca faced Mishaal, for so long the boy man he'd despaired of helping. He found he couldn't address him formally. He couldn't speak. His heart was a fist in his throat. He nodded instead.

Mishaal was swathed in a black and gold farwa coat, a thick Bedouin armour of jewelled, corded velvet, as exotic on the frosted cobbles as a leopard. He nodded back. Behind him, his big bull of a bodyguard stood in front of Beck's door, trigger hands making fists by his sides.

Mishaal stepped forwards with a swish. 'Luca, I came to make peace.'

'Is that a fact?' Luca was still eyeing the dark stable door and its beefcake doorman.

'Listen to our plea, Luca.' Signe stepped beside her husband and they held hands.

'My marriage to Atiya has made a great difference to me,' Mishaal said, raising his wife's hand to his lips. 'We have worked together on many changes, on our charitable projects and on our beloved family.' He touched her bump. 'Atiya focusses her spirituality on processes that heal.'

'Good for you.'

'I have made an inventory of all those that I have harmed and I wish to make amends to you all. I humbly ask your forgiveness.' Mishaal lowered his eyes and waited.

Luca was nonplussed. Weren't those the words of the Eighth Step so recently baulked at by himself and Pax? Had Signe plagiarised them for her healing spirituality?

He shot her a wary look.

The big blue eyes radiated back kindness. 'My husband is lifting the curse, Luca.'

'Oh, right. That's good news.' He glanced to the stable door again.

'Peace be with you, *namaste, assalamu alaikum, fred være med dog*.' Signe raised her hands to either side and let out a joyful breath.

Mishaal looked up, his face relieved. 'Is that over? Can we go now?'

'You're not going anywhere until I know this guy's safe.' Luca marched to Beck's stable.

A white face lifted in the darkness, eyes like black pearls.

Luca pressed his forehead to the bars with relief. He'd been in there all along, standing at his comfort blanket back wall. A belly roar of relief went up now, and Beck stormed across the shavings towards him. Then he stopped, throwing his head up, eyes huge.

'Which horse is this, Luca?' Mishaal was alongside.

Beck didn't move. Luca didn't move. 'You don't know him?'

The horse might have turned from gunmetal to white since Mishaal took him to deathmatch, but he was unmistakable, surely?

'They all look the same to me,' Mishaal said lightly, his all-seeing eye on the Irishman's face. 'My wife wants to buy the dun colt in the barn.'

'He's not for sale,' Luca dismissed, watching Beck still, a silver statue in the darkness.

'That is what Mrs Ledwell said.' Mishaal's monotone had a bemused uplift. 'When I said she could name her price, she told me Spirit has no price.'

'It doesn't,' Luca breathed, watching Beck, who hadn't moved, only his skin shimmering with occasional twitches belied the fact every muscle was drum-tight.

'You always were his saviour.' Mishaal offered his hand to shake. 'Mine also, as it turns out. Good bye, Luca. *Ila liqaa.*'

Luca took it. 'Indeed, until we meet again.'

The helicopter was reverberating its way over the crest, lights flashing by the time Pax finally managed to shepherd Bay outside.

'They didn't say goodbye.' He tilted his head to watch it. 'How rude.'

'Goodnight, Bay.'

'Darling one, we need that lunch.' Penhaligon's Quercus. Kisses on cheeks. Stubble. 'Bring Kes. Hugely good company. Do say goodbye to your mother from me.'

Only Ronnie, Pax reflected, could get away with recruiting the bounder who had once come between them as a babysitter.

Battery charged, she was back on the phone to Blair now, leaving Pax to throw Bay out and round up Luca. Her heart tightened at the thought.

'He won't make you happy, you know,' Bay said.

'Who?'

'Man called Horse or whatever title he gives himself. He's a chancer. Won't make you happy.'

'Who are you to judge what makes me happy?'

'Because I did once. And that means I still know what it feels like to hold it here.' He held up a closed fist.

'Goodnight, Bay.'

Head lowered, feet scuffing, he sucked a shaking breath through his teeth. 'You know my marriage has come unstuck too?'

Pax had a brief, sharp image of the stud-fringed ear, deep, distorted unhappiness. 'So go home and deal with it.'

'You're a hard taskmaster.'

'I know what's good for you.' She held up her own fist. 'I held it here.'

'You still do. For God's sake don't let go.' Two more Penhaligon cheek kisses and he was gone.

'Don't blaspheme,' she breathed after him.

She looked up at Cassiopeia and Cepheus, constant onlookers to the waxing moon, still six slices away from Wolf. Then, hugging herself for warmth, she crossed out through the yards, all the dogs at her heels. Bay's tail-lights were streaking away down the drive.

Luca was by Beck's stable as she'd known he would be, clean-shaven face still unfamiliar, taking a heartbeat to recognise. She stood beside him and he told her that Mishaal had asked forgiveness, urged on by his wife. Obsessive, driven and bulldozing as always, he couldn't leave the country without it. 'He pretended not to know Beck at all.'

'Maybe it was easier that way? You hid what you knew about his past from us.'

'Nothing's hidden now,' he promised, taking her shoulders and standing her opposite him. Letting go, he started walking backwards, counting.

'What are you doing?'

'... eight, nine, ten, eleven, twelve steps. Twelve steps between us. I'm back at Step One.'

'Admit you have a problem.'

He didn't hesitate. 'I love you. I fell in love with you the day I met you. The stroke of midnight would be an exaggeration – you were kissing another man at the time, and you weren't great company after that, to be honest – but later that day something happened. I can't tell you if it was you pulling the wires from your bra, throwing a feed scoop at me or getting the giggles because you realised you were breaking out of your marriage, but I just loved you, Just like that. That's my problem.'

Pax looked at him across the cobbles. 'We have exactly the same problem.'

'Remind me what Step Twelve is again?' he asked.

'You'd better come over here and find out.'

21

'Isn't this fecking shite?' Bridge hissed at her fellow Saddle Bags as they picked vegan *amuse bouche* crumbs from their cleavages and tried not to gawp at Mr Well Cottage's Phileas Fogg mutton chop sideburns in the next-door group, let alone the fact he was talking to a trio that looked suspiciously like Kate Moss, Damien Hirst and Stella McCartney.

The grand opening of Suzy David at The Hare in Compton had brought Cotswold and Bardswold celebrities within close reach of the villagers. There were even paparazzi outside. Petra had walked in three times so far, hoping to be snapped to no avail.

'I think it's thrilling,' she insisted. 'Well worth a night out of the shed. Look, there's that actor from... um... um, help?'

'*Fifty Shades of Grey*,' Gill obliged.

'I think he's one of the waiters, love.' Mo was still trying to get edamame and chia falafel out from between her teeth.

'*You* watched *Fifty Shades of Grey*, Gill?'

'I'll have you know I watched *Nine and a Half Weeks*, back in the day.'

'Mickey Rourke still does it for me.'

'You know the rules, ladies. No vintage fecking pin-ups.'

'Don Johnson. Speedboats and no socks, *ooh*.'

'Stop it.'

'Michael Praed. Robiiiin-da-da-da-da. The only mullet still rocking it after three decades.'

'Stop it.'

'Trevor Eve. *Shoestring*. The *Magnum PI* of Bristol.'

'That's it, I'm not listening.'

'Don't all look now, but Carla Delevingne's at eleven o'clock.'

'No, that's Carly – she's waitressing.'

'I thought it was the big fight tonight? King of the Turner Gypsies.'

'Ash won on a technicality.'

'What was that?'

'Jed's inside doing three months for hare coursing. They've rescheduled for May Bank Holiday so they can double up with the Horse Fayre.'

'Who is that coming in now? Tell me it's Prue Leith and Paul Hollywood?'

'Auriol Bullock and... d'you know, that might actually *be* Paul Hollywood. Bridge?'

'It's Bring Your *Bake Off* Judge to Work day at school. That's Kes's dad, Mack. The beard's a new thing, along with being really nice to Pax and *infiltrating the village*. Now Kes is on the school register, we can't keep him away. He's even joined the PTA and her divorce solicitor's the chair. He so wants her back. He's got stiff competition, mind you. Of which—'

'*Ladies!* Petra, you look too divine. Really, the angels are *deafening*. I'm off to the bar. Anyone want a drink?'

'We're good, Bay.'

'Good-oh. Chat later.'

'Back on the market any day now, my informants tell me. Monique's put the deposit down on a barn conversion to rent in Earls Compton.'

'It's so sad when marriages end.'

'Sometimes it's just the beginning though, isn't it?'

'Bay's one hell of a catch.'

'Put your hands down, Petra.'

'Ha ha. I killed off Father Willy, remember?'

'How's your blond Irish royalist rebel?'

'He is going to be dead on a battlefield this week if he doesn't show up here tonight.'

'Rest in peace, Luca O'Brien.'

'No! He's the only vegan in the village. He *has* to be here.'

'He's out riding. Carly told me. They've been practising all week.'

'He's *what*?'

Lester asked the taxi driver to stop halfway up the drive. He needed a moment to regroup. He hadn't anticipated that coming home would feel so overwhelming.

'Don't think you should walk from here, man. It's well dark out there, innit?'

'I think you'll find it's unusually light tonight. It's a supermoon.'

'Is that like a moon in a mask and cloak fighting the forces of evil, eh-huh, eh-huh, eh-huh?' The taxi driver had a laugh like Basil Brush.

'You can drive on, it's fine.'

Lester hadn't told anybody of his intention to discharge himself from hospital a week early. It wasn't that he wanted to stage a surprise. It was because he didn't want a fuss.

He couldn't hope to navigate the stairs in his cottage yet, but he and Ronnie had decided he was to have the run of the old housekeeper's rooms beside the back lobby, which were within short reach of kitchen, lavatory and – most importantly – a flat walk to the stable yards. There was already a day bed down there, from memory, and he could live without bedding and other flimflammeries for one night if it meant being home on the Wolf Moon.

'Man, what was that!' His driver slalomed into the arrivals

yard. 'I saw something moving. Headless ghosts on horseback or something. You hear that?' He was rigid with fear. '*Music*.'

Lester heard it. He could hardly believe his ears, but he could definitely hear it.

'Man, what is that shit?'

'*That*,' he handed several ten-pound notes across, 'Is Holst's Opus 32, fourth movement – Jupiter, to be precise. Keep the change.'

Waving the driver impatiently away with a crutch rather than accept his offers of help, Lester made his way laboriously beneath the arch. The Percys' old gramophone player was sitting on a table in the middle of the yard.

'Jupiter, Bringer of Jollity' was already launching into the section Lester couldn't help but stand to attention for: 'I Vow to Thee My Country'.

What a homecoming. *What* a homecoming!

He cocked his head and strained. Hoofbeats. Good girl. His amazing girl. His world-beater.

He limped across to greet Cruisoe who rumbled with furious delight. The white fury was now next door, he noted with disapproval. There was an overweight Shetland next to that, pulling faces at him through a sheep hurdle placed across his open door. The old point-to-pointer and his cob were missing from their boxes. The latter would never complete the task before the last violin sounded.

He strained his ears again. Had they even reached the windmill?

The French horns and strings were duetting again, the timpani dancing attendance: da da da da da da... da da da da da da-da-da.

Leaning hard on his crutches, he made his way through the second yard to the open track, thrilling at the sight and sound of the herd shifting through the straw, snorting in alarm, then recognising his call to quietness.

The hooves were coming back. Impressively fast. Not

quick enough, mind. He limped his way back, the cobbles making him unsteady. By goodness it hurt. The task ahead felt gargantuan, but he would meet it. He'd be in the saddle again by hound exercise.

Back at the gramophone, the final run of Holst's glorious little violin arpeggios was upon them. Barely a minute of music left, and still half a dozen fields to cross.

He looked up at the big white moon. It had witnessed him once before, and it had forgiven him then. Sometimes in life, one had to relive a moment to get things right.

He swiftly lifted the needle and set it back to the beginning of the track, then picked up his bag, hooked it over his crutch and set off for the house.